The Best of THE THREE STOOGES® Comicbooks

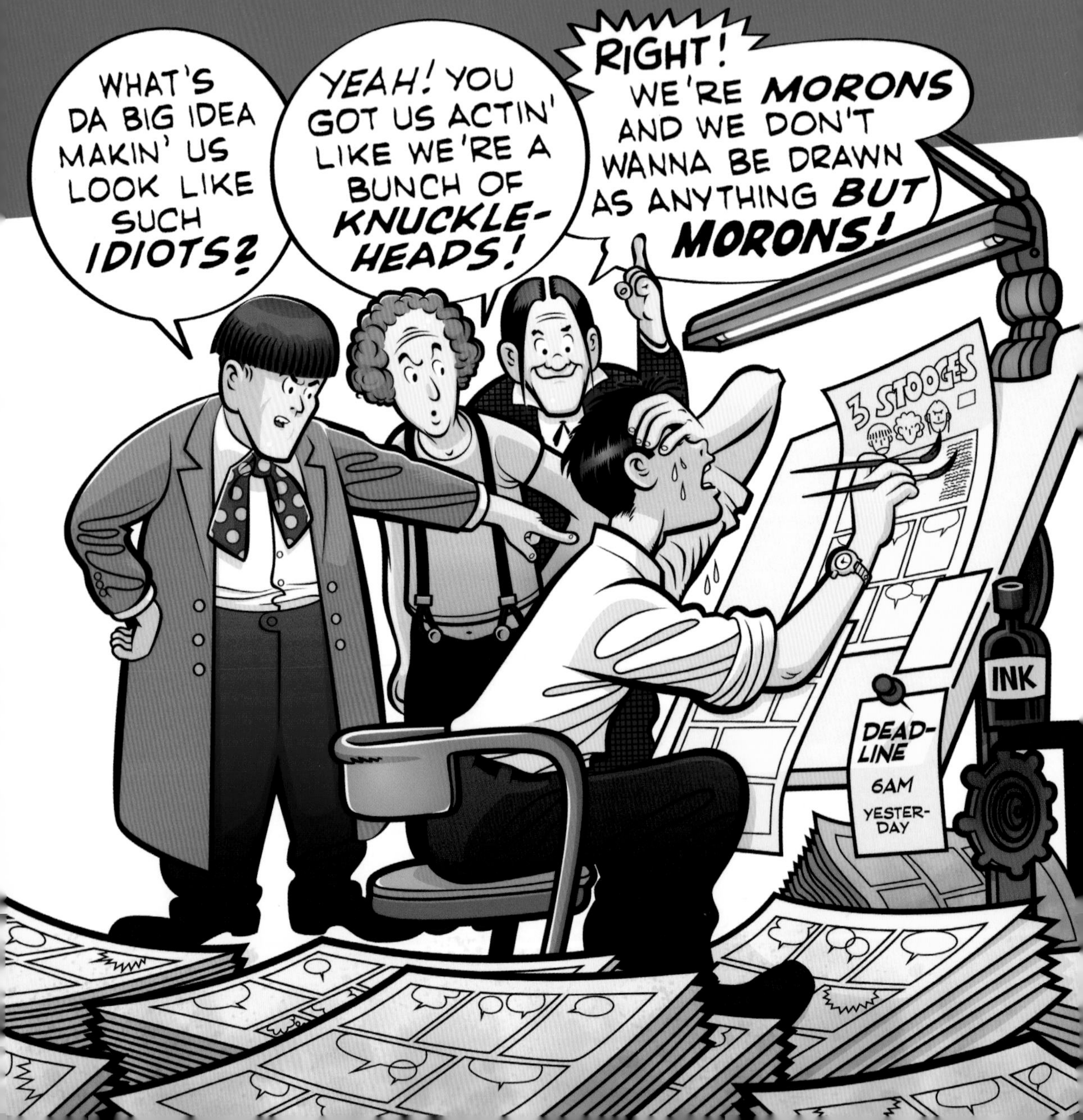
WHAT'S DA BIG IDEA MAKIN' US LOOK LIKE SUCH IDIOTS?
YEAH! YOU GOT US ACTIN' LIKE WE'RE A BUNCH OF KNUCKLE-HEADS!
RIGHT! WE'RE MORONS AND WE DON'T WANNA BE DRAWN AS ANYTHING BUT MORONS!
3 STOOGES
INK
DEAD-LINE
6AM
YESTER-DAY

The Best of THE THREE STOOGES® Comicbooks

Volume 2

Presented by C3 Entertainment, Inc.

by

NORMAN MAURER
JOE MESSERLI
PETE ALVARADO

PAPERCUTZ™
New York

THE THREE STOOGES GRAPHIC NOVELS AVAILABLE FROM PAPERCUTZ™

THE THREE STOOGES
#1 "Bed-Bugged"
All-new comics by
George Gladir,
Jim Salicrup,
& Stan Goldberg

THE THREE STOOGES
#2 "Ebenezer Stooge"
All-new comics by
George Gladir,
Stefan Petrucha,
& Stan Goldberg

THE THREE STOOGES
#3 "Cell Block-Heads"
All-new comics by
George Gladir, Jim Salicrup,
Stan Goldberg, Sid Jacobson,
Ernie Colon, and more!

THE BEST OF THE
THREE STOOGES
COMICBOOKS
Volume One
Classic Stooge comics by
Norman Maurer
& Pete Alvarado
Introduction by
Joan Maurer

THE BEST OF THE
THREE STOOGES
COMICBOOKS
Volume Two
Classic Stooge comics by
Norman Maurer, Joe
Messerli, & Pete Alvarado
Plus: Shel Dorf's Norman
Maurer Interview

THE THREE STOOGES graphic novels are available for $6.99 each in paperback, and $10.99 in hardcover. THE BEST OF THE THREE STOOGES COMICBOOKS graphic novels are only available in hardcover for $19.99 each. Available from booksellers everywhere. You can also order online from www.papercutz.com. Or call 1-800-886-1223, Monday through Fridays, 9 – 5 EST. MC, Visa, and AmEx accepted. To order by mail, please add $4.00 for postage and handling for first book ordered, $1.00 for each additional book and make check payable to NBM Publishing. Send to: Papercutz, 160 Broadway, Suite 700, East Wing, New York, NY 10038.

THE BEST OF THE THREE STOOGES COMICBOOKS are also available digitally wherever e-books are sold.

THE BEST OF THE THREE STOOGES COMICBOOKS
Volume Two

Dedicated to Joe Kubert, 1926 – 2012

By Norman Maurer, Joe Messerli, & Pete Alvarado
Norman Maurer and Joe Kubert – Original Editors (St. John comics)
Chase Craig – Original Editor (Western/Dell/Gold Key comics)
Special thanks to: Jim Burns, Shel Dorf, David Anthony Kraft,
 Brent Frankenhoff, Brent Seguine, Maggie Thompson
Ken Cooper – Art Restoration
Diego Jourdon – Cover/Title Page Illustration (after Norman Maurer)
Adam Grano – Design and Production
Michael Petranek – Associate Editor
Jim Salicrup
Editor-in-Chief

ISBN: 978-1-59707-350-9

The Norman Maurer interview is excerpted from "Shel Dorf and the Fantasy Makers: Norman Maurer," which originally ran in the November 23, 1984 issue of *Comics Buyer's Guide* and is © Copyright 1984 by Krause Publications, Inc. Used here with permission.

The Joe Kubert Interview is excerpted from "Kubert," which originally ran in the May 1984 issue of *David Anthony Kraft's COMICS INTERVIEW* and is © Copyright 1984, 2010 by Fictioneer Books Ltd. All rights reserved. Used here with permission.

Printed in China
October 2012 by New Era Printing LTD.
Unit C, 8/F Worldwide Centre
123 Cheung Tau St., Kowloon, Hong Kong

Distributed by Macmillan
First Papercutz Printing

TABLE OF CONTENTS

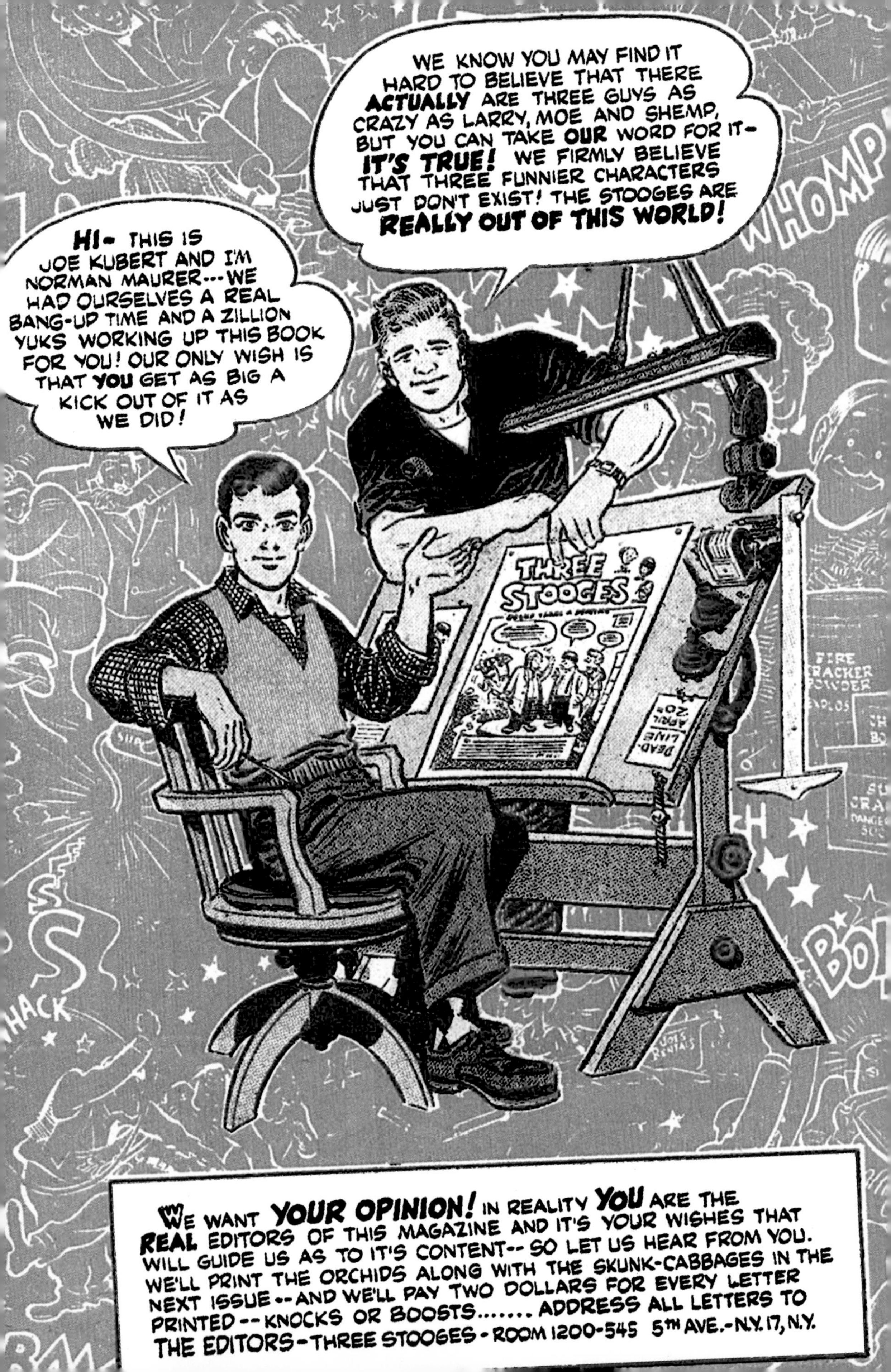
HI- THIS IS JOE KUBERT AND I'M NORMAN MAURER--- WE HAD OURSELVES A REAL BANG-UP TIME AND A ZILLION YUKS WORKING UP THIS BOOK FOR YOU! OUR ONLY WISH IS THAT YOU GET AS BIG A KICK OUT OF IT AS WE DID!
WE KNOW YOU MAY FIND IT HARD TO BELIEVE THAT THERE ACTUALLY ARE THREE GUYS AS CRAZY AS LARRY, MOE AND SHEMP, BUT YOU CAN TAKE OUR WORD FOR IT- IT'S TRUE! WE FIRMLY BELIEVE THAT THREE FUNNIER CHARACTERS JUST DON'T EXIST! THE STOOGES ARE REALLY OUT OF THIS WORLD!
THREE STOOGES
WHOMP
WE WANT YOUR OPINION! IN REALITY YOU ARE THE REAL EDITORS OF THIS MAGAZINE AND IT'S YOUR WISHES THAT WILL GUIDE US AS TO IT'S CONTENT-- SO LET US HEAR FROM YOU. WE'LL PRINT THE ORCHIDS ALONG WITH THE SKUNK-CABBAGES IN THE NEXT ISSUE--AND WE'LL PAY TWO DOLLARS FOR EVERY LETTER PRINTED--KNOCKS OR BOOSTS....... ADDRESS ALL LETTERS TO THE EDITORS-THREE STOOGES-ROOM 1200-545 5TH AVE.-N.Y. 17, N.Y.

THE NORMAN MAURER INTERVIEW

by Shel Dorf

The late Shel Dorf loved comics and the people who made them. As a co-founder of the San Diego Comic-Con, he helped create a way for comics fans to meet the writers and artists who created the comics. Comic-Con has since turned into an annual major media event. He also conducted a series of interviews entitled "Shel Dorf and the Fantasy Makers" in which he spoke to countless pop culture icons. Shel's interview with Norman Maurer was originally published in The Comics Buyer's Guide, November 23, 1984 issue. Because of Norman's unique relationship with THE THREE STOOGES, and because he was the artist, writer, and co-editor of the very first THREE STOOGES comics, as well as the co-writer, artist, and editor of the later LITTLE STOOGES comics, we're excerpting parts of that interview here…

You turn left at the 20th Century-Fox studios and enter an area called The Cheviot Hills. It is a neighborhood of large, comfortable upper-middle-class homes. At the corner where Ray Bradbury's home sits, you turn left. Soon you are at a beautiful large California-style home (swimming pool, etc.) that is the residence and studio of Norman Maurer.

Since his name stopped appearing on comicbooks some years ago, fans have wondered what happened to him. Learning he was still most definitely active in the creative field, I sought him out for readers of Comics Buyer's Guide.

It was a happy discovery to find he is (and has been for years) married to the daughter of Moe Howard of The Three Stooges. It was a double treat to visit them in their home and we are now good friends.

So, for you young historians and you slightly older fans here is a rare treat!

Shel Dorf: Norman, what have you been doing for the last 20 years? You were a superstar of comicbooks in the Forties and Fifties, and then we lost track of you.

Norman Maurer: Well, in the Fifties I was married to Joan, who was Moe's daughter, Moe Howard of The Three Stooges, and I was still doing comics for Biro-Wood and some for St. John. Joe Kubert and I were partners.

Moe used to harass me, why didn't I go into the film business because the cartoonist does everything alone that in the film business takes 100 people to do. You do the story, you design the characters, you do wardrobe dressing, layouts, the camera work, etc. I resisted for several years. Finally he got the better of me and I got a crack at it and I did independent science-fiction pictures. I was associate producer on a Fox picture called *Spacemaster X-7* and a co-producer with Sidney Pink, who did *Bwana Devil*, an early 3-D movie, who was the money man behind Arch Oboler. He got me to be his producer because he didn't know anything about film. We did a picture called *The Angry Red Planet*, which has become sort of a cult movie now. I always said about that movie "I wish they would have dubbed the reviews in Italian."

Shel: How did you learn about filmmaking? Did it come easy to you because of all the plotting you did for comicbooks?

Norman: Because of my experience in comics and art work and so forth, a fellow named Bernie Glasser got me to be his associate producer on *Spacemaster X-7*. He used to say to me, "never worry about being a producer, you get caught up in the momentum and the day-to day needs carry you along, and if you

Opposite: Norman Maurer and Joe Kubert from THE THREE STOOGES #1, the St. John comic, September 1953, by Norman Maurer.

have half a brain in your head, you can analyze it and figure it out." And that picture gave me quite a bit of experience, which got me the next picture. Shortly after that, Moe and the Stooges talked me into doing a Three Stooges feature, which I wrote and produced. *The Three Stooges Meet Hercules*, and it was and still is their most successful movie.

Shel: It's interesting that the son-in-law was coerced into the business instead of marrying into it. You sounded kind of reluctant.

Norman: I was. I grew up with Joe Kubert and we were both of the same feeling. We would like to have both spent the rest of our lives with a brush in our hands and a bottle of ink, and a slanted desk. Joe is still doing that. I don't think Joe could ever be happy if he wasn't at a slanted desk. I was the same way but, with all the pressure that Moe gave me, my father-in-law who was a marvelous guy, a marvelous father-in-law, and living in the town where all the film was going on, I figured I'd give it a try. And, once I gave it a try, I really liked it.

Shel: So what have these 20 years been like in the film business?

Norman: Well, I did *The Three Stooges Meet Hercules*, my first picture at Columbia, which was a one-picture deal, the picture was successful. They signed us up for another picture. We did *The Three Stooges in Orbit*. I wrote the story and produced it, then the studio talked me into directing another Stooge picture. I wrote the story and produced and directed the Stooge's *Around the World in a Daze*, and then wrote, produced, and directed *The Outlaws Is Coming*, another Stooge picture. And that one-picture deal with Columbia lasted nine years under exclusive contract.

Shel: When did you first get into animated film?

Norman: I have to go back to after I left comics before I even went into the films. I had developed an animation process called Artiscope at that time which produced *Prince Valiant*-style animation without artists. Frankly, I was 20 years ahead of my time and I spent two years developing it, financing it, so forth, and then ran out of money and got out of it. So, I was first in the film business at that point.

Shel: What year was this? Do you remember?

Norman: Around '53, after we left comics. Another reason I left comics was because Joe Kubert and I were partners with Arthur St. John and St. John went under.

Shel: You started with *Tor*?

Norman: 3-D comics, we did *Tor* and *The Three Stooges* in 3-D and then we tried to talk Arthur into not going full blast into 3-D books. He didn't listen

to us and pretty soon he over-produced and went bankrupt. And that's when I sort of decided, well, the comic business is going down the tubes. And, if you recall, when that 3-D book came out, the first *Mighty Mouse* was a huge success.

And then every publisher jumped into it. And at that point, I don't exactly remember how many comicbook publishers there were, but there were a lot. A year later there was just a handful, just a few could survive. I thought the whole business was going down the tubes at that time. That again got me into films.

Shel: 3-D movies sort of phased out too.

Norman: Yes, yes!

Shel: I think at the time MGM had decided to do a Cole Porter musical in 3-D. By the time *Kiss Me Kate* was finished, the 3-D craze peaked and was over, so the film was released as a flat, regular picture. It only showed in a few cities in 3-D.

Norman: Well, you could do that with a movie and release it what way, but, unfortunately, all the independent comicbook publishers jumped on the bandwagon and it was too late, and most of them went under. So, getting back to your question, about the 20-year period and how did I get into animation.

Shel: Okay. You made quite a remarkable statement. How is that possible, to do animation without people involved?

Norman: Well, by tricks and invention and makeup and wardrobe. We would shoot a normal black-and-white film with a movie camera. The actors in front of a black velvet background. By chemical and mechanical processes, we converted the reproduced images into pure outline.

So the artists had to do some touchups but it was very minor. About 1%. And, actually, interestingly enough, the more detail you put into it, the cheaper the process was to produce. I won't go into that because it gets very technical.

Shel: You said you had nine years with the Three Stooges movies?

Norman: Well, no. I had nine years at Columbia. I did four Three Stooges pictures and then I did *Who's Minding the Mint?* It had an all-star cast; Joey Bishop, Milton Berle, Jim Hutton, Walter Brennan. Jamie Farr got his first comedy role in that film. Howie Morris of the Sid Caesar show directed for me. Everybody and his uncle was in that film. And then I did *The Mad Room* with Stella Stevens and Shelley Winters and then I had a fight with Columbia and left and went over to CBS.

Shel: Had you been working as an independent producer all this time?

Norman: Well, in those nine years with Columbia I was an independent producer under exclusive contract as producer/director.

Shel: Columbia, because that's where the Stooges had their ties?

Norman: Well, that's also where I got my start. I found though, after the second Stooge picture, probably after the first, I didn't like directing. Not at all. It was too hectic.

Shel: Preferred writing?

Norman: Yes. I not only preferred it, but I have to be honest, I found that a producer, as I was, would start on a picture project and he would be a year and a half on that project. During that year and a half, your writer worked eight weeks, and went on to the next picture and the next picture and the next picture. Then I found out the writers were sitting at home, having more fun and making more money than the producers were. I'll tell you why. I feel that writing in the motion picture industry is the only area (well, I could say maybe there is one other area — that is, as music composer) where you can be like a cartoonist, be alone at your little drawing board, with nobody pushing your paint brush around. The only area in the film business where you can work alone.

Shel: Is that important to you?

Norman: Very! Very important, especially after 15-18 years of being a cartoonist, I found that as a director with 150 people asking me what to do, giving me suggestions, studio executives telling me what to do, it was like somebody was pushing that brush around — go left, go right, go in the middle. A writer can sit alone at his typewriter, turn in his script, they look at it — they hate it, they throw it out. If they like it — they buy it. But he still works alone.

Shel: How do you feel about what happens after the writer turns loose his finished script? The treatment of the writer in Hollywood has not always been the best.

Norman: No it hasn't, but I've got to look at it from the standpoint of having been a producer and as a director, and I have lived through these experiences of the writers saying, "You can't change that comma, you can't change that period, it isn't the way I meant it." I found out over the years that the input from the producers, from the studios, even from way up in the executive level, in the end, makes a better script. And that's what you see on the screen.

Shel: So being a producer made it easier for you to compromise.

Norman: It was easier for me to understand it. Even the actors, when they get on the set, can add to a script. A writer may scream bloody murder, "Hey, that's ego, I didn't write that!" But in the end, in most cases, it comes out a little better.

Shel: Since then, what has your career been like? I just thought I would like to bring this up to date, and then I want to start at the beginning.

Norman: After I left Columbia, I went over to Cinema Center, which is CBS, to do a feature and we were just about to start looking for a director, when Mr. William Paley of CBS found out that the studio lost $34,000,000 and pulled the plug. And I was out of work. That was the poverty period of my life. When I was struggling to become a writer, having very few credits, just four story credits, no screenplay credits. And of course, one of the great training grounds, just as the Catskills was for comedians, the great training ground for writers today is animated cartoons and I had some friends in the business, so I got in and started writing cartoons. *Josie and the Pussycats.* And that started a whole new career where I did better than I did as a producer. Not only financially, but I got both my sons in the business. You know, the old bit. You become a manufacturer, it's George Smith and Sons. Well, a cartoonist doesn't have that, a writer doesn't have that.

Well, I was the lucky one, I got both my kids in when they were young. I was working at Hanna-Barbera and I got them in as assistants and trained them and today they are big TV writers.

Shel: Norman, let's go back to your origin. You were born in Brooklyn — right?

Norman: Right. Crown Street — somewhere out there in that area.

Shel: What year?

Norman: 1926. Several blocks from Ebbets Field.

Shel: Were there any other artists in your family?

Norman: No, not really. Just an uncle who used to draw pictures and he'd draw a body on the page and he'd run out of space at the bottom around the body's waist so he'd turn the page over and finish the legs on the other side. Maybe that started it — I don't know.

Shel: Did you read the comics in the papers?

Norman: Sundays? I guess that was the old Saturday morning television. I couldn't wait 'til Sunday mornings. I couldn't wait to go out there and get the funnies.

Shel: What were some of your favorite strips?

Norman: My all-time favorite, as you know, was *Terry and the Pirates.*

I always liked the old adventure comics as a kid. *Flash Gordon, Terry, Prince Valiant, Brick Bradford.*

Shel: People have said that your style had sort of a Caniff look to it. Was he your "teacher," so to speak?

Norman: I never met him but I can answer that

very simply. Who, in the adventure strip field, wasn't a Caniff student?

Shel: What kind of art training did you have? Did you go to special art classes? The High School of Music and Art had some very progressive teachers and kids that came out of that school did very well.

Norman: Well, actually, I met Joe Kubert for the first time when we were both at The High School of Music and Art, taking exams. You had to draw pretty good in order to get in.

Shel: How old were you?

Norman: I guess about 14 or 15. We had just gotten out of grammar school and, all over the city, kids were going up to take the exam to get into "Music and Art," where I met Joe. We both got in and we went there for two years.

Shel: Did Joe live in Brooklyn then too?

Norman: I think he did. That was before the family moved to New Jersey.

Shel: He's still in New Jersey, isn't he?

Norman: Yes, he's still there, I've gotta tell you. As somebody that knows Joe for some 30-odd years, he hasn't changed a bit. He's still the same sweet, lovely guy.

Shel: What were your art teachers like? Did you have a natural ability which they made better or did you really learn to become an artist there?

Norman: No, I think Joe and I (it's easier to admit now), were both pretty big hooky players. We played a lot of hooky and we'd go back home, draw our little samples, and bring them over to the publishers in New York, get a little advice and go back and do new samples. I think that's the way we learned.

Shel: At 15?

Norman: Yes … Well, Joe and I were working when we were 15. We were working for a company called Denby in New York during the summer. It was like a mill. I was doing a comic strip called *Bombshell* or something and Joe was doing something else. There were 30 or 40 artists. We were getting $12.50 a week — I'll never forget it, because I got a 50¢ raise. 50¢ a week. And Joe got so mad because he didn't get it, he quit.

I have a theory on what made me an artist. It starts way back in grammar school, in the fourth or fifth grade, when your class had to draw an assignment, draw and paint a sailboat, and 40 kids painted a sailboat and they were rotten, including mine, but the teacher singled mine out and gave me a prize and I went home and I was the hero of my family. I think that's what kept me wanting to do it, not to go out to play baseball or stickball or what have you. I don't think you're born with it, I really don't. I know it's a big argument, but I just don't think you're born with it. I think it's a matter of wanting to do it bad enough and practicing a lot.

Shel: And being encouraged and praised.

Norman: And being encouraged and praised, and you could say being singled out from the mob.

Shel: You could always draw very well. I remember when I first saw your stuff, it occurred to me all the proportions were right and the line quality in your work was very special.

Norman: For 30 years my wife has always complained about my artwork, saying I draw everybody short-waisted like me.

Shel: How did you start with Lev Gleason publications?

Norman: Well, that's kind of hazy. I have to go back to when I was 14. As I said before, Joe and I used to go up to comicbook publishers in New York either together or separately, and show them our samples and the artists were always friendly and nice and gave us suggestions and directions.

Shel: Who were some of the artists working at that time?

Norman: Carl Hubbell was there. He was very helpful. Carl was a terrific guy. He did a lot of stuff for Joe and me when we did *Whack!* He was a marvelous guy. There are a lotta guys like that. Irv Novick was up there and used to give us a lot of help.

Shel: How about Jack Kirby? Was he there?

Norman: I don't remember. I just met Jack Kirby about four months ago over at Ruby-Spears productions for the first time.

I never met him when we were both working in New York. Anyway, not to my knowledge. I may have and not remembered. He was probably just on the way up then.

Shel: Was there ever a time in your life as a kid when you wanted to do anything else but cartooning?

Norman: Nothing but comicbooks. ★

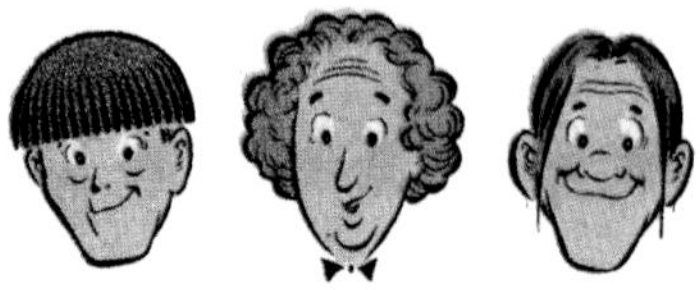

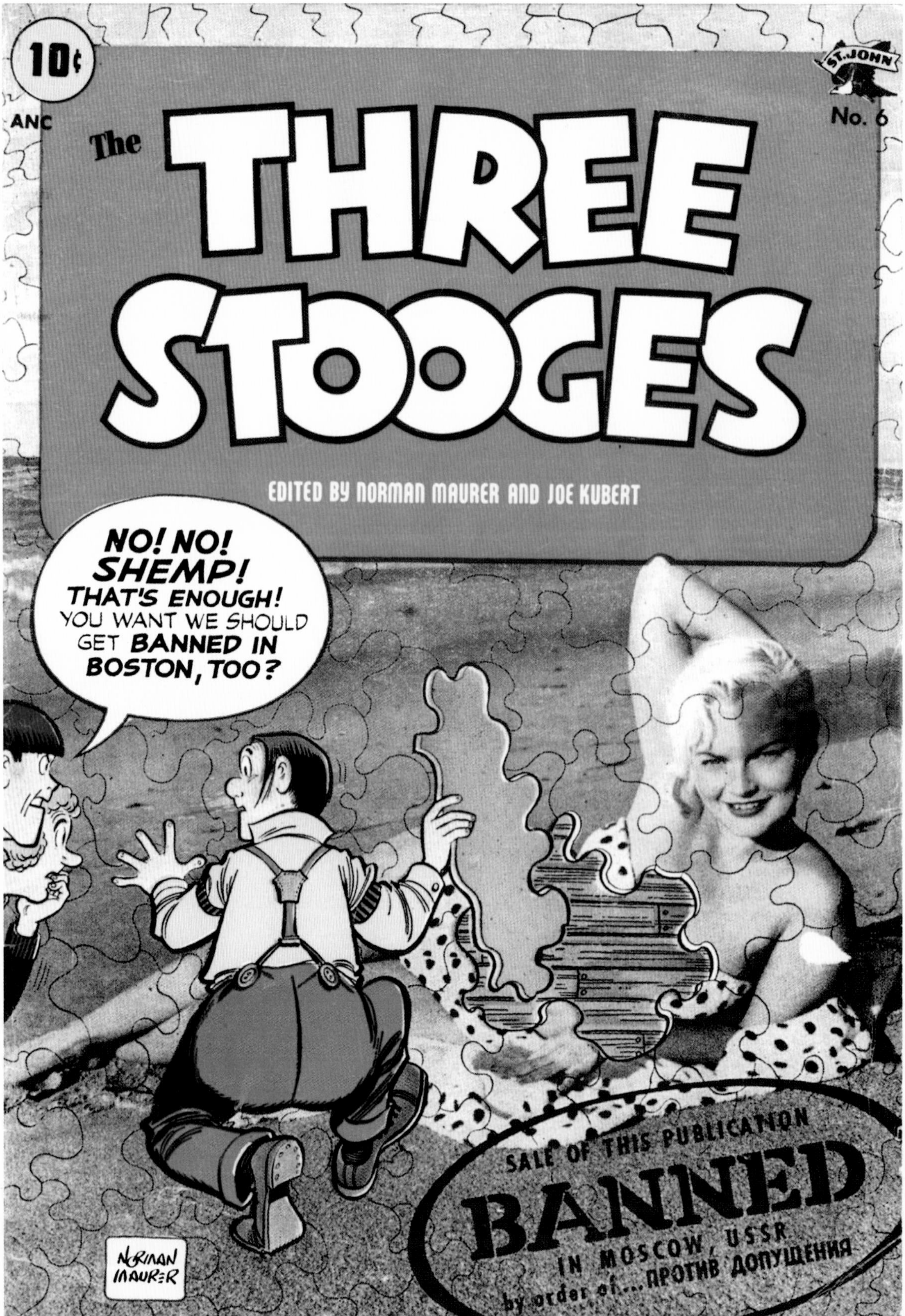
10¢
ANC
ST. JOHN
No. 6
The THREE STOOGES
EDITED BY NORMAN MAURER AND JOE KUBERT
NO! NO! SHEMP! THAT'S ENOUGH! YOU WANT WE SHOULD GET BANNED IN BOSTON, TOO?
NORMAN MAURER
SALE OF THIS PUBLICATION BANNED IN MOSCOW, USSR by order of... ПРОТИВ ДОПУЩЕНИЯ

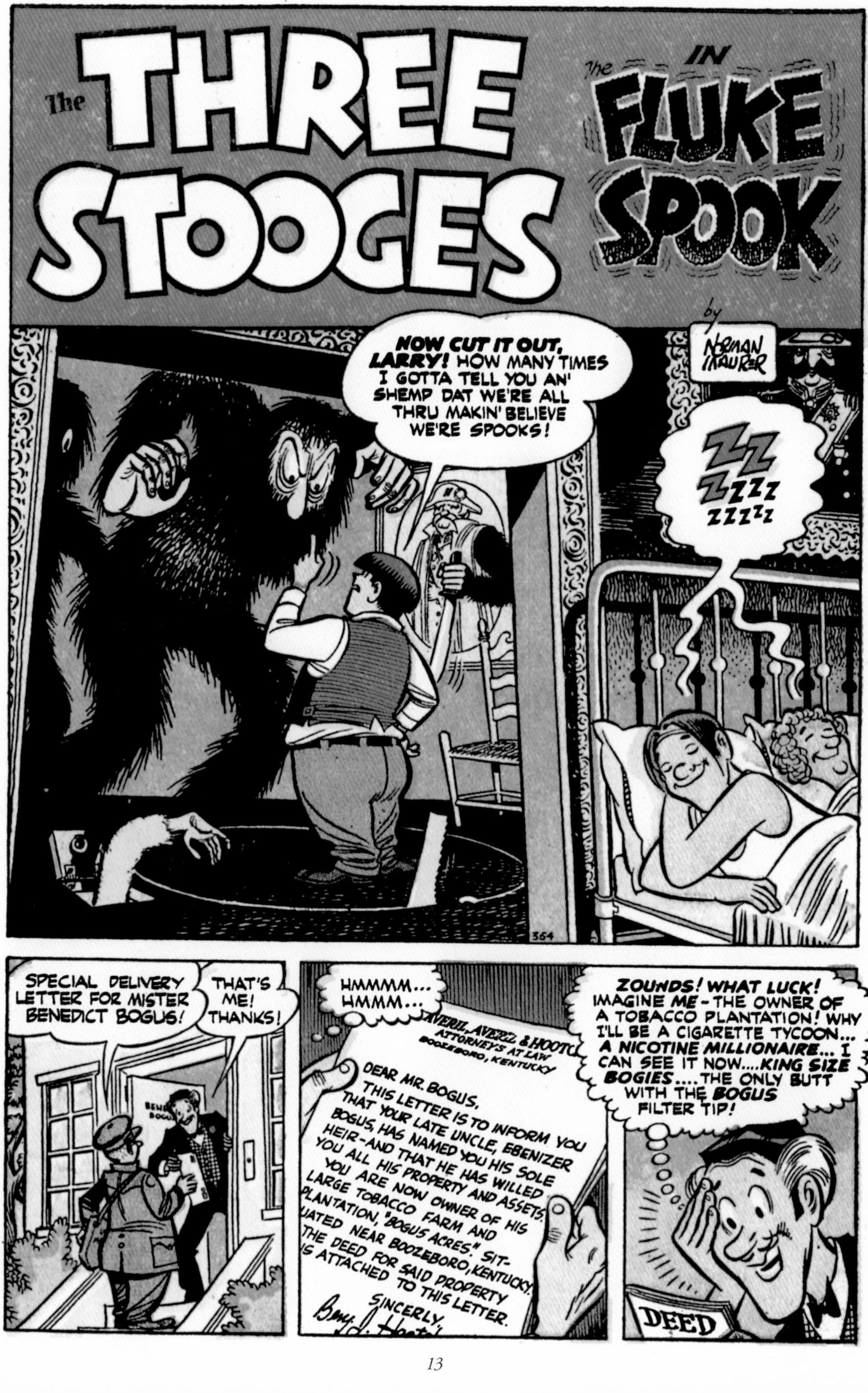
The THREE STOOGES
IN The FLUKE SPOOK
by Norman Maurer
NOW CUT IT OUT, LARRY! HOW MANY TIMES I GOTTA TELL YOU AN' SHEMP DAT WE'RE ALL THRU MAKIN' BELIEVE WE'RE SPOOKS!
ZZ ZZZZ ZZZZZ
SPECIAL DELIVERY LETTER FOR MISTER BENEDICT BOGUS!
THAT'S ME! THANKS!
HMMMM... HMMM...
AVERIL, AVERIL & HOOTCH ATTORNEYS AT LAW BOOZEBORO, KENTUCKY
DEAR MR. BOGUS, THIS LETTER IS TO INFORM YOU THAT YOUR LATE UNCLE, EBENIZER BOGUS, HAS NAMED YOU HIS SOLE HEIR–AND THAT HE HAS WILLED YOU ALL HIS PROPERTY AND ASSETS. YOU ARE NOW OWNER OF HIS LARGE TOBACCO FARM AND PLANTATION, "BOGUS ACRES." SITUATED NEAR BOOZEBORO, KENTUCKY. THE DEED FOR SAID PROPERTY IS ATTACHED TO THIS LETTER.
SINCERLY,
ZOUNDS! WHAT LUCK! IMAGINE ME – THE OWNER OF A TOBACCO PLANTATION! WHY I'LL BE A CIGARETTE TYCOON... A NICOTINE MILLIONAIRE... I CAN SEE IT NOW.... KING SIZE BOGIES..... THE ONLY BUTT WITH THE BOGUS FILTER TIP!
DEED

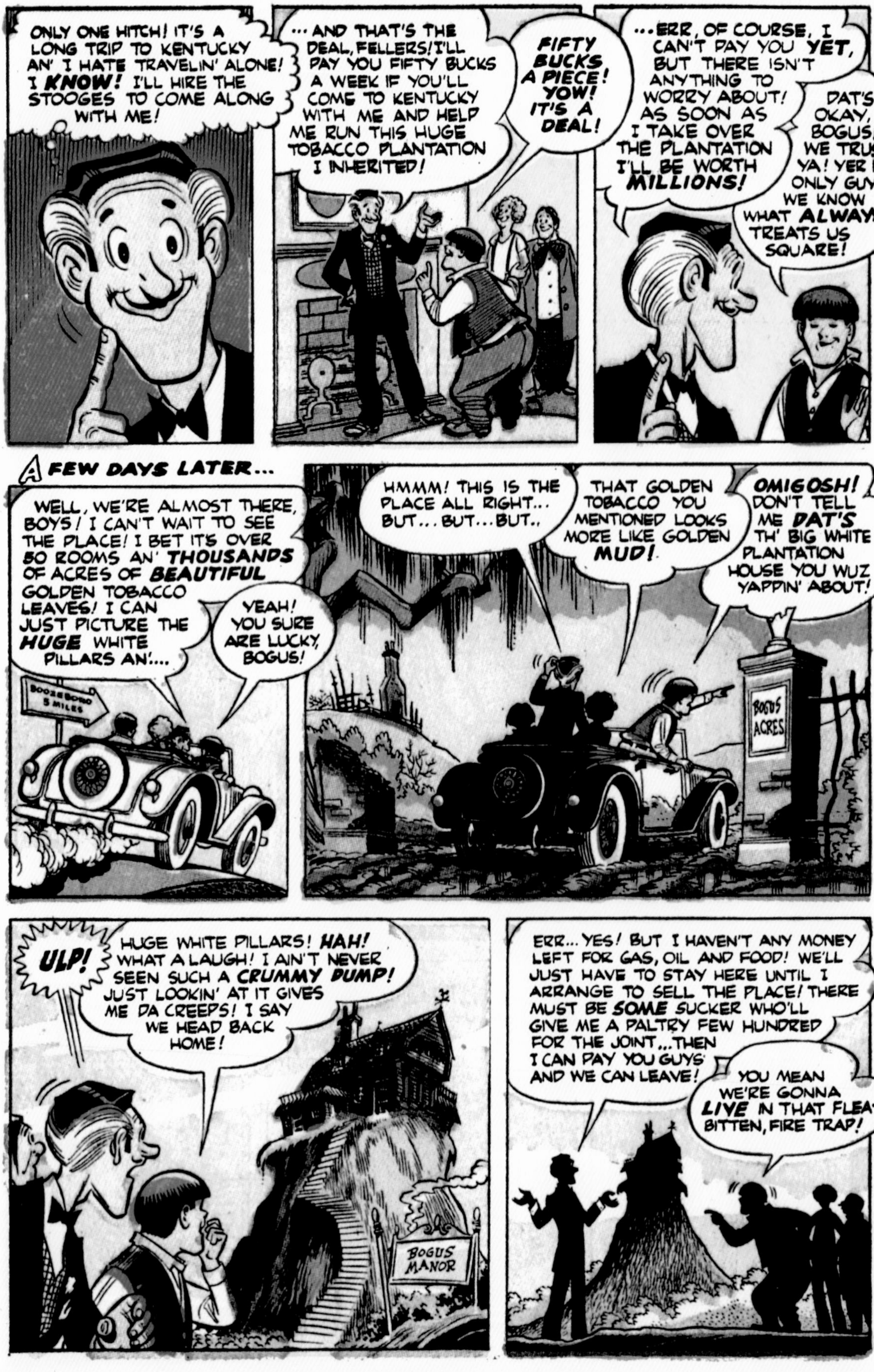
ONLY ONE HITCH! IT'S A LONG TRIP TO KENTUCKY AN' I HATE TRAVELIN' ALONE! I KNOW! I'LL HIRE THE STOOGES TO COME ALONG WITH ME!
...AND THAT'S THE DEAL, FELLERS! I'LL PAY YOU FIFTY BUCKS A WEEK IF YOU'LL COME TO KENTUCKY WITH ME AND HELP ME RUN THIS HUGE TOBACCO PLANTATION I INHERITED!
FIFTY BUCKS A PIECE! YOW! IT'S A DEAL!
...ERR, OF COURSE, I CAN'T PAY YOU YET, BUT THERE ISN'T ANYTHING TO WORRY ABOUT! AS SOON AS I TAKE OVER THE PLANTATION I'LL BE WORTH MILLIONS!
DAT'S OKAY, BOGUS! WE TRUST YA! YER DA ONLY GUY WE KNOW WHAT ALWAYS TREATS US SQUARE!
A FEW DAYS LATER...
WELL, WE'RE ALMOST THERE, BOYS! I CAN'T WAIT TO SEE THE PLACE! I BET IT'S OVER 50 ROOMS AN' THOUSANDS OF ACRES OF BEAUTIFUL GOLDEN TOBACCO LEAVES! I CAN JUST PICTURE THE HUGE WHITE PILLARS AN'...
YEAH! YOU SURE ARE LUCKY, BOGUS!
BOOZEBORO 5 MILES
HMMM! THIS IS THE PLACE ALL RIGHT... BUT... BUT... BUT..
THAT GOLDEN TOBACCO YOU MENTIONED LOOKS MORE LIKE GOLDEN MUD!
OMIGOSH! DON'T TELL ME DAT'S TH' BIG WHITE PLANTATION HOUSE YOU WUZ YAPPIN' ABOUT!
BOGUS ACRES
ULP!
HUGE WHITE PILLARS! HAH! WHAT A LAUGH! I AIN'T NEVER SEEN SUCH A CRUMMY DUMP! JUST LOOKIN' AT IT GIVES ME DA CREEPS! I SAY WE HEAD BACK HOME!
BOGUS MANOR
ERR... YES! BUT I HAVEN'T ANY MONEY LEFT FOR GAS, OIL AND FOOD! WE'LL JUST HAVE TO STAY HERE UNTIL I ARRANGE TO SELL THE PLACE! THERE MUST BE SOME SUCKER WHO'LL GIVE ME A PALTRY FEW HUNDRED FOR THE JOINT,...THEN I CAN PAY YOU GUYS AND WE CAN LEAVE!
YOU MEAN WE'RE GONNA LIVE IN THAT FLEA-BITTEN, FIRE TRAP!

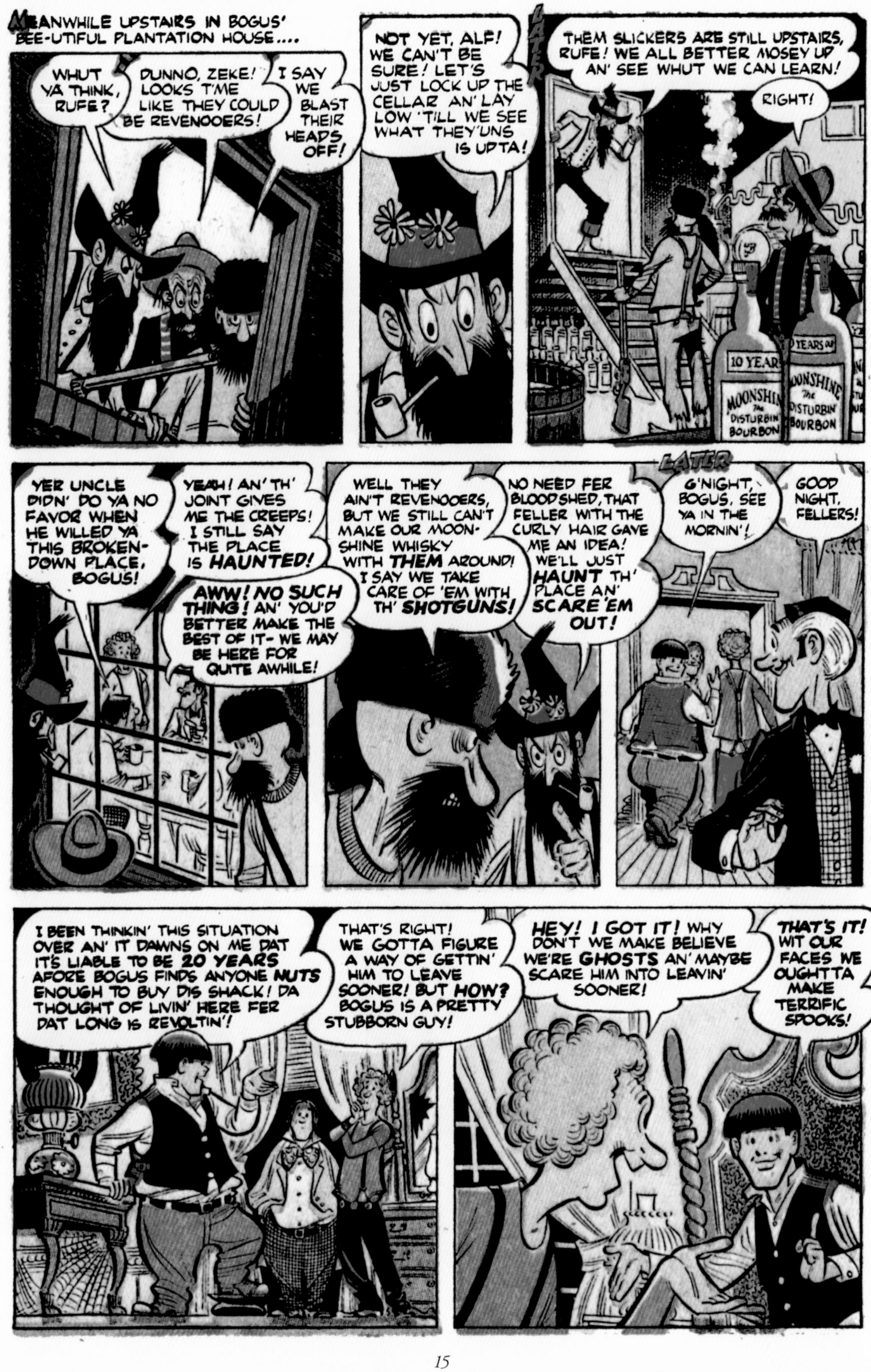
MEANWHILE UPSTAIRS IN BOGUS' BEE-UTIFUL PLANTATION HOUSE....
WHUT YA THINK, RUFE?
DUNNO, ZEKE! LOOKS T'ME LIKE THEY COULD BE REVENOOERS!
I SAY WE BLAST THEIR HEADS OFF!
NOT YET, ALF! WE CAN'T BE SURE! LET'S JUST LOCK UP THE CELLAR AN' LAY LOW 'TILL WE SEE WHAT THEY'UNS IS UPTA!
LATER
THEM SLICKERS ARE STILL UPSTAIRS, RUFE! WE ALL BETTER MOSEY UP AN' SEE WHUT WE CAN LEARN!
RIGHT!
10 YEAR MOONSHINE The DISTURBIN' BOURBON
YEARS OLD MOONSHINE The DISTURBIN' BOURBON
YER UNCLE DIDN' DO YA NO FAVOR WHEN HE WILLED YA THIS BROKEN-DOWN PLACE, BOGUS!
YEAH! AN' TH' JOINT GIVES ME THE CREEPS! I STILL SAY THE PLACE IS HAUNTED!
AWW! NO SUCH THING! AN' YOU'D BETTER MAKE THE BEST OF IT- WE MAY BE HERE FOR QUITE AWHILE!
WELL THEY AIN'T REVENOOERS, BUT WE STILL CAN'T MAKE OUR MOON-SHINE WHISKY WITH THEM AROUND! I SAY WE TAKE CARE OF 'EM WITH TH' SHOTGUNS!
NO NEED FER BLOODSHED, THAT FELLER WITH THE CURLY HAIR GAVE ME AN IDEA! WE'LL JUST HAUNT TH' PLACE AN' SCARE 'EM OUT!
LATER
G'NIGHT, BOGUS, SEE YA IN THE MORNIN'!
GOOD NIGHT, FELLERS!
I BEEN THINKIN' THIS SITUATION OVER AN' IT DAWNS ON ME DAT IT'S LIABLE TO BE 20 YEARS AFORE BOGUS FINDS ANYONE NUTS ENOUGH TO BUY DIS SHACK! DA THOUGHT OF LIVIN' HERE FER DAT LONG IS REVOLTIN'!
THAT'S RIGHT! WE GOTTA FIGURE A WAY OF GETTIN' HIM TO LEAVE SOONER! BUT HOW? BOGUS IS A PRETTY STUBBORN GUY!
HEY! I GOT IT! WHY DON'T WE MAKE BELIEVE WE'RE GHOSTS AN' MAYBE SCARE HIM INTO LEAVIN' SOONER!
THAT'S IT! WIT OUR FACES WE OUGHTTA MAKE TERRIFIC SPOOKS!

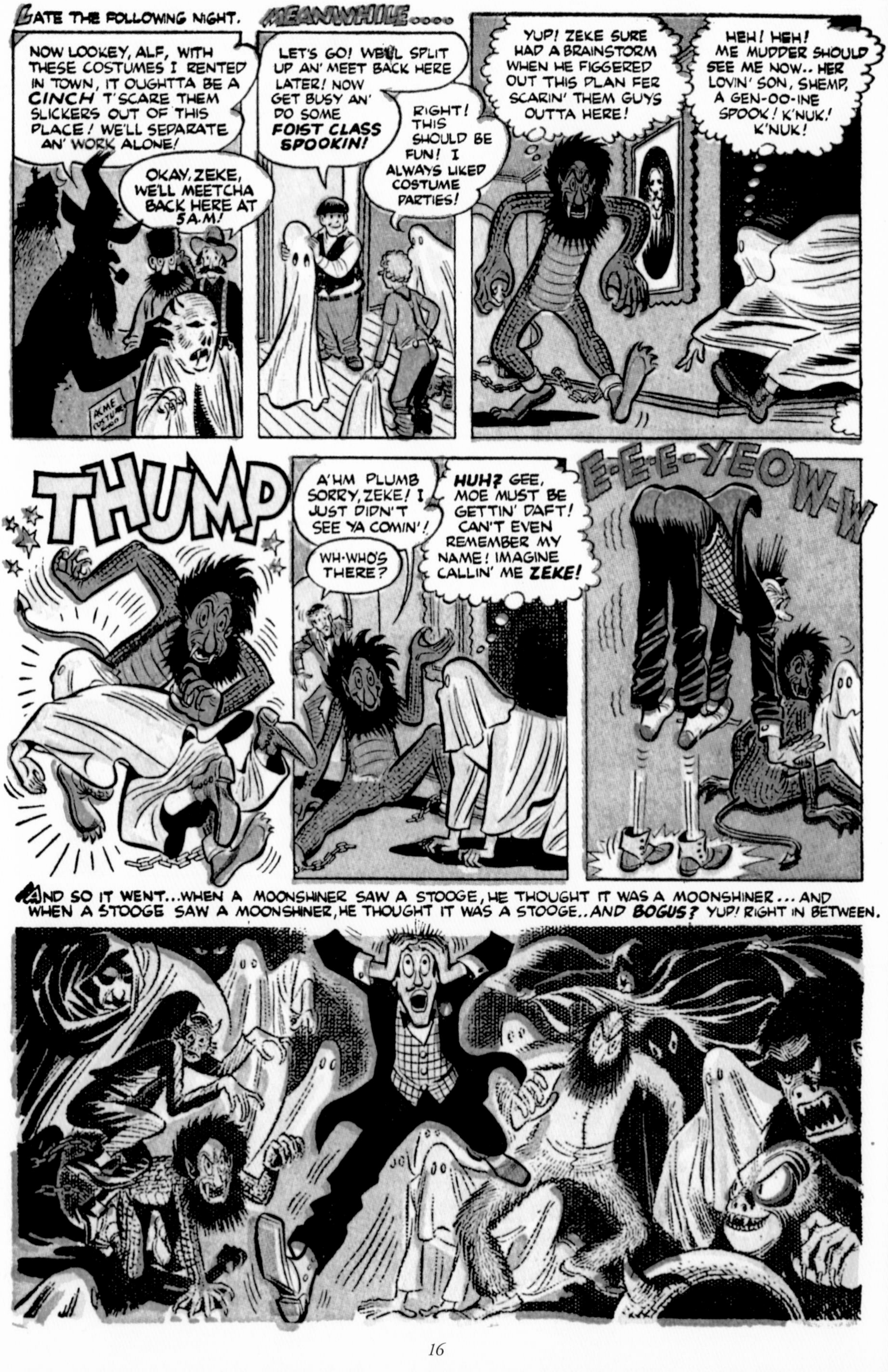
LATE THE FOLLOWING NIGHT.
NOW LOOKEY, ALF, WITH THESE COSTUMES I RENTED IN TOWN, IT OUGHTTA BE A CINCH T'SCARE THEM SLICKERS OUT OF THIS PLACE! WE'LL SEPARATE AN' WORK ALONE!
OKAY, ZEKE, WE'LL MEETCHA BACK HERE AT 5 A.M!
MEANWHILE....
LET'S GO! WE'LL SPLIT UP AN' MEET BACK HERE LATER! NOW GET BUSY AN' DO SOME FOIST CLASS SPOOKIN!
RIGHT! THIS SHOULD BE FUN! I ALWAYS LIKED COSTUME PARTIES!
YUP! ZEKE SURE HAD A BRAINSTORM WHEN HE FIGGERED OUT THIS PLAN FER SCARIN' THEM GUYS OUTTA HERE!
HEH! HEH! ME MUDDER SHOULD SEE ME NOW.. HER LOVIN' SON, SHEMP, A GEN-OO-INE SPOOK! K'NUK! K'NUK!
THUMP
A'HM PLUMB SORRY, ZEKE! I JUST DIDN'T SEE YA COMIN'!
WH-WHO'S THERE?
HUH? GEE, MOE MUST BE GETTIN' DAFT! CAN'T EVEN REMEMBER MY NAME! IMAGINE CALLIN' ME ZEKE!
E-E-E-YEOW-W
AND SO IT WENT...WHEN A MOONSHINER SAW A STOOGE, HE THOUGHT IT WAS A MOONSHINER... AND WHEN A STOOGE SAW A MOONSHINER, HE THOUGHT IT WAS A STOOGE.. AND BOGUS? YUP! RIGHT IN BETWEEN.

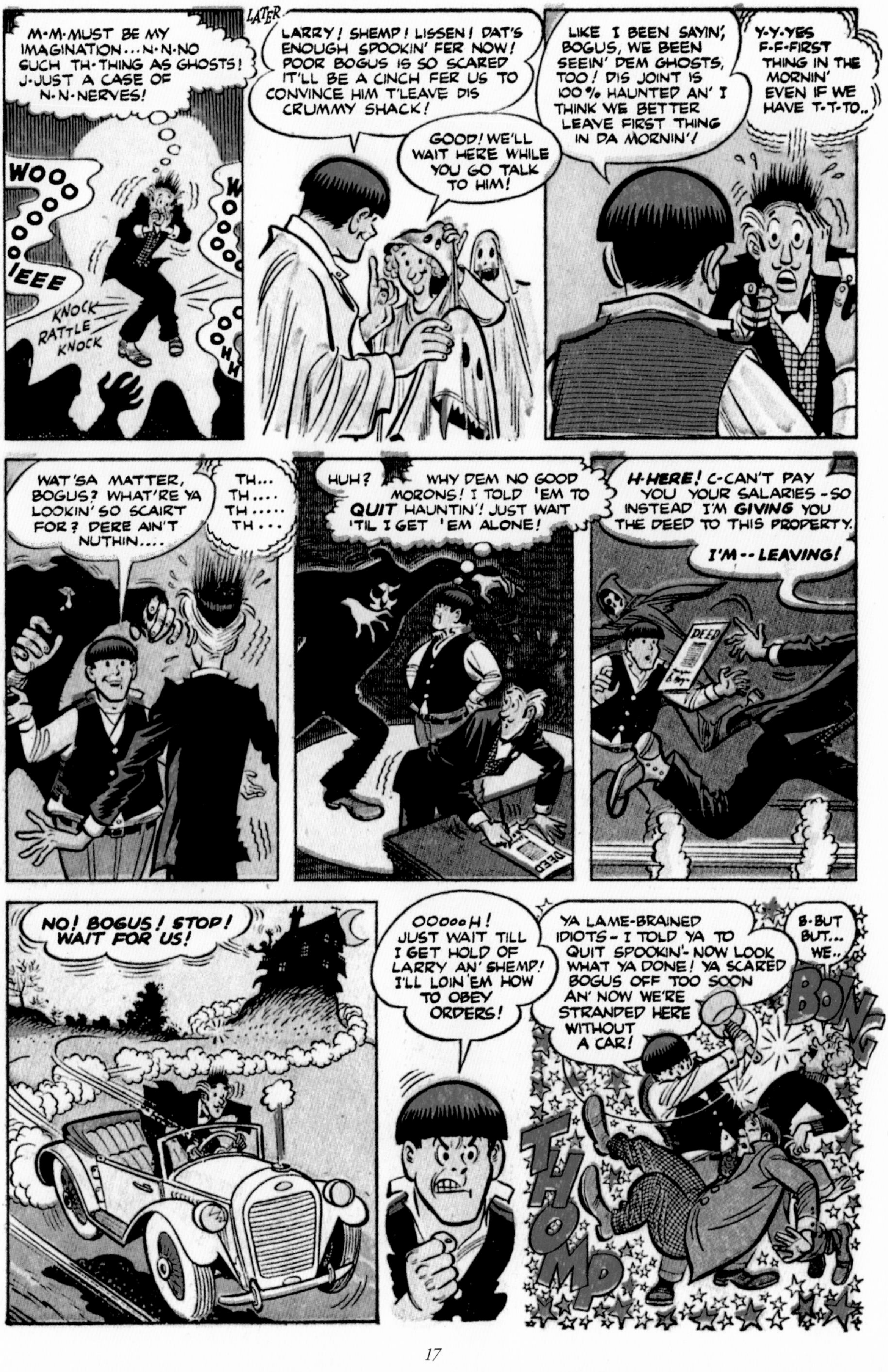
M-M-MUST BE MY IMAGINATION...N-N-NO SUCH TH-THING AS GHOSTS! J-JUST A CASE OF N-N-NERVES!
WOOOOOOOIEEE
WOOOOOOOHH
KNOCK RATTLE KNOCK
LATER
LARRY! SHEMP! LISSEN! DAT'S ENOUGH SPOOKIN' FER NOW! POOR BOGUS IS SO SCARED IT'LL BE A CINCH FER US TO CONVINCE HIM T'LEAVE DIS CRUMMY SHACK!
GOOD! WE'LL WAIT HERE WHILE YOU GO TALK TO HIM!
LIKE I BEEN SAYIN', BOGUS, WE BEEN SEEIN' DEM GHOSTS, TOO! DIS JOINT IS 100% HAUNTED AN' I THINK WE BETTER LEAVE FIRST THING IN DA MORNIN'!
Y-Y-YES F-F-FIRST THING IN THE MORNIN' EVEN IF WE HAVE T-T-TO..
WAT'SA MATTER, BOGUS? WHAT'RE YA LOOKIN' SO SCAIRT FOR? DERE AIN'T NUTHIN....
TH... TH.... TH..... TH...
HUH? WHY DEM NO GOOD MORONS! I TOLD 'EM TO QUIT HAUNTIN'! JUST WAIT 'TIL I GET 'EM ALONE!
DEED
H-HERE! C-CAN'T PAY YOU YOUR SALARIES - SO INSTEAD I'M GIVING YOU THE DEED TO THIS PROPERTY.
I'M -- LEAVING!
DEED
NO! BOGUS! STOP! WAIT FOR US!
OOOooH! JUST WAIT TILL I GET HOLD OF LARRY AN' SHEMP! I'LL LOIN 'EM HOW TO OBEY ORDERS!
YA LAME-BRAINED IDIOTS - I TOLD YA TO QUIT SPOOKIN' - NOW LOOK WHAT YA DONE! YA SCARED BOGUS OFF TOO SOON AN' NOW WE'RE STRANDED HERE WITHOUT A CAR!
B-BUT BUT... WE..
BONG
THOMP

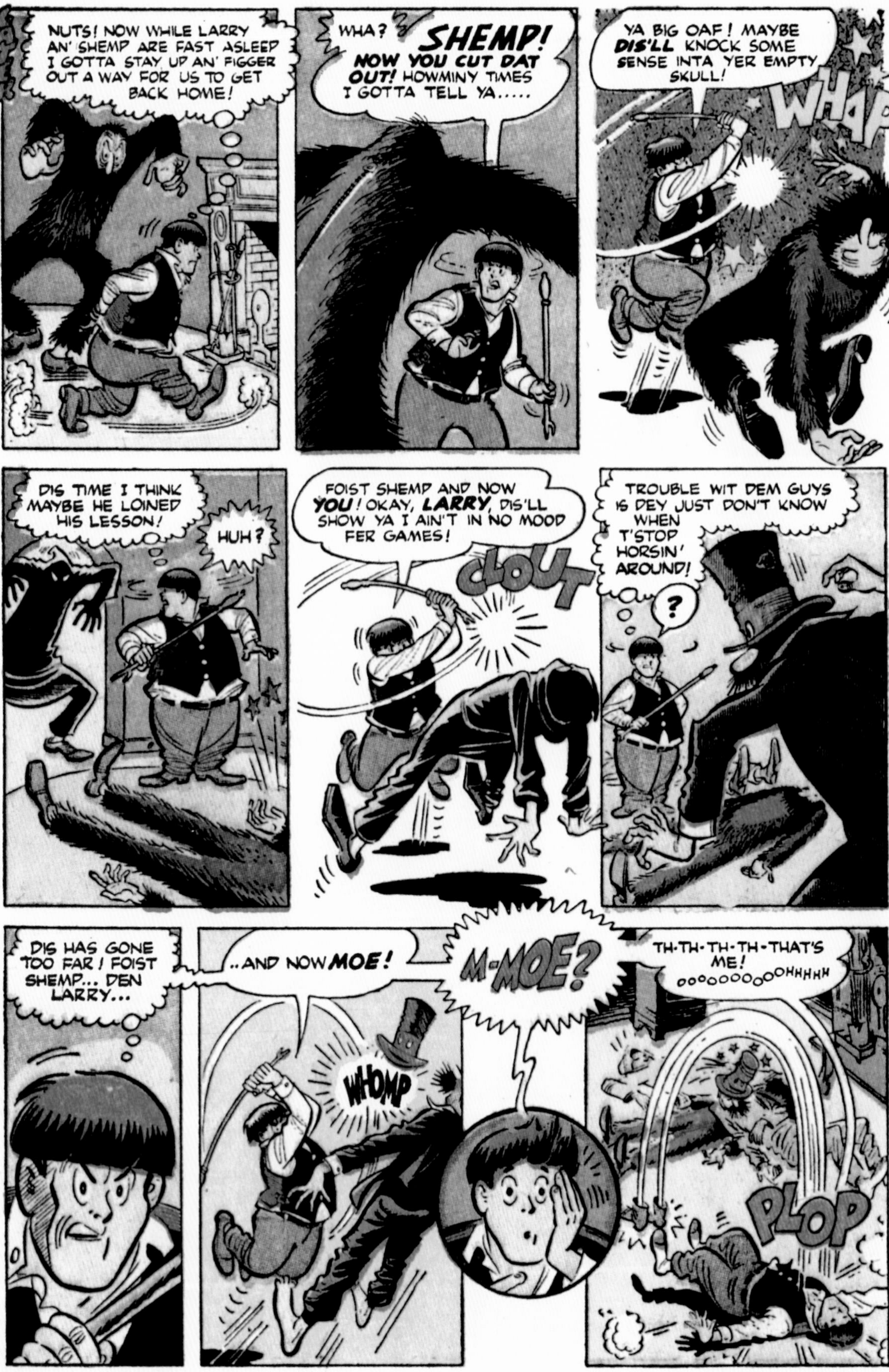
NUTS! NOW WHILE LARRY AN' SHEMP ARE FAST ASLEEP I GOTTA STAY UP AN' FIGGER OUT A WAY FOR US TO GET BACK HOME!
WHA?
SHEMP! NOW YOU CUT DAT OUT! HOWMINY TIMES I GOTTA TELL YA.....
YA BIG OAF! MAYBE DIS'LL KNOCK SOME SENSE INTA YER EMPTY SKULL!
WHAP
DIS TIME I THINK MAYBE HE LOINED HIS LESSON!
HUH?
FOIST SHEMP AND NOW YOU! OKAY, LARRY, DIS'LL SHOW YA I AIN'T IN NO MOOD FER GAMES!
CLOUT
TROUBLE WIT DEM GUYS IS DEY JUST DON'T KNOW WHEN T'STOP HORSIN' AROUND!
?
DIS HAS GONE TOO FAR! FOIST SHEMP... DEN LARRY...
..AND NOW MOE!
M-MOE?
WHOMP
TH-TH-TH-TH-THAT'S ME! OOOOOOOOOOHHHHHH
PLOP

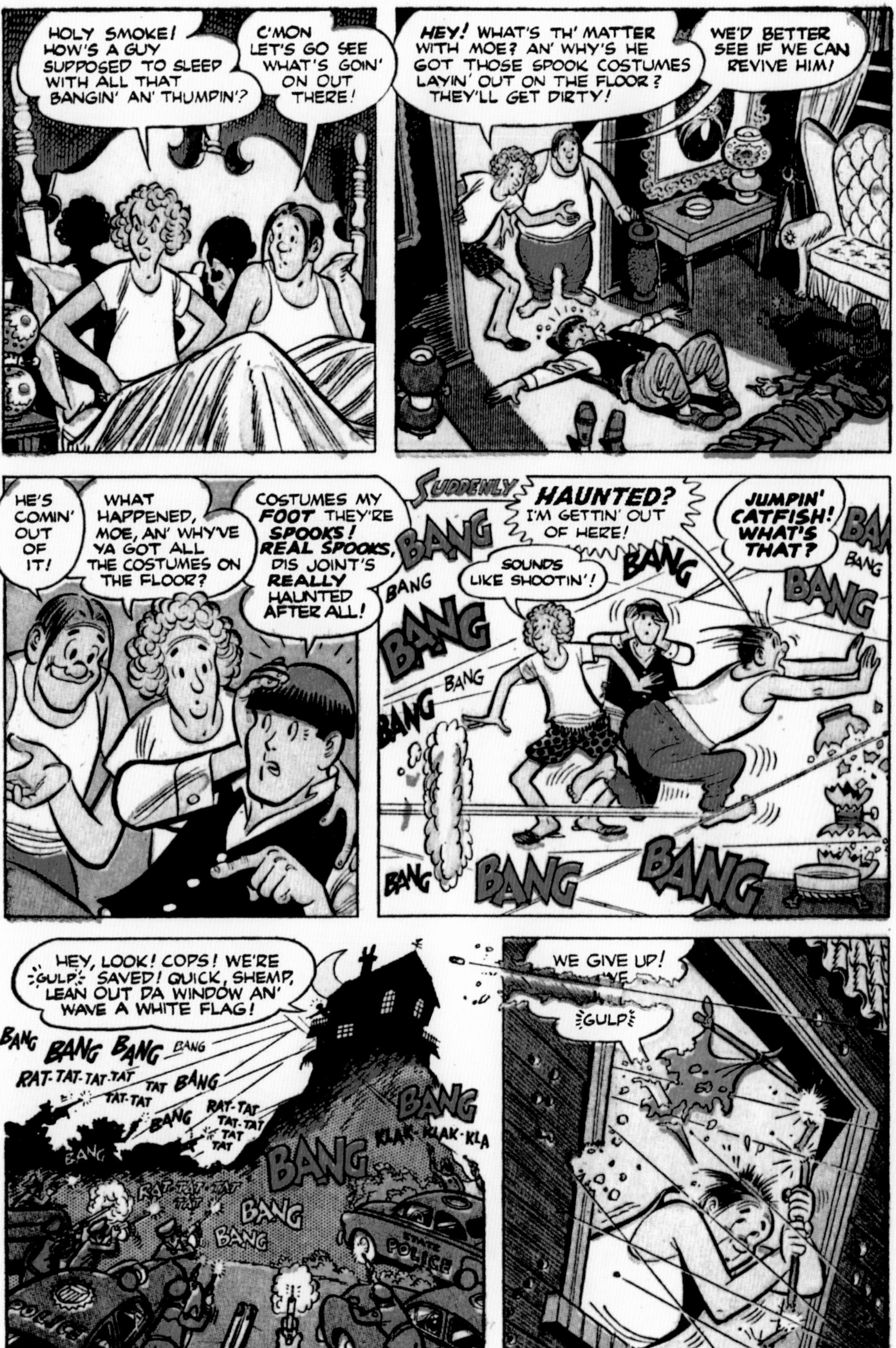
HOLY SMOKE! HOW'S A GUY SUPPOSED TO SLEEP WITH ALL THAT BANGIN' AN' THUMPIN'?
C'MON LET'S GO SEE WHAT'S GOIN' ON OUT THERE!
HEY! WHAT'S TH' MATTER WITH MOE? AN' WHY'S HE GOT THOSE SPOOK COSTUMES LAYIN' OUT ON THE FLOOR? THEY'LL GET DIRTY!
WE'D BETTER SEE IF WE CAN REVIVE HIM!
HE'S COMIN' OUT OF IT!
WHAT HAPPENED, MOE, AN' WHY'VE YA GOT ALL THE COSTUMES ON THE FLOOR?
COSTUMES MY FOOT THEY'RE SPOOKS! REAL SPOOKS, DIS JOINT'S REALLY HAUNTED AFTER ALL!
SUDDENLY
HAUNTED? I'M GETTIN' OUT OF HERE!
JUMPIN' CATFISH! WHAT'S THAT?
SOUNDS LIKE SHOOTIN'!
BANG BANG BANG BANG BANG BANG BANG BANG BANG BANG BANG
HEY, LOOK! COPS! WE'RE GULP SAVED! QUICK, SHEMP, LEAN OUT DA WINDOW AN' WAVE A WHITE FLAG!
BANG BANG BANG BANG
RAT-TAT-TAT-TAT TAT BANG
TAT-TAT
BANG
RAT-TAT TAT-TAT TAT TAT
BANG
BANG
KLAK-KLAK-KLA
BANG
BANG
BANG
BANG
STATE POLICE
WE GIVE UP! WE
GULP

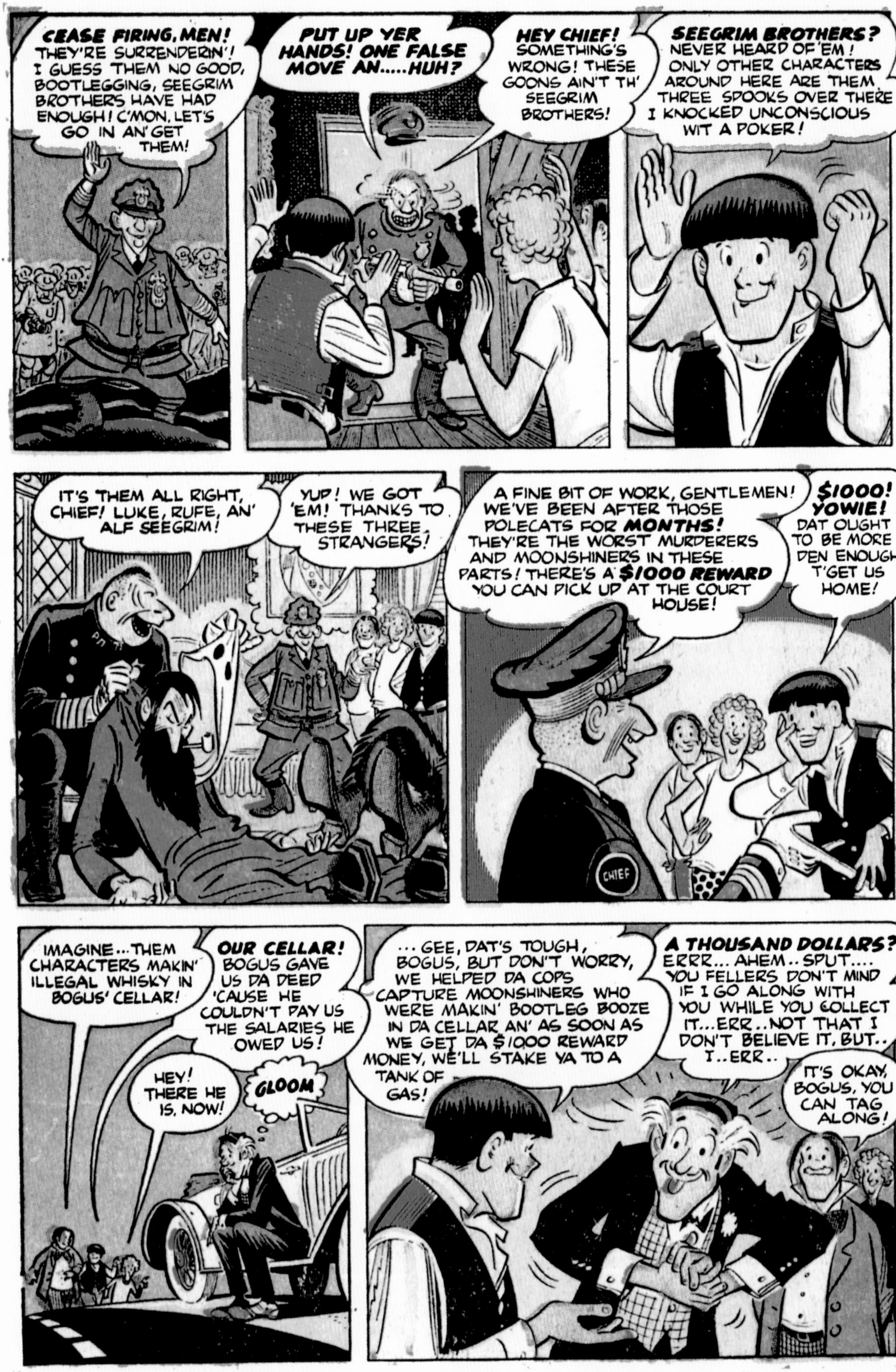
CEASE FIRING, MEN! THEY'RE SURRENDERIN'! I GUESS THEM NO GOOD, BOOTLEGGING, SEEGRIM BROTHERS HAVE HAD ENOUGH! C'MON, LET'S GO IN AN' GET THEM!
PUT UP YER HANDS! ONE FALSE MOVE AN.....HUH?
HEY CHIEF! SOMETHING'S WRONG! THESE GOONS AIN'T TH' SEEGRIM BROTHERS!
SEEGRIM BROTHERS? NEVER HEARD OF 'EM! ONLY OTHER CHARACTERS AROUND HERE ARE THEM THREE SPOOKS OVER THERE I KNOCKED UNCONSCIOUS WIT A POKER!
IT'S THEM ALL RIGHT, CHIEF! LUKE, RUFE, AN' ALF SEEGRIM!
YUP! WE GOT 'EM! THANKS TO THESE THREE STRANGERS!
A FINE BIT OF WORK, GENTLEMEN! WE'VE BEEN AFTER THOSE POLECATS FOR MONTHS! THEY'RE THE WORST MURDERERS AND MOONSHINERS IN THESE PARTS! THERE'S A $1000 REWARD YOU CAN PICK UP AT THE COURT HOUSE!
$1000! YOWIE! DAT OUGHT TO BE MORE DEN ENOUGH T'GET US HOME!
CHIEF
IMAGINE...THEM CHARACTERS MAKIN' ILLEGAL WHISKY IN BOGUS' CELLAR!
OUR CELLAR! BOGUS GAVE US DA DEED 'CAUSE HE COULDN'T PAY US THE SALARIES HE OWED US!
HEY! THERE HE IS, NOW!
GLOOM
... GEE, DAT'S TOUGH, BOGUS, BUT DON'T WORRY, WE HELPED DA COPS CAPTURE MOONSHINERS WHO WERE MAKIN' BOOTLEG BOOZE IN DA CELLAR AN' AS SOON AS WE GET DA $1000 REWARD MONEY, WE'LL STAKE YA TO A TANK OF GAS!
A THOUSAND DOLLARS? ERRR... AHEM.. SPUT.... YOU FELLERS DON'T MIND IF I GO ALONG WITH YOU WHILE YOU COLLECT IT...ERR..NOT THAT I DON'T BELIEVE IT, BUT.. I..ERR..
IT'S OKAY, BOGUS, YOU CAN TAG ALONG!

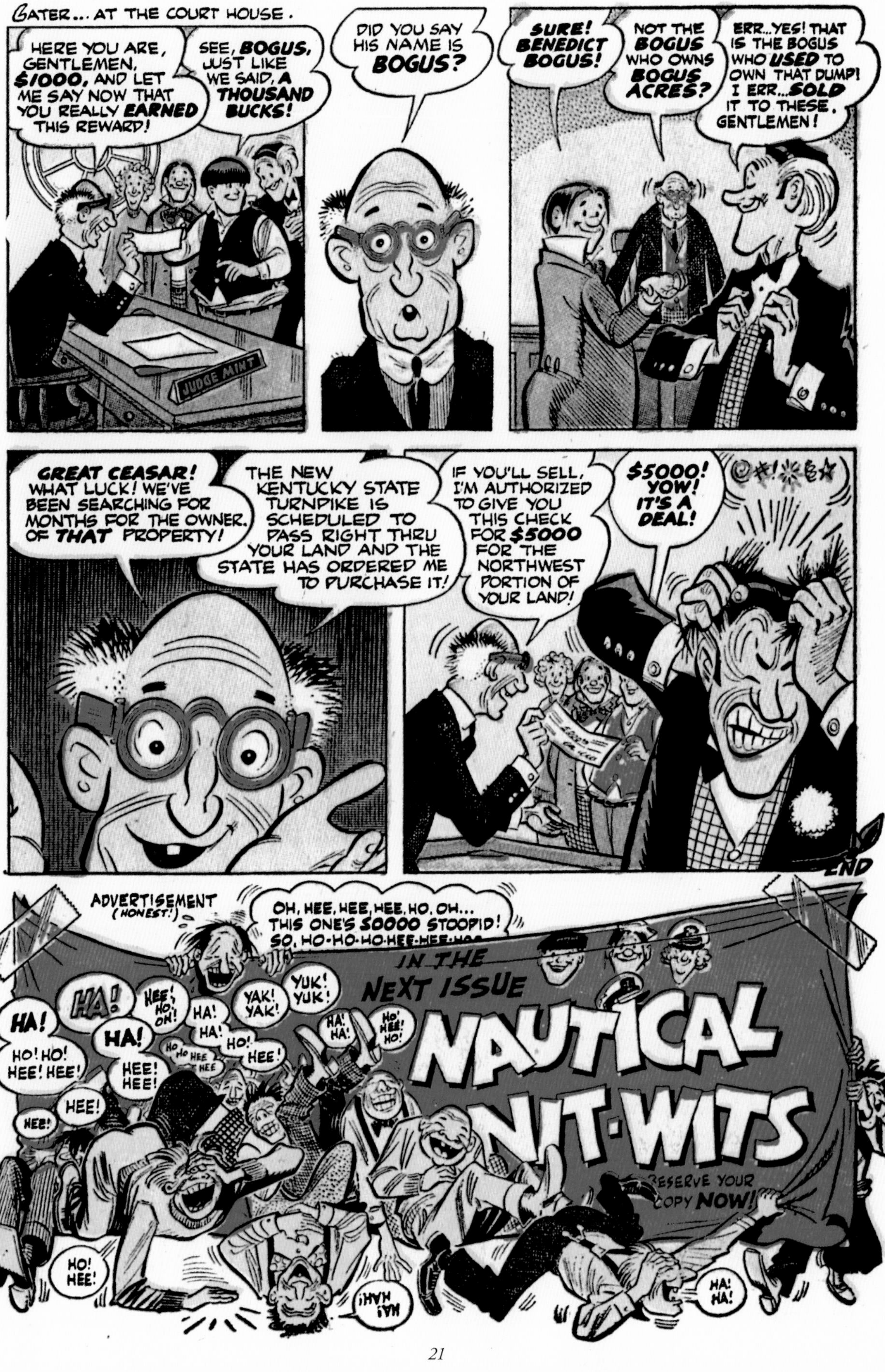
LATER... AT THE COURT HOUSE.
HERE YOU ARE, GENTLEMEN, $1000, AND LET ME SAY NOW THAT YOU REALLY EARNED THIS REWARD!
SEE, BOGUS, JUST LIKE WE SAID, A THOUSAND BUCKS!
JUDGE MINT
DID YOU SAY HIS NAME IS BOGUS?
SURE! BENEDICT BOGUS!
NOT THE BOGUS WHO OWNS BOGUS ACRES?
ERR...YES! THAT IS THE BOGUS WHO USED TO OWN THAT DUMP! I ERR...SOLD IT TO THESE. GENTLEMEN!
GREAT CEASAR! WHAT LUCK! WE'VE BEEN SEARCHING FOR MONTHS FOR THE OWNER. OF THAT PROPERTY!
THE NEW KENTUCKY STATE TURNPIKE IS SCHEDULED TO PASS RIGHT THRU YOUR LAND AND THE STATE HAS ORDERED ME TO PURCHASE IT!
IF YOU'LL SELL, I'M AUTHORIZED TO GIVE YOU THIS CHECK FOR $5000 FOR THE NORTHWEST PORTION OF YOUR LAND!
$5000! YOW! IT'S A DEAL!
END
ADVERTISEMENT (HONEST!)
OH, HEE, HEE, HEE, HO, OH... THIS ONE'S SOOOO STOOPID! SO, HO-HO-HO-HEE-HEE-HAR
HA!
HA!
HEE! HO, OH!
HA! HA!
YAK! YAK!
YUK! YUK!
HA! HA!
HO! HEE! HO!
HO! HO! HEE! HEE!
HA!
HO!
HEE!
HEE! HEE!
HEE!
HEE!
IN THE NEXT ISSUE
NAUTICAL NIT-WITS
RESERVE YOUR COPY NOW!
HO! HEE!
HA! HAH!
HA! HA!

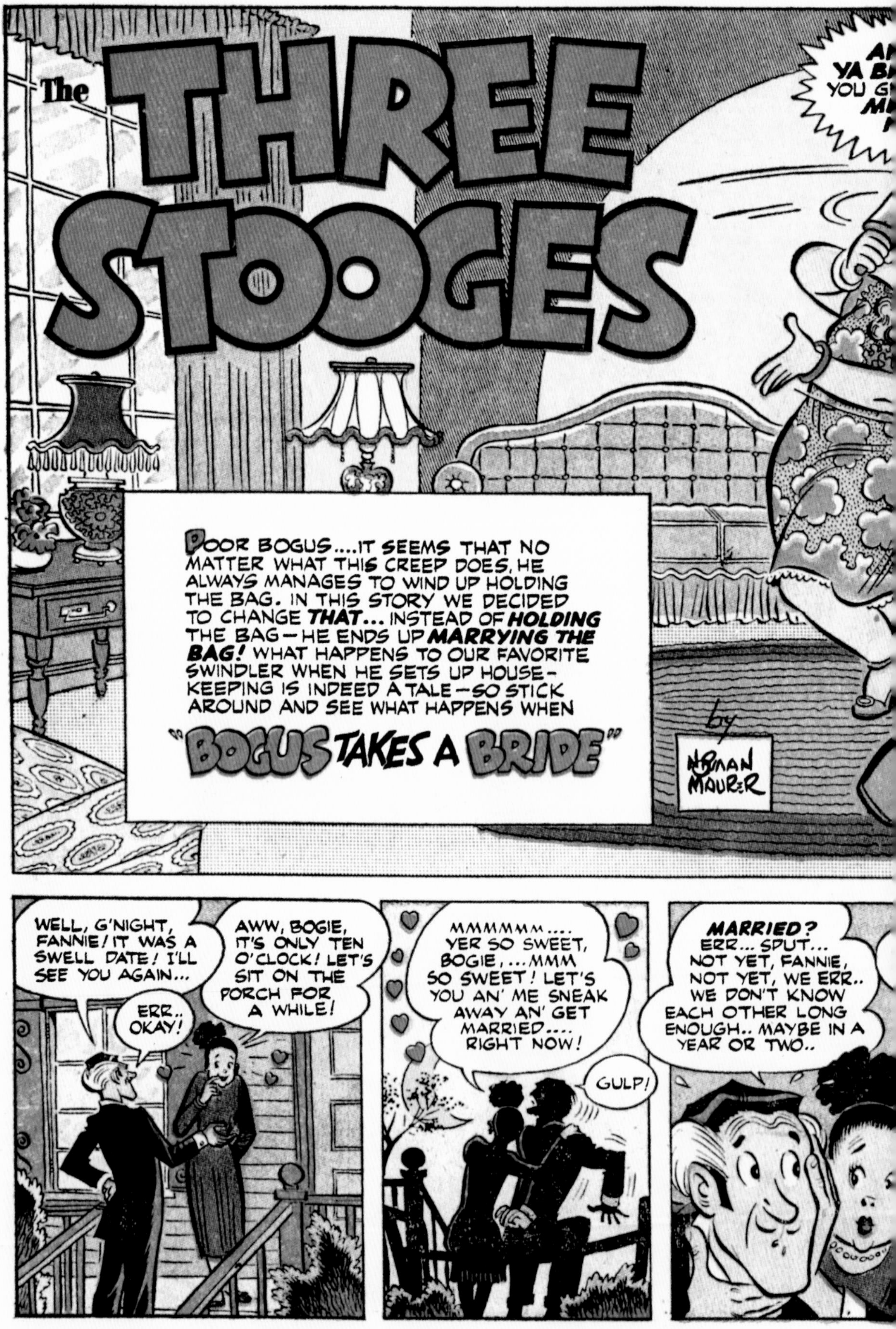
The THREE STOOGES
POOR BOGUS....IT SEEMS THAT NO MATTER WHAT THIS CREEP DOES, HE ALWAYS MANAGES TO WIND UP HOLDING THE BAG. IN THIS STORY WE DECIDED TO CHANGE THAT... INSTEAD OF HOLDING THE BAG—HE ENDS UP MARRYING THE BAG! WHAT HAPPENS TO OUR FAVORITE SWINDLER WHEN HE SETS UP HOUSE-KEEPING IS INDEED A TALE—SO STICK AROUND AND SEE WHAT HAPPENS WHEN
"BOGUS TAKES A BRIDE"
by NORMAN MAURER
WELL, G'NIGHT, FANNIE! IT WAS A SWELL DATE! I'LL SEE YOU AGAIN...
AWW, BOGIE, IT'S ONLY TEN O'CLOCK! LET'S SIT ON THE PORCH FOR A WHILE!
ERR.. OKAY!
MMMMMM.... YER SO SWEET, BOGIE, ...MMM SO SWEET! LET'S YOU AN' ME SNEAK AWAY AN' GET MARRIED.... RIGHT NOW!
GULP!
MARRIED? ERR... SPUT... NOT YET, FANNIE, NOT YET, WE ERR.. WE DON'T KNOW EACH OTHER LONG ENOUGH.. MAYBE IN A YEAR OR TWO..

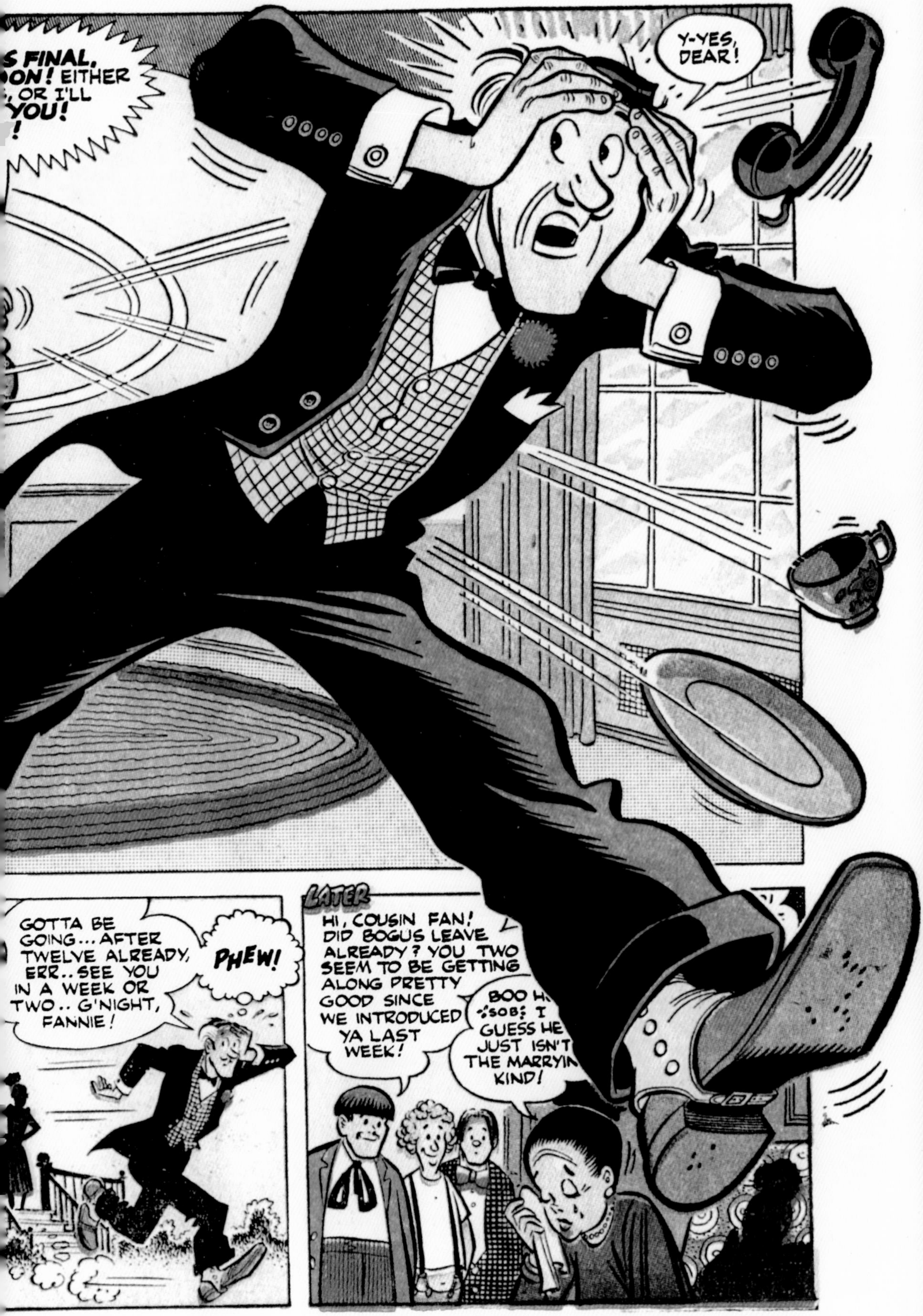

S FINAL, ON! EITHER , OR I'LL YOU! !
Y-YES, DEAR!
GOTTA BE GOING... AFTER TWELVE ALREADY, ERR.. SEE YOU IN A WEEK OR TWO.. G'NIGHT, FANNIE!
PHEW!
LATER
HI, COUSIN FAN! DID BOGUS LEAVE ALREADY? YOU TWO SEEM TO BE GETTING ALONG PRETTY GOOD SINCE WE INTRODUCED YA LAST WEEK!
BOO H SOB I GUESS HE JUST ISN'T THE MARRYIN KIND!

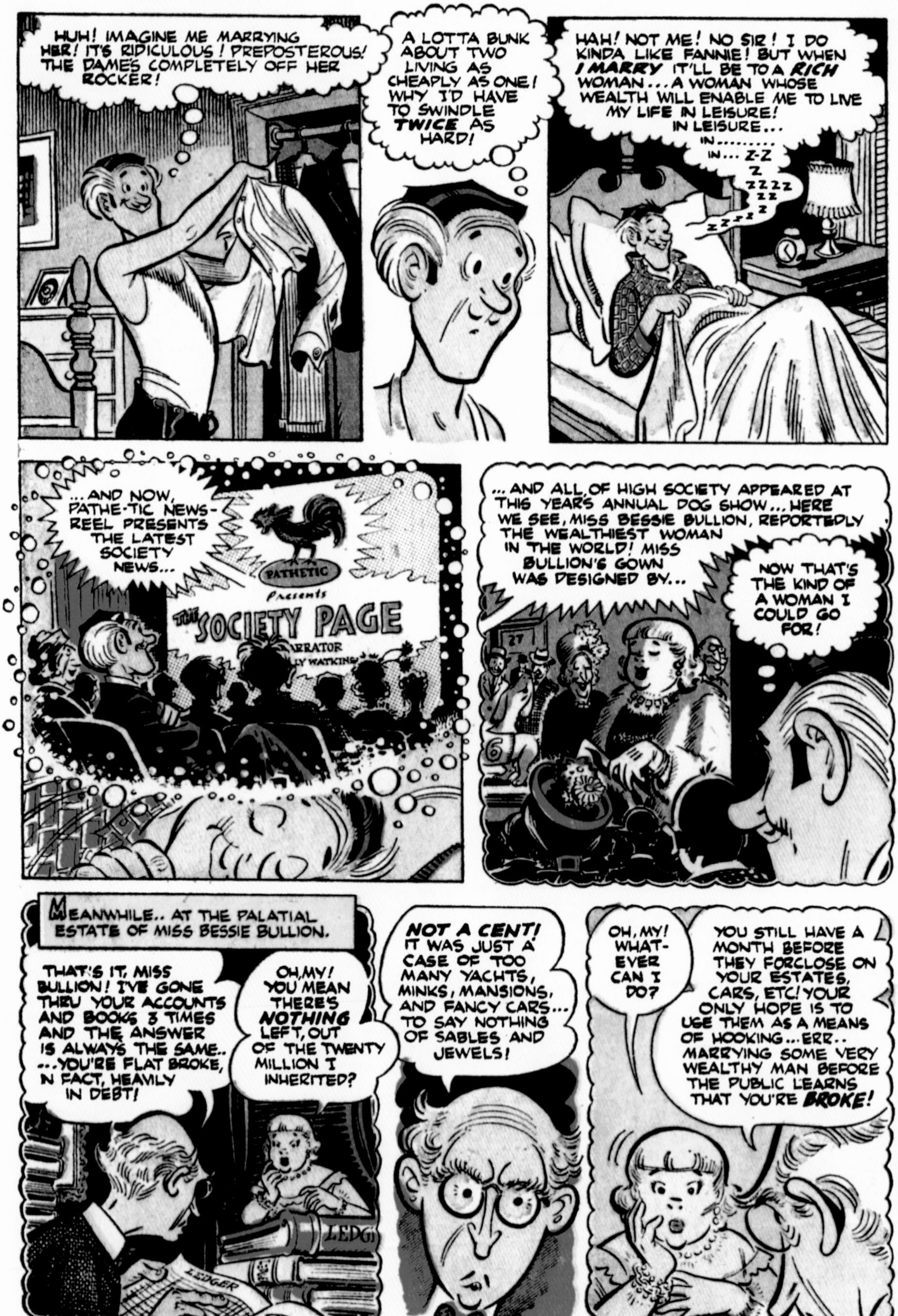
HUH! IMAGINE ME MARRYING HER! IT'S RIDICULOUS! PREPOSTEROUS! THE DAME'S COMPLETELY OFF HER ROCKER!
A LOTTA BUNK ABOUT TWO LIVING AS CHEAPLY AS ONE! WHY I'D HAVE TO SWINDLE TWICE AS HARD!
HAH! NOT ME! NO SIR! I DO KINDA LIKE FANNIE! BUT WHEN I MARRY IT'LL BE TO A RICH WOMAN... A WOMAN WHOSE WEALTH WILL ENABLE ME TO LIVE MY LIFE IN LEISURE! IN LEISURE... IN......... IN... Z-Z Z ZZZZ ZZ Z
ZZZZZ
...AND NOW, PATHE-TIC NEWS-REEL PRESENTS THE LATEST SOCIETY NEWS...
PATHETIC
Presents
THE SOCIETY PAGE
...AND ALL, OF HIGH SOCIETY APPEARED AT THIS YEAR'S ANNUAL DOG SHOW... HERE WE SEE, MISS BESSIE BULLION, REPORTEDLY THE WEALTHIEST WOMAN IN THE WORLD! MISS BULLION'S GOWN WAS DESIGNED BY...
NOW THAT'S THE KIND OF A WOMAN I COULD GO FOR!
27
6
MEANWHILE.. AT THE PALATIAL ESTATE OF MISS BESSIE BULLION.
THAT'S IT, MISS BULLION! I'VE GONE THRU YOUR ACCOUNTS AND BOOKS 3 TIMES AND THE ANSWER IS ALWAYS THE SAME.. ...YOU'RE FLAT BROKE, IN FACT, HEAVILY IN DEBT!
OH, MY! YOU MEAN THERE'S NOTHING LEFT, OUT OF THE TWENTY MILLION I INHERITED?
LEDGER
NOT A CENT! IT WAS JUST A CASE OF TOO MANY YACHTS, MINKS, MANSIONS, AND FANCY CARS... TO SAY NOTHING OF SABLES AND JEWELS!
OH, MY! WHAT-EVER CAN I DO?
YOU STILL HAVE A MONTH BEFORE THEY FORCLOSE ON YOUR ESTATES, CARS, ETC! YOUR ONLY HOPE IS TO USE THEM AS A MEANS OF HOOKING...ERR.. MARRYING SOME VERY WEALTHY MAN BEFORE THE PUBLIC LEARNS THAT YOU'RE BROKE!

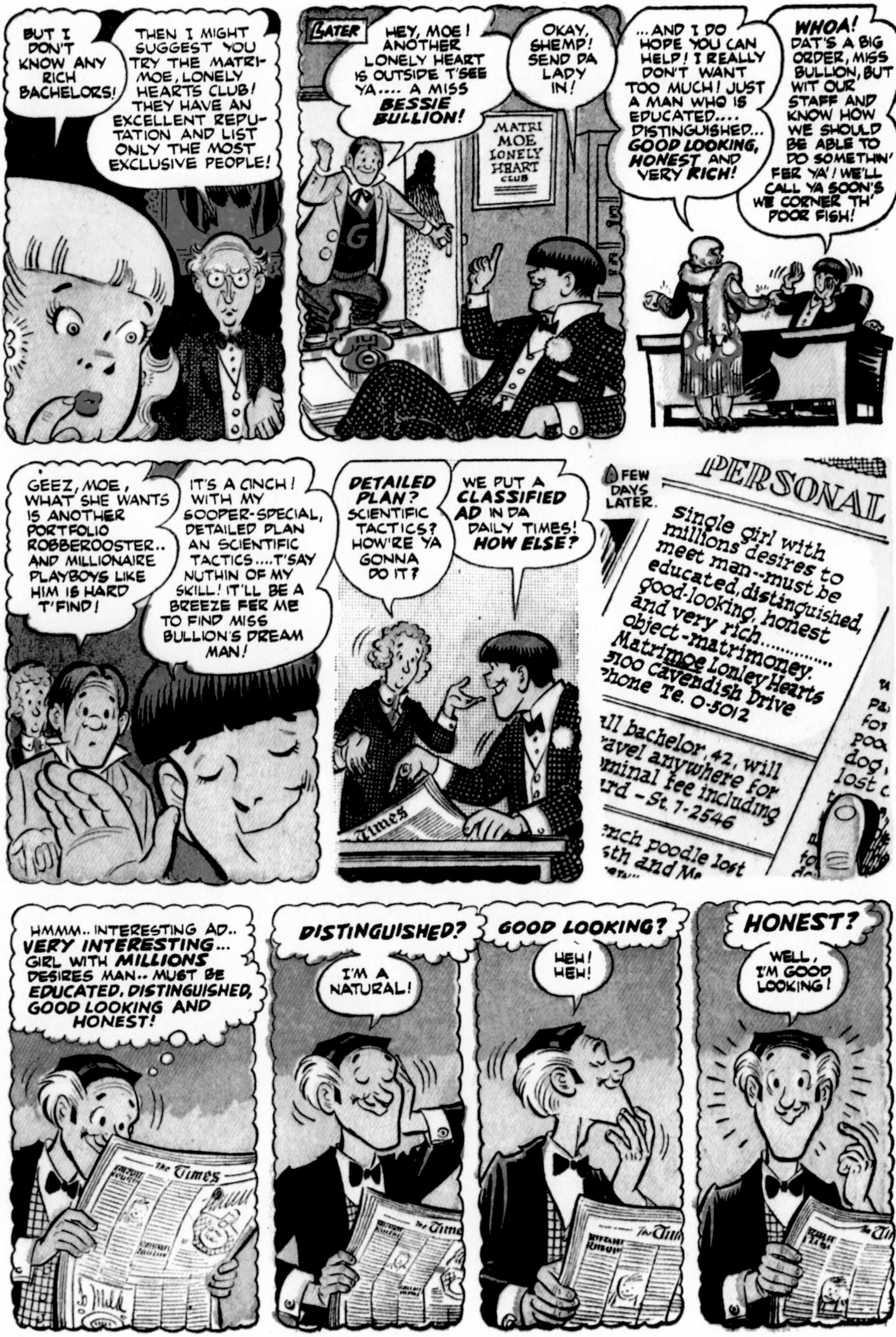
BUT I DON'T KNOW ANY RICH BACHELORS!
THEN I MIGHT SUGGEST YOU TRY THE MATRI-MOE, LONELY HEARTS CLUB! THEY HAVE AN EXCELLENT REPUTATION AND LIST ONLY THE MOST EXCLUSIVE PEOPLE!
LATER
HEY, MOE! ANOTHER LONELY HEART IS OUTSIDE T'SEE YA.... A MISS BESSIE BULLION!
OKAY, SHEMP! SEND DA LADY IN!
MATRI MOE LONELY HEART CLUB
...AND I DO HOPE YOU CAN HELP! I REALLY DON'T WANT TOO MUCH! JUST A MAN WHO IS EDUCATED.... DISTINGUISHED... GOOD LOOKING, HONEST AND VERY RICH!
WHOA! DAT'S A BIG ORDER, MISS BULLION, BUT WIT OUR STAFF AND KNOW HOW WE SHOULD BE ABLE TO DO SOMETHIN' FER YA'! WE'LL CALL YA SOON'S WE CORNER TH' POOR FISH!
GEEZ, MOE, WHAT SHE WANTS IS ANOTHER PORTFOLIO ROBBEROOSTER.. AND MILLIONAIRE PLAYBOYS LIKE HIM IS HARD T'FIND!
IT'S A CINCH! WITH MY SOOPER-SPECIAL, DETAILED PLAN AN SCIENTIFIC TACTICS....T'SAY NUTHIN OF MY SKILL! IT'LL BE A BREEZE FER ME TO FIND MISS BULLION'S DREAM MAN!
DETAILED PLAN? SCIENTIFIC TACTICS? HOW'RE YA GONNA DO IT?
WE PUT A CLASSIFIED AD IN DA DAILY TIMES! HOW ELSE?
Times
A FEW DAYS LATER.
PERSONAL
single girl with millions desires to meet man--must be educated, distinguished, good-looking, honest and very rich............ object-matrimoney. Matrimoe Lonley Hearts 5100 Cavendish Drive Phone Te. 0-5012
ll bachelor, 42, will ravel anywhere for minal fee including rd – St. 7-2546
nch poodle lost sth and Ma
HMMM.. INTERESTING AD.. VERY INTERESTING... GIRL WITH MILLIONS DESIRES MAN.. MUST BE EDUCATED, DISTINGUISHED, GOOD LOOKING AND HONEST!
The Times
DISTINGUISHED?
I'M A NATURAL!
GOOD LOOKING?
HEH! HEH!
HONEST?
WELL, I'M GOOD LOOKING!

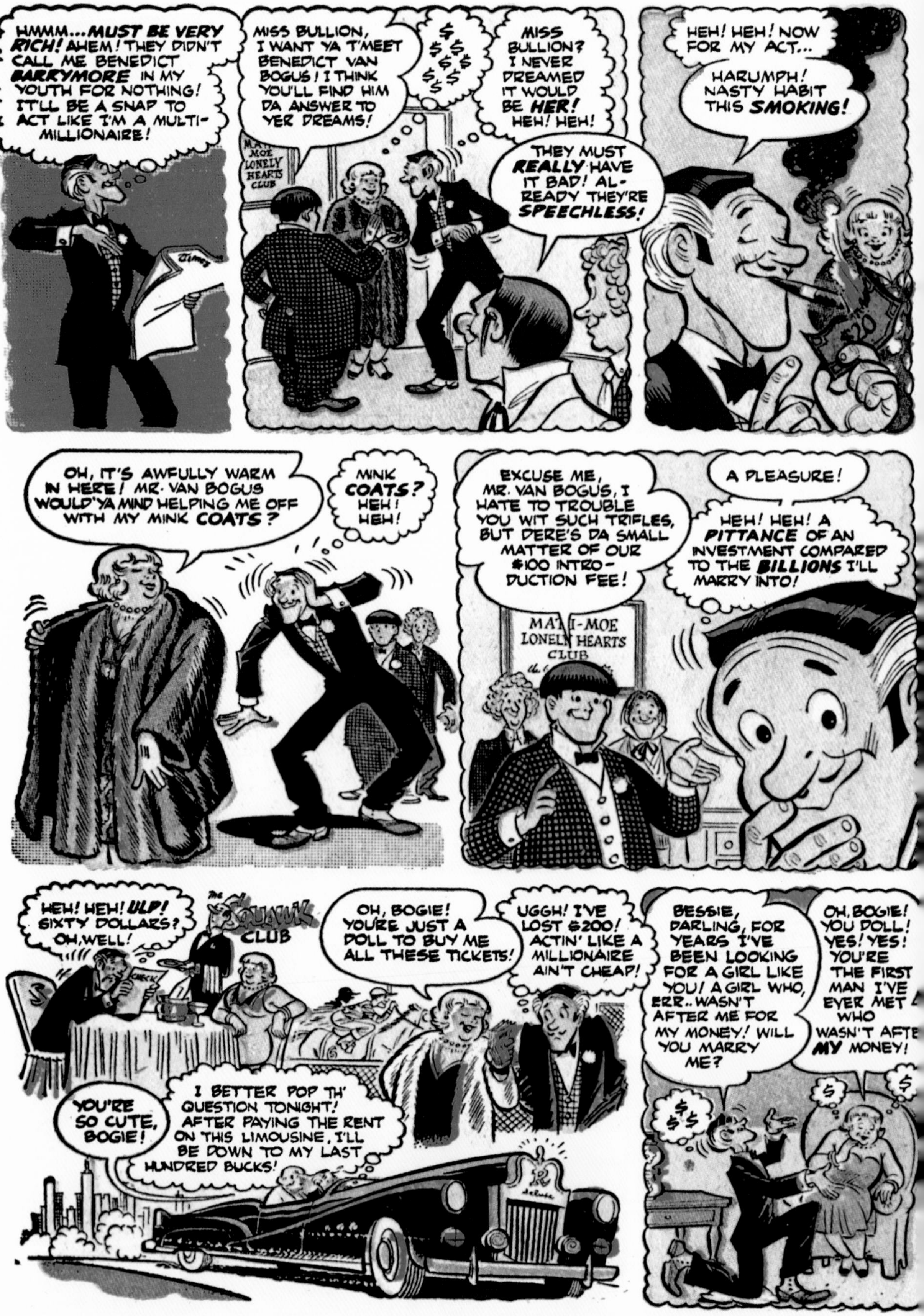
HMMM... MUST BE VERY RICH! AHEM! THEY DIDN'T CALL ME BENEDICT BARRYMORE IN MY YOUTH FOR NOTHING! IT'LL BE A SNAP TO ACT LIKE I'M A MULTI-MILLIONAIRE!
MISS BULLION, I WANT YA T'MEET BENEDICT VAN BOGUS! I THINK YOU'LL FIND HIM DA ANSWER TO YER DREAMS!
$ $ $ $ $ $ $ $
MISS BULLION? I NEVER DREAMED IT WOULD BE HER! HEH! HEH!
MATI-MOE LONELY HEARTS CLUB
THEY MUST REALLY HAVE IT BAD! AL-READY THEY'RE SPEECHLESS!
HEH! HEH! NOW FOR MY ACT...
HARUMPH! NASTY HABIT THIS SMOKING!
OH, IT'S AWFULLY WARM IN HERE! MR. VAN BOGUS WOULD'YA MIND HELPING ME OFF WITH MY MINK COATS?
MINK COATS? HEH! HEH!
EXCUSE ME, MR. VAN BOGUS, I HATE TO TROUBLE YOU WIT SUCH TRIFLES, BUT DERE'S DA SMALL MATTER OF OUR $100 INTRO-DUCTION FEE!
A PLEASURE!
HEH! HEH! A PITTANCE OF AN INVESTMENT COMPARED TO THE BILLIONS I'LL MARRY INTO!
MATI-MOE LONELY HEARTS CLUB
HEH! HEH! ULP! SIXTY DOLLARS? OH, WELL!
THE SQUAWK CLUB
CHECK
OH, BOGIE! YOU'RE JUST A DOLL TO BUY ME ALL THESE TICKETS!
UGGH! I'VE LOST $200! ACTIN' LIKE A MILLIONAIRE AIN'T CHEAP!
YOU'RE SO CUTE, BOGIE!
I BETTER POP TH' QUESTION TONIGHT! AFTER PAYING THE RENT ON THIS LIMOUSINE, I'LL BE DOWN TO MY LAST HUNDRED BUCKS!
deluxe
BESSIE, DARLING, FOR YEARS I'VE BEEN LOOKING FOR A GIRL LIKE YOU! A GIRL WHO, ERR.. WASN'T AFTER ME FOR MY MONEY! WILL YOU MARRY ME?
OH, BOGIE! YOU DOLL! YES! YES! YOU'RE THE FIRST MAN I'VE EVER MET WHO WASN'T AFTE MY MONEY!
$ $ $
$
$

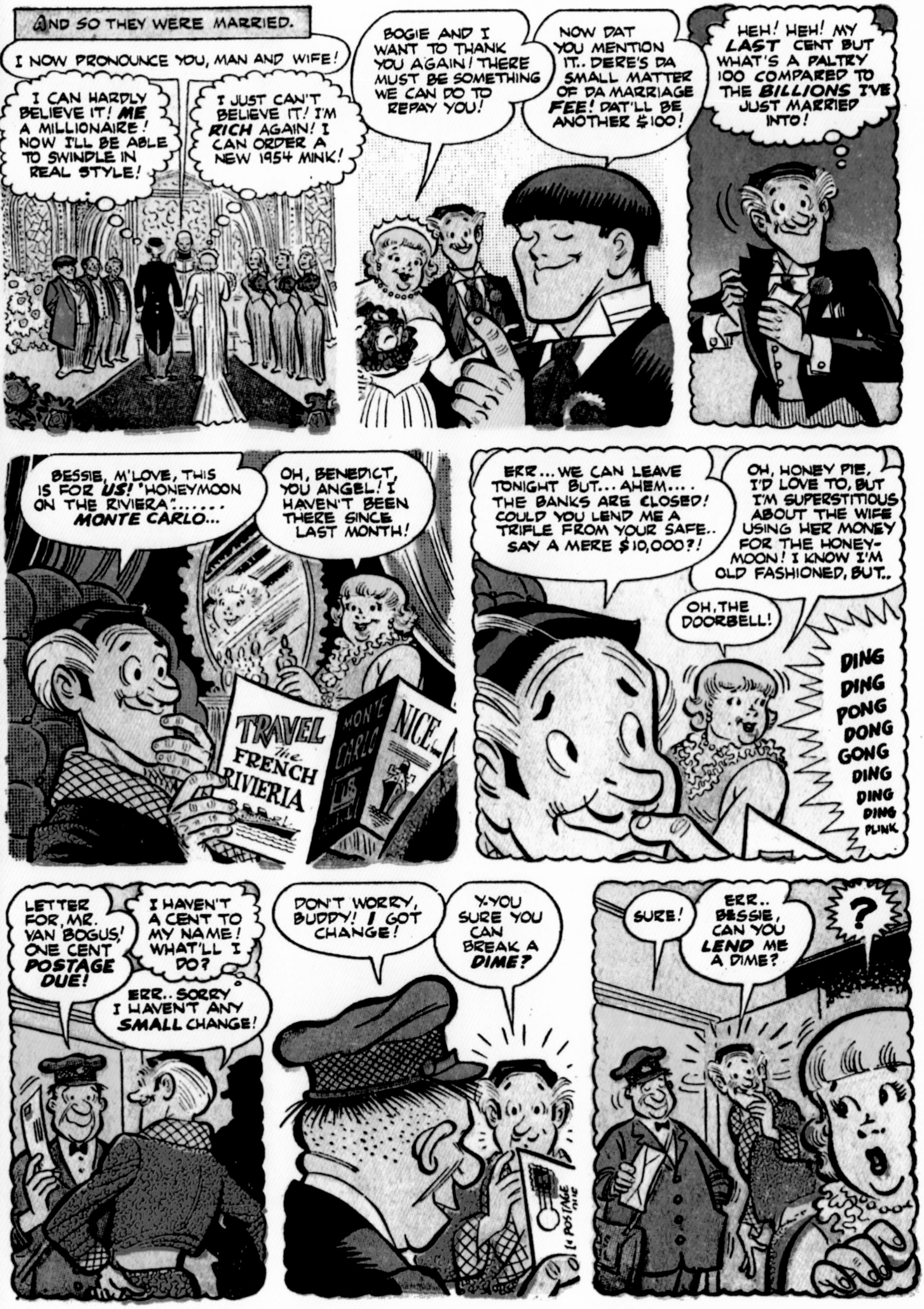
AND SO THEY WERE MARRIED.
I NOW PRONOUNCE YOU, MAN AND WIFE!
I CAN HARDLY BELIEVE IT! ME A MILLIONAIRE! NOW I'LL BE ABLE TO SWINDLE IN REAL STYLE!
I JUST CAN'T BELIEVE IT! I'M RICH AGAIN! I CAN ORDER A NEW 1954 MINK!
BOGIE AND I WANT TO THANK YOU AGAIN! THERE MUST BE SOMETHING WE CAN DO TO REPAY YOU!
NOW DAT YOU MENTION IT.. DERE'S DA SMALL MATTER OF DA MARRIAGE FEE! DAT'LL BE ANOTHER $100!
HEH! HEH! MY LAST CENT BUT WHAT'S A PALTRY 100 COMPARED TO THE BILLIONS I'VE JUST MARRIED INTO!
BESSIE, M'LOVE, THIS IS FOR US! 'HONEYMOON ON THE RIVIERA'...... MONTE CARLO...
OH, BENEDICT, YOU ANGEL! I HAVEN'T BEEN THERE SINCE LAST MONTH!
TRAVEL the FRENCH RIVIERA
MONTE CARLO
NICE
ERR... WE CAN LEAVE TONIGHT BUT... AHEM.... THE BANKS ARE CLOSED! COULD YOU LEND ME A TRIFLE FROM YOUR SAFE.. SAY A MERE $10,000?!
OH, HONEY PIE, I'D LOVE TO, BUT I'M SUPERSTITIOUS ABOUT THE WIFE USING HER MONEY FOR THE HONEY-MOON! I KNOW I'M OLD FASHIONED, BUT..
OH, THE DOORBELL!
DING DING PONG DONG GONG DING DING DING PLINK
LETTER FOR, MR. VAN BOGUS! ONE CENT POSTAGE DUE!
I HAVEN'T A CENT TO MY NAME! WHAT'LL I DO?
ERR.. SORRY I HAVENT ANY SMALL CHANGE!
DON'T WORRY, BUDDY! I GOT CHANGE!
Y-YOU SURE YOU CAN BREAK A DIME?
1¢ POSTAGE DUE
SURE!
ERR.. BESSIE, CAN YOU LEND ME A DIME?
?

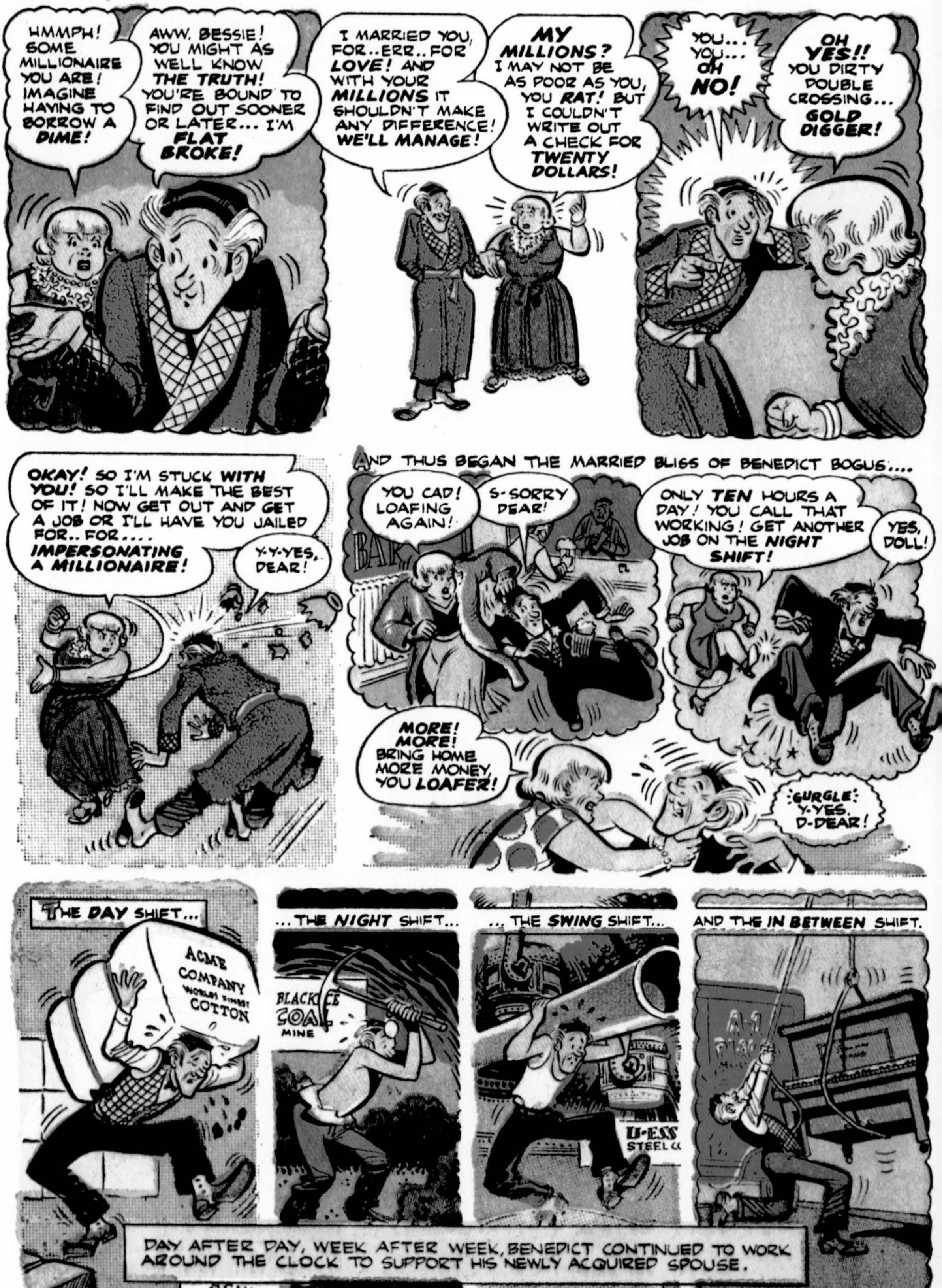
HMMPH! SOME MILLIONAIRE YOU ARE! IMAGINE HAVING TO BORROW A DIME!
AWW, BESSIE! YOU MIGHT AS WELL KNOW THE TRUTH! YOU'RE BOUND TO FIND OUT SOONER OR LATER... I'M FLAT BROKE!
I MARRIED YOU, FOR..ERR..FOR LOVE! AND WITH YOUR MILLIONS IT SHOULDN'T MAKE ANY DIFFERENCE! WE'LL MANAGE!
MY MILLIONS? I MAY NOT BE AS POOR AS YOU, YOU RAT! BUT I COULDN'T WRITE OUT A CHECK FOR TWENTY DOLLARS!
YOU... YOU... OH NO!
OH YES!! YOU DIRTY DOUBLE CROSSING... GOLD DIGGER!
OKAY! SO I'M STUCK WITH YOU! SO I'LL MAKE THE BEST OF IT! NOW GET OUT AND GET A JOB OR I'LL HAVE YOU JAILED FOR.. FOR.... IMPERSONATING A MILLIONAIRE!
Y-Y-YES, DEAR!
AND THUS BEGAN THE MARRIED BLISS OF BENEDICT BOGUS....
YOU CAD! LOAFING AGAIN!
S-SORRY DEAR!
BAR
ONLY TEN HOURS A DAY! YOU CALL THAT WORKING! GET ANOTHER JOB ON THE NIGHT SHIFT!
YES, DOLL!
MORE! MORE! BRING HOME MORE MONEY, YOU LOAFER!
GURGLE! Y-YES, D-DEAR!
THE DAY SHIFT...
ACME COMPANY WORLDS FINEST COTTON
... THE NIGHT SHIFT...
BLACK ICE COAL MINE
... THE SWING SHIFT...
U-ESS STEEL CO
AND THE IN BETWEEN SHIFT.
A-1 PIANO
DAY AFTER DAY, WEEK AFTER WEEK, BENEDICT CONTINUED TO WORK AROUND THE CLOCK TO SUPPORT HIS NEWLY ACQUIRED SPOUSE.
ACME CO..

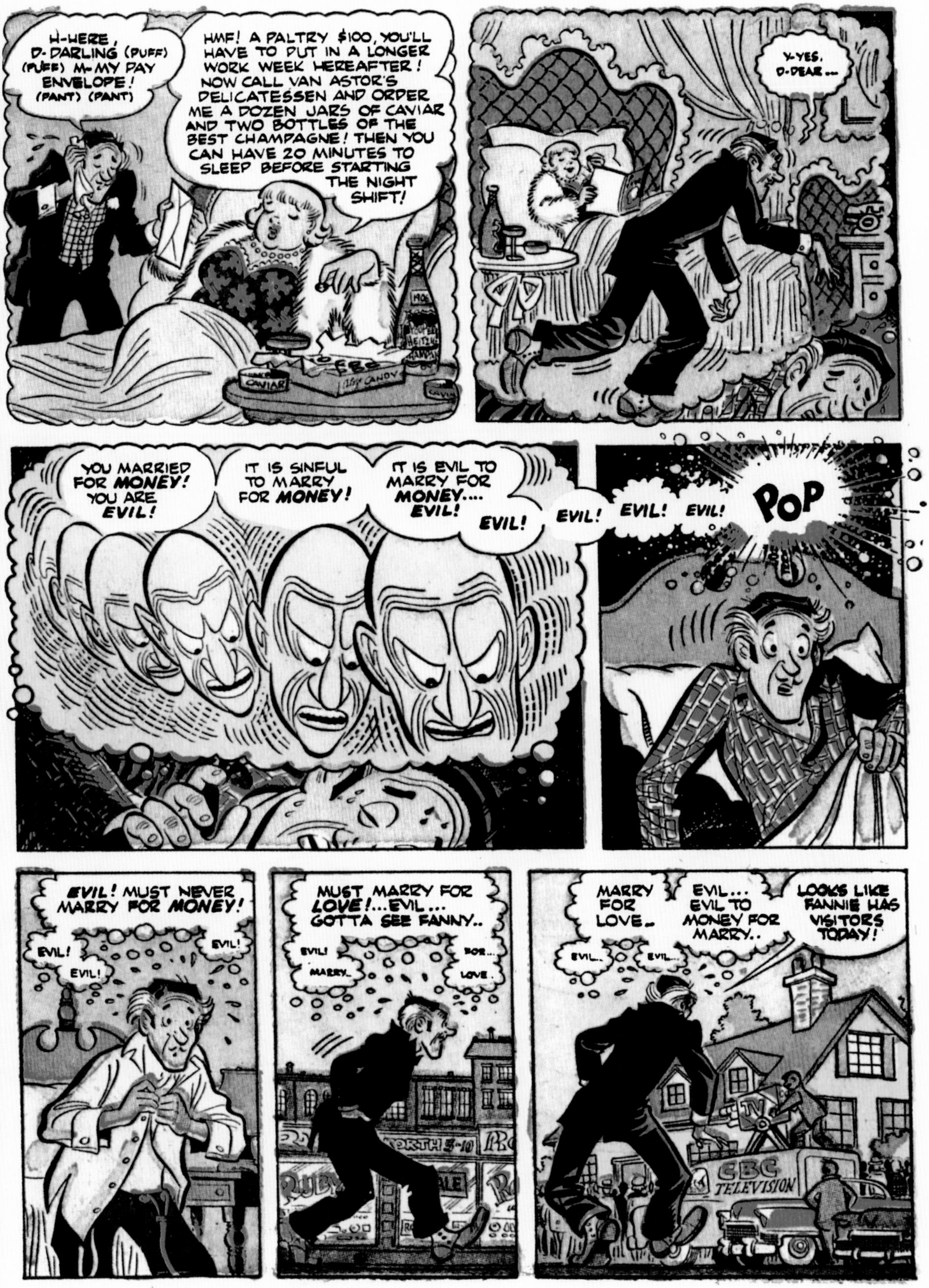
H-HERE, D-DARLING (PUFF) (PUFF) M-MY PAY ENVELOPE! (PANT) (PANT)
HMF! A PALTRY $100, YOU'LL HAVE TO PUT IN A LONGER WORK WEEK HEREAFTER! NOW CALL VAN ASTOR'S DELICATESSEN AND ORDER ME A DOZEN JARS OF CAVIAR AND TWO BOTTLES OF THE BEST CHAMPAGNE! THEN YOU CAN HAVE 20 MINUTES TO SLEEP BEFORE STARTING THE NIGHT SHIFT!
CAVIAR
CANDY
Y-YES, D-DEAR...
YOU MARRIED FOR MONEY! YOU ARE EVIL!
IT IS SINFUL TO MARRY FOR MONEY!
IT IS EVIL TO MARRY FOR MONEY.... EVIL!
EVIL!
EVIL!
EVIL!
EVIL!
POP
EVIL! MUST NEVER MARRY FOR MONEY!
EVIL!
EVIL!
EVIL!
MUST MARRY FOR LOVE!...EVIL... GOTTA SEE FANNY..
EVIL!
MARRY..
FOR...
LOVE.
MARRY FOR LOVE..
EVIL... EVIL TO MONEY FOR MARRY..
EVIL..
EVIL..
LOOKS LIKE FANNIE HAS VISITORS TODAY!
TV
CBC TELEVISION

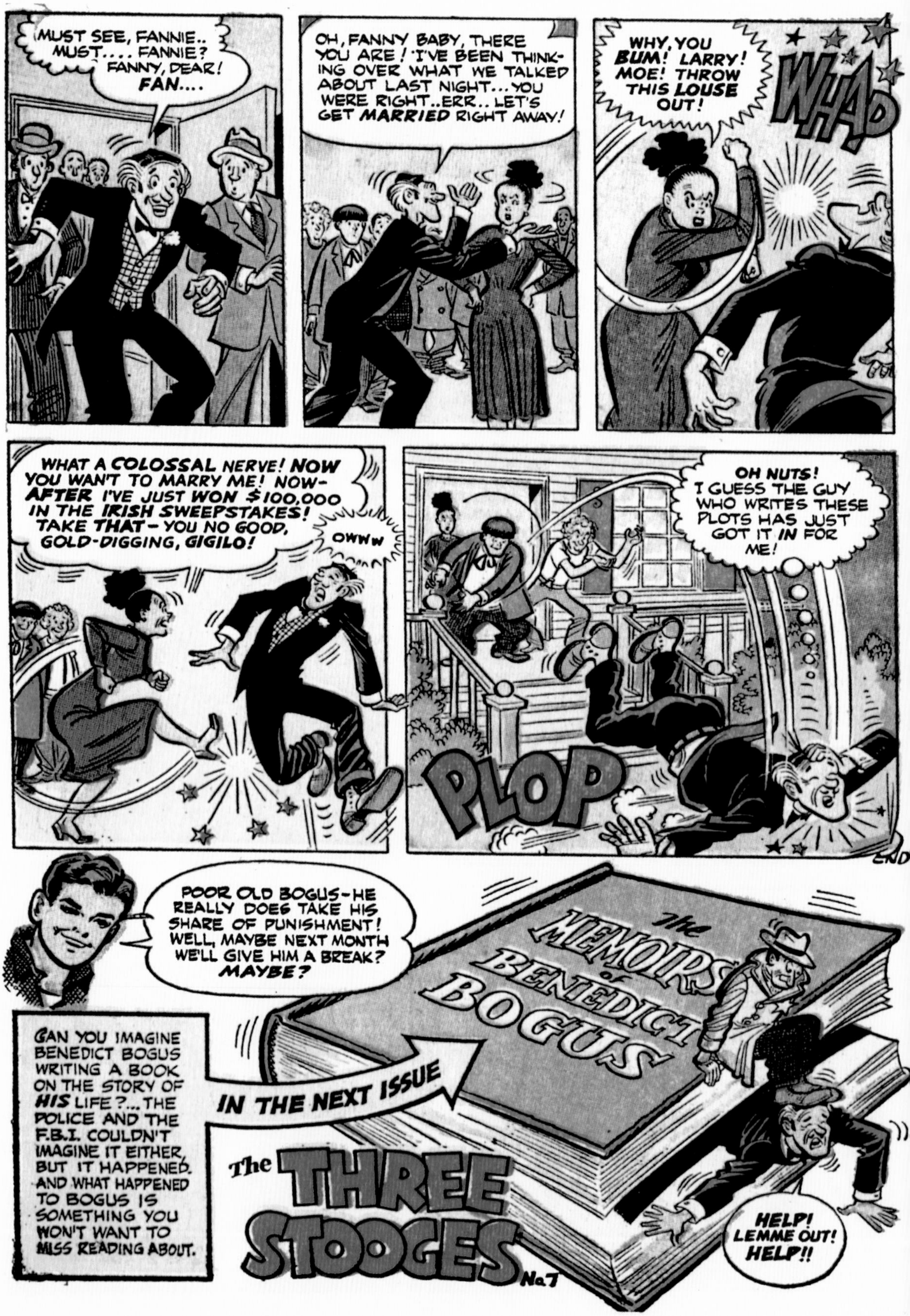
MUST SEE, FANNIE.. MUST.... FANNIE? FANNY, DEAR! FAN....
OH, FANNY BABY, THERE YOU ARE! I'VE BEEN THINKING OVER WHAT WE TALKED ABOUT LAST NIGHT... YOU WERE RIGHT..ERR.. LET'S GET MARRIED RIGHT AWAY!
WHY, YOU BUM! LARRY! MOE! THROW THIS LOUSE OUT!
WHAP
WHAT A COLOSSAL NERVE! NOW YOU WAN'T TO MARRY ME! NOW-AFTER I'VE JUST WON $100,000 IN THE IRISH SWEEPSTAKES! TAKE THAT-YOU NO GOOD, GOLD-DIGGING, GIGILO!
OWWW
OH NUTS! I GUESS THE GUY WHO WRITES THESE PLOTS HAS JUST GOT IT IN FOR ME!
PLOP
END
POOR OLD BOGUS-HE REALLY DOES TAKE HIS SHARE OF PUNISHMENT! WELL, MAYBE NEXT MONTH WE'LL GIVE HIM A BREAK? MAYBE?
The MEMOIRS of BENEDICT BOGUS
CAN YOU IMAGINE BENEDICT BOGUS WRITING A BOOK ON THE STORY OF HIS LIFE?... THE POLICE AND THE F.B.I. COULDN'T IMAGINE IT EITHER, BUT IT HAPPENED. AND WHAT HAPPENED TO BOGUS IS SOMETHING YOU WON'T WANT TO MISS READING ABOUT.
IN THE NEXT ISSUE
The THREE STOOGES No.7
HELP! LEMME OUT! HELP!!

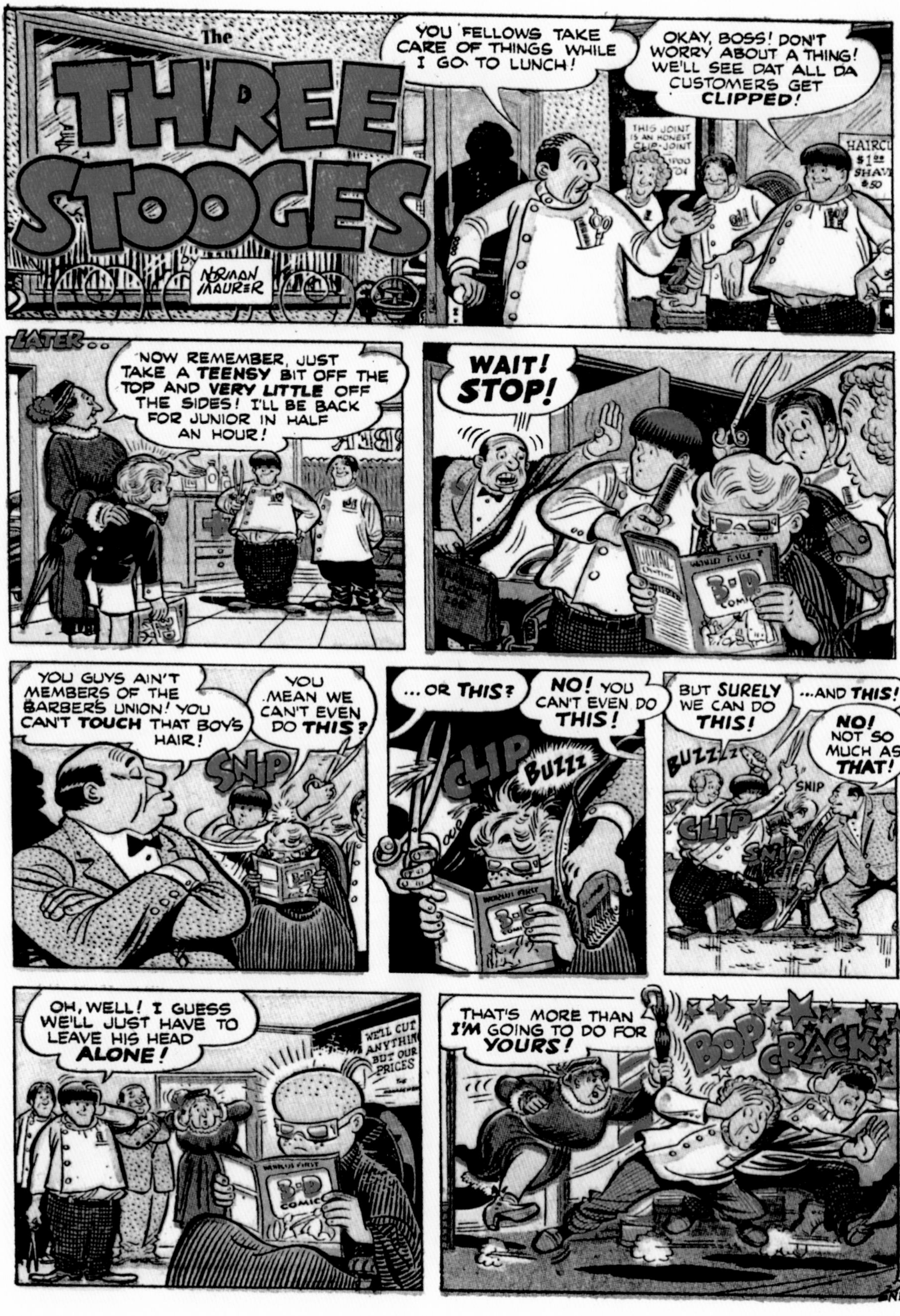
The THREE STOOGES
by NORMAN MAURER
YOU FELLOWS TAKE CARE OF THINGS WHILE I GO TO LUNCH!
OKAY, BOSS! DON'T WORRY ABOUT A THING! WE'LL SEE DAT ALL DA CUSTOMERS GET CLIPPED!
THIS JOINT IS AN HONEST CLIP-JOINT
HAIRCU $1.00 SHAVE $.50
LATER...
NOW REMEMBER, JUST TAKE A TEENSY BIT OFF THE TOP AND VERY LITTLE OFF THE SIDES! I'LL BE BACK FOR JUNIOR IN HALF AN HOUR!
WAIT! STOP!
YOU GUYS AIN'T MEMBERS OF THE BARBER'S UNION! YOU CAN'T TOUCH THAT BOY'S HAIR!
YOU MEAN WE CAN'T EVEN DO THIS?
SNIP
...OR THIS?
NO! YOU CAN'T EVEN DO THIS!
CLIP
BUZZZ
BUT SURELY WE CAN DO THIS!
...AND THIS!
NO! NOT SO MUCH AS THAT!
BUZZZZ
SNIP
CLIP
SNIP
OH, WELL! I GUESS WE'LL JUST HAVE TO LEAVE HIS HEAD ALONE!
WE'LL CUT ANYTHING BUT OUR PRICES
THAT'S MORE THAN I'M GOING TO DO FOR YOURS!
BOP
CRACK
END

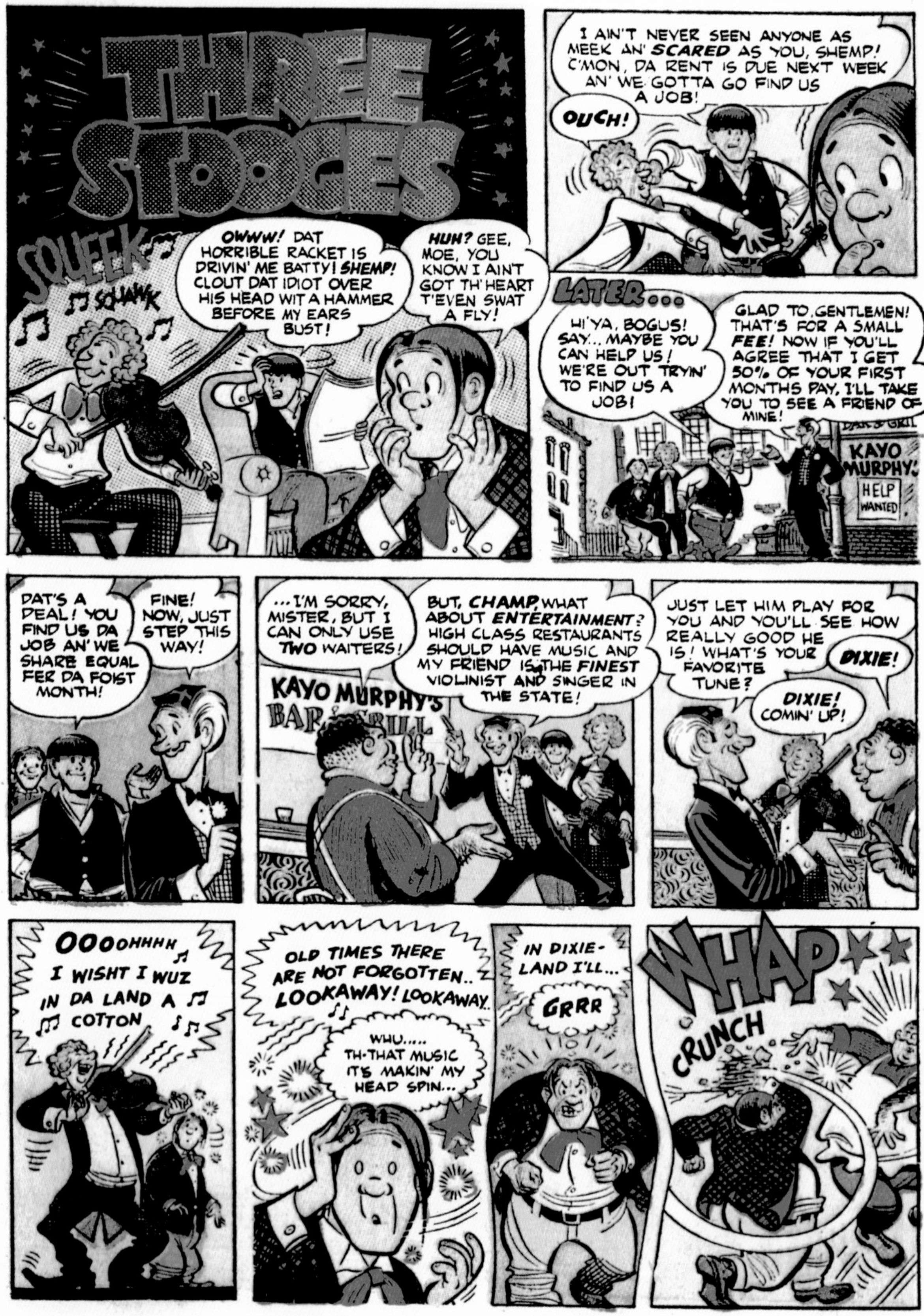
THREE STOOGES
SQUEEK
SQUAWK
OWWW! DAT HORRIBLE RACKET IS DRIVIN' ME BATTY! SHEMP! CLOUT DAT IDIOT OVER HIS HEAD WIT A HAMMER BEFORE MY EARS BUST!
HUH? GEE, MOE, YOU KNOW I AIN'T GOT TH' HEART T'EVEN SWAT A FLY!
I AIN'T NEVER SEEN ANYONE AS MEEK AN' SCARED AS YOU, SHEMP! C'MON, DA RENT IS DUE NEXT WEEK AN' WE GOTTA GO FIND US A JOB!
OUCH!
LATER...
HI'YA, BOGUS! SAY... MAYBE YOU CAN HELP US! WE'RE OUT TRYIN' TO FIND US A JOB!
GLAD TO, GENTLEMEN! THAT'S FOR A SMALL FEE! NOW IF YOU'LL AGREE THAT I GET 50% OF YOUR FIRST MONTHS PAY, I'LL TAKE YOU TO SEE A FRIEND OF MINE!
KAYO MURPHY'S
HELP WANTED
DAT'S A DEAL! YOU FIND US DA JOB AN' WE SHARE EQUAL FER DA FOIST MONTH!
FINE! NOW, JUST STEP THIS WAY!
...I'M SORRY, MISTER, BUT I CAN ONLY USE TWO WAITERS!
BUT, CHAMP, WHAT ABOUT ENTERTAINMENT? HIGH CLASS RESTAURANTS SHOULD HAVE MUSIC AND MY FRIEND IS THE FINEST VIOLINIST AND SINGER IN THE STATE!
KAYO MURPHY'S BAR & GRILL
JUST LET HIM PLAY FOR YOU AND YOU'LL SEE HOW REALLY GOOD HE IS! WHAT'S YOUR FAVORITE TUNE?
DIXIE!
DIXIE! COMIN' UP!
OOOOHHHH I WISHT I WUZ IN DA LAND A COTTON
OLD TIMES THERE ARE NOT FORGOTTEN.. LOOKAWAY! LOOKAWAY..
WHU..... TH-THAT MUSIC IT'S MAKIN' MY HEAD SPIN...
IN DIXIE-LAND I'LL...
GRRR
WHAP
CRUNCH

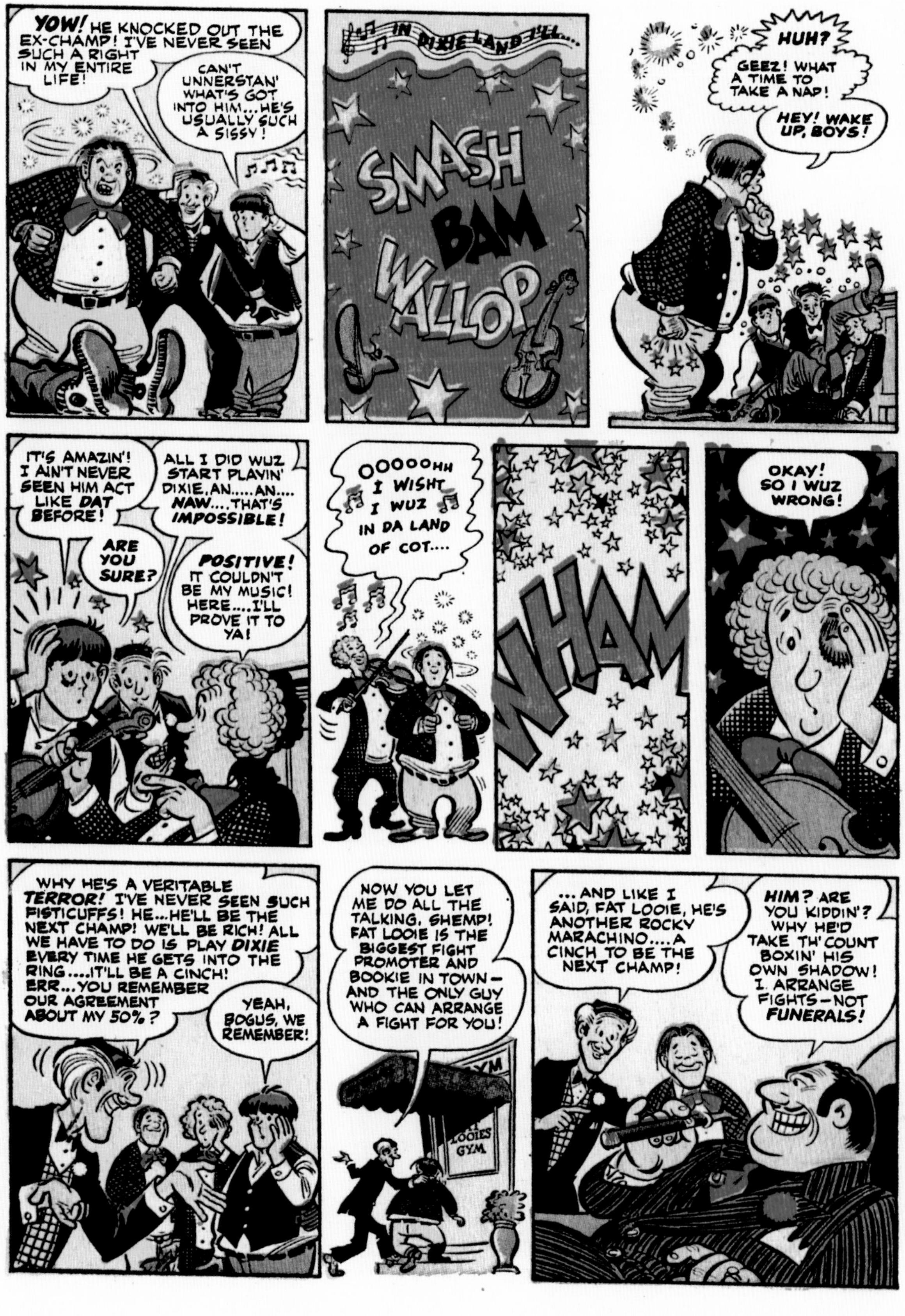
YOW! HE KNOCKED OUT THE EX-CHAMP! I'VE NEVER SEEN SUCH A RIGHT IN MY ENTIRE LIFE!
CAN'T UNNERSTAN' WHAT'S GOT INTO HIM... HE'S USUALLY SUCH A SISSY!
IN DIXIE LAND I'LL....
SMASH
BAM
WALLOP
HUH?
GEEZ! WHAT A TIME TO TAKE A NAP!
HEY! WAKE UP, BOYS!
IT'S AMAZIN'! I AIN'T NEVER SEEN HIM ACT LIKE DAT BEFORE!
ALL I DID WUZ START PLAYIN' DIXIE, AN.....AN.... NAW....THAT'S IMPOSSIBLE!
ARE YOU SURE?
POSITIVE! IT COULDN'T BE MY MUSIC! HERE....I'LL PROVE IT TO YA!
OOOOOHH I WISHT I WUZ IN DA LAND OF COT....
WHAM
OKAY! SO I WUZ WRONG!
WHY HE'S A VERITABLE TERROR! I'VE NEVER SEEN SUCH FISTICUFFS! HE...HE'LL BE THE NEXT CHAMP! WE'LL BE RICH! ALL WE HAVE TO DO IS PLAY DIXIE EVERY TIME HE GETS INTO THE RING....IT'LL BE A CINCH! ERR...YOU REMEMBER OUR AGREEMENT ABOUT MY 50%?
YEAH, BOGUS, WE REMEMBER!
NOW YOU LET ME DO ALL THE TALKING, SHEMP! FAT LOOIE IS THE BIGGEST FIGHT PROMOTER AND BOOKIE IN TOWN— AND THE ONLY GUY WHO CAN ARRANGE A FIGHT FOR YOU!
LOOIES GYM
...AND LIKE I SAID, FAT LOOIE, HE'S ANOTHER ROCKY MARACHINO....A CINCH TO BE THE NEXT CHAMP!
HIM? ARE YOU KIDDIN'? WHY HE'D TAKE TH' COUNT BOXIN' HIS OWN SHADOW! I ARRANGE FIGHTS—NOT FUNERALS!

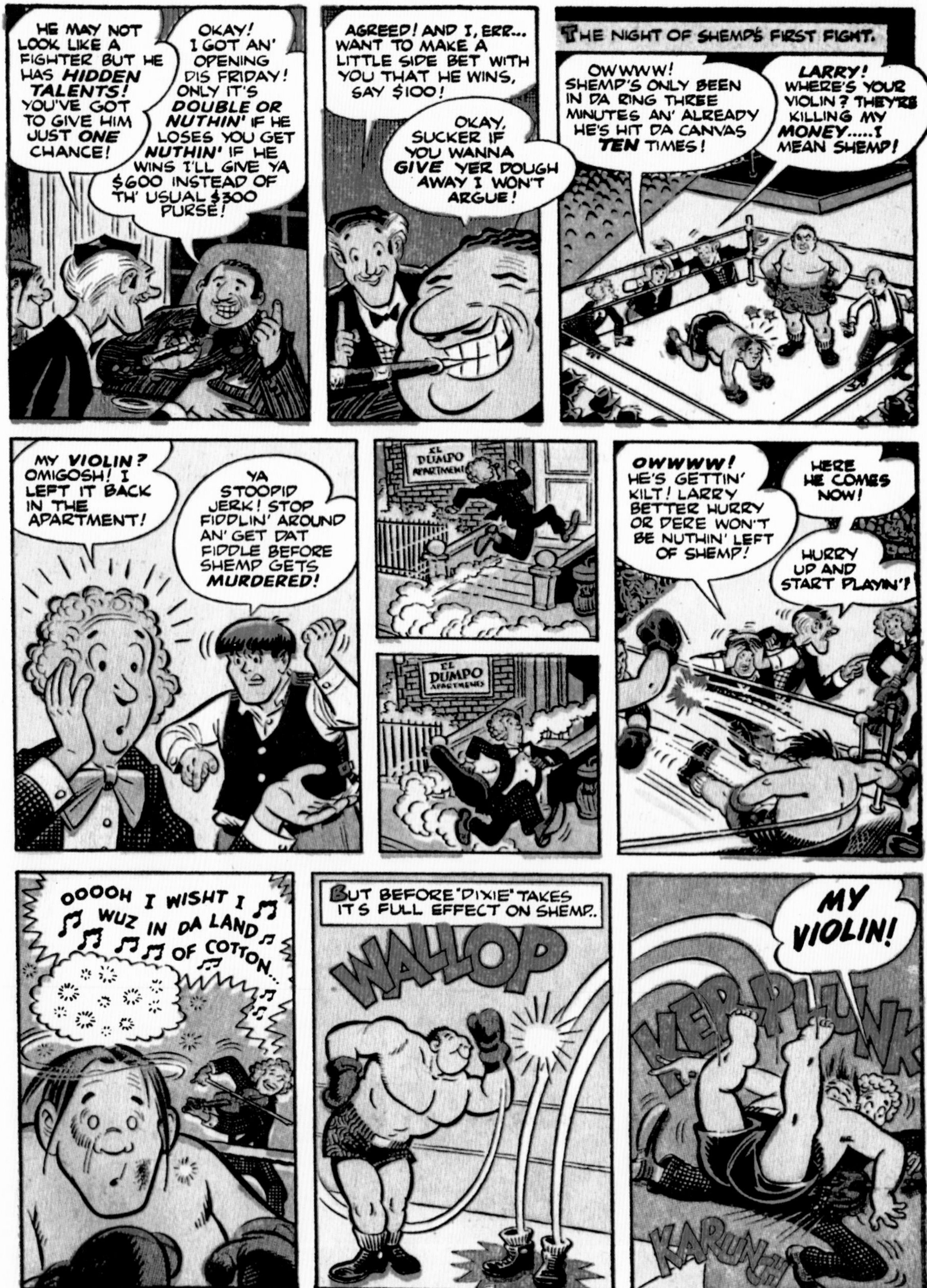
HE MAY NOT LOOK LIKE A FIGHTER BUT HE HAS HIDDEN TALENTS! YOU'VE GOT TO GIVE HIM JUST ONE CHANCE!
OKAY! I GOT AN' OPENING DIS FRIDAY! ONLY IT'S DOUBLE OR NUTHIN' IF HE LOSES YOU GET NUTHIN' IF HE WINS I'LL GIVE YA $600 INSTEAD OF TH' USUAL $300 PURSE!
AGREED! AND I, ERR... WANT TO MAKE A LITTLE SIDE BET WITH YOU THAT HE WINS, SAY $100!
OKAY, SUCKER IF YOU WANNA GIVE YER DOUGH AWAY I WON'T ARGUE!
THE NIGHT OF SHEMP'S FIRST FIGHT.
OWWWW! SHEMP'S ONLY BEEN IN DA RING THREE MINUTES AN' ALREADY HE'S HIT DA CANVAS TEN TIMES!
LARRY! WHERE'S YOUR VIOLIN? THEY'RE KILLING MY MONEY.....I MEAN SHEMP!
MY VIOLIN? OMIGOSH! I LEFT IT BACK IN THE APARTMENT!
YA STOOPID JERK! STOP FIDDLIN' AROUND AN' GET DAT FIDDLE BEFORE SHEMP GETS MURDERED!
EL DUMPO APARTMENT
EL DUMPO APARTMENTS
OWWWW! HE'S GETTIN' KILT! LARRY BETTER HURRY OR DERE WON'T BE NUTHIN' LEFT OF SHEMP!
HERE HE COMES NOW!
HURRY UP AND START PLAYIN'!
OOOOH I WISHT I WUZ IN DA LAND OF COTTON...
BUT BEFORE "DIXIE" TAKES ITS FULL EFFECT ON SHEMP..
WALLOP
MY VIOLIN!
KER-PLUNK
KARUNCH!

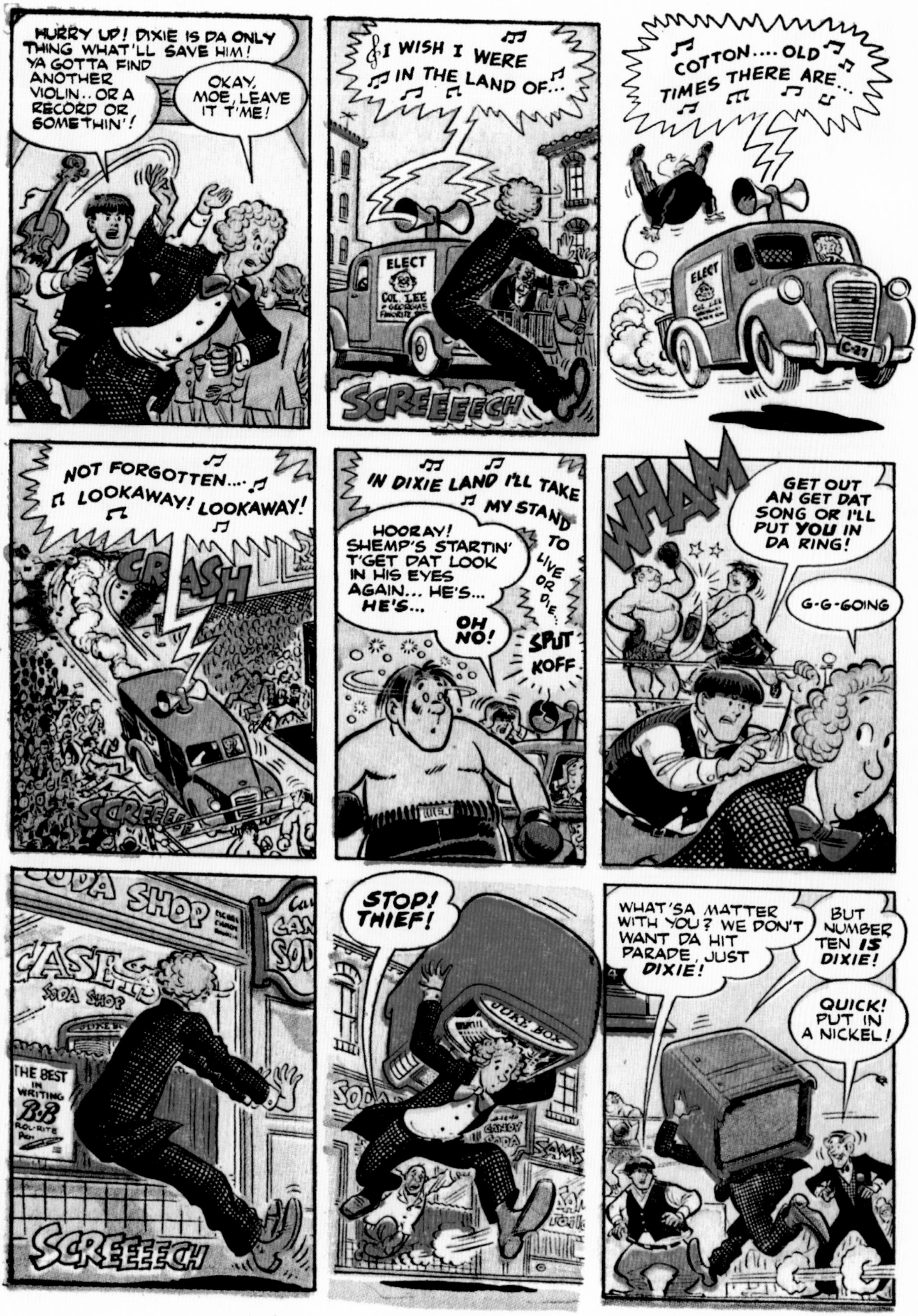
HURRY UP! DIXIE IS DA ONLY THING WHAT'LL SAVE HIM! YA GOTTA FIND ANOTHER VIOLIN..OR A RECORD OR SOMETHIN'!
OKAY, MOE, LEAVE IT T'ME!
I WISH I WERE IN THE LAND OF...
ELECT
COL. LEE
SCREEEECH
COTTON.... OLD TIMES THERE ARE...
ELECT
C-27
NOT FORGOTTEN.... LOOKAWAY! LOOKAWAY!
CRASH
IN DIXIE LAND I'LL TAKE MY STAND TO LIVE OR DIE...
HOORAY! SHEMP'S STARTIN' T'GET DAT LOOK IN HIS EYES AGAIN... HE'S... HE'S...
OH NO!
SPUT
KOFF
WHAM
GET OUT AN GET DAT SONG OR I'LL PUT YOU IN DA RING!
G-G-GOING
SODA SHOP
SODA SHOP
THE BEST IN WRITING
B-B
ROL-RITE PEN
SCREEEECH
STOP! THIEF!
JUKE BOX
WHAT'SA MATTER WITH YOU? WE DON'T WANT DA HIT PARADE, JUST DIXIE!
BUT NUMBER TEN IS DIXIE!
QUICK! PUT IN A NICKEL!

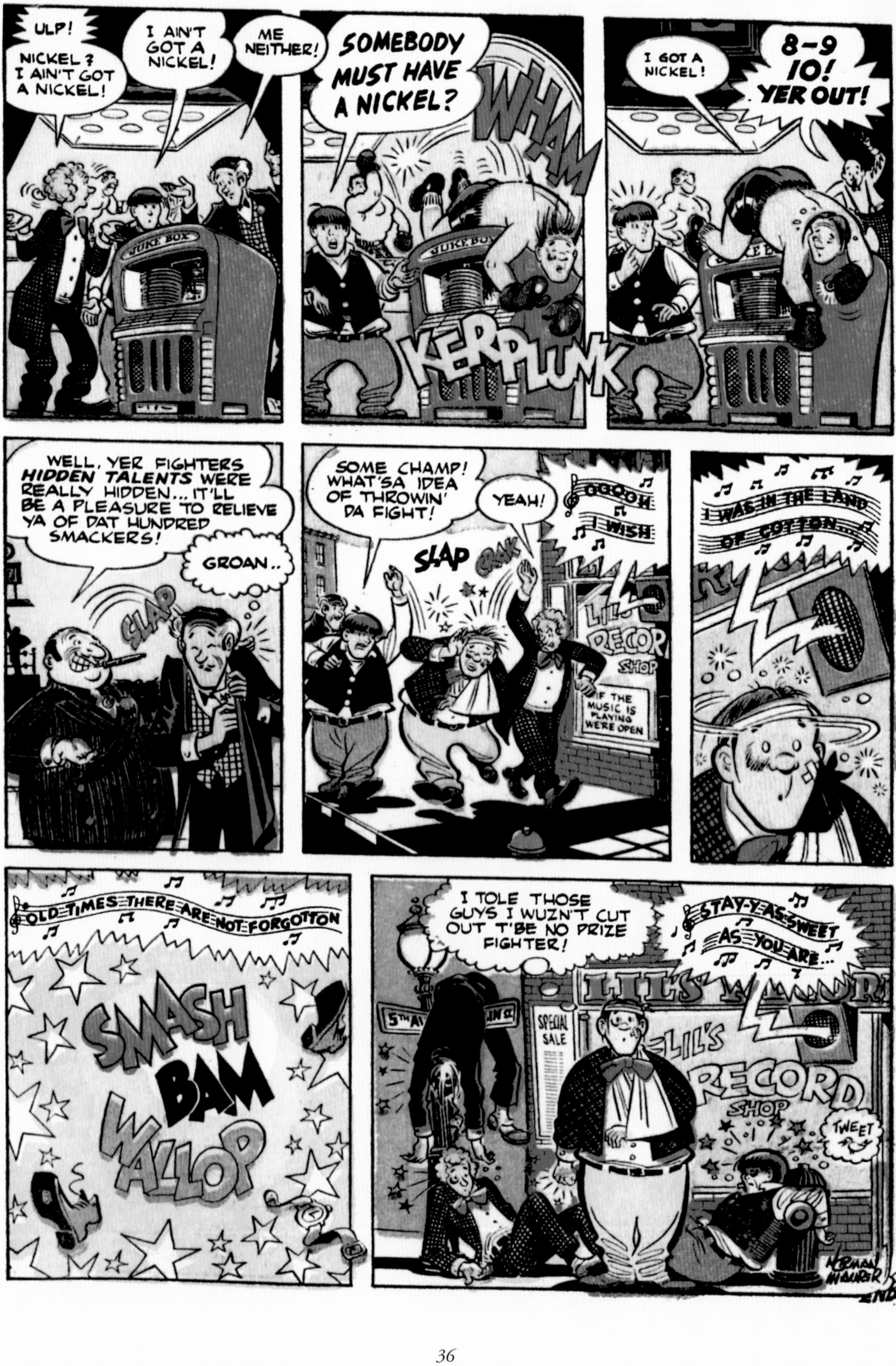
ULP!
NICKEL? I AIN'T GOT A NICKEL!
I AIN'T GOT A NICKEL!
ME NEITHER!
SOMEBODY MUST HAVE A NICKEL?
WHAM
KERPLUNK
I GOT A NICKEL!
8-9 10! YER OUT!
WELL, YER FIGHTERS HIDDEN TALENTS WERE REALLY HIDDEN... IT'LL BE A PLEASURE TO RELIEVE YA OF DAT HUNDRED SMACKERS!
GROAN..
SLAP
SOME CHAMP! WHAT'SA IDEA OF THROWIN' DA FIGHT!
YEAH!
SLAP
OOOOH I WISH
IF THE MUSIC IS PLAYING WE'RE OPEN
I WAS IN THE LAND OF COTTON...
OLD TIMES THERE ARE NOT FORGOTTON
SMASH
BAM
WALLOP
I TOLE THOSE GUYS I WUZN'T CUT OUT T'BE NO PRIZE FIGHTER!
STAY-Y AS SWEET AS YOU ARE...
5TH AV
SPECIAL SALE
LIL'S RECORD SHOP
TWEET
NORMAN MAURER
END

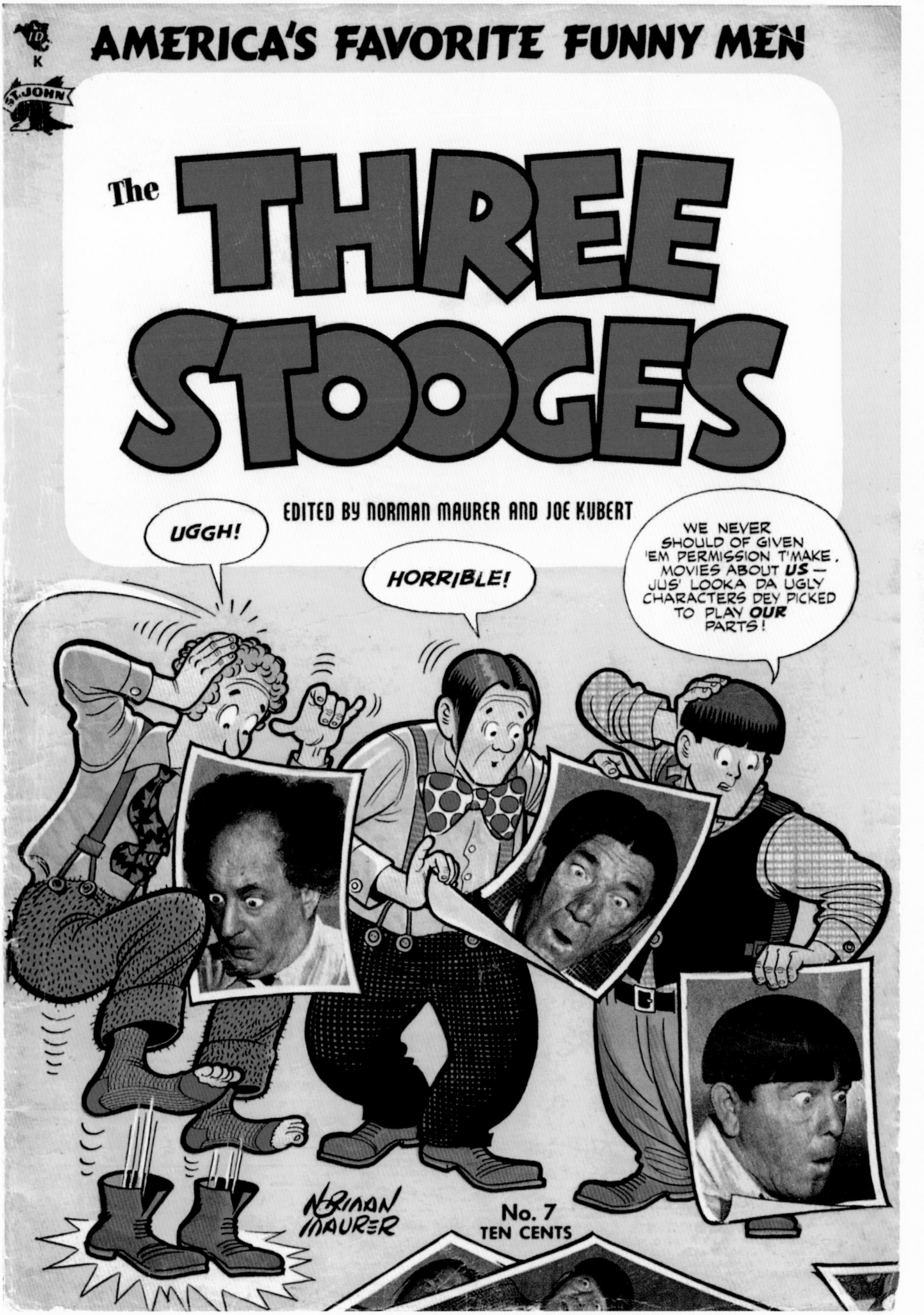
AMERICA'S FAVORITE FUNNY MEN
ST. JOHN
The THREE STOOGES
EDITED BY NORMAN MAURER AND JOE KUBERT
UGGH!
HORRIBLE!
WE NEVER SHOULD OF GIVEN 'EM PERMISSION T'MAKE MOVIES ABOUT US — JUS' LOOKA DA UGLY CHARACTERS DEY PICKED TO PLAY OUR PARTS!
NORMAN MAURER
No. 7
TEN CENTS

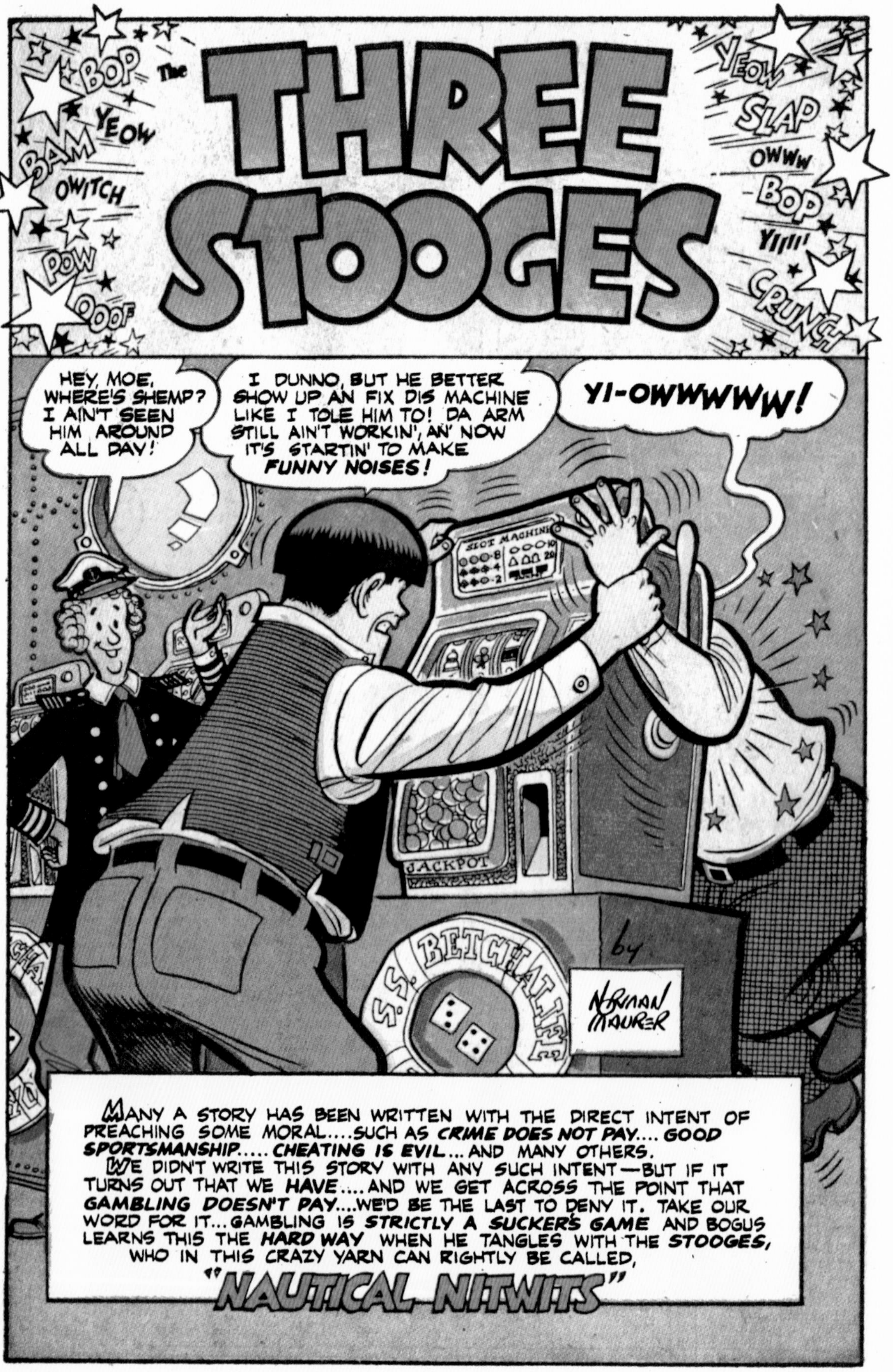

The THREE STOOGES
BOP
YEOW
BAM
OWITCH
POW
OOOF
YEOW
SLAP
OWWW
BOP
YIII
CRUNCH
HEY, MOE, WHERE'S SHEMP? I AIN'T SEEN HIM AROUND ALL DAY!
I DUNNO, BUT HE BETTER SHOW UP AN FIX DIS MACHINE LIKE I TOLE HIM TO! DA ARM STILL AIN'T WORKIN', AN' NOW IT'S STARTIN' TO MAKE FUNNY NOISES!
YI-OWWWWW!
SLOT MACHINE
JACKPOT
S.S. BETCHALIFE
by NORMAN MAURER
MANY A STORY HAS BEEN WRITTEN WITH THE DIRECT INTENT OF PREACHING SOME MORAL....SUCH AS CRIME DOES NOT PAY.... GOOD SPORTSMANSHIP..... CHEATING IS EVIL... AND MANY OTHERS.
WE DIDN'T WRITE THIS STORY WITH ANY SUCH INTENT—BUT IF IT TURNS OUT THAT WE HAVE....AND WE GET ACROSS THE POINT THAT GAMBLING DOESN'T PAY....WE'D BE THE LAST TO DENY IT. TAKE OUR WORD FOR IT...GAMBLING IS STRICTLY A SUCKER'S GAME AND BOGUS LEARNS THIS THE HARD WAY WHEN HE TANGLES WITH THE STOOGES, WHO IN THIS CRAZY YARN CAN RIGHTLY BE CALLED,
"NAUTICAL NITWITS"

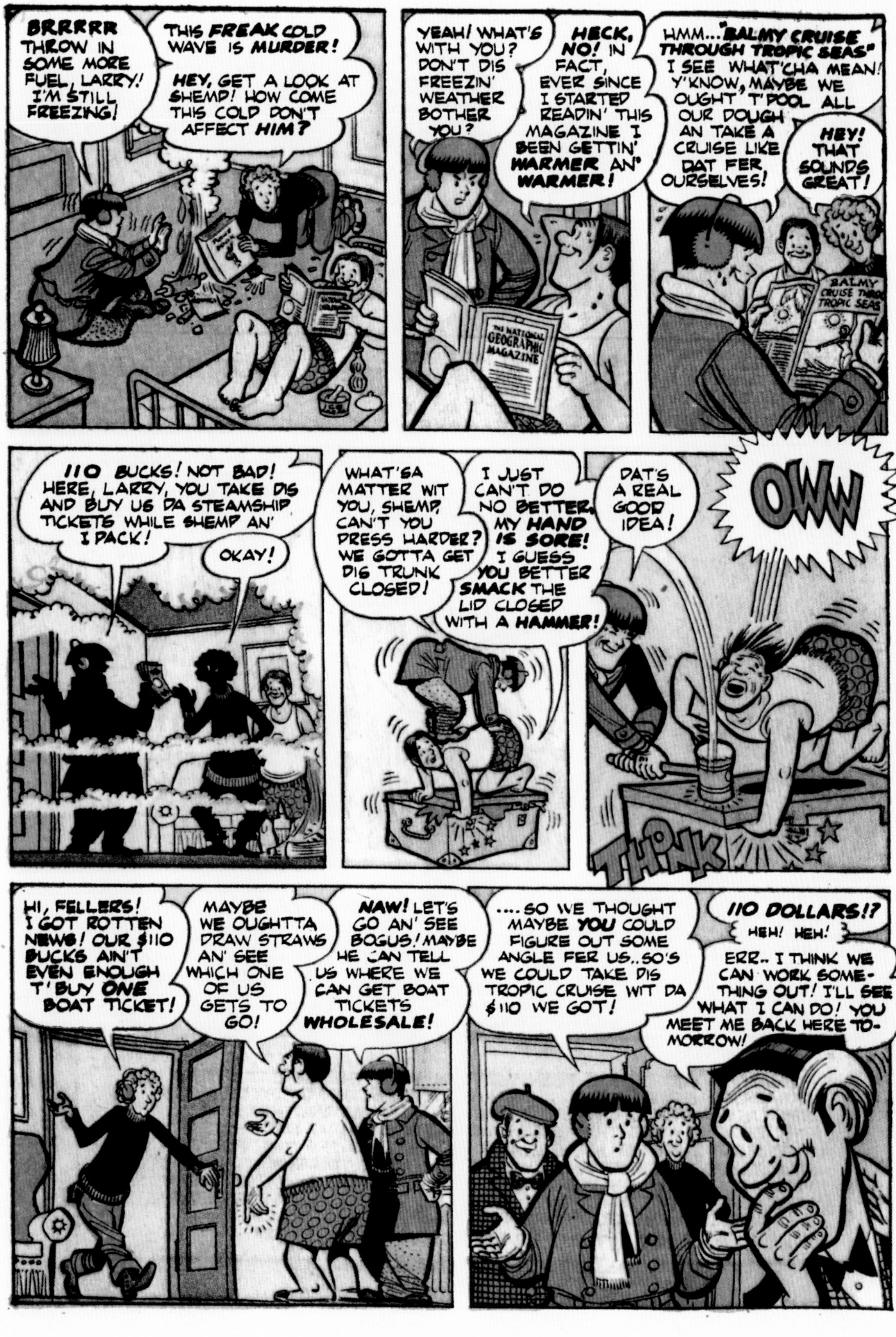
BRRRRR THROW IN SOME MORE FUEL, LARRY! I'M STILL FREEZING!
THIS FREAK COLD WAVE IS MURDER!
HEY, GET A LOOK AT SHEMP! HOW COME THIS COLD DON'T AFFECT HIM?
YEAH! WHAT'S WITH YOU? DON'T DIS FREEZIN' WEATHER BOTHER YOU?
HECK, NO! IN FACT, EVER SINCE I STARTED READIN' THIS MAGAZINE I BEEN GETTIN' WARMER AN' WARMER!
THE NATIONAL GEOGRAPHIC MAGAZINE
HMM... "BALMY CRUISE THROUGH TROPIC SEAS" I SEE WHAT'CHA MEAN! Y'KNOW, MAYBE WE OUGHT T'POOL ALL OUR DOUGH AN TAKE A CRUISE LIKE DAT FER OURSELVES!
HEY! THAT SOUNDS GREAT!
110 BUCKS! NOT BAD! HERE, LARRY, YOU TAKE DIS AND BUY US DA STEAMSHIP TICKETS WHILE SHEMP AN' I PACK!
OKAY!
WHAT'SA MATTER WIT YOU, SHEMP, CAN'T YOU PRESS HARDER? WE GOTTA GET DIS TRUNK CLOSED!
I JUST CAN'T DO NO BETTER. MY HAND IS SORE! I GUESS YOU BETTER SMACK THE LID CLOSED WITH A HAMMER!
DAT'S A REAL GOOD IDEA!
OWW
THONK
HI, FELLERS! I GOT ROTTEN NEWS! OUR $110 BUCKS AIN'T EVEN ENOUGH T' BUY ONE BOAT TICKET!
MAYBE WE OUGHTTA DRAW STRAWS AN' SEE WHICH ONE OF US GETS TO GO!
NAW! LET'S GO AN' SEE BOGUS! MAYBE HE CAN TELL US WHERE WE CAN GET BOAT TICKETS WHOLESALE!
....SO WE THOUGHT MAYBE YOU COULD FIGURE OUT SOME ANGLE FER US..SO'S WE COULD TAKE DIS TROPIC CRUISE WIT DA $110 WE GOT!
110 DOLLARS!? HEH! HEH!
ERR.. I THINK WE CAN WORK SOME-THING OUT! I'LL SEE WHAT I CAN DO! YOU MEET ME BACK HERE TO-MORROW!

...YOU MEAN TO TELL ME YOU WANT TO CHARGE ME $200 FOR *THAT* BROKEN DOWN TUB? THE SUMMER IS OVER AND BOATS ARE TOUGH TO SELL NOW! I'LL GIVE YA *FIFTY* BUCKS FOR IT!

I'LL TAKE IT!

HEH-HEH! NOT BAD FOR *FIFTY* BUCKS! WHEN I GET FINISHED IT'LL LOOK LIKE IT'S WORTH $500!

THERE! FINISHED! LET'S SEE...THE BOAT COST ME $50!...LUMBER, $6.....PAINT $4...HARDWARE... $2.....TOTAL $62⁰⁰... AND I SELL IT TO THE STOOGES FOR $110, A NICE PROFIT OF $48... NOT BAD.. HEH! HEH!

WELL, I DID IT, BOYS! I FOUND YOU A *BEAUTIFUL YACHT* TO TAKE YOUR TROPIC CRUISE IN! IT'S A DREAM AN' ALL YOURS FOR A MERE $110!

I KNEW YOU'D COME THRU, BOGUS! IT SOUNDS *GREAT!* HERE'S TH' DOUGH! WHERE DO WE FIND DA YACHT?

HEH-HEH! YOU'LL FIND IT AT CARSON'S COVE, JUST OUTSIDE THE CITY LIMIT— CAN'T MISS IT— IT'S TIED TO BUOY 13!

THANKS! WE'LL SEE YA SOON, BOGUS!

MEANWHILE.. AT CARSON'S COVE....

WHAT IN BLAZES!? NOW WHO LEFT THAT BROKEN-DOWN TUB TIED TO MY PRIVATE BUOY?

YA GOT ME, BOSS!

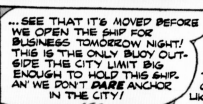

...SEE THAT IT'S MOVED BEFORE WE OPEN THE SHIP FOR BUSINESS TOMORROW NIGHT! THIS IS THE ONLY BUOY OUT-SIDE THE CITY LIMIT BIG ENOUGH TO HOLD THIS SHIP. AN' WE DON'T *DARE* ANCHOR IN THE CITY!

YOU SAID IT! THE CITY COPS ARE PRETTY TOUGH ABOUT GAMBLIN' SHIPS LIKE DIS COMIN' IN DA HARBOR!

BEFORE WE GO ASHORE FER TH' NIGHT I WANT TO BE SURE YOU GOT ALL THE SLOT-MACHINES *FIXED*...ADJUSTED SO THEY PAY-OFF ONLY ONCE IN EVERY 200 TIMES!

THEY'RE ALL SET, SNAKEYE! WIT DESE LITTLE STICKERS WE HAD PRINTED, IT WUZ A CINCH! ALL I HADDA DO WUZ PASTE DA RIGHT ONES IN DA RIGHT PLACES AN' DA MACHINES DO JUST LIKE WE WANT 'EM TO!

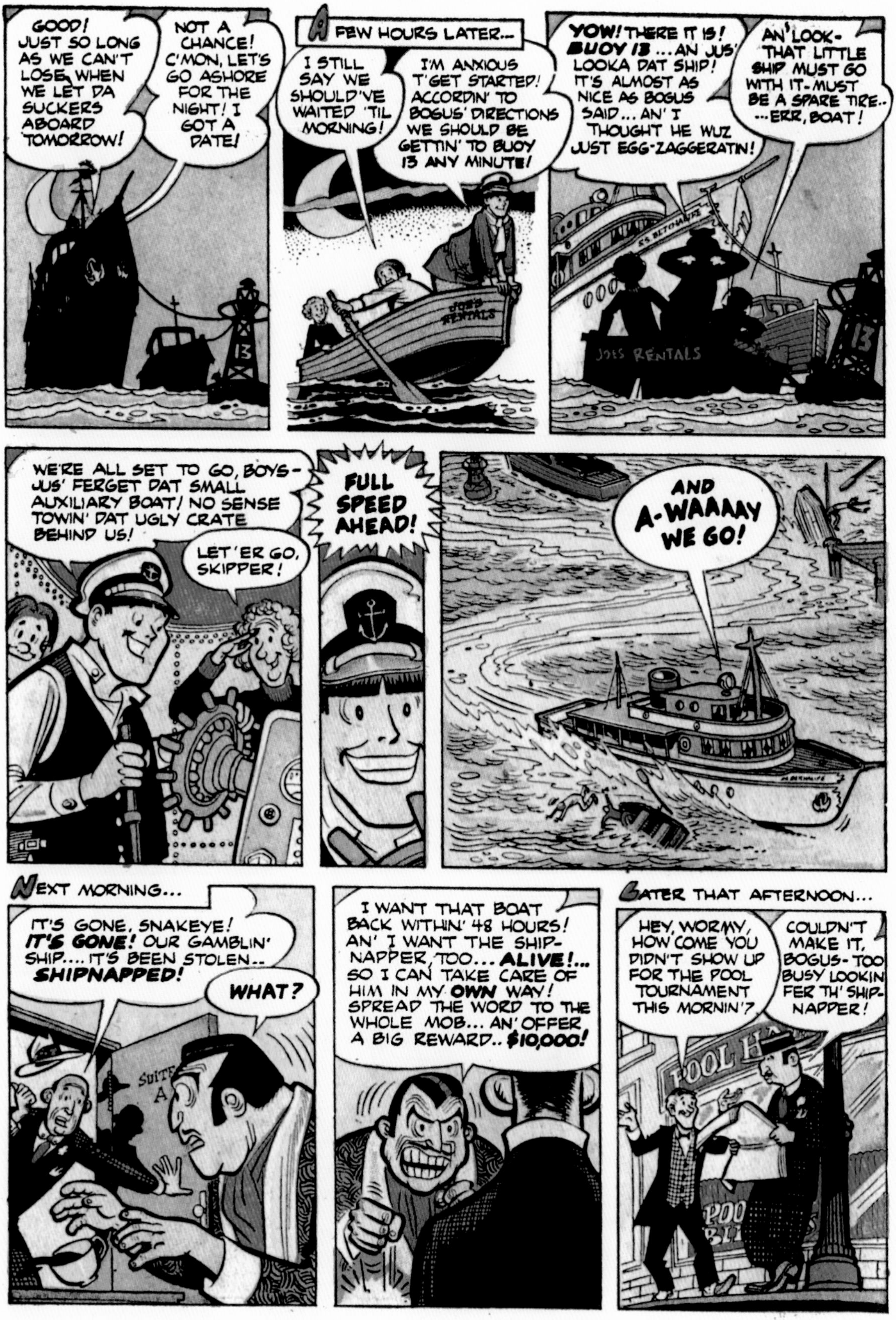
GOOD! JUST SO LONG AS WE CAN'T LOSE, WHEN WE LET DA SUCKERS ABOARD TOMORROW!
NOT A CHANCE! C'MON, LET'S GO ASHORE FOR THE NIGHT! I GOT A DATE!
A FEW HOURS LATER...
I STILL SAY WE SHOULD'VE WAITED 'TIL MORNING!
I'M ANXIOUS T'GET STARTED! ACCORDIN' TO BOGUS' DIRECTIONS WE SHOULD BE GETTIN' TO BUOY 13 ANY MINUTE!
JOE'S RENTALS
YOW! THERE IT IS! BUOY 13 ... AN JUS' LOOKA DAT SHIP! IT'S ALMOST AS NICE AS BOGUS SAID... AN' I THOUGHT HE WUZ JUST EGG-ZAGGERATIN!
AN' LOOK- THAT LITTLE SHIP MUST GO WITH IT- MUST BE A SPARE TIRE.. ...ERR, BOAT!
JOE'S RENTALS
WE'RE ALL SET TO GO, BOYS- JUS' FERGET DAT SMALL AUXILIARY BOAT! NO SENSE TOWIN' DAT UGLY CRATE BEHIND US!
LET 'ER GO, SKIPPER!
FULL SPEED AHEAD!
AND A-WAAAAY WE GO!
NEXT MORNING...
IT'S GONE, SNAKEYE! IT'S GONE! OUR GAMBLIN' SHIP.... IT'S BEEN STOLEN.. SHIPNAPPED!
WHAT?
I WANT THAT BOAT BACK WITHIN' 48 HOURS! AN' I WANT THE SHIP-NAPPER, TOO... ALIVE!... SO I CAN TAKE CARE OF HIM IN MY OWN WAY! SPREAD THE WORD TO THE WHOLE MOB... AN' OFFER A BIG REWARD.. $10,000!
LATER THAT AFTERNOON...
HEY, WORMY, HOW COME YOU DIDN'T SHOW UP FOR THE POOL TOURNAMENT THIS MORNIN'?
COULDN'T MAKE IT, BOGUS- TOO BUSY LOOKIN FER TH' SHIP-NAPPER!

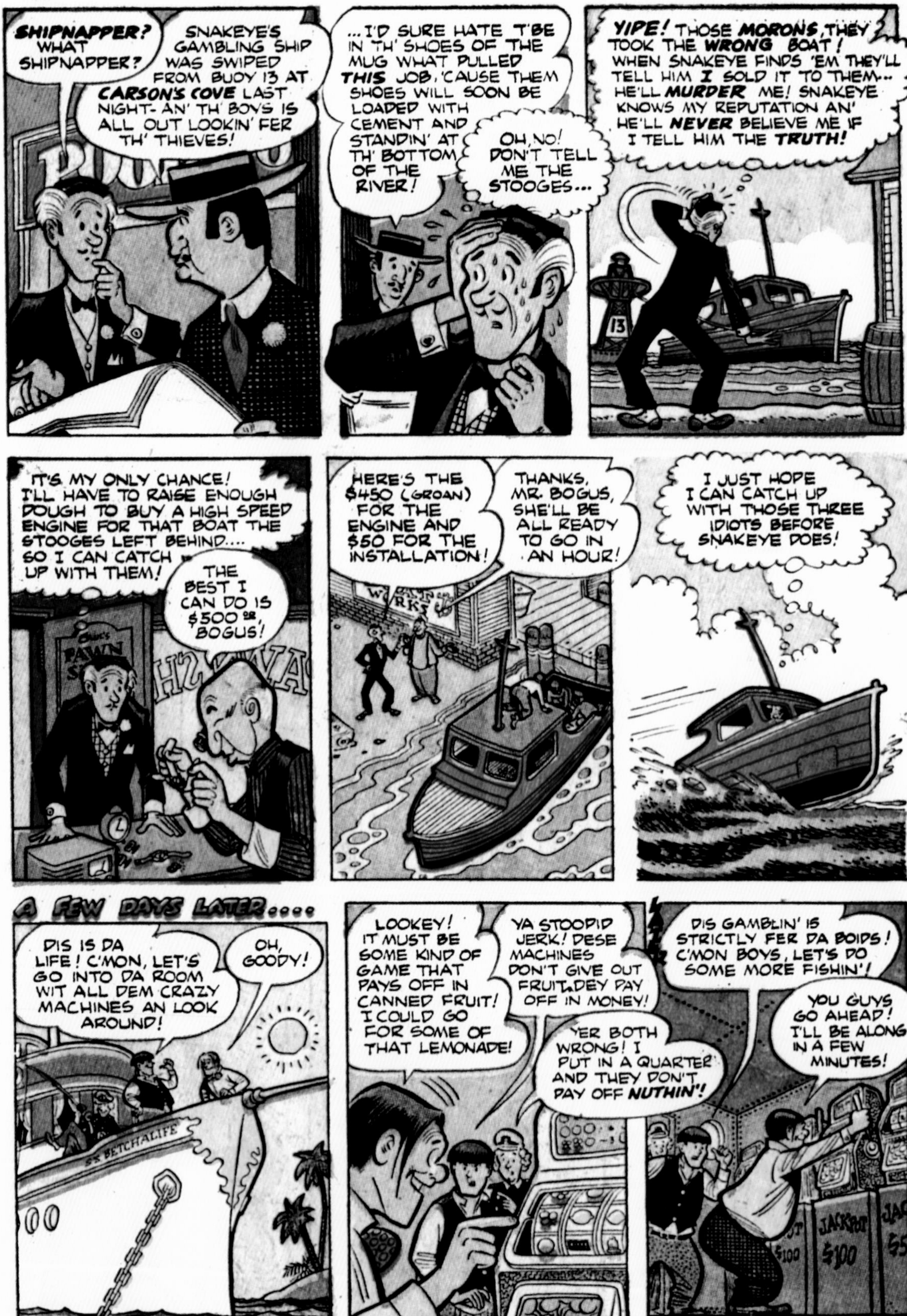
SHIPNAPPER? WHAT SHIPNAPPER?
SNAKEYE'S GAMBLING SHIP WAS SWIPED FROM BUOY 13 AT CARSON'S COVE LAST NIGHT- AN' TH' BOYS IS ALL OUT LOOKIN' FER TH' THIEVES!
...I'D SURE HATE T'BE IN TH' SHOES OF THE MUG WHAT PULLED THIS JOB, 'CAUSE THEM SHOES WILL SOON BE LOADED WITH CEMENT AND STANDIN' AT TH' BOTTOM OF THE RIVER!
OH, NO! DON'T TELL ME THE STOOGES...
YIPE! THOSE MORONS, THEY TOOK THE WRONG BOAT! WHEN SNAKEYE FINDS 'EM THEY'LL TELL HIM I SOLD IT TO THEM.. HE'LL MURDER ME! SNAKEYE KNOWS MY REPUTATION AN' HE'LL NEVER BELIEVE ME IF I TELL HIM THE TRUTH!
13
IT'S MY ONLY CHANCE! I'LL HAVE TO RAISE ENOUGH DOUGH TO BUY A HIGH SPEED ENGINE FOR THAT BOAT THE STOOGES LEFT BEHIND.... SO I CAN CATCH UP WITH THEM!
THE BEST I CAN DO IS $500 OR BOGUS!
PAWN
HERE'S THE $450 (GROAN) FOR THE ENGINE AND $50 FOR THE INSTALLATION!
THANKS, MR. BOGUS, SHE'LL BE ALL READY TO GO IN AN HOUR!
I JUST HOPE I CAN CATCH UP WITH THOSE THREE IDIOTS BEFORE SNAKEYE DOES!
A FEW DAYS LATER....
DIS IS DA LIFE! C'MON, LET'S GO INTO DA ROOM WIT ALL DEM CRAZY MACHINES AN LOOK AROUND!
OH, GOODY!
S.S. BETCHALIFE
LOOKEY! IT MUST BE SOME KIND OF GAME THAT PAYS OFF IN CANNED FRUIT! I COULD GO FOR SOME OF THAT LEMONADE!
YA STOOPID JERK! DESE MACHINES DON'T GIVE OUT FRUIT-DEY PAY OFF IN MONEY!
YER BOTH WRONG! I PUT IN A QUARTER AND THEY DON'T PAY OFF NUTHIN'!
DIS GAMBLIN' IS STRICTLY FER DA BOIDS! C'MON BOYS, LET'S DO SOME MORE FISHIN'!
YOU GUYS GO AHEAD! I'LL BE ALONG IN A FEW MINUTES!
JACKPOT $100
$100

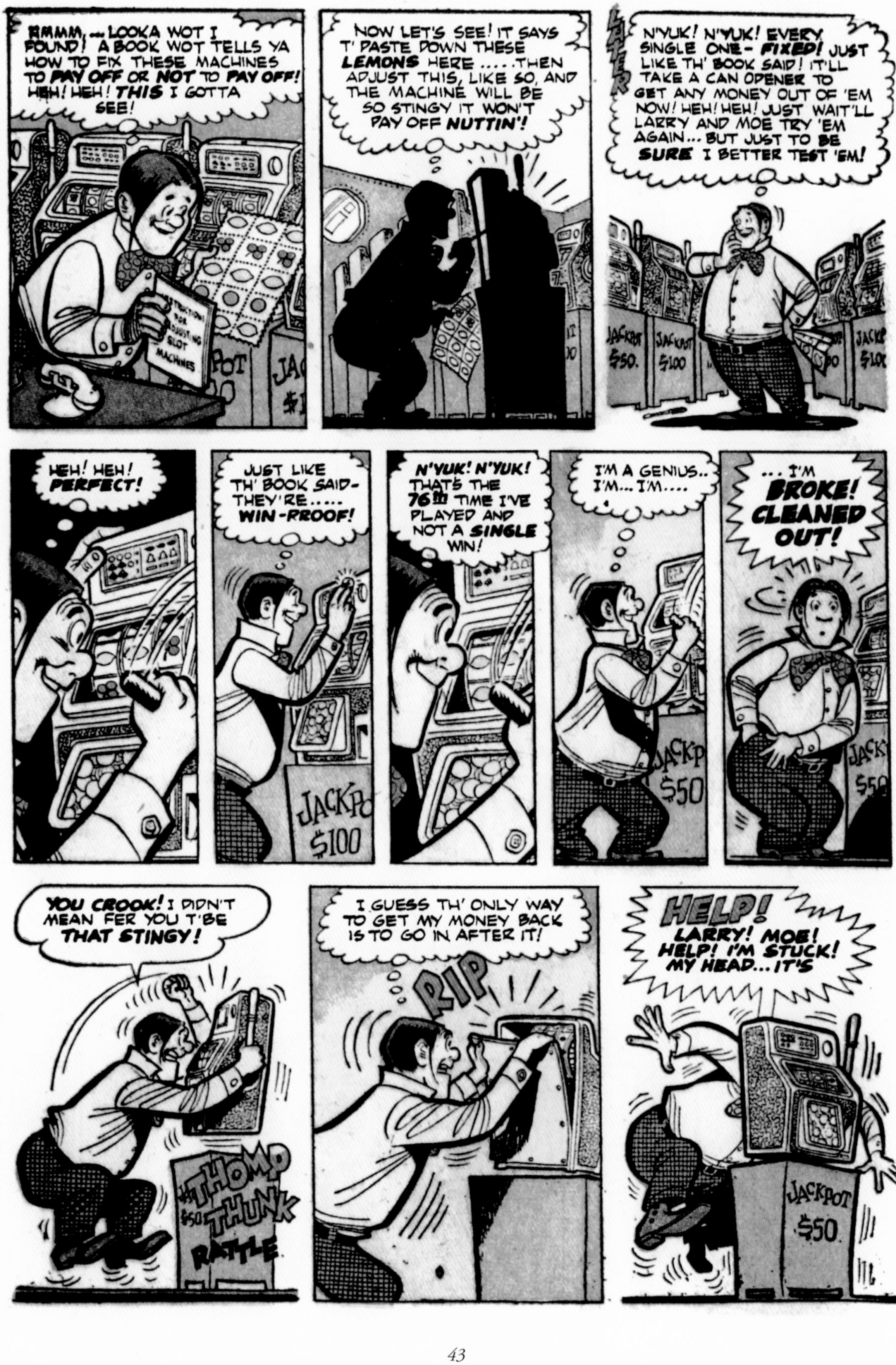
HMMM, ... LOOKA WOT I FOUND! A BOOK WOT TELLS YA HOW TO FIX THESE MACHINES TO PAY OFF OR NOT TO PAY OFF! HEH! HEH! THIS I GOTTA SEE!
INSTRUCTIONS FOR ADJUSTING SLOT MACHINES
NOW LET'S SEE! IT SAYS T' PASTE DOWN THESE LEMONS HERE .....THEN ADJUST THIS, LIKE SO, AND THE MACHINE WILL BE SO STINGY IT WON'T PAY OFF NUTTIN'!
LATER
N'YUK! N'YUK! EVERY SINGLE ONE- FIXED! JUST LIKE TH' BOOK SAID! IT'LL TAKE A CAN OPENER TO GET ANY MONEY OUT OF 'EM NOW! HEH! HEH! JUST WAIT'LL LARRY AND MOE TRY 'EM AGAIN... BUT JUST TO BE SURE I BETTER TEST 'EM!
JACKPOT $50.
JACKPOT $100
HEH! HEH! PERFECT!
JUST LIKE TH' BOOK SAID- THEY'RE..... WIN-PROOF!
JACKPOT $100
N'YUK! N'YUK! THAT'S THE 76TH TIME I'VE PLAYED AND NOT A SINGLE WIN!
I'M A GENIUS.. I'M... I'M....
JACKPOT $50
... I'M BROKE! CLEANED OUT!
YOU CROOK! I DIDN'T MEAN FER YOU T'BE THAT STINGY!
THOMP THUNK RATTLE
I GUESS TH' ONLY WAY TO GET MY MONEY BACK IS TO GO IN AFTER IT!
RIP
HELP! LARRY! MOE! HELP! I'M STUCK! MY HEAD... IT'S
JACKPOT $50

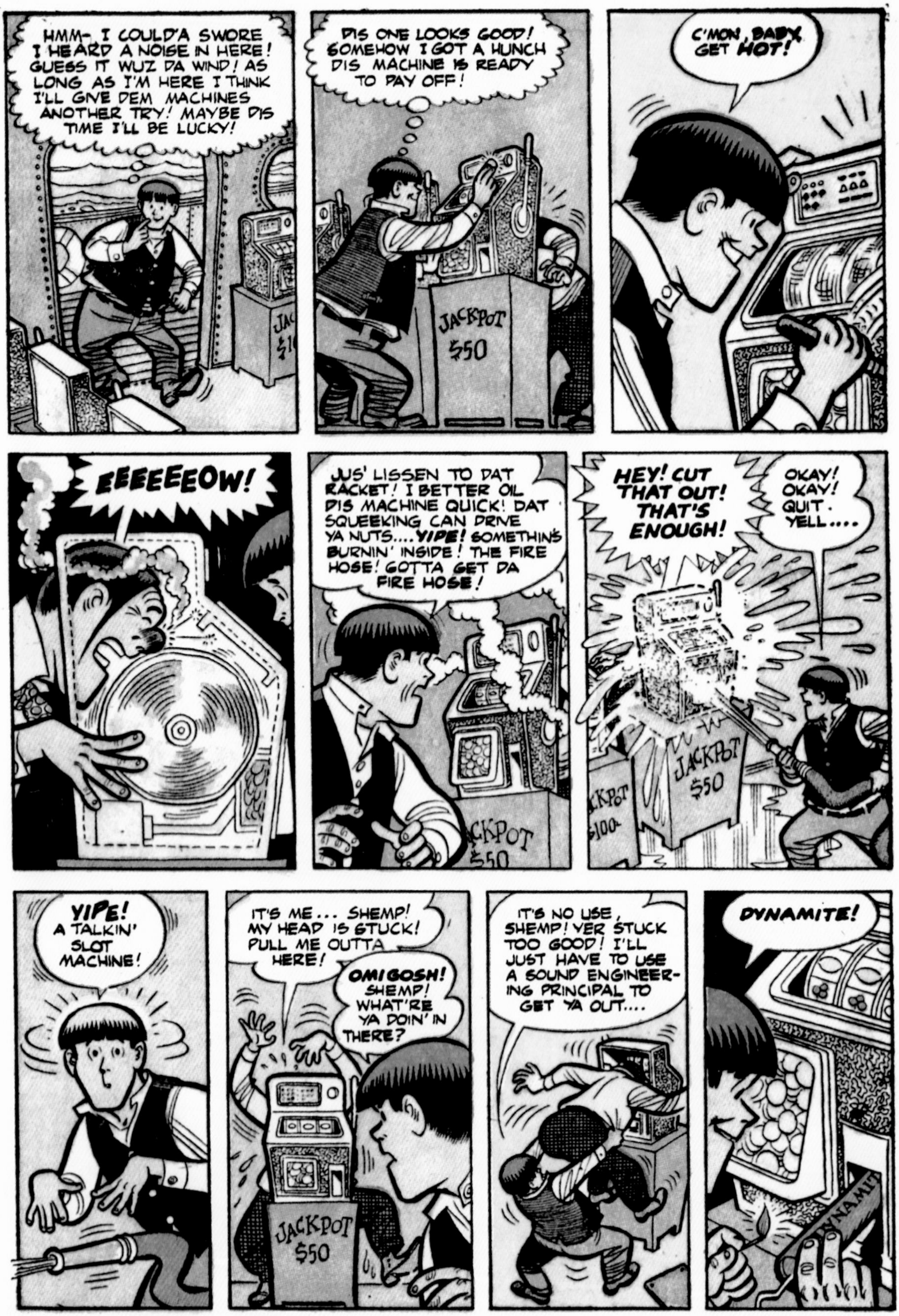
HMM- I COULD'A SWORE I HEARD A NOISE IN HERE! GUESS IT WUZ DA WIND! AS LONG AS I'M HERE I THINK I'LL GIVE DEM MACHINES ANOTHER TRY! MAYBE DIS TIME I'LL BE LUCKY!
DIS ONE LOOKS GOOD! SOMEHOW I GOT A HUNCH DIS MACHINE IS READY TO PAY OFF!
JACKPOT $50
C'MON, BABY, GET HOT!
EEEEEEOW!
JUS' LISSEN TO DAT RACKET! I BETTER OIL DIS MACHINE QUICK! DAT SQUEEKING CAN DRIVE YA NUTS....YIPE! SOMETHIN'S BURNIN' INSIDE! THE FIRE HOSE! GOTTA GET DA FIRE HOSE!
HEY! CUT THAT OUT! THAT'S ENOUGH!
OKAY! OKAY! QUIT YELL....
JACKPOT $50
YIPE! A TALKIN' SLOT MACHINE!
IT'S ME... SHEMP! MY HEAD IS STUCK! PULL ME OUTTA HERE!
OMIGOSH! SHEMP! WHAT'RE YA DOIN' IN THERE?
JACKPOT $50
IT'S NO USE, SHEMP! YER STUCK TOO GOOD! I'LL JUST HAVE TO USE A SOUND ENGINEERING PRINCIPAL TO GET YA OUT....
DYNAMITE!

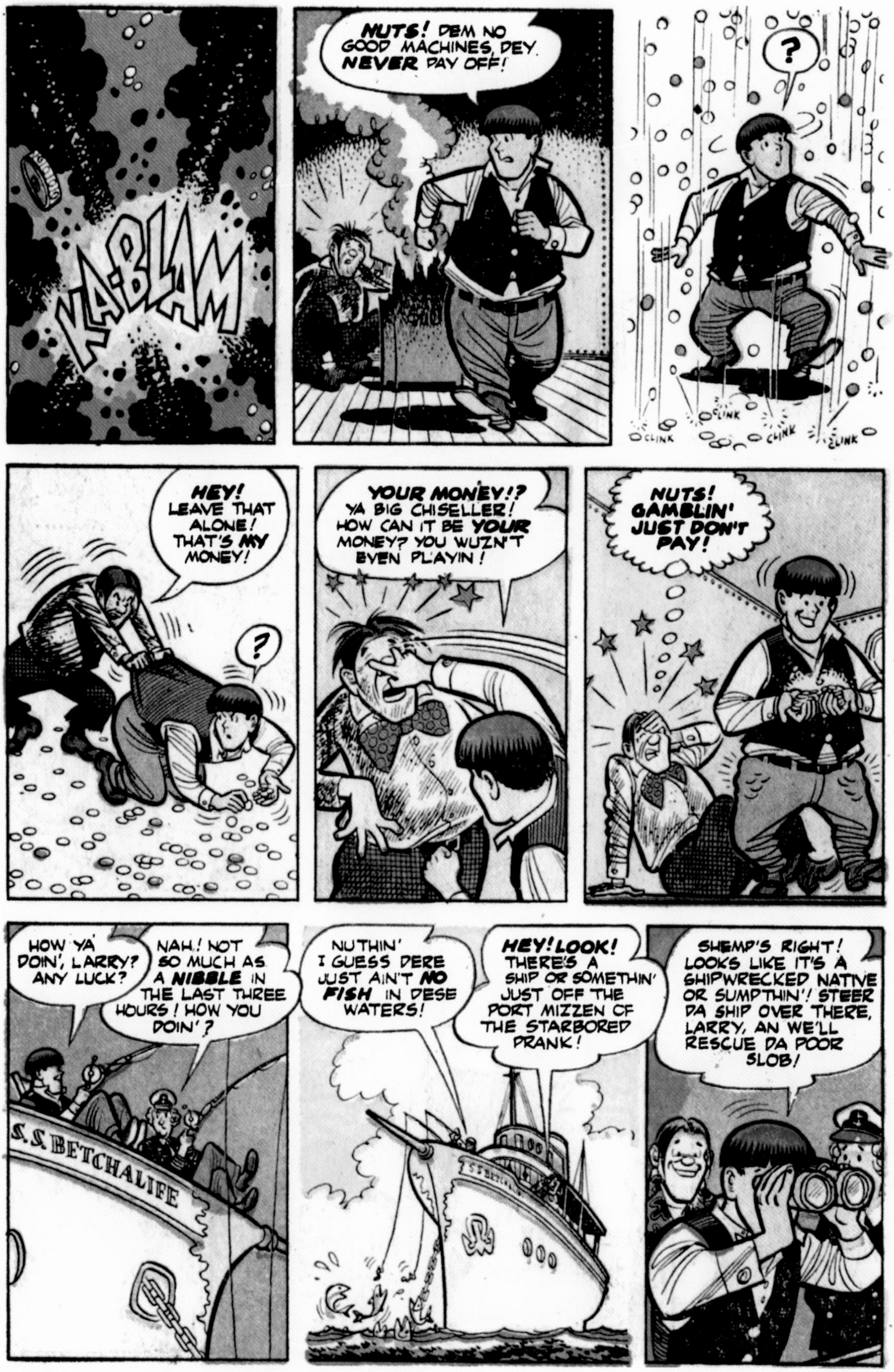
KA-BLAM
NUTS! DEM NO GOOD MACHINES, DEY NEVER PAY OFF!
?
CLINK
CLINK
CLINK
CLINK
HEY! LEAVE THAT ALONE! THAT'S MY MONEY!
?
YOUR MONEY!? YA BIG CHISELLER! HOW CAN IT BE YOUR MONEY? YOU WUZN'T EVEN PLAYIN!
NUTS! GAMBLIN' JUST DON'T PAY!
HOW YA' DOIN', LARRY? ANY LUCK?
NAH! NOT SO MUCH AS A NIBBLE IN THE LAST THREE HOURS! HOW YOU DOIN'?
S.S. BETCHALIFE
NUTHIN' I GUESS DERE JUST AIN'T NO FISH IN DESE WATERS!
HEY! LOOK! THERE'S A SHIP OR SOMETHIN' JUST OFF THE PORT MIZZEN OF THE STARBORED PRANK!
SHEMP'S RIGHT! LOOKS LIKE IT'S A SHIPWRECKED NATIVE OR SUMPTHIN'! STEER DA SHIP OVER THERE, LARRY, AN WE'LL RESCUE DA POOR SLOB!

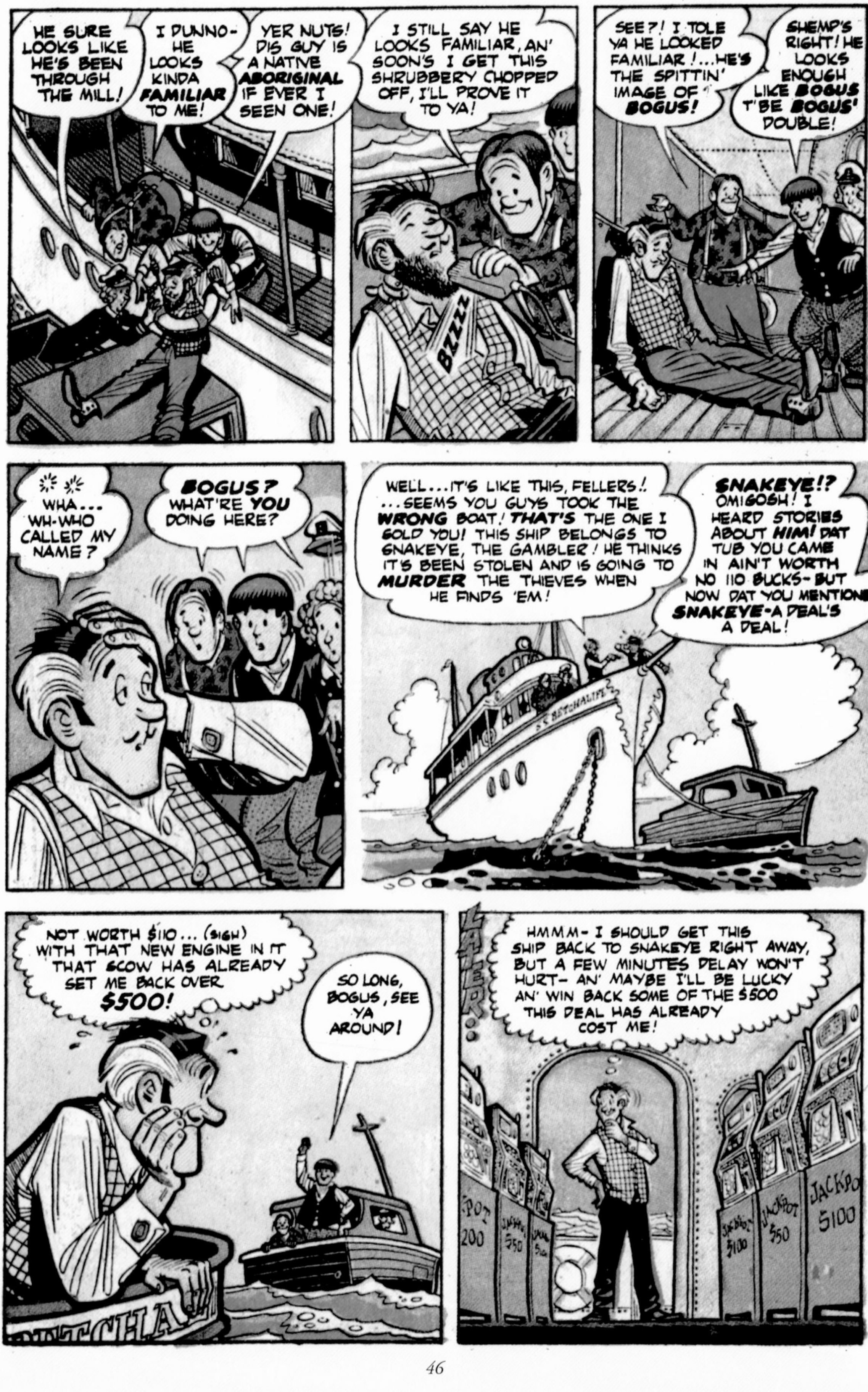
HE SURE LOOKS LIKE HE'S BEEN THROUGH THE MILL!
I DUNNO- HE LOOKS KINDA **FAMILIAR** TO ME!
YER NUTS! DIS GUY IS A NATIVE **ABORIGINAL** IF EVER I SEEN ONE!
I STILL SAY HE LOOKS FAMILIAR, AN' SOON'S I GET THIS SHRUBBERY CHOPPED OFF, I'LL PROVE IT TO YA!
BZZZZ
SEE?! I TOLE YA HE LOOKED FAMILIAR!...HE'S THE SPITTIN' IMAGE OF **BOGUS!**
SHEMP'S RIGHT! HE LOOKS ENOUGH LIKE **BOGUS** T'BE **BOGUS'** DOUBLE!
WHA... WH-WHO CALLED MY NAME?
BOGUS? WHAT'RE **YOU** DOING HERE?
WELL...IT'S LIKE THIS, FELLERS!...SEEMS YOU GUYS TOOK THE **WRONG** BOAT! **THAT'S** THE ONE I SOLD YOU! THIS SHIP BELONGS TO SNAKEYE, THE GAMBLER! HE THINKS IT'S BEEN STOLEN AND IS GOING TO **MURDER** THE THIEVES WHEN HE FINDS 'EM!
SNAKEYE!? OMIGOSH! I HEARD STORIES ABOUT **HIM!** DAT TUB YOU CAME IN AIN'T WORTH NO 110 BUCKS- BUT NOW DAT YOU MENTIONED **SNAKEYE**- A DEAL'S A DEAL!
S.S. BETCHALIFE
NOT WORTH $110... (SIGH) WITH THAT NEW ENGINE IN IT THAT SCOW HAS ALREADY SET ME BACK OVER **$500!**
SO LONG, BOGUS, SEE YA AROUND!
LATER
HMMM- I SHOULD GET THIS SHIP BACK TO SNAKEYE RIGHT AWAY, BUT A FEW MINUTES DELAY WON'T HURT- AN' MAYBE I'LL BE LUCKY AN' WIN BACK SOME OF THE $500 THIS DEAL HAS ALREADY COST ME!
JACKPOT $100

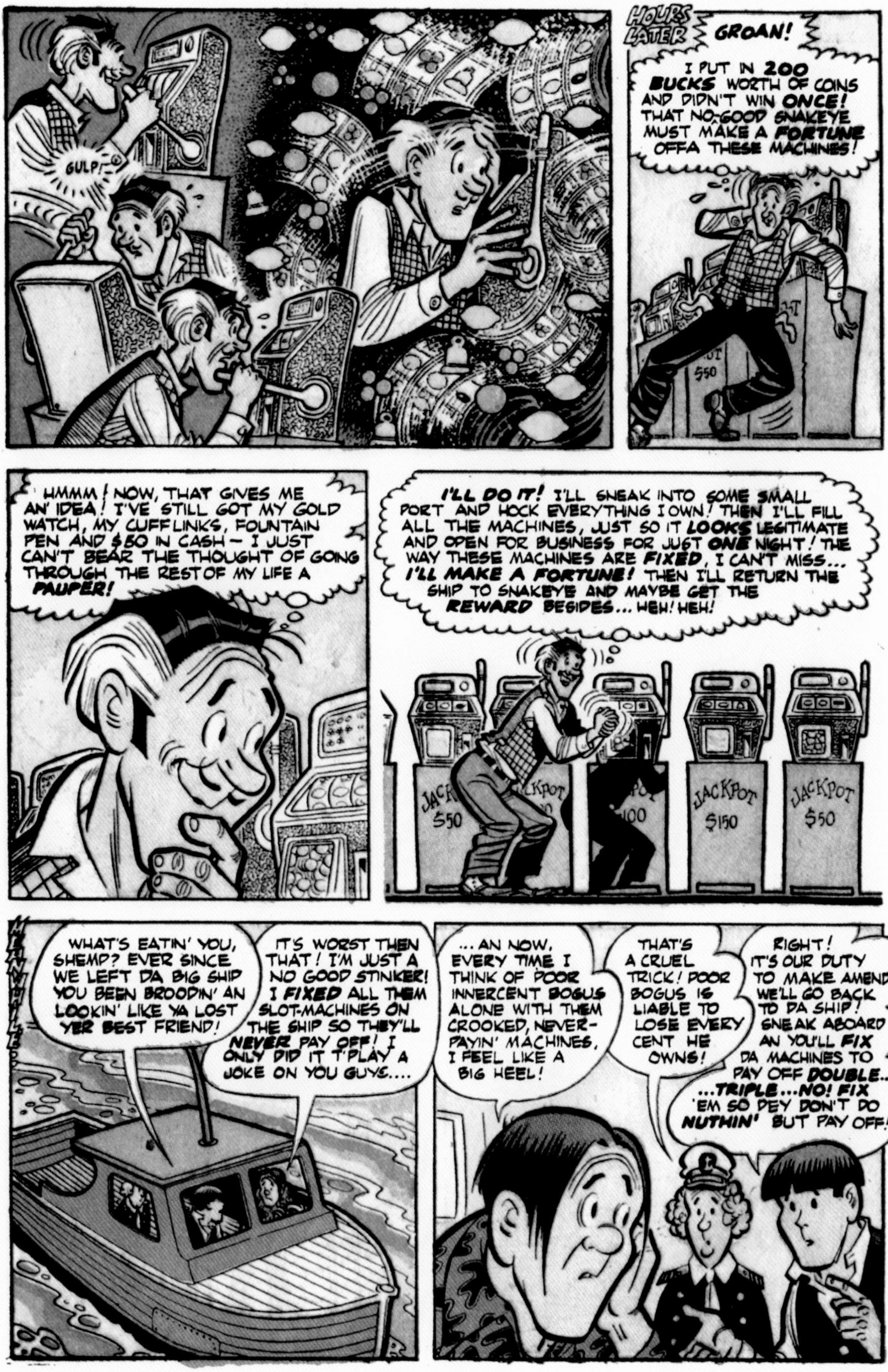
GULP!
HOURS LATER
GROAN!
I PUT IN 200 BUCKS WORTH OF COINS AND DIDN'T WIN ONCE! THAT NO-GOOD SNAKEYE MUST MAKE A FORTUNE OFFA THESE MACHINES!
HMMM! NOW, THAT GIVES ME AN' IDEA! I'VE STILL GOT MY GOLD WATCH, MY CUFFLINKS, FOUNTAIN PEN AND $50 IN CASH — I JUST CAN'T BEAR THE THOUGHT OF GOING THROUGH THE REST OF MY LIFE A PAUPER!
I'LL DO IT! I'LL SNEAK INTO SOME SMALL PORT AND HOCK EVERYTHING I OWN! THEN I'LL FILL ALL THE MACHINES, JUST SO IT LOOKS LEGITIMATE AND OPEN FOR BUSINESS FOR JUST ONE NIGHT! THE WAY THESE MACHINES ARE FIXED, I CAN'T MISS... I'LL MAKE A FORTUNE! THEN I'LL RETURN THE SHIP TO SNAKEYE AND MAYBE GET THE REWARD BESIDES... HEH! HEH!
JACKPOT $50
JACKPOT $150
JACKPOT $50
MEANWHILE
WHAT'S EATIN' YOU, SHEMP? EVER SINCE WE LEFT DA BIG SHIP YOU BEEN BROODIN' AN LOOKIN' LIKE YA LOST YER BEST FRIEND!
IT'S WORST THEN THAT! I'M JUST A NO GOOD STINKER! I FIXED ALL THEM SLOT-MACHINES ON THE SHIP SO THEY'LL NEVER PAY OFF! I ONLY DID IT T'PLAY A JOKE ON YOU GUYS....
...AN NOW, EVERY TIME I THINK OF POOR INNERCENT BOGUS ALONE WITH THEM CROOKED, NEVER-PAYIN' MACHINES, I FEEL LIKE A BIG HEEL!
THAT'S A CRUEL TRICK! POOR BOGUS IS LIABLE TO LOSE EVERY CENT HE OWNS!
RIGHT! IT'S OUR DUTY TO MAKE AMENDS! WE'LL GO BACK TO DA SHIP! SNEAK ABOARD AN YOU'LL FIX DA MACHINES TO PAY OFF DOUBLE... ...TRIPLE...NO! FIX 'EM SO DEY DON'T DO NUTHIN' BUT PAY OFF!

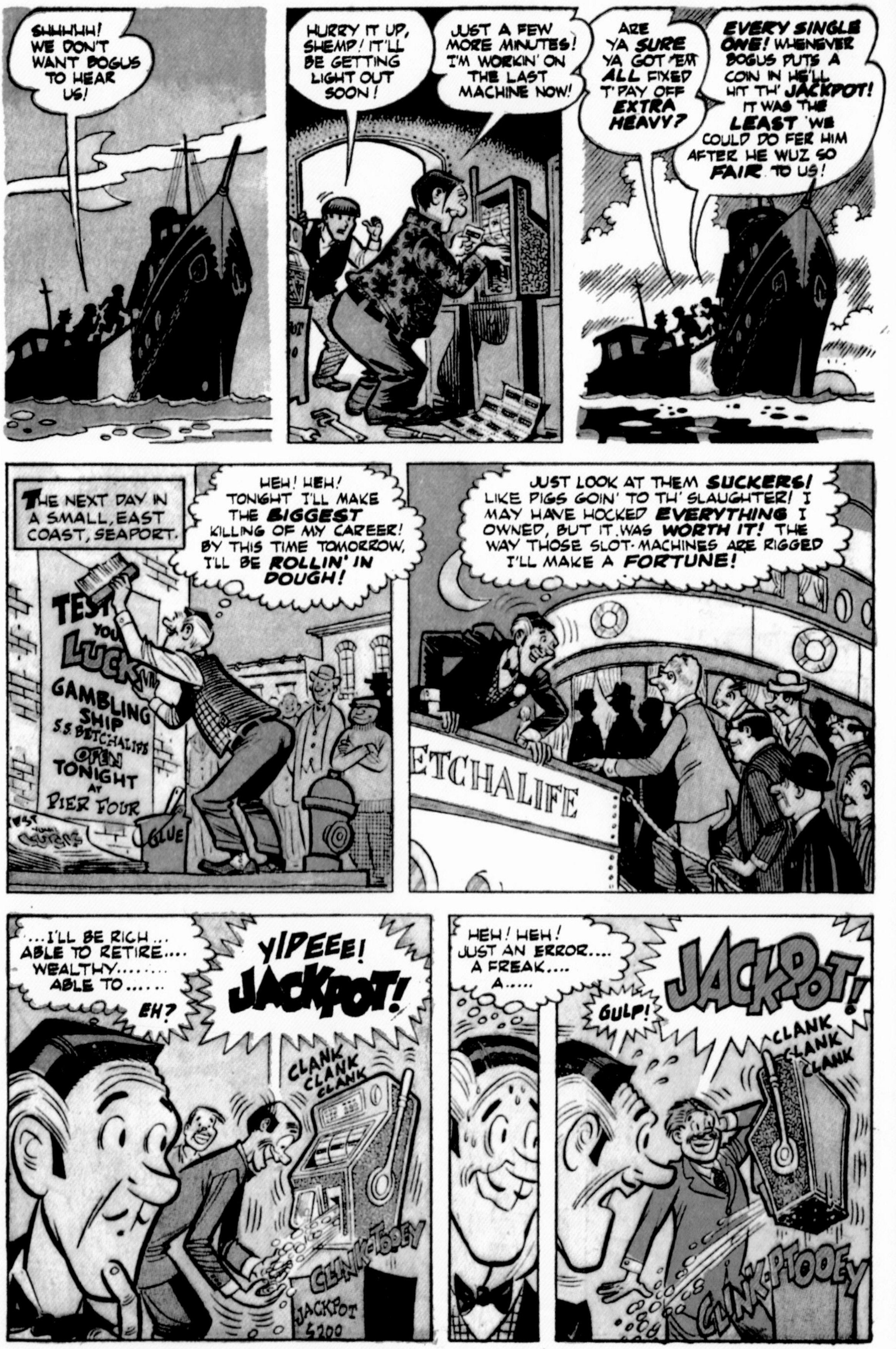
SHHHHH! WE DON'T WANT BOGUS TO HEAR US!
HURRY IT UP, SHEMP! IT'LL BE GETTING LIGHT OUT SOON!
JUST A FEW MORE MINUTES! I'M WORKIN' ON THE LAST MACHINE NOW!
ARE YA SURE YA GOT 'EM ALL FIXED T' PAY OFF EXTRA HEAVY?
EVERY SINGLE ONE! WHENEVER BOGUS PUTS A COIN IN HE'LL HIT TH' JACKPOT! IT WAS THE LEAST WE COULD DO FER HIM AFTER HE WUZ SO FAIR TO US!
THE NEXT DAY IN A SMALL, EAST COAST, SEAPORT.
HEH! HEH! TONIGHT I'LL MAKE THE BIGGEST KILLING OF MY CAREER! BY THIS TIME TOMORROW, I'LL BE ROLLIN' IN DOUGH!
TEST YOUR LUCK
GAMBLING SHIP
S.S. BETCHALIFE
OPEN TONIGHT AT PIER FOUR
GLUE
JUST LOOK AT THEM SUCKERS! LIKE PIGS GOIN' TO TH' SLAUGHTER! I MAY HAVE HOCKED EVERYTHING I OWNED, BUT IT WAS WORTH IT! THE WAY THOSE SLOT-MACHINES ARE RIGGED I'LL MAKE A FORTUNE!
ETCHALIFE
...I'LL BE RICH ... ABLE TO RETIRE.... WEALTHY........ ABLE TO ......
EH?
YIPEEE! JACKPOT!
CLANK CLANK CLANK
CLINK-TOOEY
JACKPOT $200
HEH! HEH! JUST AN ERROR.... A FREAK.... A.....
GULP!
JACKPOT!
CLANK CLANK CLANK
CLINK-PTOOEY

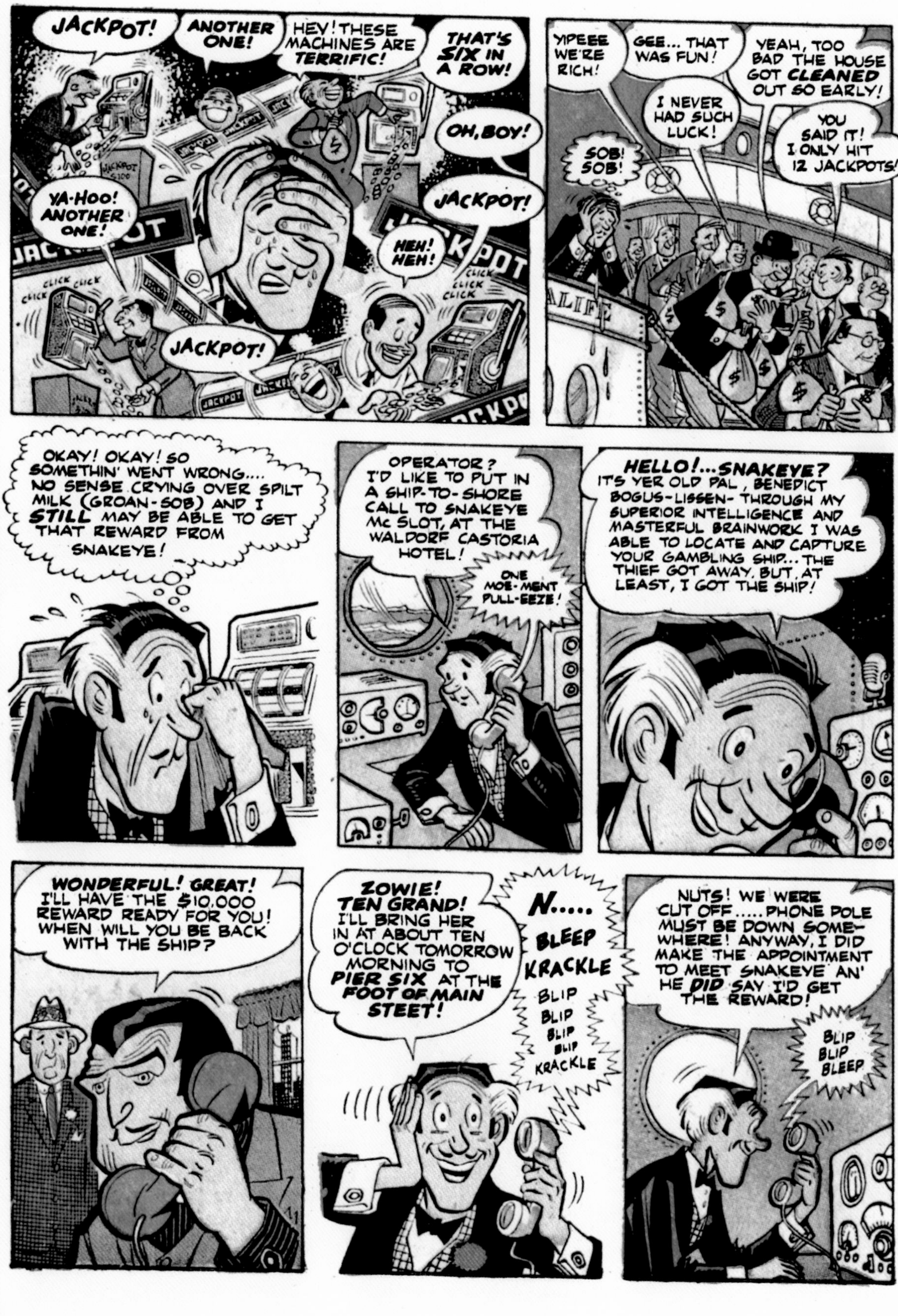
JACKPOT!
ANOTHER ONE!
HEY! THESE MACHINES ARE TERRIFIC!
THAT'S SIX IN A ROW!
OH, BOY!
YA-HOO! ANOTHER ONE!
JACKPOT!
HEH! HEH!
CLICK CLICK CLICK
CLICK CLICK CLICK
JACKPOT!
YIPEEE WE'RE RICH!
GEE... THAT WAS FUN!
YEAH, TOO BAD THE HOUSE GOT CLEANED OUT SO EARLY!
I NEVER HAD SUCH LUCK!
YOU SAID IT! I ONLY HIT 12 JACKPOTS!
SOB! SOB!
OKAY! OKAY! SO SOMETHIN' WENT WRONG.... NO SENSE CRYING OVER SPILT MILK (GROAN-SOB) AND I STILL MAY BE ABLE TO GET THAT REWARD FROM SNAKEYE!
OPERATOR? I'D LIKE TO PUT IN A SHIP-TO-SHORE CALL TO SNAKEYE Mc SLOT, AT THE WALDORF CASTORIA HOTEL!
ONE MOE-MENT PULL-EEZE!
HELLO!...SNAKEYE? IT'S YER OLD PAL, BENEDICT BOGUS-LISSEN-THROUGH MY SUPERIOR INTELLIGENCE AND MASTERFUL BRAINWORK I WAS ABLE TO LOCATE AND CAPTURE YOUR GAMBLING SHIP... THE THIEF GOT AWAY. BUT, AT LEAST, I GOT THE SHIP!
WONDERFUL! GREAT! I'LL HAVE THE $10,000 REWARD READY FOR YOU! WHEN WILL YOU BE BACK WITH THE SHIP?
ZOWIE! TEN GRAND! I'LL BRING HER IN AT ABOUT TEN O'CLOCK TOMORROW MORNING TO PIER SIX AT THE FOOT OF MAIN STEET!
N.....
BLEEP
KRACKLE
BLIP
BLIP
BLIP
BLIP
KRACKLE
NUTS! WE WERE CUT OFF.....PHONE POLE MUST BE DOWN SOME-WHERE! ANYWAY, I DID MAKE THE APPOINTMENT TO MEET SNAKEYE AN' HE DID SAY I'D GET THE REWARD!
BLIP BLIP BLEEP

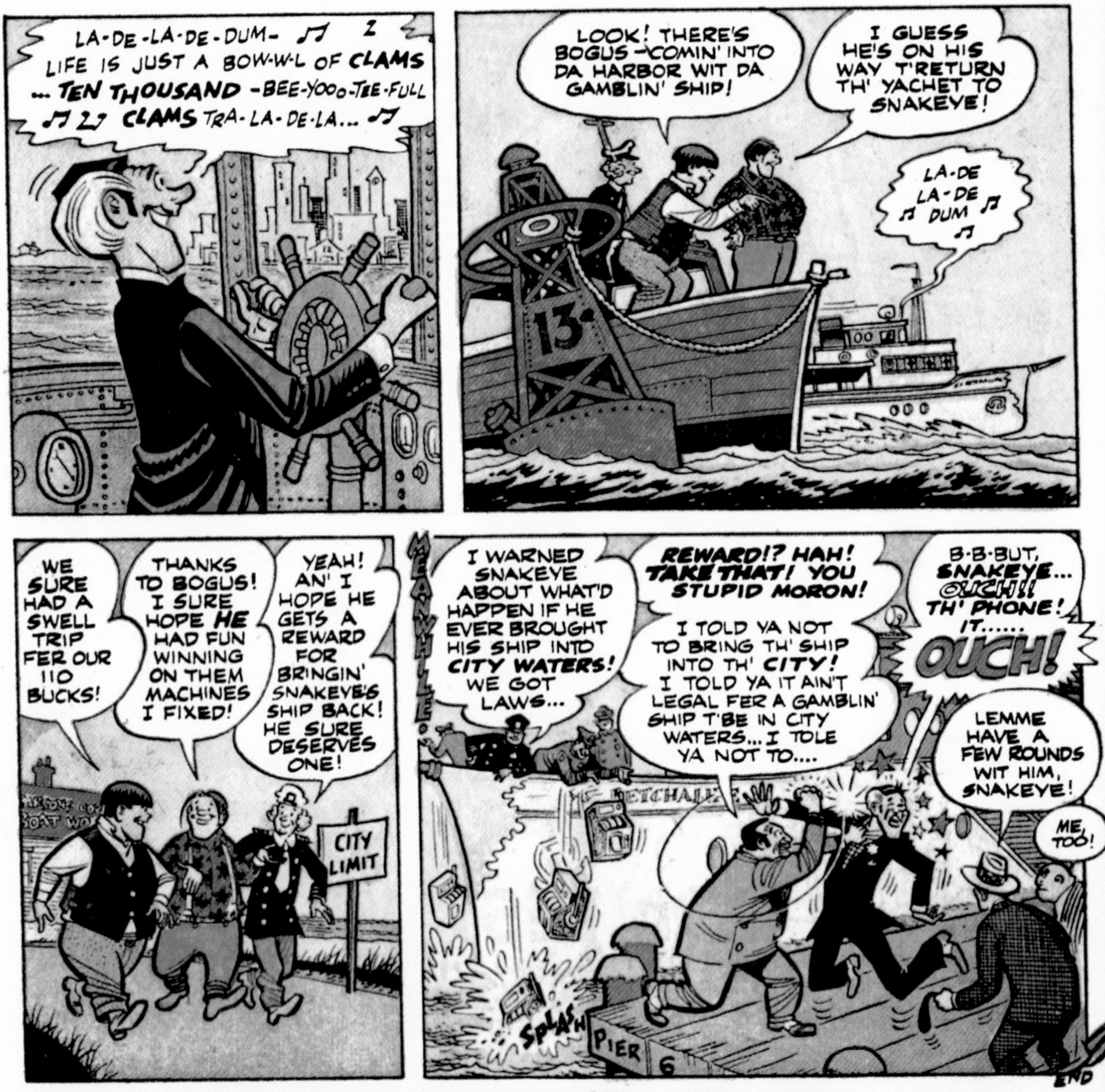
LA-DE-LA-DE-DUM- Z
LIFE IS JUST A BOW-W-L OF CLAMS
... TEN THOUSAND -BEE-YOOo-TEE-FULL
CLAMS TRA-LA-DE-LA...
LOOK! THERE'S BOGUS—COMIN' INTO DA HARBOR WIT DA GAMBLIN' SHIP!
I GUESS HE'S ON HIS WAY T'RETURN TH' YACHET TO SNAKEYE!
LA-DE LA-DE DUM
13
WE SURE HAD A SWELL TRIP FER OUR 110 BUCKS!
THANKS TO BOGUS! I SURE HOPE HE HAD FUN WINNING ON THEM MACHINES I FIXED!
YEAH! AN' I HOPE HE GETS A REWARD FOR BRINGIN' SNAKEYE'S SHIP BACK! HE SURE DESERVES ONE!
CITY LIMIT
MEANWHILE...
I WARNED SNAKEYE ABOUT WHAT'D HAPPEN IF HE EVER BROUGHT HIS SHIP INTO CITY WATERS! WE GOT LAWS...
REWARD!? HAH! TAKE THAT! YOU STUPID MORON!
I TOLD YA NOT TO BRING TH' SHIP INTO TH' CITY! I TOLD YA IT AIN'T LEGAL FER A GAMBLIN' SHIP T'BE IN CITY WATERS... I TOLE YA NOT TO....
B-B-BUT, SNAKEYE... OUCH!! TH' PHONE! IT......
OUCH!
LEMME HAVE A FEW ROUNDS WIT HIM, SNAKEYE!
ME, TOO!
SPLASH
PIER 6
END

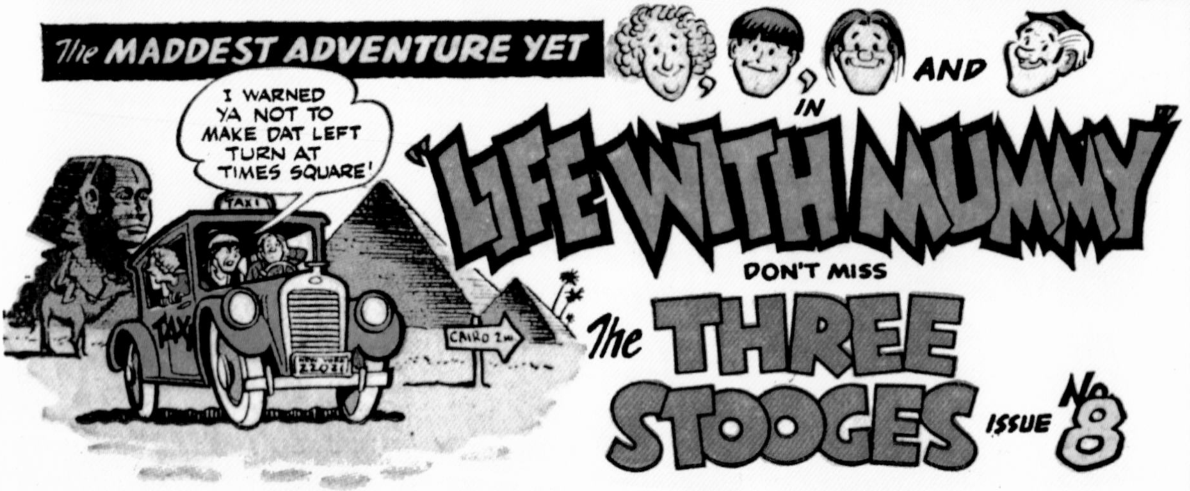
The MADDEST ADVENTURE YET
, , AND
IN
I WARNED YA NOT TO MAKE DAT LEFT TURN AT TIMES SQUARE!
TAXI
CAIRO 2 mi.
"LIFE WITH MUMMY"
DON'T MISS
The THREE STOOGES ISSUE No. 8

Editor's Note: Despite the ads, alas, there never was an eighth St. John Three Stooges comic.
(But Benedict Bogus would return 18 years later—see THE LITTLE STOOGES #1.)

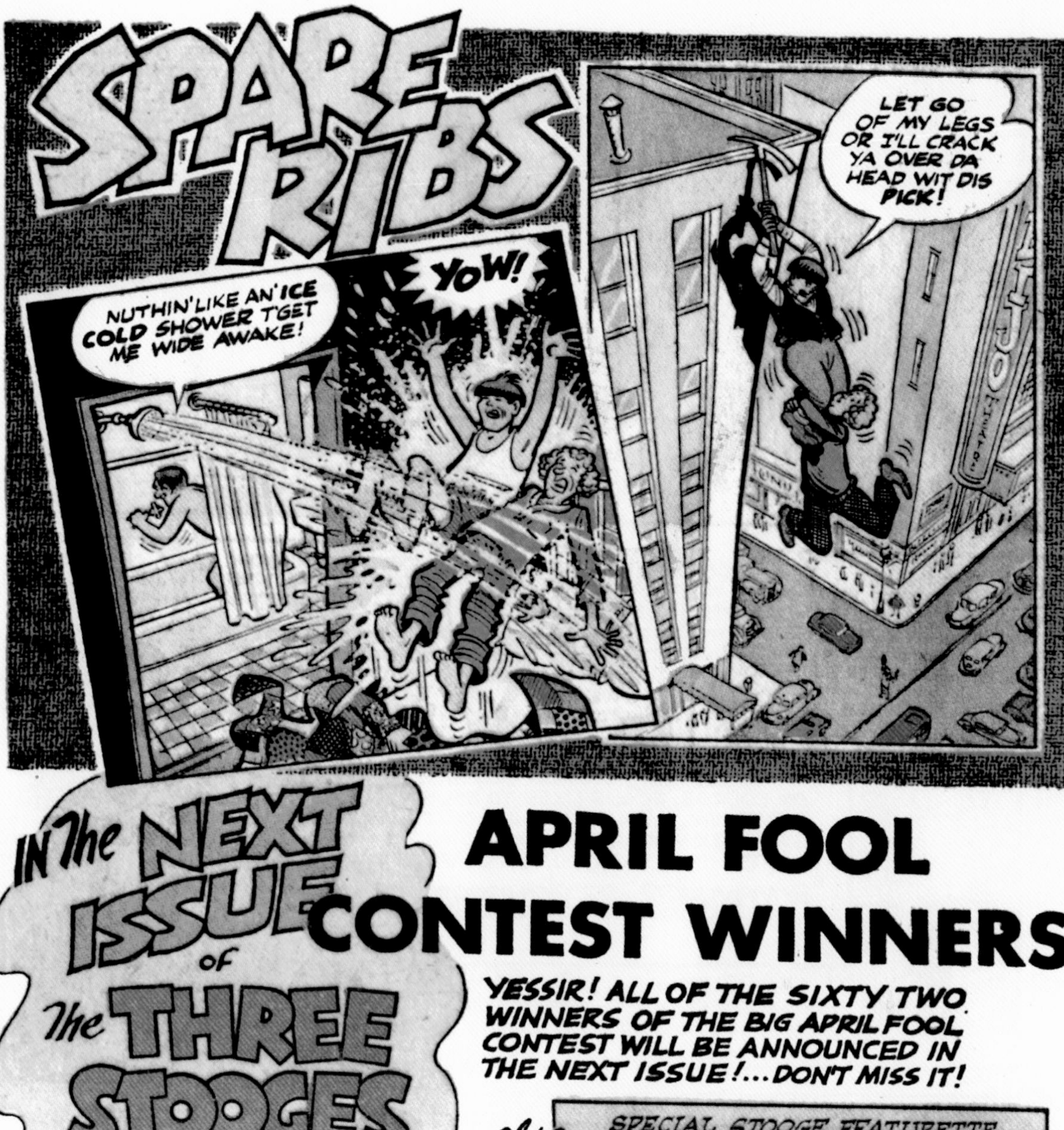
SPARE RIBS
NUTHIN' LIKE AN' ICE COLD SHOWER T'GET ME WIDE AWAKE!
YOW!
LET GO OF MY LEGS OR I'LL CRACK YA OVER DA HEAD WIT DIS PICK!
IN The NEXT ISSUE of The THREE STOOGES
APRIL FOOL CONTEST WINNERS
YESSIR! ALL OF THE SIXTY TWO WINNERS OF THE BIG APRIL FOOL CONTEST WILL BE ANNOUNCED IN THE NEXT ISSUE!... DON'T MISS IT!
also
SPECIAL STOOGE FEATURETTE
"ALI BAB-O" AND The GREASY THIEVES
ON-SALE-SOON!
HI, THERE! JOE KUBERT AND I WANT TO TAKE THIS OPPORTUNITY TO THANK ALL YOU SWELL GUYS AND GALS FOR YOUR CONTINUED SUPPORT OF OUR MAGAZINES. WE GIVE YOU OUR WORD THAT WE'LL KEEP ON TRYING TO GIVE YOU THE VERY BEST PRODUCT WE ARE CAPABLE OF PRODUCING. OUR THANKS, ALSO, FOR YOUR MANY SWELL LETTERS-WHICH ARE WRITTEN PROOF THAT OUR EFFORTS TO BRING YOU GOOD-CLEAN-WHOLESOME COMICS HAVE NOT BEEN IN VAIN! WE'LL BE LOOKING FOWARD TO HAVING YOU WITH US AGAIN IN THE COMING ISSUES OF "TOR" AND THE "THREE STOOGES"!

Editor's Note: Sorry, contest winners. There never was an eighth issue. April Fools!

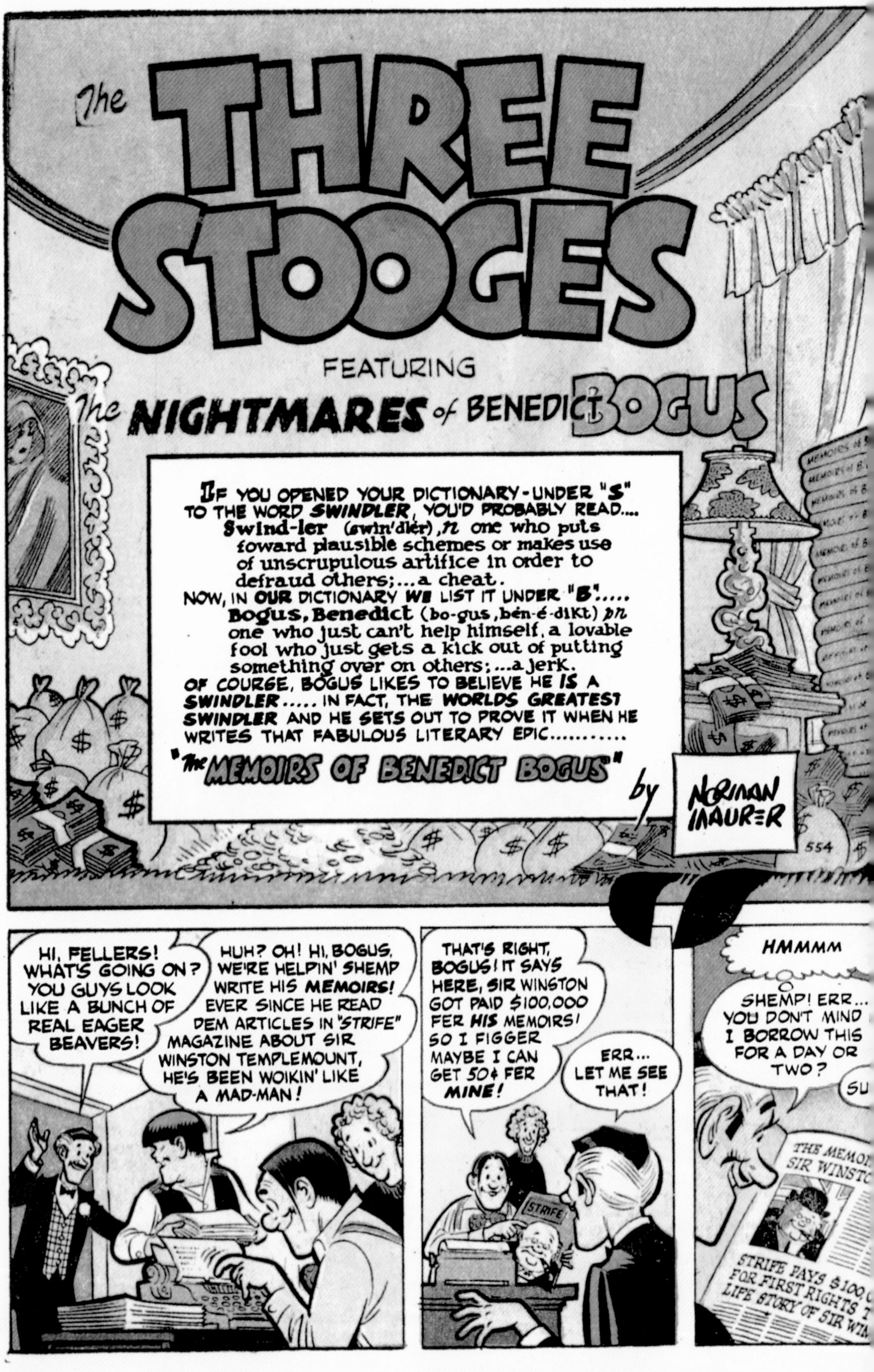

The THREE STOOGES
FEATURING
The NIGHTMARES of BENEDICT BOGUS
IF YOU OPENED YOUR DICTIONARY - UNDER "S" TO THE WORD SWINDLER, YOU'D PROBABLY READ.... Swind-ler (swin'dlér), n one who puts foward plausible schemes or makes use of unscrupulous artifice in order to defraud others;...a cheat.
NOW, IN OUR DICTIONARY WE LIST IT UNDER "B"..... Bogus, Benedict (bo-gus, bén-é-dikt) pn one who just can't help himself, a lovable fool who just gets a kick out of putting something over on others;...a jerk.
OF COURSE, BOGUS LIKES TO BELIEVE HE IS A SWINDLER..... IN FACT, THE WORLDS GREATEST SWINDLER AND HE SETS OUT TO PROVE IT WHEN HE WRITES THAT FABULOUS LITERARY EPIC..........
"The MEMOIRS OF BENEDICT BOGUS"
by NORMAN MAURER
554
HI, FELLERS! WHAT'S GOING ON? YOU GUYS LOOK LIKE A BUNCH OF REAL EAGER BEAVERS!
HUH? OH! HI, BOGUS. WE'RE HELPIN' SHEMP WRITE HIS MEMOIRS! EVER SINCE HE READ DEM ARTICLES IN "STRIFE" MAGAZINE ABOUT SIR WINSTON TEMPLEMOUNT, HE'S BEEN WOIKIN' LIKE A MAD-MAN!
THAT'S RIGHT, BOGUS! IT SAYS HERE, SIR WINSTON GOT PAID $100,000 FER HIS MEMOIRS! SO I FIGGER MAYBE I CAN GET 50¢ FER MINE!
ERR... LET ME SEE THAT!
STRIFE
HMMMM
SHEMP! ERR... YOU DON'T MIND I BORROW THIS FOR A DAY OR TWO?
SU
THE MEMOI
SIR WINSTO
STRIFE PAYS $100,0
FOR FIRST RIGHTS T
LIFE STORY OF SIR WIN

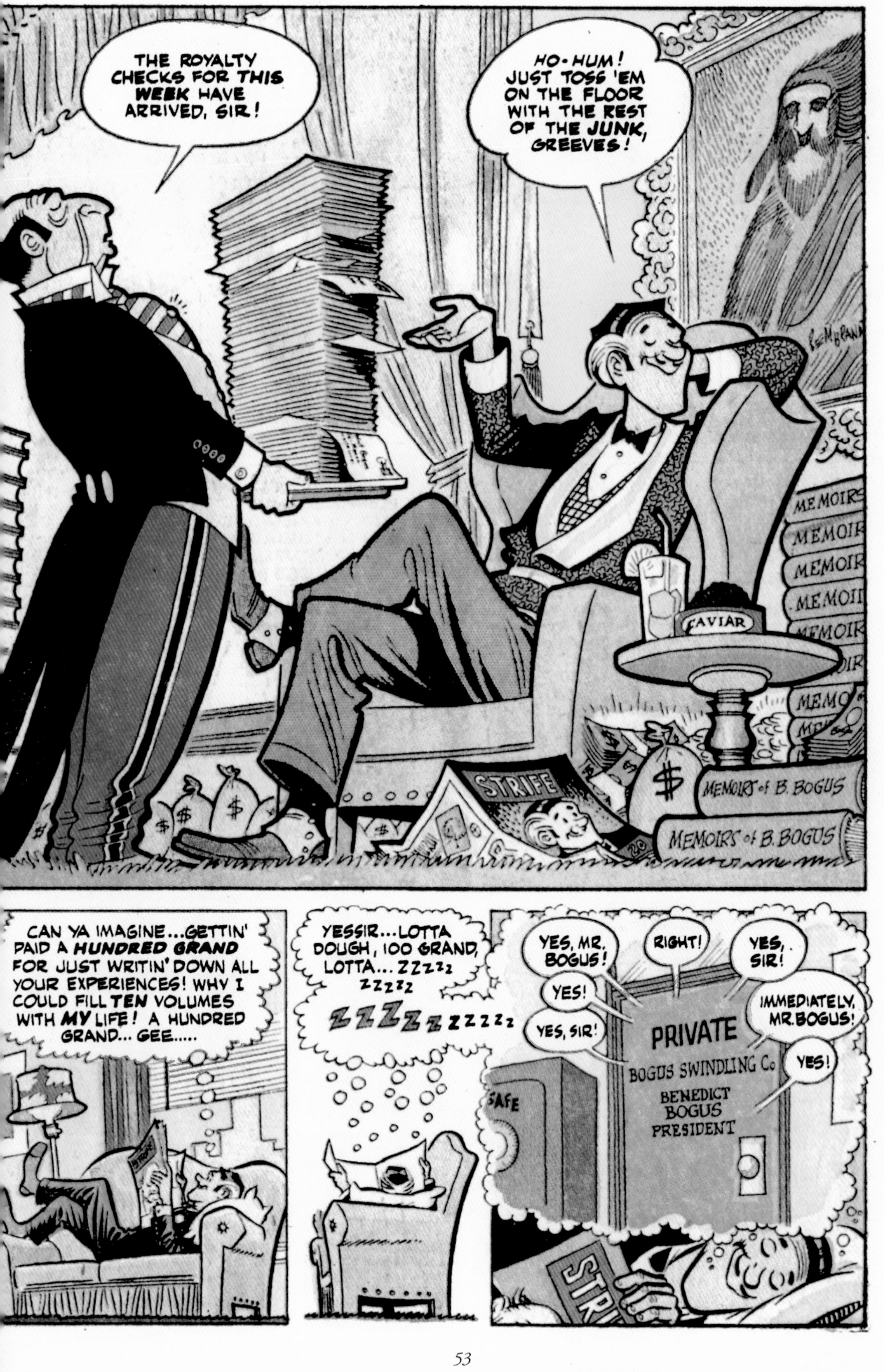
THE ROYALTY CHECKS FOR THIS WEEK HAVE ARRIVED, SIR!
HO-HUM! JUST TOSS 'EM ON THE FLOOR WITH THE REST OF THE JUNK, GREEVES!
CAVIAR
STRIFE
MEMOIRS of B. BOGUS
MEMOIRS of B. BOGUS
CAN YA IMAGINE...GETTIN' PAID A HUNDRED GRAND FOR JUST WRITIN' DOWN ALL YOUR EXPERIENCES! WHY I COULD FILL TEN VOLUMES WITH MY LIFE! A HUNDRED GRAND... GEE.....
YESSIR...LOTTA DOUGH, 100 GRAND, LOTTA... ZZZZZ ZZZZZ
ZZZZZZZZZZ
YES, MR. BOGUS!
RIGHT!
YES, SIR!
YES!
YES, SIR!
IMMEDIATELY, MR. BOGUS!
YES!
PRIVATE
BOGUS SWINDLING Co
BENEDICT BOGUS PRESIDENT
SAFE

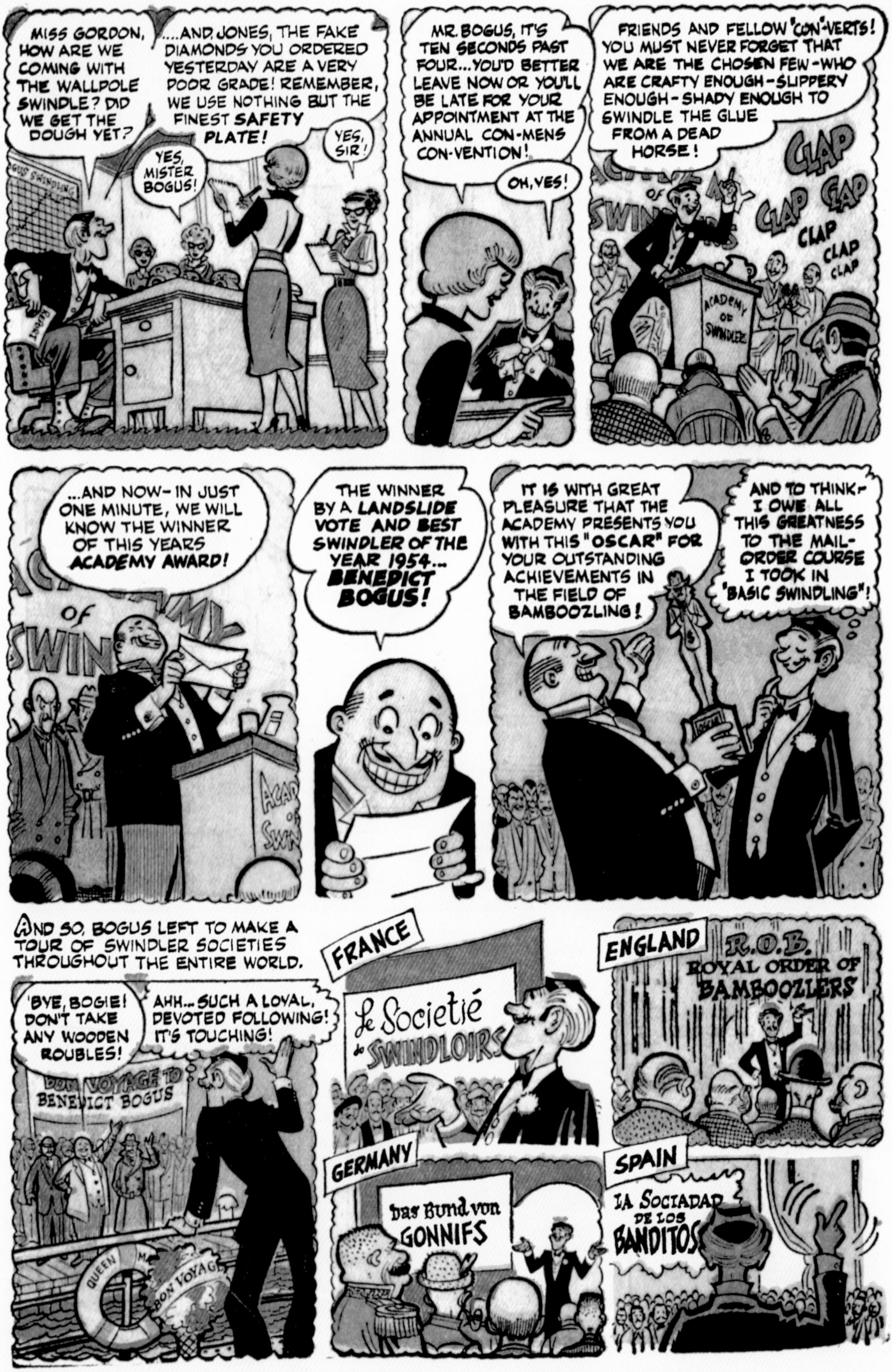

MISS GORDON, HOW ARE WE COMING WITH THE WALLPOLE SWINDLE? DID WE GET THE DOUGH YET?
....AND, JONES, THE FAKE DIAMONDS YOU ORDERED YESTERDAY ARE A VERY POOR GRADE! REMEMBER, WE USE NOTHING BUT THE FINEST SAFETY PLATE!
YES, MISTER BOGUS!
YES, SIR!
MR. BOGUS, IT'S TEN SECONDS PAST FOUR...YOU'D BETTER LEAVE NOW OR YOU'LL BE LATE FOR YOUR APPOINTMENT AT THE ANNUAL CON-MENS CON-VENTION!
OH, YES!
FRIENDS AND FELLOW "CON"-VERTS! YOU MUST NEVER FORGET THAT WE ARE THE CHOSEN FEW-WHO ARE CRAFTY ENOUGH-SLIPPERY ENOUGH-SHADY ENOUGH TO SWINDLE THE GLUE FROM A DEAD HORSE!
CLAP CLAP CLAP CLAP CLAP CLAP
ACADEMY OF SWINDLERS
...AND NOW-IN JUST ONE MINUTE, WE WILL KNOW THE WINNER OF THIS YEARS ACADEMY AWARD!
THE WINNER BY A LANDSLIDE VOTE AND BEST SWINDLER OF THE YEAR 1954... BENEDICT BOGUS!
IT IS WITH GREAT PLEASURE THAT THE ACADEMY PRESENTS YOU WITH THIS "OSCAR" FOR YOUR OUTSTANDING ACHIEVEMENTS IN THE FIELD OF BAMBOOZLING!
AND TO THINK-I OWE ALL THIS GREATNESS TO THE MAIL-ORDER COURSE I TOOK IN "BASIC SWINDLING"!
OSCAR
AND SO, BOGUS LEFT TO MAKE A TOUR OF SWINDLER SOCIETIES THROUGHOUT THE ENTIRE WORLD.
'BYE, BOGIE! DON'T TAKE ANY WOODEN ROUBLES!
AHH... SUCH A LOYAL, DEVOTED FOLLOWING! IT'S TOUCHING!
BON VOYAGE TO BENEDICT BOGUS
QUEEN MA
BON VOYAGE
FRANCE
Le Societié de SWINDLOIRS
ENGLAND
R.O.B. ROYAL ORDER OF BAMBOOZLERS
GERMANY
Das Bund von GONNIFS
SPAIN
LA SOCIADAD DE LOS BANDITOS

GATER .... BACK IN THE U.S.A.

EDITOR'S NOTE: NOT BAD DRAWING! JUST A SWELLED HEAD!

HEH! HEH! Y'KNOW — I'M BEGINNING TO THINK I'M TERRIFIC!!

The Cheaters Digest
BOGUS ACCLAIMED FOREMOST SWINDLER OF ALL TIME

YES, SIR! A REAL SENSATIONAL CHARACTER.... I MUST TELL THE ENTIRE WORLD OF MY GREATNESS! IT IS MY DUTY TO MANKIND TO WRITE THE FULL STORY OF MY LIFE!

WHY DIDN'T I THINK OF THIS BEFORE? THE MEMOIRS OF BENEDICT BOGUS WILL BE THE LITERARY MASTERPIECE OF ALL TIME!

LATER

THERE YOU ARE, MR. BOGUS, YOUR ADVANCE ROYALTY CHECK FOR $100,000! YOUR MEMOIRS ARE THE HOTTEST THING SINCE 3-D COMICS!

HEH! HEH! NATURALLY! I JUST HOPE YOU'LL BE ABLE TO BUY ENOUGH PAPER FOR ALL THE RE-PRINTS!

STRIFE

EDITOR-STRIFE INC.

HMM! NOT BAD! NOT BAD AT ALL .... I LOOK A LITTLE LIKE HUMPHRY BOGUS... ERR, BOGURT!

STRIFE

...AND THE WINNER OF THE 1954 "BULLITZER" PRIZE, FOR LITERATURE...BENEDICT BOGUS! HERE, SIR, IS YOUR AWARD CHECK FOR $50,000, FOR WRITING THE GREATEST MEMOIRS OF ALL TIME!

IT WAS NOTHIN'!

BULLITZER 1954

YOUR ROYALTY CHECKS FOR THIS WEEK HAVE ARRIVED, SIR!

JUST TOSS 'EM ON THE FLOOR WITH THE REST OF THE JUNK, GREEVES!

HEH! HEH! I'M GETTING RICHER EVERY DAY!

MEMOIRS

STRIFE

RICHER... RICHER...

POP

YOW!

STRIFE

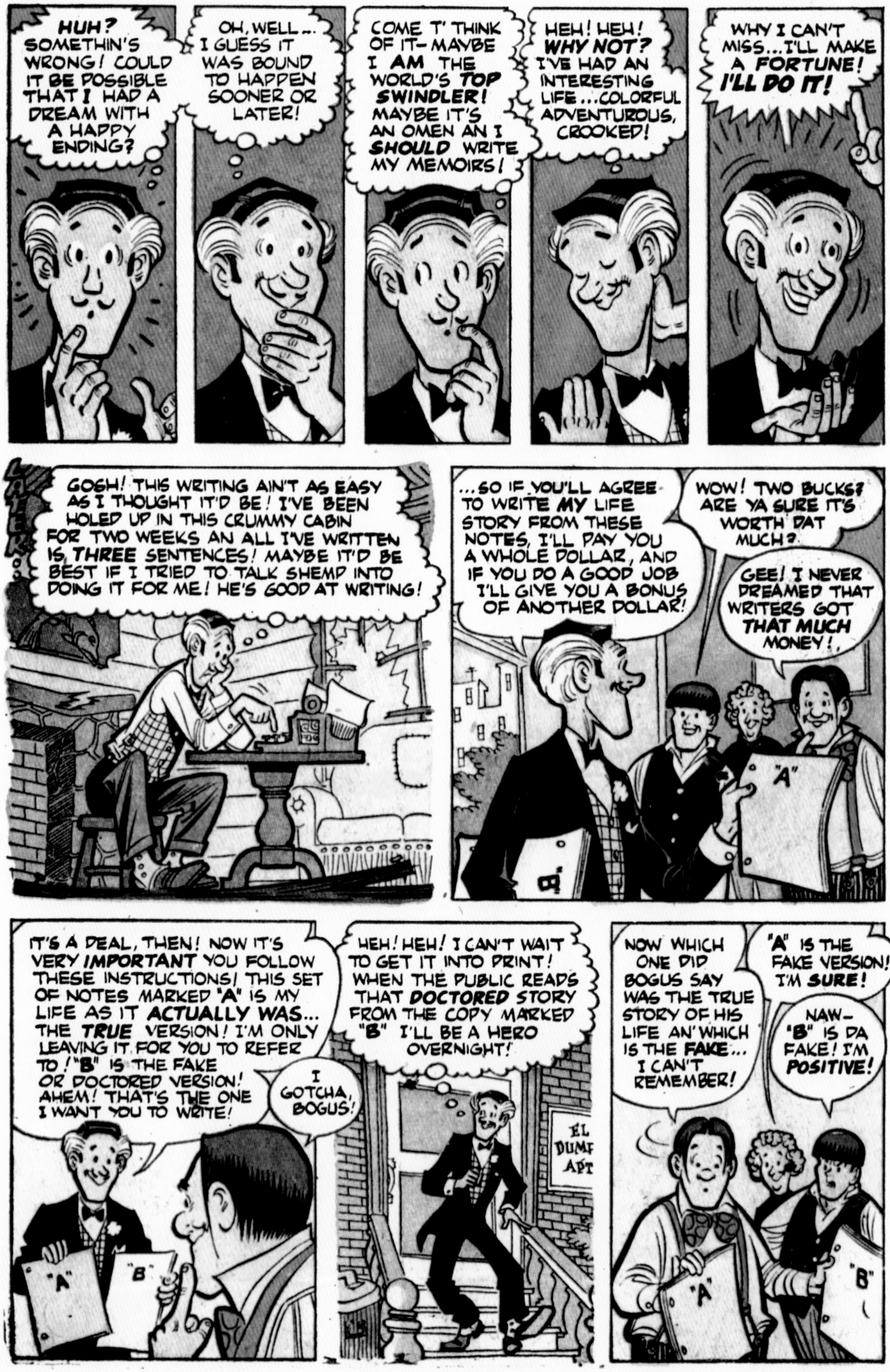
HUH? SOMETHIN'S WRONG! COULD IT BE POSSIBLE THAT I HAD A DREAM WITH A HAPPY ENDING?
OH, WELL... I GUESS IT WAS BOUND TO HAPPEN SOONER OR LATER!
COME T' THINK OF IT- MAYBE I AM THE WORLD'S TOP SWINDLER! MAYBE IT'S AN OMEN AN I SHOULD WRITE MY MEMOIRS!
HEH! HEH! WHY NOT? I'VE HAD AN INTERESTING LIFE... COLORFUL ADVENTUROUS, CROOKED!
WHY I CAN'T MISS... I'LL MAKE A FORTUNE! I'LL DO IT!
LATER...
GOSH! THIS WRITING AIN'T AS EASY AS I THOUGHT IT'D BE! I'VE BEEN HOLED UP IN THIS CRUMMY CABIN FOR TWO WEEKS AN ALL I'VE WRITTEN IS THREE SENTENCES! MAYBE IT'D BE BEST IF I TRIED TO TALK SHEMP INTO DOING IT FOR ME! HE'S GOOD AT WRITING!
...SO IF YOU'LL AGREE TO WRITE MY LIFE STORY FROM THESE NOTES, I'LL PAY YOU A WHOLE DOLLAR, AND IF YOU DO A GOOD JOB I'LL GIVE YOU A BONUS OF ANOTHER DOLLAR!
WOW! TWO BUCKS? ARE YA SURE IT'S WORTH DAT MUCH?
GEE! I NEVER DREAMED THAT WRITERS GOT THAT MUCH MONEY!
"A"
"B"
IT'S A DEAL, THEN! NOW IT'S VERY IMPORTANT YOU FOLLOW THESE INSTRUCTIONS! THIS SET OF NOTES MARKED "A" IS MY LIFE AS IT ACTUALLY WAS... THE TRUE VERSION! I'M ONLY LEAVING IT FOR YOU TO REFER TO! "B" IS THE FAKE OR DOCTORED VERSION! AHEM! THAT'S THE ONE I WANT YOU TO WRITE!
I GOTCHA, BOGUS!
"A"
"B"
HEH! HEH! I CAN'T WAIT TO GET IT INTO PRINT! WHEN THE PUBLIC READS THAT DOCTORED STORY FROM THE COPY MARKED "B" I'LL BE A HERO OVERNIGHT!
EL DUMP APT
NOW WHICH ONE DID BOGUS SAY WAS THE TRUE STORY OF HIS LIFE AN' WHICH IS THE FAKE... I CAN'T REMEMBER!
"A" IS THE FAKE VERSION! I'M SURE!
NAW- "B" IS DA FAKE! I'M POSITIVE!
"A"
"B"

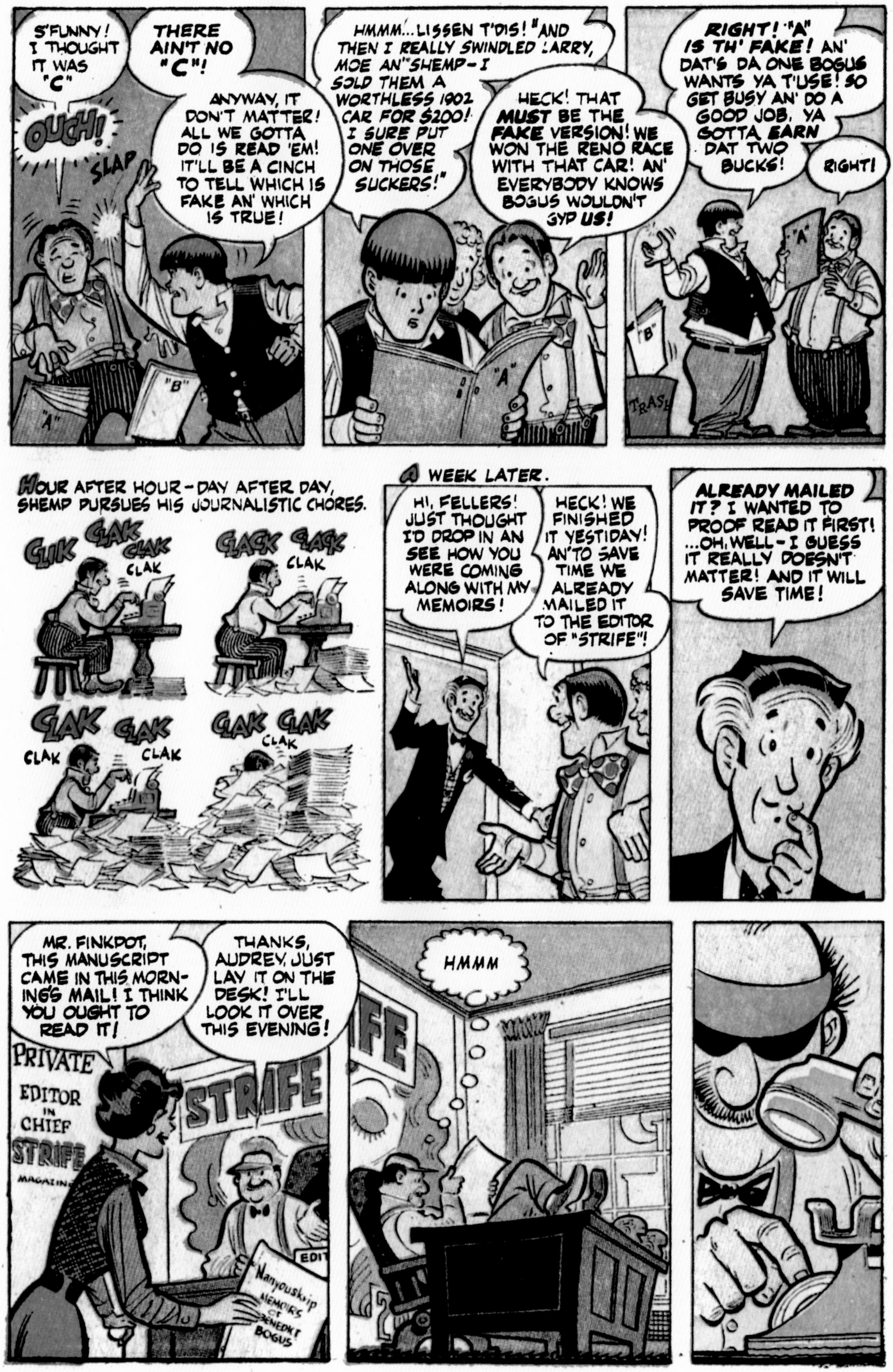
S'FUNNY! I THOUGHT IT WAS "C"
THERE AIN'T NO "C"!
OUCH!
SLAP
ANYWAY, IT DON'T MATTER! ALL WE GOTTA DO IS READ 'EM! IT'LL BE A CINCH TO TELL WHICH IS FAKE AN' WHICH IS TRUE!
"B"
"A"
HMMM...LISSEN T'DIS! "AND THEN I REALLY SWINDLED LARRY, MOE AN' SHEMP - I SOLD THEM A WORTHLESS 1902 CAR FOR $200! I SURE PUT ONE OVER ON THOSE SUCKERS!"
HECK! THAT MUST BE THE FAKE VERSION! WE WON THE RENO RACE WITH THAT CAR! AN' EVERYBODY KNOWS BOGUS WOULDN'T GYP US!
"A"
RIGHT! "A" IS TH' FAKE! AN' DAT'S DA ONE BOGUS WANTS YA T'USE! SO GET BUSY AN' DO A GOOD JOB, YA GOTTA EARN DAT TWO BUCKS!
RIGHT!
"A"
"B"
TRASH
HOUR AFTER HOUR - DAY AFTER DAY, SHEMP PURSUES HIS JOURNALISTIC CHORES.
CLIK CLAK CLAK CLAK
CLACK CLACK CLAK
CLAK CLAK CLAK CLAK
CLAK CLAK CLAK
A WEEK LATER.
HI, FELLERS! JUST THOUGHT I'D DROP IN AN SEE HOW YOU WERE COMING ALONG WITH MY MEMOIRS!
HECK! WE FINISHED IT YESTIDAY! AN' TO SAVE TIME WE ALREADY MAILED IT TO THE EDITOR OF "STRIFE"!
ALREADY MAILED IT? I WANTED TO PROOF READ IT FIRST! ...OH, WELL - I GUESS IT REALLY DOESN'T MATTER! AND IT WILL SAVE TIME!
MR. FINKPOT, THIS MANUSCRIPT CAME IN THIS MORNING'S MAIL! I THINK YOU OUGHT TO READ IT!
THANKS, AUDREY, JUST LAY IT ON THE DESK! I'LL LOOK IT OVER THIS EVENING!
PRIVATE
EDITOR IN CHIEF
STRIFE
STRIFE
EDIT
MEMOIRS OF
BOGUS
HMMM
IFE

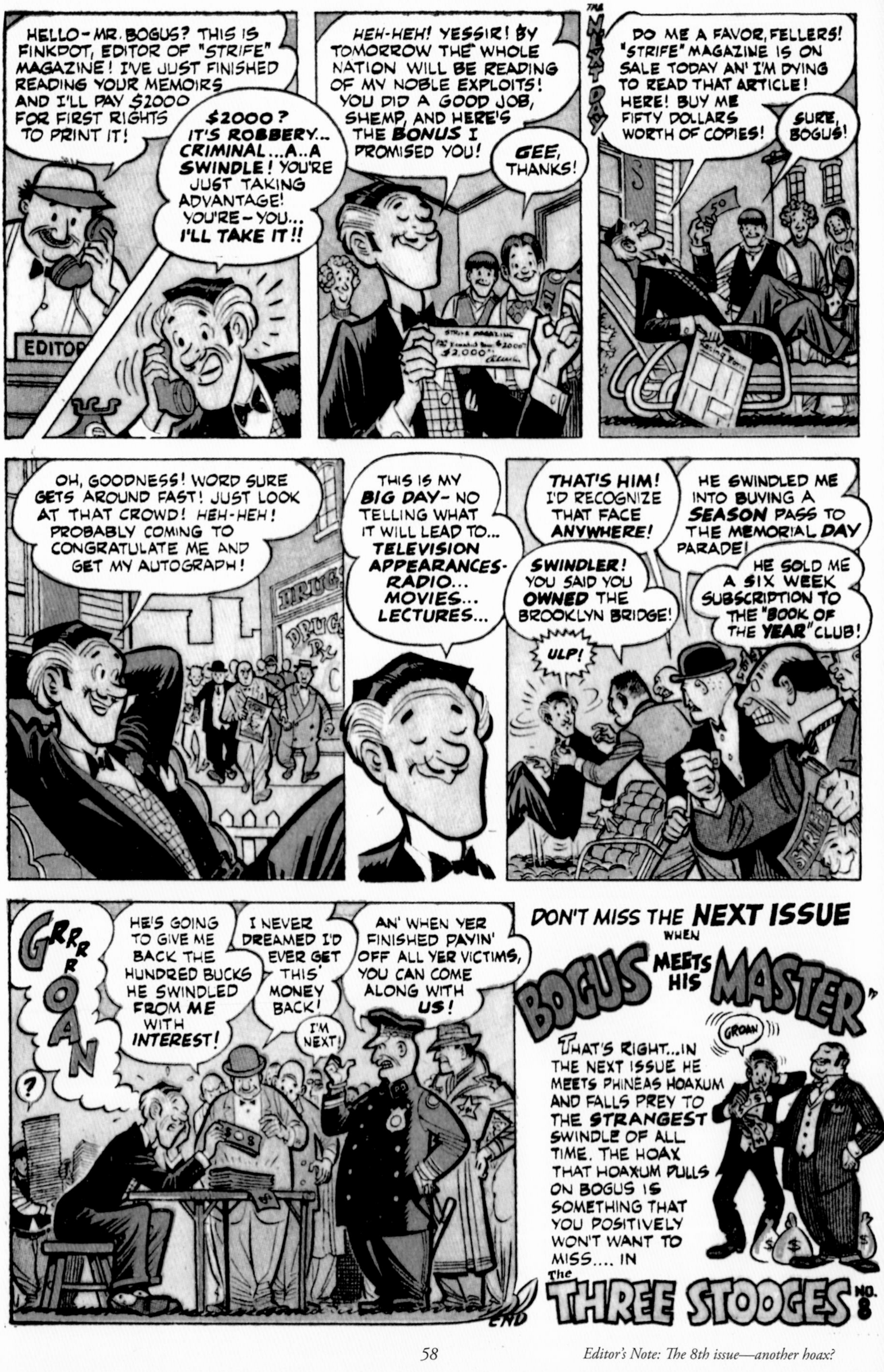
HELLO–MR. BOGUS? THIS IS FINKDOT, EDITOR OF "STRIFE" MAGAZINE! I'VE JUST FINISHED READING YOUR MEMOIRS AND I'LL PAY $2000 FOR FIRST RIGHTS TO PRINT IT!
EDITOR
$2000? IT'S ROBBERY... CRIMINAL...A..A SWINDLE! YOU'RE JUST TAKING ADVANTAGE! YOU'RE–YOU... I'LL TAKE IT!!
HEH-HEH! YESSIR! BY TOMORROW THE WHOLE NATION WILL BE READING OF MY NOBLE EXPLOITS! YOU DID A GOOD JOB, SHEMP, AND HERE'S THE BONUS I PROMISED YOU!
GEE, THANKS!
$2,000
THE NEXT DAY
DO ME A FAVOR, FELLERS! "STRIFE" MAGAZINE IS ON SALE TODAY AN' I'M DYING TO READ THAT ARTICLE! HERE! BUY ME FIFTY DOLLARS WORTH OF COPIES!
SURE, BOGUS!
OH, GOODNESS! WORD SURE GETS AROUND FAST! JUST LOOK AT THAT CROWD! HEH-HEH! PROBABLY COMING TO CONGRATULATE ME AND GET MY AUTOGRAPH!
DRUGS
THIS IS MY BIG DAY–NO TELLING WHAT IT WILL LEAD TO... TELEVISION APPEARANCES-RADIO... MOVIES... LECTURES...
THAT'S HIM! I'D RECOGNIZE THAT FACE ANYWHERE!
HE SWINDLED ME INTO BUYING A SEASON PASS TO THE MEMORIAL DAY PARADE!
SWINDLER! YOU SAID YOU OWNED THE BROOKLYN BRIDGE!
HE SOLD ME A SIX WEEK SUBSCRIPTION TO THE "BOOK OF THE YEAR" CLUB!
ULP!
STRIFE
GRRRR ROAN
?
HE'S GOING TO GIVE ME BACK THE HUNDRED BUCKS HE SWINDLED FROM ME WITH INTEREST!
I NEVER DREAMED I'D EVER GET THIS MONEY BACK!
AN' WHEN YER FINISHED PAYIN' OFF ALL YER VICTIMS, YOU CAN COME ALONG WITH US!
I'M NEXT!
END
DON'T MISS THE NEXT ISSUE WHEN
"BOGUS MEETS HIS MASTER"
GROAN
THAT'S RIGHT...IN THE NEXT ISSUE HE MEETS PHINEAS HOAXUM AND FALLS PREY TO THE STRANGEST SWINDLE OF ALL TIME. THE HOAX THAT HOAXUM PULLS ON BOGUS IS SOMETHING THAT YOU POSITIVELY WON'T WANT TO MISS.... IN
The THREE STOOGES NO. 8

Editor's Note: The 8th issue—another hoax?

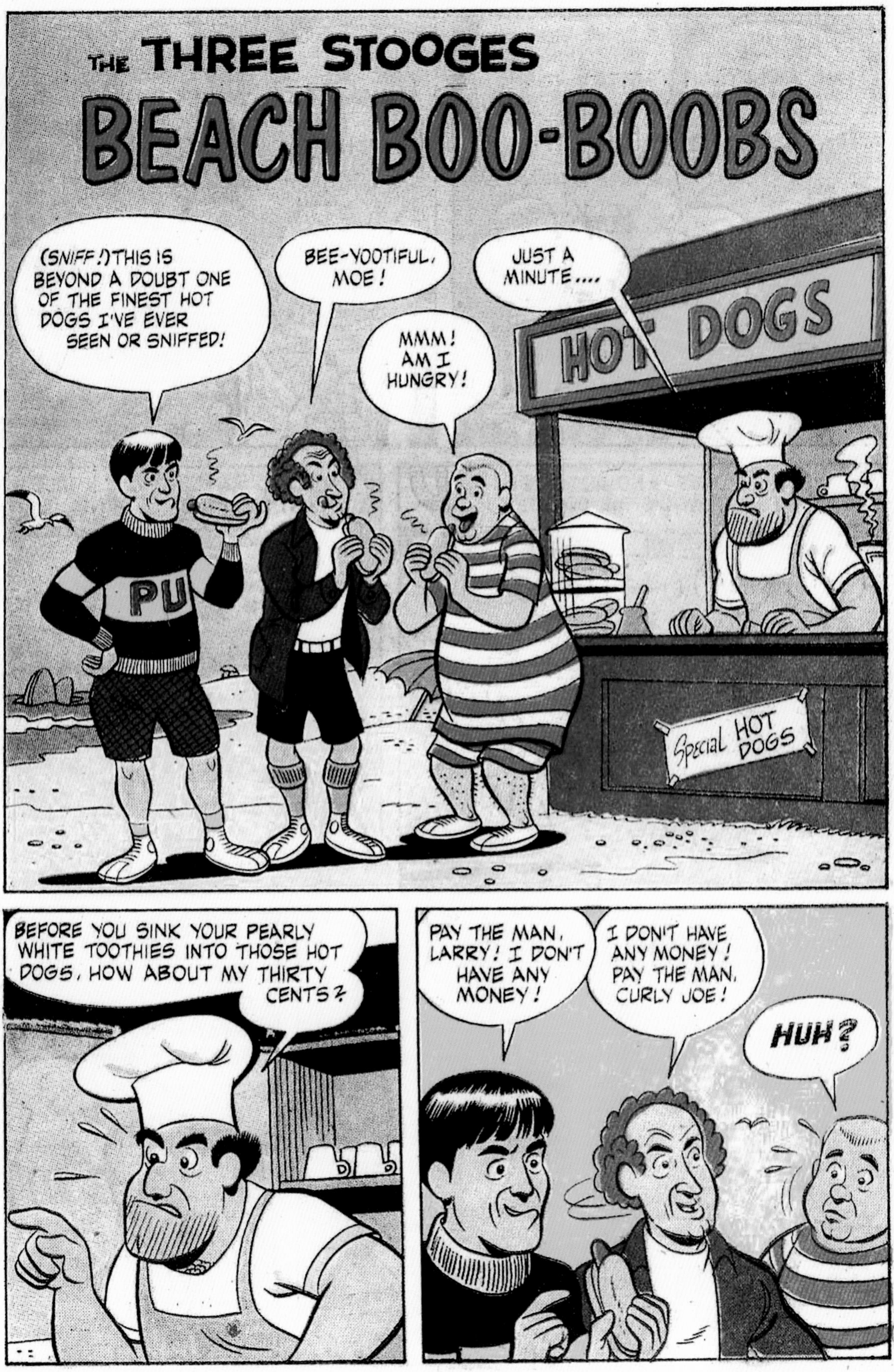
THE THREE STOOGES
BEACH BOO-BOOBS
(SNIFF!) THIS IS BEYOND A DOUBT ONE OF THE FINEST HOT DOGS I'VE EVER SEEN OR SNIFFED!
BEE-YOOTIFUL, MOE!
MMM! AM I HUNGRY!
JUST A MINUTE....
HOT DOGS
PU
Special HOT DOGS
BEFORE YOU SINK YOUR PEARLY WHITE TOOTHIES INTO THOSE HOT DOGS, HOW ABOUT MY THIRTY CENTS?
PAY THE MAN, LARRY! I DON'T HAVE ANY MONEY!
I DON'T HAVE ANY MONEY! PAY THE MAN, CURLY JOE!
HUH?

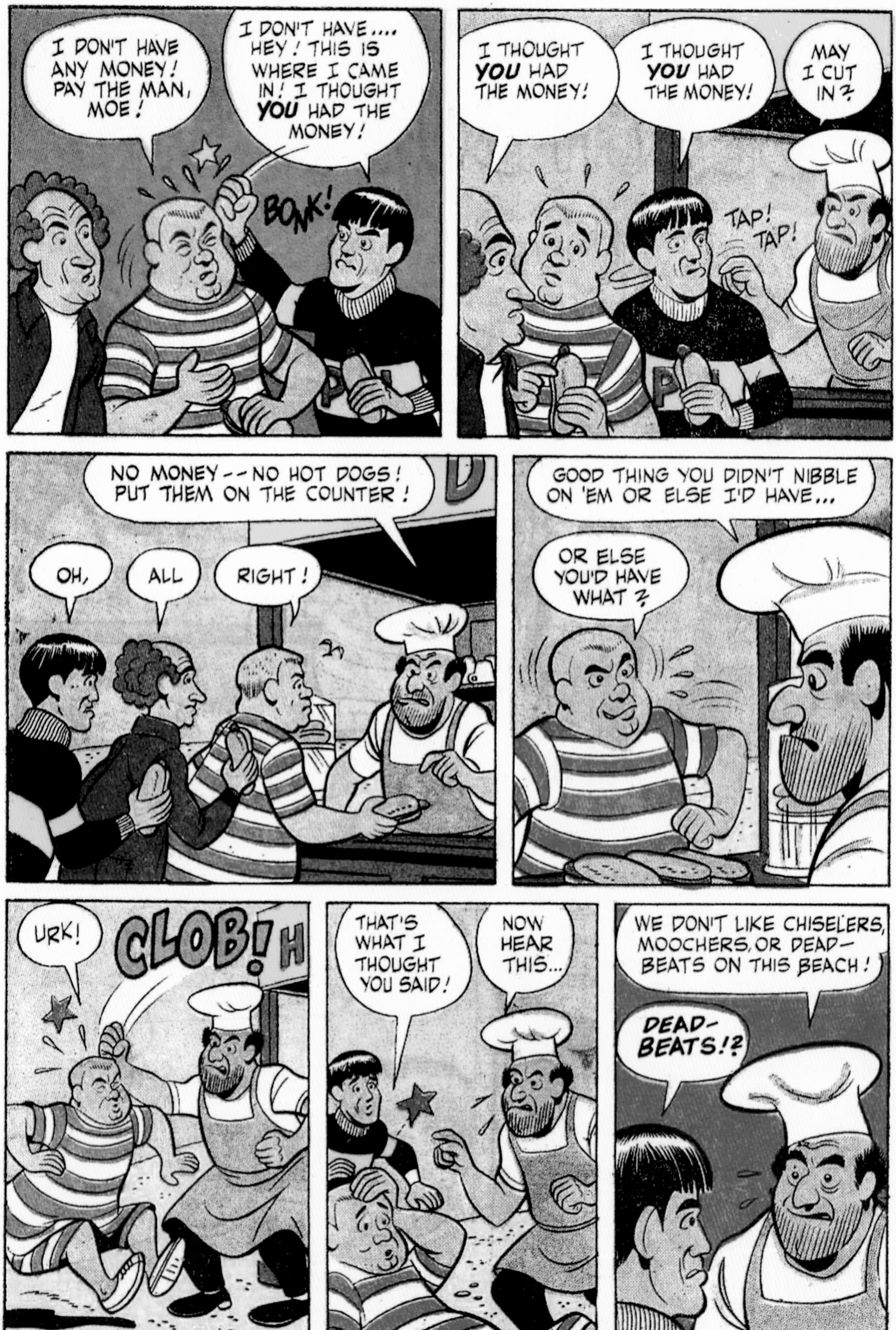
I DON'T HAVE ANY MONEY! PAY THE MAN, MOE!
I DON'T HAVE.... HEY! THIS IS WHERE I CAME IN! I THOUGHT YOU HAD THE MONEY!
BONK!
I THOUGHT YOU HAD THE MONEY!
I THOUGHT YOU HAD THE MONEY!
MAY I CUT IN?
TAP! TAP!
NO MONEY--NO HOT DOGS! PUT THEM ON THE COUNTER!
OH,
ALL
RIGHT!
GOOD THING YOU DIDN'T NIBBLE ON 'EM OR ELSE I'D HAVE...
OR ELSE YOU'D HAVE WHAT?
URK!
CLOB!
THAT'S WHAT I THOUGHT YOU SAID!
NOW HEAR THIS...
WE DON'T LIKE CHISELERS, MOOCHERS, OR DEAD-BEATS ON THIS BEACH!
DEAD-BEATS!?

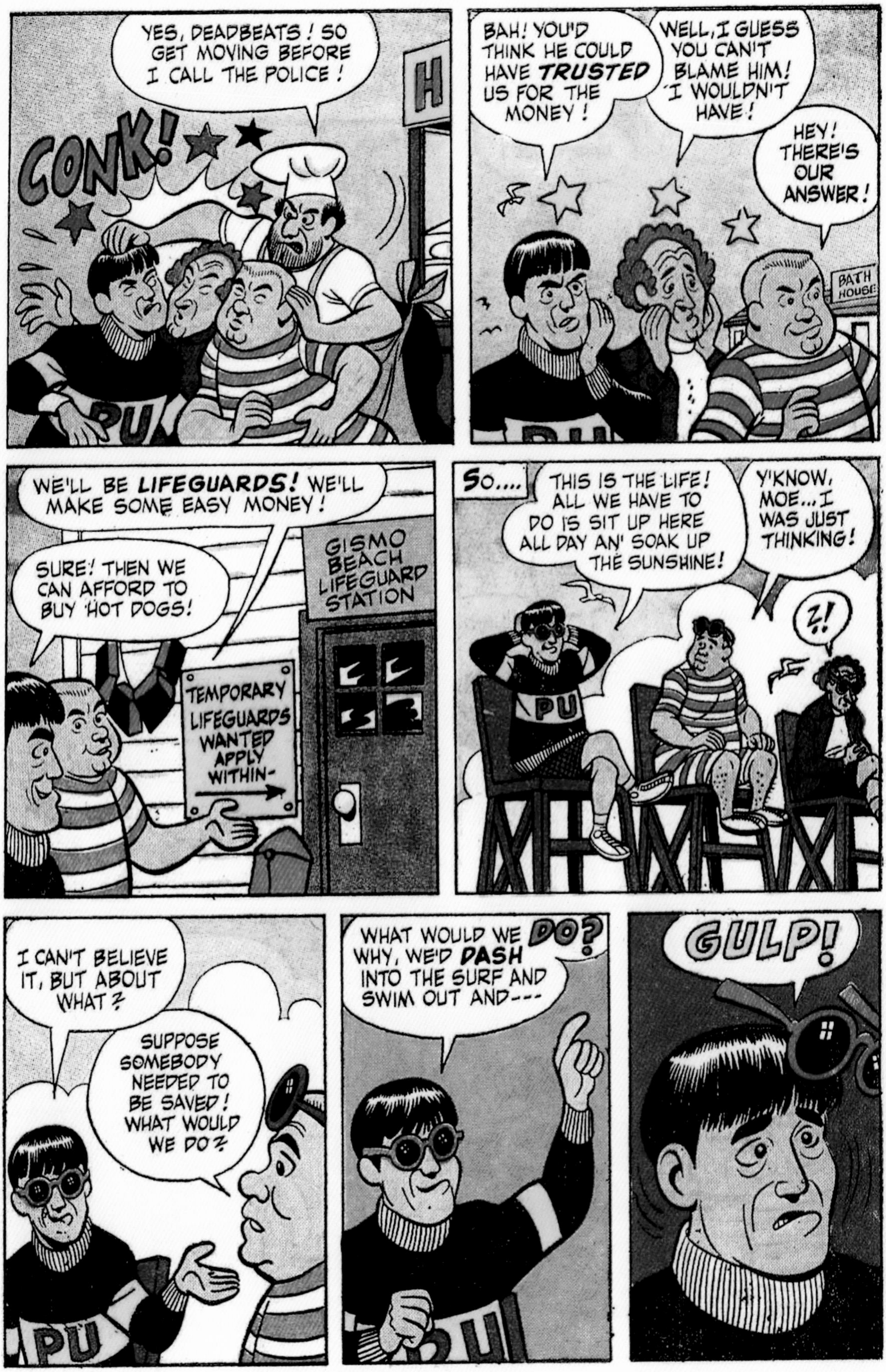
YES, DEADBEATS! SO GET MOVING BEFORE I CALL THE POLICE!
CONK!
H
BAH! YOU'D THINK HE COULD HAVE TRUSTED US FOR THE MONEY!
WELL, I GUESS YOU CAN'T BLAME HIM! I WOULDN'T HAVE!
HEY! THERE'S OUR ANSWER!
BATH HOUSE
PU
WE'LL BE LIFEGUARDS! WE'LL MAKE SOME EASY MONEY!
SURE! THEN WE CAN AFFORD TO BUY HOT DOGS!
GISMO BEACH LIFEGUARD STATION
TEMPORARY LIFEGUARDS WANTED APPLY WITHIN-
SO....
THIS IS THE LIFE! ALL WE HAVE TO DO IS SIT UP HERE ALL DAY AN' SOAK UP THE SUNSHINE!
Y'KNOW, MOE...I WAS JUST THINKING!
?!
I CAN'T BELIEVE IT, BUT ABOUT WHAT?
SUPPOSE SOMEBODY NEEDED TO BE SAVED! WHAT WOULD WE DO?
WHAT WOULD WE DO? WHY, WE'D DASH INTO THE SURF AND SWIM OUT AND---
GULP!

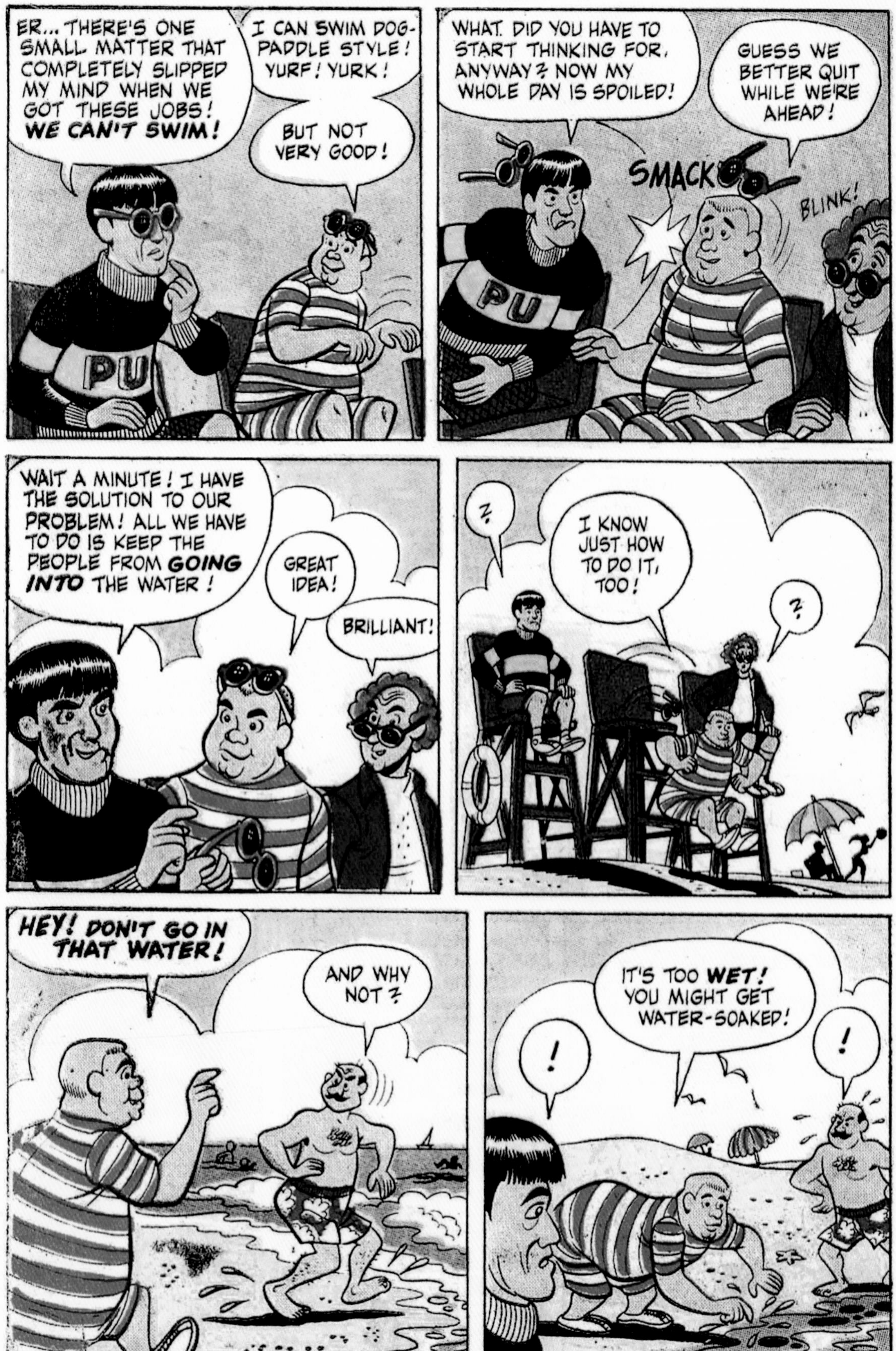
ER... THERE'S ONE SMALL MATTER THAT COMPLETELY SLIPPED MY MIND WHEN WE GOT THESE JOBS! WE CAN'T SWIM!
I CAN SWIM DOG-PADDLE STYLE! YURF! YURK!
BUT NOT VERY GOOD!
WHAT. DID YOU HAVE TO START THINKING FOR, ANYWAY? NOW MY WHOLE DAY IS SPOILED!
GUESS WE BETTER QUIT WHILE WE'RE AHEAD!
SMACK
BLINK!
WAIT A MINUTE! I HAVE THE SOLUTION TO OUR PROBLEM! ALL WE HAVE TO DO IS KEEP THE PEOPLE FROM GOING INTO THE WATER!
GREAT IDEA!
BRILLIANT!
?
I KNOW JUST HOW TO DO IT, TOO!
?
HEY! DON'T GO IN THAT WATER!
AND WHY NOT?
!
IT'S TOO WET! YOU MIGHT GET WATER-SOAKED!
!

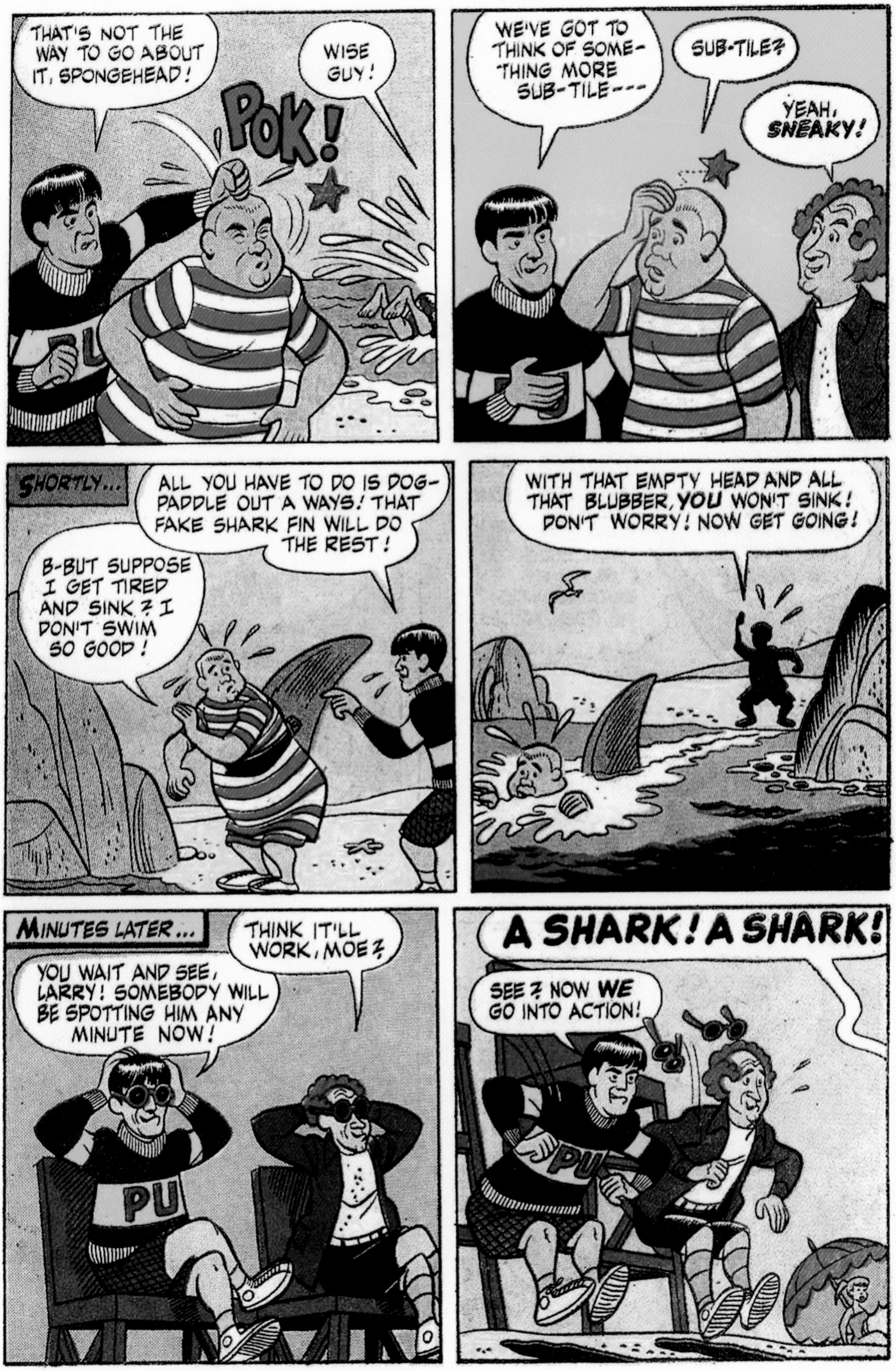
THAT'S NOT THE WAY TO GO ABOUT IT, SPONGEHEAD!
WISE GUY!
POK!
WE'VE GOT TO THINK OF SOME-THING MORE SUB-TILE---
SUB-TILE?
YEAH, SNEAKY!
SHORTLY...
ALL YOU HAVE TO DO IS DOG-PADDLE OUT A WAYS! THAT FAKE SHARK FIN WILL DO THE REST!
B-BUT SUPPOSE I GET TIRED AND SINK? I DON'T SWIM SO GOOD!
WITH THAT EMPTY HEAD AND ALL THAT BLUBBER, YOU WON'T SINK! DON'T WORRY! NOW GET GOING!
MINUTES LATER...
THINK IT'LL WORK, MOE?
YOU WAIT AND SEE, LARRY! SOMEBODY WILL BE SPOTTING HIM ANY MINUTE NOW!
PU
A SHARK! A SHARK!
SEE? NOW WE GO INTO ACTION!
PU

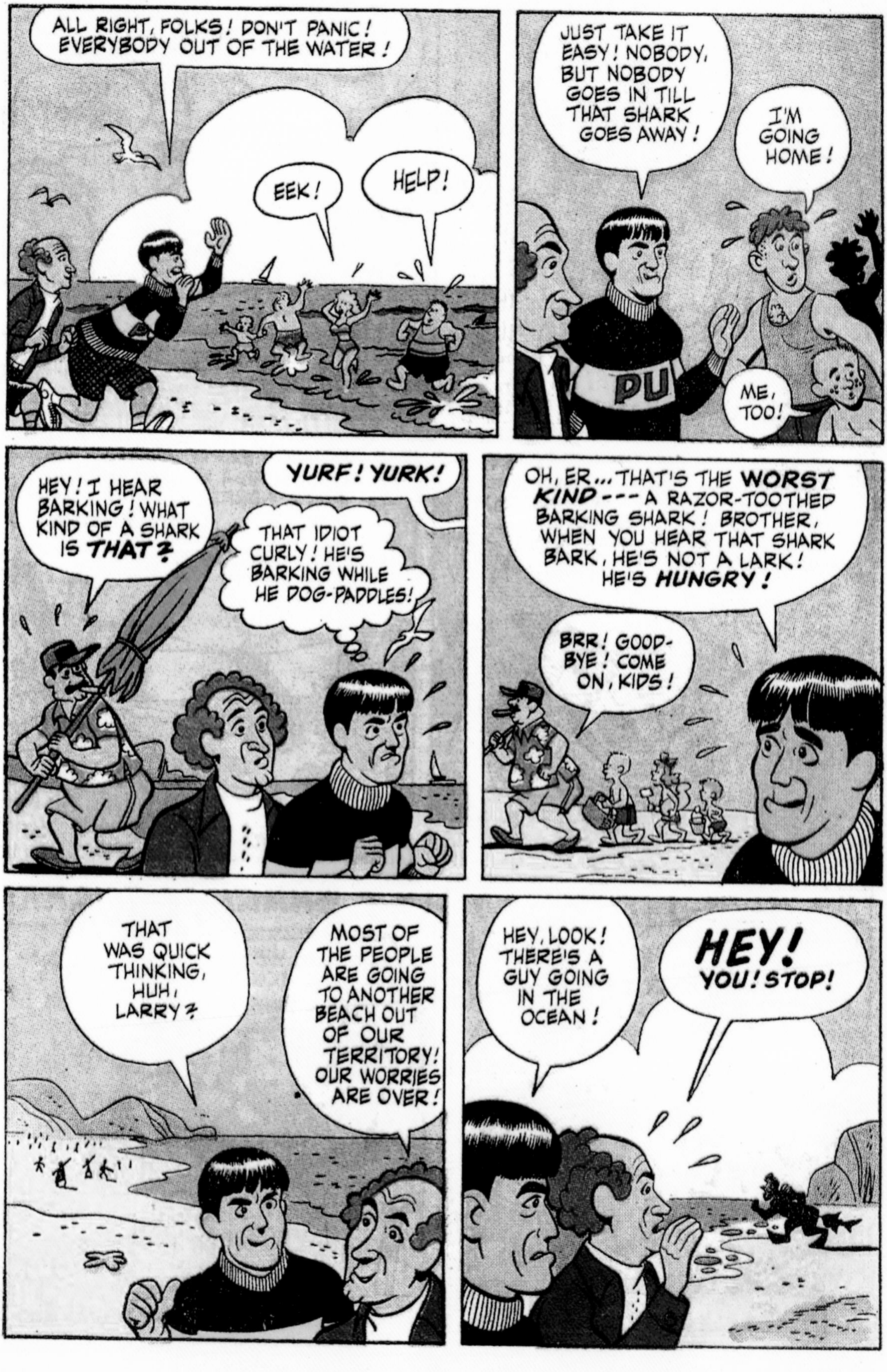
ALL RIGHT, FOLKS! DON'T PANIC! EVERYBODY OUT OF THE WATER!
EEK!
HELP!
JUST TAKE IT EASY! NOBODY, BUT NOBODY GOES IN TILL THAT SHARK GOES AWAY!
I'M GOING HOME!
PU
ME, TOO!
HEY! I HEAR BARKING! WHAT KIND OF A SHARK IS THAT?
YURF! YURK!
THAT IDIOT CURLY! HE'S BARKING WHILE HE DOG-PADDLES!
OH, ER... THAT'S THE WORST KIND--- A RAZOR-TOOTHED BARKING SHARK! BROTHER, WHEN YOU HEAR THAT SHARK BARK, HE'S NOT A LARK! HE'S HUNGRY!
BRR! GOOD-BYE! COME ON, KIDS!
THAT WAS QUICK THINKING, HUH, LARRY?
MOST OF THE PEOPLE ARE GOING TO ANOTHER BEACH OUT OF OUR TERRITORY! OUR WORRIES ARE OVER!
HEY, LOOK! THERE'S A GUY GOING IN THE OCEAN!
HEY! YOU! STOP!

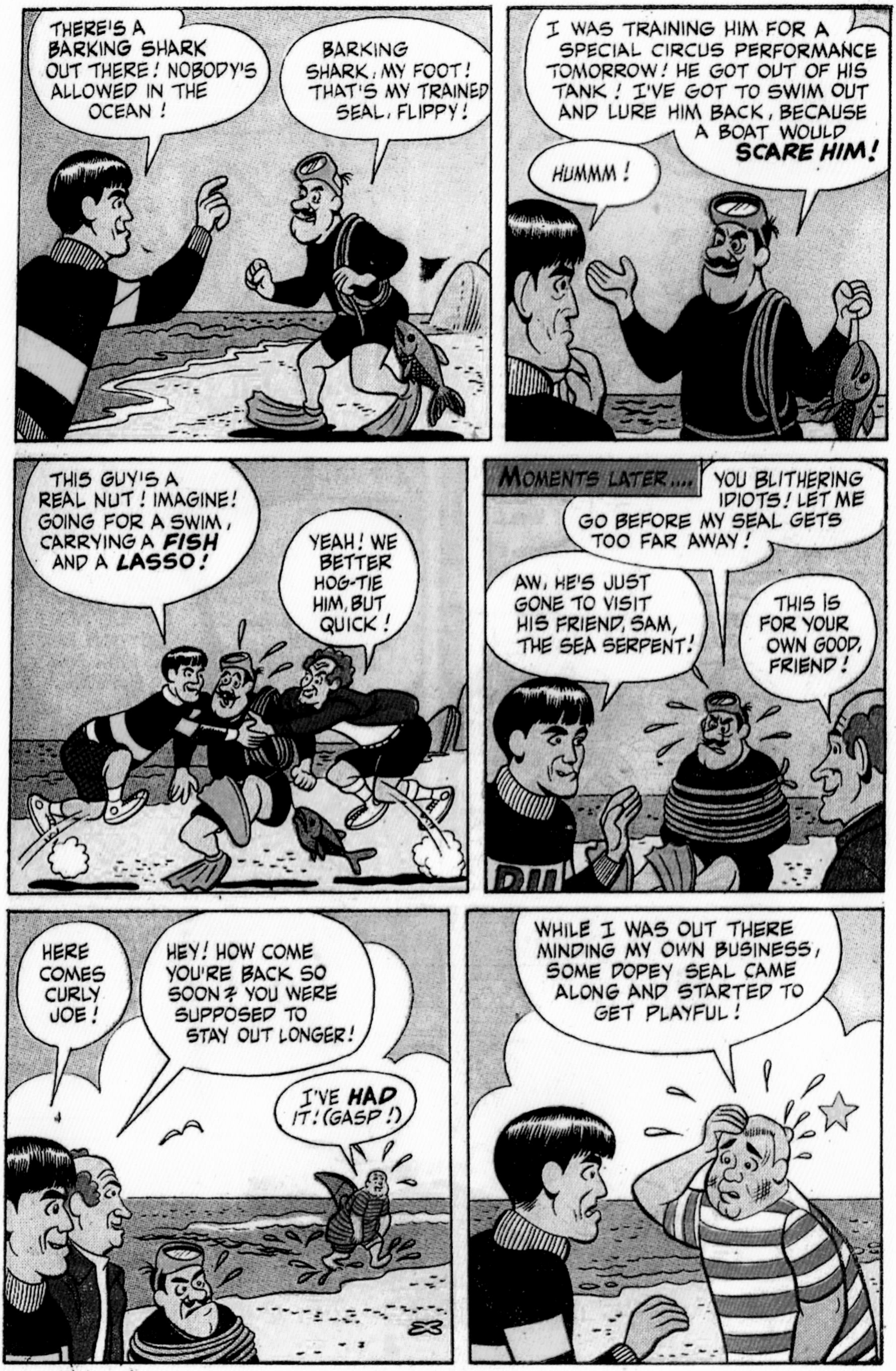
THERE'S A BARKING SHARK OUT THERE! NOBODY'S ALLOWED IN THE OCEAN!
BARKING SHARK, MY FOOT! THAT'S MY TRAINED SEAL, FLIPPY!
I WAS TRAINING HIM FOR A SPECIAL CIRCUS PERFORMANCE TOMORROW! HE GOT OUT OF HIS TANK! I'VE GOT TO SWIM OUT AND LURE HIM BACK, BECAUSE A BOAT WOULD SCARE HIM!
HUMMM!
THIS GUY'S A REAL NUT! IMAGINE! GOING FOR A SWIM, CARRYING A FISH AND A LASSO!
YEAH! WE BETTER HOG-TIE HIM, BUT QUICK!
MOMENTS LATER....
YOU BLITHERING IDIOTS! LET ME GO BEFORE MY SEAL GETS TOO FAR AWAY!
AW, HE'S JUST GONE TO VISIT HIS FRIEND, SAM, THE SEA SERPENT!
THIS IS FOR YOUR OWN GOOD, FRIEND!
HERE COMES CURLY JOE!
HEY! HOW COME YOU'RE BACK SO SOON? YOU WERE SUPPOSED TO STAY OUT LONGER!
I'VE HAD IT! (GASP!)
WHILE I WAS OUT THERE MINDING MY OWN BUSINESS, SOME DOPEY SEAL CAME ALONG AND STARTED TO GET PLAYFUL!

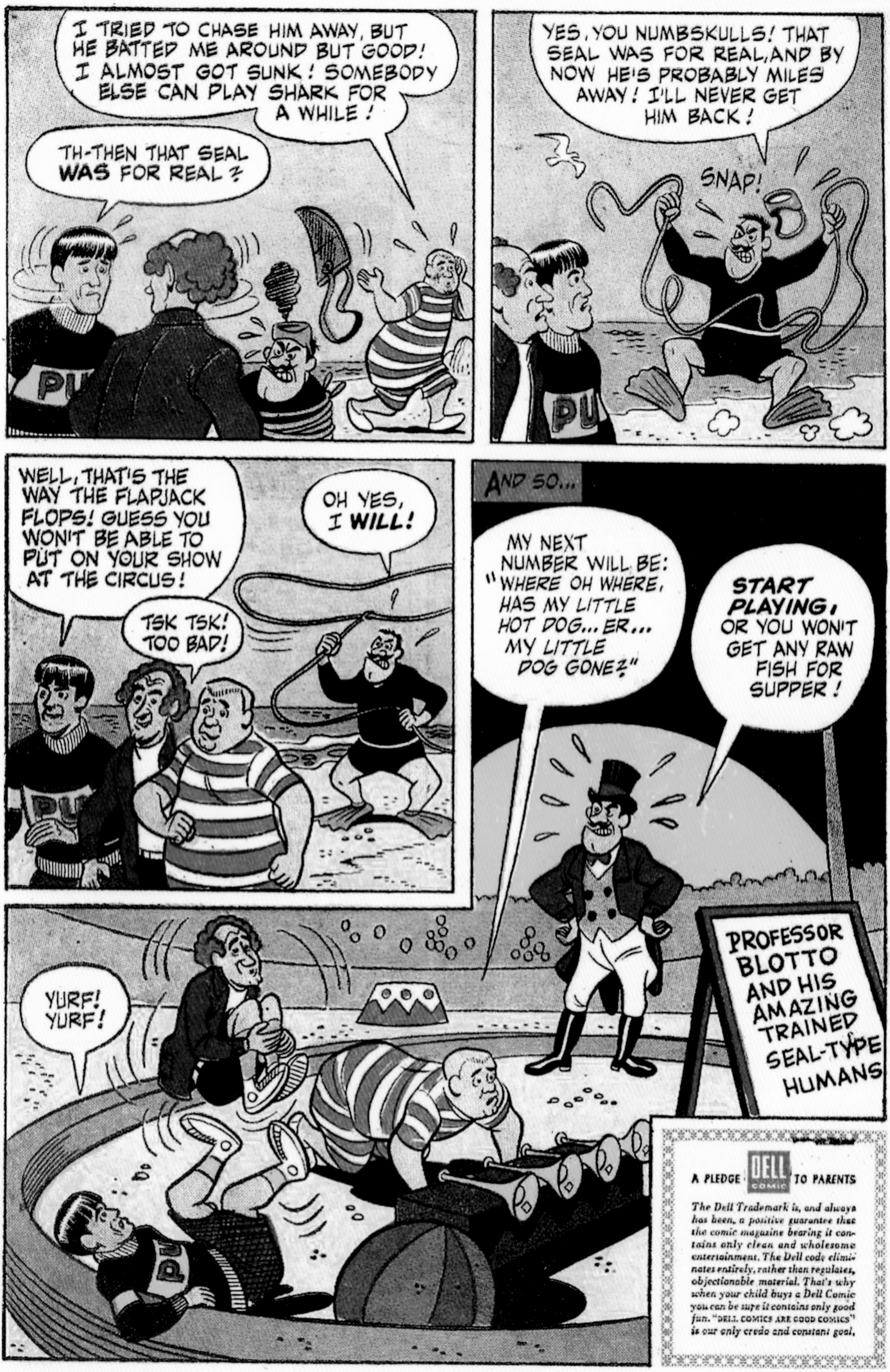
I TRIED TO CHASE HIM AWAY, BUT HE BATTED ME AROUND BUT GOOD! I ALMOST GOT SUNK! SOMEBODY ELSE CAN PLAY SHARK FOR A WHILE!
TH-THEN THAT SEAL **WAS** FOR REAL?
YES, YOU NUMBSKULLS! THAT SEAL WAS FOR REAL, AND BY NOW HE'S PROBABLY MILES AWAY! I'LL NEVER GET HIM BACK!
SNAP!
WELL, THAT'S THE WAY THE FLAPJACK FLOPS! GUESS YOU WON'T BE ABLE TO PUT ON YOUR SHOW AT THE CIRCUS!
OH YES, I **WILL**!
TSK TSK! TOO BAD!
AND SO...
MY NEXT NUMBER WILL BE: "WHERE OH WHERE, HAS MY LITTLE HOT DOG... ER... MY LITTLE DOG GONE?"
START PLAYING, OR YOU WON'T GET ANY RAW FISH FOR SUPPER!
YURF! YURF!
PROFESSOR BLOTTO AND HIS AMAZING TRAINED SEAL-TYPE HUMANS
A PLEDGE DELL COMIC TO PARENTS
The Dell Trademark is, and always has been, a positive guarantee that the comic magazine bearing it contains only clean and wholesome entertainment. The Dell code eliminates entirely, rather than regulates, objectionable material. That's why when your child buys a Dell Comic you can be sure it contains only good fun. "DELL COMICS ARE GOOD COMICS" is our only credo and constant goal.

THE THREE STOOGES

MAY

15¢

NO. 1170

FUN-nee!
Larry, Moe
and Curly
Joe!

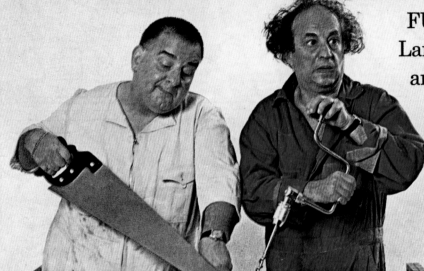

© 1961, NORMAN MAUREK
PRODUCTIONS, INC.

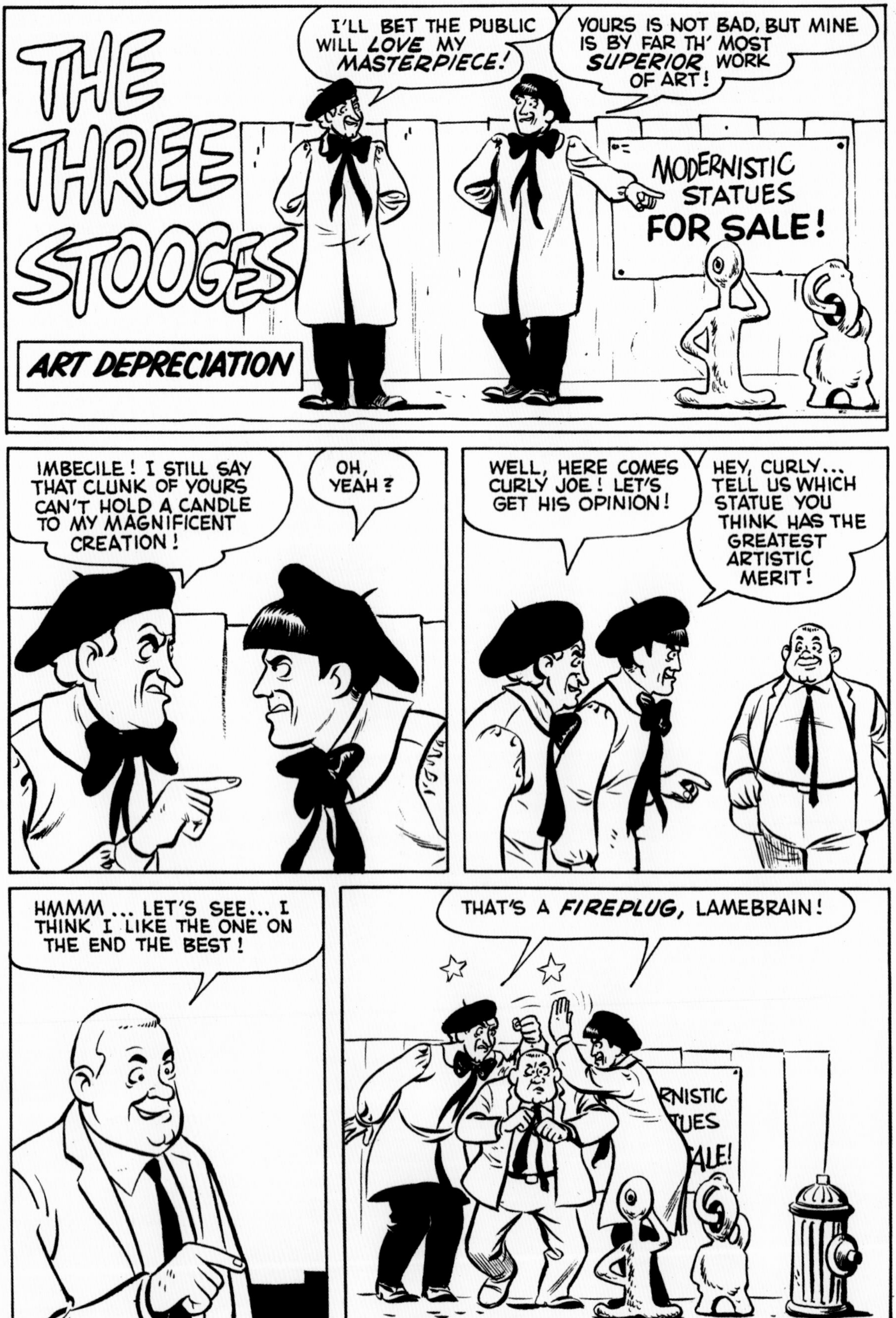
THE THREE STOOGES
ART DEPRECIATION
I'LL BET THE PUBLIC WILL LOVE MY MASTERPIECE!
YOURS IS NOT BAD, BUT MINE IS BY FAR TH' MOST SUPERIOR WORK OF ART!
MODERNISTIC STATUES FOR SALE!
IMBECILE! I STILL SAY THAT CLUNK OF YOURS CAN'T HOLD A CANDLE TO MY MAGNIFICENT CREATION!
OH, YEAH?
WELL, HERE COMES CURLY JOE! LET'S GET HIS OPINION!
HEY, CURLY... TELL US WHICH STATUE YOU THINK HAS THE GREATEST ARTISTIC MERIT!
HMMM... LET'S SEE... I THINK I LIKE THE ONE ON THE END THE BEST!
THAT'S A FIREPLUG, LAMEBRAIN!

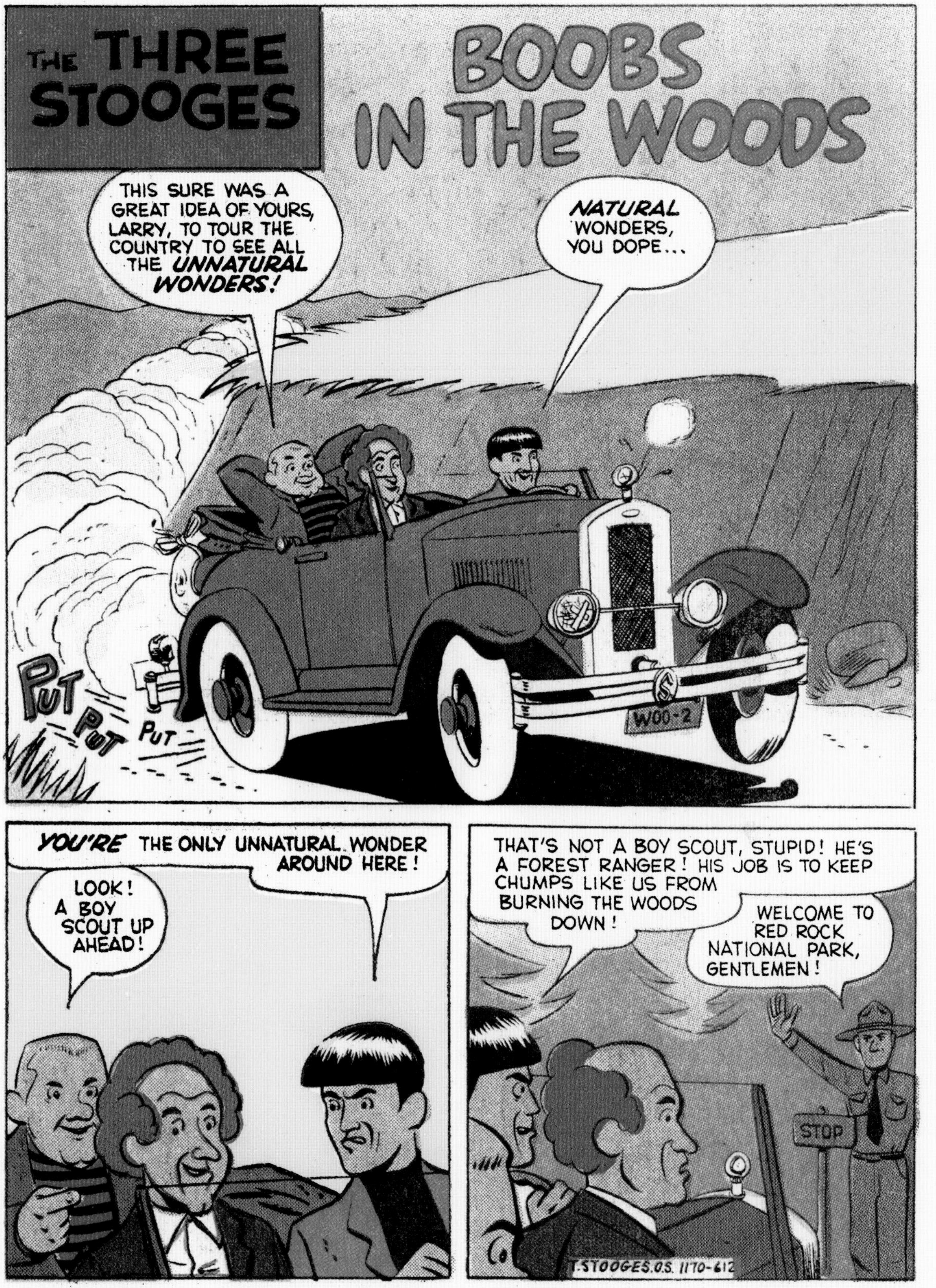
THE THREE STOOGES
BOOBS IN THE WOODS
THIS SURE WAS A GREAT IDEA OF YOURS, LARRY, TO TOUR THE COUNTRY TO SEE ALL THE *UNNATURAL WONDERS!*
NATURAL WONDERS, YOU DOPE...
PUT PUT PUT
WOO-2
YOU'RE THE ONLY UNNATURAL WONDER AROUND HERE!
LOOK! A BOY SCOUT UP AHEAD!
THAT'S NOT A BOY SCOUT, STUPID! HE'S A FOREST RANGER! HIS JOB IS TO KEEP CHUMPS LIKE US FROM BURNING THE WOODS DOWN!
WELCOME TO RED ROCK NATIONAL PARK, GENTLEMEN!
STOP
T. STOOGES. O.S. 1170-612

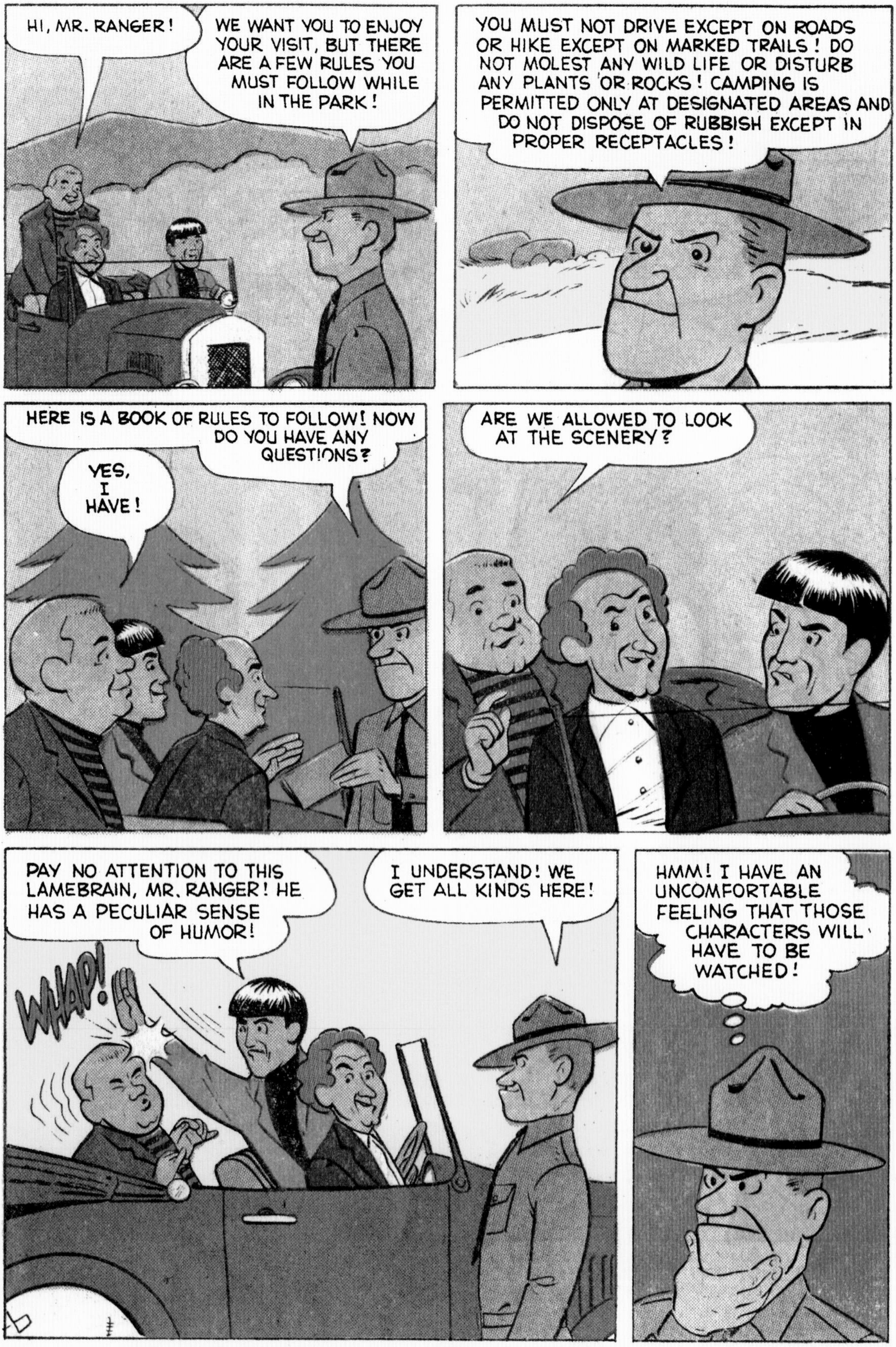
HI, MR. RANGER!
WE WANT YOU TO ENJOY YOUR VISIT, BUT THERE ARE A FEW RULES YOU MUST FOLLOW WHILE IN THE PARK!
YOU MUST NOT DRIVE EXCEPT ON ROADS OR HIKE EXCEPT ON MARKED TRAILS! DO NOT MOLEST ANY WILD LIFE OR DISTURB ANY PLANTS OR ROCKS! CAMPING IS PERMITTED ONLY AT DESIGNATED AREAS AND DO NOT DISPOSE OF RUBBISH EXCEPT IN PROPER RECEPTACLES!
HERE IS A BOOK OF RULES TO FOLLOW! NOW DO YOU HAVE ANY QUESTIONS?
YES, I HAVE!
ARE WE ALLOWED TO LOOK AT THE SCENERY?
PAY NO ATTENTION TO THIS LAMEBRAIN, MR. RANGER! HE HAS A PECULIAR SENSE OF HUMOR!
I UNDERSTAND! WE GET ALL KINDS HERE!
WHAP!
HMM! I HAVE AN UNCOMFORTABLE FEELING THAT THOSE CHARACTERS WILL HAVE TO BE WATCHED!

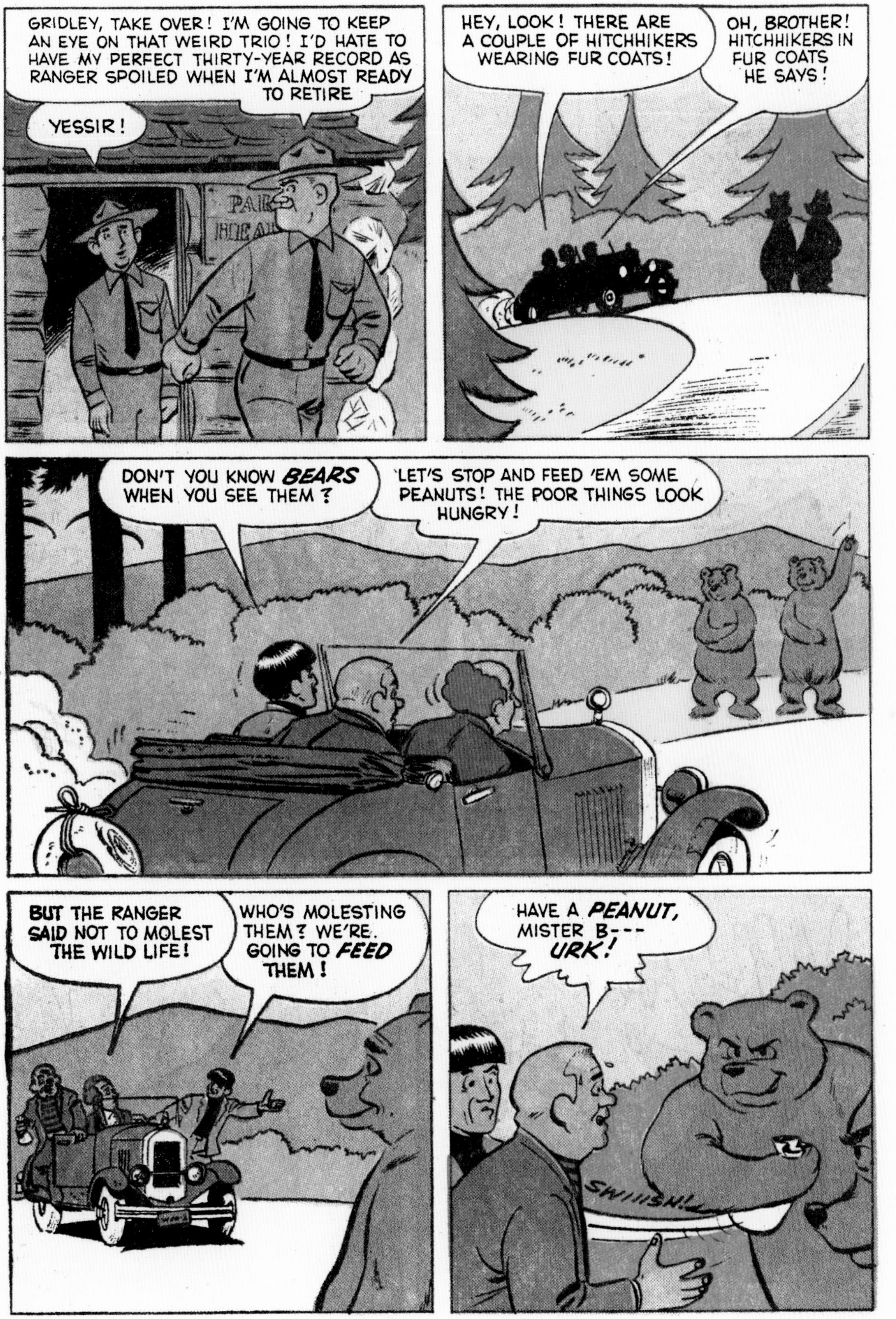
GRIDLEY, TAKE OVER! I'M GOING TO KEEP AN EYE ON THAT WEIRD TRIO! I'D HATE TO HAVE MY PERFECT THIRTY-YEAR RECORD AS RANGER SPOILED WHEN I'M ALMOST READY TO RETIRE
YESSIR!
HEY, LOOK! THERE ARE A COUPLE OF HITCHHIKERS WEARING FUR COATS!
OH, BROTHER! HITCHHIKERS IN FUR COATS HE SAYS!
DON'T YOU KNOW BEARS WHEN YOU SEE THEM?
LET'S STOP AND FEED 'EM SOME PEANUTS! THE POOR THINGS LOOK HUNGRY!
BUT THE RANGER SAID NOT TO MOLEST THE WILD LIFE!
WHO'S MOLESTING THEM? WE'RE. GOING TO FEED THEM!
HAVE A PEANUT, MISTER B--- URK!
SWIIISH!

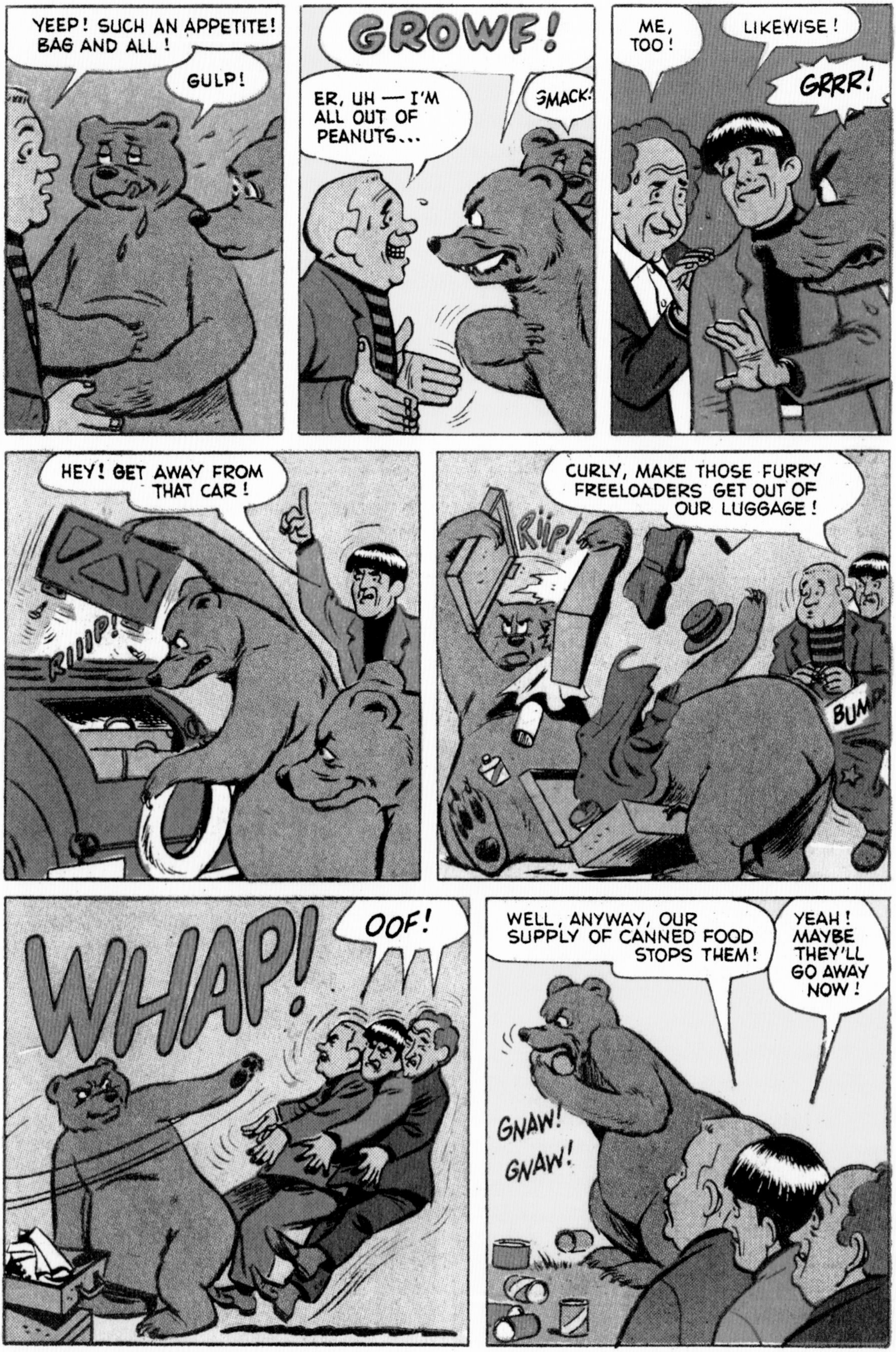
YEEP! SUCH AN APPETITE! BAG AND ALL!
GULP!
GROWF!
ER, UH — I'M ALL OUT OF PEANUTS...
SMACK!
ME, TOO!
LIKEWISE!
GRRR!
HEY! GET AWAY FROM THAT CAR!
RIIIP!
CURLY, MAKE THOSE FURRY FREELOADERS GET OUT OF OUR LUGGAGE!
RIIP!
BUMP!
WHAP!
OOF!
WELL, ANYWAY, OUR SUPPLY OF CANNED FOOD STOPS THEM!
YEAH! MAYBE THEY'LL GO AWAY NOW!
GNAW! GNAW!

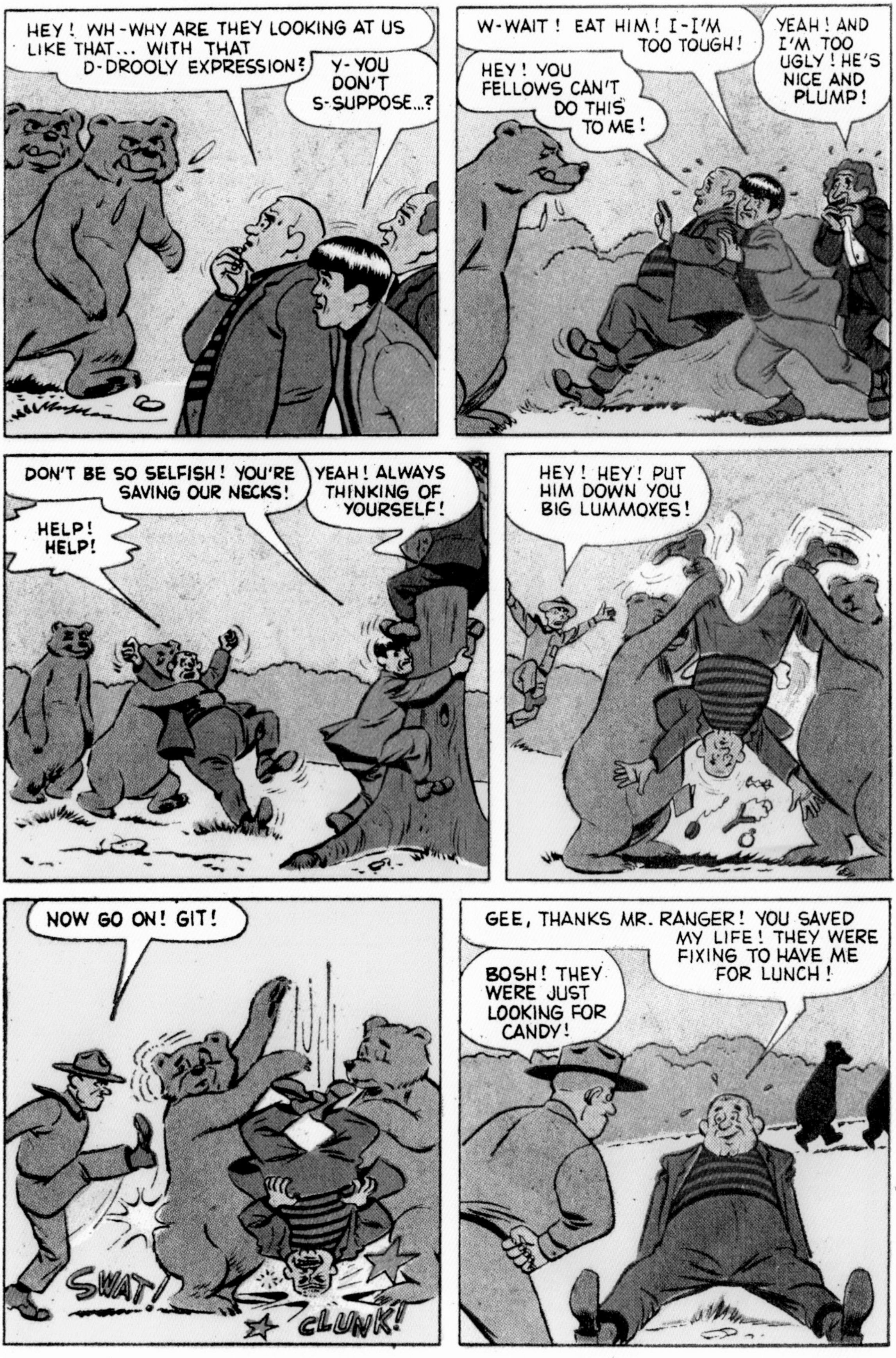
HEY! WH-WHY ARE THEY LOOKING AT US LIKE THAT... WITH THAT D-DROOLY EXPRESSION?
Y-YOU DON'T S-SUPPOSE...?
W-WAIT! EAT HIM! I-I'M TOO TOUGH!
HEY! YOU FELLOWS CAN'T DO THIS TO ME!
YEAH! AND I'M TOO UGLY! HE'S NICE AND PLUMP!
DON'T BE SO SELFISH! YOU'RE SAVING OUR NECKS!
YEAH! ALWAYS THINKING OF YOURSELF!
HELP! HELP!
HEY! HEY! PUT HIM DOWN YOU BIG LUMMOXES!
NOW GO ON! GIT!
SWAT!
CLUNK!
GEE, THANKS MR. RANGER! YOU SAVED MY LIFE! THEY WERE FIXING TO HAVE ME FOR LUNCH!
BOSH! THEY WERE JUST LOOKING FOR CANDY!

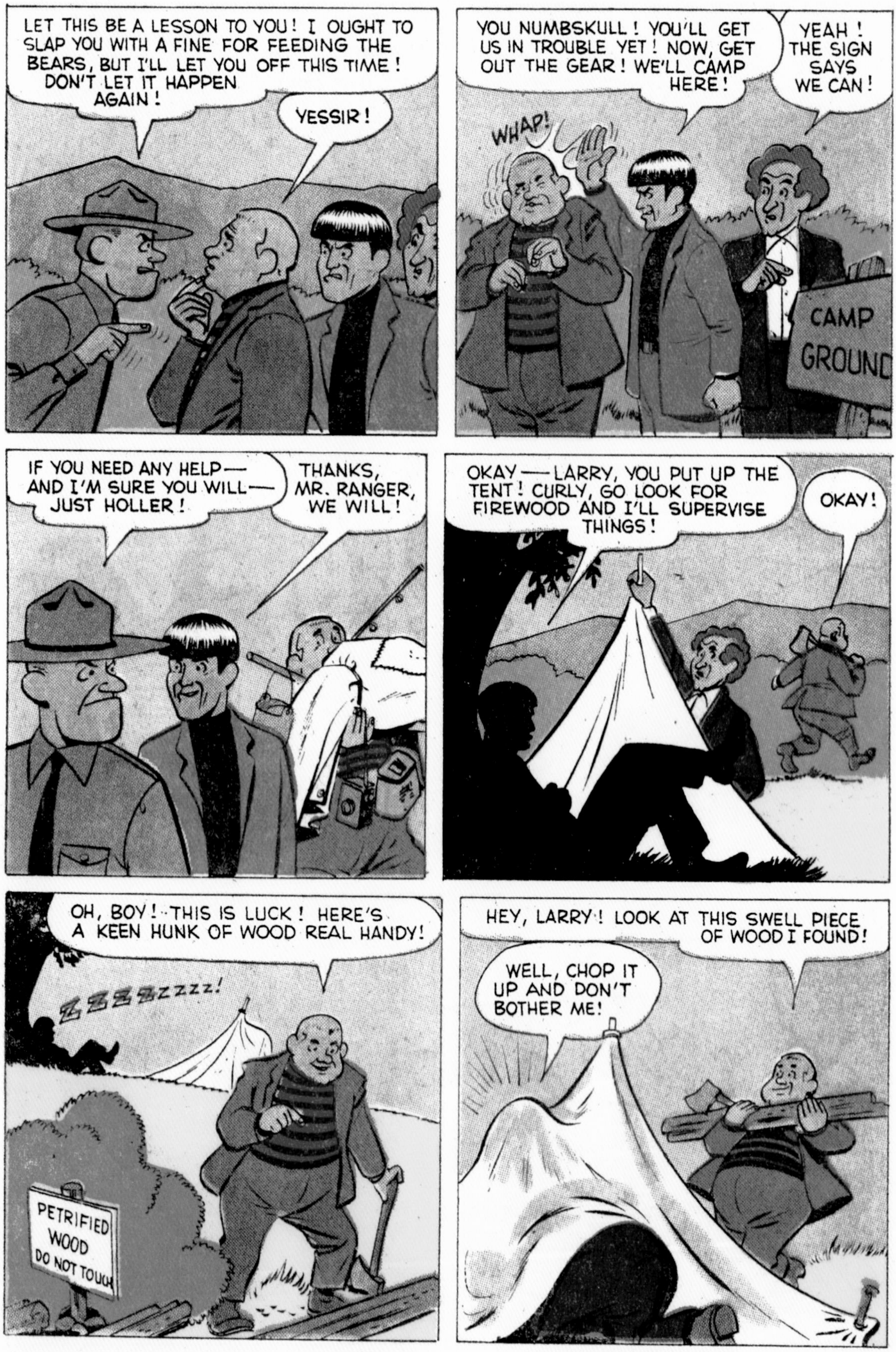
LET THIS BE A LESSON TO YOU! I OUGHT TO SLAP YOU WITH A FINE FOR FEEDING THE BEARS, BUT I'LL LET YOU OFF THIS TIME! DON'T LET IT HAPPEN AGAIN!
YESSIR!
YOU NUMBSKULL! YOU'LL GET US IN TROUBLE YET! NOW, GET OUT THE GEAR! WE'LL CAMP HERE!
YEAH! THE SIGN SAYS WE CAN!
WHAP!
CAMP GROUND
IF YOU NEED ANY HELP— AND I'M SURE YOU WILL— JUST HOLLER!
THANKS, MR. RANGER, WE WILL!
OKAY — LARRY, YOU PUT UP THE TENT! CURLY, GO LOOK FOR FIREWOOD AND I'LL SUPERVISE THINGS!
OKAY!
OH, BOY! THIS IS LUCK! HERE'S A KEEN HUNK OF WOOD REAL HANDY!
ZZZZzzzz!
PETRIFIED WOOD DO NOT TOUCH
HEY, LARRY! LOOK AT THIS SWELL PIECE OF WOOD I FOUND!
WELL, CHOP IT UP AND DON'T BOTHER ME!

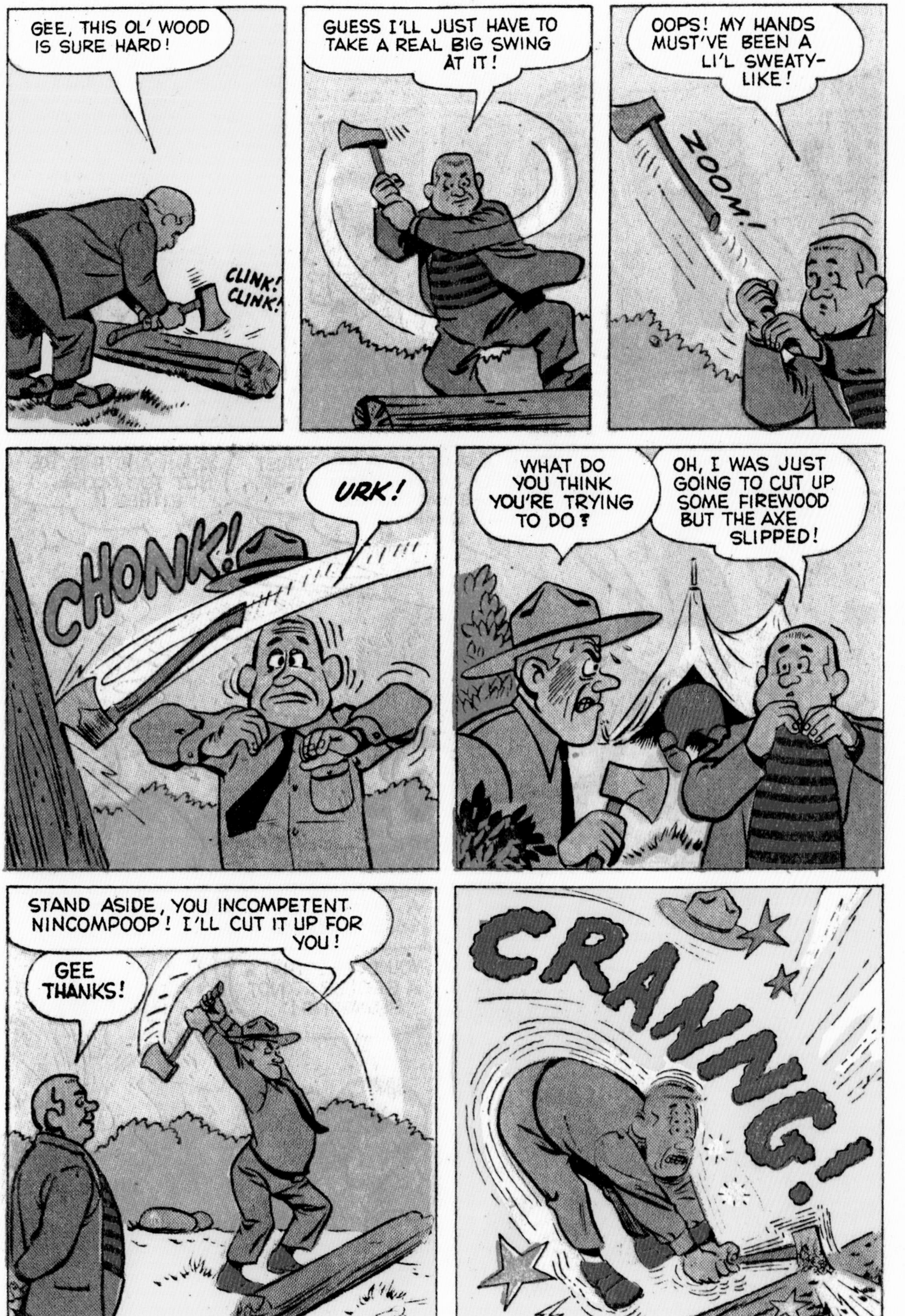
GEE, THIS OL' WOOD IS SURE HARD!
CLINK! CLINK!
GUESS I'LL JUST HAVE TO TAKE A REAL BIG SWING AT IT!
OOPS! MY HANDS MUST'VE BEEN A LI'L SWEATY-LIKE!
ZOOM!
URK!
CHONK!
WHAT DO YOU THINK YOU'RE TRYING TO DO?
OH, I WAS JUST GOING TO CUT UP SOME FIREWOOD BUT THE AXE SLIPPED!
STAND ASIDE, YOU INCOMPETENT NINCOMPOOP! I'LL CUT IT UP FOR YOU!
GEE THANKS!
CRANNG!

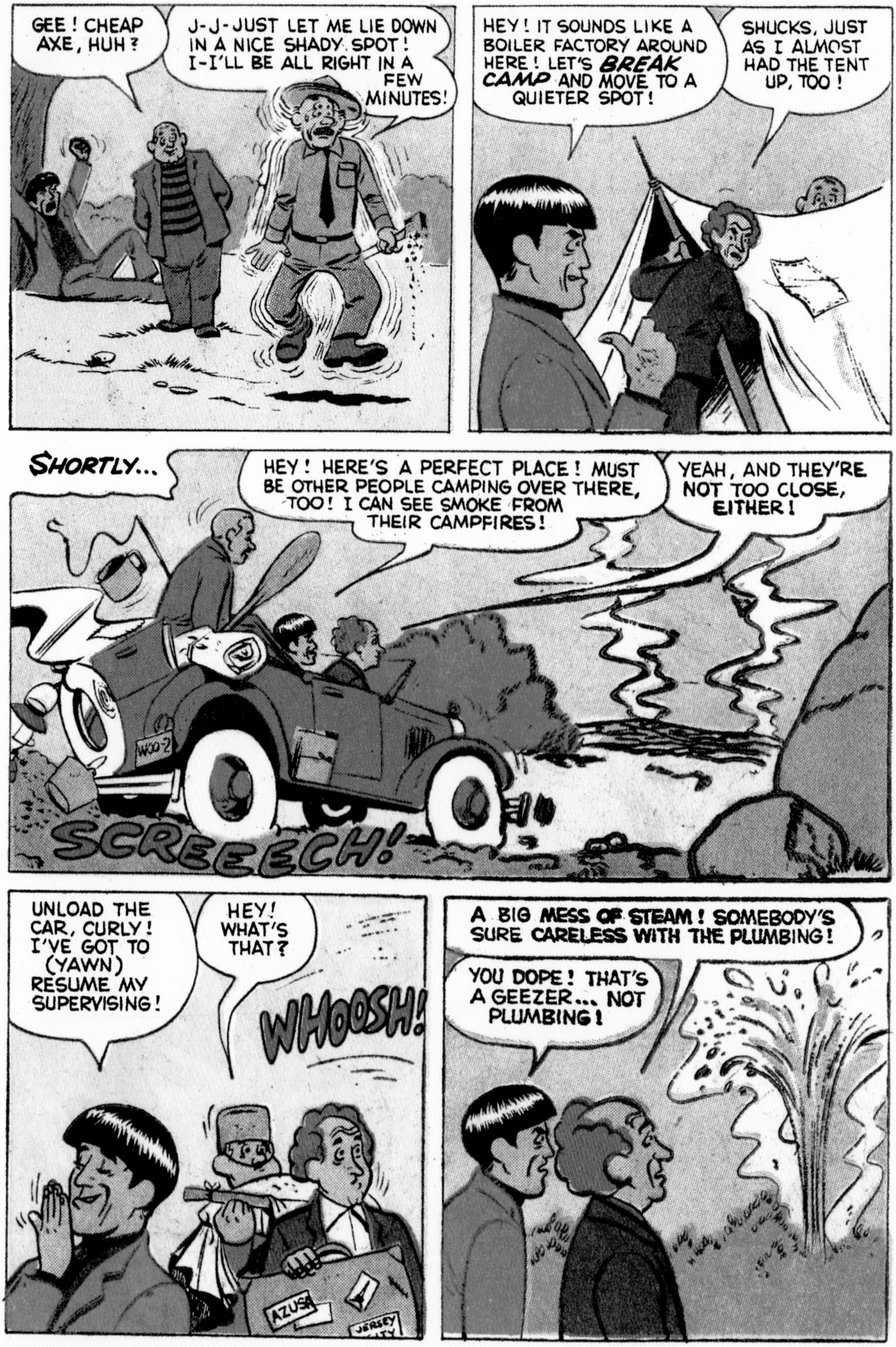
GEE! CHEAP AXE, HUH?
J-J-JUST LET ME LIE DOWN IN A NICE SHADY SPOT! I-I'LL BE ALL RIGHT IN A FEW MINUTES!
HEY! IT SOUNDS LIKE A BOILER FACTORY AROUND HERE! LET'S BREAK CAMP AND MOVE TO A QUIETER SPOT!
SHUCKS, JUST AS I ALMOST HAD THE TENT UP, TOO!
SHORTLY...
HEY! HERE'S A PERFECT PLACE! MUST BE OTHER PEOPLE CAMPING OVER THERE, TOO! I CAN SEE SMOKE FROM THEIR CAMPFIRES!
YEAH, AND THEY'RE NOT TOO CLOSE, EITHER!
WOO-2
SCREEECH!
UNLOAD THE CAR, CURLY! I'VE GOT TO (YAWN) RESUME MY SUPERVISING!
HEY! WHAT'S THAT?
WHOOSH!
AZUSA
JERSEY CITY
A BIG MESS OF STEAM! SOMEBODY'S SURE CARELESS WITH THE PLUMBING!
YOU DOPE! THAT'S A GEEZER... NOT PLUMBING!

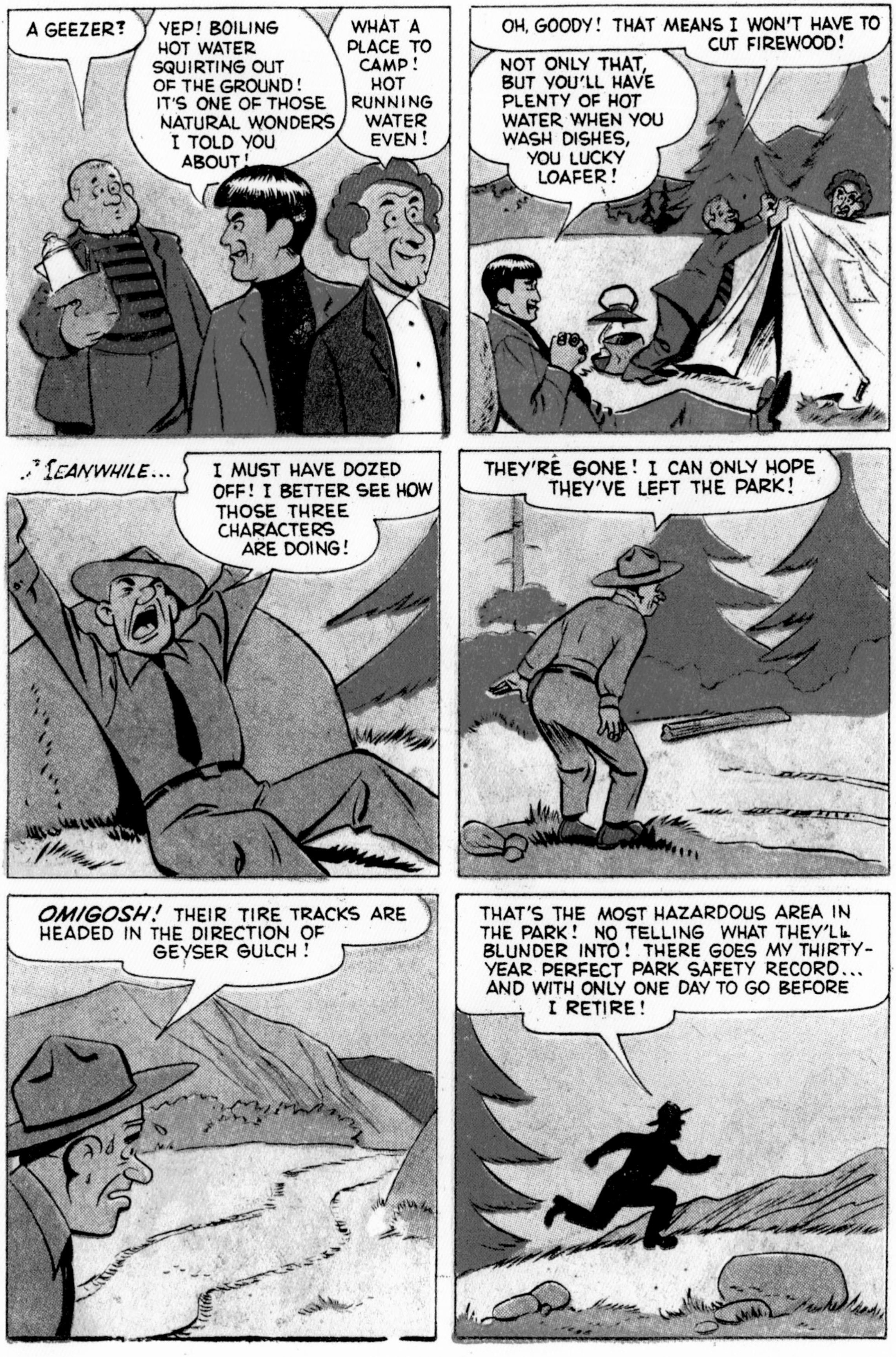
A GEEZER?
YEP! BOILING HOT WATER SQUIRTING OUT OF THE GROUND! IT'S ONE OF THOSE NATURAL WONDERS I TOLD YOU ABOUT!
WHAT A PLACE TO CAMP! HOT RUNNING WATER EVEN!
OH, GOODY! THAT MEANS I WON'T HAVE TO CUT FIREWOOD!
NOT ONLY THAT, BUT YOU'LL HAVE PLENTY OF HOT WATER WHEN YOU WASH DISHES, YOU LUCKY LOAFER!
MEANWHILE...
I MUST HAVE DOZED OFF! I BETTER SEE HOW THOSE THREE CHARACTERS ARE DOING!
THEY'RE GONE! I CAN ONLY HOPE THEY'VE LEFT THE PARK!
OMIGOSH! THEIR TIRE TRACKS ARE HEADED IN THE DIRECTION OF GEYSER GULCH!
THAT'S THE MOST HAZARDOUS AREA IN THE PARK! NO TELLING WHAT THEY'LL BLUNDER INTO! THERE GOES MY THIRTY-YEAR PERFECT PARK SAFETY RECORD... AND WITH ONLY ONE DAY TO GO BEFORE I RETIRE!

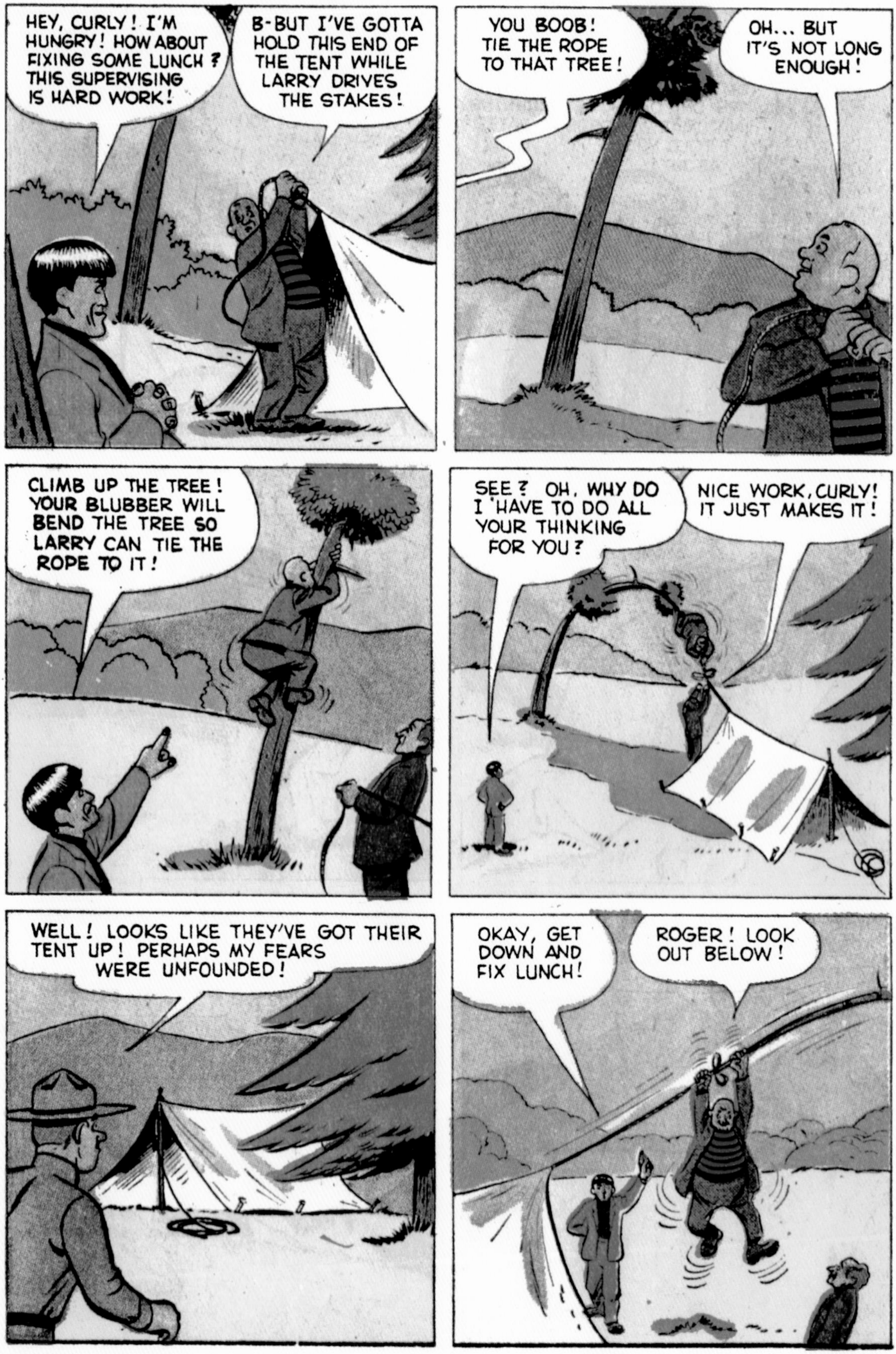
HEY, CURLY! I'M HUNGRY! HOW ABOUT FIXING SOME LUNCH? THIS SUPERVISING IS HARD WORK!
B-BUT I'VE GOTTA HOLD THIS END OF THE TENT WHILE LARRY DRIVES THE STAKES!
YOU BOOB! TIE THE ROPE TO THAT TREE!
OH... BUT IT'S NOT LONG ENOUGH!
CLIMB UP THE TREE! YOUR BLUBBER WILL BEND THE TREE SO LARRY CAN TIE THE ROPE TO IT!
SEE? OH, WHY DO I HAVE TO DO ALL YOUR THINKING FOR YOU?
NICE WORK, CURLY! IT JUST MAKES IT!
WELL! LOOKS LIKE THEY'VE GOT THEIR TENT UP! PERHAPS MY FEARS WERE UNFOUNDED!
OKAY, GET DOWN AND FIX LUNCH!
ROGER! LOOK OUT BELOW!

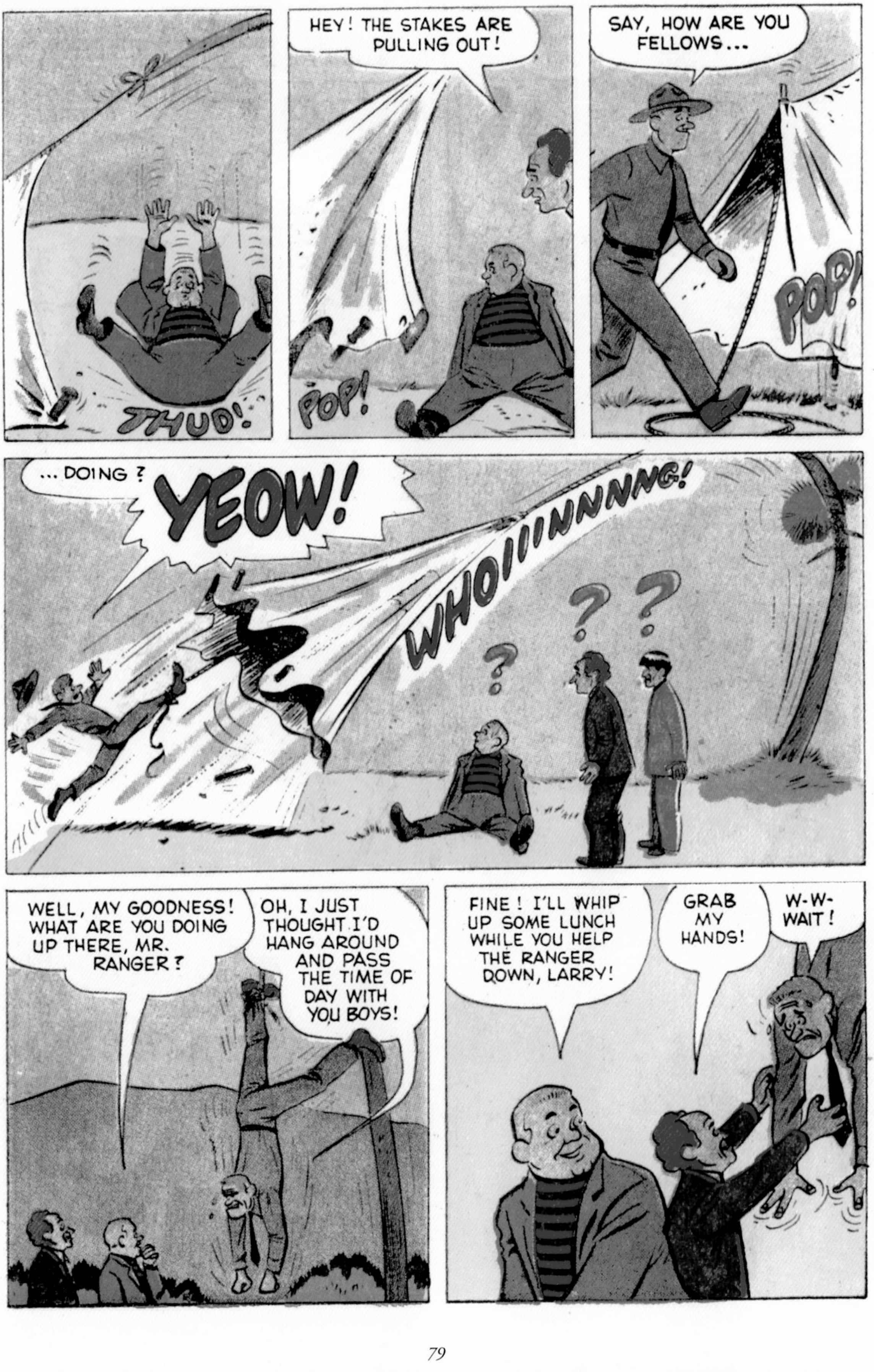
THUD!
HEY! THE STAKES ARE PULLING OUT!
POP!
SAY, HOW ARE YOU FELLOWS...
POP!
... DOING ?
YEOW!
WHOIIINNNNG!
WELL, MY GOODNESS! WHAT ARE YOU DOING UP THERE, MR. RANGER?
OH, I JUST THOUGHT I'D HANG AROUND AND PASS THE TIME OF DAY WITH YOU BOYS!
FINE! I'LL WHIP UP SOME LUNCH WHILE YOU HELP THE RANGER DOWN, LARRY!
GRAB MY HANDS!
W-W-WAIT!

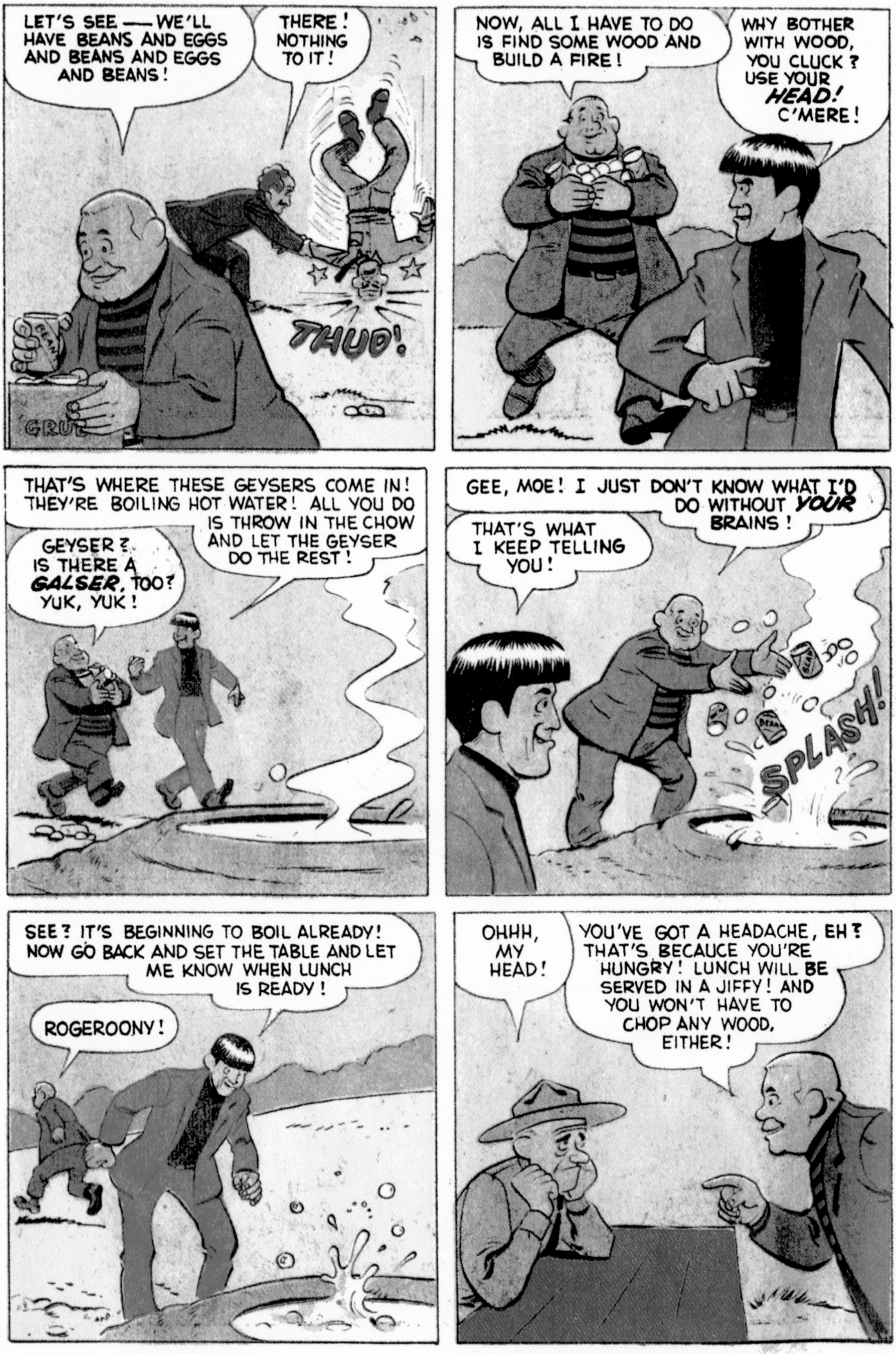
LET'S SEE — WE'LL HAVE BEANS AND EGGS AND BEANS AND EGGS AND BEANS!
THERE! NOTHING TO IT!
BEAN
GRUB
THUD!
NOW, ALL I HAVE TO DO IS FIND SOME WOOD AND BUILD A FIRE!
WHY BOTHER WITH WOOD, YOU CLUCK? USE YOUR HEAD! C'MERE!
THAT'S WHERE THESE GEYSERS COME IN! THEY'RE BOILING HOT WATER! ALL YOU DO IS THROW IN THE CHOW AND LET THE GEYSER DO THE REST!
GEYSER? IS THERE A GALSER, TOO? YUK, YUK!
GEE, MOE! I JUST DON'T KNOW WHAT I'D DO WITHOUT YOUR BRAINS!
THAT'S WHAT I KEEP TELLING YOU!
SPLASH!
SEE? IT'S BEGINNING TO BOIL ALREADY! NOW GO BACK AND SET THE TABLE AND LET ME KNOW WHEN LUNCH IS READY!
ROGEROONY!
OHHH, MY HEAD!
YOU'VE GOT A HEADACHE, EH? THAT'S BECAUCE YOU'RE HUNGRY! LUNCH WILL BE SERVED IN A JIFFY! AND YOU WON'T HAVE TO CHOP ANY WOOD, EITHER!

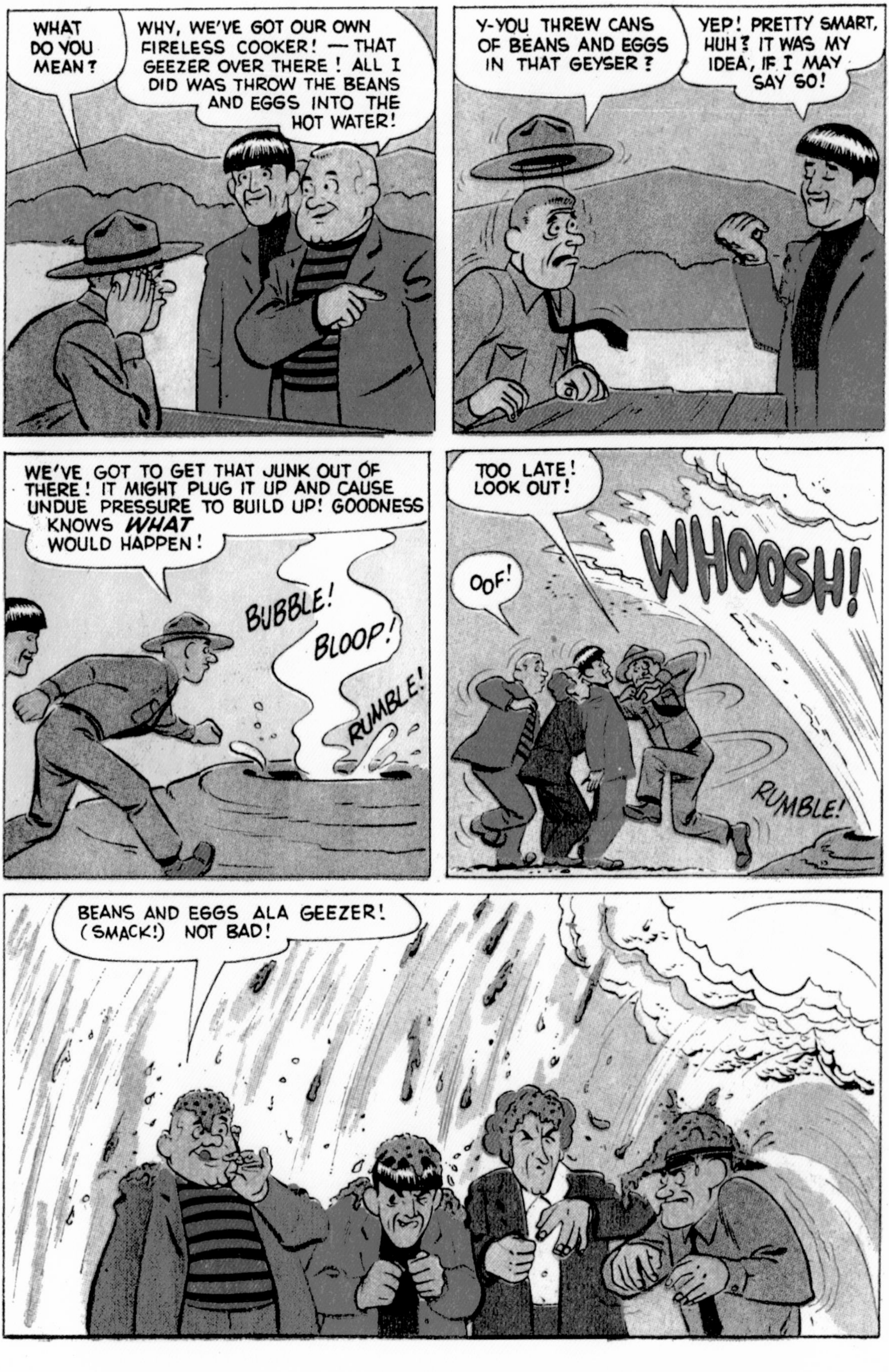
WHAT DO YOU MEAN?
WHY, WE'VE GOT OUR OWN FIRELESS COOKER! —THAT GEEZER OVER THERE! ALL I DID WAS THROW THE BEANS AND EGGS INTO THE HOT WATER!
Y-YOU THREW CANS OF BEANS AND EGGS IN THAT GEYSER?
YEP! PRETTY SMART, HUH? IT WAS MY IDEA, IF I MAY SAY SO!
WE'VE GOT TO GET THAT JUNK OUT OF THERE! IT MIGHT PLUG IT UP AND CAUSE UNDUE PRESSURE TO BUILD UP! GOODNESS KNOWS *WHAT* WOULD HAPPEN!
BUBBLE!
BLOOP!
RUMBLE!
TOO LATE! LOOK OUT!
OOF!
WHOOSH!
RUMBLE!
BEANS AND EGGS ALA GEEZER! (SMACK!) NOT BAD!

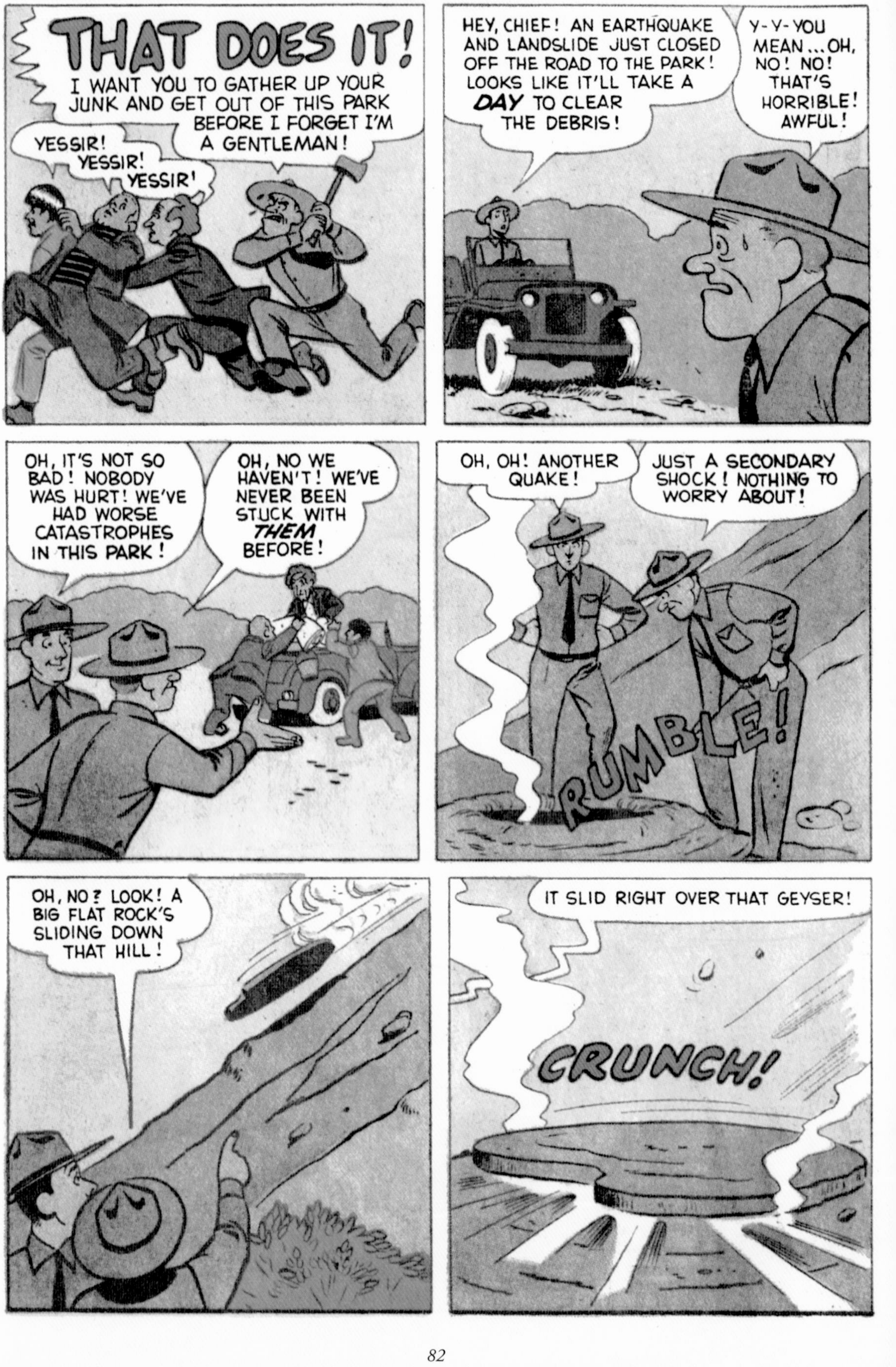
THAT DOES IT!
I WANT YOU TO GATHER UP YOUR JUNK AND GET OUT OF THIS PARK BEFORE I FORGET I'M A GENTLEMAN!
YESSIR! YESSIR! YESSIR!
HEY, CHIEF! AN EARTHQUAKE AND LANDSLIDE JUST CLOSED OFF THE ROAD TO THE PARK! LOOKS LIKE IT'LL TAKE A DAY TO CLEAR THE DEBRIS!
Y-Y-YOU MEAN...OH, NO! NO! THAT'S HORRIBLE! AWFUL!
OH, IT'S NOT SO BAD! NOBODY WAS HURT! WE'VE HAD WORSE CATASTROPHES IN THIS PARK!
OH, NO WE HAVEN'T! WE'VE NEVER BEEN STUCK WITH THEM BEFORE!
OH, OH! ANOTHER QUAKE!
JUST A SECONDARY SHOCK! NOTHING TO WORRY ABOUT!
RUMBLE!
OH, NO? LOOK! A BIG FLAT ROCK'S SLIDING DOWN THAT HILL!
IT SLID RIGHT OVER THAT GEYSER!
CRUNCH!

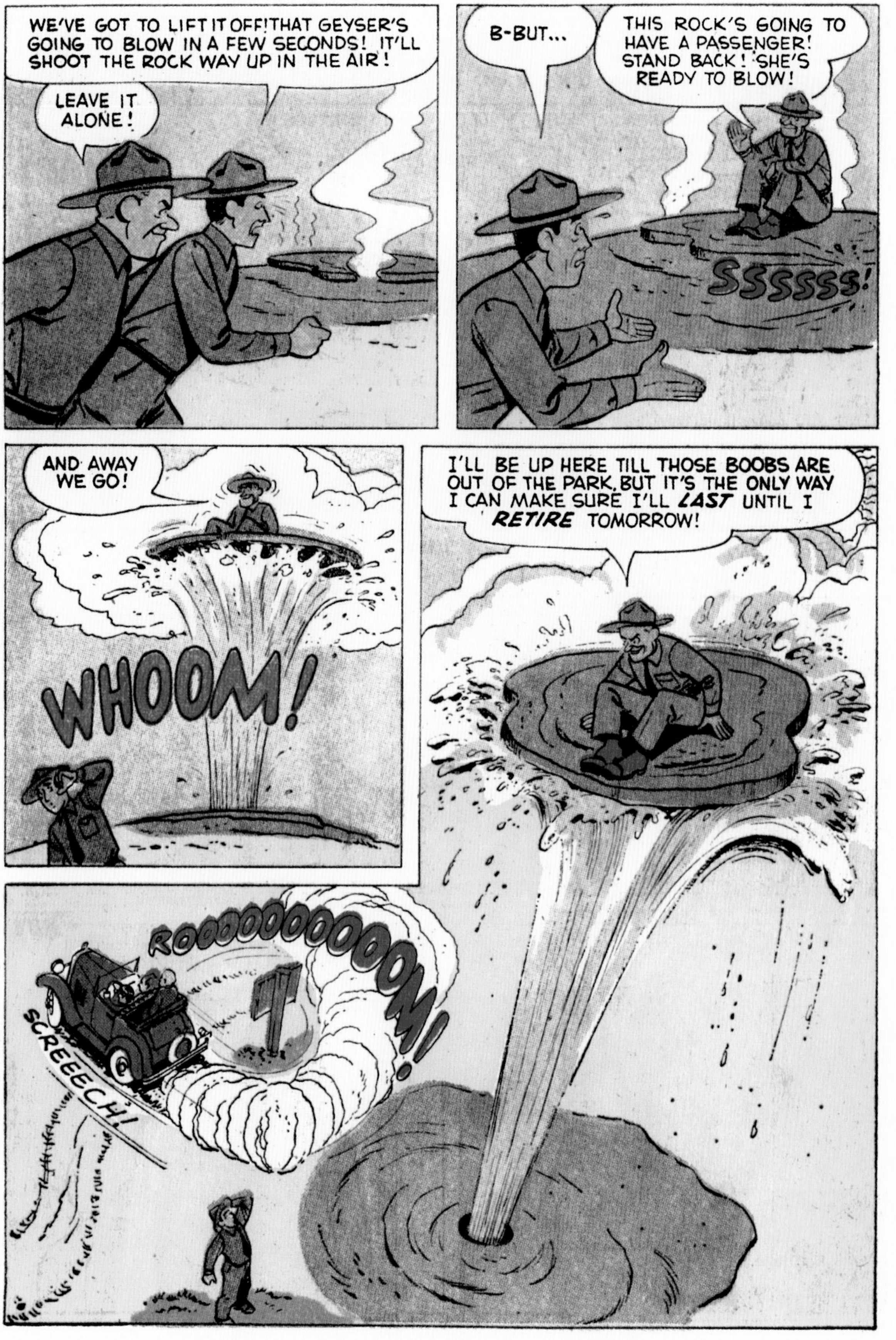
WE'VE GOT TO LIFT IT OFF! THAT GEYSER'S GOING TO BLOW IN A FEW SECONDS! IT'LL SHOOT THE ROCK WAY UP IN THE AIR!
LEAVE IT ALONE!
B-BUT...
THIS ROCK'S GOING TO HAVE A PASSENGER! STAND BACK! SHE'S READY TO BLOW!
SSSSSS!
AND AWAY WE GO!
WHOOM!
I'LL BE UP HERE TILL THOSE BOOBS ARE OUT OF THE PARK, BUT IT'S THE ONLY WAY I CAN MAKE SURE I'LL LAST UNTIL I RETIRE TOMORROW!
ROOOOOOOOOOOM!
SCREEECH!

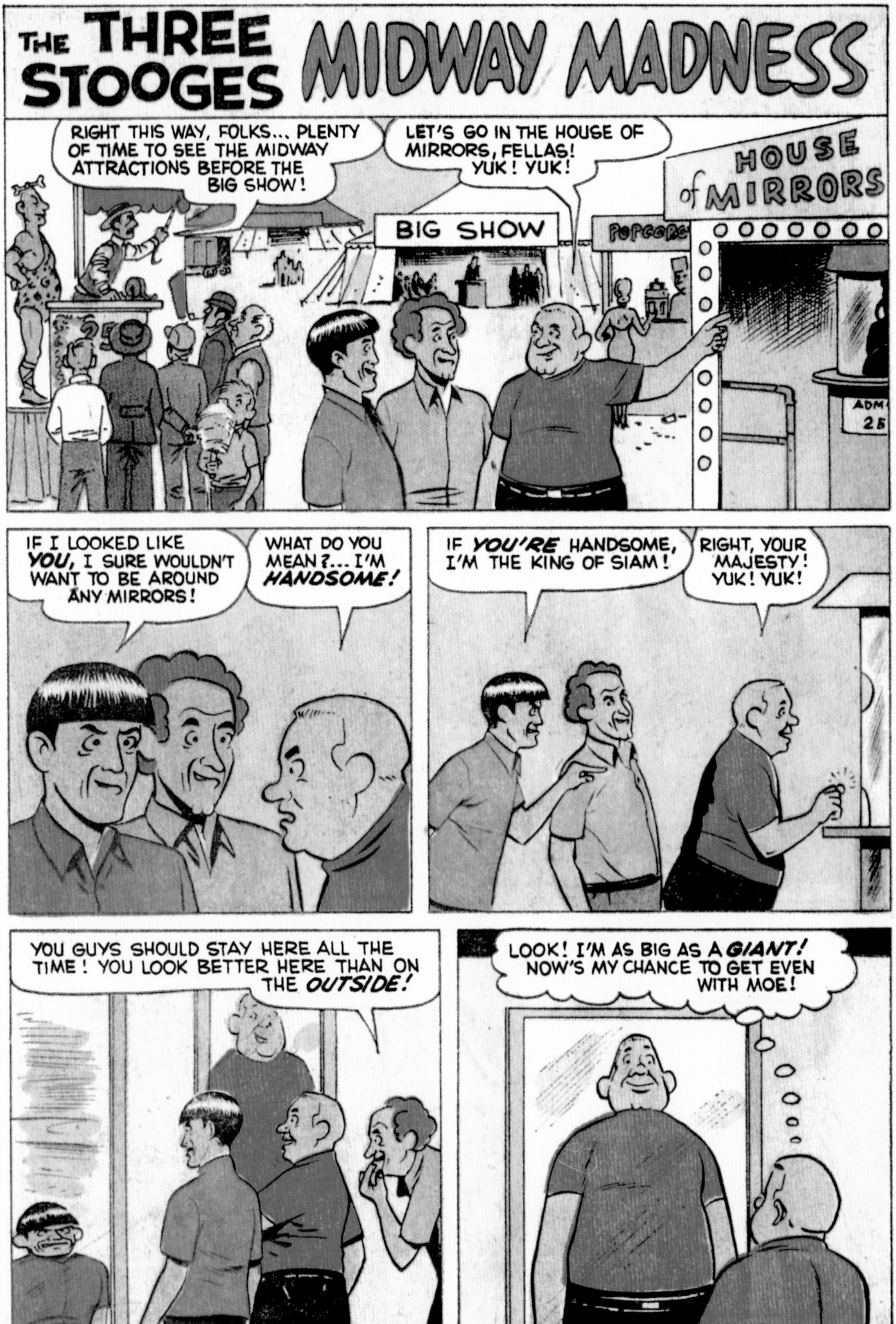
THE THREE STOOGES
MIDWAY MADNESS
RIGHT THIS WAY, FOLKS... PLENTY OF TIME TO SEE THE MIDWAY ATTRACTIONS BEFORE THE BIG SHOW!
LET'S GO IN THE HOUSE OF MIRRORS, FELLAS! YUK! YUK!
HOUSE of MIRRORS
BIG SHOW
ADM 25
IF I LOOKED LIKE YOU, I SURE WOULDN'T WANT TO BE AROUND ANY MIRRORS!
WHAT DO YOU MEAN?... I'M HANDSOME!
IF YOU'RE HANDSOME, I'M THE KING OF SIAM!
RIGHT, YOUR MAJESTY! YUK! YUK!
YOU GUYS SHOULD STAY HERE ALL THE TIME! YOU LOOK BETTER HERE THAN ON THE OUTSIDE!
LOOK! I'M AS BIG AS A GIANT! NOW'S MY CHANCE TO GET EVEN WITH MOE!

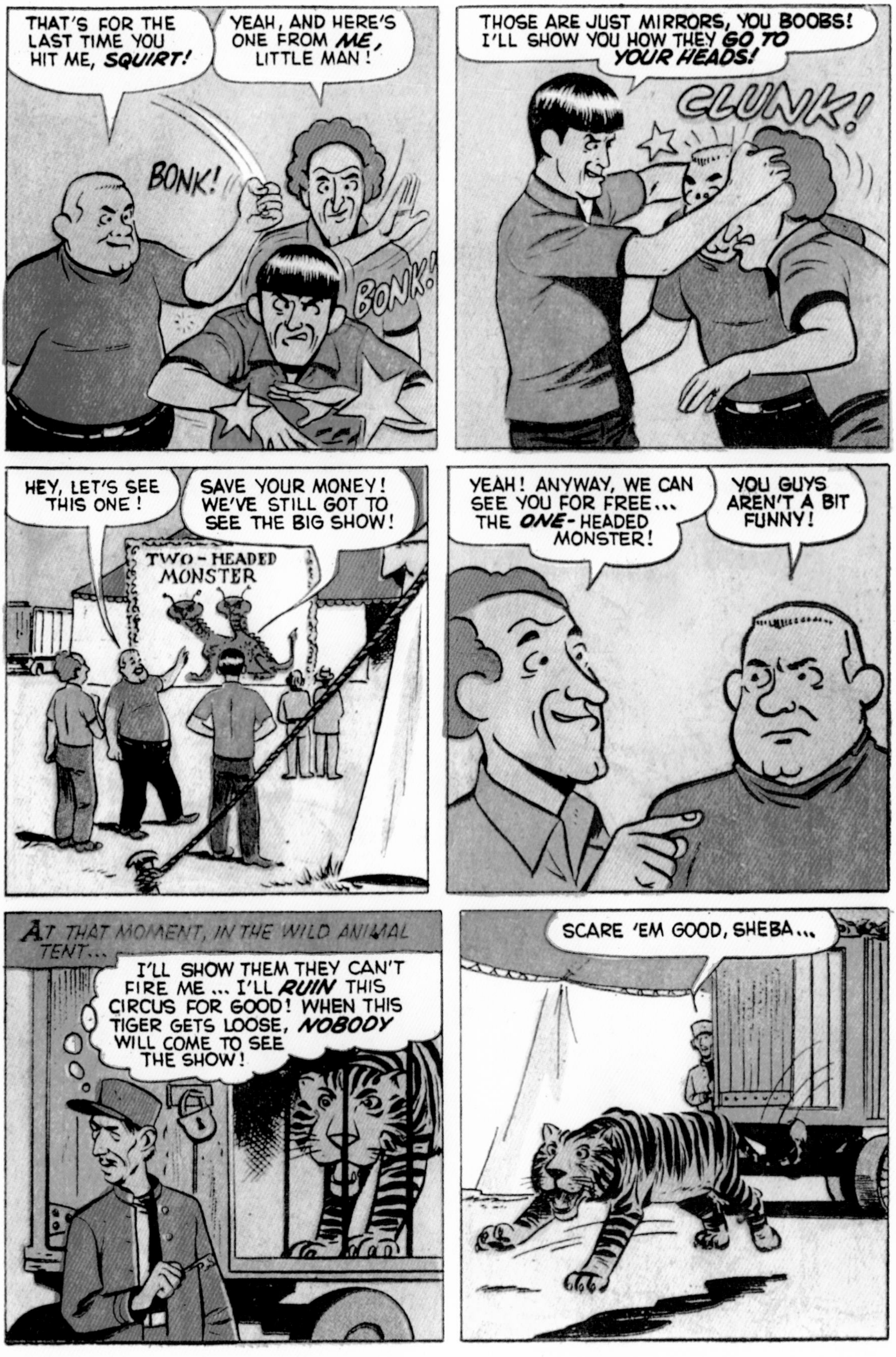

THAT'S FOR THE LAST TIME YOU HIT ME, SQUIRT!
YEAH, AND HERE'S ONE FROM ME, LITTLE MAN!
BONK!
BONK!
THOSE ARE JUST MIRRORS, YOU BOOBS! I'LL SHOW YOU HOW THEY GO TO YOUR HEADS!
CLUNK!
HEY, LET'S SEE THIS ONE!
SAVE YOUR MONEY! WE'VE STILL GOT TO SEE THE BIG SHOW!
TWO-HEADED MONSTER
YEAH! ANYWAY, WE CAN SEE YOU FOR FREE... THE ONE-HEADED MONSTER!
YOU GUYS AREN'T A BIT FUNNY!
AT THAT MOMENT, IN THE WILD ANIMAL TENT...
I'LL SHOW THEM THEY CAN'T FIRE ME... I'LL RUIN THIS CIRCUS FOR GOOD! WHEN THIS TIGER GETS LOOSE, NOBODY WILL COME TO SEE THE SHOW!
SCARE 'EM GOOD, SHEBA...

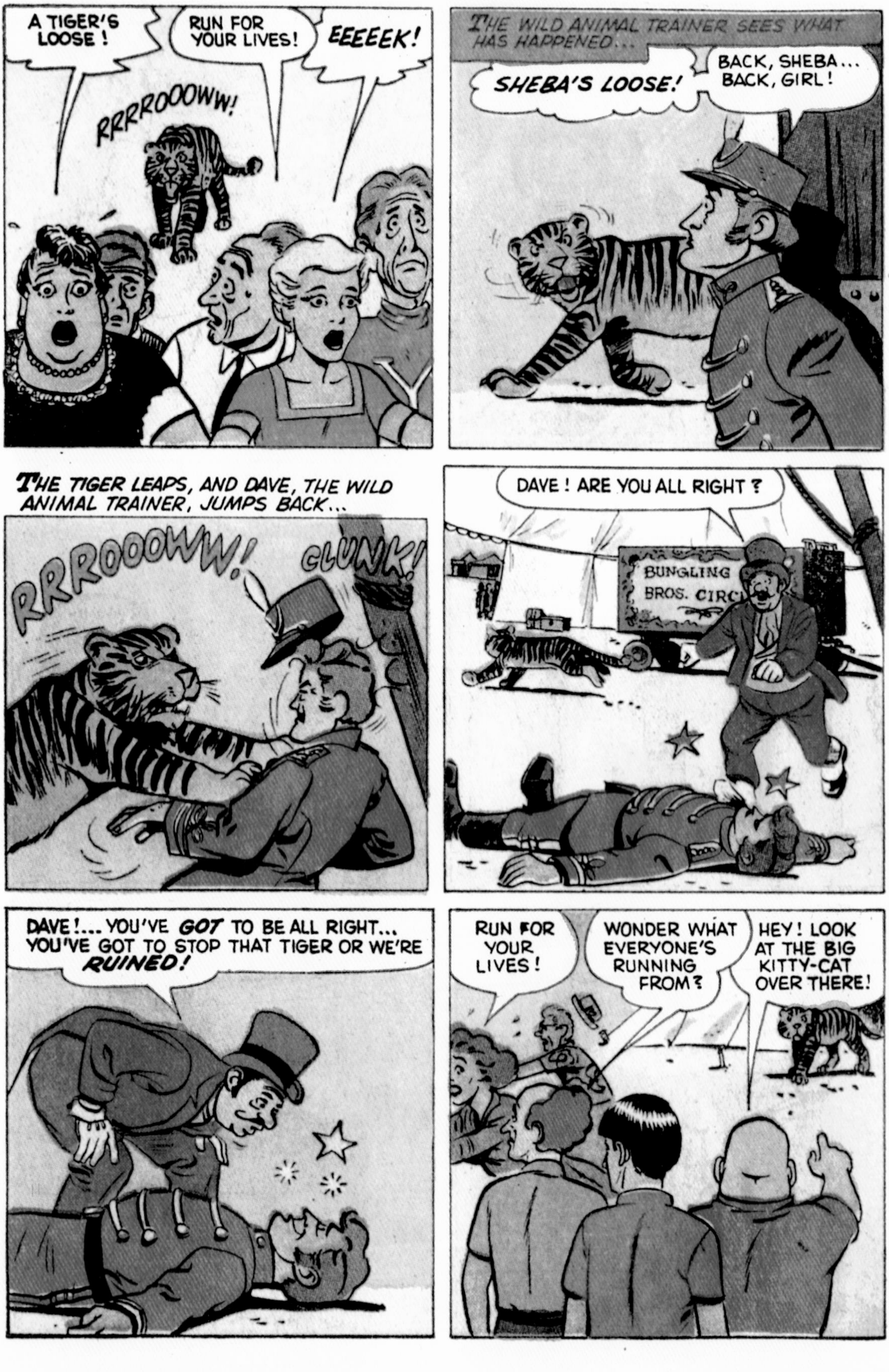
A TIGER'S LOOSE!
RUN FOR YOUR LIVES!
EEEEEK!
RRRROOOWW!
THE WILD ANIMAL TRAINER SEES WHAT HAS HAPPENED...
SHEBA'S LOOSE!
BACK, SHEBA... BACK, GIRL!
THE TIGER LEAPS, AND DAVE, THE WILD ANIMAL TRAINER, JUMPS BACK...
RRROOOWW!
GLUNK!
DAVE! ARE YOU ALL RIGHT?
BUNGLING BROS. CIRC
DAVE!... YOU'VE GOT TO BE ALL RIGHT... YOU'VE GOT TO STOP THAT TIGER OR WE'RE RUINED!
RUN FOR YOUR LIVES!
WONDER WHAT EVERYONE'S RUNNING FROM?
HEY! LOOK AT THE BIG KITTY-CAT OVER THERE!

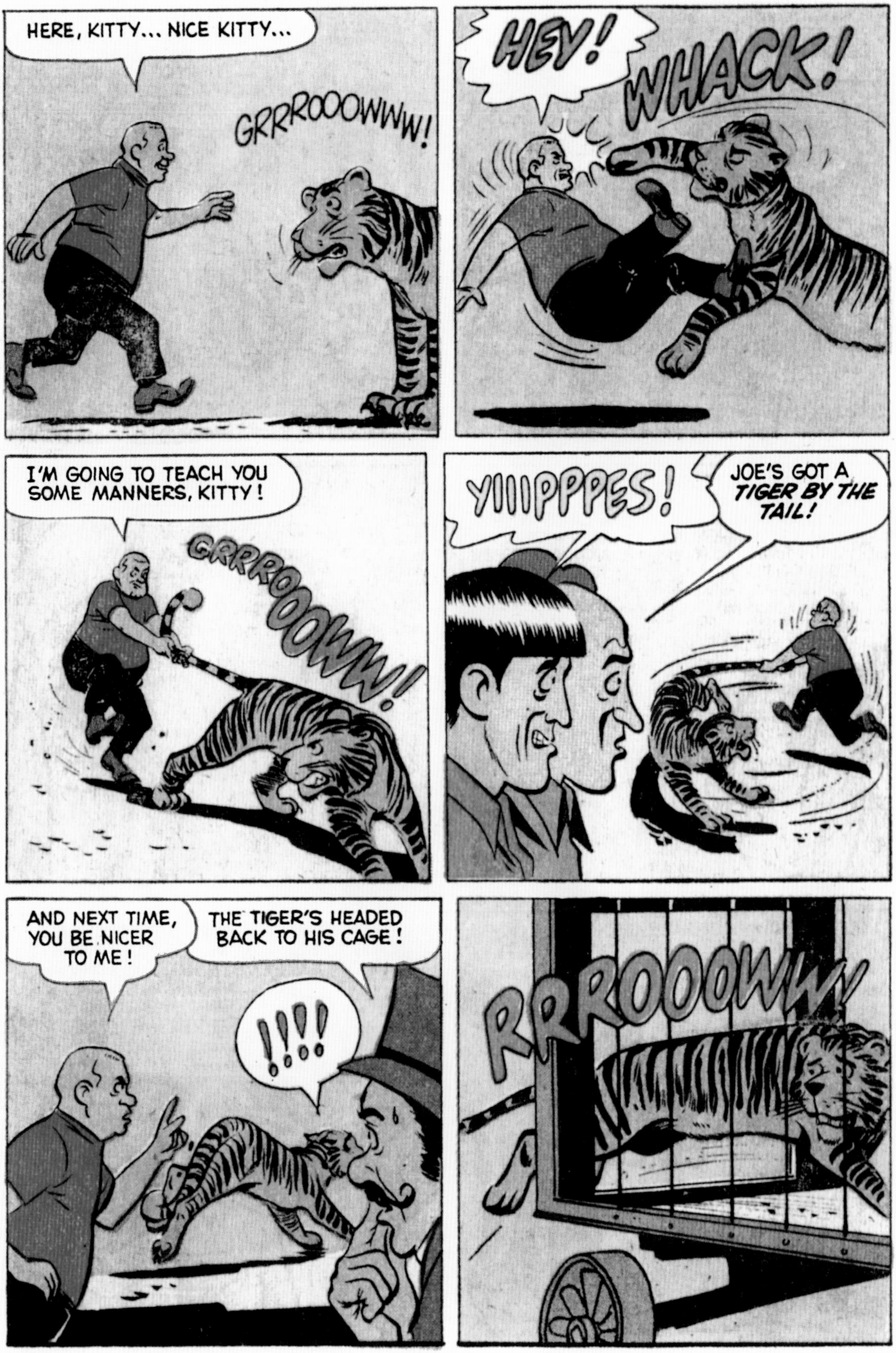

HERE, KITTY... NICE KITTY...
GRRROOOWWW!
HEY!
WHACK!
I'M GOING TO TEACH YOU SOME MANNERS, KITTY!
GRRROOOWW!
YIIIPPPES!
JOE'S GOT A TIGER BY THE TAIL!
AND NEXT TIME, YOU BE NICER TO ME!
THE TIGER'S HEADED BACK TO HIS CAGE!
!!!!
RRROOOWW!

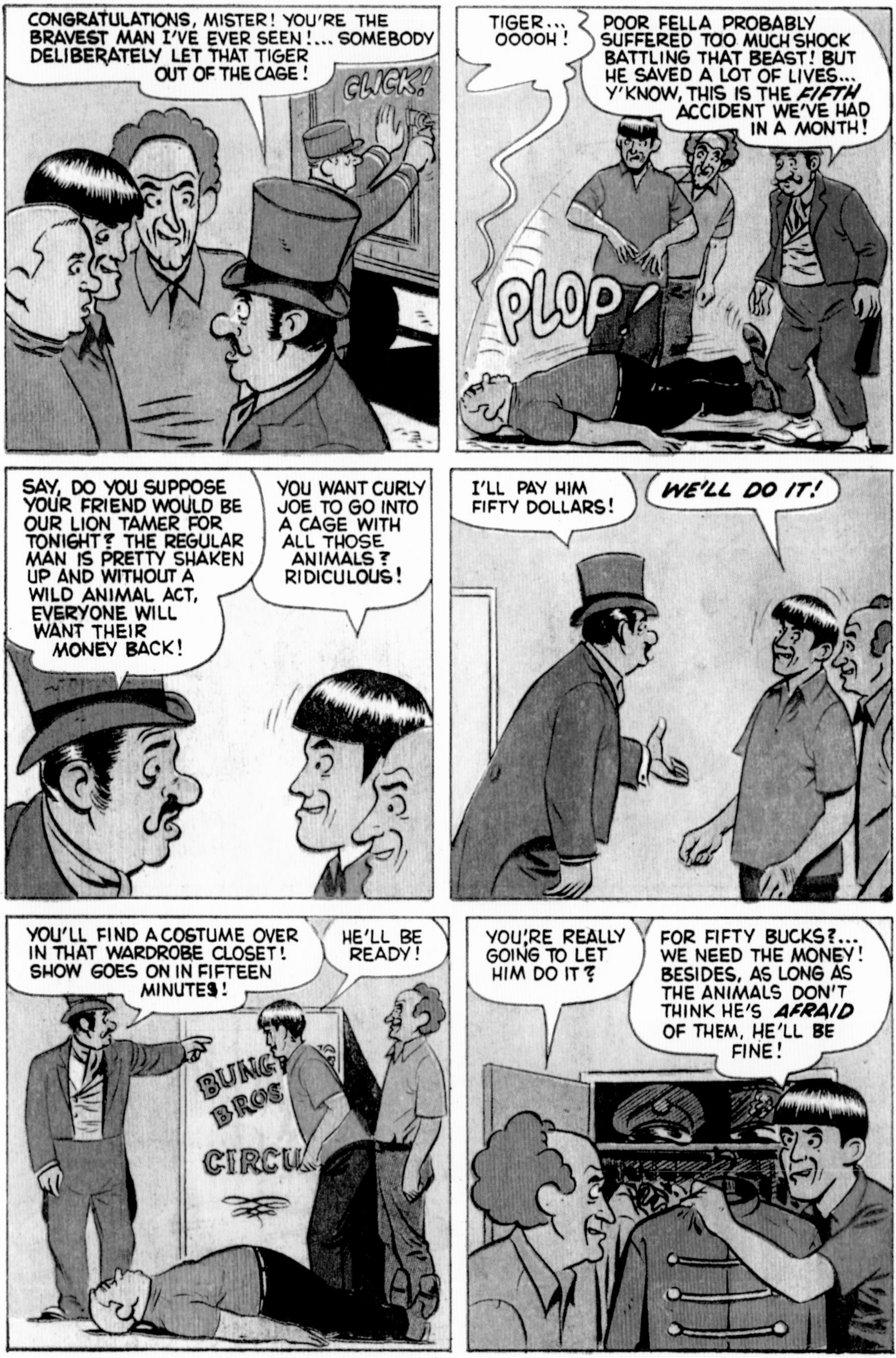
CONGRATULATIONS, MISTER! YOU'RE THE BRAVEST MAN I'VE EVER SEEN!... SOMEBODY DELIBERATELY LET THAT TIGER OUT OF THE CAGE!
CLICK!
TIGER... OOOOH!
POOR FELLA PROBABLY SUFFERED TOO MUCH SHOCK BATTLING THAT BEAST! BUT HE SAVED A LOT OF LIVES... Y'KNOW, THIS IS THE FIFTH ACCIDENT WE'VE HAD IN A MONTH!
PLOP!
SAY, DO YOU SUPPOSE YOUR FRIEND WOULD BE OUR LION TAMER FOR TONIGHT? THE REGULAR MAN IS PRETTY SHAKEN UP AND WITHOUT A WILD ANIMAL ACT, EVERYONE WILL WANT THEIR MONEY BACK!
YOU WANT CURLY JOE TO GO INTO A CAGE WITH ALL THOSE ANIMALS? RIDICULOUS!
I'LL PAY HIM FIFTY DOLLARS!
WE'LL DO IT!
YOU'LL FIND A COSTUME OVER IN THAT WARDROBE CLOSET! SHOW GOES ON IN FIFTEEN MINUTES!
HE'LL BE READY!
BUNG BROS CIRCU
YOU'RE REALLY GOING TO LET HIM DO IT?
FOR FIFTY BUCKS?... WE NEED THE MONEY! BESIDES, AS LONG AS THE ANIMALS DON'T THINK HE'S AFRAID OF THEM, HE'LL BE FINE!

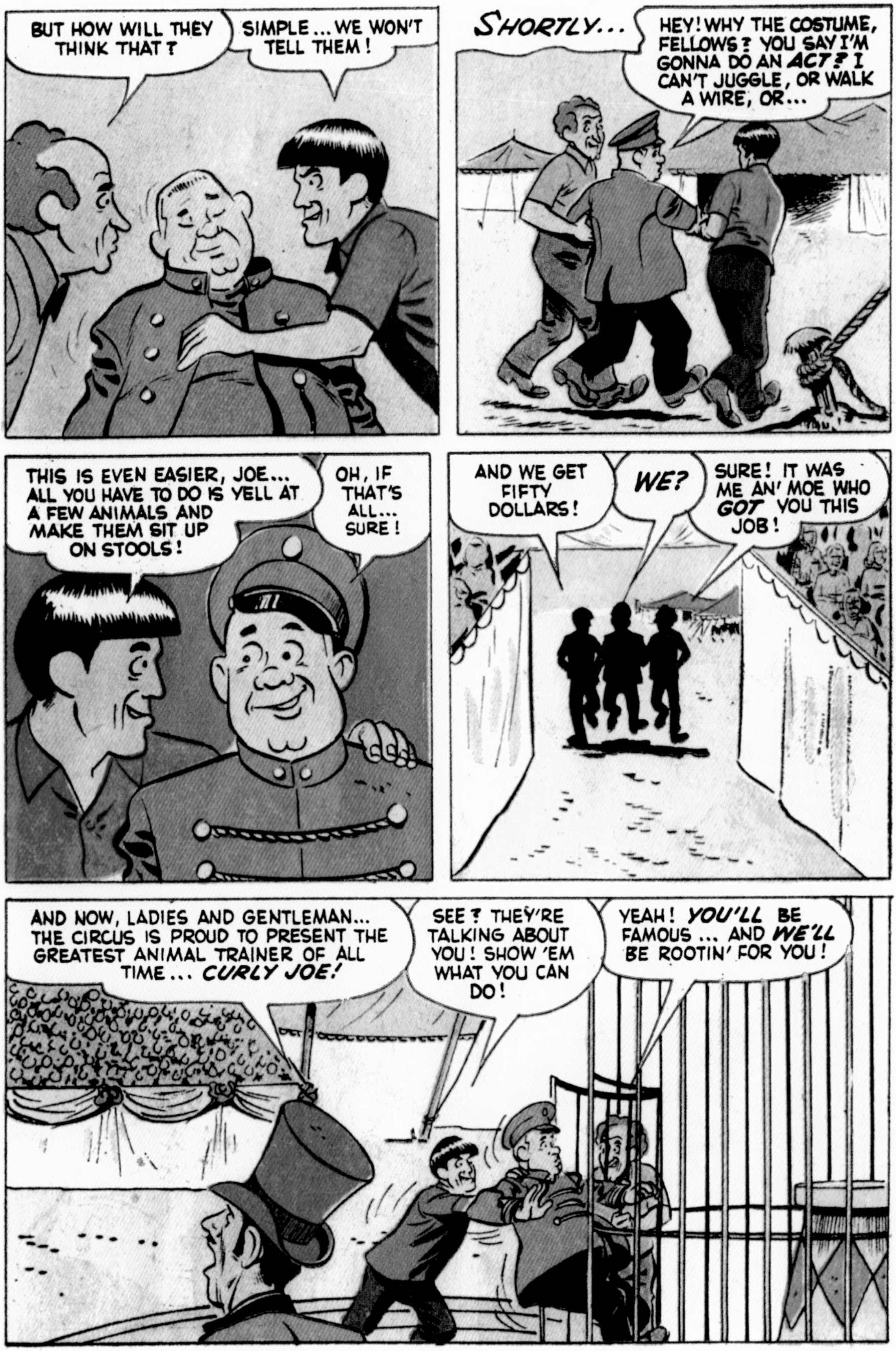
BUT HOW WILL THEY THINK THAT?
SIMPLE... WE WON'T TELL THEM!
SHORTLY...
HEY! WHY THE COSTUME, FELLOWS? YOU SAY I'M GONNA DO AN ACT? I CAN'T JUGGLE, OR WALK A WIRE, OR...
THIS IS EVEN EASIER, JOE... ALL YOU HAVE TO DO IS YELL AT A FEW ANIMALS AND MAKE THEM SIT UP ON STOOLS!
OH, IF THAT'S ALL... SURE!
AND WE GET FIFTY DOLLARS!
WE?
SURE! IT WAS ME AN' MOE WHO GOT YOU THIS JOB!
AND NOW, LADIES AND GENTLEMAN... THE CIRCUS IS PROUD TO PRESENT THE GREATEST ANIMAL TRAINER OF ALL TIME... CURLY JOE!
SEE? THEY'RE TALKING ABOUT YOU! SHOW 'EM WHAT YOU CAN DO!
YEAH! YOU'LL BE FAMOUS ... AND WE'LL BE ROOTIN' FOR YOU!

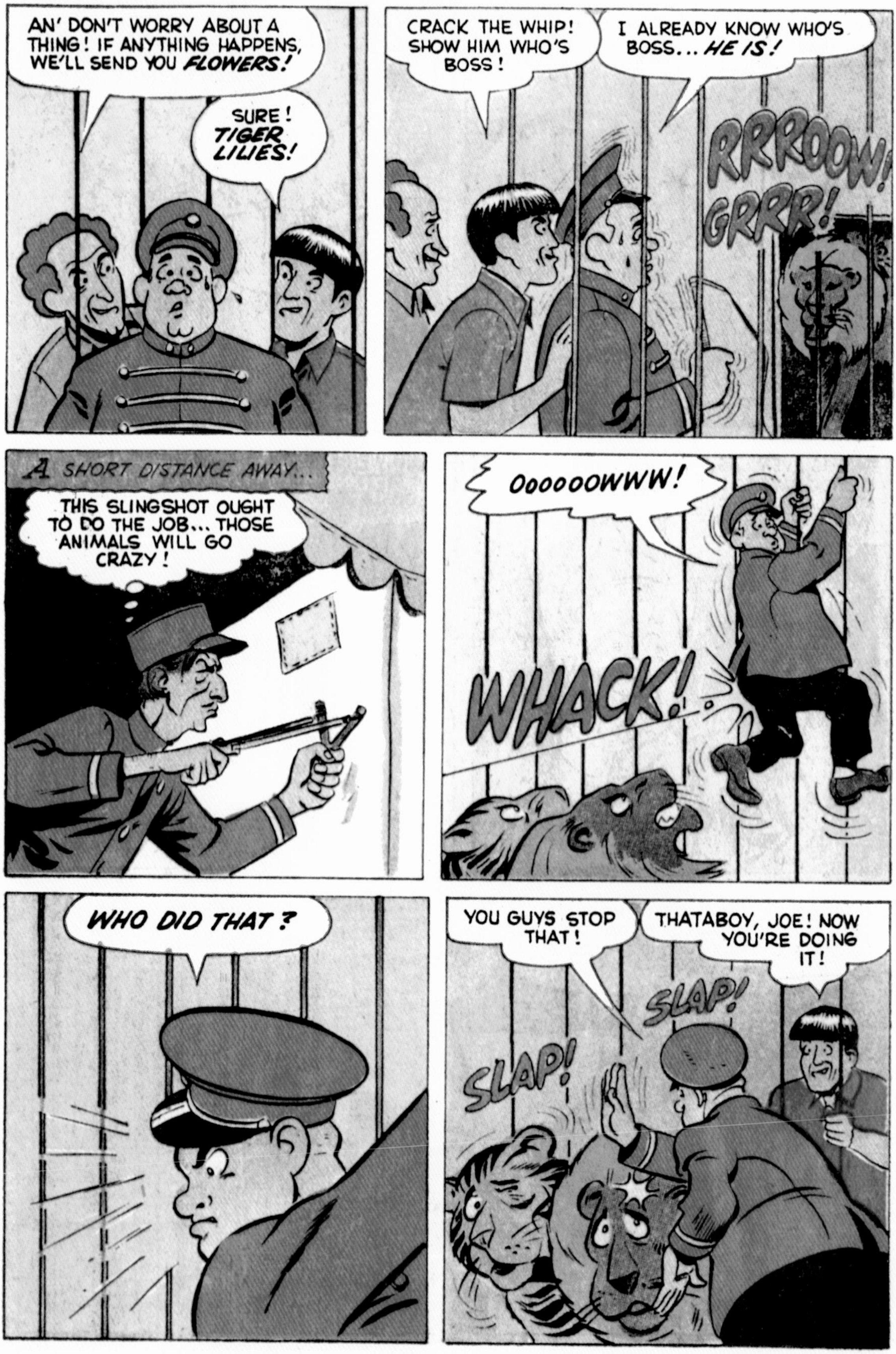
AN' DON'T WORRY ABOUT A THING! IF ANYTHING HAPPENS, WE'LL SEND YOU FLOWERS!
SURE! TIGER LILIES!
CRACK THE WHIP! SHOW HIM WHO'S BOSS!
I ALREADY KNOW WHO'S BOSS... HE IS!
RRROOW!
GRRR!
A SHORT DISTANCE AWAY...
THIS SLINGSHOT OUGHT TO DO THE JOB... THOSE ANIMALS WILL GO CRAZY!
OOOOOOWWW!
WHACK!
WHO DID THAT?
YOU GUYS STOP THAT!
THATABOY, JOE! NOW YOU'RE DOING IT!
SLAP!
SLAP!

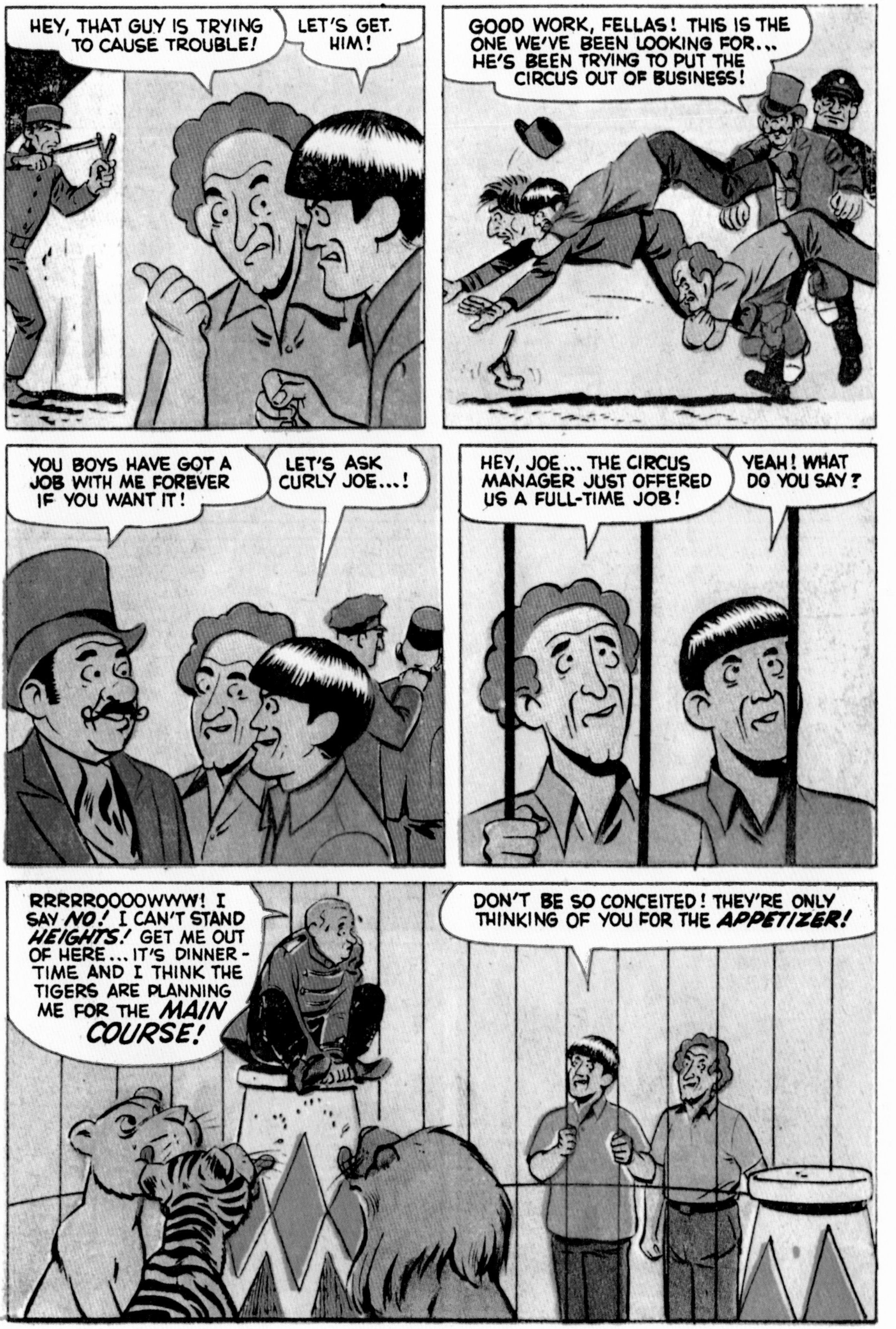
HEY, THAT GUY IS TRYING TO CAUSE TROUBLE!
LET'S GET. HIM!
GOOD WORK, FELLAS! THIS IS THE ONE WE'VE BEEN LOOKING FOR... HE'S BEEN TRYING TO PUT THE CIRCUS OUT OF BUSINESS!
YOU BOYS HAVE GOT A JOB WITH ME FOREVER IF YOU WANT IT!
LET'S ASK CURLY JOE...!
HEY, JOE... THE CIRCUS MANAGER JUST OFFERED US A FULL-TIME JOB!
YEAH! WHAT DO YOU SAY?
RRRRROOOOWWW! I SAY NO! I CAN'T STAND HEIGHTS! GET ME OUT OF HERE... IT'S DINNER-TIME AND I THINK THE TIGERS ARE PLANNING ME FOR THE MAIN COURSE!
DON'T BE SO CONCEITED! THEY'RE ONLY THINKING OF YOU FOR THE APPETIZER!

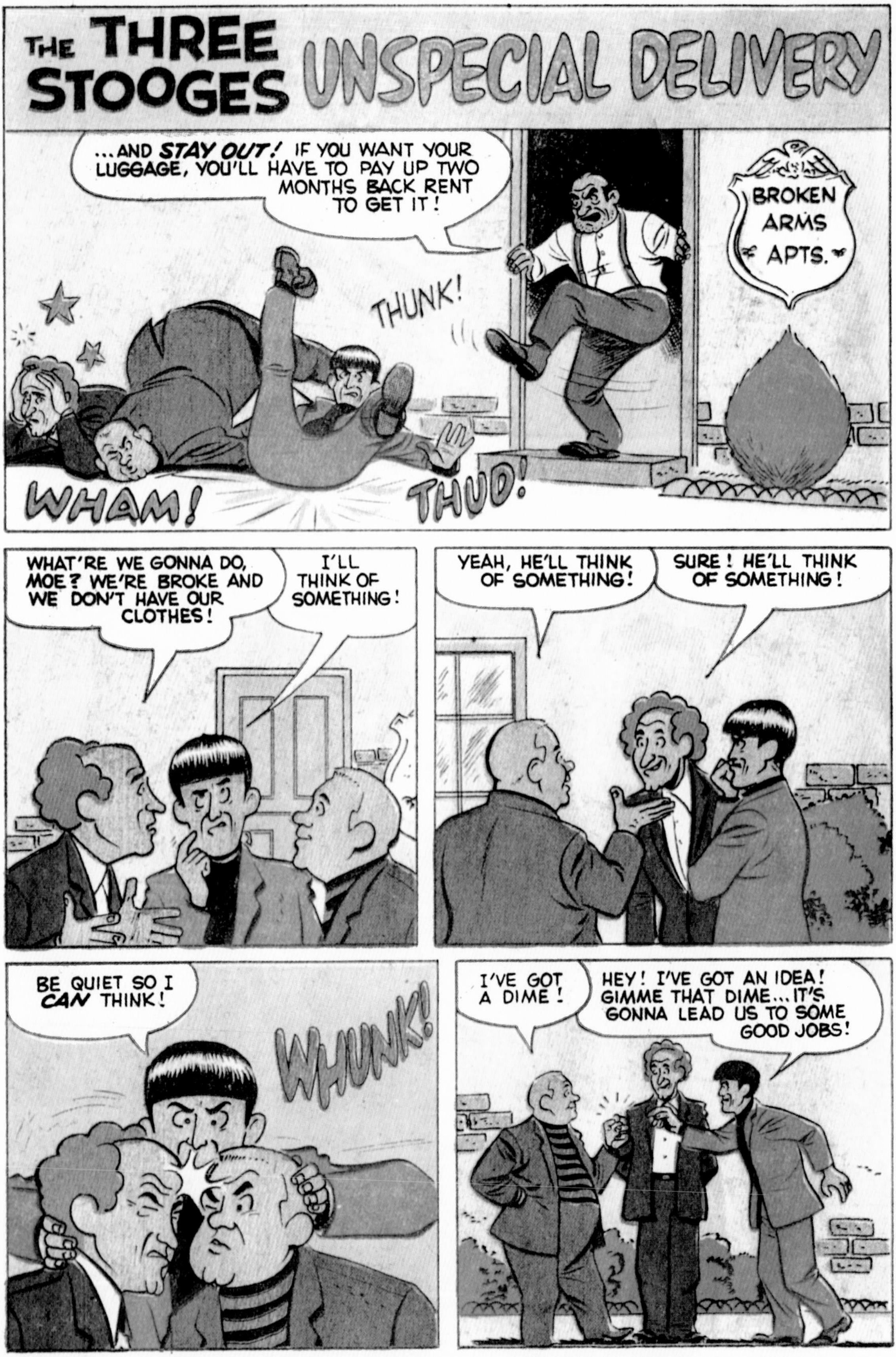
THE THREE STOOGES
UNSPECIAL DELIVERY
...AND STAY OUT! IF YOU WANT YOUR LUGGAGE, YOU'LL HAVE TO PAY UP TWO MONTHS BACK RENT TO GET IT!
BROKEN ARMS APTS.
THUNK!
WHAM!
THUD!
WHAT'RE WE GONNA DO, MOE? WE'RE BROKE AND WE DON'T HAVE OUR CLOTHES!
I'LL THINK OF SOMETHING!
YEAH, HE'LL THINK OF SOMETHING!
SURE! HE'LL THINK OF SOMETHING!
BE QUIET SO I CAN THINK!
WHUNK!
I'VE GOT A DIME!
HEY! I'VE GOT AN IDEA! GIMME THAT DIME... IT'S GONNA LEAD US TO SOME GOOD JOBS!

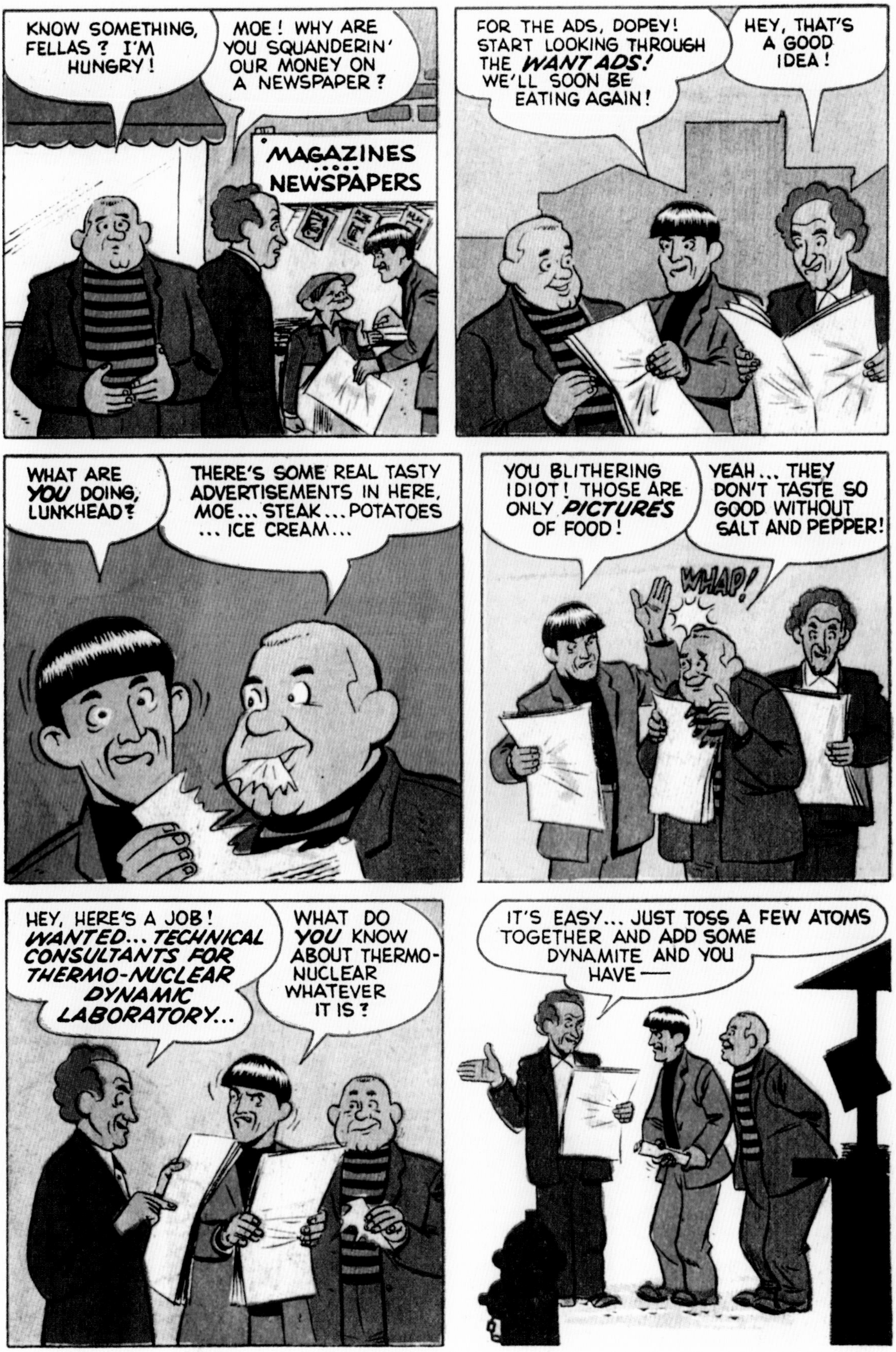
KNOW SOMETHING, FELLAS? I'M HUNGRY!
MOE! WHY ARE YOU SQUANDERIN' OUR MONEY ON A NEWSPAPER?
MAGAZINES .... NEWSPAPERS
FOR THE ADS, DOPEY! START LOOKING THROUGH THE WANT ADS! WE'LL SOON BE EATING AGAIN!
HEY, THAT'S A GOOD IDEA!
WHAT ARE YOU DOING, LUNKHEAD?
THERE'S SOME REAL TASTY ADVERTISEMENTS IN HERE, MOE... STEAK... POTATOES ... ICE CREAM...
YOU BLITHERING IDIOT! THOSE ARE ONLY PICTURES OF FOOD!
YEAH... THEY DON'T TASTE SO GOOD WITHOUT SALT AND PEPPER!
WHAP!
HEY, HERE'S A JOB! WANTED... TECHNICAL CONSULTANTS FOR THERMO-NUCLEAR DYNAMIC LABORATORY...
WHAT DO YOU KNOW ABOUT THERMO-NUCLEAR WHATEVER IT IS?
IT'S EASY... JUST TOSS A FEW ATOMS TOGETHER AND ADD SOME DYNAMITE AND YOU HAVE—

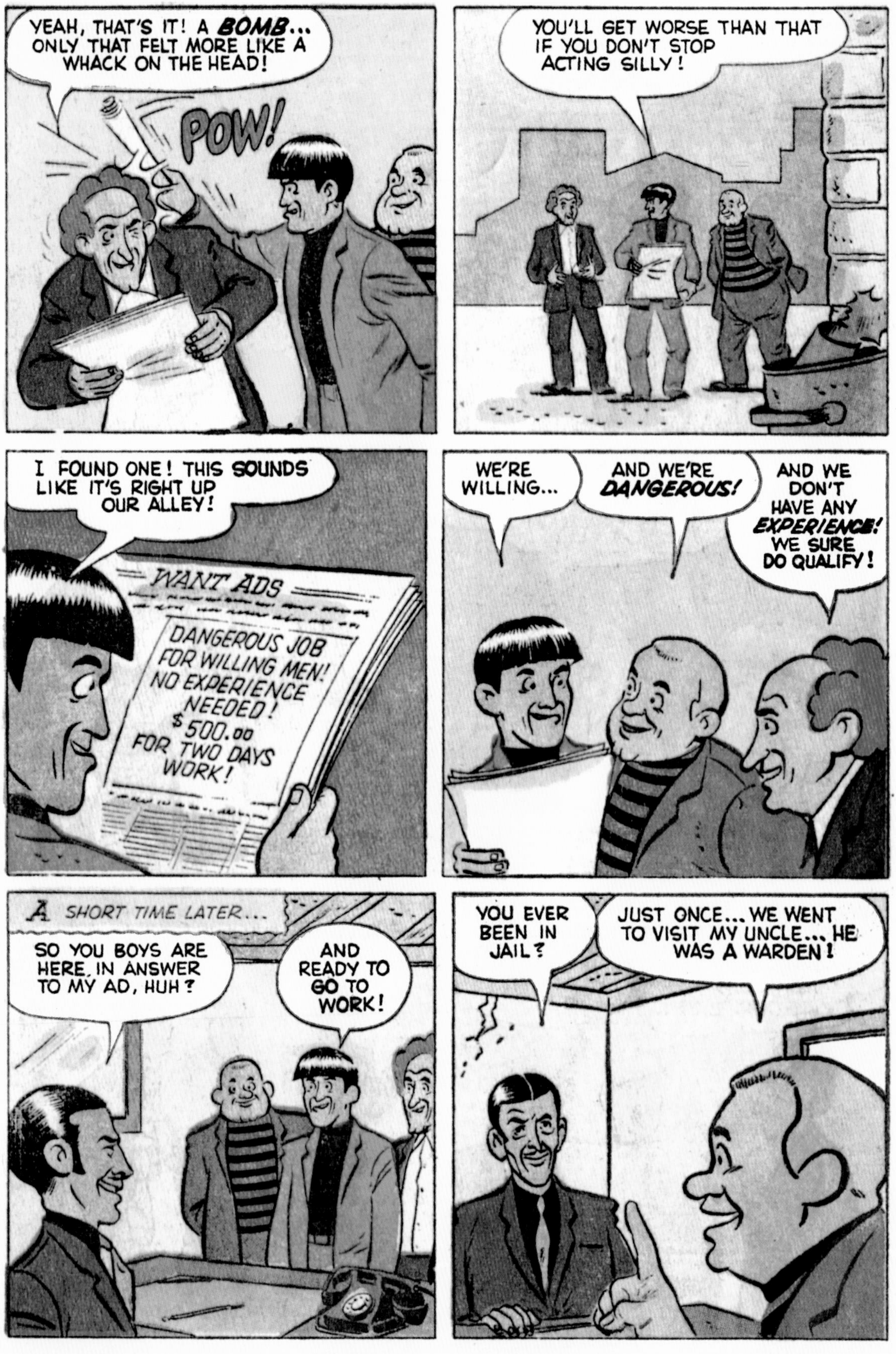
YEAH, THAT'S IT! A BOMB... ONLY THAT FELT MORE LIKE A WHACK ON THE HEAD!
POW!
YOU'LL GET WORSE THAN THAT IF YOU DON'T STOP ACTING SILLY!
I FOUND ONE! THIS SOUNDS LIKE IT'S RIGHT UP OUR ALLEY!
WANT ADS
DANGEROUS JOB FOR WILLING MEN! NO EXPERIENCE NEEDED! $500.00 FOR TWO DAYS WORK!
WE'RE WILLING...
AND WE'RE DANGEROUS!
AND WE DON'T HAVE ANY EXPERIENCE! WE SURE DO QUALIFY!
A SHORT TIME LATER...
SO YOU BOYS ARE HERE IN ANSWER TO MY AD, HUH?
AND READY TO GO TO WORK!
YOU EVER BEEN IN JAIL?
JUST ONCE... WE WENT TO VISIT MY UNCLE... HE WAS A WARDEN!

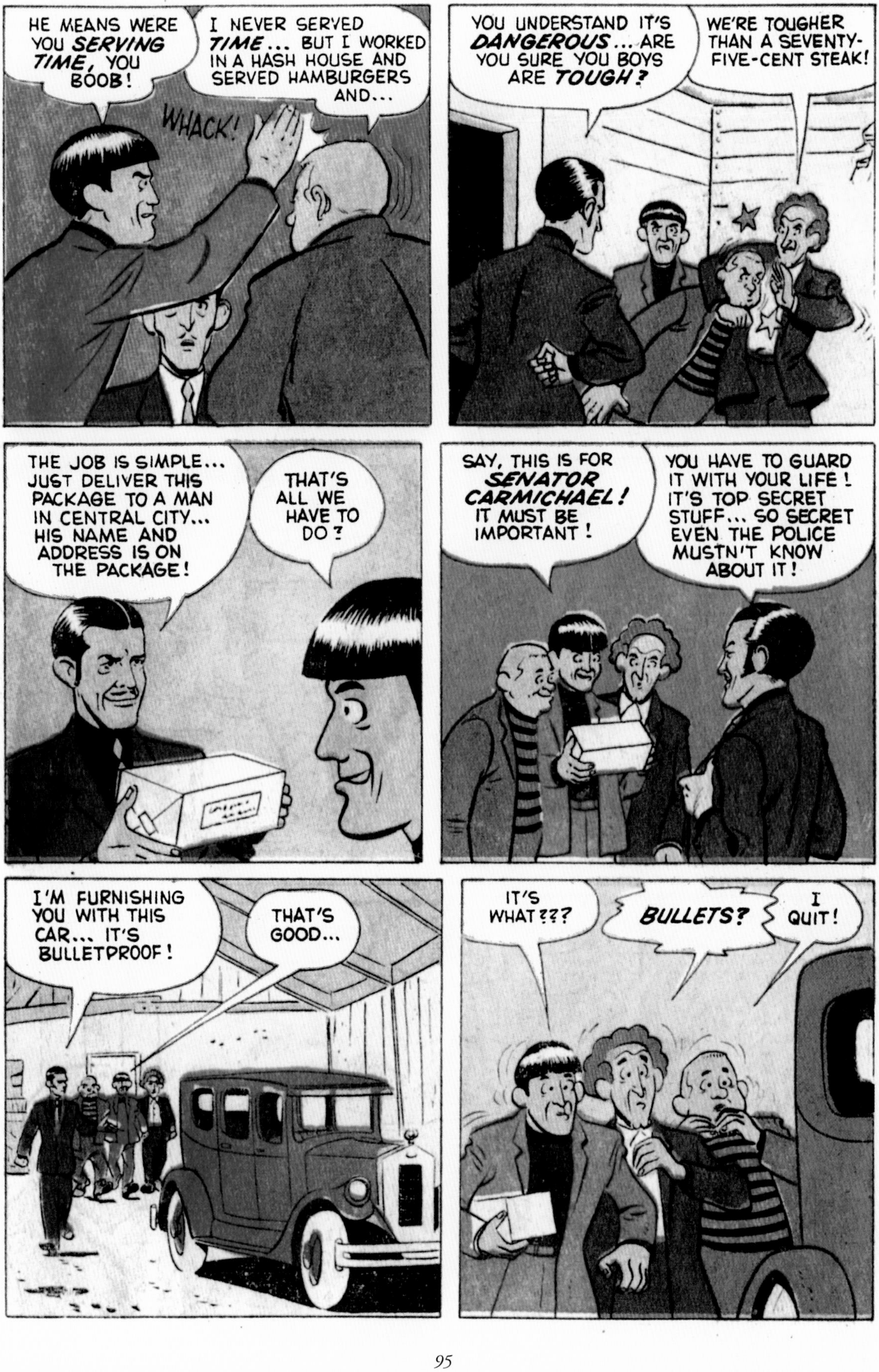
HE MEANS WERE YOU SERVING TIME, YOU BOOB!
I NEVER SERVED TIME... BUT I WORKED IN A HASH HOUSE AND SERVED HAMBURGERS AND...
WHACK!
YOU UNDERSTAND IT'S DANGEROUS... ARE YOU SURE YOU BOYS ARE TOUGH?
WE'RE TOUGHER THAN A SEVENTY-FIVE-CENT STEAK!
THE JOB IS SIMPLE... JUST DELIVER THIS PACKAGE TO A MAN IN CENTRAL CITY... HIS NAME AND ADDRESS IS ON THE PACKAGE!
THAT'S ALL WE HAVE TO DO?
SAY, THIS IS FOR SENATOR CARMICHAEL! IT MUST BE IMPORTANT!
YOU HAVE TO GUARD IT WITH YOUR LIFE! IT'S TOP SECRET STUFF... SO SECRET EVEN THE POLICE MUSTN'T KNOW ABOUT IT!
I'M FURNISHING YOU WITH THIS CAR... IT'S BULLETPROOF!
THAT'S GOOD...
IT'S WHAT???
BULLETS?
I QUIT!

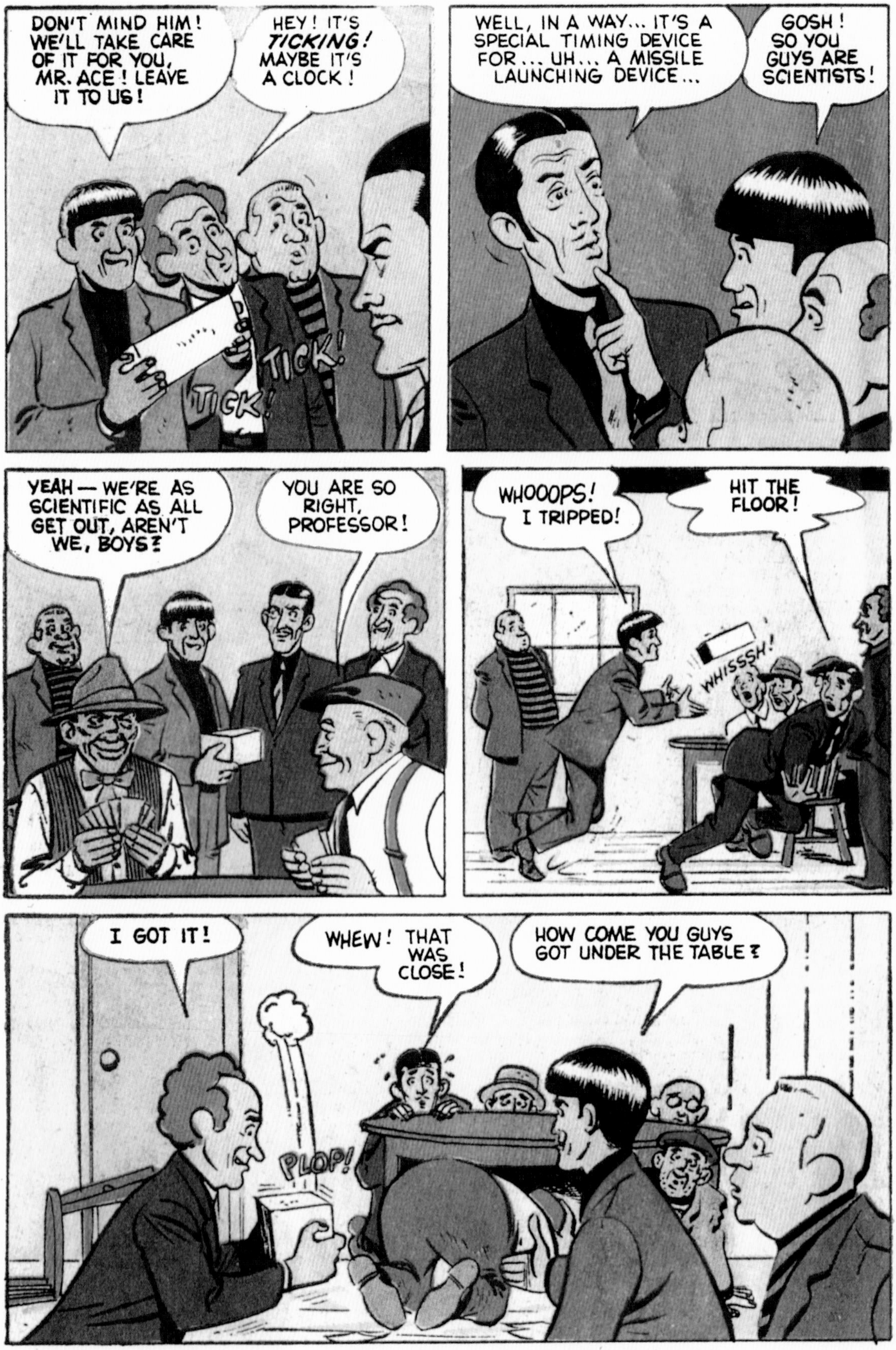

DON'T MIND HIM! WE'LL TAKE CARE OF IT FOR YOU, MR. ACE! LEAVE IT TO US!
HEY! IT'S TICKING! MAYBE IT'S A CLOCK!
TICK! TICK!
WELL, IN A WAY... IT'S A SPECIAL TIMING DEVICE FOR... UH... A MISSILE LAUNCHING DEVICE...
GOSH! SO YOU GUYS ARE SCIENTISTS!
YEAH — WE'RE AS SCIENTIFIC AS ALL GET OUT, AREN'T WE, BOYS?
YOU ARE SO RIGHT, PROFESSOR!
WHOOOPS! I TRIPPED!
HIT THE FLOOR!
WHISSSH!
I GOT IT!
WHEW! THAT WAS CLOSE!
HOW COME YOU GUYS GOT UNDER THE TABLE?
PLOP!

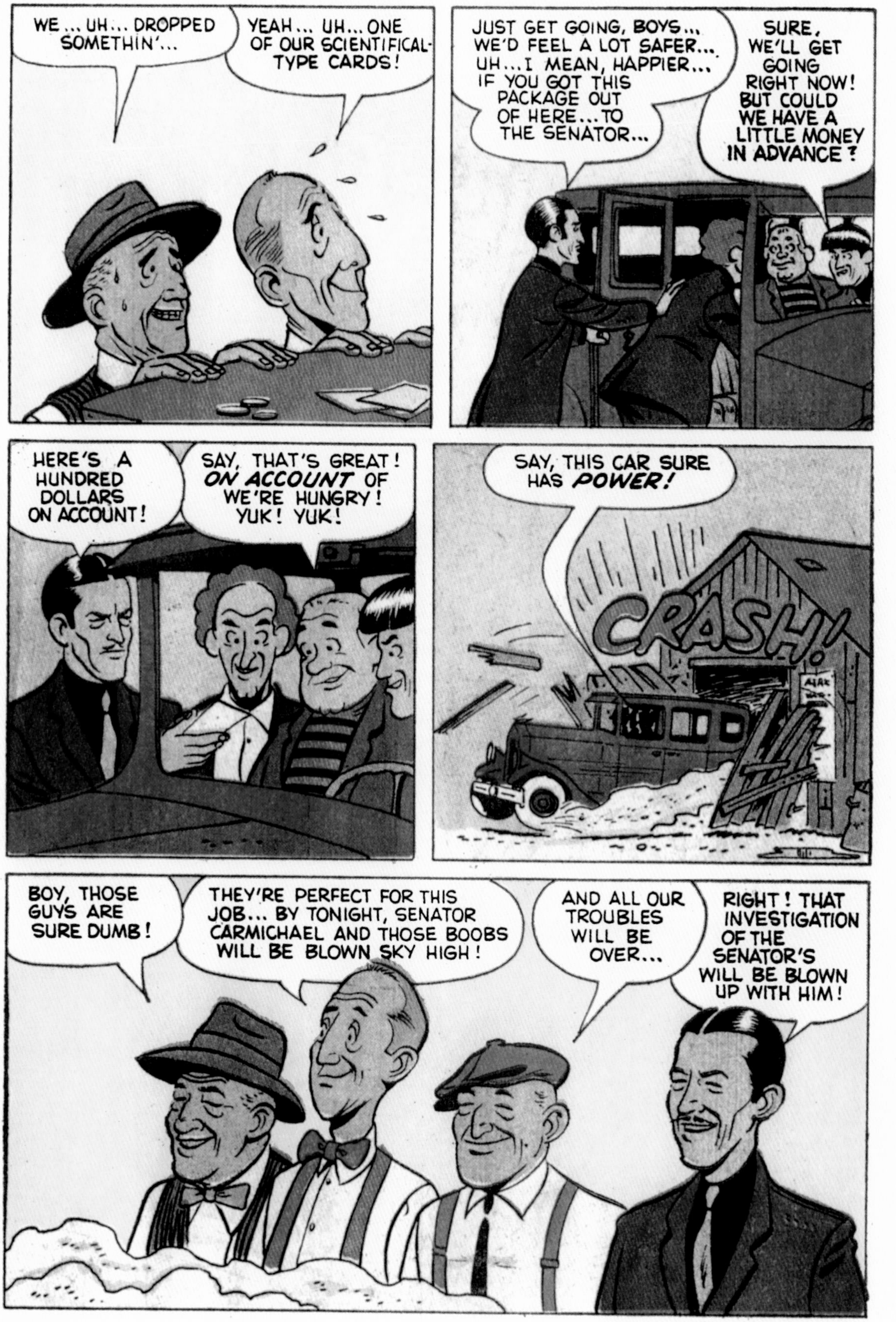
WE ... UH ... DROPPED SOMETHIN'...
YEAH ... UH ... ONE OF OUR SCIENTIFICAL-TYPE CARDS!
JUST GET GOING, BOYS... WE'D FEEL A LOT SAFER... UH ... I MEAN, HAPPIER... IF YOU GOT THIS PACKAGE OUT OF HERE... TO THE SENATOR...
SURE, WE'LL GET GOING RIGHT NOW! BUT COULD WE HAVE A LITTLE MONEY IN ADVANCE?
HERE'S A HUNDRED DOLLARS ON ACCOUNT!
SAY, THAT'S GREAT! *ON ACCOUNT* OF WE'RE HUNGRY! YUK! YUK!
SAY, THIS CAR SURE HAS *POWER!*
CRASH!
BOY, THOSE GUYS ARE SURE DUMB!
THEY'RE PERFECT FOR THIS JOB... BY TONIGHT, SENATOR CARMICHAEL AND THOSE BOOBS WILL BE BLOWN SKY HIGH!
AND ALL OUR TROUBLES WILL BE OVER...
RIGHT! THAT INVESTIGATION OF THE SENATOR'S WILL BE BLOWN UP WITH HIM!

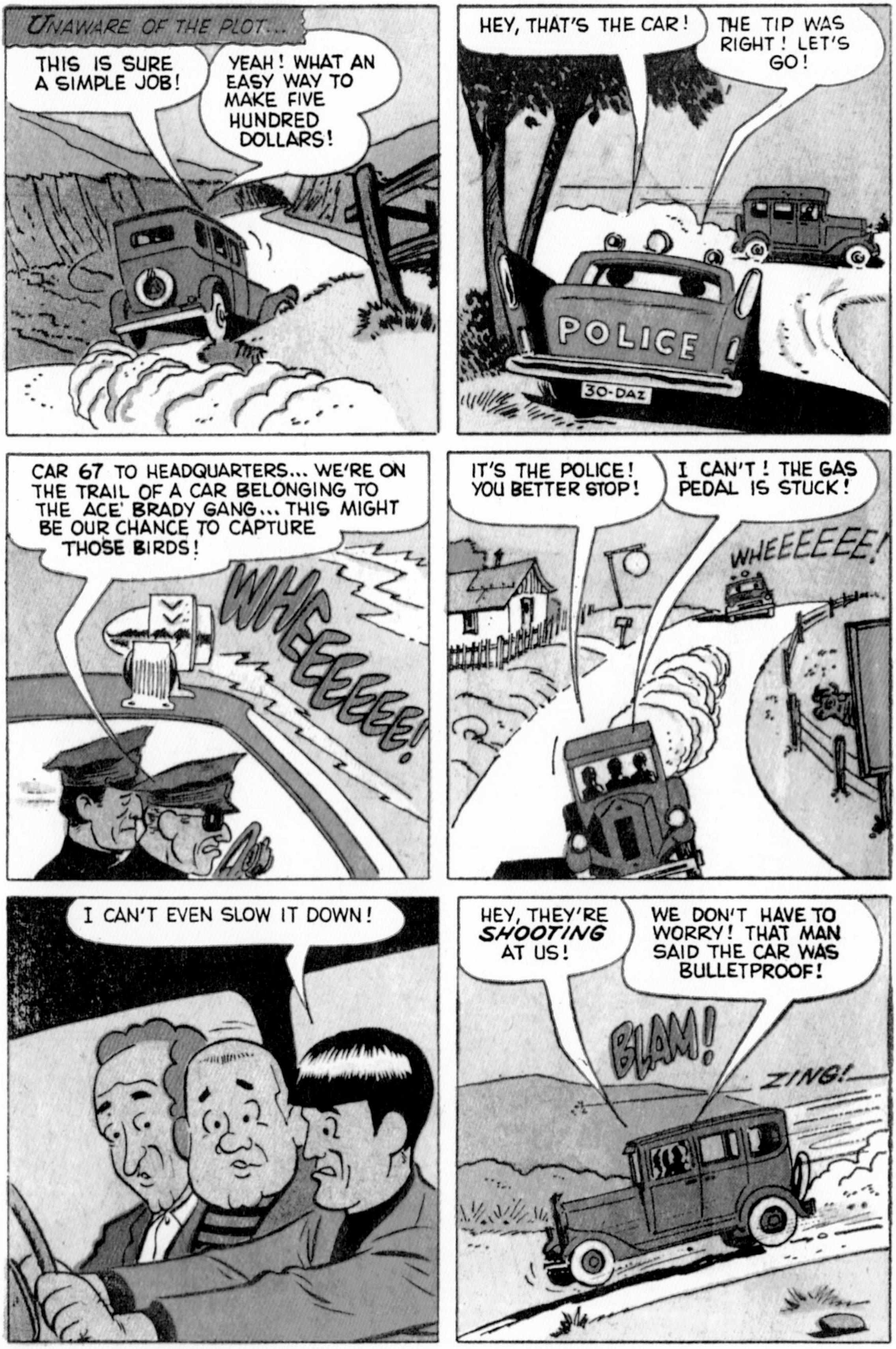

UNAWARE OF THE PLOT...
THIS IS SURE A SIMPLE JOB!
YEAH! WHAT AN EASY WAY TO MAKE FIVE HUNDRED DOLLARS!
HEY, THAT'S THE CAR!
THE TIP WAS RIGHT! LET'S GO!
POLICE
30-DAZ
CAR 67 TO HEADQUARTERS... WE'RE ON THE TRAIL OF A CAR BELONGING TO THE ACE' BRADY GANG... THIS MIGHT BE OUR CHANCE TO CAPTURE THOSE BIRDS!
WHEEEEEEE!
IT'S THE POLICE! YOU BETTER STOP!
I CAN'T! THE GAS PEDAL IS STUCK!
WHEEEEEEE!
I CAN'T EVEN SLOW IT DOWN!
HEY, THEY'RE *SHOOTING* AT US!
WE DON'T HAVE TO WORRY! THAT MAN SAID THE CAR WAS BULLETPROOF!
BLAM!
ZING!

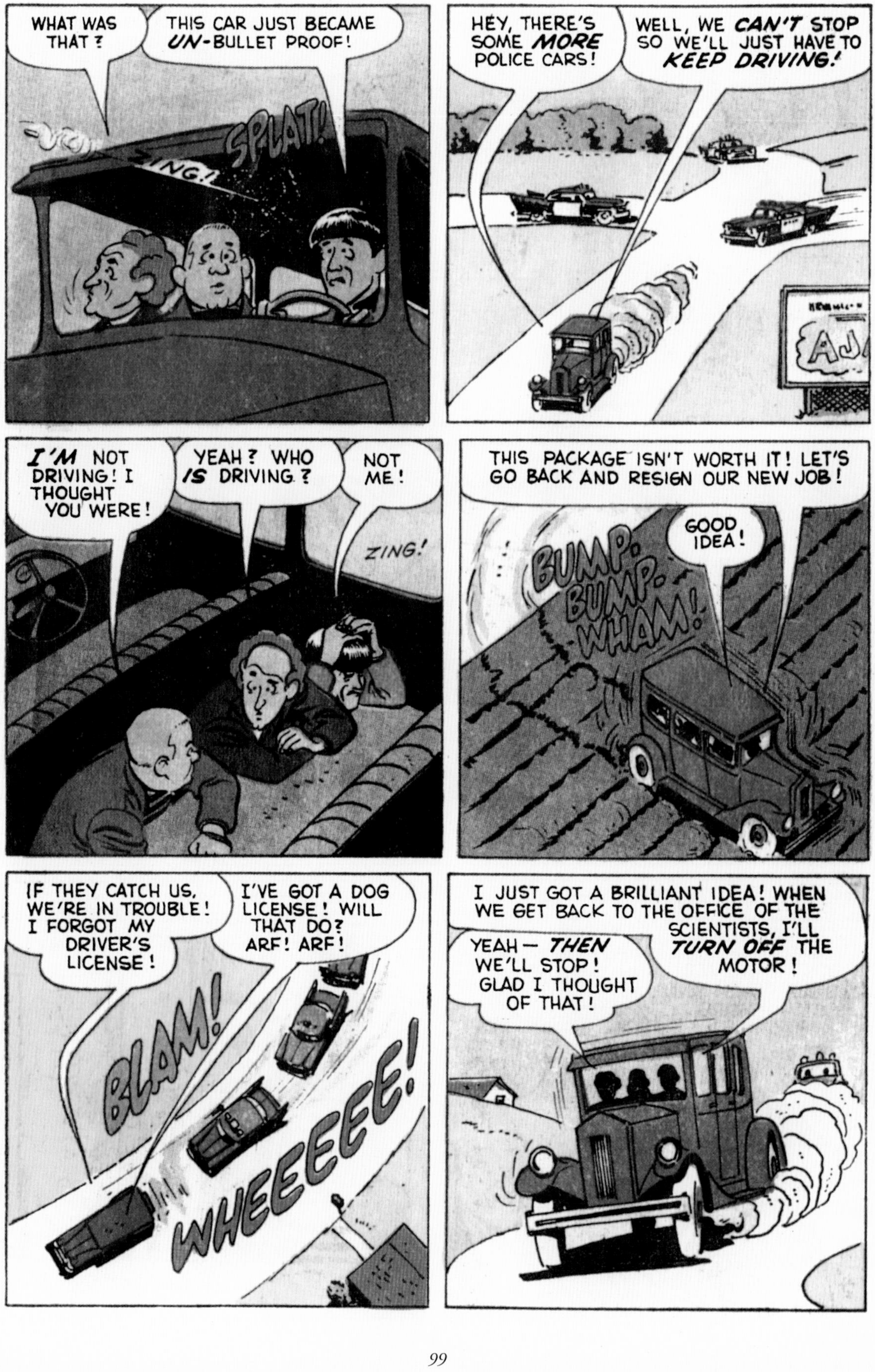
WHAT WAS THAT?
THIS CAR JUST BECAME *UN*-BULLET PROOF!
SPLAT!
HEY, THERE'S SOME *MORE* POLICE CARS!
WELL, WE *CAN'T* STOP SO WE'LL JUST HAVE TO *KEEP DRIVING!*
I'M NOT DRIVING! I THOUGHT YOU WERE!
YEAH? WHO *IS* DRIVING?
NOT ME!
ZING!
THIS PACKAGE ISN'T WORTH IT! LET'S GO BACK AND RESIGN OUR NEW JOB!
GOOD IDEA!
BUMP-BUMP-WHAM!
IF THEY CATCH US, WE'RE IN TROUBLE! I FORGOT MY DRIVER'S LICENSE!
I'VE GOT A DOG LICENSE! WILL THAT DO? ARF! ARF!
BLAM!
WHEEEEEE!
I JUST GOT A BRILLIANT IDEA! WHEN WE GET BACK TO THE OFFICE OF THE SCIENTISTS, I'LL *TURN OFF* THE MOTOR!
YEAH — *THEN* WE'LL STOP! GLAD I THOUGHT OF THAT!

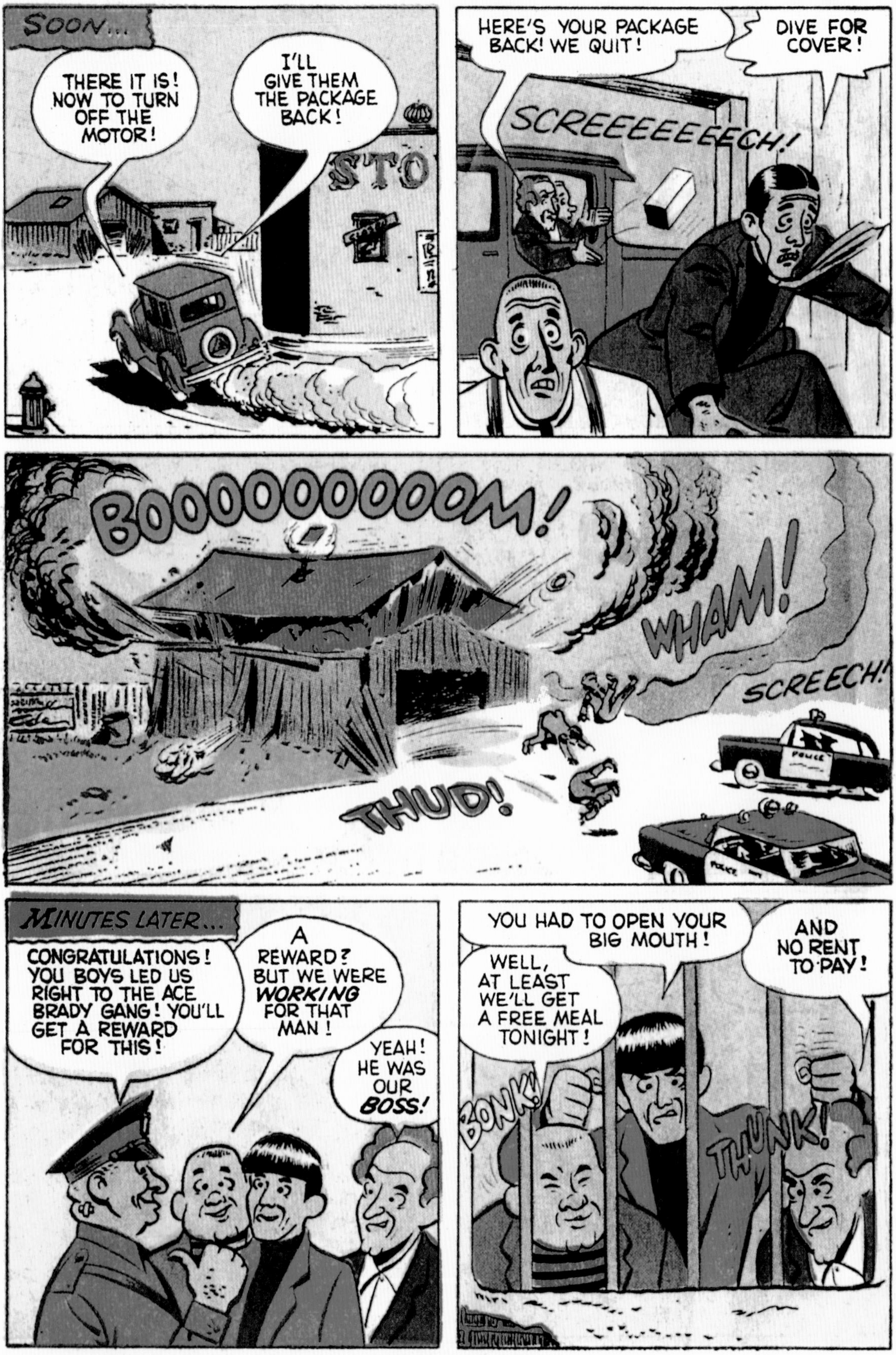

SOON...
THERE IT IS! NOW TO TURN OFF THE MOTOR!
I'LL GIVE THEM THE PACKAGE BACK!
HERE'S YOUR PACKAGE BACK! WE QUIT!
DIVE FOR COVER!
SCREEEEEEEECH!
BOOOOOOOOOM!
WHAM!
SCREECH!
THUD!
MINUTES LATER...
CONGRATULATIONS! YOU BOYS LED US RIGHT TO THE ACE BRADY GANG! YOU'LL GET A REWARD FOR THIS!
A REWARD? BUT WE WERE *WORKING* FOR THAT MAN!
YEAH! HE WAS OUR *BOSS!*
YOU HAD TO OPEN YOUR BIG MOUTH!
WELL, AT LEAST WE'LL GET A FREE MEAL TONIGHT!
AND NO RENT TO PAY!
BONK!
THUNK!

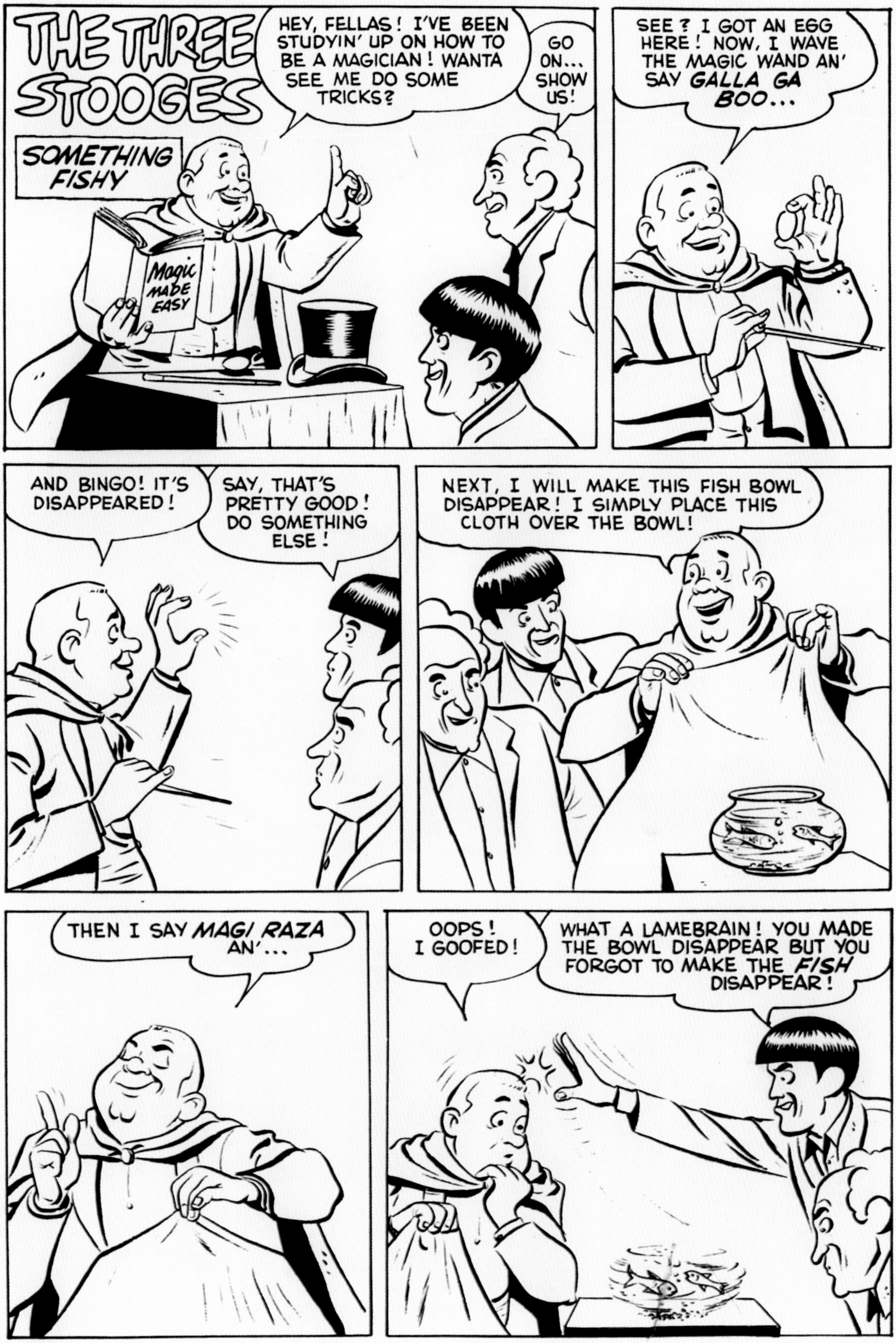
THE THREE STOOGES
SOMETHING FISHY
HEY, FELLAS! I'VE BEEN STUDYIN' UP ON HOW TO BE A MAGICIAN! WANTA SEE ME DO SOME TRICKS?
GO ON... SHOW US!
Magic MADE EASY
SEE? I GOT AN EGG HERE! NOW, I WAVE THE MAGIC WAND AN' SAY GALLA GA BOO...
AND BINGO! IT'S DISAPPEARED!
SAY, THAT'S PRETTY GOOD! DO SOMETHING ELSE!
NEXT, I WILL MAKE THIS FISH BOWL DISAPPEAR! I SIMPLY PLACE THIS CLOTH OVER THE BOWL!
THEN I SAY MAGI RAZA AN'...
OOPS! I GOOFED!
WHAT A LAMEBRAIN! YOU MADE THE BOWL DISAPPEAR BUT YOU FORGOT TO MAKE THE FISH DISAPPEAR!

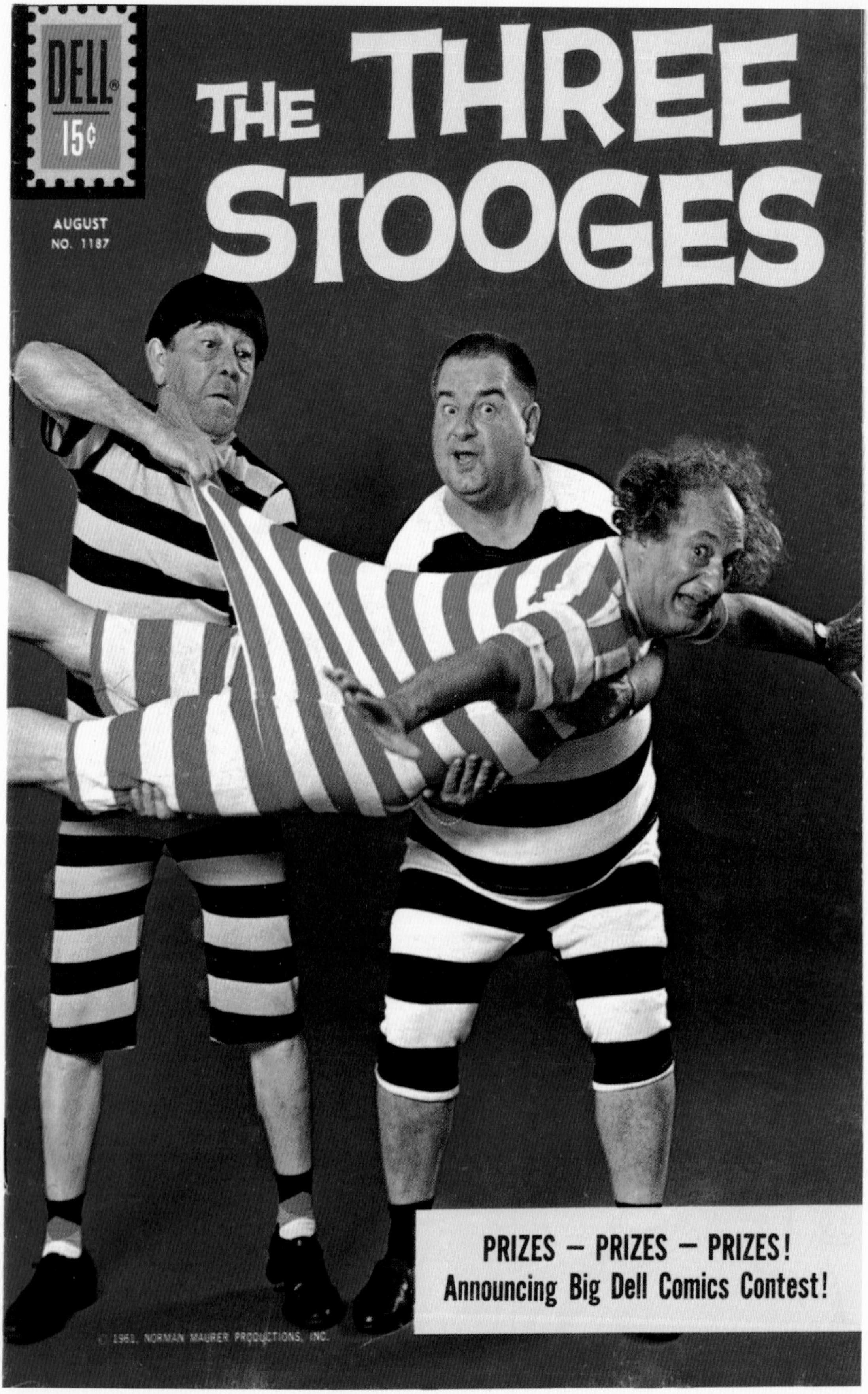
DELL
15¢
THE THREE STOOGES
AUGUST
NO. 1187
PRIZES – PRIZES – PRIZES!
Announcing Big Dell Comics Contest!
© 1961, NORMAN MAURER PRODUCTIONS, INC.

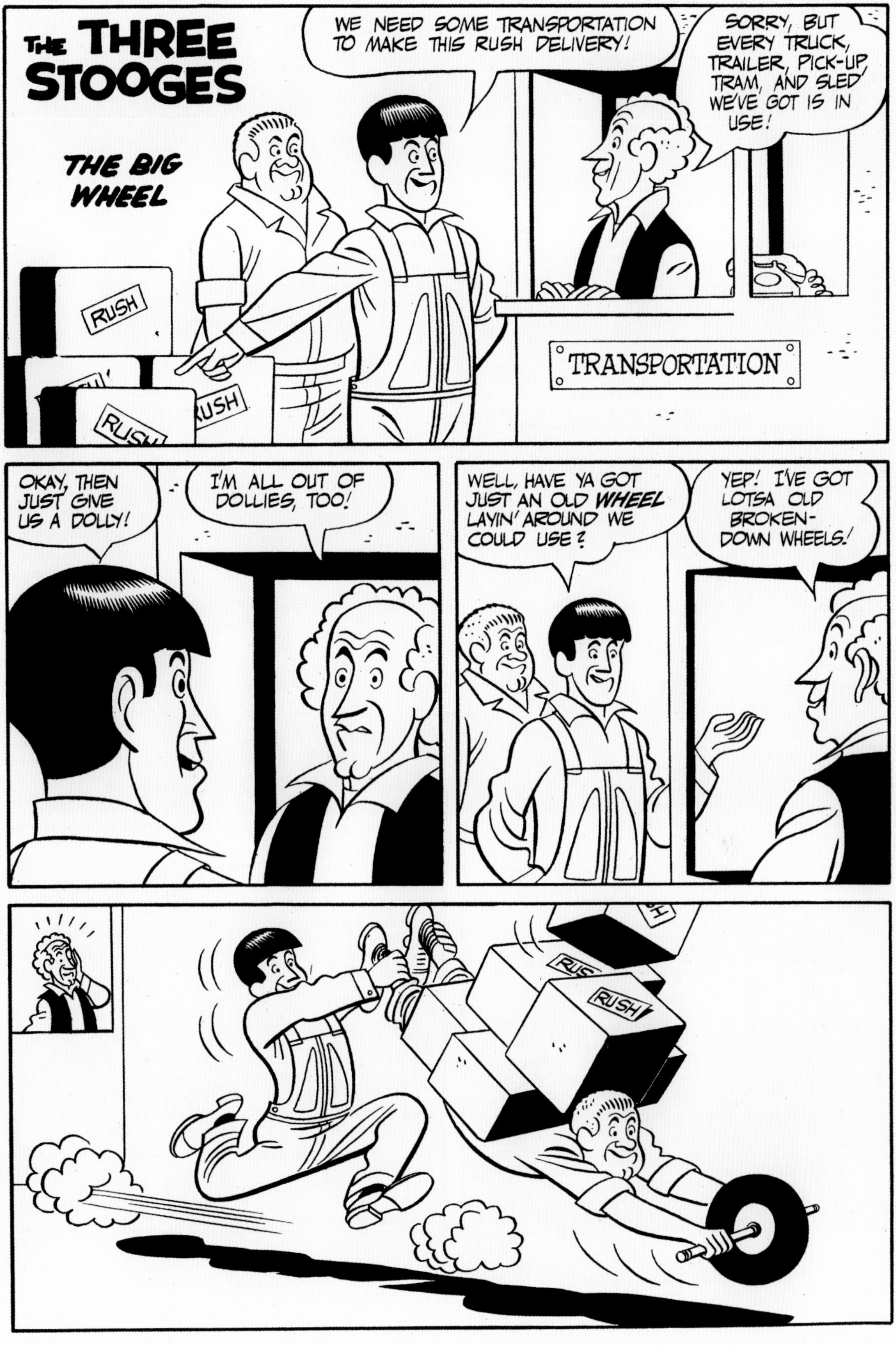
THE THREE STOOGES
THE BIG WHEEL
WE NEED SOME TRANSPORTATION TO MAKE THIS RUSH DELIVERY!
SORRY, BUT EVERY TRUCK, TRAILER, PICK-UP, TRAM, AND SLED WE'VE GOT IS IN USE!
RUSH
RUSH
RUSH
TRANSPORTATION
OKAY, THEN JUST GIVE US A DOLLY!
I'M ALL OUT OF DOLLIES, TOO!
WELL, HAVE YA GOT JUST AN OLD WHEEL LAYIN' AROUND WE COULD USE?
YEP! I'VE GOT LOTSA OLD BROKEN-DOWN WHEELS!
RUSH
RUSH

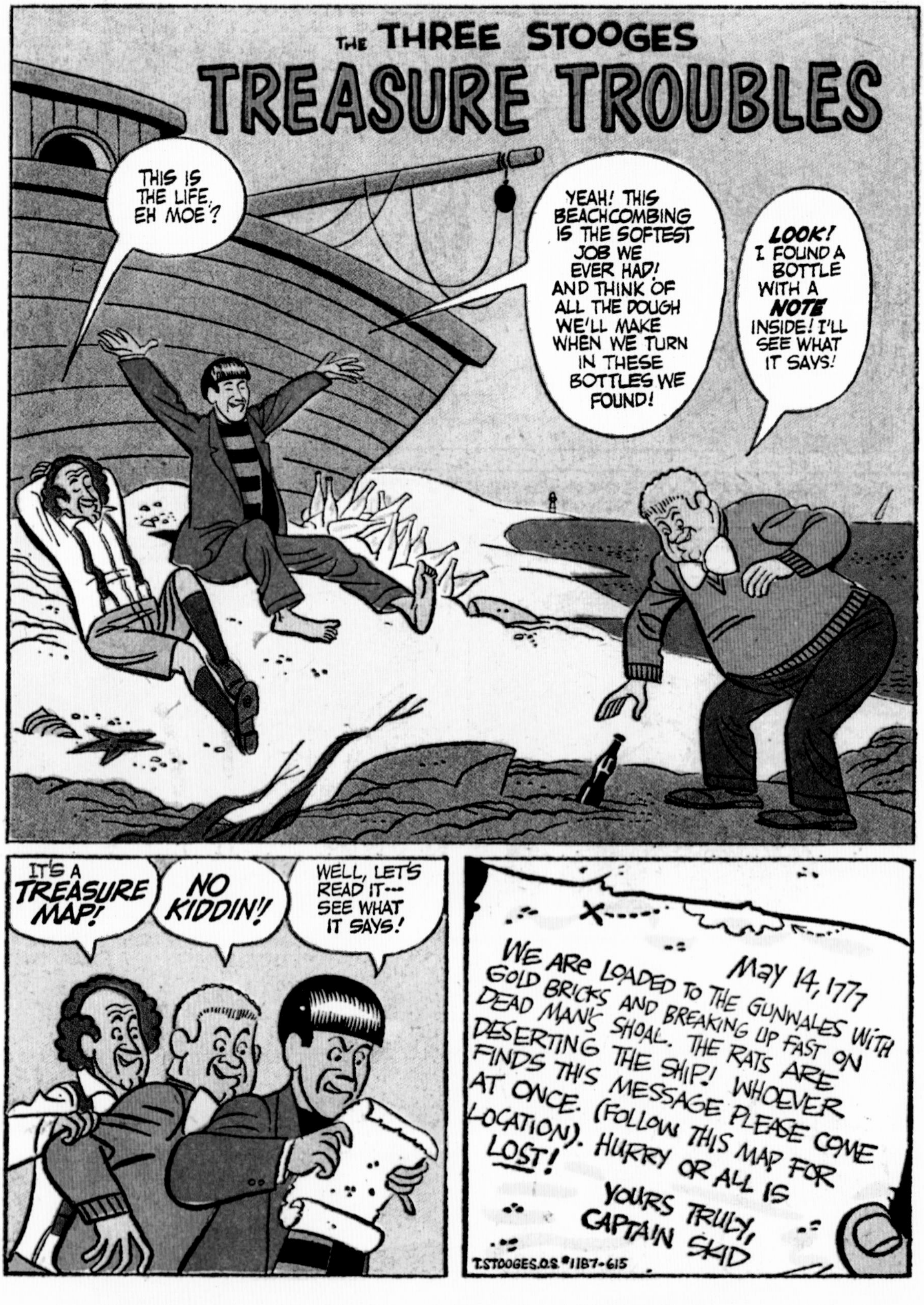
THE THREE STOOGES
TREASURE TROUBLES
THIS IS THE LIFE, EH MOE'?
YEAH! THIS BEACHCOMBING IS THE SOFTEST JOB WE EVER HAD! AND THINK OF ALL THE DOUGH WE'LL MAKE WHEN WE TURN IN THESE BOTTLES WE FOUND!
LOOK! I FOUND A BOTTLE WITH A NOTE INSIDE! I'LL SEE WHAT IT SAYS!
IT'S A TREASURE MAP!
NO KIDDIN'!
WELL, LET'S READ IT--- SEE WHAT IT SAYS!
May 14, 1777
WE ARE LOADED TO THE GUNWALES WITH GOLD BRICKS AND BREAKING UP FAST ON DEAD MAN'S SHOAL. THE RATS ARE DESERTING THE SHIP! WHOEVER FINDS THIS MESSAGE PLEASE COME AT ONCE. (FOLLOW THIS MAP FOR LOCATION). HURRY OR ALL IS LOST!
YOURS TRULY, CAPTAIN SKID
T.STOOGES.O.S. #1187-615

Editor's Note: Unlike many other comics published by Western Publishing/Gold Key that were based on movies and TV shows that used either publicity photos or stills for their covers, THE THREE STOOGES photo covers (like the one on the previous page) were photographed and created exclusively for the comicbooks.

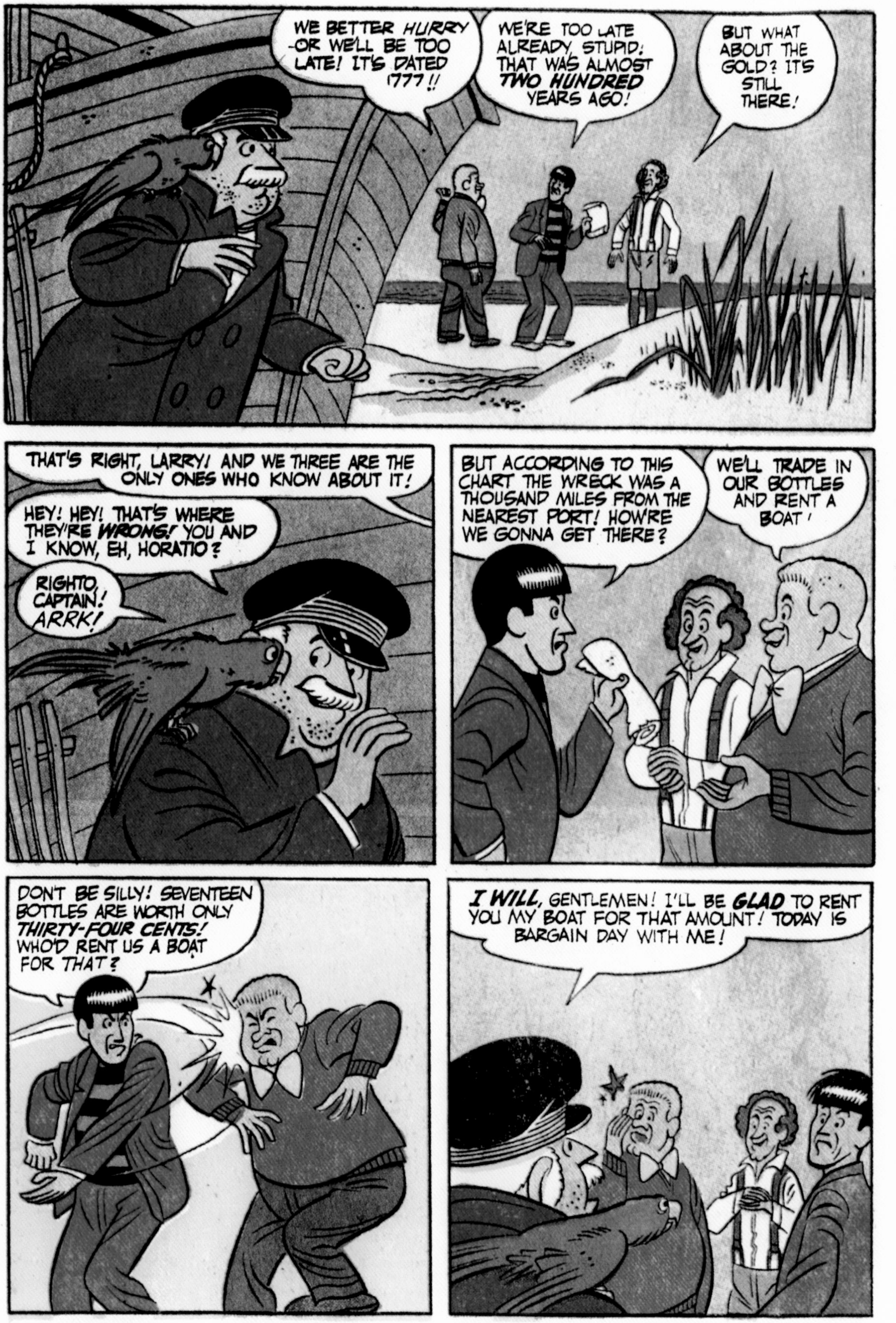
WE BETTER HURRY -OR WE'LL BE TOO LATE! IT'S DATED 1777!!
WE'RE TOO LATE ALREADY, STUPID! THAT WAS ALMOST TWO HUNDRED YEARS AGO!
BUT WHAT ABOUT THE GOLD? IT'S STILL THERE!
THAT'S RIGHT, LARRY! AND WE THREE ARE THE ONLY ONES WHO KNOW ABOUT IT!
HEY! HEY! THAT'S WHERE THEY'RE WRONG! YOU AND I KNOW, EH, HORATIO?
RIGHTO, CAPTAIN! ARRK!
BUT ACCORDING TO THIS CHART THE WRECK WAS A THOUSAND MILES FROM THE NEAREST PORT! HOW'RE WE GONNA GET THERE?
WE'LL TRADE IN OUR BOTTLES AND RENT A BOAT!
DON'T BE SILLY! SEVENTEEN BOTTLES ARE WORTH ONLY THIRTY-FOUR CENTS! WHO'D RENT US A BOAT FOR THAT?
I WILL, GENTLEMEN! I'LL BE GLAD TO RENT YOU MY BOAT FOR THAT AMOUNT! TODAY IS BARGAIN DAY WITH ME!

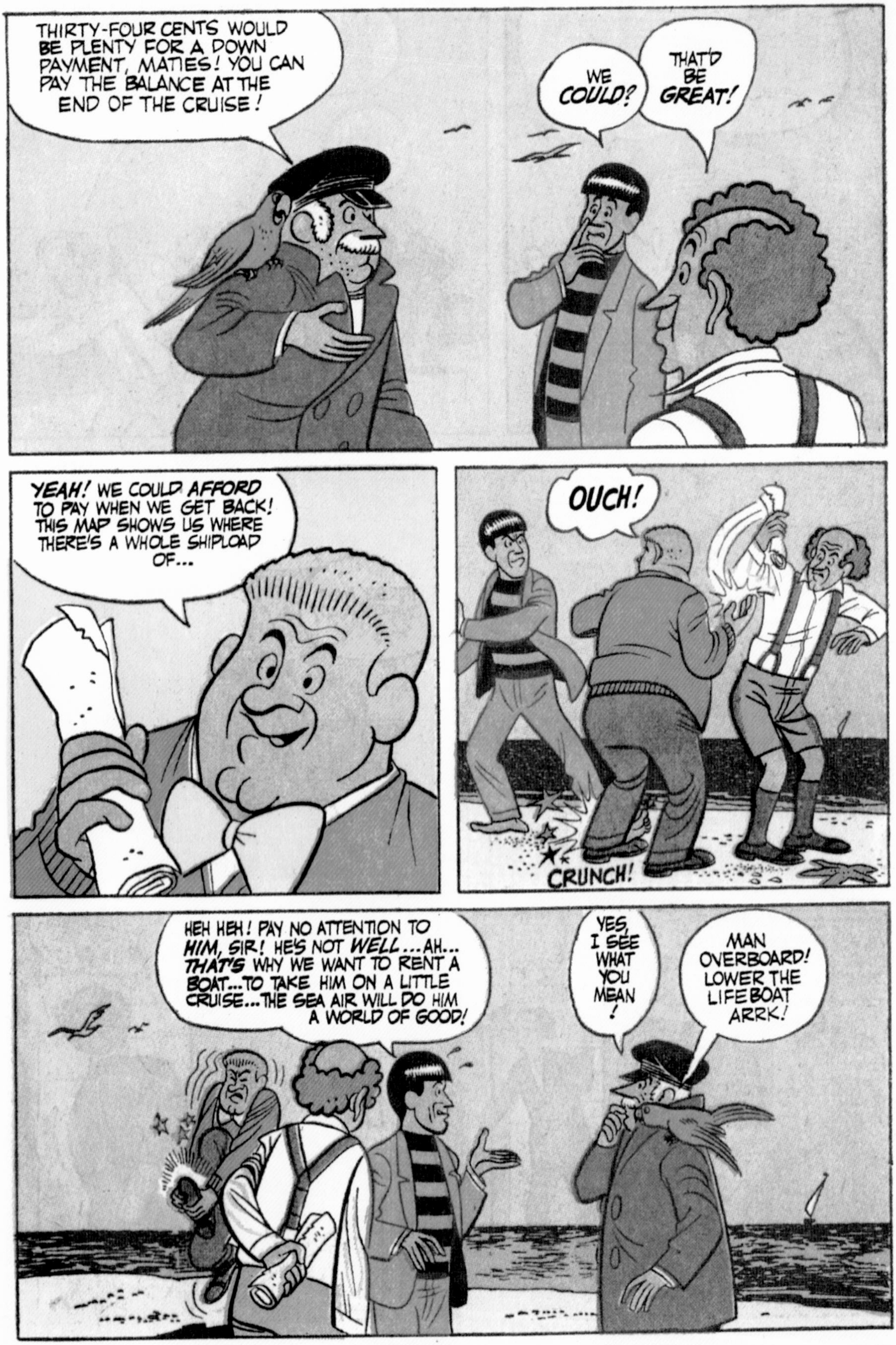
THIRTY-FOUR CENTS WOULD BE PLENTY FOR A DOWN PAYMENT, MATIES! YOU CAN PAY THE BALANCE AT THE END OF THE CRUISE!
WE COULD?
THAT'D BE GREAT!
YEAH! WE COULD AFFORD TO PAY WHEN WE GET BACK! THIS MAP SHOWS US WHERE THERE'S A WHOLE SHIPLOAD OF...
OUCH!
CRUNCH!
HEH HEH! PAY NO ATTENTION TO HIM, SIR! HE'S NOT WELL...AH... THAT'S WHY WE WANT TO RENT A BOAT...TO TAKE HIM ON A LITTLE CRUISE...THE SEA AIR WILL DO HIM A WORLD OF GOOD!
YES, I SEE WHAT YOU MEAN!
MAN OVERBOARD! LOWER THE LIFEBOAT ARRK!

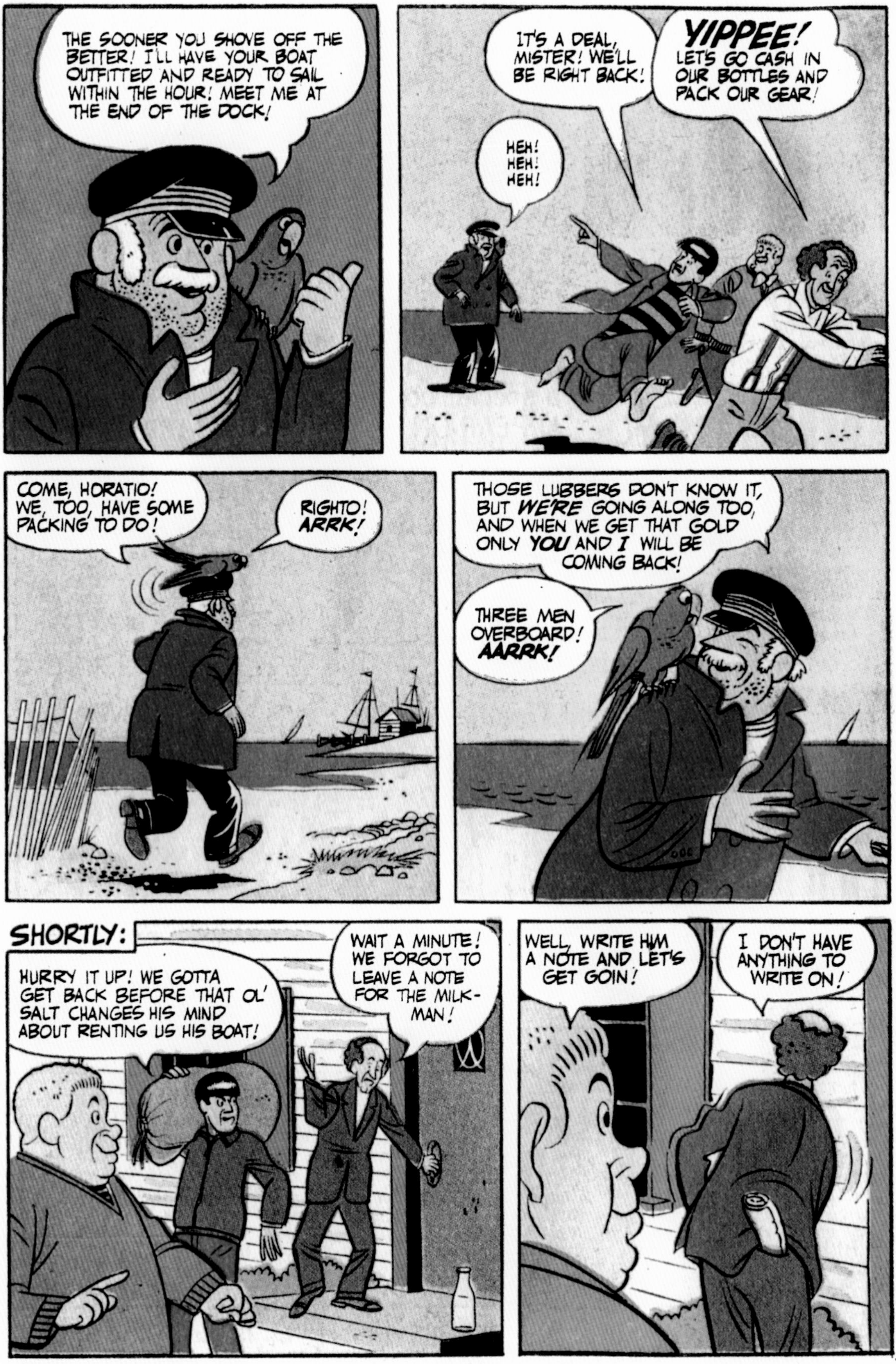
THE SOONER YOU SHOVE OFF THE BETTER! I'LL HAVE YOUR BOAT OUTFITTED AND READY TO SAIL WITHIN THE HOUR! MEET ME AT THE END OF THE DOCK!
IT'S A DEAL, MISTER! WE'LL BE RIGHT BACK!
YIPPEE! LET'S GO CASH IN OUR BOTTLES AND PACK OUR GEAR!
HEH! HEH! HEH!
COME, HORATIO! WE, TOO, HAVE SOME PACKING TO DO!
RIGHTO! ARRK!
THOSE LUBBERS DON'T KNOW IT, BUT WE'RE GOING ALONG TOO, AND WHEN WE GET THAT GOLD ONLY YOU AND I WILL BE COMING BACK!
THREE MEN OVERBOARD! AARRK!
SHORTLY:
HURRY IT UP! WE GOTTA GET BACK BEFORE THAT OL' SALT CHANGES HIS MIND ABOUT RENTING US HIS BOAT!
WAIT A MINUTE! WE FORGOT TO LEAVE A NOTE FOR THE MILK-MAN!
WELL, WRITE HIM A NOTE AND LET'S GET GOIN'!
I DON'T HAVE ANYTHING TO WRITE ON!

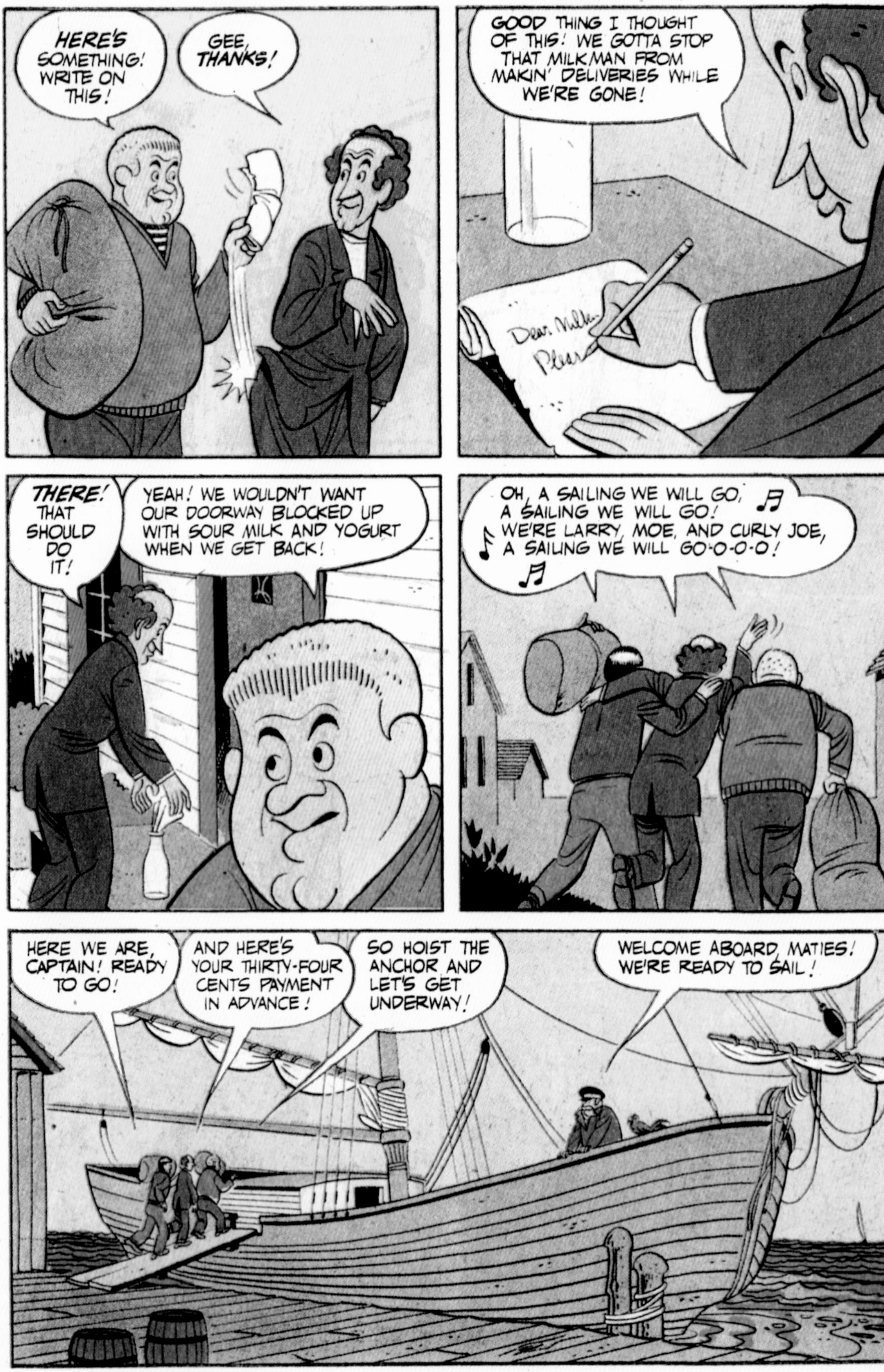
HERE'S SOMETHING! WRITE ON THIS!
GEE, THANKS!
GOOD THING I THOUGHT OF THIS! WE GOTTA STOP THAT MILKMAN FROM MAKIN' DELIVERIES WHILE WE'RE GONE!
THERE! THAT SHOULD DO IT!
YEAH! WE WOULDN'T WANT OUR DOORWAY BLOCKED UP WITH SOUR MILK AND YOGURT WHEN WE GET BACK!
OH, A SAILING WE WILL GO, A SAILING WE WILL GO! WE'RE LARRY, MOE, AND CURLY JOE, A SAILING WE WILL GO-O-O-O!
HERE WE ARE, CAPTAIN! READY TO GO!
AND HERE'S YOUR THIRTY-FOUR CENTS PAYMENT IN ADVANCE!
SO HOIST THE ANCHOR AND LET'S GET UNDERWAY!
WELCOME ABOARD, MATIES! WE'RE READY TO SAIL!

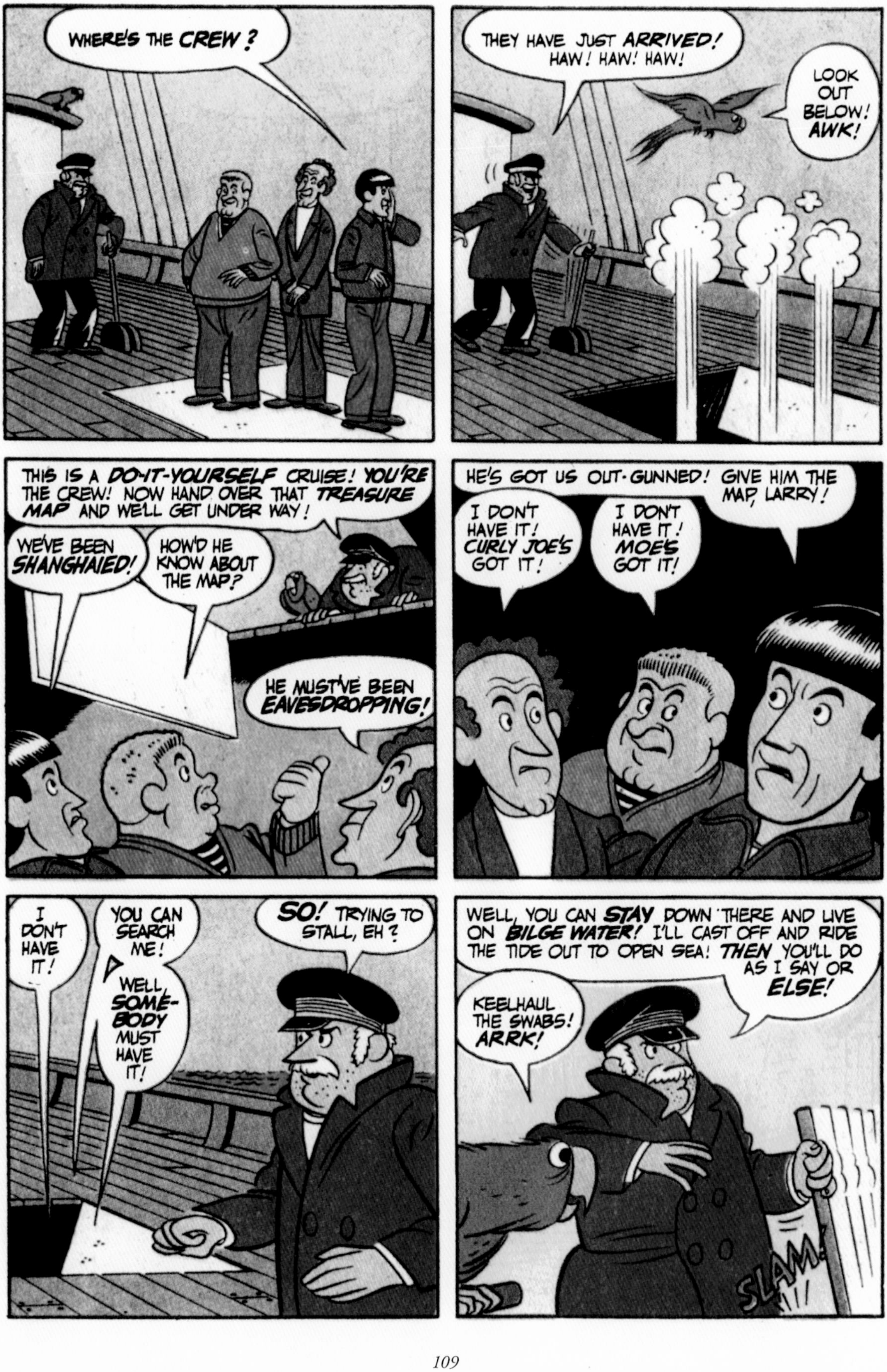
WHERE'S THE CREW?
THEY HAVE JUST ARRIVED! HAW! HAW! HAW!
LOOK OUT BELOW! AWK!
THIS IS A DO-IT-YOURSELF CRUISE! YOU'RE THE CREW! NOW HAND OVER THAT TREASURE MAP AND WE'LL GET UNDER WAY!
WE'VE BEEN SHANGHAIED!
HOW'D HE KNOW ABOUT THE MAP?
HE MUST'VE BEEN EAVESDROPPING!
HE'S GOT US OUT-GUNNED! GIVE HIM THE MAP, LARRY!
I DON'T HAVE IT! CURLY JOE'S GOT IT!
I DON'T HAVE IT! MOE'S GOT IT!
I DON'T HAVE IT!
YOU CAN SEARCH ME!
WELL SOMEBODY MUST HAVE IT!
SO! TRYING TO STALL, EH?
WELL, YOU CAN STAY DOWN THERE AND LIVE ON BILGE WATER! I'LL CAST OFF AND RIDE THE TIDE OUT TO OPEN SEA! THEN YOU'LL DO AS I SAY OR ELSE!
KEELHAUL THE SWABS! ARRK!
SLAM!

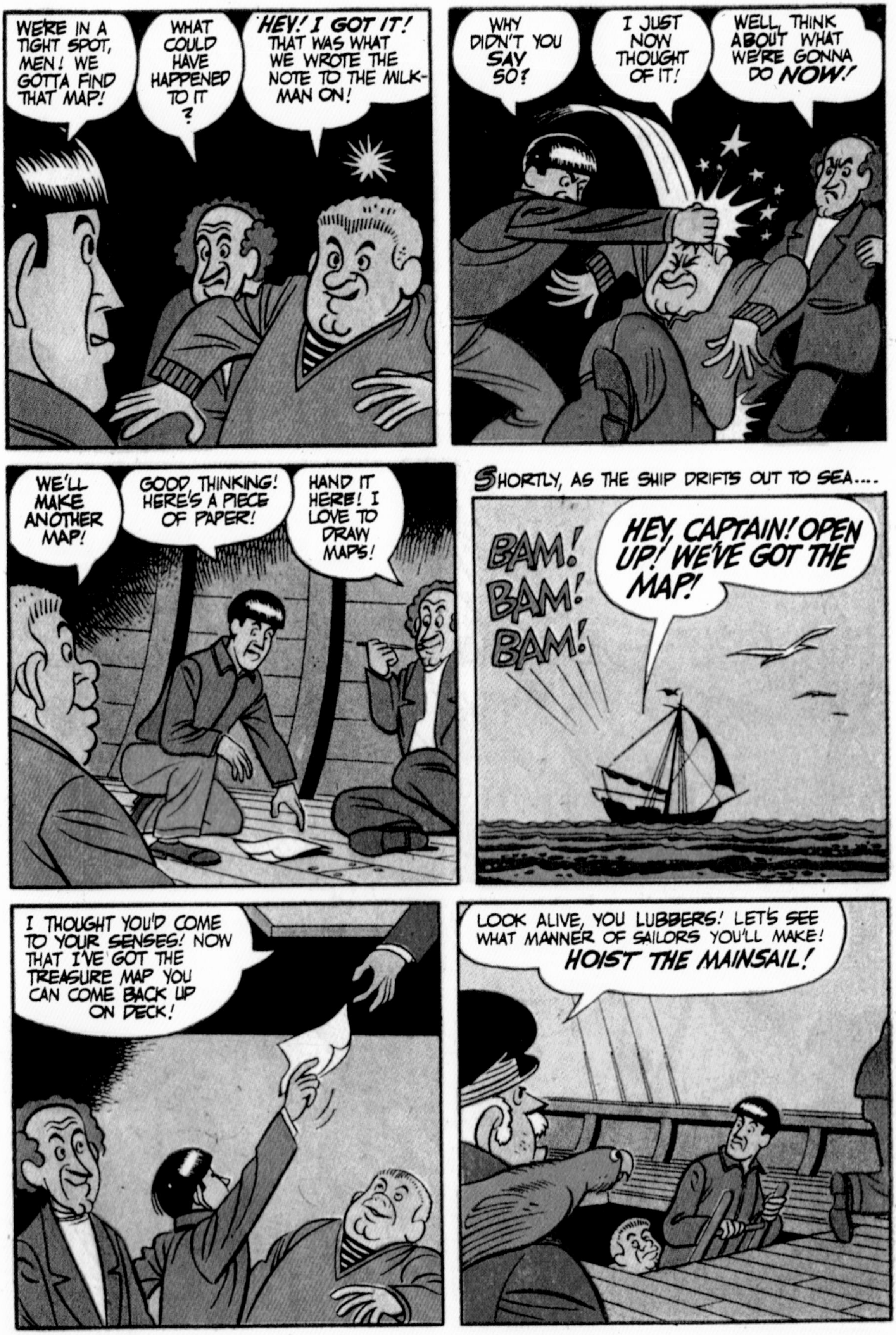
WE'RE IN A TIGHT SPOT, MEN! WE GOTTA FIND THAT MAP!
WHAT COULD HAVE HAPPENED TO IT?
HEY! I GOT IT! THAT WAS WHAT WE WROTE THE NOTE TO THE MILK-MAN ON!
WHY DIDN'T YOU SAY SO?
I JUST NOW THOUGHT OF IT!
WELL, THINK ABOUT WHAT WE'RE GONNA DO NOW!
WE'LL MAKE ANOTHER MAP!
GOOD THINKING! HERE'S A PIECE OF PAPER!
HAND IT HERE! I LOVE TO DRAW MAPS!
SHORTLY, AS THE SHIP DRIFTS OUT TO SEA....
BAM! BAM! BAM!
HEY, CAPTAIN! OPEN UP! WE'VE GOT THE MAP!
I THOUGHT YOU'D COME TO YOUR SENSES! NOW THAT I'VE GOT THE TREASURE MAP YOU CAN COME BACK UP ON DECK!
LOOK ALIVE, YOU LUBBERS! LET'S SEE WHAT MANNER OF SAILORS YOU'LL MAKE! HOIST THE MAINSAIL!

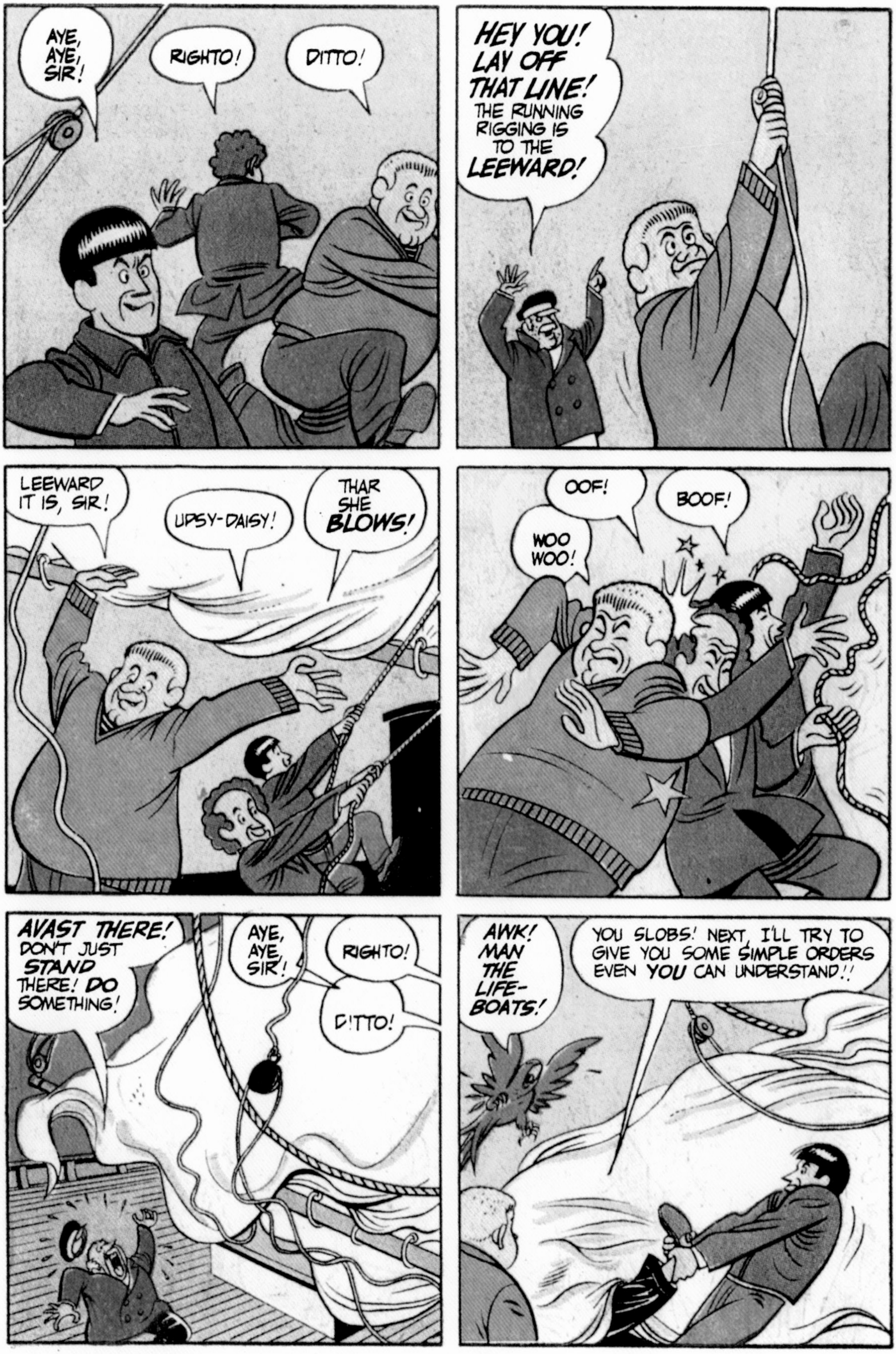
AYE, AYE, SIR!
RIGHTO!
DITTO!
HEY YOU! LAY OFF THAT LINE! THE RUNNING RIGGING IS TO THE LEEWARD!
LEEWARD IT IS, SIR!
UPSY-DAISY!
THAR SHE BLOWS!
OOF!
BOOF!
WOO WOO!
AVAST THERE! DON'T JUST STAND THERE! DO SOMETHING!
AYE, AYE, SIR!
RIGHTO!
DITTO!
AWK! MAN THE LIFE-BOATS!
YOU SLOBS! NEXT, I'LL TRY TO GIVE YOU SOME SIMPLE ORDERS EVEN YOU CAN UNDERSTAND!!

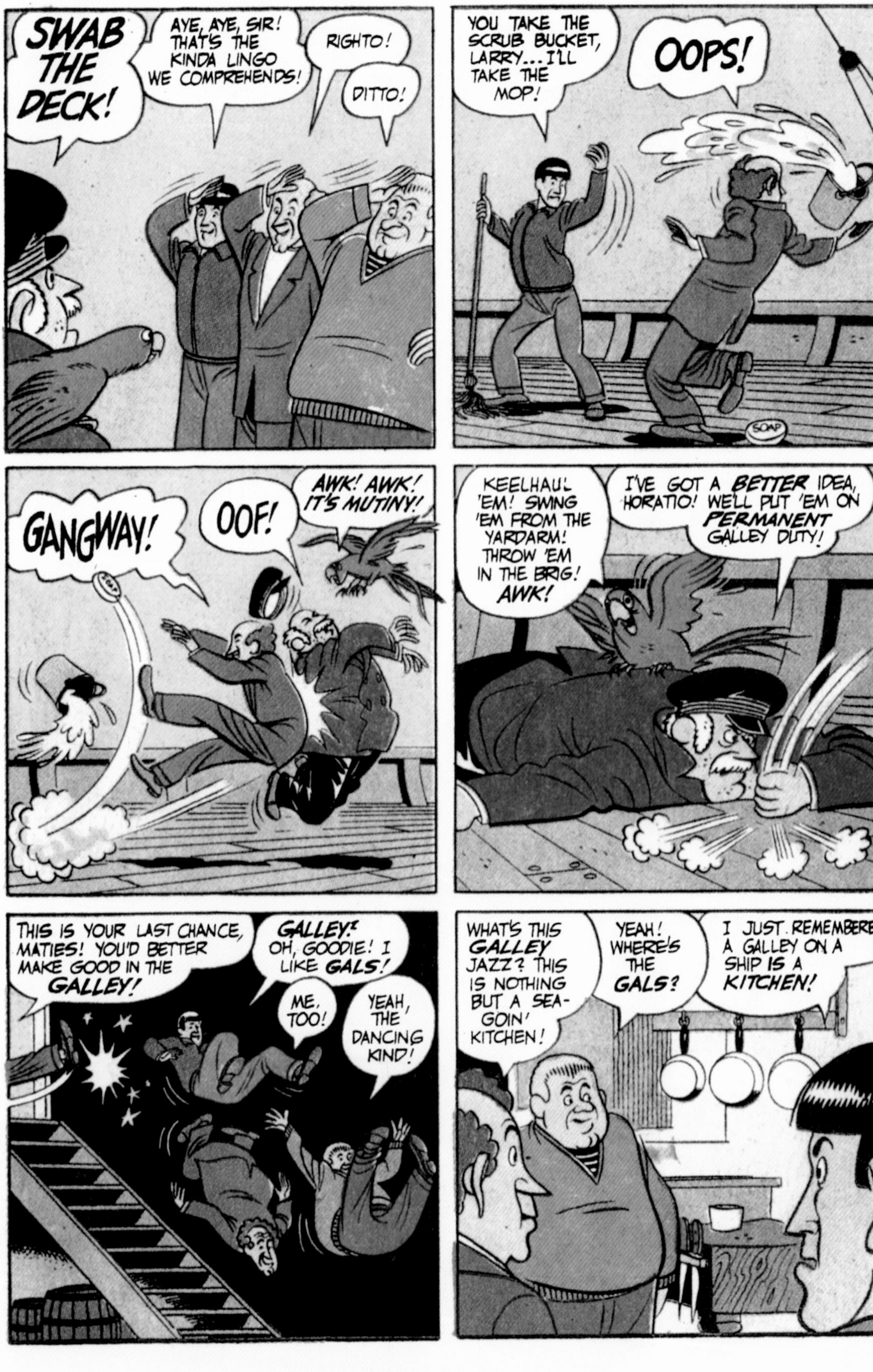
SWAB THE DECK!
AYE, AYE, SIR! THAT'S THE KINDA LINGO WE COMPREHENDS!
RIGHTO!
DITTO!
YOU TAKE THE SCRUB BUCKET, LARRY... I'LL TAKE THE MOP!
OOPS!
SOAP
GANGWAY!
OOF!
AWK! AWK! IT'S MUTINY!
KEELHAUL 'EM! SWING 'EM FROM THE YARDARM! THROW 'EM IN THE BRIG! AWK!
I'VE GOT A BETTER IDEA, HORATIO! WE'LL PUT 'EM ON PERMANENT GALLEY DUTY!
SOAP
THIS IS YOUR LAST CHANCE, MATIES! YOU'D BETTER MAKE GOOD IN THE GALLEY!
GALLEY! OH, GOODIE! I LIKE GALS!
ME, TOO!
YEAH, THE DANCING KIND!
WHAT'S THIS GALLEY JAZZ? THIS IS NOTHING BUT A SEA-GOIN' KITCHEN!
YEAH! WHERE'S THE GALS?
I JUST REMEMBERED. A GALLEY ON A SHIP IS A KITCHEN!

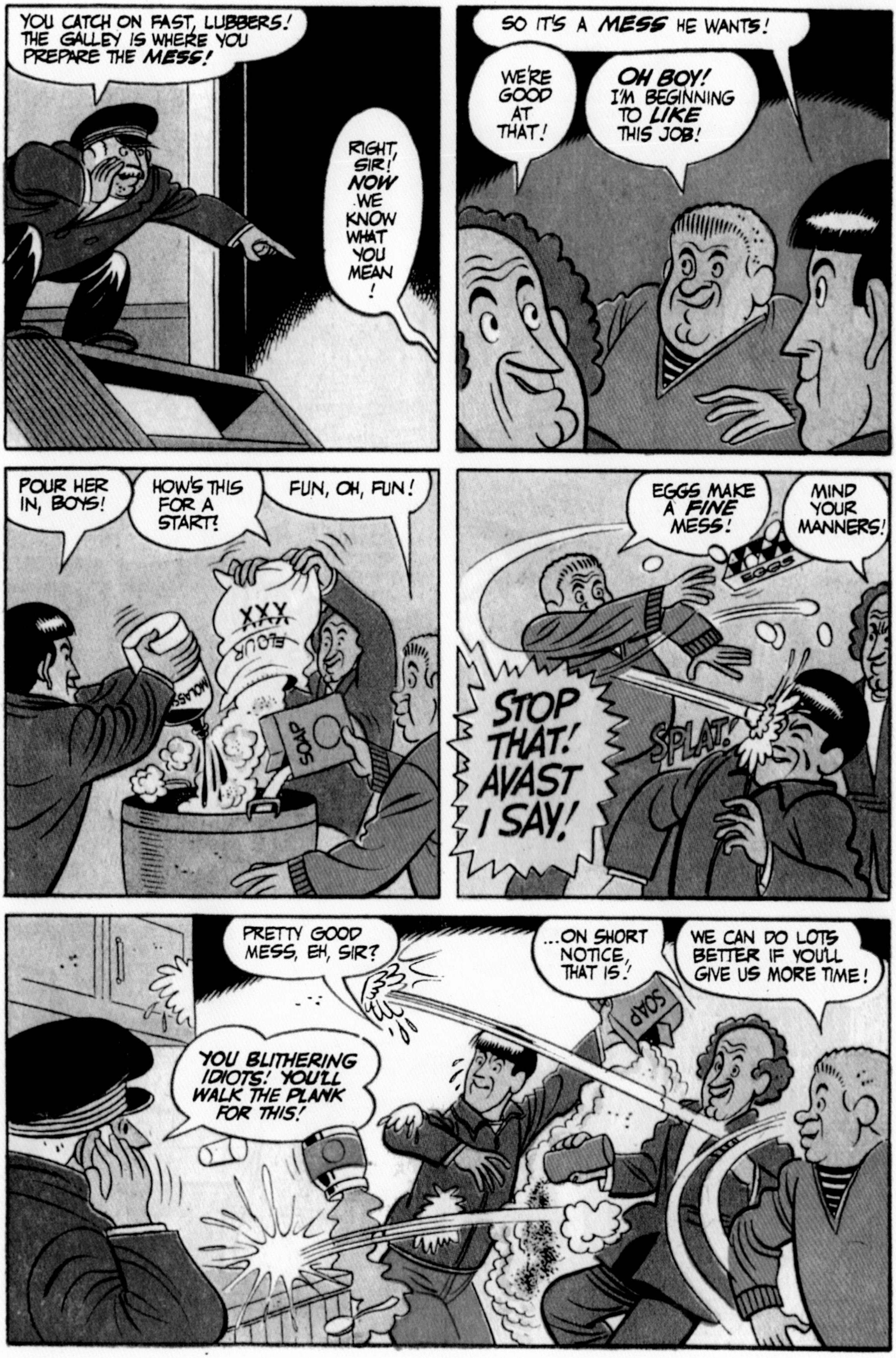
YOU CATCH ON FAST, LUBBERS! THE GALLEY IS WHERE YOU PREPARE THE MESS!
RIGHT, SIR! NOW WE KNOW WHAT YOU MEAN!
SO IT'S A MESS HE WANTS!
WE'RE GOOD AT THAT!
OH BOY! I'M BEGINNING TO LIKE THIS JOB!
POUR HER IN, BOYS!
HOW'S THIS FOR A START?
FUN, OH, FUN!
XXX
FLOUR
MOLASS
SOAP
EGGS MAKE A FINE MESS!
MIND YOUR MANNERS!
EGGS
STOP THAT! AVAST I SAY!
SPLAT!
PRETTY GOOD MESS, EH, SIR?
...ON SHORT NOTICE, THAT IS!
WE CAN DO LOTS BETTER IF YOU'LL GIVE US MORE TIME!
SOAP
YOU BLITHERING IDIOTS! YOU'LL WALK THE PLANK FOR THIS!

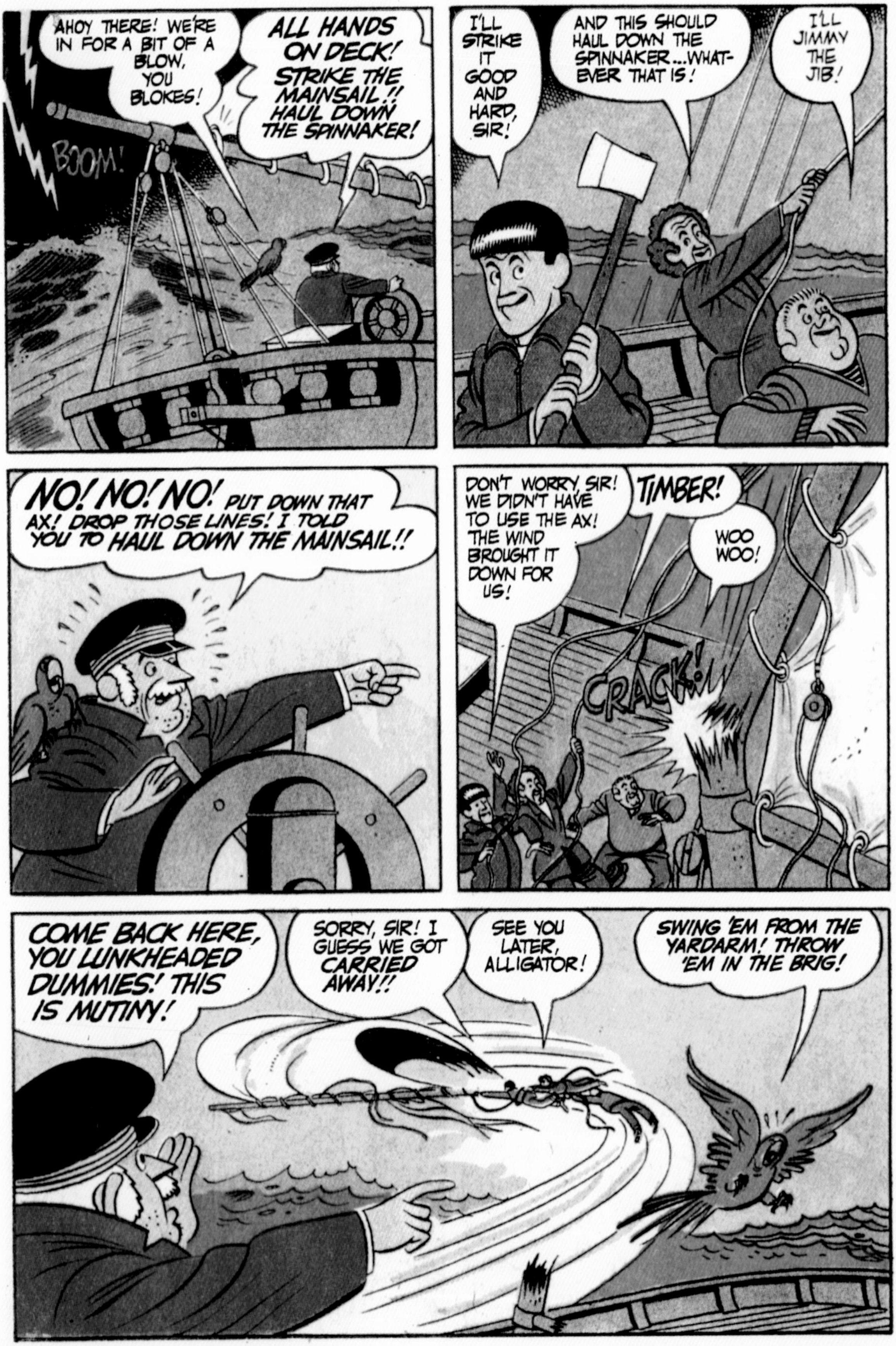
AHOY THERE! WE'RE IN FOR A BIT OF A BLOW, YOU BLOKES!
ALL HANDS ON DECK! STRIKE THE MAINSAIL!! HAUL DOWN THE SPINNAKER!
BOOM!
I'LL STRIKE IT GOOD AND HARD, SIR!
AND THIS SHOULD HAUL DOWN THE SPINNAKER...WHATEVER THAT IS!
I'LL JIMMY THE JIB!
NO! NO! NO! PUT DOWN THAT AX! DROP THOSE LINES! I TOLD YOU TO HAUL DOWN THE MAINSAIL!!
DON'T WORRY, SIR! WE DIDN'T HAVE TO USE THE AX! THE WIND BROUGHT IT DOWN FOR US!
TIMBER!
WOO WOO!
CRACK!
COME BACK HERE, YOU LUNKHEADED DUMMIES! THIS IS MUTINY!
SORRY, SIR! I GUESS WE GOT CARRIED AWAY!!
SEE YOU LATER, ALLIGATOR!
SWING 'EM FROM THE YARDARM! THROW 'EM IN THE BRIG!

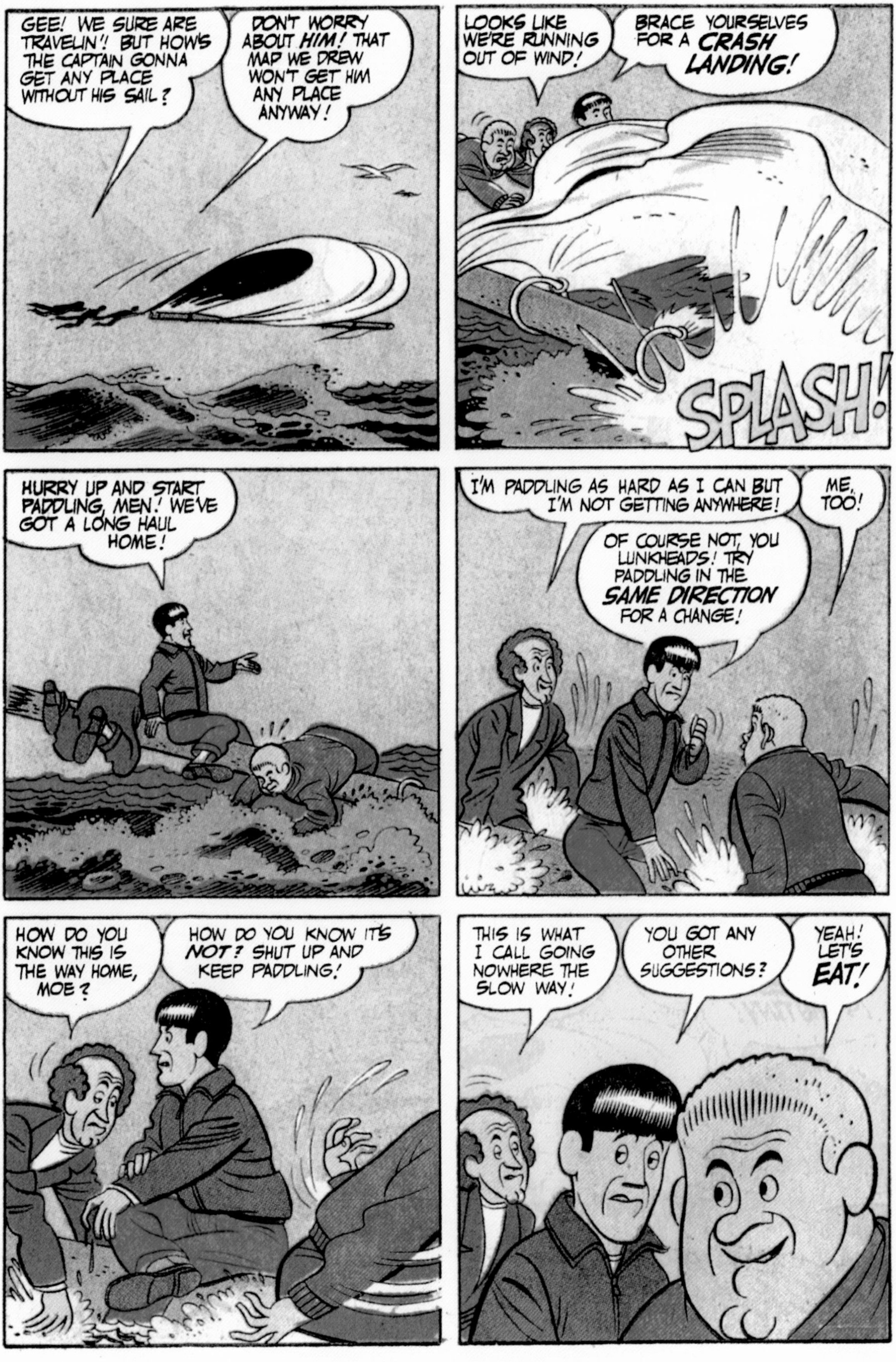
GEE! WE SURE ARE TRAVELIN'! BUT HOW'S THE CAPTAIN GONNA GET ANY PLACE WITHOUT HIS SAIL?
DON'T WORRY ABOUT HIM! THAT MAP WE DREW WON'T GET HIM ANY PLACE ANYWAY!
LOOKS LIKE WE'RE RUNNING OUT OF WIND!
BRACE YOURSELVES FOR A CRASH LANDING!
SPLASH!
HURRY UP AND START PADDLING, MEN! WE'VE GOT A LONG HAUL HOME!
I'M PADDLING AS HARD AS I CAN BUT I'M NOT GETTING ANYWHERE!
ME, TOO!
OF COURSE NOT, YOU LUNKHEADS! TRY PADDLING IN THE SAME DIRECTION FOR A CHANGE!
HOW DO YOU KNOW THIS IS THE WAY HOME, MOE?
HOW DO YOU KNOW IT'S NOT? SHUT UP AND KEEP PADDLING!
THIS IS WHAT I CALL GOING NOWHERE THE SLOW WAY!
YOU GOT ANY OTHER SUGGESTIONS?
YEAH! LET'S EAT!

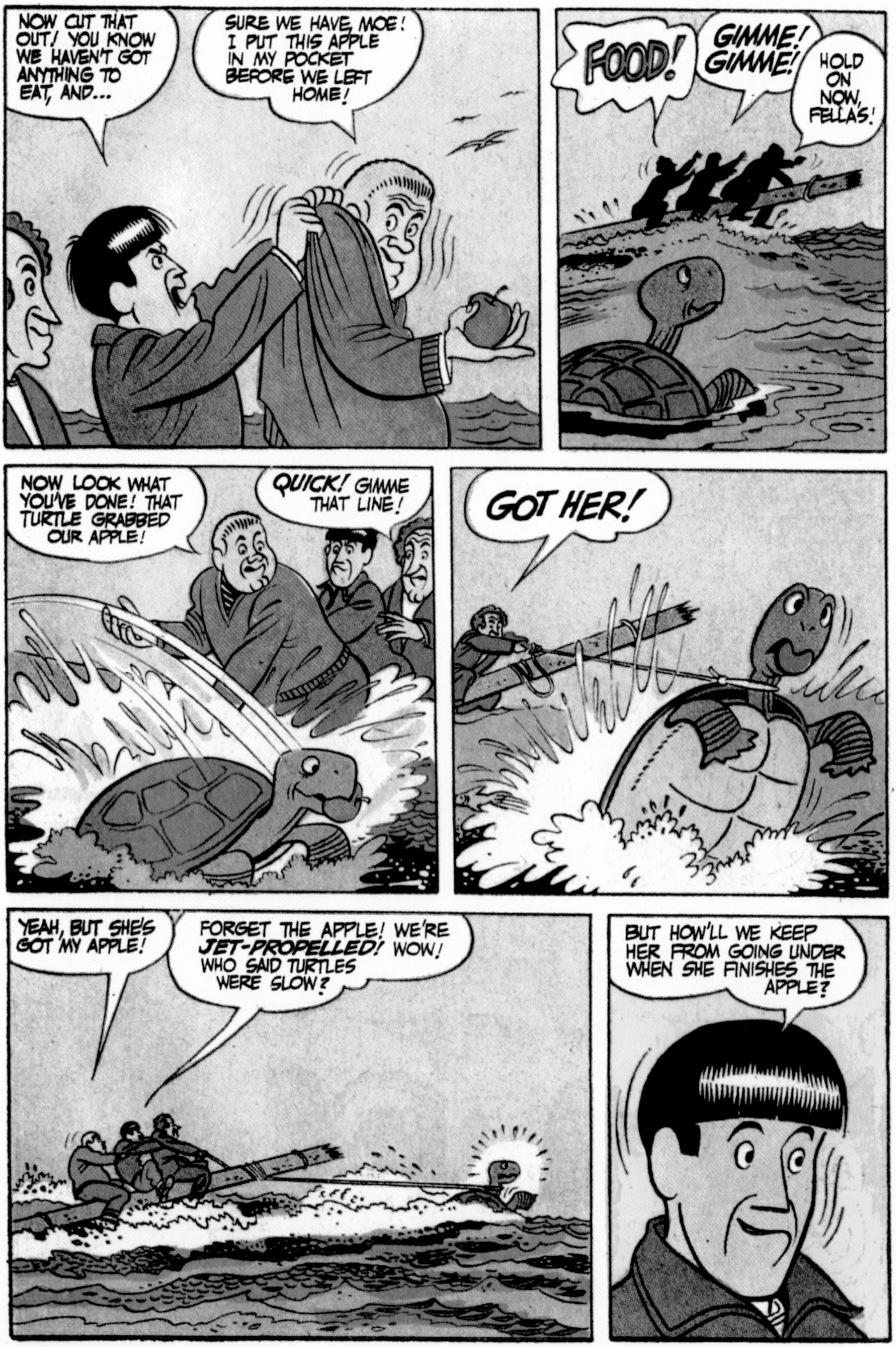
NOW CUT THAT OUT! YOU KNOW WE HAVEN'T GOT ANYTHING TO EAT, AND...
SURE WE HAVE, MOE! I PUT THIS APPLE IN MY POCKET BEFORE WE LEFT HOME!
FOOD!
GIMME! GIMME!
HOLD ON NOW, FELLAS!
NOW LOOK WHAT YOU'VE DONE! THAT TURTLE GRABBED OUR APPLE!
QUICK! GIMME THAT LINE!
GOT HER!
YEAH, BUT SHE'S GOT MY APPLE!
FORGET THE APPLE! WE'RE JET-PROPELLED! WOW! WHO SAID TURTLES WERE SLOW?
BUT HOW'LL WE KEEP HER FROM GOING UNDER WHEN SHE FINISHES THE APPLE?

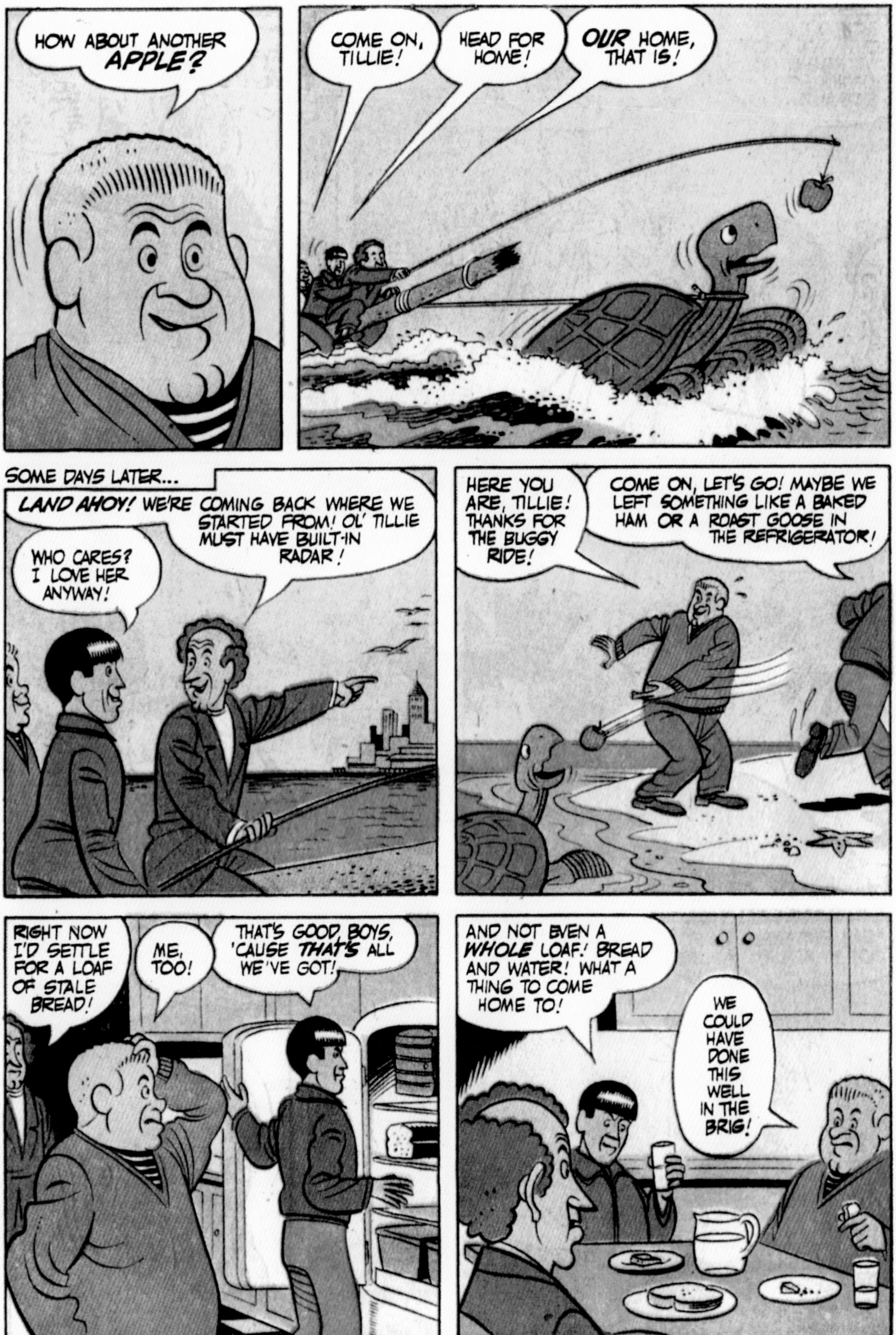
HOW ABOUT ANOTHER APPLE?
COME ON, TILLIE!
HEAD FOR HOME!
OUR HOME, THAT IS!
SOME DAYS LATER...
LAND AHOY! WE'RE COMING BACK WHERE WE STARTED FROM! OL' TILLIE MUST HAVE BUILT-IN RADAR!
WHO CARES? I LOVE HER ANYWAY!
HERE YOU ARE, TILLIE! THANKS FOR THE BUGGY RIDE!
COME ON, LET'S GO! MAYBE WE LEFT SOMETHING LIKE A BAKED HAM OR A ROAST GOOSE IN THE REFRIGERATOR!
RIGHT NOW I'D SETTLE FOR A LOAF OF STALE BREAD!
ME, TOO!
THAT'S GOOD, BOYS, 'CAUSE THAT'S ALL WE'VE GOT!
AND NOT EVEN A WHOLE LOAF! BREAD AND WATER! WHAT A THING TO COME HOME TO!
WE COULD HAVE DONE THIS WELL IN THE BRIG!

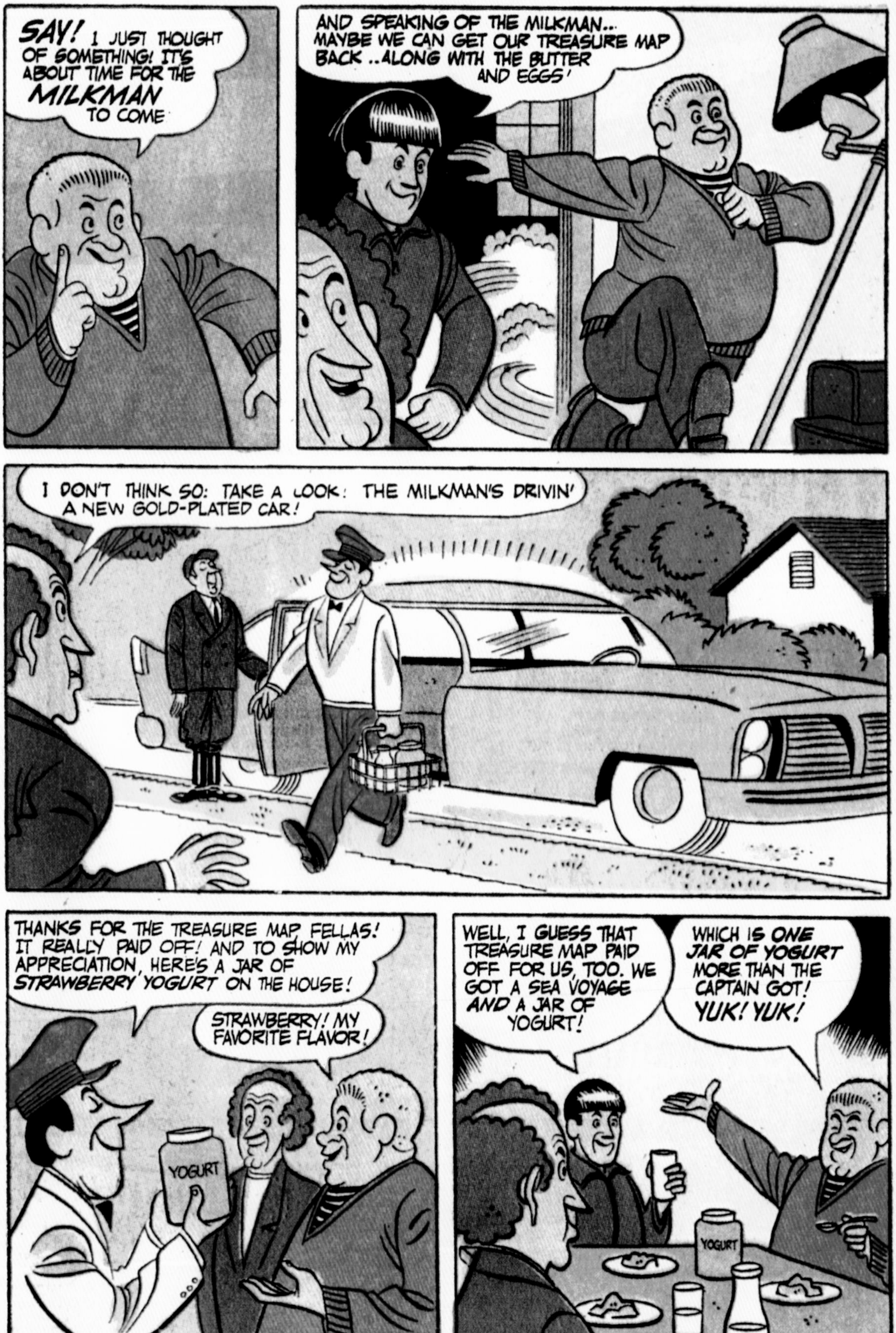
SAY! I JUST THOUGHT OF SOMETHING! IT'S ABOUT TIME FOR THE MILKMAN TO COME
AND SPEAKING OF THE MILKMAN... MAYBE WE CAN GET OUR TREASURE MAP BACK ..ALONG WITH THE BUTTER AND EGGS!
I DON'T THINK SO: TAKE A LOOK: THE MILKMAN'S DRIVIN' A NEW GOLD-PLATED CAR!
THANKS FOR THE TREASURE MAP FELLAS! IT REALLY PAID OFF! AND TO SHOW MY APPRECIATION, HERE'S A JAR OF STRAWBERRY YOGURT ON THE HOUSE!
STRAWBERRY! MY FAVORITE FLAVOR!
YOGURT
WELL, I GUESS THAT TREASURE MAP PAID OFF FOR US, TOO. WE GOT A SEA VOYAGE AND A JAR OF YOGURT!
WHICH IS ONE JAR OF YOGURT MORE THAN THE CAPTAIN GOT! YUK! YUK!
YOGURT

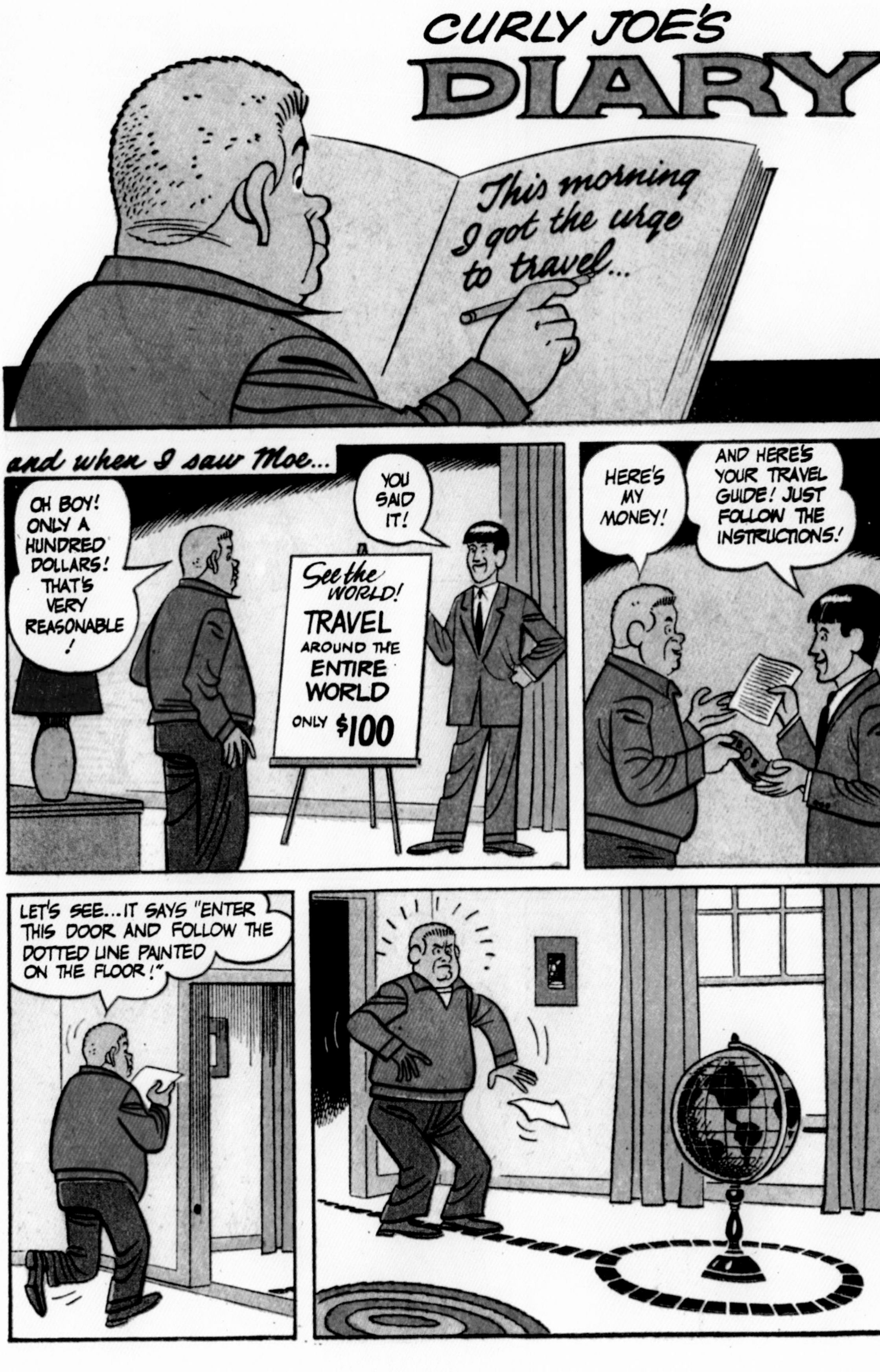
CURLY JOE'S
DIARY
This morning I got the urge to travel...
and when I saw Moe...
OH BOY! ONLY A HUNDRED DOLLARS! THAT'S VERY REASONABLE!
YOU SAID IT!
See the WORLD! TRAVEL AROUND THE ENTIRE WORLD ONLY $100
HERE'S MY MONEY!
AND HERE'S YOUR TRAVEL GUIDE! JUST FOLLOW THE INSTRUCTIONS!
LET'S SEE...IT SAYS "ENTER THIS DOOR AND FOLLOW THE DOTTED LINE PAINTED ON THE FLOOR!"

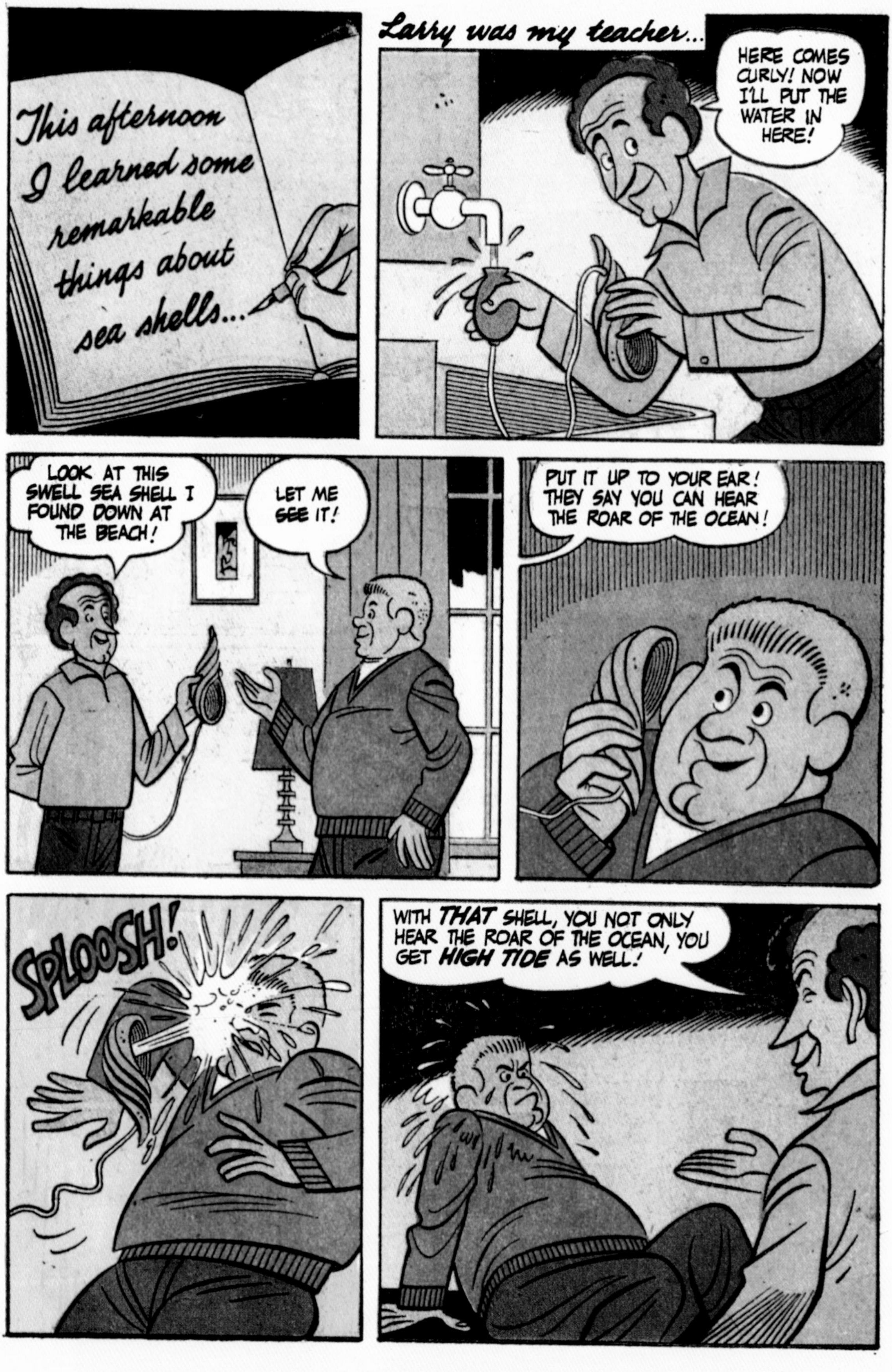
This afternoon I learned some remarkable things about sea shells...
Larry was my teacher...
HERE COMES CURLY! NOW I'LL PUT THE WATER IN HERE!
LOOK AT THIS SWELL SEA SHELL I FOUND DOWN AT THE BEACH!
LET ME SEE IT!
PUT IT UP TO YOUR EAR! THEY SAY YOU CAN HEAR THE ROAR OF THE OCEAN!
SPLOOSH!
WITH THAT SHELL, YOU NOT ONLY HEAR THE ROAR OF THE OCEAN, YOU GET HIGH TIDE AS WELL!

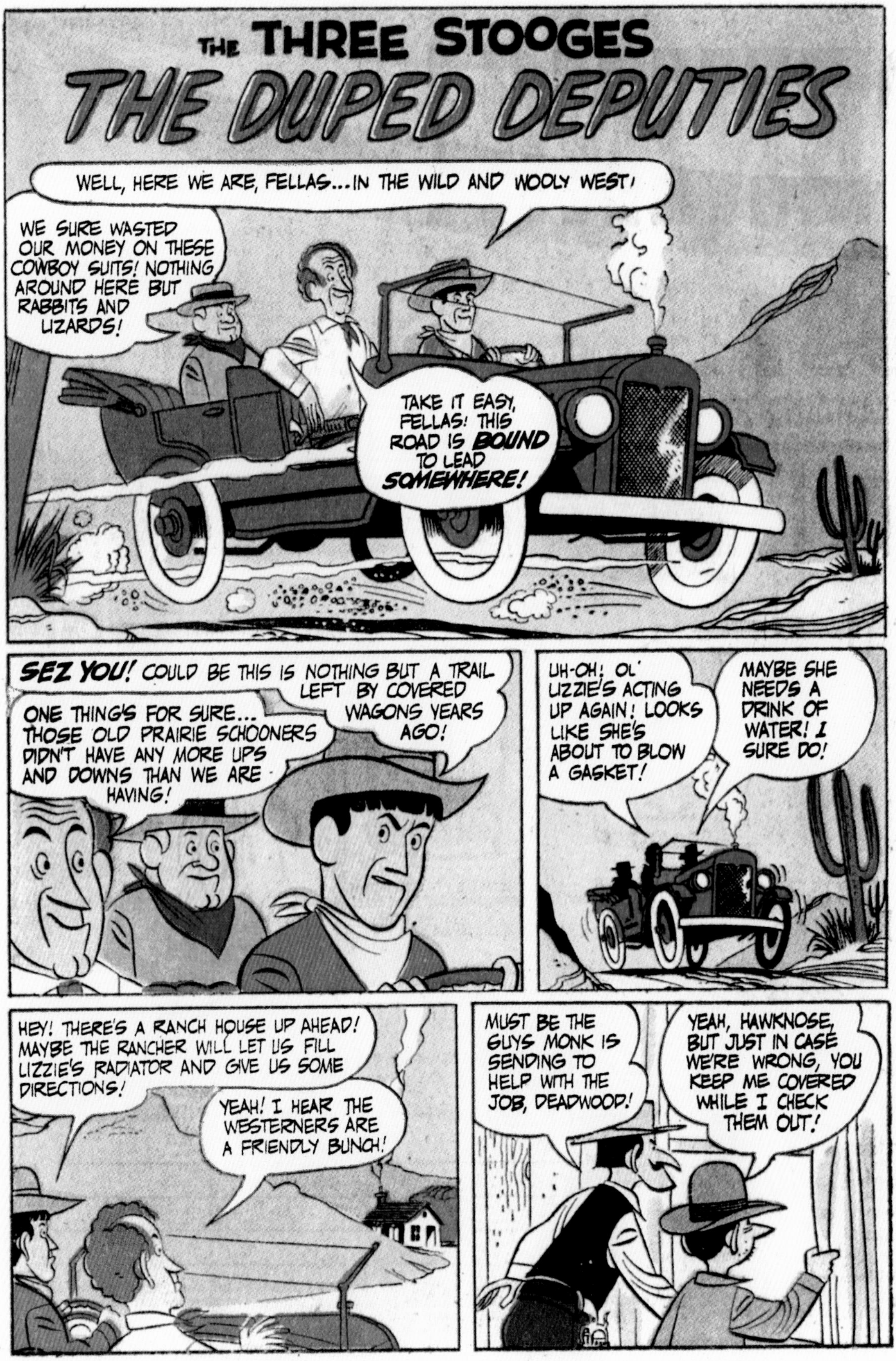
THE THREE STOOGES
THE DUPED DEPUTIES
WELL, HERE WE ARE, FELLAS...IN THE WILD AND WOOLY WEST!
WE SURE WASTED OUR MONEY ON THESE COWBOY SUITS! NOTHING AROUND HERE BUT RABBITS AND LIZARDS!
TAKE IT EASY, FELLAS! THIS ROAD IS BOUND TO LEAD SOMEWHERE!
SEZ YOU! COULD BE THIS IS NOTHING BUT A TRAIL LEFT BY COVERED WAGONS YEARS AGO!
ONE THING'S FOR SURE... THOSE OLD PRAIRIE SCHOONERS DIDN'T HAVE ANY MORE UPS AND DOWNS THAN WE ARE HAVING!
UH-OH! OL' LIZZIE'S ACTING UP AGAIN! LOOKS LIKE SHE'S ABOUT TO BLOW A GASKET!
MAYBE SHE NEEDS A DRINK OF WATER! I SURE DO!
HEY! THERE'S A RANCH HOUSE UP AHEAD! MAYBE THE RANCHER WILL LET US FILL LIZZIE'S RADIATOR AND GIVE US SOME DIRECTIONS!
YEAH! I HEAR THE WESTERNERS ARE A FRIENDLY BUNCH!
MUST BE THE GUYS MONK IS SENDING TO HELP WITH THE JOB, DEADWOOD!
YEAH, HAWKNOSE, BUT JUST IN CASE WE'RE WRONG, YOU KEEP ME COVERED WHILE I CHECK THEM OUT!

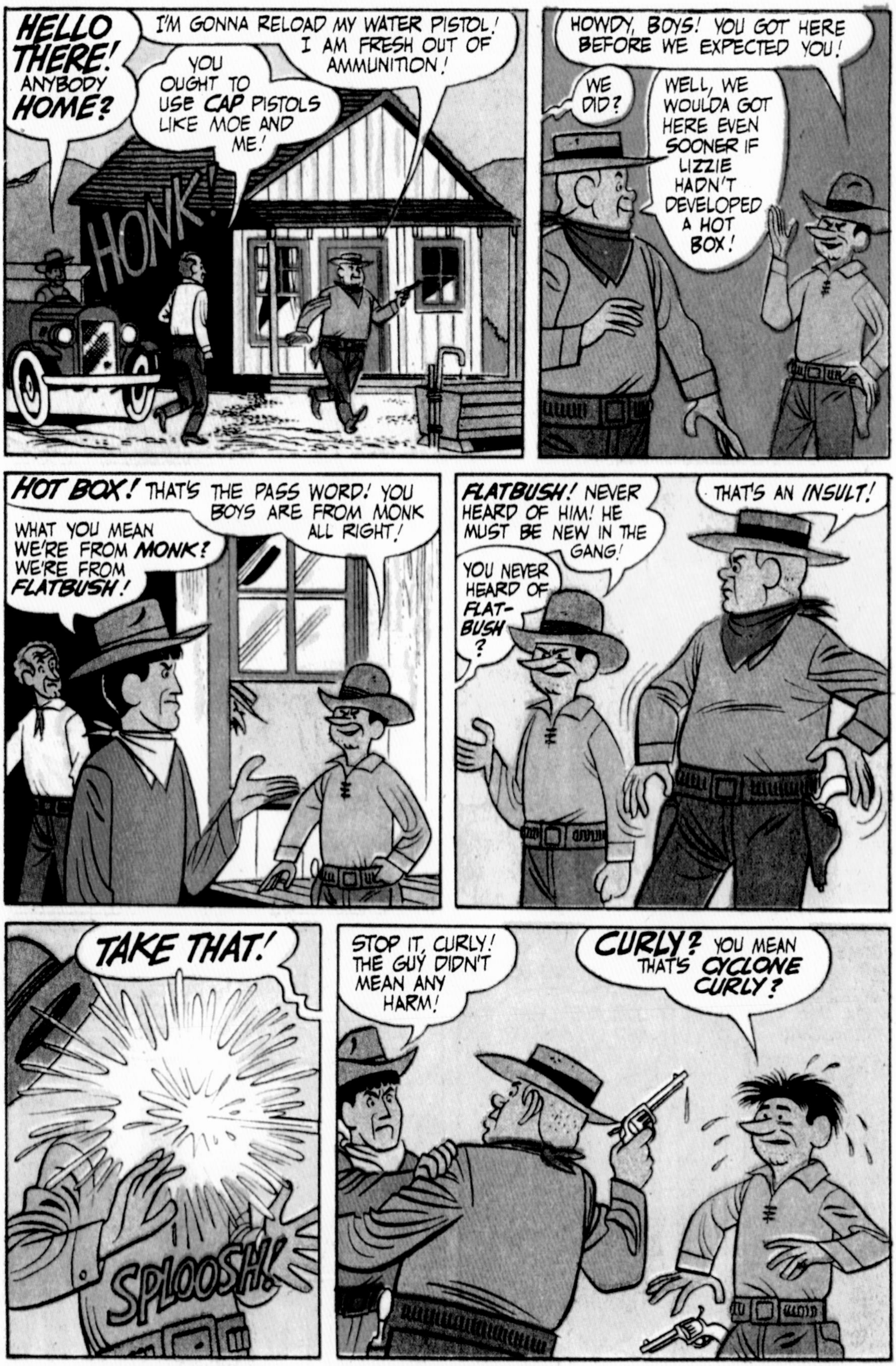
HELLO THERE! ANYBODY HOME?
I'M GONNA RELOAD MY WATER PISTOL! I AM FRESH OUT OF AMMUNITION!
YOU OUGHT TO USE CAP PISTOLS LIKE MOE AND ME!
HONK!
HOWDY, BOYS! YOU GOT HERE BEFORE WE EXPECTED YOU!
WE DID?
WELL, WE WOULDA GOT HERE EVEN SOONER IF LIZZIE HADN'T DEVELOPED A HOT BOX!
HOT BOX! THAT'S THE PASS WORD! YOU BOYS ARE FROM MONK ALL RIGHT!
WHAT YOU MEAN WE'RE FROM MONK? WE'RE FROM FLATBUSH!
FLATBUSH! NEVER HEARD OF HIM! HE MUST BE NEW IN THE GANG!
THAT'S AN INSULT!
YOU NEVER HEARD OF FLAT-BUSH?
TAKE THAT!
SPLOOSH!
STOP IT, CURLY! THE GUY DIDN'T MEAN ANY HARM!
CURLY? YOU MEAN THAT'S CYCLONE CURLY?

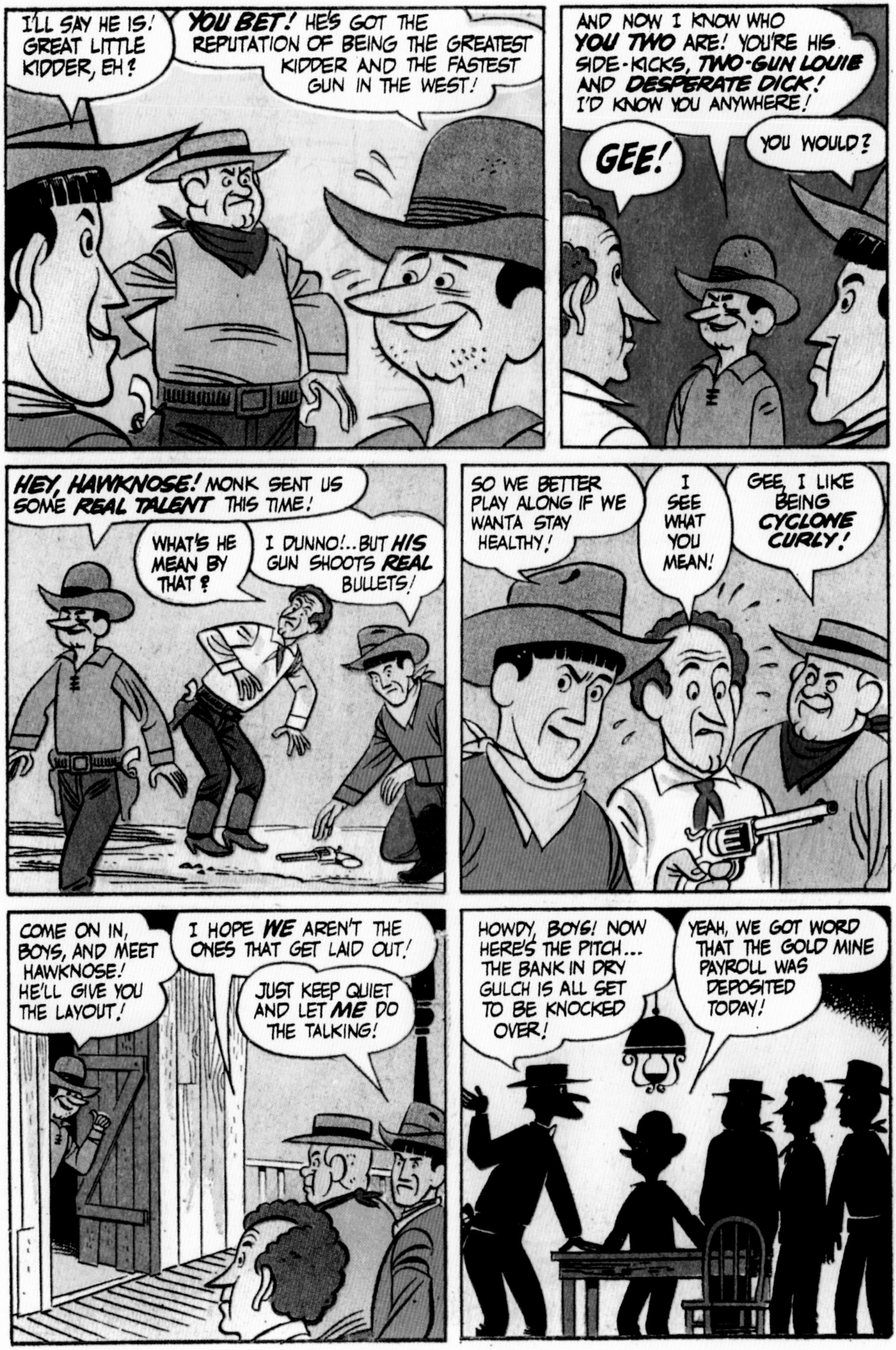
I'LL SAY HE IS! GREAT LITTLE KIDDER, EH?
YOU BET! HE'S GOT THE REPUTATION OF BEING THE GREATEST KIDDER AND THE FASTEST GUN IN THE WEST!
AND NOW I KNOW WHO YOU TWO ARE! YOU'RE HIS SIDE-KICKS, TWO-GUN LOUIE AND DESPERATE DICK! I'D KNOW YOU ANYWHERE!
GEE!
YOU WOULD?
HEY, HAWKNOSE! MONK SENT US SOME REAL TALENT THIS TIME!
WHAT'S HE MEAN BY THAT?
I DUNNO!... BUT HIS GUN SHOOTS REAL BULLETS!
SO WE BETTER PLAY ALONG IF WE WANTA STAY HEALTHY!
I SEE WHAT YOU MEAN!
GEE, I LIKE BEING CYCLONE CURLY!
COME ON IN, BOYS, AND MEET HAWKNOSE! HE'LL GIVE YOU THE LAYOUT!
I HOPE WE AREN'T THE ONES THAT GET LAID OUT!
JUST KEEP QUIET AND LET ME DO THE TALKING!
HOWDY, BOYS! NOW HERE'S THE PITCH... THE BANK IN DRY GULCH IS ALL SET TO BE KNOCKED OVER!
YEAH, WE GOT WORD THAT THE GOLD MINE PAYROLL WAS DEPOSITED TODAY!

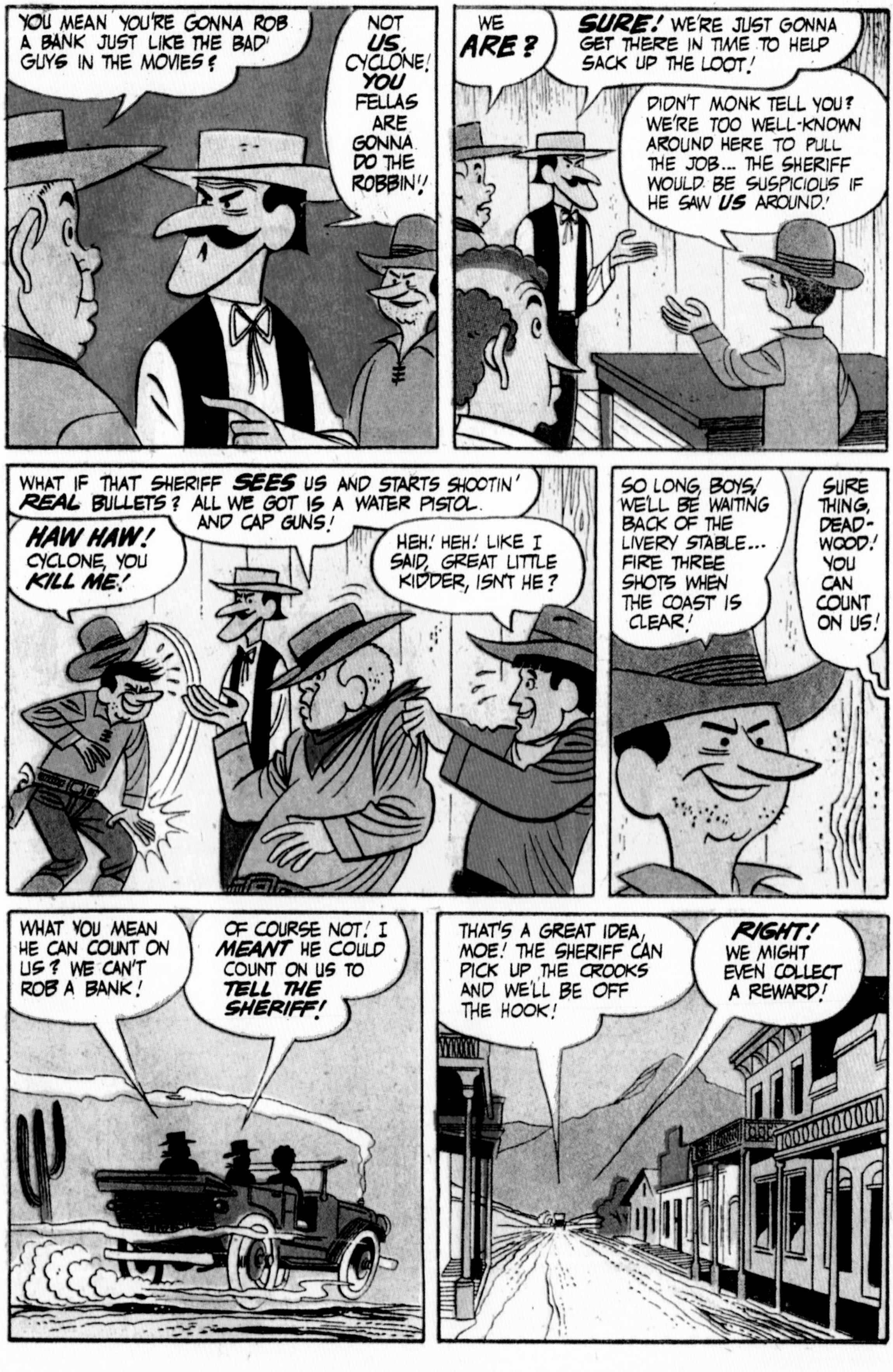
YOU MEAN YOU'RE GONNA ROB A BANK JUST LIKE THE BAD GUYS IN THE MOVIES?
NOT US, CYCLONE! YOU FELLAS ARE GONNA DO THE ROBBIN'!
WE ARE?
SURE! WE'RE JUST GONNA GET THERE IN TIME TO HELP SACK UP THE LOOT!
DIDN'T MONK TELL YOU? WE'RE TOO WELL-KNOWN AROUND HERE TO PULL THE JOB... THE SHERIFF WOULD BE SUSPICIOUS IF HE SAW US AROUND!
WHAT IF THAT SHERIFF SEES US AND STARTS SHOOTIN' REAL BULLETS? ALL WE GOT IS A WATER PISTOL AND CAP GUNS!
HAW HAW! CYCLONE, YOU KILL ME!
HEH! HEH! LIKE I SAID, GREAT LITTLE KIDDER, ISN'T HE?
SO LONG, BOYS! WE'LL BE WAITING BACK OF THE LIVERY STABLE... FIRE THREE SHOTS WHEN THE COAST IS CLEAR!
SURE THING, DEAD-WOOD! YOU CAN COUNT ON US!
WHAT YOU MEAN HE CAN COUNT ON US? WE CAN'T ROB A BANK!
OF COURSE NOT! I MEANT HE COULD COUNT ON US TO TELL THE SHERIFF!
THAT'S A GREAT IDEA, MOE! THE SHERIFF CAN PICK UP THE CROOKS AND WE'LL BE OFF THE HOOK!
RIGHT! WE MIGHT EVEN COLLECT A REWARD!

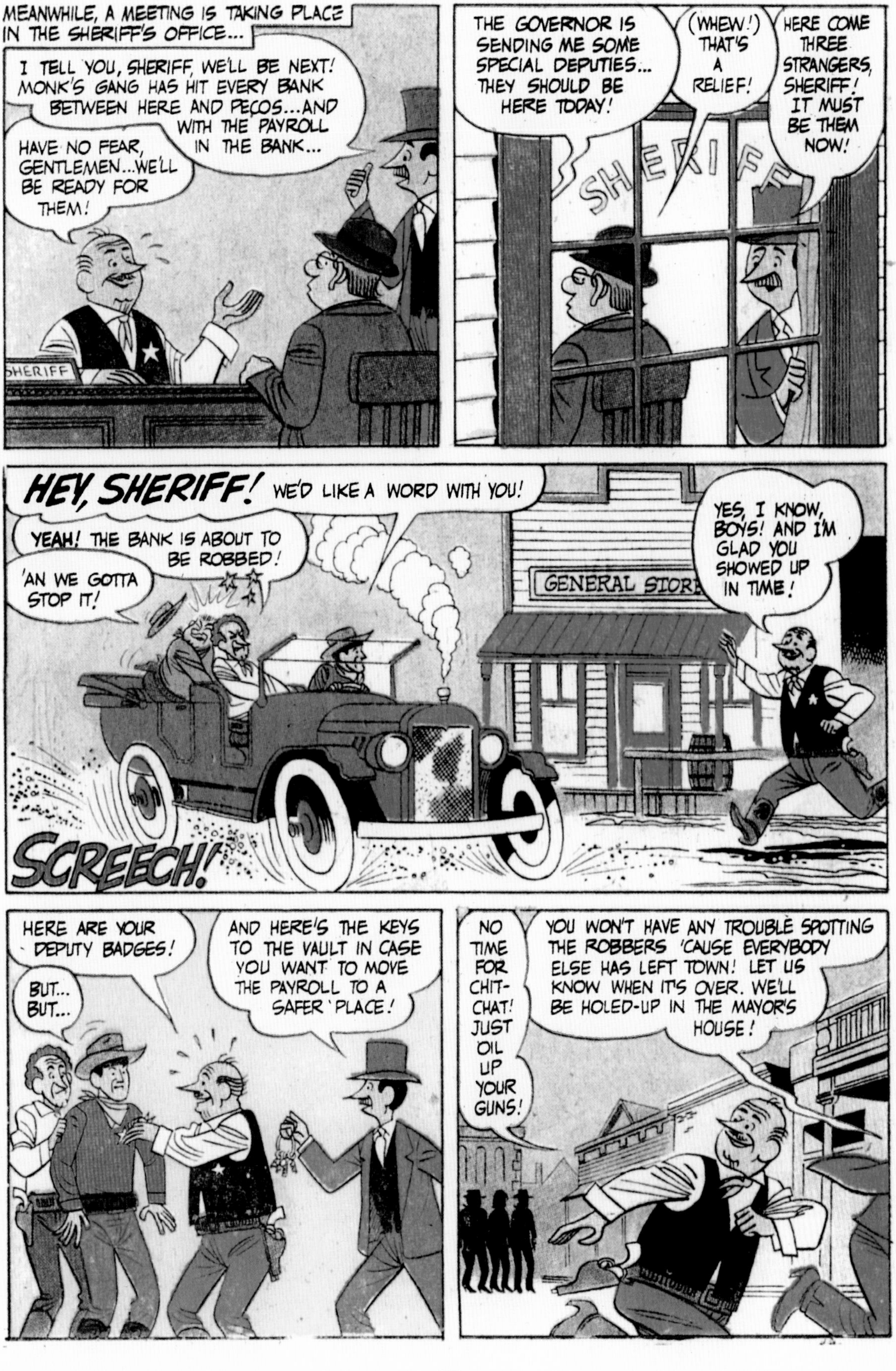
MEANWHILE, A MEETING IS TAKING PLACE IN THE SHERIFF'S OFFICE...
I TELL YOU, SHERIFF, WE'LL BE NEXT! MONK'S GANG HAS HIT EVERY BANK BETWEEN HERE AND PECOS...AND WITH THE PAYROLL IN THE BANK...
HAVE NO FEAR, GENTLEMEN...WE'LL BE READY FOR THEM!
SHERIFF
THE GOVERNOR IS SENDING ME SOME SPECIAL DEPUTIES... THEY SHOULD BE HERE TODAY!
(WHEW!) THAT'S A RELIEF!
HERE COME THREE STRANGERS, SHERIFF! IT MUST BE THEM NOW!
SHERIFF
HEY, SHERIFF! WE'D LIKE A WORD WITH YOU!
YEAH! THE BANK IS ABOUT TO BE ROBBED!
'AN WE GOTTA STOP IT!
GENERAL STORE
YES, I KNOW, BOYS! AND I'M GLAD YOU SHOWED UP IN TIME!
SCREECH!
HERE ARE YOUR DEPUTY BADGES!
BUT... BUT...
AND HERE'S THE KEYS TO THE VAULT IN CASE YOU WANT TO MOVE THE PAYROLL TO A SAFER PLACE!
NO TIME FOR CHIT-CHAT! JUST OIL UP YOUR GUNS!
YOU WON'T HAVE ANY TROUBLE SPOTTING THE ROBBERS 'CAUSE EVERYBODY ELSE HAS LEFT TOWN! LET US KNOW WHEN IT'S OVER. WE'LL BE HOLED-UP IN THE MAYOR'S HOUSE!

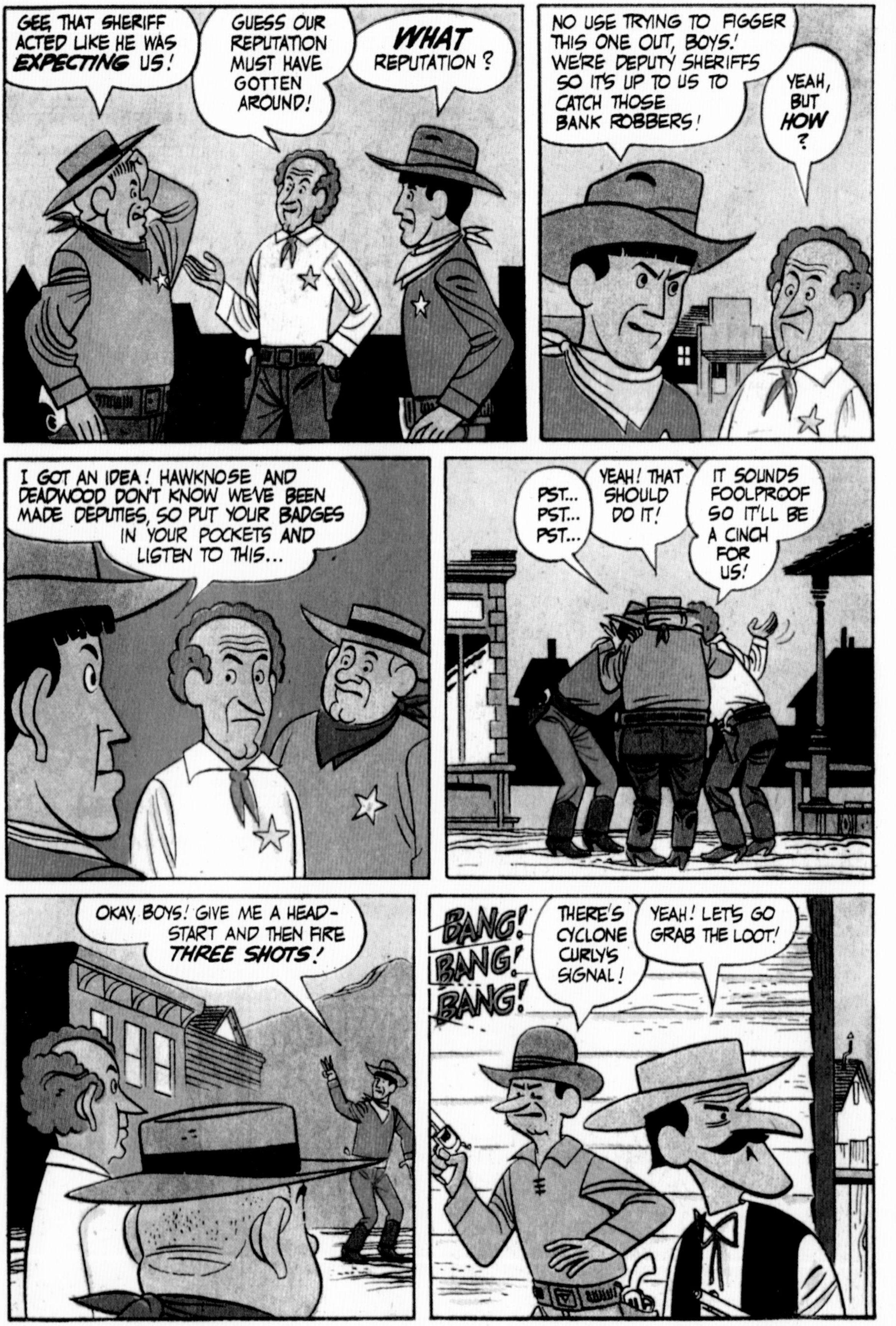
GEE, THAT SHERIFF ACTED LIKE HE WAS EXPECTING US!
GUESS OUR REPUTATION MUST HAVE GOTTEN AROUND!
WHAT REPUTATION?
NO USE TRYING TO FIGGER THIS ONE OUT, BOYS! WE'RE DEPUTY SHERIFFS SO IT'S UP TO US TO CATCH THOSE BANK ROBBERS!
YEAH, BUT HOW?
I GOT AN IDEA! HAWKNOSE AND DEADWOOD DON'T KNOW WE'VE BEEN MADE DEPUTIES, SO PUT YOUR BADGES IN YOUR POCKETS AND LISTEN TO THIS...
PST... PST... PST...
YEAH! THAT SHOULD DO IT!
IT SOUNDS FOOLPROOF SO IT'LL BE A CINCH FOR US!
OKAY, BOYS! GIVE ME A HEAD-START AND THEN FIRE THREE SHOTS!
BANG! BANG! BANG!
THERE'S CYCLONE CURLY'S SIGNAL!
YEAH! LET'S GO GRAB THE LOOT!

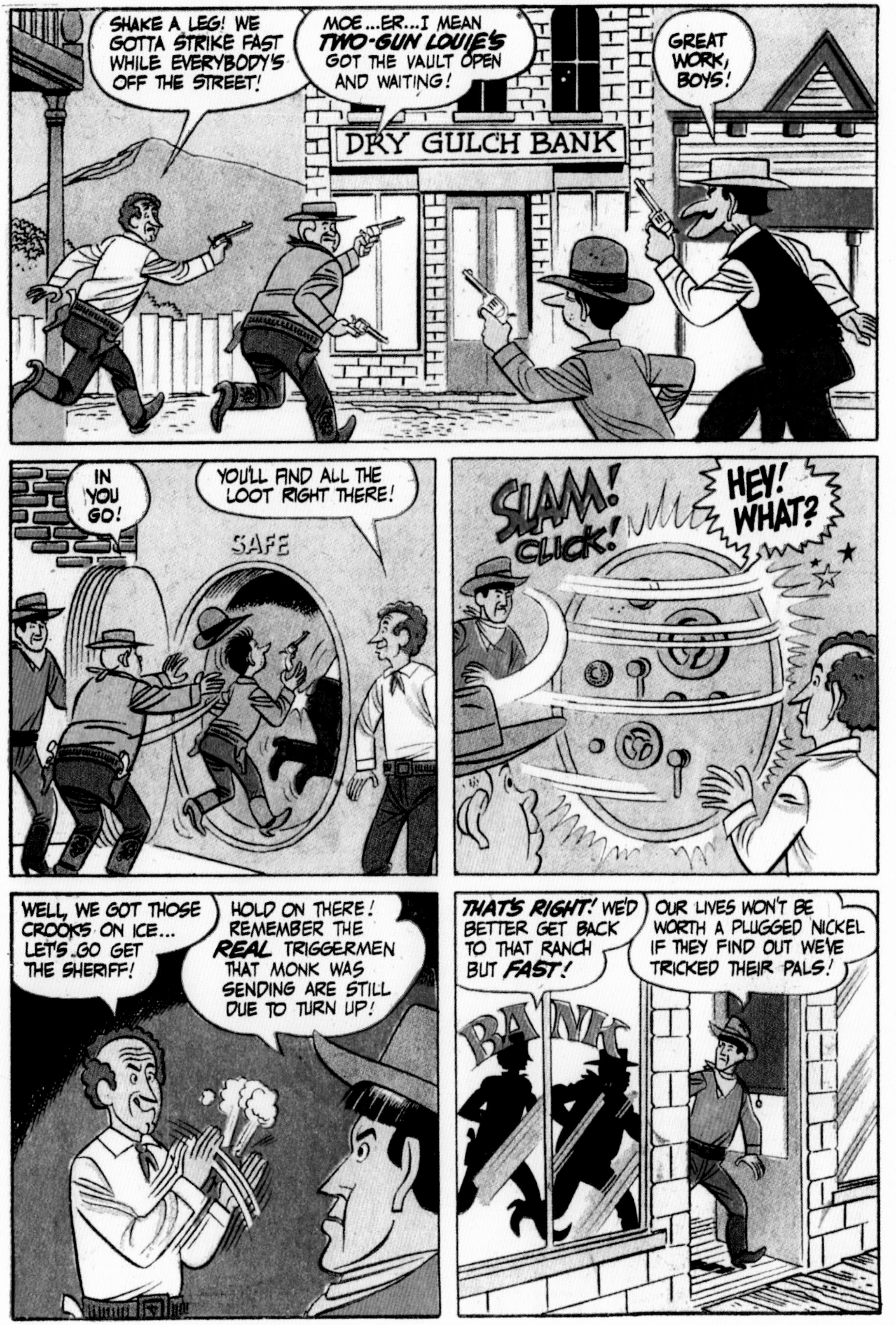
SHAKE A LEG! WE GOTTA STRIKE FAST WHILE EVERYBODY'S OFF THE STREET!
MOE...ER...I MEAN TWO-GUN LOUIE'S GOT THE VAULT OPEN AND WAITING!
DRY GULCH BANK
GREAT WORK, BOYS!
IN YOU GO!
YOU'LL FIND ALL THE LOOT RIGHT THERE!
SAFE
SLAM! CLICK!
HEY! WHAT?
WELL, WE GOT THOSE CROOKS ON ICE... LET'S GO GET THE SHERIFF!
HOLD ON THERE! REMEMBER THE REAL TRIGGERMEN THAT MONK WAS SENDING ARE STILL DUE TO TURN UP!
THAT'S RIGHT! WE'D BETTER GET BACK TO THAT RANCH BUT FAST!
OUR LIVES WON'T BE WORTH A PLUGGED NICKEL IF THEY FIND OUT WE'VE TRICKED THEIR PALS!
BANK

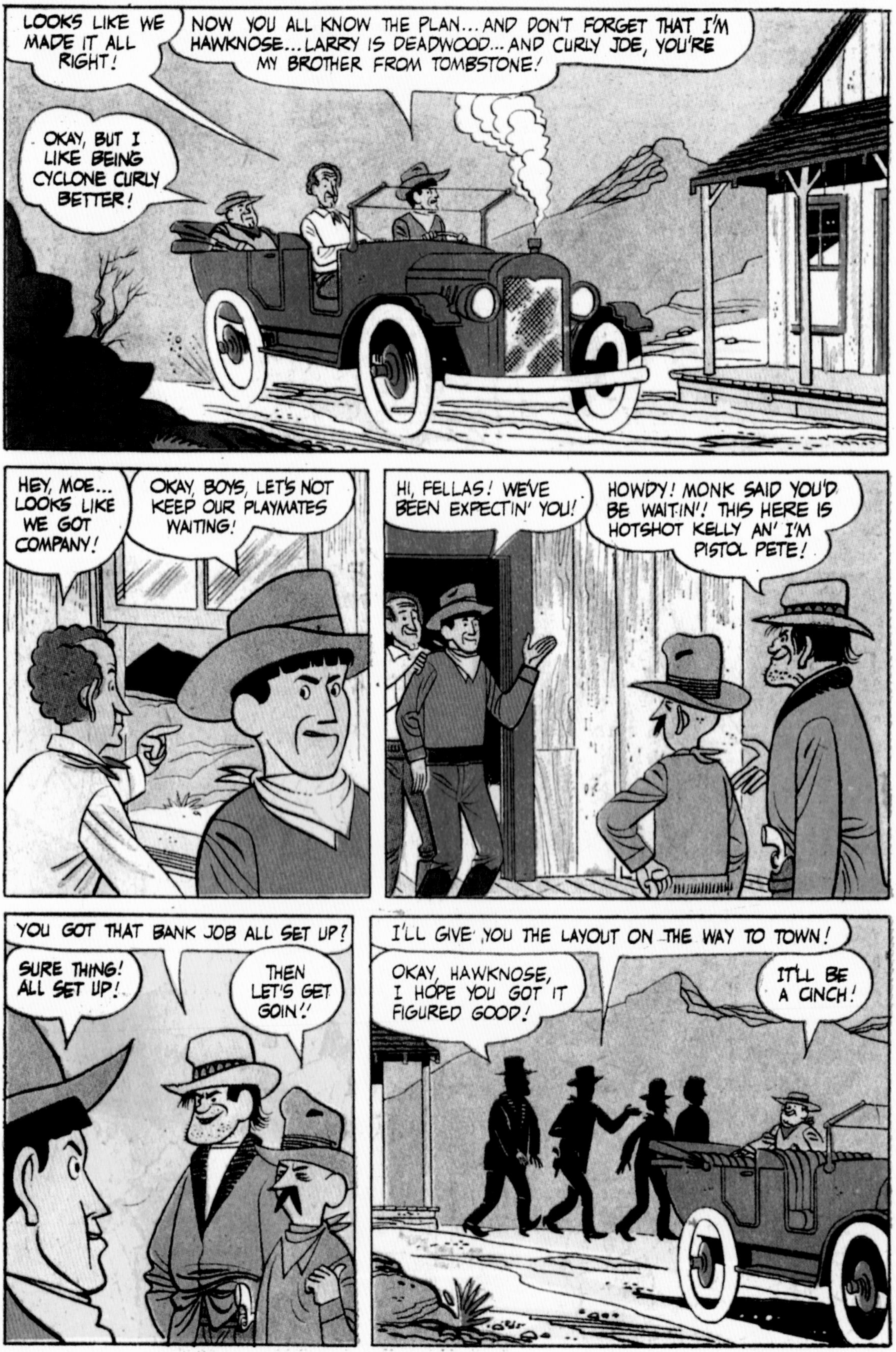
LOOKS LIKE WE MADE IT ALL RIGHT!
NOW YOU ALL KNOW THE PLAN... AND DON'T FORGET THAT I'M HAWKNOSE... LARRY IS DEADWOOD... AND CURLY JOE, YOU'RE MY BROTHER FROM TOMBSTONE!
OKAY, BUT I LIKE BEING CYCLONE CURLY BETTER!
HEY, MOE... LOOKS LIKE WE GOT COMPANY!
OKAY, BOYS, LET'S NOT KEEP OUR PLAYMATES WAITING!
HI, FELLAS! WE'VE BEEN EXPECTIN' YOU!
HOWDY! MONK SAID YOU'D BE WAITIN'! THIS HERE IS HOTSHOT KELLY AN' I'M PISTOL PETE!
YOU GOT THAT BANK JOB ALL SET UP?
SURE THING! ALL SET UP!
THEN LET'S GET GOIN'!
I'LL GIVE YOU THE LAYOUT ON THE WAY TO TOWN!
OKAY, HAWKNOSE, I HOPE YOU GOT IT FIGURED GOOD!
IT'LL BE A CINCH!

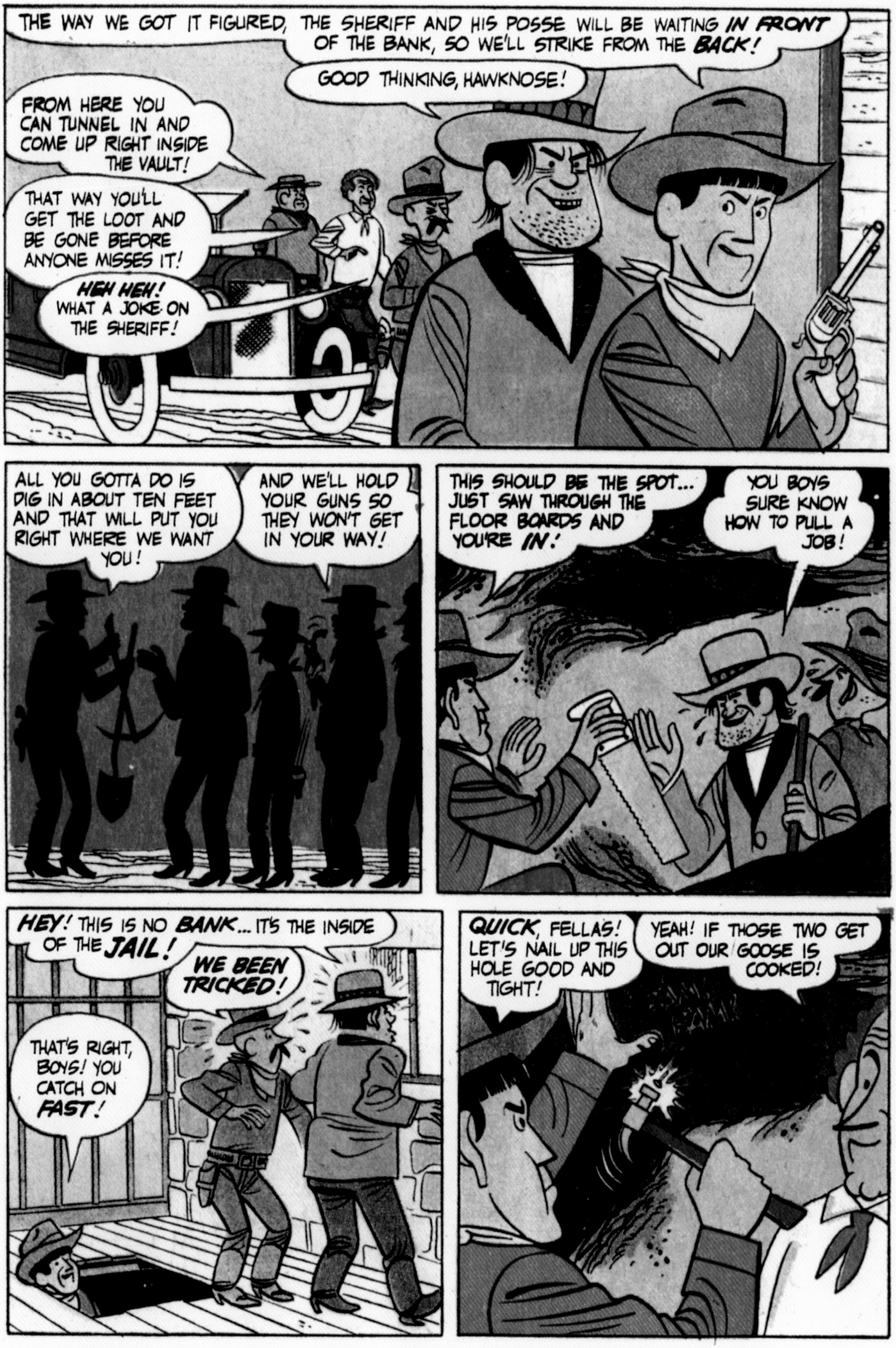
THE WAY WE GOT IT FIGURED, THE SHERIFF AND HIS POSSE WILL BE WAITING IN FRONT OF THE BANK, SO WE'LL STRIKE FROM THE BACK!
GOOD THINKING, HAWKNOSE!
FROM HERE YOU CAN TUNNEL IN AND COME UP RIGHT INSIDE THE VAULT!
THAT WAY YOU'LL GET THE LOOT AND BE GONE BEFORE ANYONE MISSES IT!
HEH HEH! WHAT A JOKE ON THE SHERIFF!
ALL YOU GOTTA DO IS DIG IN ABOUT TEN FEET AND THAT WILL PUT YOU RIGHT WHERE WE WANT YOU!
AND WE'LL HOLD YOUR GUNS SO THEY WON'T GET IN YOUR WAY!
THIS SHOULD BE THE SPOT... JUST SAW THROUGH THE FLOOR BOARDS AND YOU'RE IN!
YOU BOYS SURE KNOW HOW TO PULL A JOB!
HEY! THIS IS NO BANK... IT'S THE INSIDE OF THE JAIL!
WE BEEN TRICKED!
THAT'S RIGHT, BOYS! YOU CATCH ON FAST!
QUICK, FELLAS! LET'S NAIL UP THIS HOLE GOOD AND TIGHT!
YEAH! IF THOSE TWO GET OUT OUR GOOSE IS COOKED!

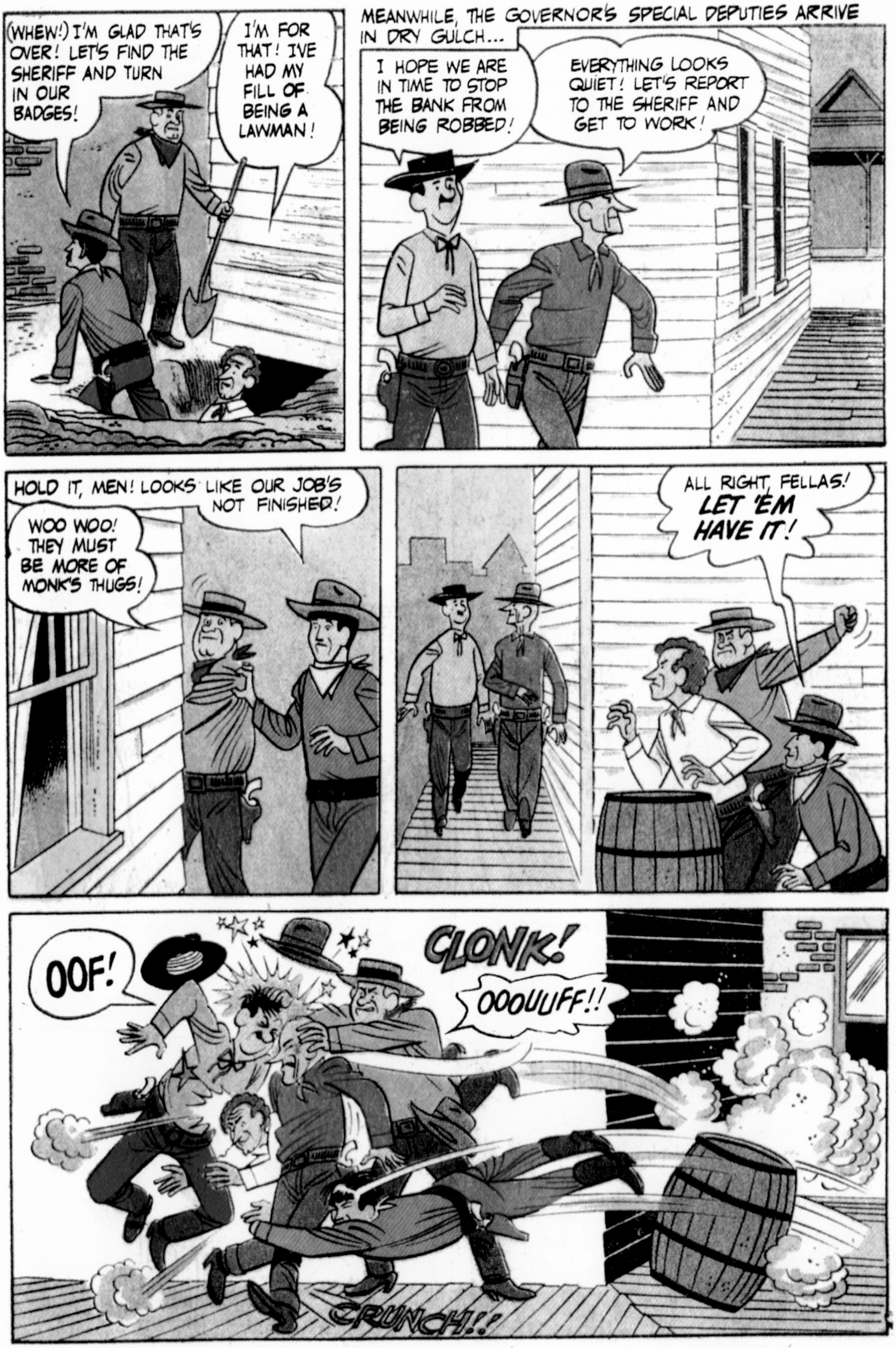
(WHEW!) I'M GLAD THAT'S OVER! LET'S FIND THE SHERIFF AND TURN IN OUR BADGES!
I'M FOR THAT! I'VE HAD MY FILL OF BEING A LAWMAN!
MEANWHILE, THE GOVERNOR'S SPECIAL DEPUTIES ARRIVE IN DRY GULCH...
I HOPE WE ARE IN TIME TO STOP THE BANK FROM BEING ROBBED!
EVERYTHING LOOKS QUIET! LET'S REPORT TO THE SHERIFF AND GET TO WORK!
HOLD IT, MEN! LOOKS LIKE OUR JOB'S NOT FINISHED!
WOO WOO! THEY MUST BE MORE OF MONK'S THUGS!
ALL RIGHT, FELLAS! LET 'EM HAVE IT!
OOF!
CLONK!
OOOUUFF!!
CRUNCH!!

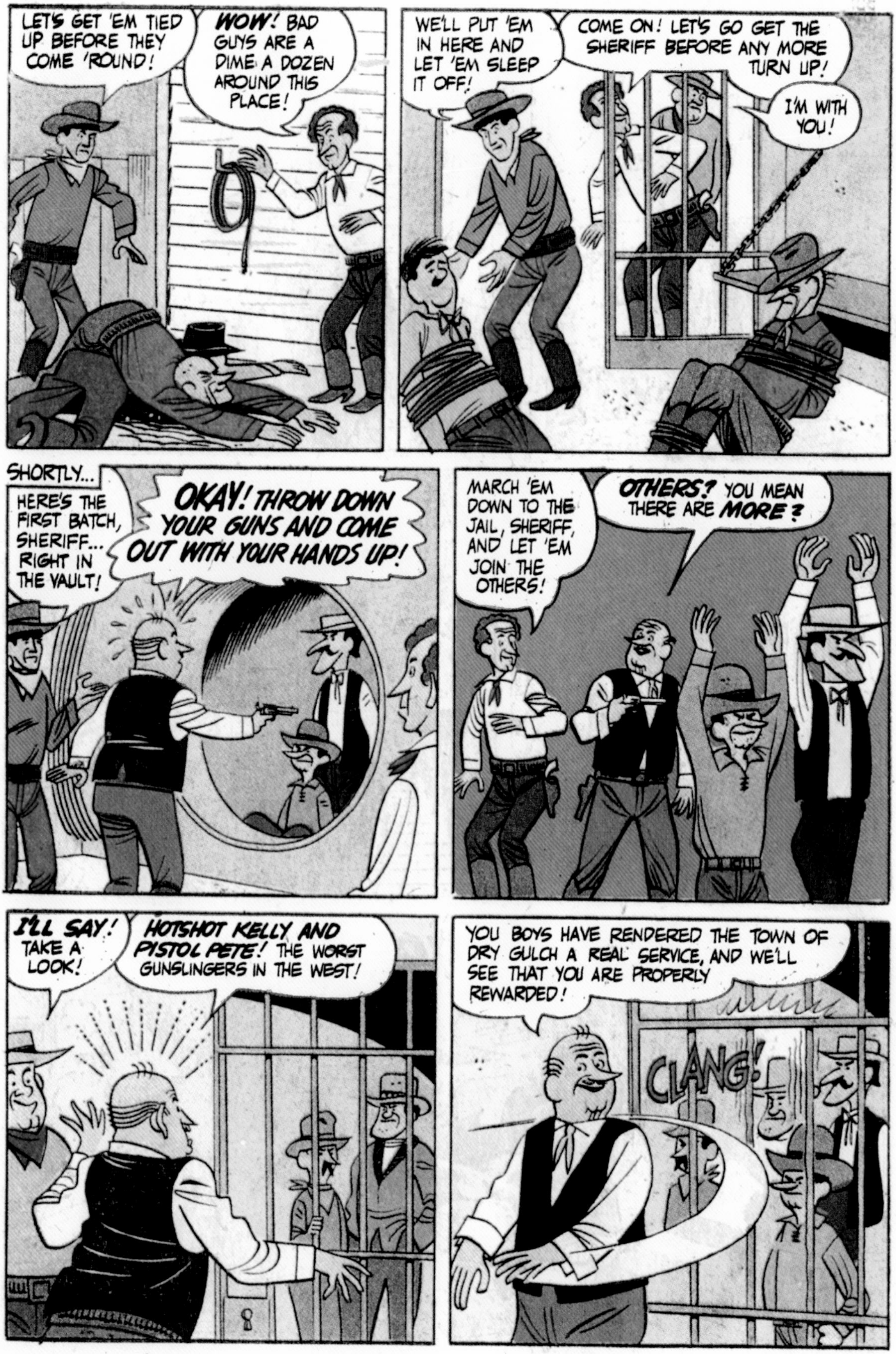
LET'S GET 'EM TIED UP BEFORE THEY COME 'ROUND!
WOW! BAD GUYS ARE A DIME A DOZEN AROUND THIS PLACE!
WE'LL PUT 'EM IN HERE AND LET 'EM SLEEP IT OFF!
COME ON! LET'S GO GET THE SHERIFF BEFORE ANY MORE TURN UP!
I'M WITH YOU!
SHORTLY...
HERE'S THE FIRST BATCH, SHERIFF... RIGHT IN THE VAULT!
OKAY! THROW DOWN YOUR GUNS AND COME OUT WITH YOUR HANDS UP!
MARCH 'EM DOWN TO THE JAIL, SHERIFF, AND LET 'EM JOIN THE OTHERS!
OTHERS? YOU MEAN THERE ARE MORE?
I'LL SAY! TAKE A LOOK!
HOTSHOT KELLY AND PISTOL PETE! THE WORST GUNSLINGERS IN THE WEST!
YOU BOYS HAVE RENDERED THE TOWN OF DRY GULCH A REAL SERVICE, AND WE'LL SEE THAT YOU ARE PROPERLY REWARDED!
CLANG!

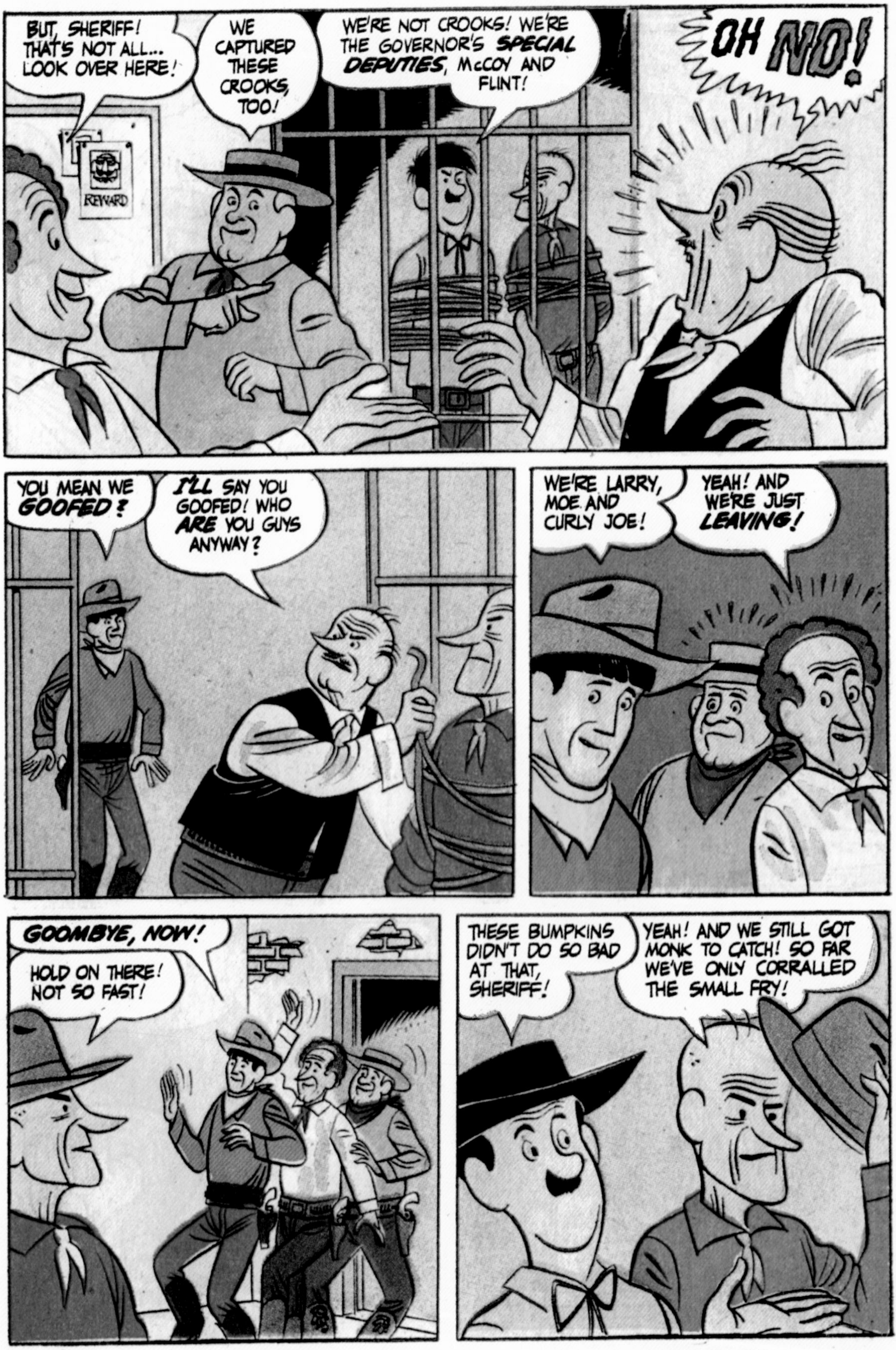
BUT, SHERIFF! THAT'S NOT ALL... LOOK OVER HERE!
WE CAPTURED THESE CROOKS, TOO!
REWARD
WE'RE NOT CROOKS! WE'RE THE GOVERNOR'S SPECIAL DEPUTIES, McCOY AND FLINT!
OH NO!
YOU MEAN WE GOOFED?
I'LL SAY YOU GOOFED! WHO ARE YOU GUYS ANYWAY?
WE'RE LARRY, MOE AND CURLY JOE!
YEAH! AND WE'RE JUST LEAVING!
GOOMBYE, NOW!
HOLD ON THERE! NOT SO FAST!
THESE BUMPKINS DIDN'T DO SO BAD AT THAT, SHERIFF!
YEAH! AND WE STILL GOT MONK TO CATCH! SO FAR WE'VE ONLY CORRALLED THE SMALL FRY!

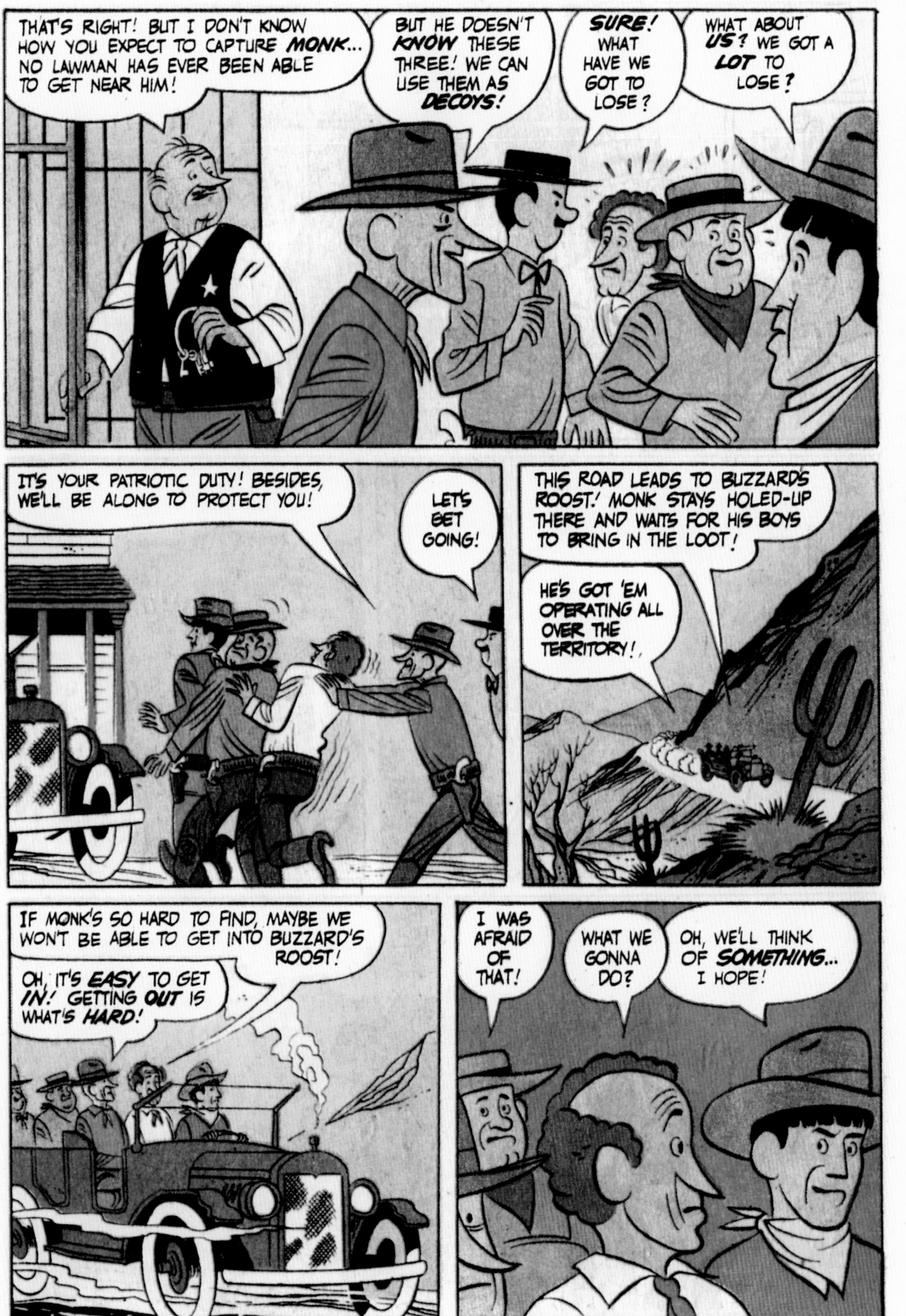
THAT'S RIGHT! BUT I DON'T KNOW HOW YOU EXPECT TO CAPTURE MONK... NO LAWMAN HAS EVER BEEN ABLE TO GET NEAR HIM!
BUT HE DOESN'T KNOW THESE THREE! WE CAN USE THEM AS DECOYS!
SURE! WHAT HAVE WE GOT TO LOSE?
WHAT ABOUT US? WE GOT A LOT TO LOSE?
IT'S YOUR PATRIOTIC DUTY! BESIDES, WE'LL BE ALONG TO PROTECT YOU!
LET'S GET GOING!
THIS ROAD LEADS TO BUZZARD'S ROOST! MONK STAYS HOLED-UP THERE AND WAITS FOR HIS BOYS TO BRING IN THE LOOT!
HE'S GOT 'EM OPERATING ALL OVER THE TERRITORY!
IF MONK'S SO HARD TO FIND, MAYBE WE WON'T BE ABLE TO GET INTO BUZZARD'S ROOST!
OH, IT'S EASY TO GET IN! GETTING OUT IS WHAT'S HARD!
I WAS AFRAID OF THAT!
WHAT WE GONNA DO?
OH, WE'LL THINK OF SOMETHING... I HOPE!

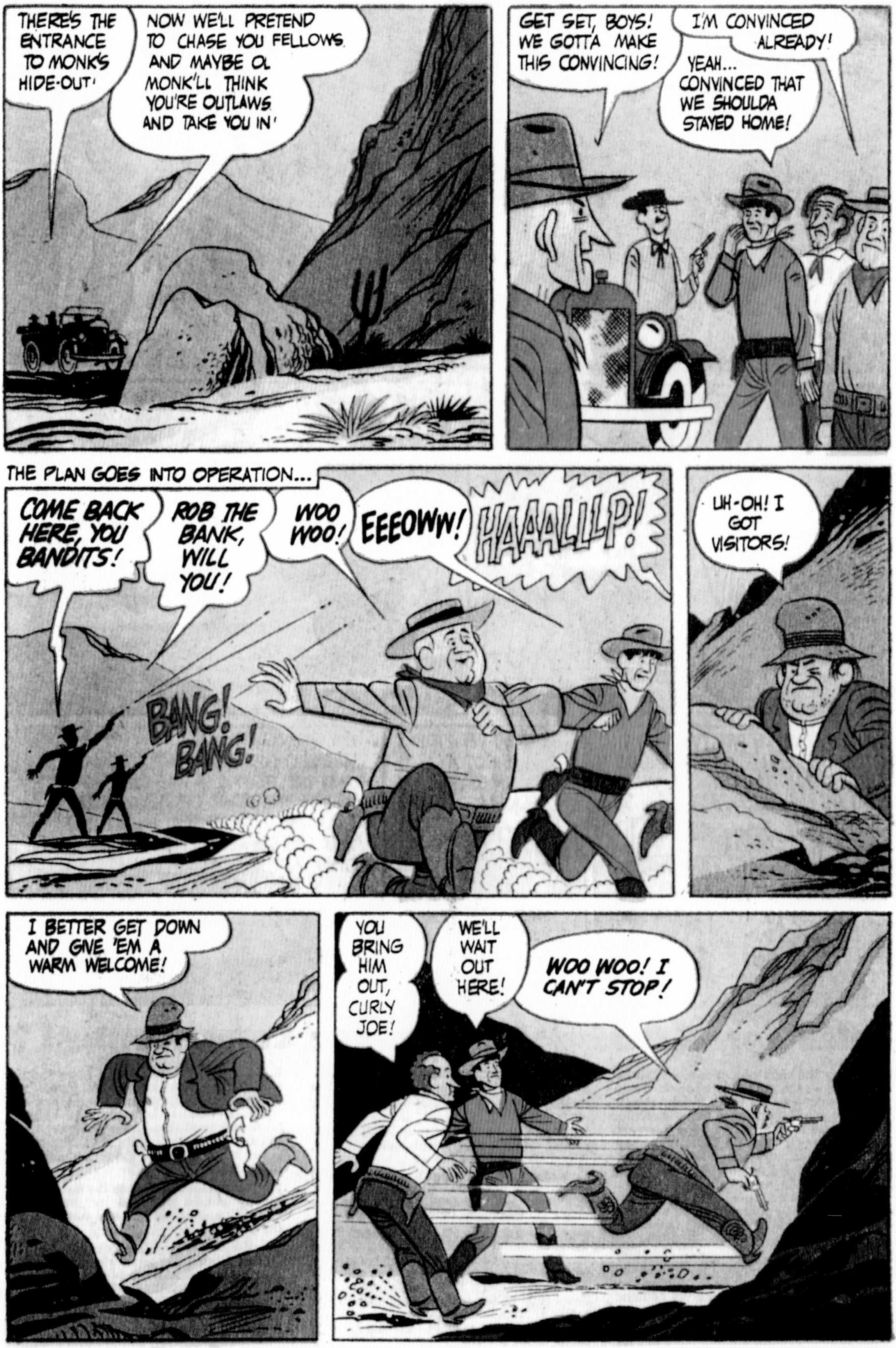

THERE'S THE ENTRANCE TO MONK'S HIDE-OUT!
NOW WE'LL PRETEND TO CHASE YOU FELLOWS AND MAYBE OL MONK'LL THINK YOU'RE OUTLAWS AND TAKE YOU IN!
GET SET, BOYS! WE GOTTA MAKE THIS CONVINCING!
I'M CONVINCED ALREADY!
YEAH... CONVINCED THAT WE SHOULDA STAYED HOME!
THE PLAN GOES INTO OPERATION...
COME BACK HERE, YOU BANDITS!
ROB THE BANK, WILL YOU!
WOO WOO!
EEEOWW!
HAAALLLP!
BANG! BANG!
UH-OH! I GOT VISITORS!
I BETTER GET DOWN AND GIVE 'EM A WARM WELCOME!
YOU BRING HIM OUT, CURLY JOE!
WE'LL WAIT OUT HERE!
WOO WOO! I CAN'T STOP!

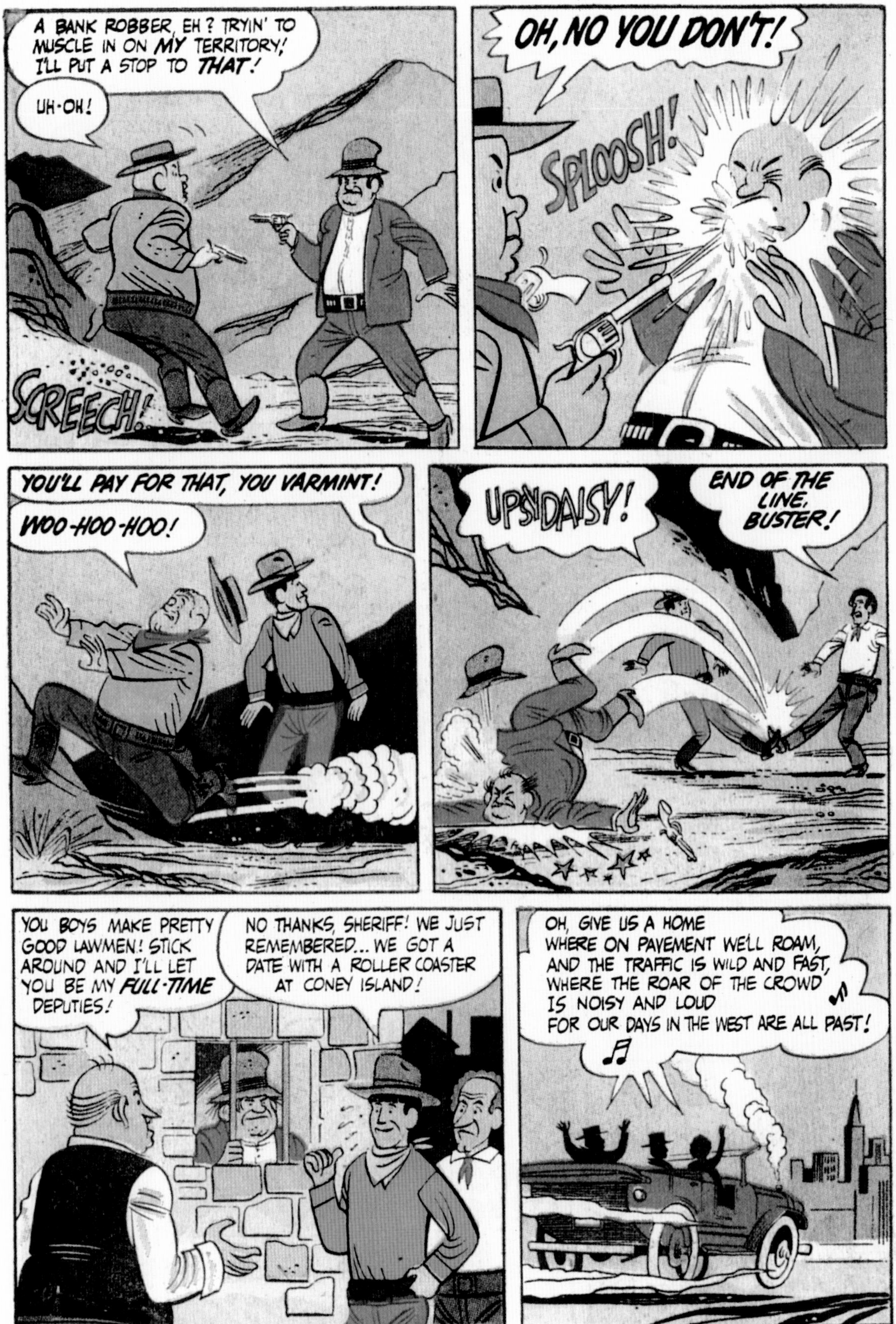
A BANK ROBBER, EH? TRYIN' TO MUSCLE IN ON MY TERRITORY! I'LL PUT A STOP TO THAT!
UH-OH!
SCREECH!
OH, NO YOU DON'T!
SPLOOSH!
YOU'LL PAY FOR THAT, YOU VARMINT!
WOO-HOO-HOO!
UPSYDAISY!
END OF THE LINE, BUSTER!
YOU BOYS MAKE PRETTY GOOD LAWMEN! STICK AROUND AND I'LL LET YOU BE MY FULL-TIME DEPUTIES!
NO THANKS, SHERIFF! WE JUST REMEMBERED... WE GOT A DATE WITH A ROLLER COASTER AT CONEY ISLAND!
OH, GIVE US A HOME
WHERE ON PAVEMENT WE'LL ROAM,
AND THE TRAFFIC IS WILD AND FAST,
WHERE THE ROAR OF THE CROWD
IS NOISY AND LOUD
FOR OUR DAYS IN THE WEST ARE ALL PAST!

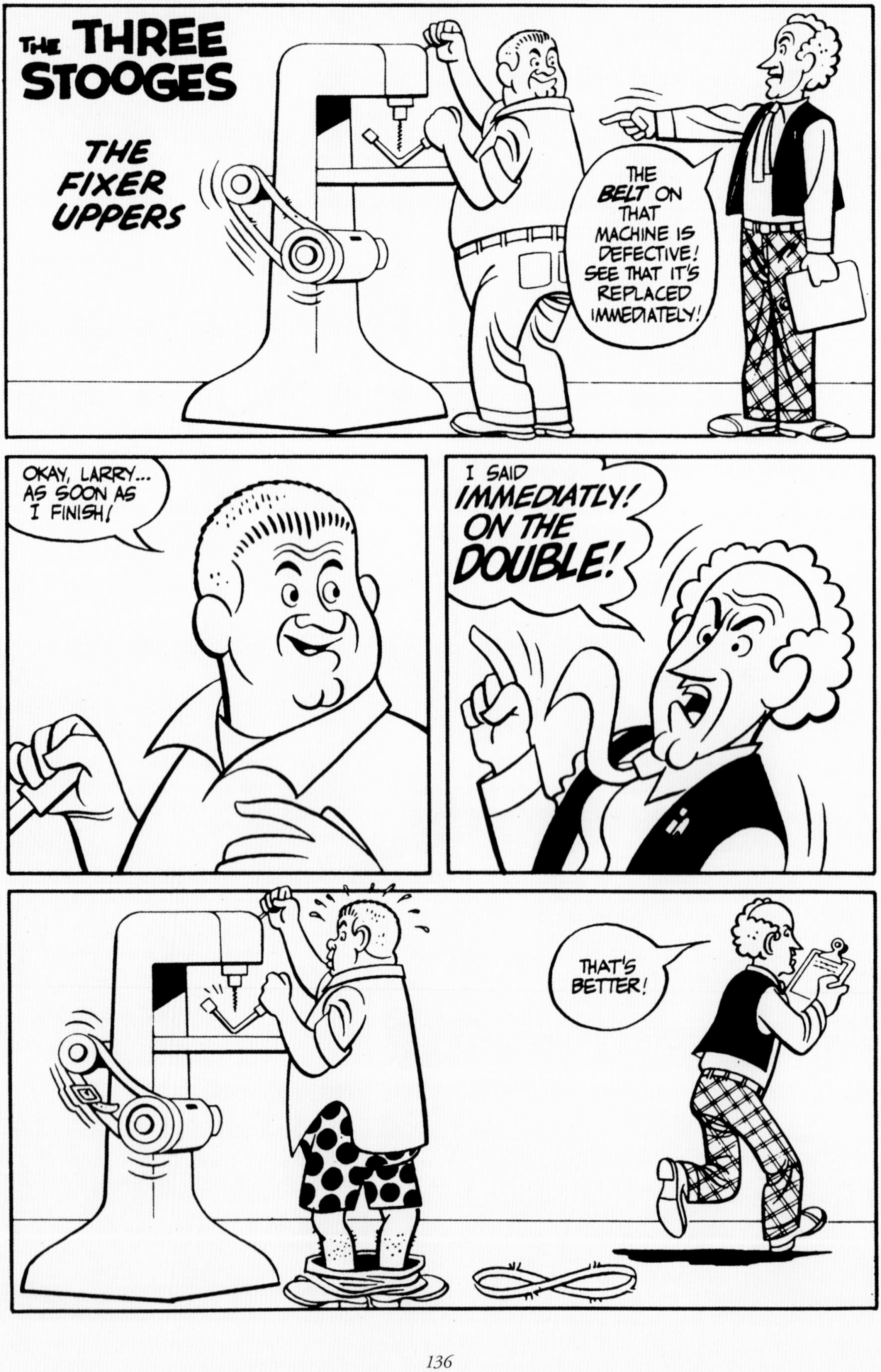
THE THREE STOOGES
THE FIXER UPPERS
THE BELT ON THAT MACHINE IS DEFECTIVE! SEE THAT IT'S REPLACED IMMEDIATELY!
OKAY, LARRY... AS SOON AS I FINISH!
I SAID IMMEDIATLY! ON THE DOUBLE!
THAT'S BETTER!

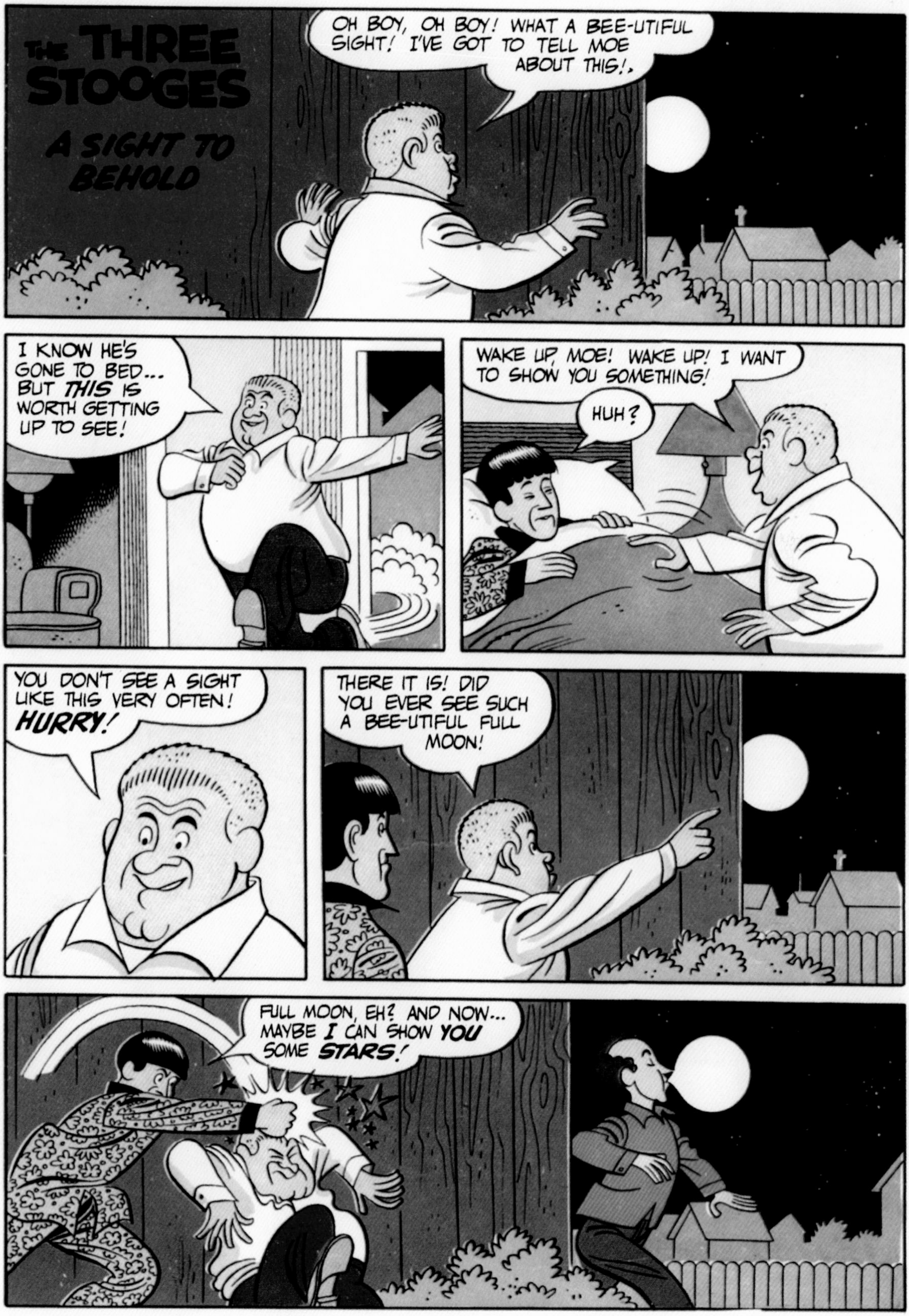
THE THREE STOOGES
A SIGHT TO BEHOLD
OH BOY, OH BOY! WHAT A BEE-UTIFUL SIGHT! I'VE GOT TO TELL MOE ABOUT THIS!.
I KNOW HE'S GONE TO BED... BUT THIS IS WORTH GETTING UP TO SEE!
WAKE UP, MOE! WAKE UP! I WANT TO SHOW YOU SOMETHING!
HUH?
YOU DON'T SEE A SIGHT LIKE THIS VERY OFTEN! HURRY!
THERE IT IS! DID YOU EVER SEE SUCH A BEE-UTIFUL FULL MOON!
FULL MOON, EH? AND NOW... MAYBE I CAN SHOW YOU SOME STARS!

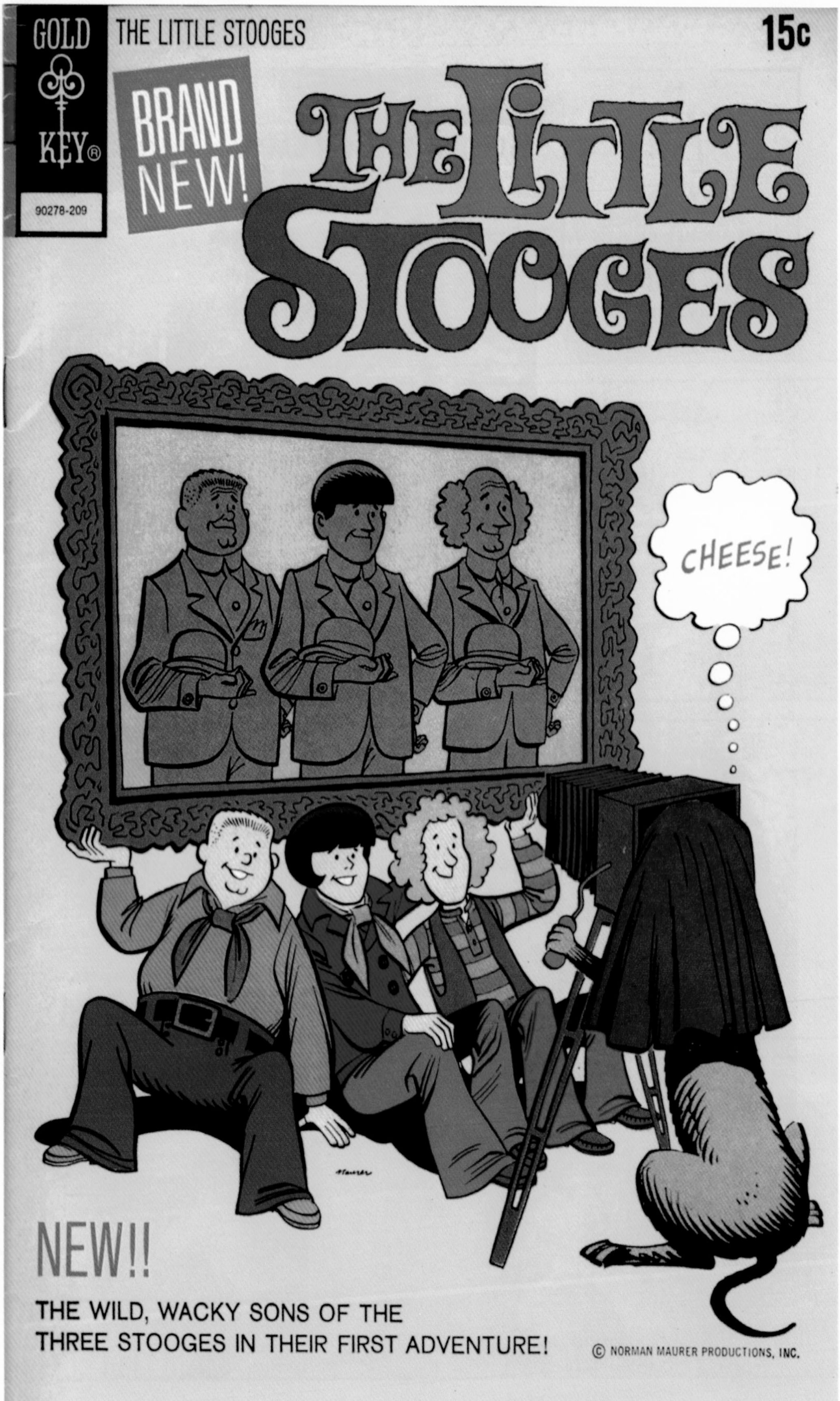
GOLD KEY®
90278-209
THE LITTLE STOOGES
15c
BRAND NEW!
THE LITTLE STOOGES
CHEESE!
NEW!!
THE WILD, WACKY SONS OF THE
THREE STOOGES IN THEIR FIRST ADVENTURE!
© NORMAN MAURER PRODUCTIONS, INC.

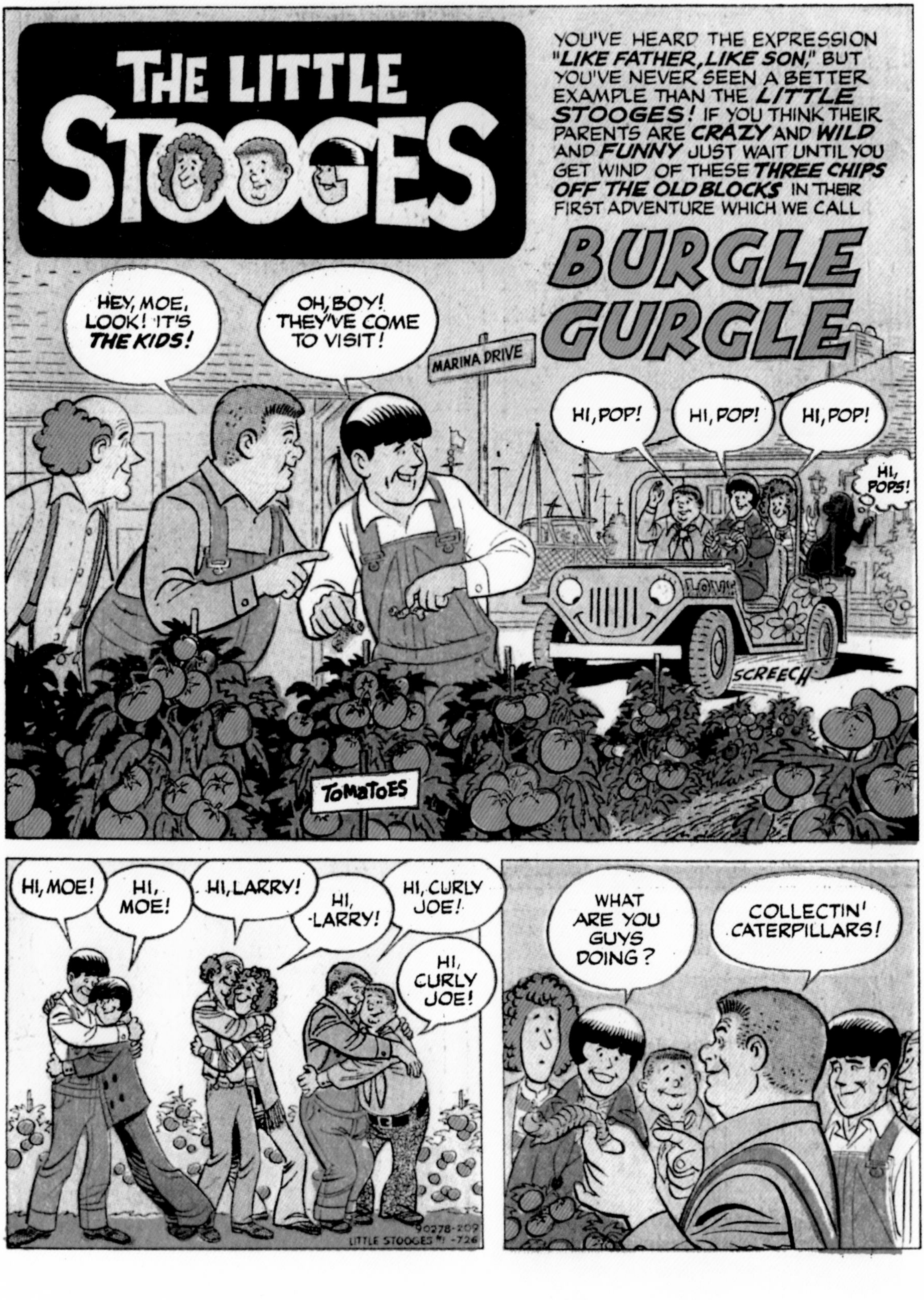
THE LITTLE STOOGES
YOU'VE HEARD THE EXPRESSION "LIKE FATHER, LIKE SON," BUT YOU'VE NEVER SEEN A BETTER EXAMPLE THAN THE LITTLE STOOGES! IF YOU THINK THEIR PARENTS ARE CRAZY AND WILD AND FUNNY JUST WAIT UNTIL YOU GET WIND OF THESE THREE CHIPS OFF THE OLD BLOCKS IN THEIR FIRST ADVENTURE WHICH WE CALL
BURGLE GURGLE
HEY, MOE, LOOK! IT'S THE KIDS!
OH, BOY! THEY'VE COME TO VISIT!
MARINA DRIVE
HI, POP!
HI, POP!
HI, POP!
HI, POPS!
SCREECH
TOMATOES
HI, MOE!
HI, MOE!
HI, LARRY!
HI, LARRY!
HI, CURLY JOE!
HI, CURLY JOE!
90278-209
LITTLE STOOGES #1 -726
WHAT ARE YOU GUYS DOING?
COLLECTIN' CATERPILLARS!

Editor's Note: After eighteen years, Norman Maurer returned, with his son Jeffrey Maurer, to create a new THREE STOOGES comicbook series starring not only the three sons of Moe, Larry, and Curly-Joe, but Benedict Bogus's near identical son as well.

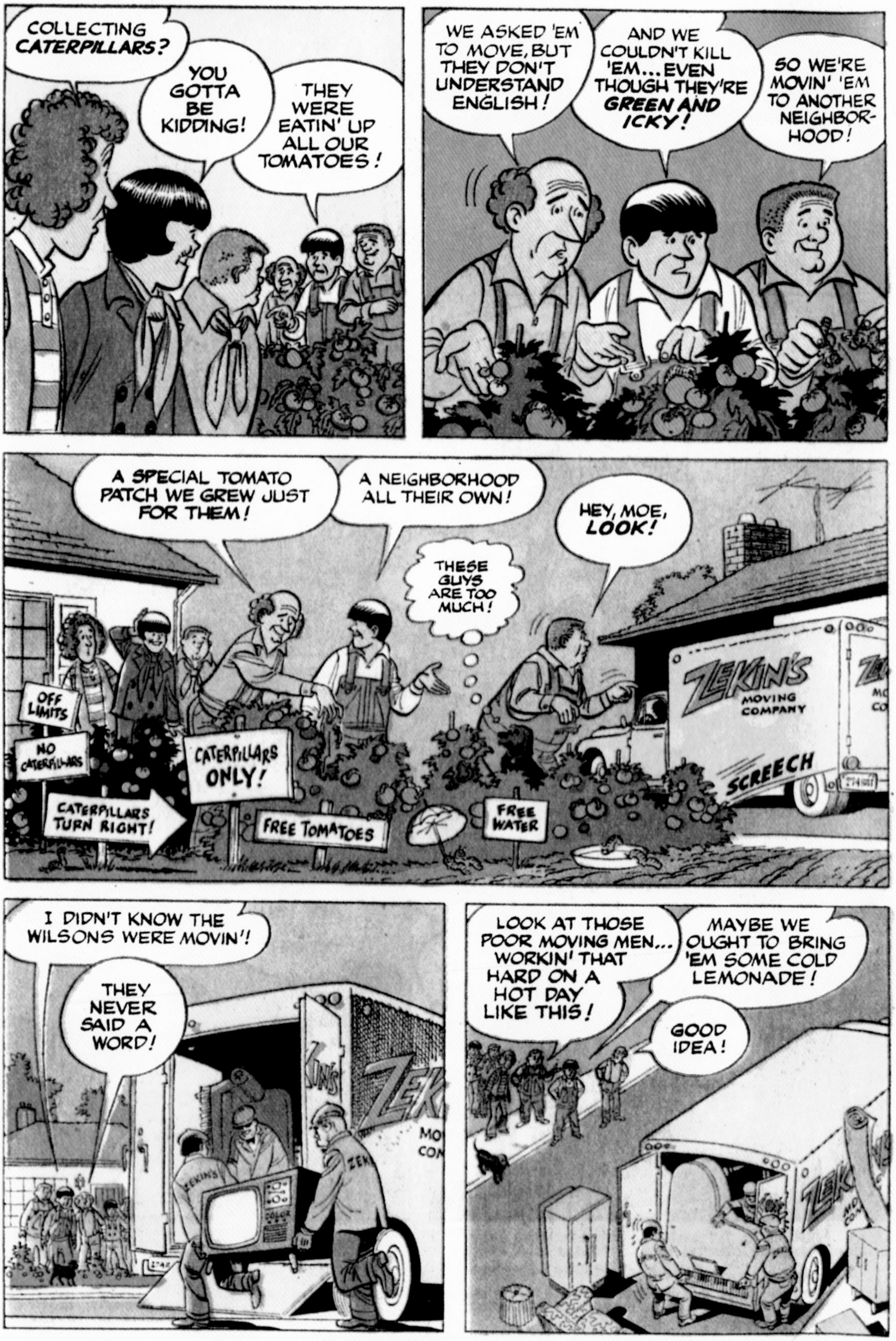
COLLECTING CATERPILLARS?
YOU GOTTA BE KIDDING!
THEY WERE EATIN' UP ALL OUR TOMATOES!
WE ASKED 'EM TO MOVE, BUT THEY DON'T UNDERSTAND ENGLISH!
AND WE COULDN'T KILL 'EM... EVEN THOUGH THEY'RE GREEN AND ICKY!
SO WE'RE MOVIN' 'EM TO ANOTHER NEIGHBOR-HOOD!
A SPECIAL TOMATO PATCH WE GREW JUST FOR THEM!
A NEIGHBORHOOD ALL THEIR OWN!
THESE GUYS ARE TOO MUCH!
HEY, MOE, LOOK!
OFF LIMITS
NO CATERPILLARS
CATERPILLARS ONLY!
CATERPILLARS TURN RIGHT!
FREE TOMATOES
FREE WATER
ZEKIN'S MOVING COMPANY
SCREECH
I DIDN'T KNOW THE WILSONS WERE MOVIN'!
THEY NEVER SAID A WORD!
LOOK AT THOSE POOR MOVING MEN... WORKIN' THAT HARD ON A HOT DAY LIKE THIS!
MAYBE WE OUGHT TO BRING 'EM SOME COLD LEMONADE!
GOOD IDEA!

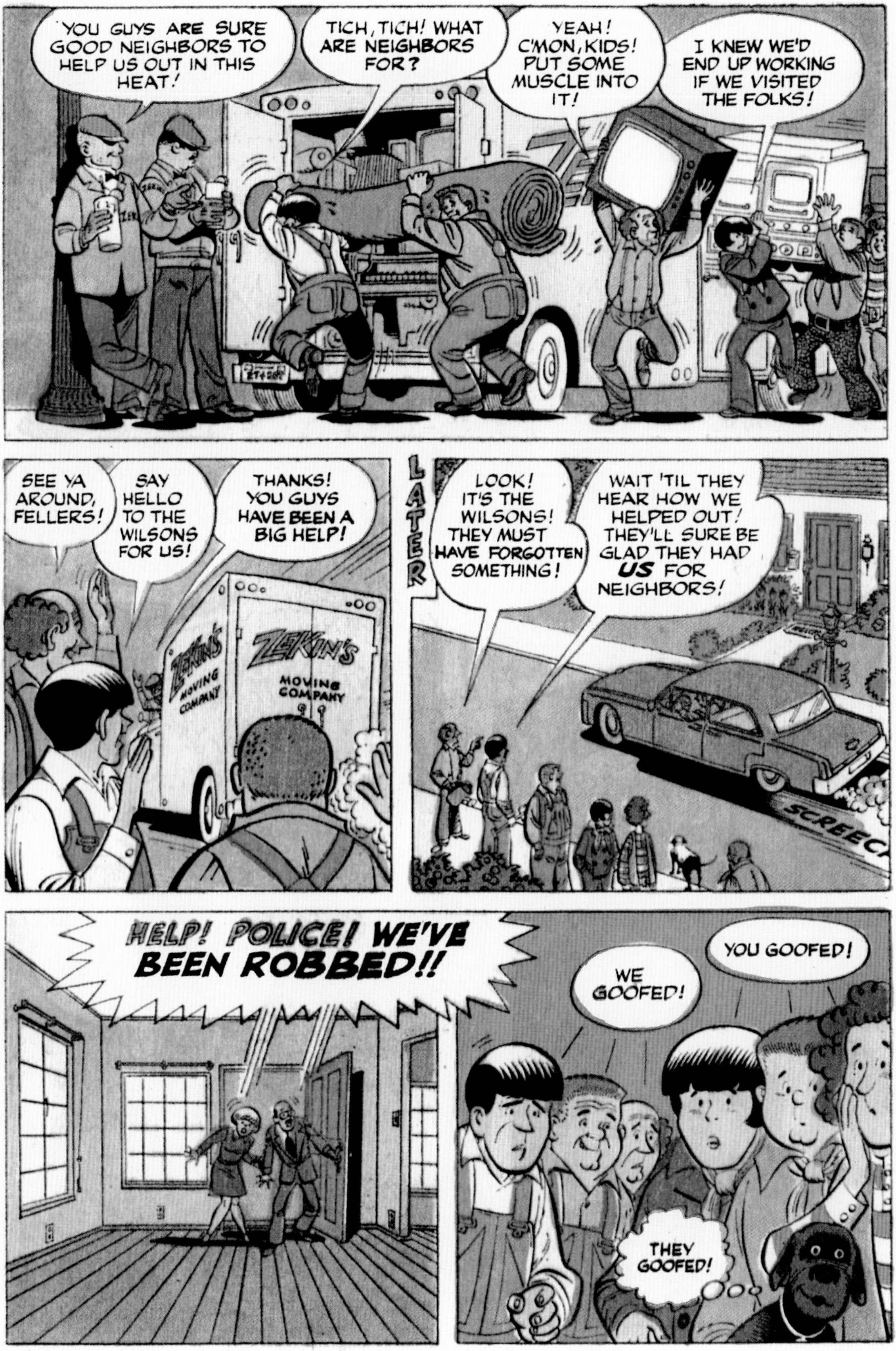
YOU GUYS ARE SURE GOOD NEIGHBORS TO HELP US OUT IN THIS HEAT!
TICH, TICH! WHAT ARE NEIGHBORS FOR?
YEAH! C'MON, KIDS! PUT SOME MUSCLE INTO IT!
I KNEW WE'D END UP WORKING IF WE VISITED THE FOLKS!
SEE YA AROUND, FELLERS!
SAY HELLO TO THE WILSONS FOR US!
THANKS! YOU GUYS HAVE BEEN A BIG HELP!
ZEKIN'S MOVING COMPANY
LATER
LOOK! IT'S THE WILSONS! THEY MUST HAVE FORGOTTEN SOMETHING!
WAIT 'TIL THEY HEAR HOW WE HELPED OUT! THEY'LL SURE BE GLAD THEY HAD US FOR NEIGHBORS!
SCREECH
HELP! POLICE! WE'VE BEEN ROBBED!!
WE GOOFED!
YOU GOOFED!
THEY GOOFED!

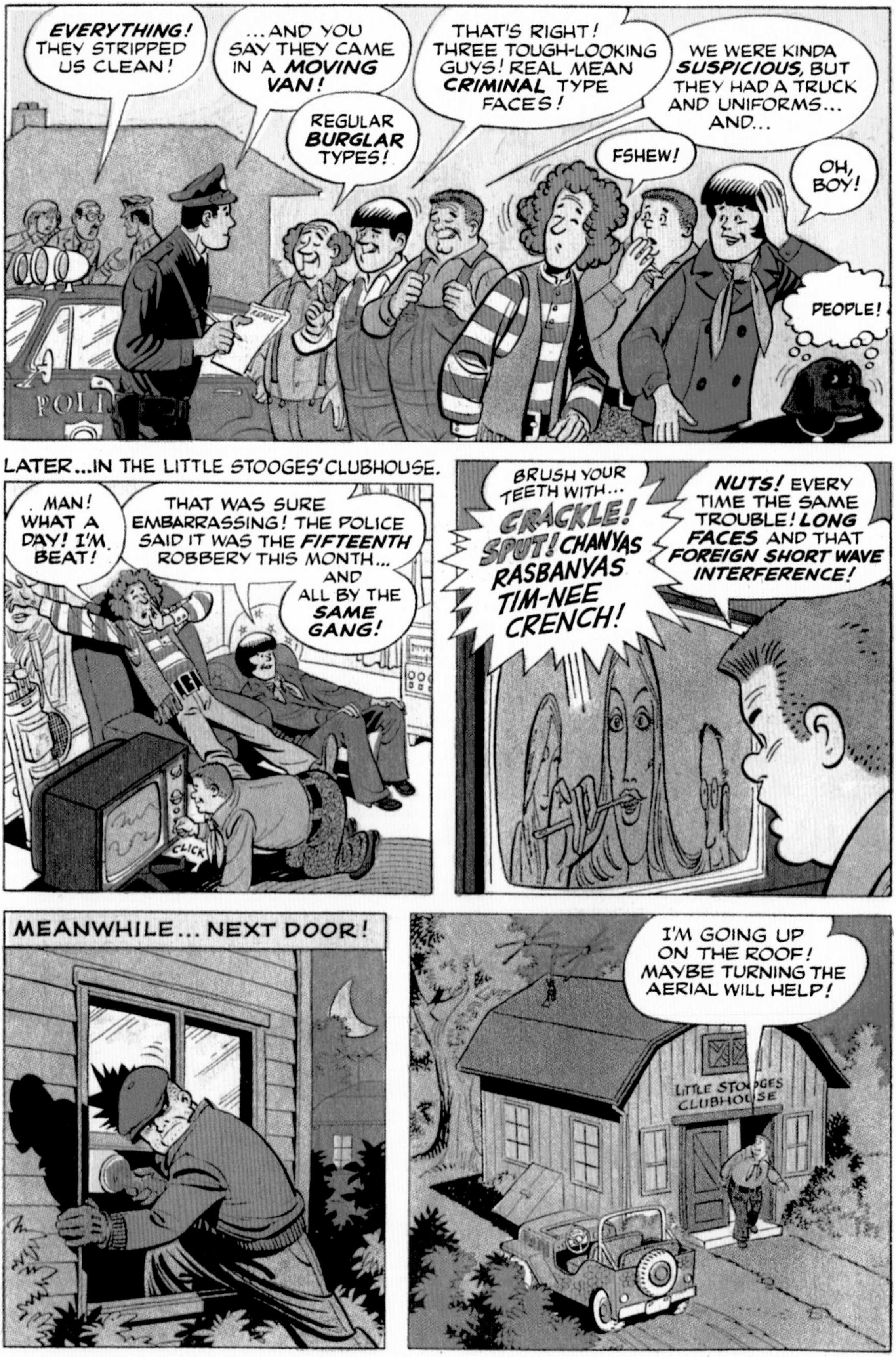

EVERYTHING! THEY STRIPPED US CLEAN!
...AND YOU SAY THEY CAME IN A MOVING VAN!
REGULAR BURGLAR TYPES!
THAT'S RIGHT! THREE TOUGH-LOOKING GUYS! REAL MEAN CRIMINAL TYPE FACES!
WE WERE KINDA SUSPICIOUS, BUT THEY HAD A TRUCK AND UNIFORMS... AND...
FSHEW!
OH, BOY!
PEOPLE!
REPORT
POLI
LATER...IN THE LITTLE STOOGES' CLUBHOUSE.
MAN! WHAT A DAY! I'M BEAT!
THAT WAS SURE EMBARRASSING! THE POLICE SAID IT WAS THE FIFTEENTH ROBBERY THIS MONTH... AND ALL BY THE SAME GANG!
CLICK
BRUSH YOUR TEETH WITH... CRACKLE! SPUT! CHANYAS RASBANYAS TIM-NEE CRENCH!
NUTS! EVERY TIME THE SAME TROUBLE! LONG FACES AND THAT FOREIGN SHORT WAVE INTERFERENCE!
MEANWHILE... NEXT DOOR!
I'M GOING UP ON THE ROOF! MAYBE TURNING THE AERIAL WILL HELP!
LITTLE STOOGES CLUBHOUSE

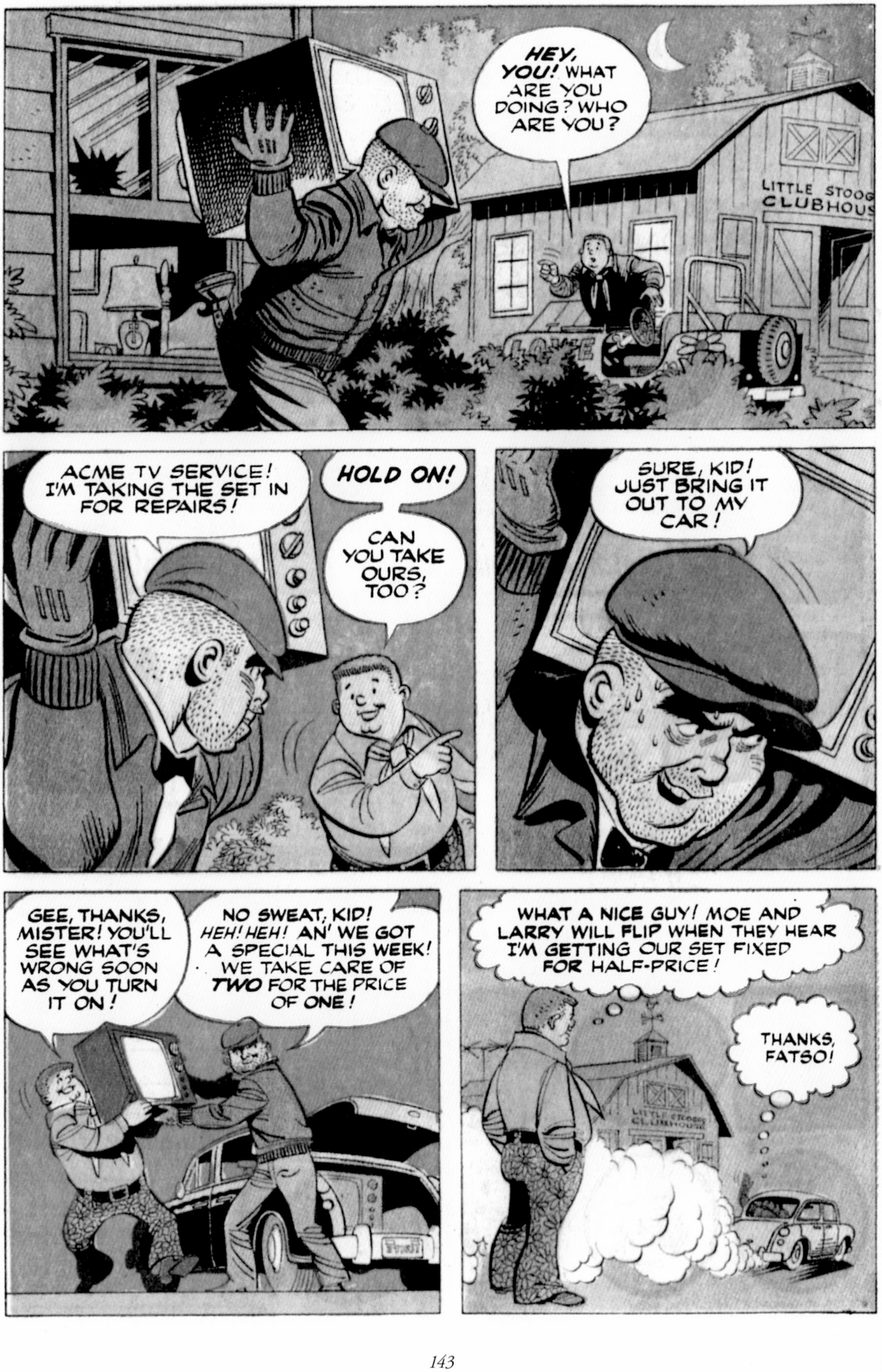
HEY, YOU! WHAT ARE YOU DOING? WHO ARE YOU?
LITTLE STOOG CLUBHOUS
ACME TV SERVICE! I'M TAKING THE SET IN FOR REPAIRS!
HOLD ON!
CAN YOU TAKE OURS, TOO?
SURE, KID! JUST BRING IT OUT TO MY CAR!
GEE, THANKS, MISTER! YOU'LL SEE WHAT'S WRONG SOON AS YOU TURN IT ON!
NO SWEAT, KID! HEH! HEH! AN' WE GOT A SPECIAL THIS WEEK! WE TAKE CARE OF TWO FOR THE PRICE OF ONE!
WHAT A NICE GUY! MOE AND LARRY WILL FLIP WHEN THEY HEAR I'M GETTING OUR SET FIXED FOR HALF-PRICE!
THANKS, FATSO!

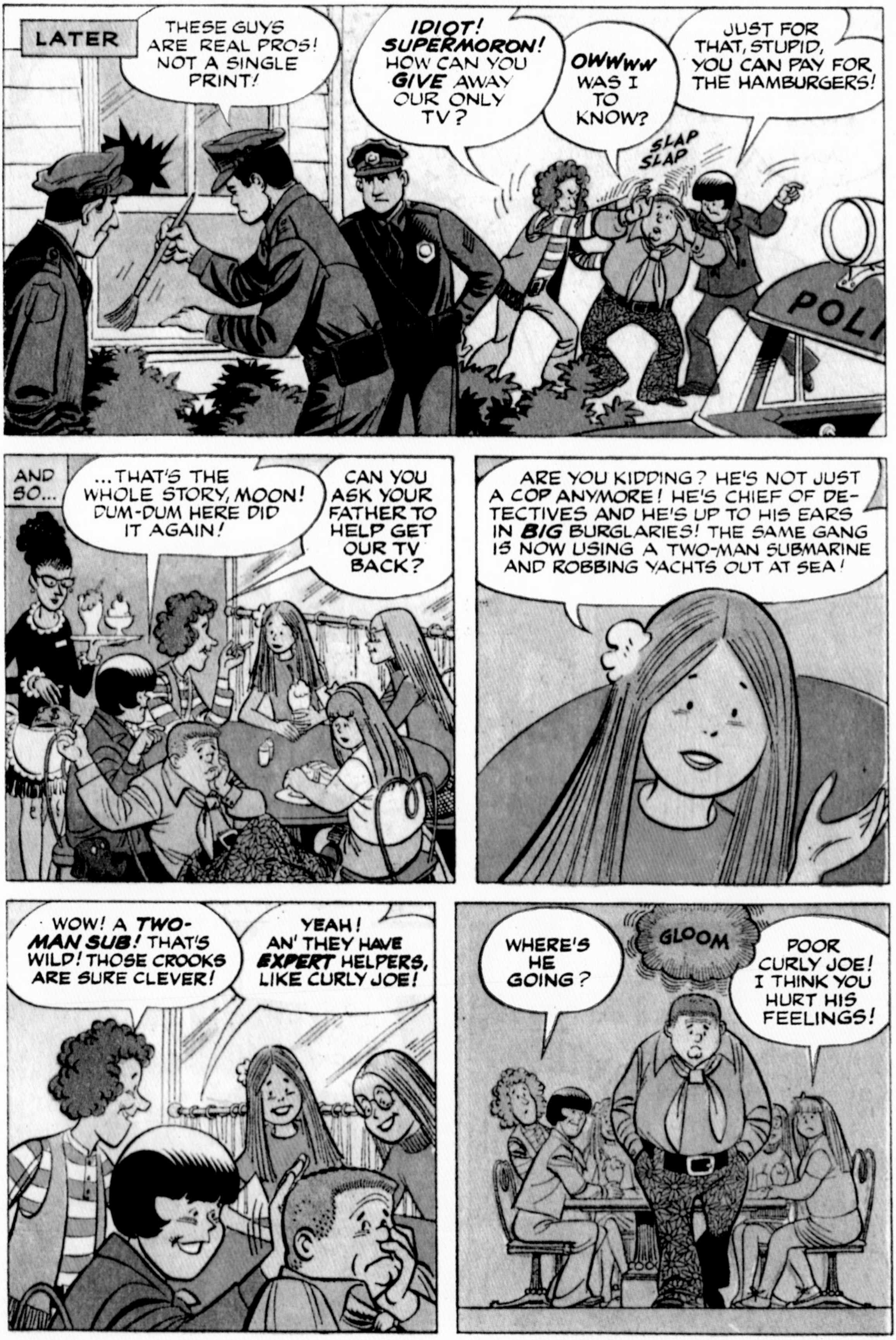
LATER
THESE GUYS ARE REAL PROS! NOT A SINGLE PRINT!
IDIOT! SUPERMORON! HOW CAN YOU GIVE AWAY OUR ONLY TV?
OWWWW WAS I TO KNOW?
SLAP SLAP
JUST FOR THAT, STUPID, YOU CAN PAY FOR THE HAMBURGERS!
POLI
AND SO...
...THAT'S THE WHOLE STORY, MOON! DUM-DUM HERE DID IT AGAIN!
CAN YOU ASK YOUR FATHER TO HELP GET OUR TV BACK?
ARE YOU KIDDING? HE'S NOT JUST A COP ANYMORE! HE'S CHIEF OF DETECTIVES AND HE'S UP TO HIS EARS IN BIG BURGLARIES! THE SAME GANG IS NOW USING A TWO-MAN SUBMARINE AND ROBBING YACHTS OUT AT SEA!
WOW! A TWO-MAN SUB! THAT'S WILD! THOSE CROOKS ARE SURE CLEVER!
YEAH! AN' THEY HAVE EXPERT HELPERS, LIKE CURLY JOE!
WHERE'S HE GOING?
GLOOM
POOR CURLY JOE! I THINK YOU HURT HIS FEELINGS!

POOR CURLY JOE LEFT HIS PALS, DETERMINED TO REDEEM HIMSELF, AND WALKED STRAIGHT INTO THE SLIPPERY HANDS OF **BENEDICT BOGUS**... THE TRICKIEST, SHARPEST CON-KID IN TOWN!

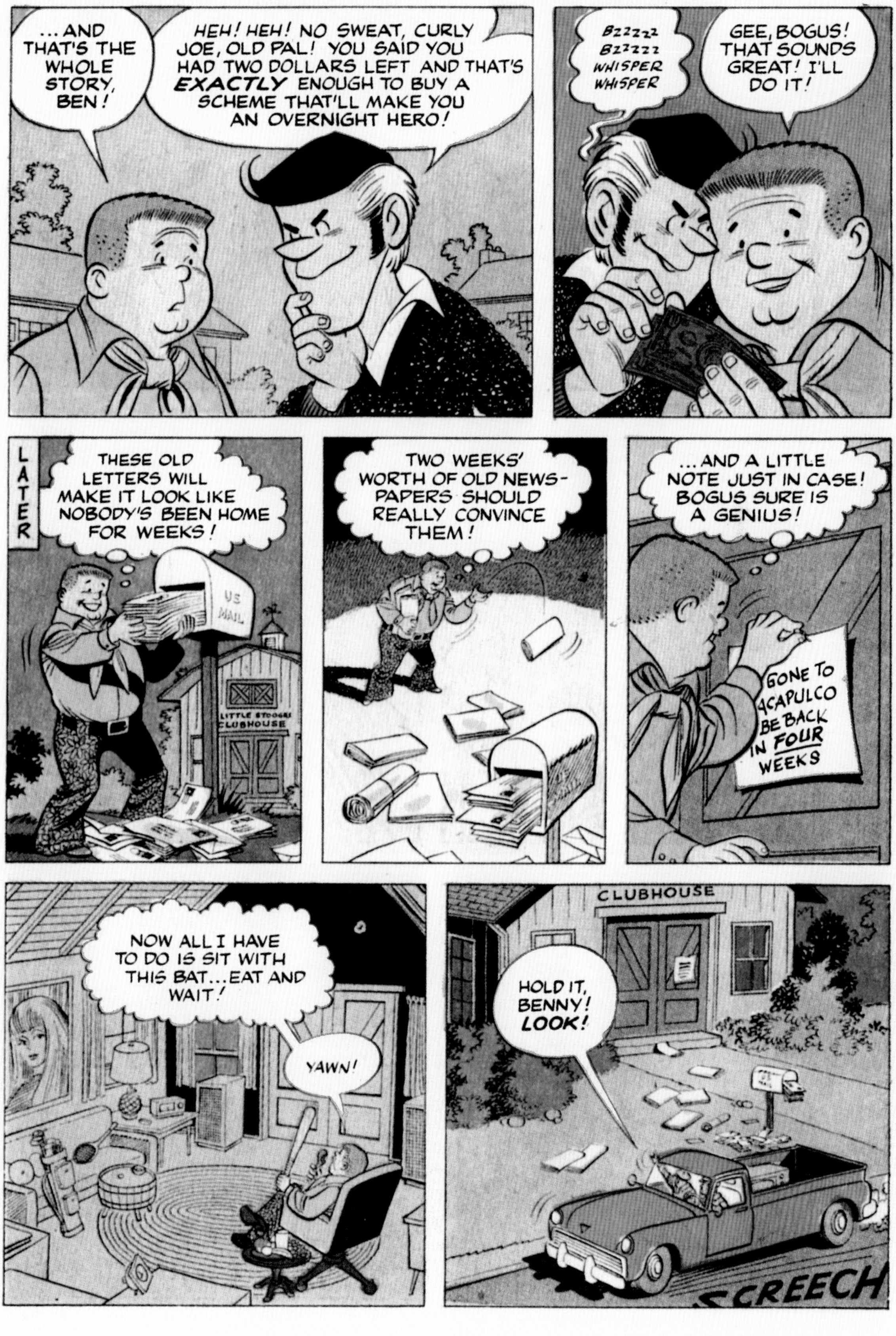
...AND THAT'S THE WHOLE STORY, BEN!
HEH! HEH! NO SWEAT, CURLY JOE, OLD PAL! YOU SAID YOU HAD TWO DOLLARS LEFT AND THAT'S EXACTLY ENOUGH TO BUY A SCHEME THAT'LL MAKE YOU AN OVERNIGHT HERO!
BZZZZZ BZZZZZ WHISPER WHISPER
GEE, BOGUS! THAT SOUNDS GREAT! I'LL DO IT!
LATER
THESE OLD LETTERS WILL MAKE IT LOOK LIKE NOBODY'S BEEN HOME FOR WEEKS!
US MAIL
LITTLE STOOGES CLUBHOUSE
TWO WEEKS' WORTH OF OLD NEWS-PAPERS SHOULD REALLY CONVINCE THEM!
...AND A LITTLE NOTE JUST IN CASE! BOGUS SURE IS A GENIUS!
GONE TO ACAPULCO BE BACK IN FOUR WEEKS
NOW ALL I HAVE TO DO IS SIT WITH THIS BAT...EAT AND WAIT!
YAWN!
CLUBHOUSE
HOLD IT, BENNY! LOOK!
SCREECH

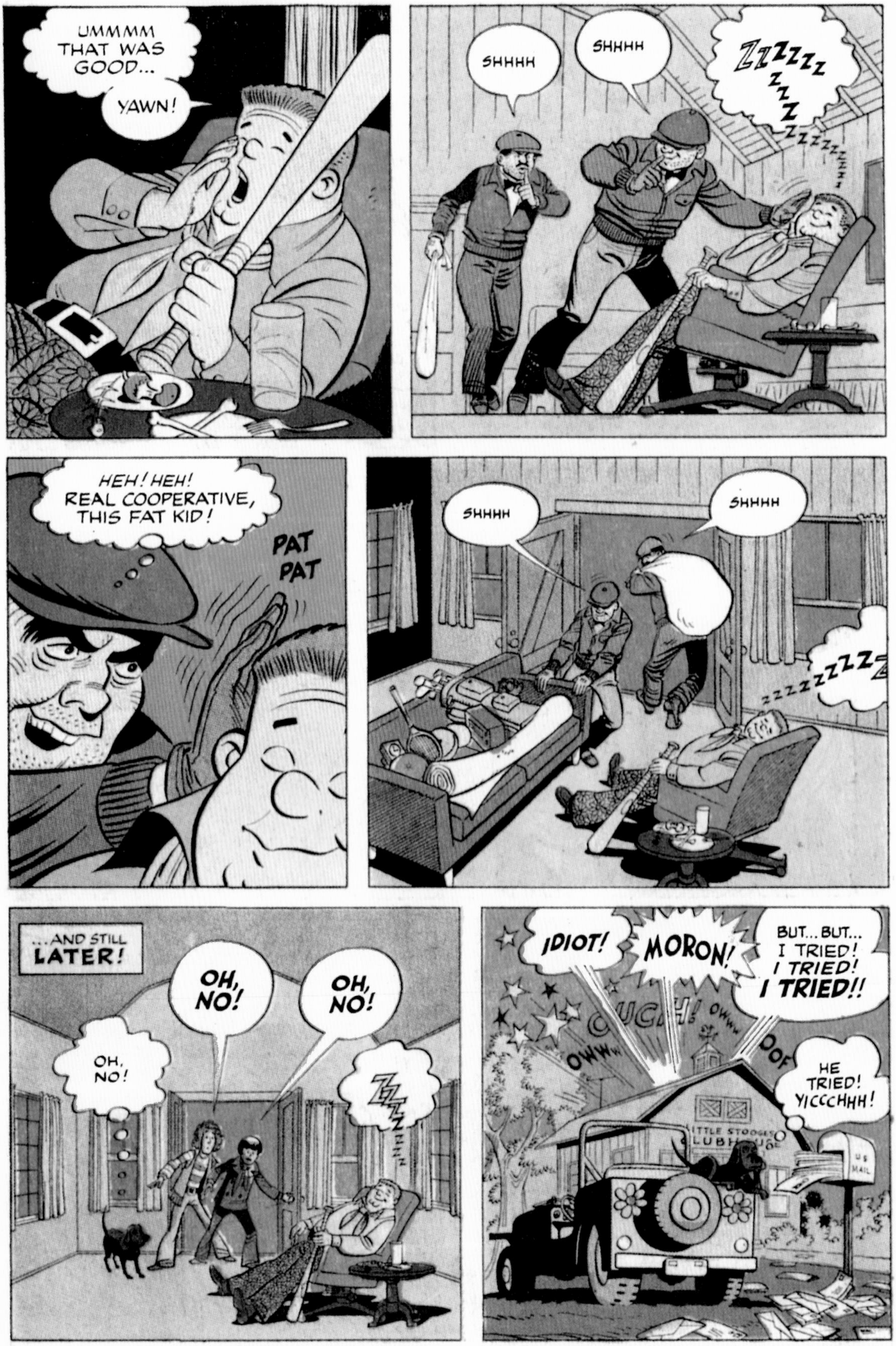
UMMMM THAT WAS GOOD...
YAWN!
SHHHH
SHHHH
ZZZZZZ
HEH! HEH! REAL COOPERATIVE, THIS FAT KID!
PAT PAT
SHHHH
SHHHH
...AND STILL LATER!
OH, NO!
OH, NO!
OH, NO!
IDIOT!
MORON!
BUT... BUT... I TRIED! I TRIED! I TRIED!!
OWWW
OOF
HE TRIED! YICCCHHH!
US MAIL

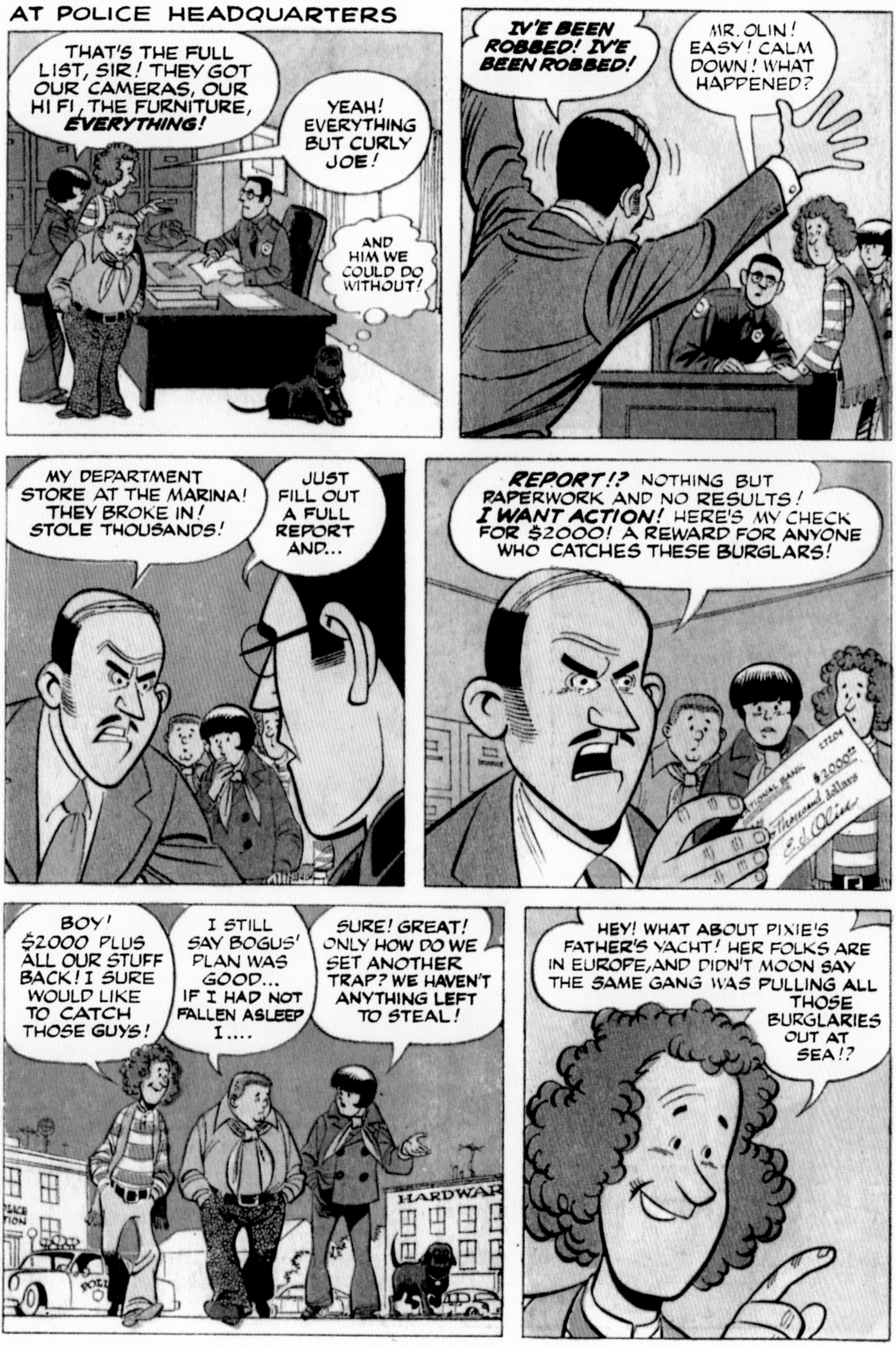
AT POLICE HEADQUARTERS
THAT'S THE FULL LIST, SIR! THEY GOT OUR CAMERAS, OUR HI FI, THE FURNITURE, EVERYTHING!
YEAH! EVERYTHING BUT CURLY JOE!
AND HIM WE COULD DO WITHOUT!
IV'E BEEN ROBBED! IV'E BEEN ROBBED!
MR. OLIN! EASY! CALM DOWN! WHAT HAPPENED?
MY DEPARTMENT STORE AT THE MARINA! THEY BROKE IN! STOLE THOUSANDS!
JUST FILL OUT A FULL REPORT AND...
REPORT!? NOTHING BUT PAPERWORK AND NO RESULTS! I WANT ACTION! HERE'S MY CHECK FOR $2000! A REWARD FOR ANYONE WHO CATCHES THESE BURGLARS!
BOY! $2000 PLUS ALL OUR STUFF BACK! I SURE WOULD LIKE TO CATCH THOSE GUYS!
I STILL SAY BOGUS' PLAN WAS GOOD... IF I HAD NOT FALLEN ASLEEP I....
SURE! GREAT! ONLY HOW DO WE SET ANOTHER TRAP? WE HAVEN'T ANYTHING LEFT TO STEAL!
HARDWAR
HEY! WHAT ABOUT PIXIE'S FATHER'S YACHT! HER FOLKS ARE IN EUROPE, AND DIDN'T MOON SAY THE SAME GANG WAS PULLING ALL THOSE BURGLARIES OUT AT SEA!?

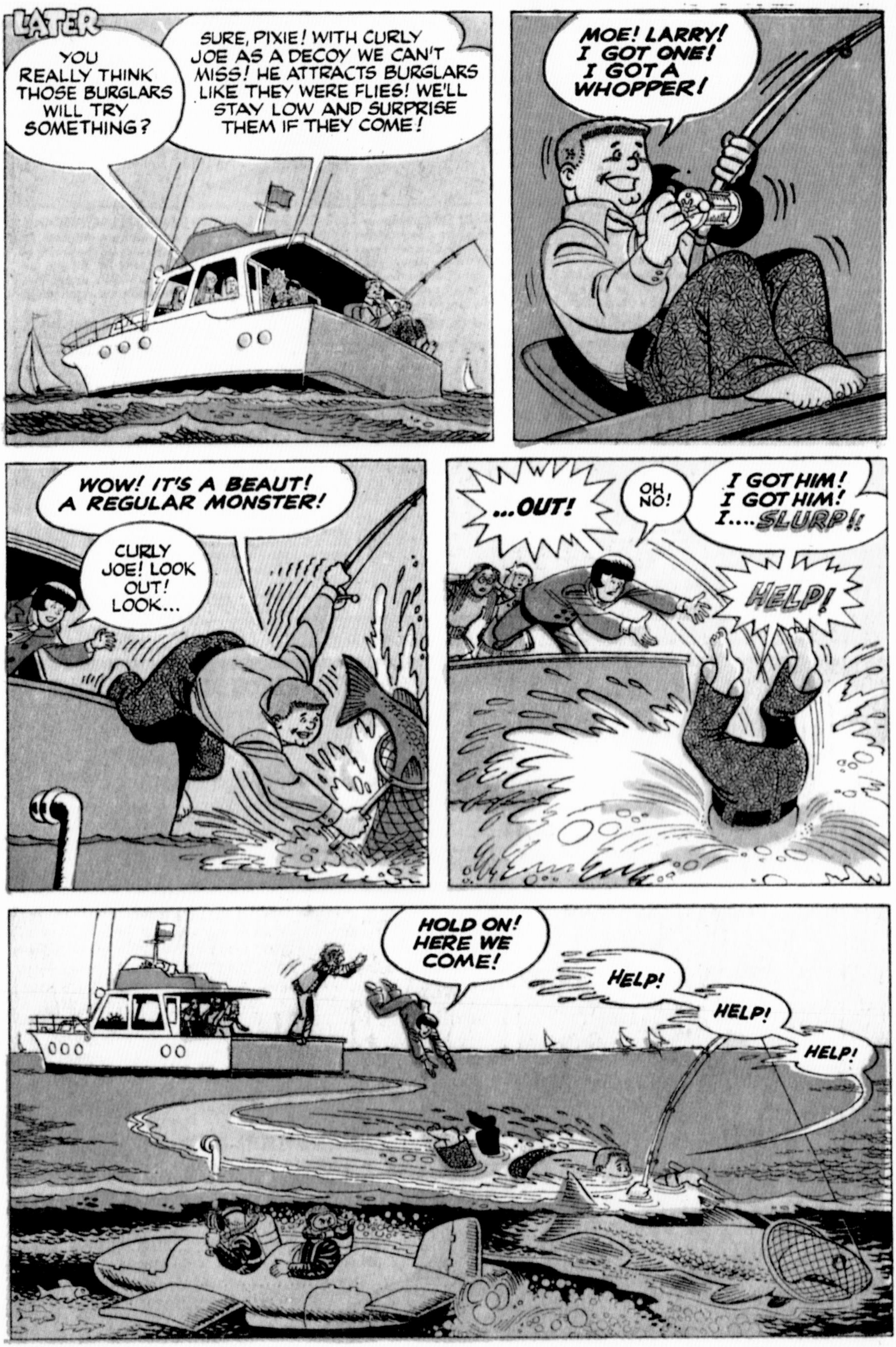
LATER
YOU REALLY THINK THOSE BURGLARS WILL TRY SOMETHING?
SURE, PIXIE! WITH CURLY JOE AS A DECOY WE CAN'T MISS! HE ATTRACTS BURGLARS LIKE THEY WERE FLIES! WE'LL STAY LOW AND SURPRISE THEM IF THEY COME!
MOE! LARRY! I GOT ONE! I GOT A WHOPPER!
WOW! IT'S A BEAUT! A REGULAR MONSTER!
CURLY JOE! LOOK OUT! LOOK...
...OUT!
OH NO!
I GOT HIM! I GOT HIM! I.... SLURP!!
HELP!
HOLD ON! HERE WE COME!
HELP!
HELP!
HELP!

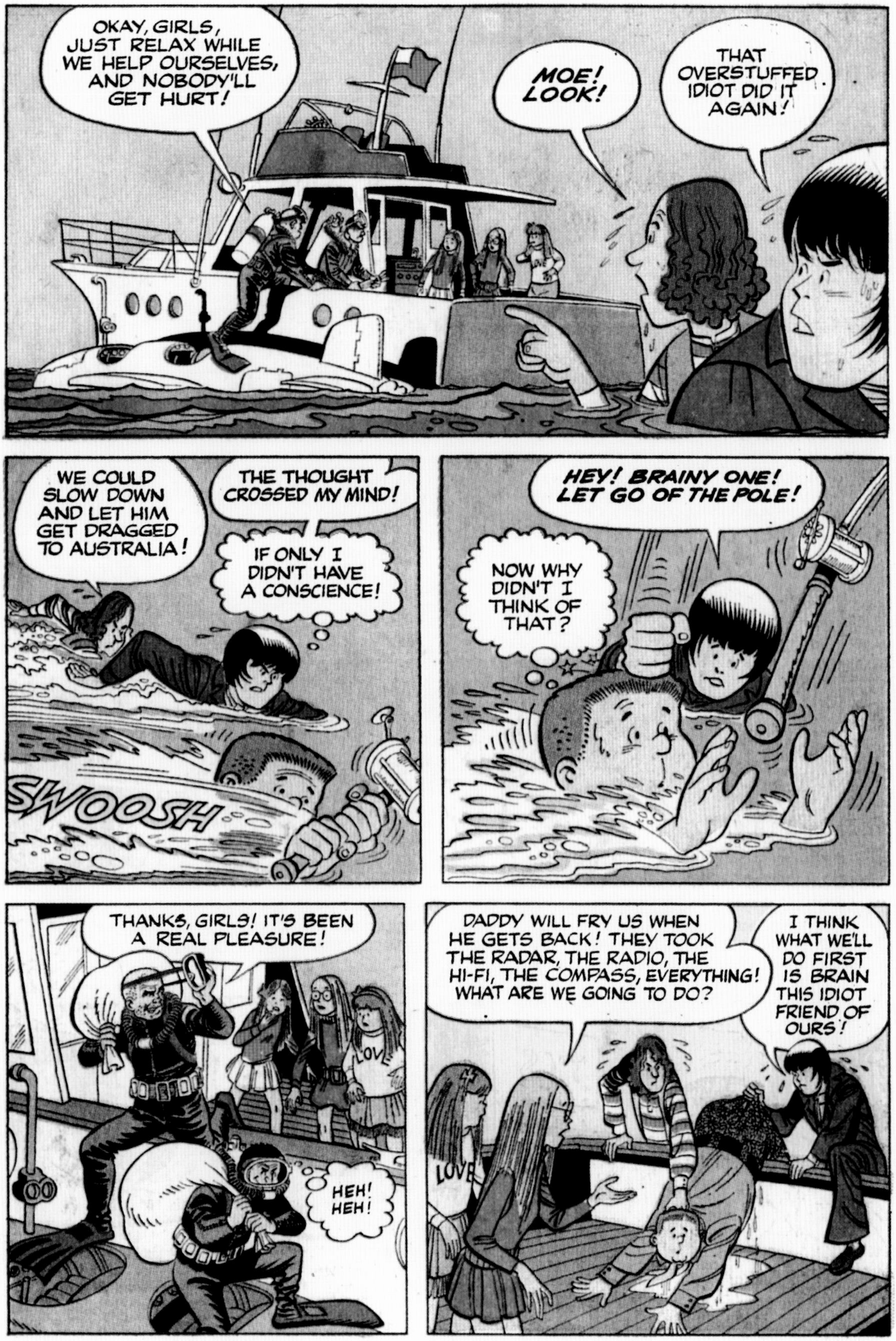
OKAY, GIRLS, JUST RELAX WHILE WE HELP OURSELVES, AND NOBODY'LL GET HURT!
MOE! LOOK!
THAT OVERSTUFFED IDIOT DID IT AGAIN!
WE COULD SLOW DOWN AND LET HIM GET DRAGGED TO AUSTRALIA!
THE THOUGHT CROSSED MY MIND!
IF ONLY I DIDN'T HAVE A CONSCIENCE!
SWOOSH
HEY! BRAINY ONE! LET GO OF THE POLE!
NOW WHY DIDN'T I THINK OF THAT?
THANKS, GIRLS! IT'S BEEN A REAL PLEASURE!
HEH! HEH!
LOVE
DADDY WILL FRY US WHEN HE GETS BACK! THEY TOOK THE RADAR, THE RADIO, THE HI-FI, THE COMPASS, EVERYTHING! WHAT ARE WE GOING TO DO?
I THINK WHAT WE'LL DO FIRST IS BRAIN THIS IDIOT FRIEND OF OURS!
LOVE

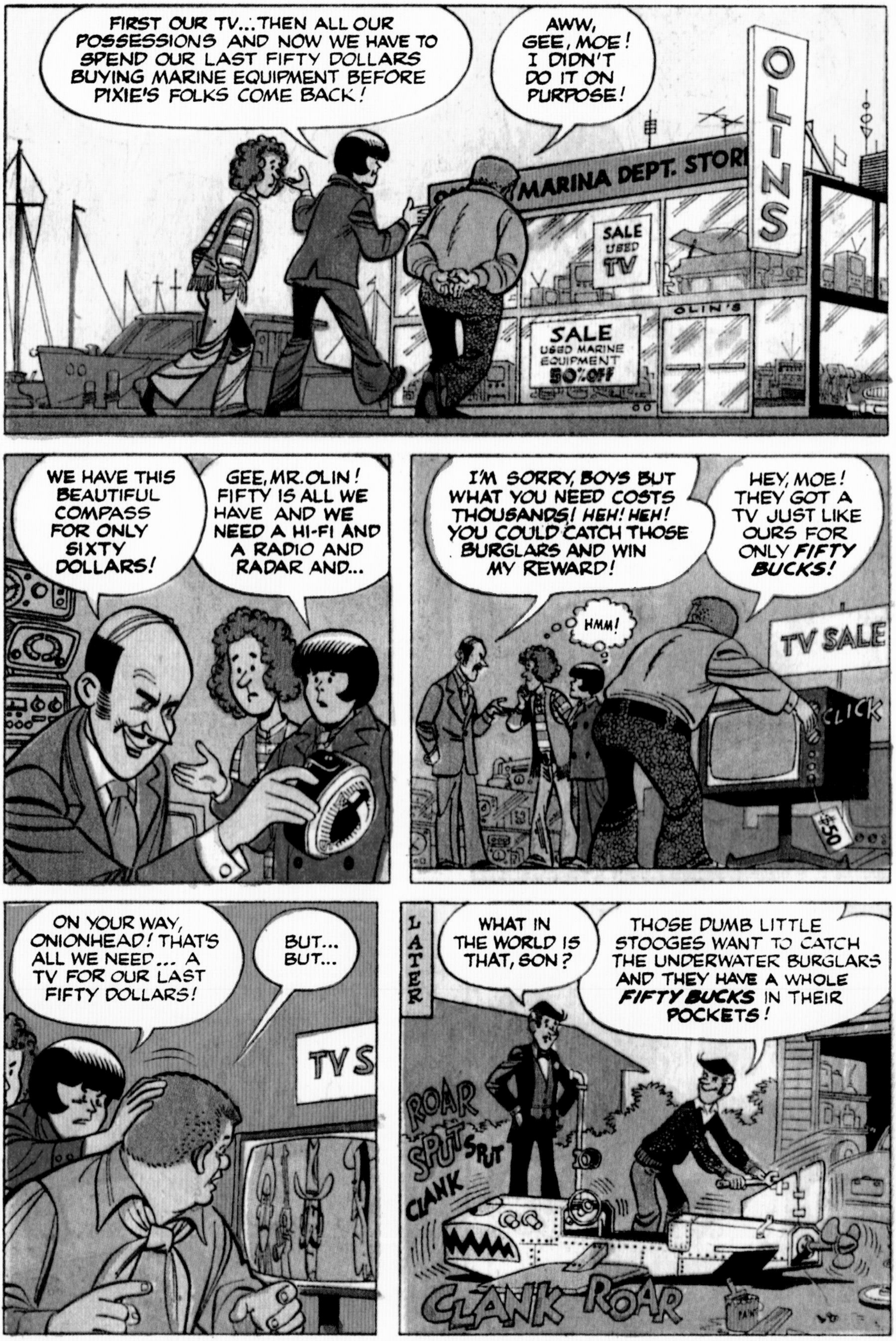
FIRST OUR TV... THEN ALL OUR POSSESSIONS AND NOW WE HAVE TO SPEND OUR LAST FIFTY DOLLARS BUYING MARINE EQUIPMENT BEFORE PIXIE'S FOLKS COME BACK!
AWW, GEE, MOE! I DIDN'T DO IT ON PURPOSE!
OLINS
MARINA DEPT. STOR
SALE USED TV
OLIN'S
SALE USED MARINE EQUIPMENT 50% OFF
WE HAVE THIS BEAUTIFUL COMPASS FOR ONLY SIXTY DOLLARS!
GEE, MR. OLIN! FIFTY IS ALL WE HAVE AND WE NEED A HI-FI AND A RADIO AND RADAR AND...
I'M SORRY, BOYS BUT WHAT YOU NEED COSTS THOUSANDS! HEH! HEH! YOU COULD CATCH THOSE BURGLARS AND WIN MY REWARD!
HEY, MOE! THEY GOT A TV JUST LIKE OURS FOR ONLY FIFTY BUCKS!
HMM!
TV SALE
CLICK
$50
ON YOUR WAY, ONIONHEAD! THAT'S ALL WE NEED... A TV FOR OUR LAST FIFTY DOLLARS!
BUT... BUT...
TV S
LATER
WHAT IN THE WORLD IS THAT, SON?
THOSE DUMB LITTLE STOOGES WANT TO CATCH THE UNDERWATER BURGLARS AND THEY HAVE A WHOLE FIFTY BUCKS IN THEIR POCKETS!
ROAR
SPUT SPUT
CLANK
CLANK ROAR

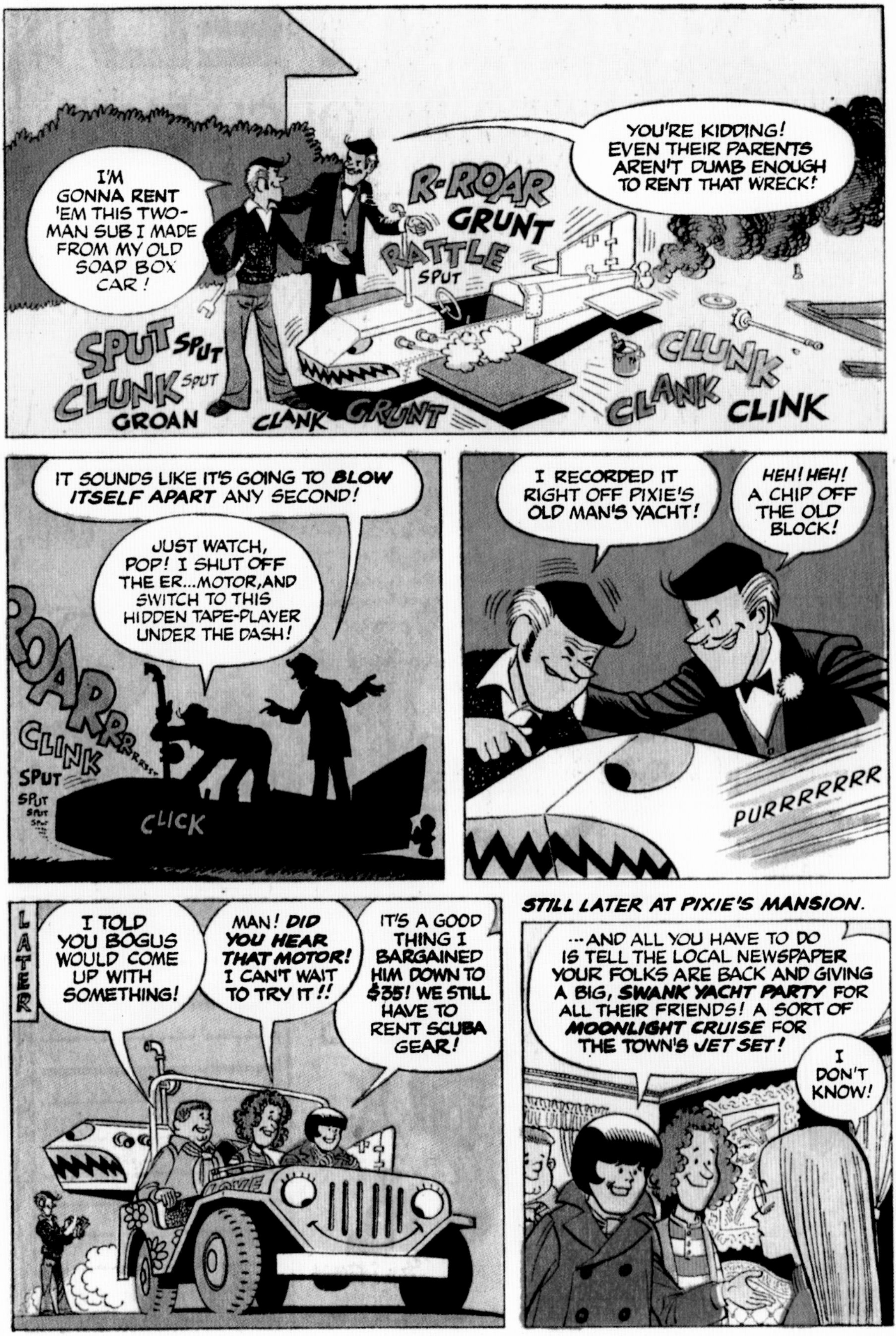
I'M GONNA RENT 'EM THIS TWO-MAN SUB I MADE FROM MY OLD SOAP BOX CAR!
YOU'RE KIDDING! EVEN THEIR PARENTS AREN'T DUMB ENOUGH TO RENT THAT WRECK!
R-ROAR
GRUNT
RATTLE
SPUT
SPUT SPUT
CLUNK SPUT
GROAN
CLANK
GRUNT
CLUNK
CLANK
CLINK
IT SOUNDS LIKE IT'S GOING TO BLOW ITSELF APART ANY SECOND!
JUST WATCH, POP! I SHUT OFF THE ER...MOTOR, AND SWITCH TO THIS HIDDEN TAPE-PLAYER UNDER THE DASH!
ROARRRr
CLINK
SPUT
CLICK
I RECORDED IT RIGHT OFF PIXIE'S OLD MAN'S YACHT!
HEH! HEH! A CHIP OFF THE OLD BLOCK!
PURRRRRRR
LATER
I TOLD YOU BOGUS WOULD COME UP WITH SOMETHING!
MAN! DID YOU HEAR THAT MOTOR! I CAN'T WAIT TO TRY IT!!
IT'S A GOOD THING I BARGAINED HIM DOWN TO $35! WE STILL HAVE TO RENT SCUBA GEAR!
LOVE
STILL LATER AT PIXIE'S MANSION.
...AND ALL YOU HAVE TO DO IS TELL THE LOCAL NEWSPAPER YOUR FOLKS ARE BACK AND GIVING A BIG, SWANK YACHT PARTY FOR ALL THEIR FRIENDS! A SORT OF MOONLIGHT CRUISE FOR THE TOWN'S JET SET!
I DON'T KNOW!

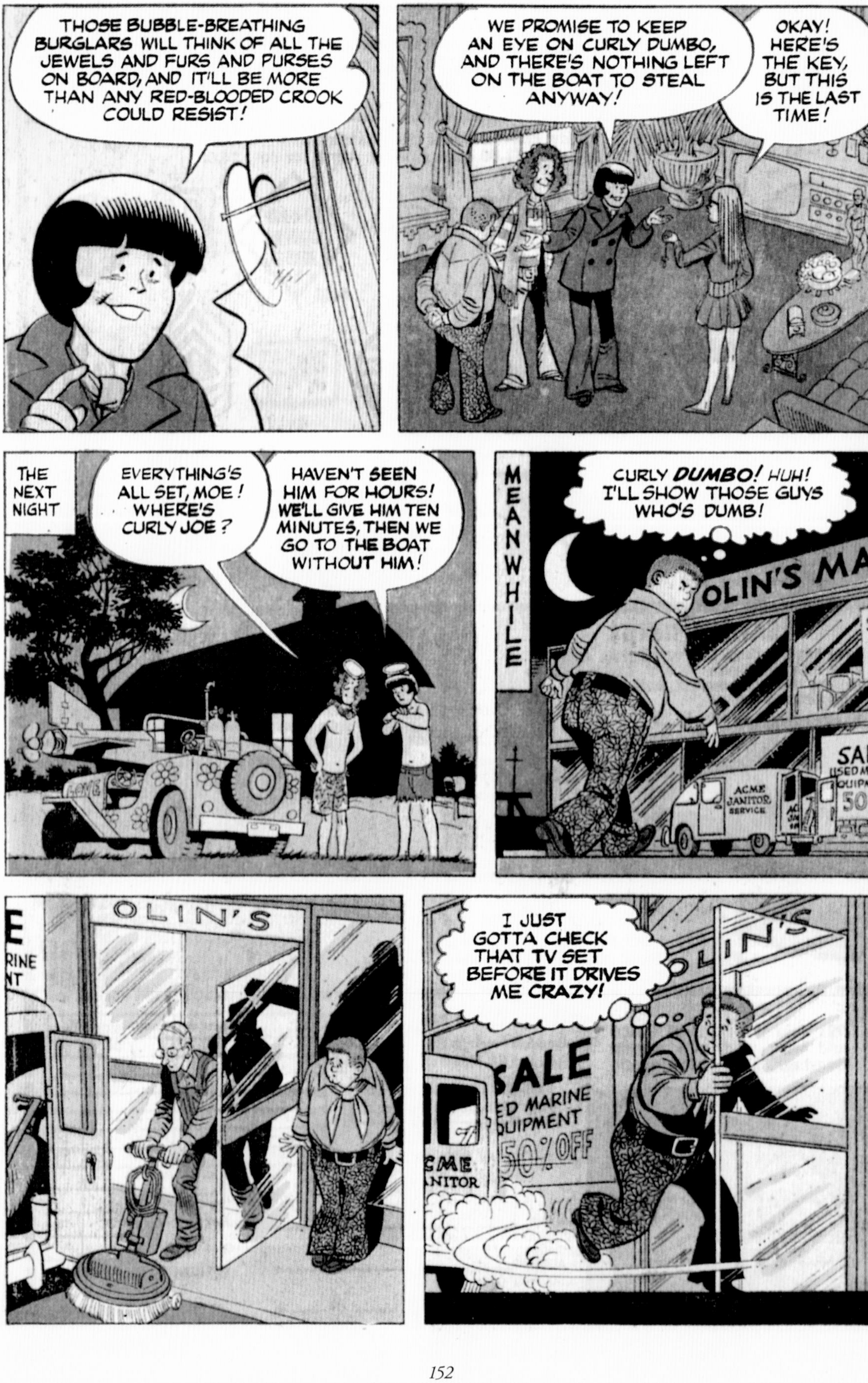
THOSE BUBBLE-BREATHING BURGLARS WILL THINK OF ALL THE JEWELS AND FURS AND PURSES ON BOARD, AND IT'LL BE MORE THAN ANY RED-BLOODED CROOK COULD RESIST!
WE PROMISE TO KEEP AN EYE ON CURLY DUMBO, AND THERE'S NOTHING LEFT ON THE BOAT TO STEAL ANYWAY!
OKAY! HERE'S THE KEY, BUT THIS IS THE LAST TIME!
THE NEXT NIGHT
EVERYTHING'S ALL SET, MOE! WHERE'S CURLY JOE?
HAVEN'T SEEN HIM FOR HOURS! WE'LL GIVE HIM TEN MINUTES, THEN WE GO TO THE BOAT WITHOUT HIM!
MEANWHILE
CURLY DUMBO! HUH! I'LL SHOW THOSE GUYS WHO'S DUMB!
ACME JANITOR SERVICE
OLIN'S
I JUST GOTTA CHECK THAT TV SET BEFORE IT DRIVES ME CRAZY!
SALE
ED MARINE
QUIPMENT
50% OFF

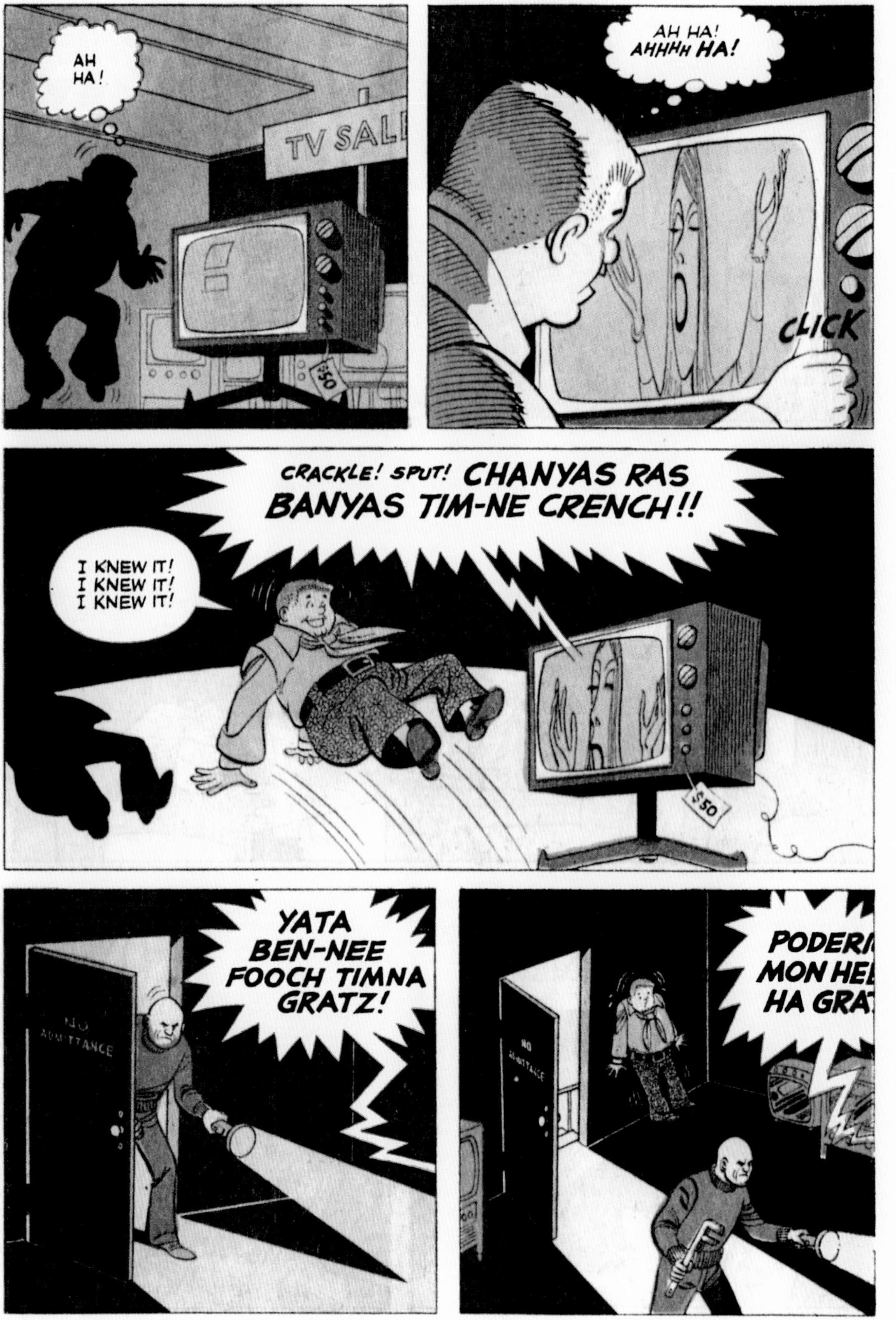
AH HA!
TV SAL
$50
AH HA! AHHHH HA!
CLICK
CRACKLE! SPUT! CHANYAS RAS BANYAS TIM-NE CRENCH!!
I KNEW IT! I KNEW IT! I KNEW IT!
$50
YATA BEN-NEE FOOCH TIMNA GRATZ!
NO ADMITTANCE
NO ADMITTANCE

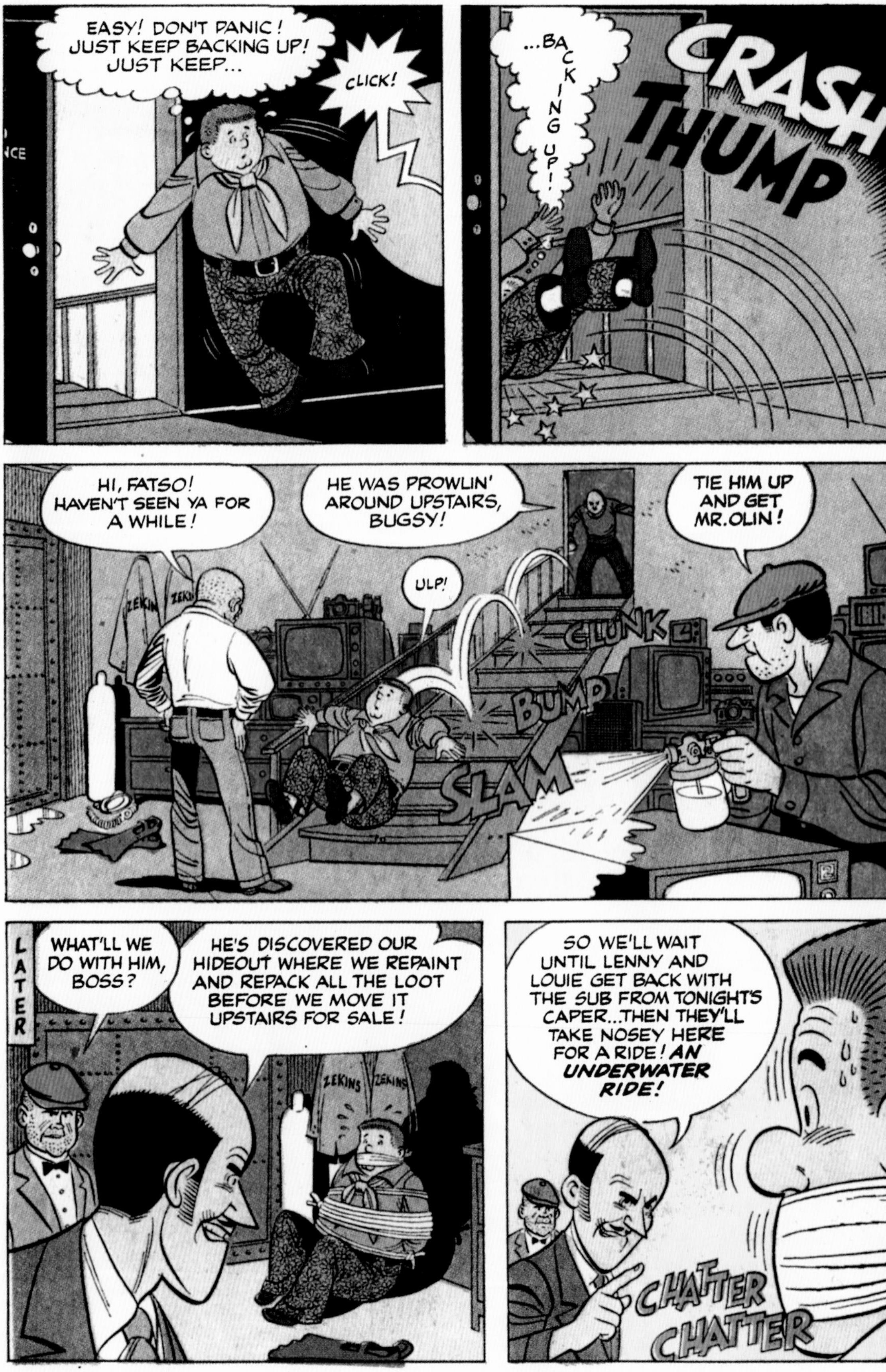
EASY! DON'T PANIC! JUST KEEP BACKING UP! JUST KEEP...
CLICK!
...BACKING UP!
CRASH
THUMP
HI, FATSO! HAVEN'T SEEN YA FOR A WHILE!
HE WAS PROWLIN' AROUND UPSTAIRS, BUGSY!
TIE HIM UP AND GET MR.OLIN!
ULP!
ZEKINS
CLUNK
BUMP
SLAM
LATER
WHAT'LL WE DO WITH HIM, BOSS?
HE'S DISCOVERED OUR HIDEOUT WHERE WE REPAINT AND REPACK ALL THE LOOT BEFORE WE MOVE IT UPSTAIRS FOR SALE!
ZEKINS
SO WE'LL WAIT UNTIL LENNY AND LOUIE GET BACK WITH THE SUB FROM TONIGHT'S CAPER...THEN THEY'LL TAKE NOSEY HERE FOR A RIDE! AN UNDERWATER RIDE!
CHATTER
CHATTER

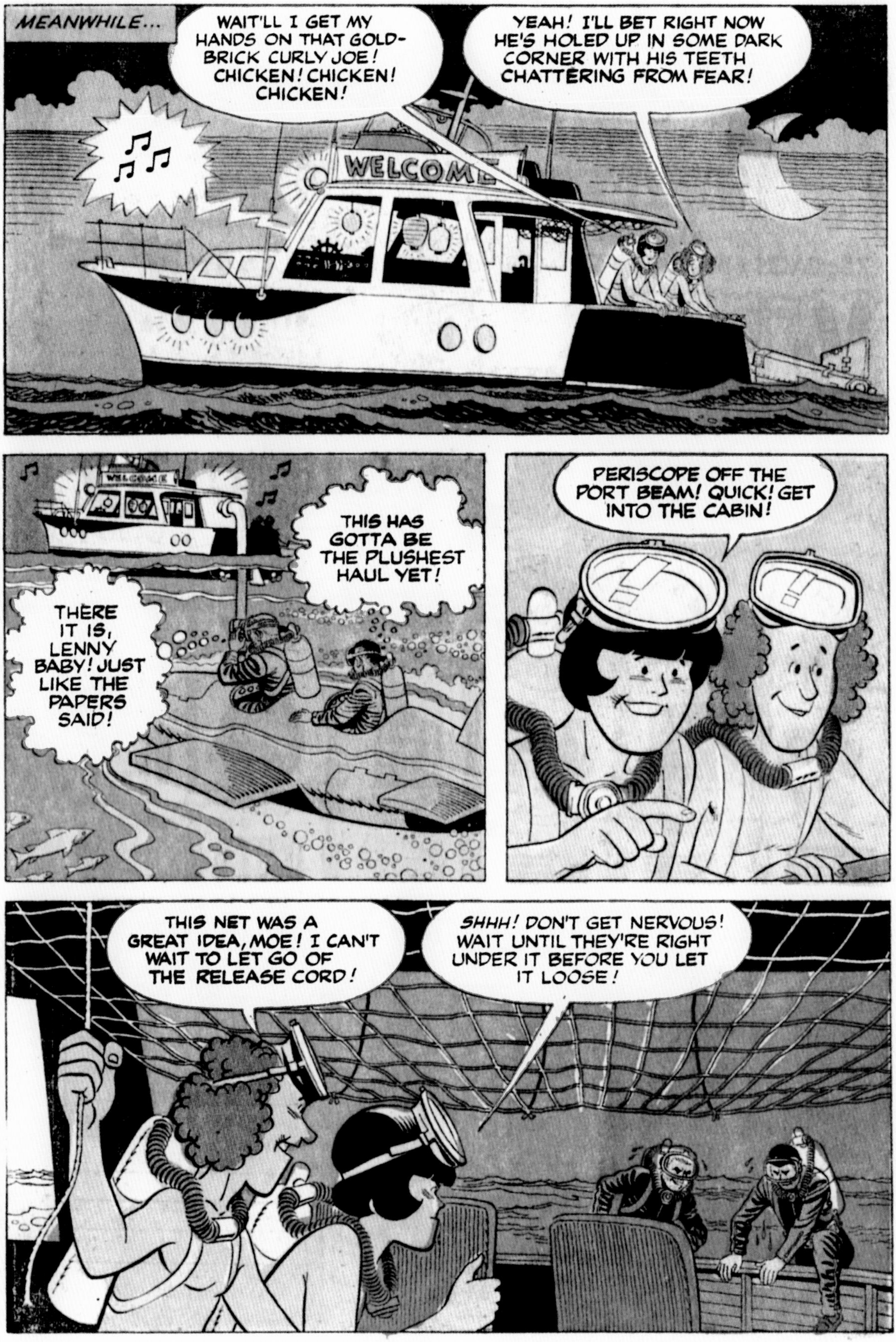
MEANWHILE...
WAIT'LL I GET MY HANDS ON THAT GOLD-BRICK CURLY JOE! CHICKEN! CHICKEN! CHICKEN!
YEAH! I'LL BET RIGHT NOW HE'S HOLED UP IN SOME DARK CORNER WITH HIS TEETH CHATTERING FROM FEAR!
WELCOME
THIS HAS GOTTA BE THE PLUSHEST HAUL YET!
THERE IT IS, LENNY BABY! JUST LIKE THE PAPERS SAID!
PERISCOPE OFF THE PORT BEAM! QUICK! GET INTO THE CABIN!
THIS NET WAS A GREAT IDEA, MOE! I CAN'T WAIT TO LET GO OF THE RELEASE CORD!
SHHH! DON'T GET NERVOUS! WAIT UNTIL THEY'RE RIGHT UNDER IT BEFORE YOU LET IT LOOSE!

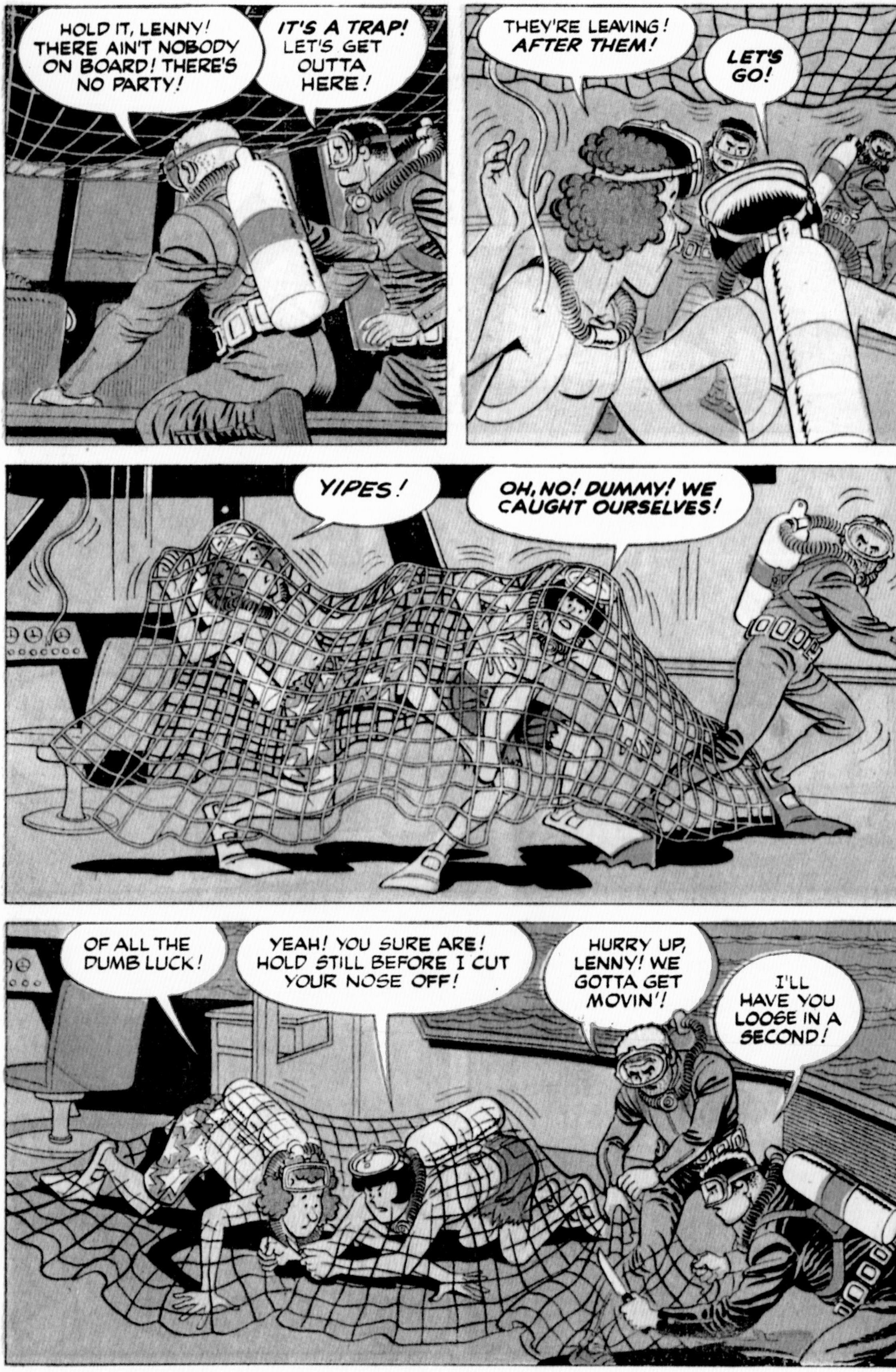
HOLD IT, LENNY! THERE AIN'T NOBODY ON BOARD! THERE'S NO PARTY!
IT'S A TRAP! LET'S GET OUTTA HERE!
THEY'RE LEAVING! AFTER THEM!
LET'S GO!
YIPES!
OH, NO! DUMMY! WE CAUGHT OURSELVES!
OF ALL THE DUMB LUCK!
YEAH! YOU SURE ARE! HOLD STILL BEFORE I CUT YOUR NOSE OFF!
HURRY UP, LENNY! WE GOTTA GET MOVIN'!
I'LL HAVE YOU LOOSE IN A SECOND!

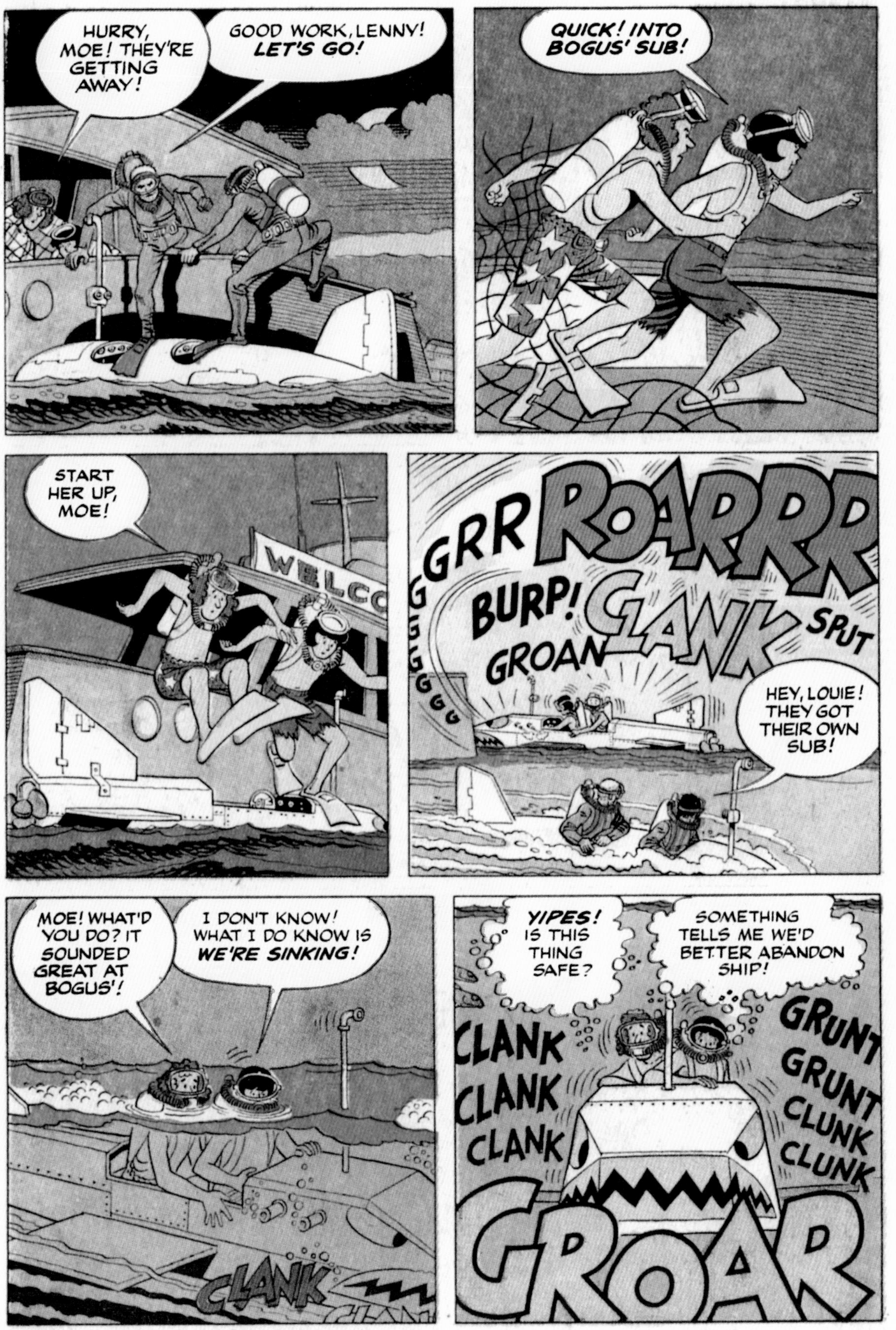
HURRY, MOE! THEY'RE GETTING AWAY!
GOOD WORK, LENNY! LET'S GO!
QUICK! INTO BOGUS' SUB!
START HER UP, MOE!
WELCO
GGGRR ROARRR
BURP!
CLANK
SPUT
GROAN
GGGGGG
HEY, LOUIE! THEY GOT THEIR OWN SUB!
MOE! WHAT'D YOU DO? IT SOUNDED GREAT AT BOGUS'!
I DON'T KNOW! WHAT I DO KNOW IS WE'RE SINKING!
CLANK
YIPES! IS THIS THING SAFE?
SOMETHING TELLS ME WE'D BETTER ABANDON SHIP!
CLANK
CLANK
CLANK
GRUNT
GRUNT
CLUNK
CLUNK
GROAR

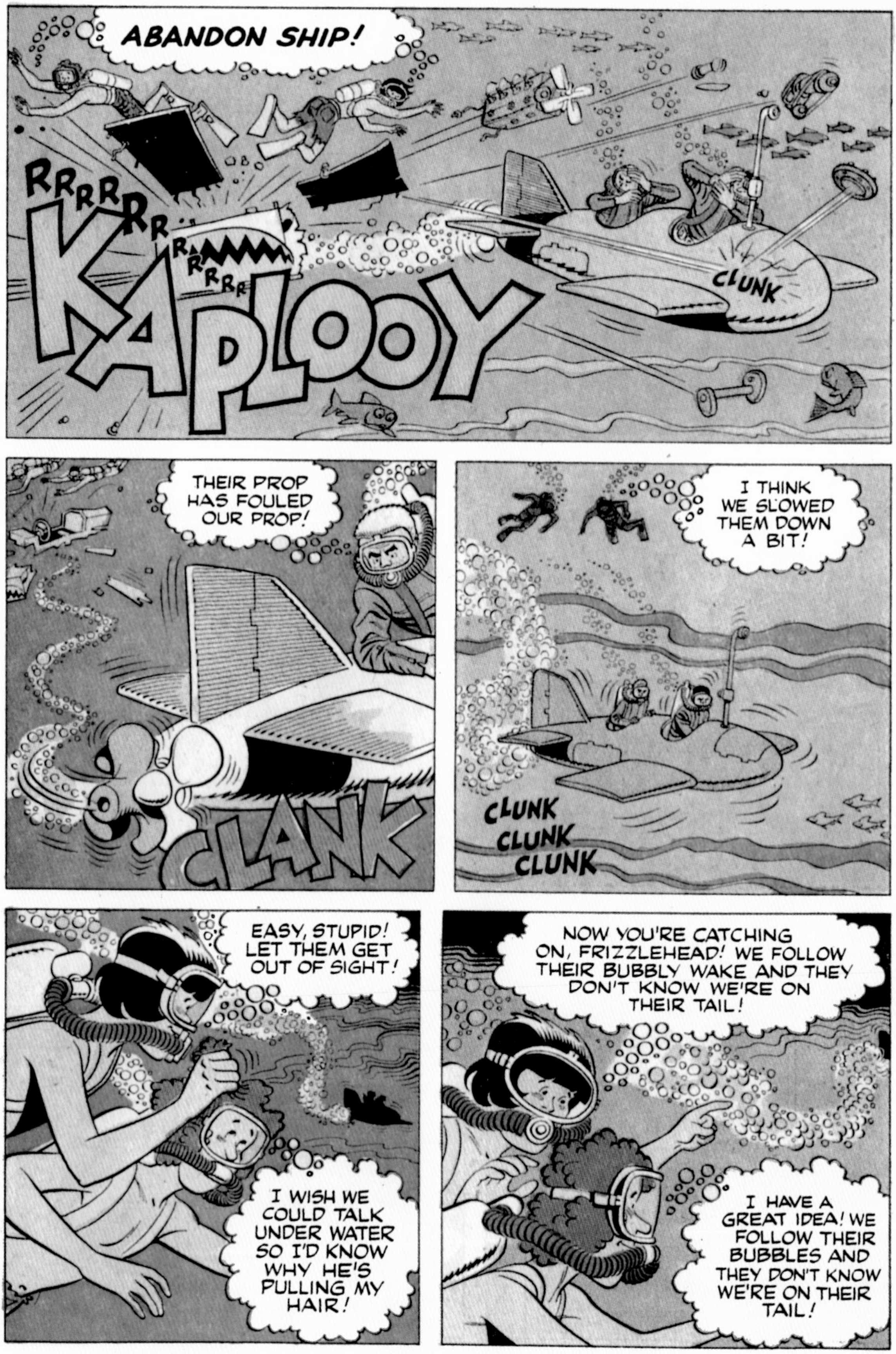
ABANDON SHIP!
KAPLOOY
CLUNK
THEIR PROP HAS FOULED OUR PROP!
CLANK
I THINK WE SLOWED THEM DOWN A BIT!
CLUNK
CLUNK
CLUNK
EASY, STUPID! LET THEM GET OUT OF SIGHT!
I WISH WE COULD TALK UNDER WATER SO I'D KNOW WHY HE'S PULLING MY HAIR!
NOW YOU'RE CATCHING ON, FRIZZLEHEAD! WE FOLLOW THEIR BUBBLY WAKE AND THEY DON'T KNOW WE'RE ON THEIR TAIL!
I HAVE A GREAT IDEA! WE FOLLOW THEIR BUBBLES AND THEY DON'T KNOW WE'RE ON THEIR TAIL!

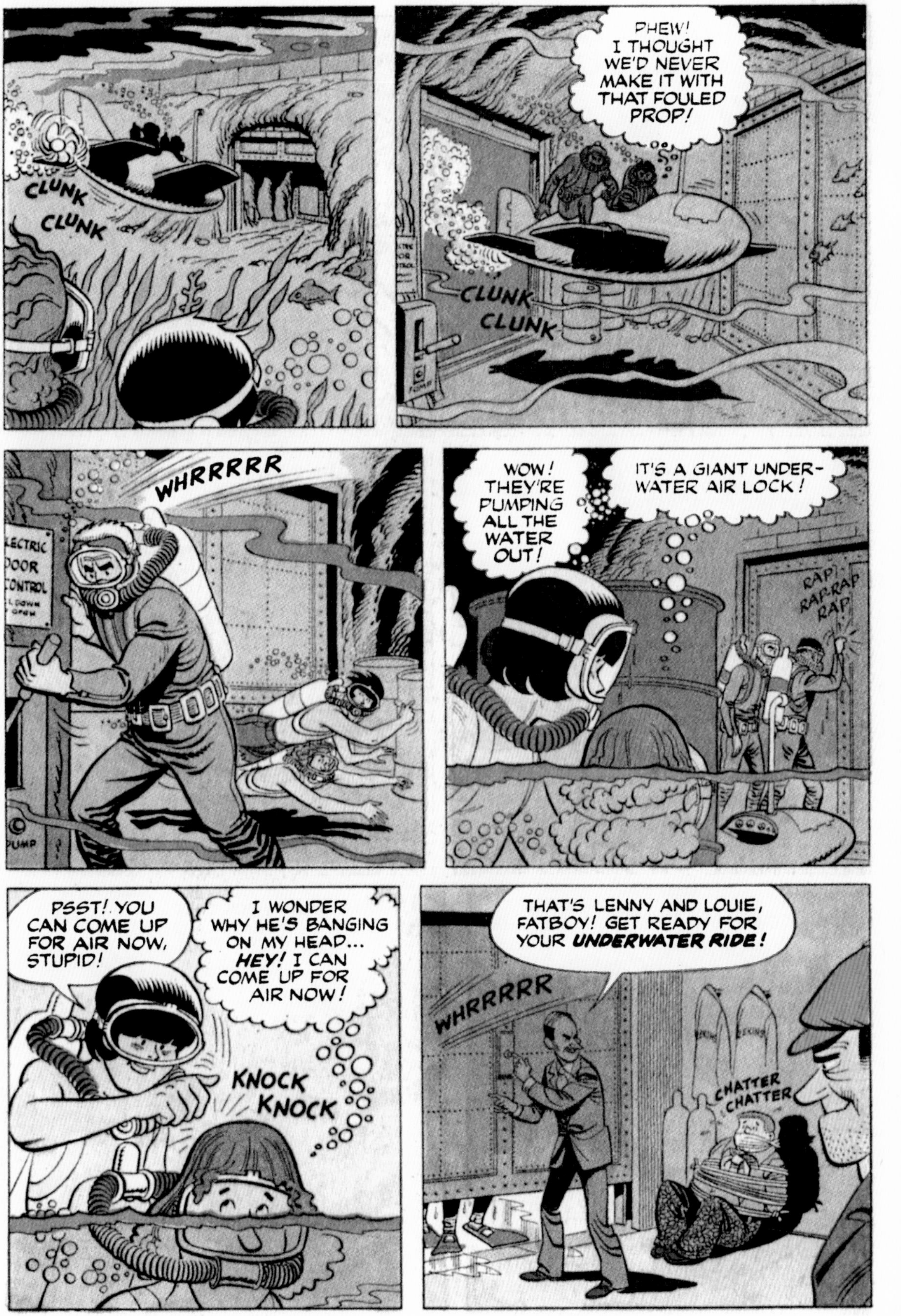
CLUNK
CLUNK
PHEW! I THOUGHT WE'D NEVER MAKE IT WITH THAT FOULED PROP!
CLUNK
CLUNK
WHRRRRR
LECTRIC DOOR CONTROL
PUMP
WOW! THEY'RE PUMPING ALL THE WATER OUT!
IT'S A GIANT UNDER-WATER AIR LOCK!
RAP RAP-RAP RAP
PSST! YOU CAN COME UP FOR AIR NOW, STUPID!
I WONDER WHY HE'S BANGING ON MY HEAD... HEY! I CAN COME UP FOR AIR NOW!
KNOCK KNOCK
THAT'S LENNY AND LOUIE, FATBOY! GET READY FOR YOUR UNDERWATER RIDE!
WHRRRRR
CHATTER CHATTER

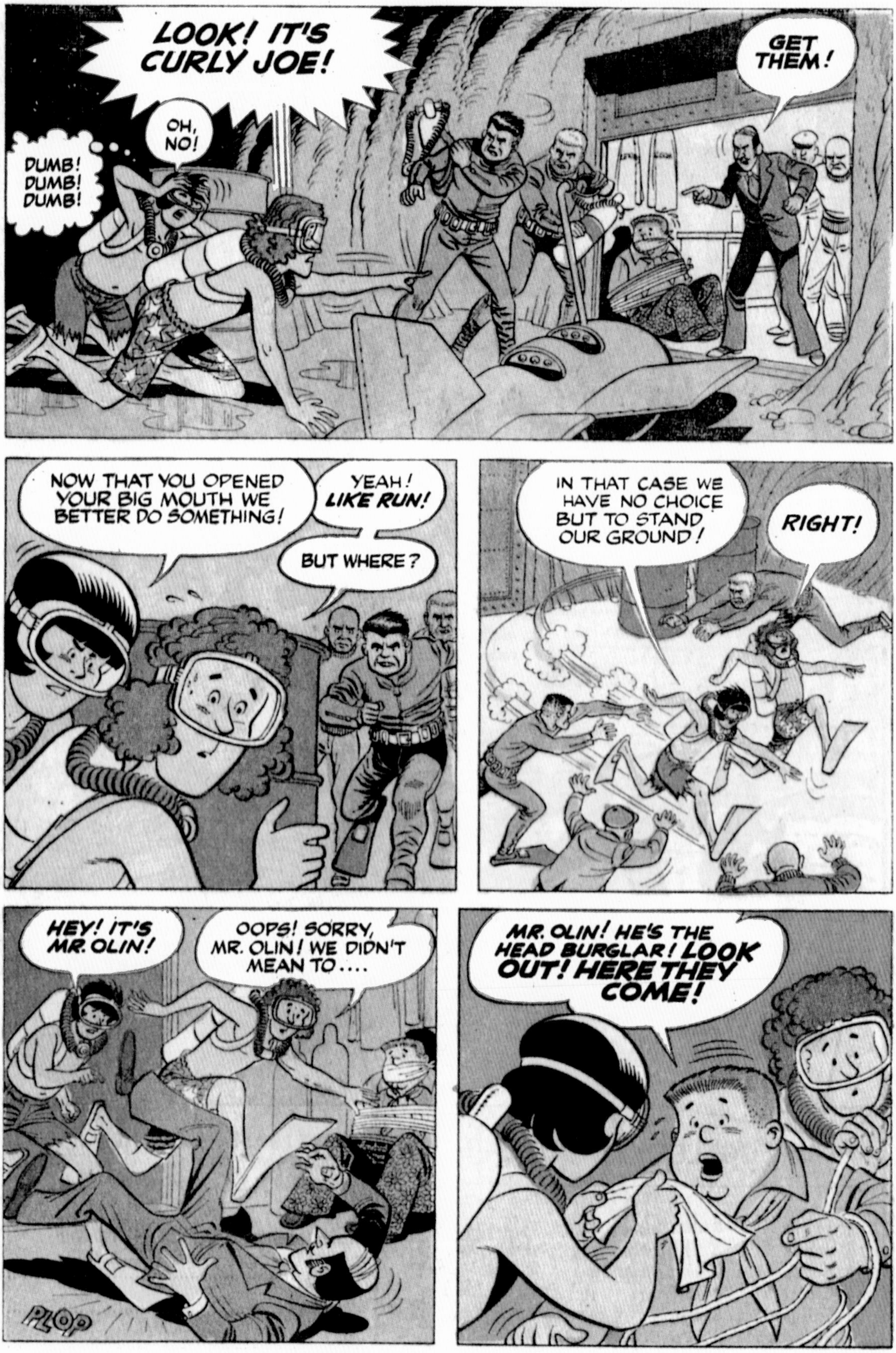
LOOK! IT'S CURLY JOE!
DUMB! DUMB! DUMB!
OH, NO!
GET THEM!
NOW THAT YOU OPENED YOUR BIG MOUTH WE BETTER DO SOMETHING!
YEAH! LIKE RUN!
BUT WHERE?
IN THAT CASE WE HAVE NO CHOICE BUT TO STAND OUR GROUND!
RIGHT!
HEY! IT'S MR. OLIN!
OOPS! SORRY, MR. OLIN! WE DIDN'T MEAN TO....
PLOP
MR. OLIN! HE'S THE HEAD BURGLAR! LOOK OUT! HERE THEY COME!

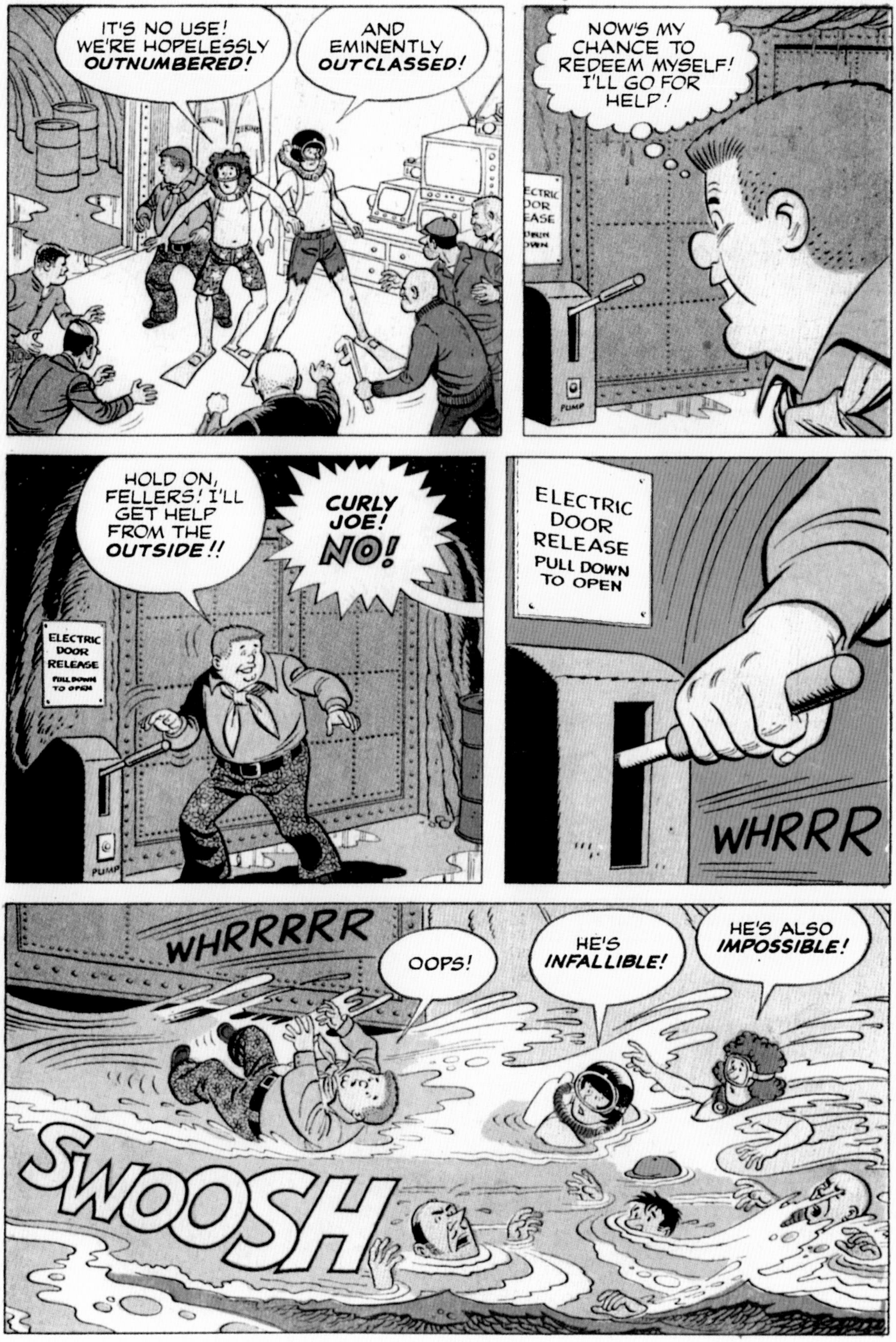
IT'S NO USE! WE'RE HOPELESSLY OUTNUMBERED!
AND EMINENTLY OUTCLASSED!
NOW'S MY CHANCE TO REDEEM MYSELF! I'LL GO FOR HELP!
HOLD ON, FELLERS! I'LL GET HELP FROM THE OUTSIDE!!
CURLY JOE! NO!
ELECTRIC DOOR RELEASE PULL DOWN TO OPEN
PUMP
ELECTRIC DOOR RELEASE PULL DOWN TO OPEN
WHRRR
WHRRRRR
OOPS!
HE'S INFALLIBLE!
HE'S ALSO IMPOSSIBLE!
SWOOSH

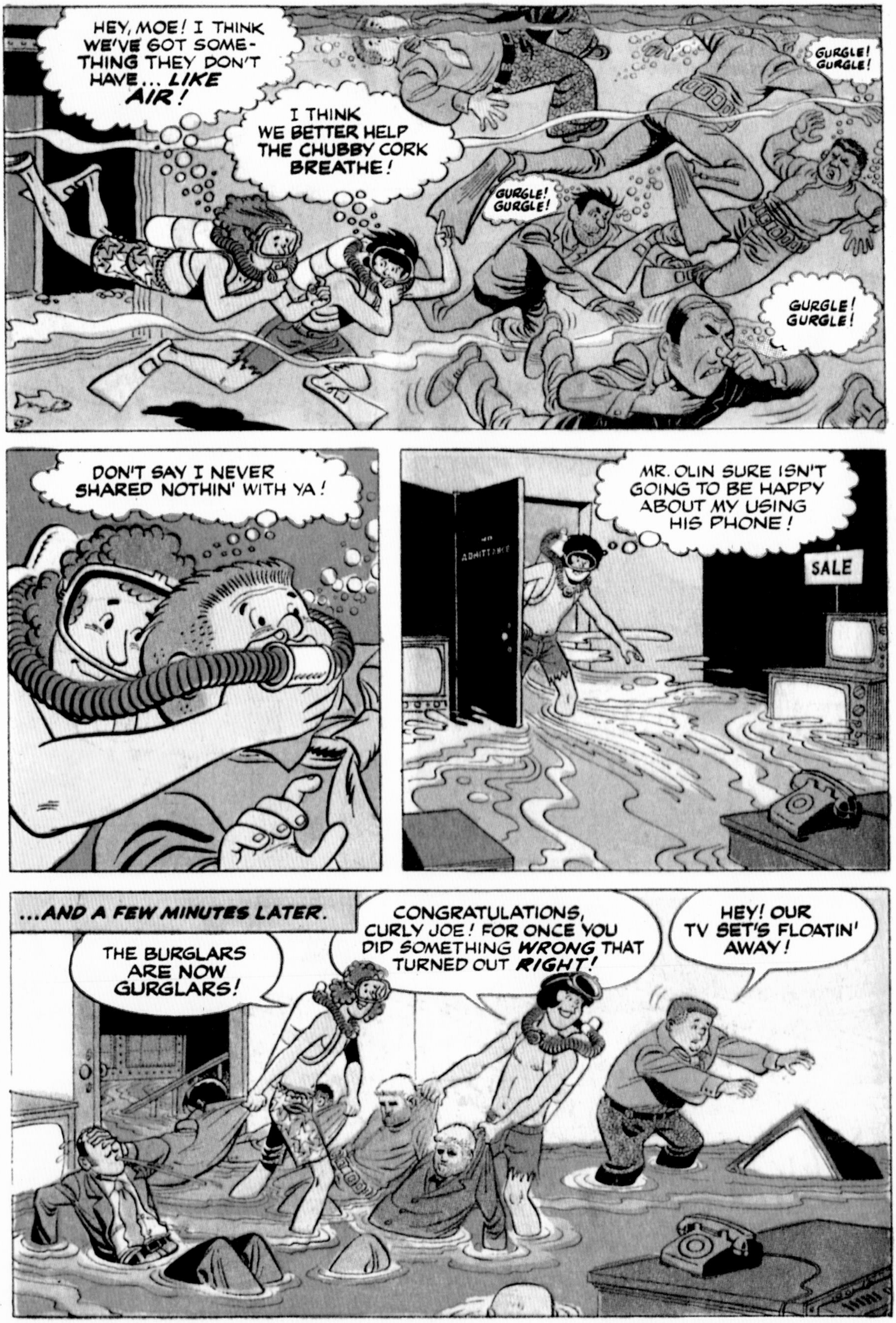
HEY, MOE! I THINK WE'VE GOT SOME-THING THEY DON'T HAVE... LIKE AIR!
I THINK WE BETTER HELP THE CHUBBY CORK BREATHE!
GURGLE! GURGLE!
GURGLE! GURGLE!
GURGLE! GURGLE!
DON'T SAY I NEVER SHARED NOTHIN' WITH YA!
MR. OLIN SURE ISN'T GOING TO BE HAPPY ABOUT MY USING HIS PHONE!
SALE
...AND A FEW MINUTES LATER.
THE BURGLARS ARE NOW GURGLARS!
CONGRATULATIONS, CURLY JOE! FOR ONCE YOU DID SOMETHING WRONG THAT TURNED OUT RIGHT!
HEY! OUR TV SET'S FLOATIN' AWAY!

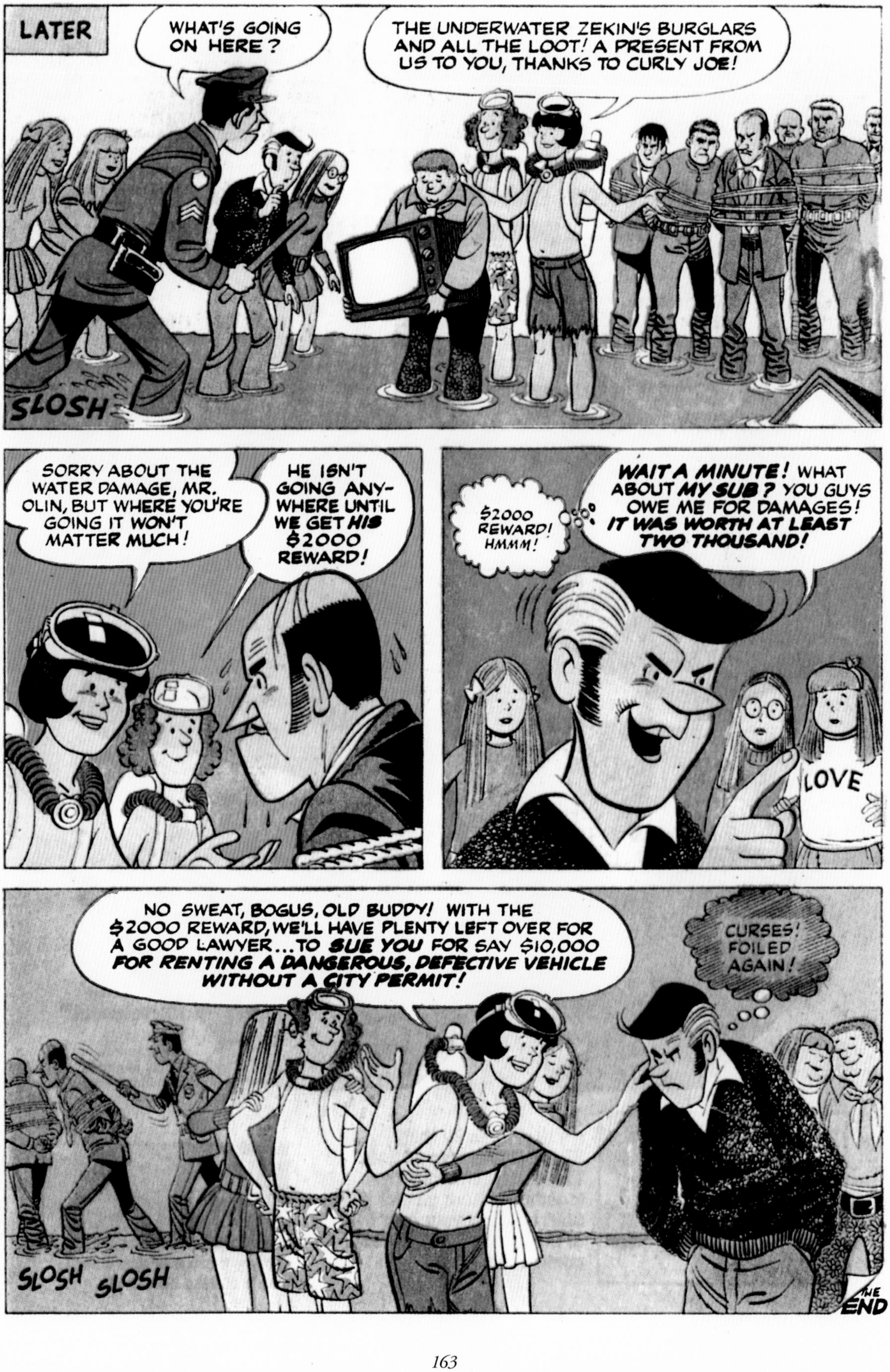
LATER
WHAT'S GOING ON HERE?
THE UNDERWATER ZEKIN'S BURGLARS AND ALL THE LOOT! A PRESENT FROM US TO YOU, THANKS TO CURLY JOE!
SLOSH
SORRY ABOUT THE WATER DAMAGE, MR. OLIN, BUT WHERE YOU'RE GOING IT WON'T MATTER MUCH!
HE ISN'T GOING ANYWHERE UNTIL WE GET HIS $2000 REWARD!
$2000 REWARD! HMMM!
WAIT A MINUTE! WHAT ABOUT MY SUB? YOU GUYS OWE ME FOR DAMAGES! IT WAS WORTH AT LEAST TWO THOUSAND!
LOVE
NO SWEAT, BOGUS, OLD BUDDY! WITH THE $2000 REWARD, WE'LL HAVE PLENTY LEFT OVER FOR A GOOD LAWYER...TO SUE YOU FOR SAY $10,000 FOR RENTING A DANGEROUS, DEFECTIVE VEHICLE WITHOUT A CITY PERMIT!
CURSES! FOILED AGAIN!
SLOSH SLOSH
THE END

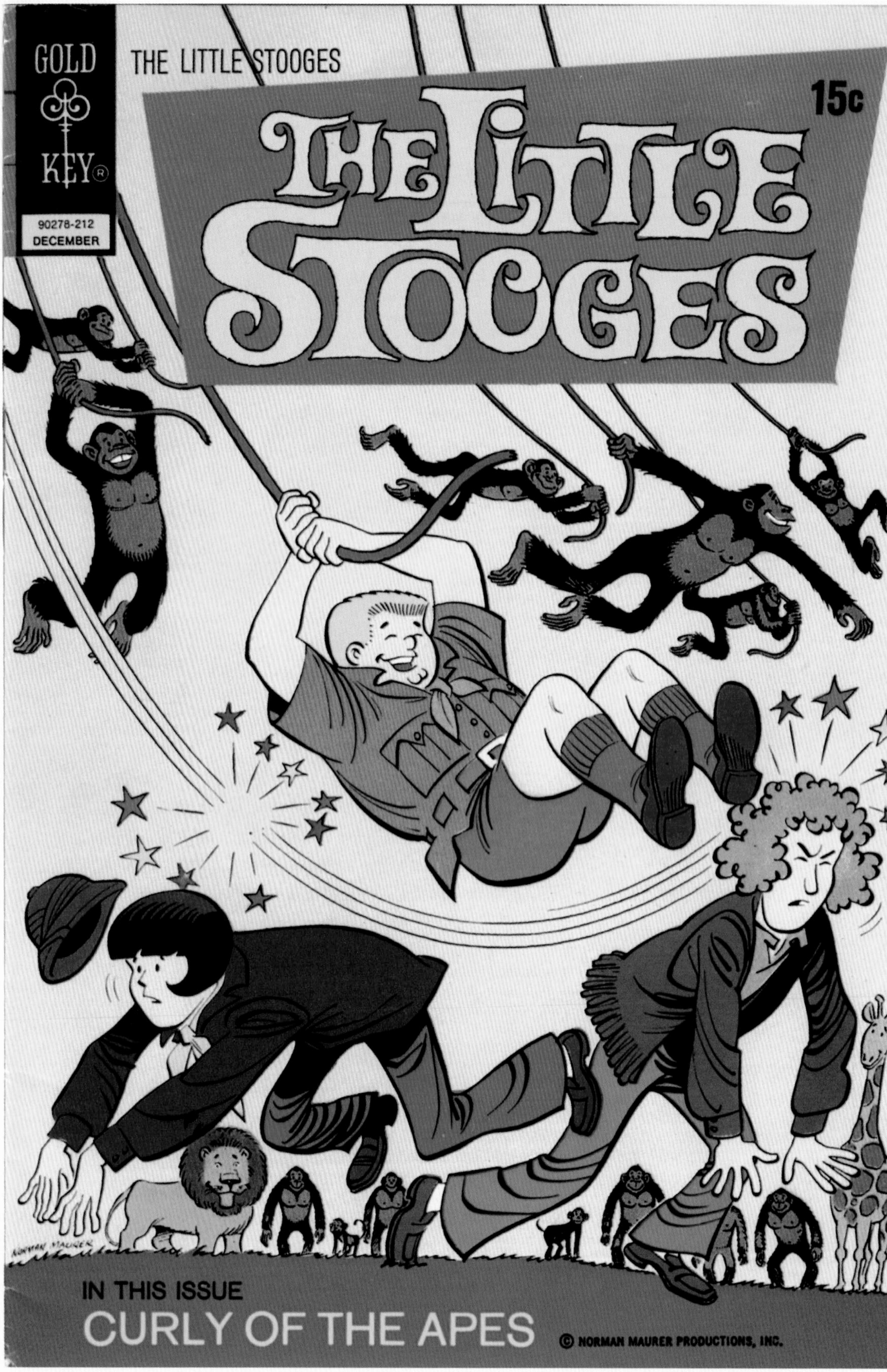
GOLD KEY
90278-212
DECEMBER
THE LITTLE STOOGES
15c
THE LITTLE STOOGES
NORMAN MAURER
IN THIS ISSUE
CURLY OF THE APES
© NORMAN MAURER PRODUCTIONS, INC.

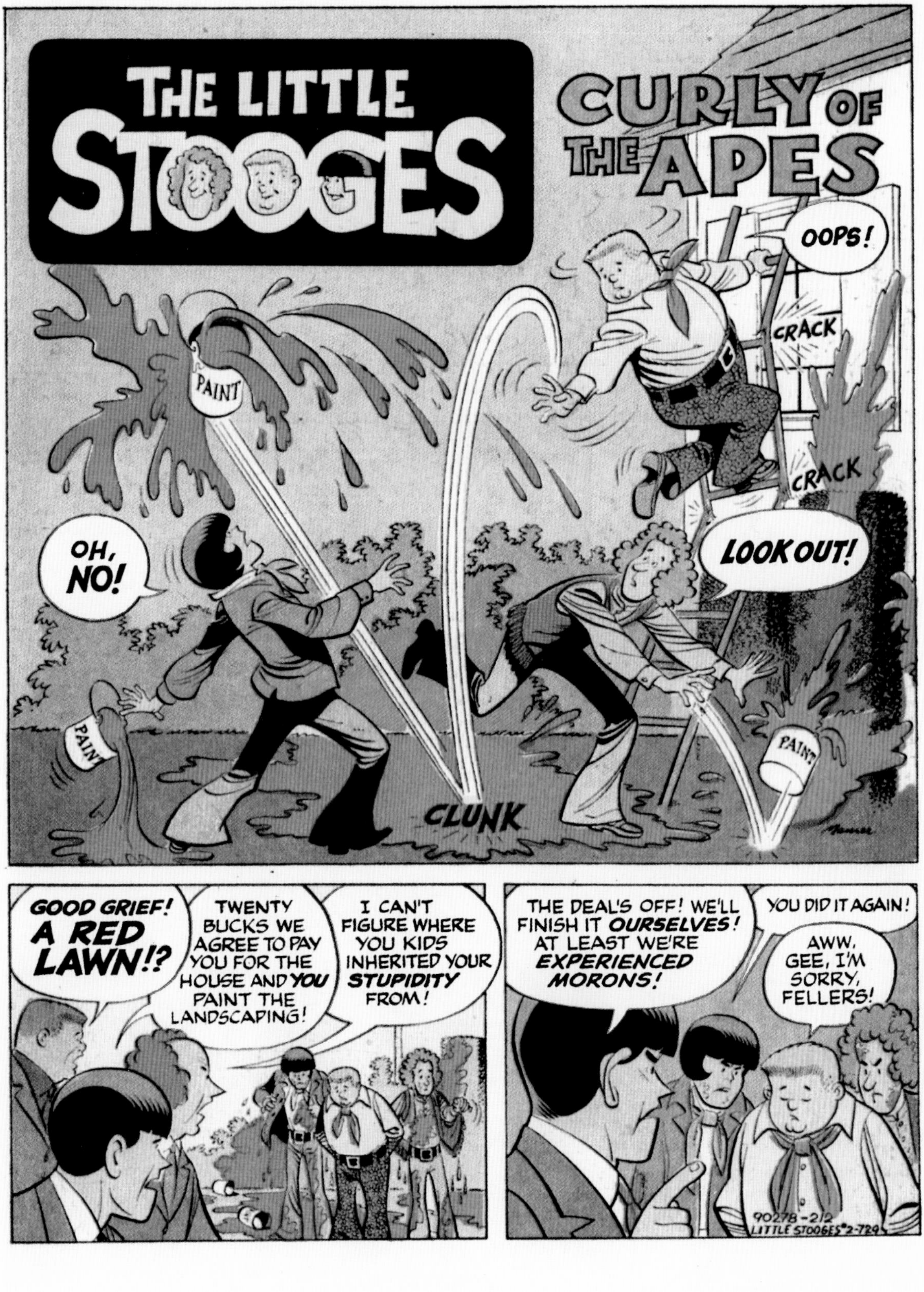
THE LITTLE STOOGES
CURLY OF THE APES
OOPS!
CRACK
CRACK
PAINT
OH, NO!
LOOK OUT!
PAINT
PAINT
CLUNK
GOOD GRIEF! A RED LAWN!?
TWENTY BUCKS WE AGREE TO PAY YOU FOR THE HOUSE AND YOU PAINT THE LANDSCAPING!
I CAN'T FIGURE WHERE YOU KIDS INHERITED YOUR STUPIDITY FROM!
THE DEAL'S OFF! WE'LL FINISH IT OURSELVES! AT LEAST WE'RE EXPERIENCED MORONS!
YOU DID IT AGAIN!
AWW, GEE, I'M SORRY, FELLERS!
90278-212
LITTLE STOOGES #2-729

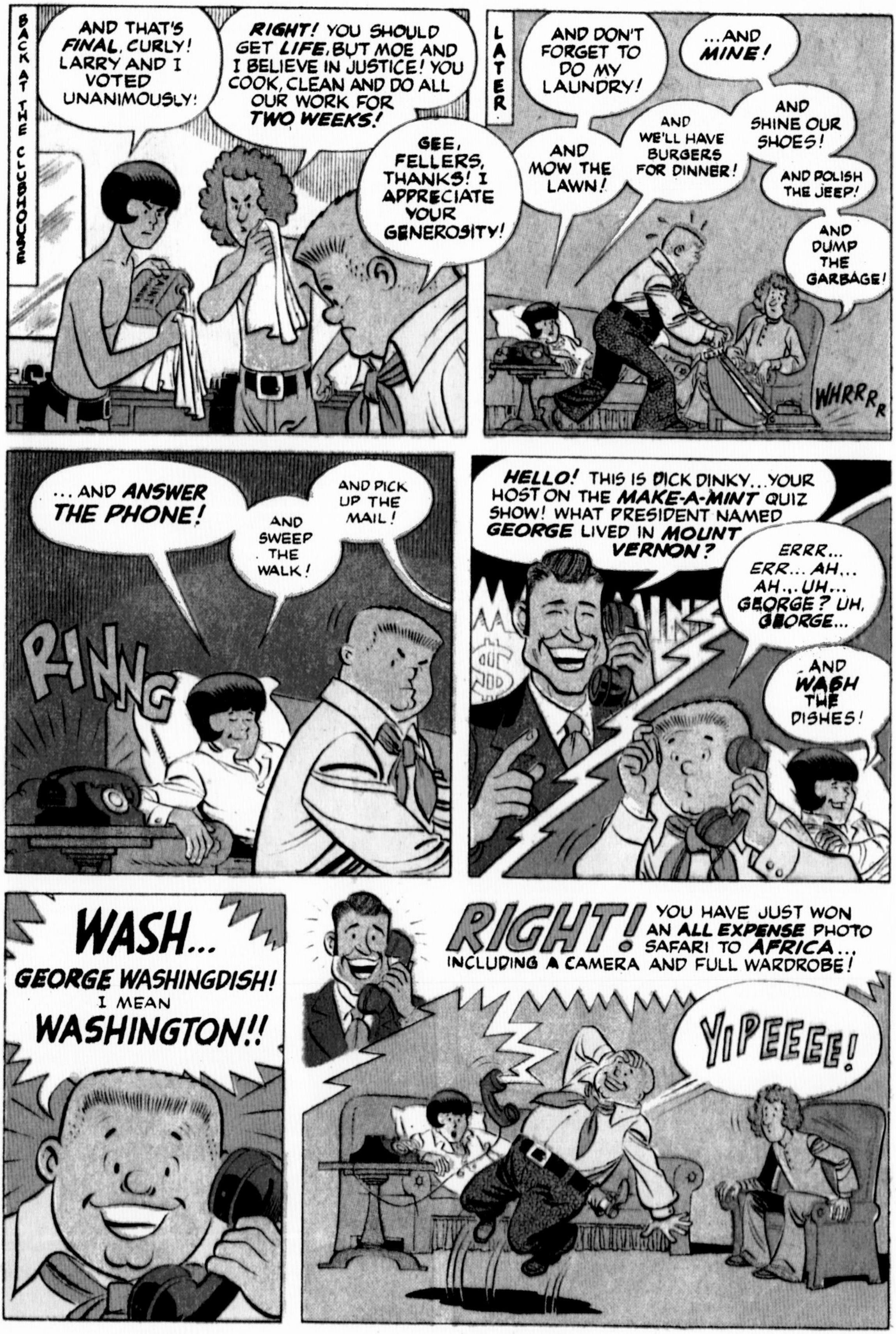
BACK AT THE CLUBHOUSE
AND THAT'S FINAL, CURLY! LARRY AND I VOTED UNANIMOUSLY!
RIGHT! YOU SHOULD GET LIFE, BUT MOE AND I BELIEVE IN JUSTICE! YOU COOK, CLEAN AND DO ALL OUR WORK FOR TWO WEEKS!
GEE, FELLERS, THANKS! I APPRECIATE YOUR GENEROSITY!
LATER
AND DON'T FORGET TO DO MY LAUNDRY!
...AND MINE!
AND MOW THE LAWN!
AND WE'LL HAVE BURGERS FOR DINNER!
AND SHINE OUR SHOES!
AND POLISH THE JEEP!
AND DUMP THE GARBAGE!
WHRRRR
... AND ANSWER THE PHONE!
AND SWEEP THE WALK!
AND PICK UP THE MAIL!
RINNG
HELLO! THIS IS DICK DINKY... YOUR HOST ON THE MAKE-A-MINT QUIZ SHOW! WHAT PRESIDENT NAMED GEORGE LIVED IN MOUNT VERNON?
ERRR... ERR... AH... AH... UH... GEORGE? UH, GEORGE...
...AND WASH THE DISHES!
WASH... GEORGE WASHINGDISH! I MEAN WASHINGTON!!
RIGHT! YOU HAVE JUST WON AN ALL EXPENSE PHOTO SAFARI TO AFRICA... INCLUDING A CAMERA AND FULL WARDROBE!
YIPEEEE!

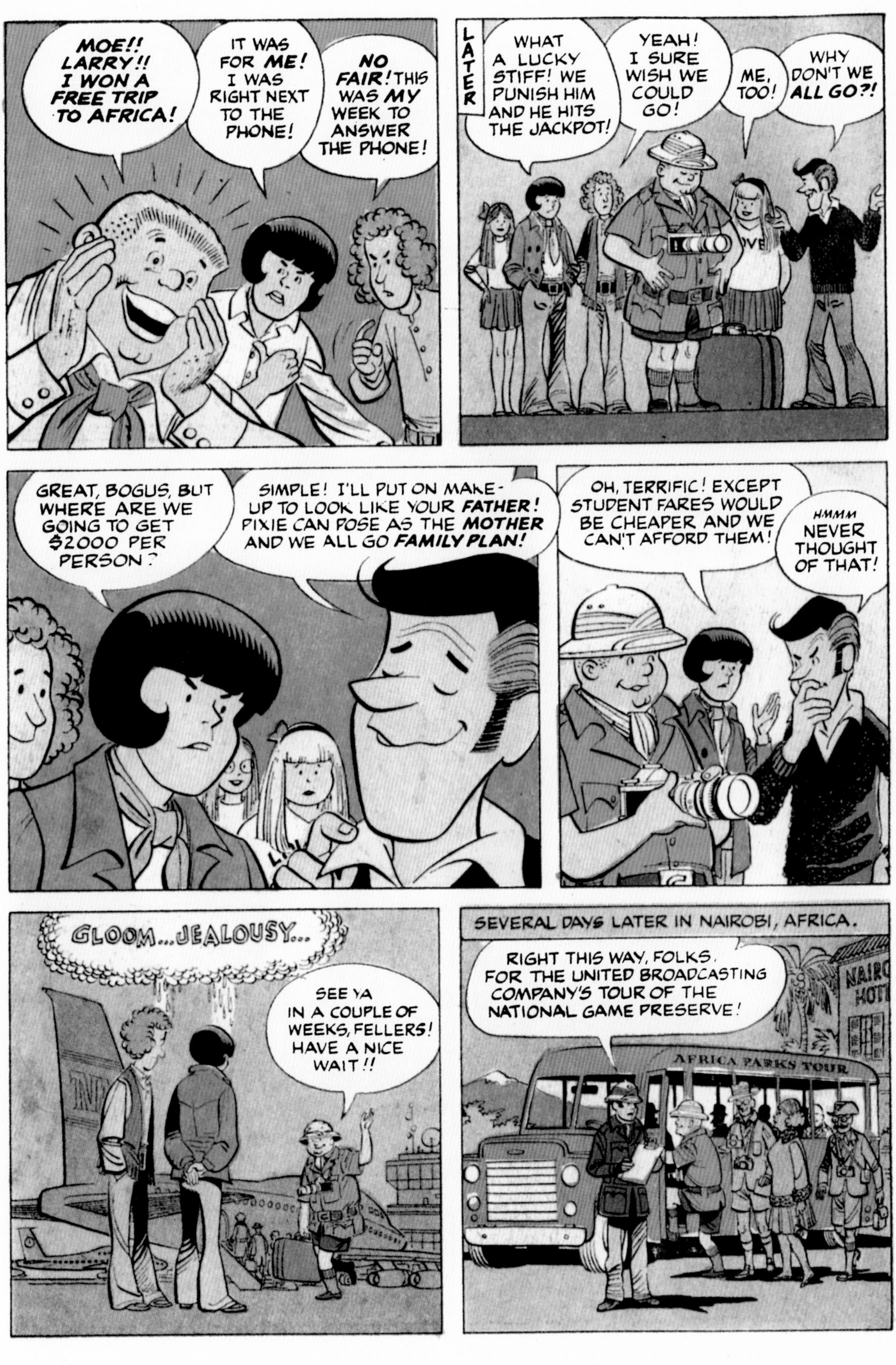

MOE!! LARRY!! I WON A FREE TRIP TO AFRICA!
IT WAS FOR ME! I WAS RIGHT NEXT TO THE PHONE!
NO FAIR! THIS WAS MY WEEK TO ANSWER THE PHONE!
LATER
WHAT A LUCKY STIFF! WE PUNISH HIM AND HE HITS THE JACKPOT!
YEAH! I SURE WISH WE COULD GO!
ME, TOO!
WHY DON'T WE ALL GO?!
GREAT, BOGUS, BUT WHERE ARE WE GOING TO GET $2000 PER PERSON?
SIMPLE! I'LL PUT ON MAKE-UP TO LOOK LIKE YOUR FATHER! PIXIE CAN POSE AS THE MOTHER AND WE ALL GO FAMILY PLAN!
OH, TERRIFIC! EXCEPT STUDENT FARES WOULD BE CHEAPER AND WE CAN'T AFFORD THEM!
HMMM NEVER THOUGHT OF THAT!
GLOOM...JEALOUSY...
SEE YA IN A COUPLE OF WEEKS, FELLERS! HAVE A NICE WAIT!!
SEVERAL DAYS LATER IN NAIROBI, AFRICA.
RIGHT THIS WAY, FOLKS. FOR THE UNITED BROADCASTING COMPANY'S TOUR OF THE NATIONAL GAME PRESERVE!
AFRICA PARKS TOUR

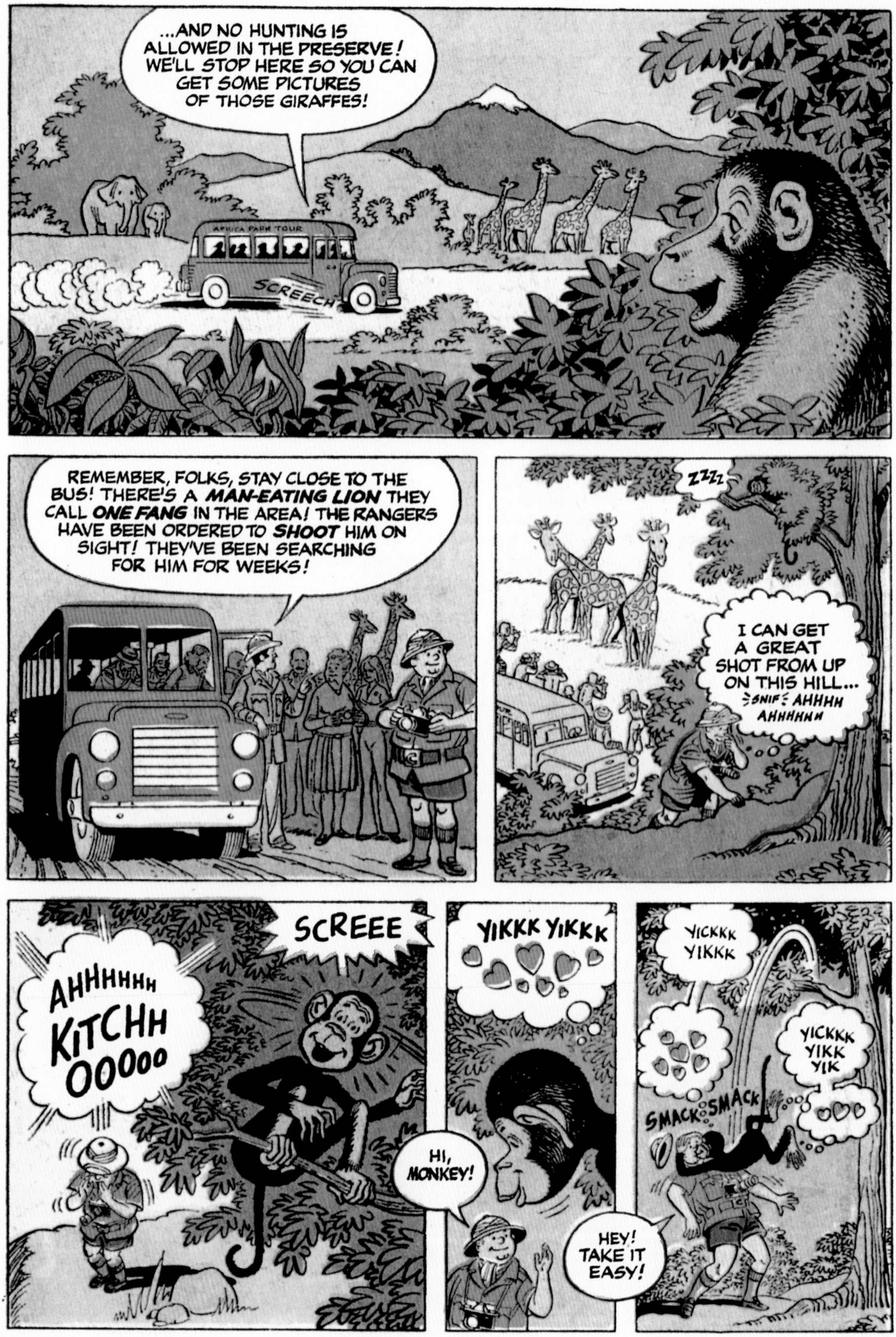
...AND NO HUNTING IS ALLOWED IN THE PRESERVE! WE'LL STOP HERE SO YOU CAN GET SOME PICTURES OF THOSE GIRAFFES!
AFRICA PARK TOUR
SCREECH
REMEMBER, FOLKS, STAY CLOSE TO THE BUS! THERE'S A MAN-EATING LION THEY CALL ONE FANG IN THE AREA! THE RANGERS HAVE BEEN ORDERED TO SHOOT HIM ON SIGHT! THEY'VE BEEN SEARCHING FOR HIM FOR WEEKS!
ZZZZ
I CAN GET A GREAT SHOT FROM UP ON THIS HILL... SNIF AHHHH AHHHHHH
SCREEE
AHHHHHH KITCHH OOOOO
YIKKK YIKKK
HI, MONKEY!
YICKKK YIKKK
YICKKK YIKK YIK
SMACK SMACK
HEY! TAKE IT EASY!

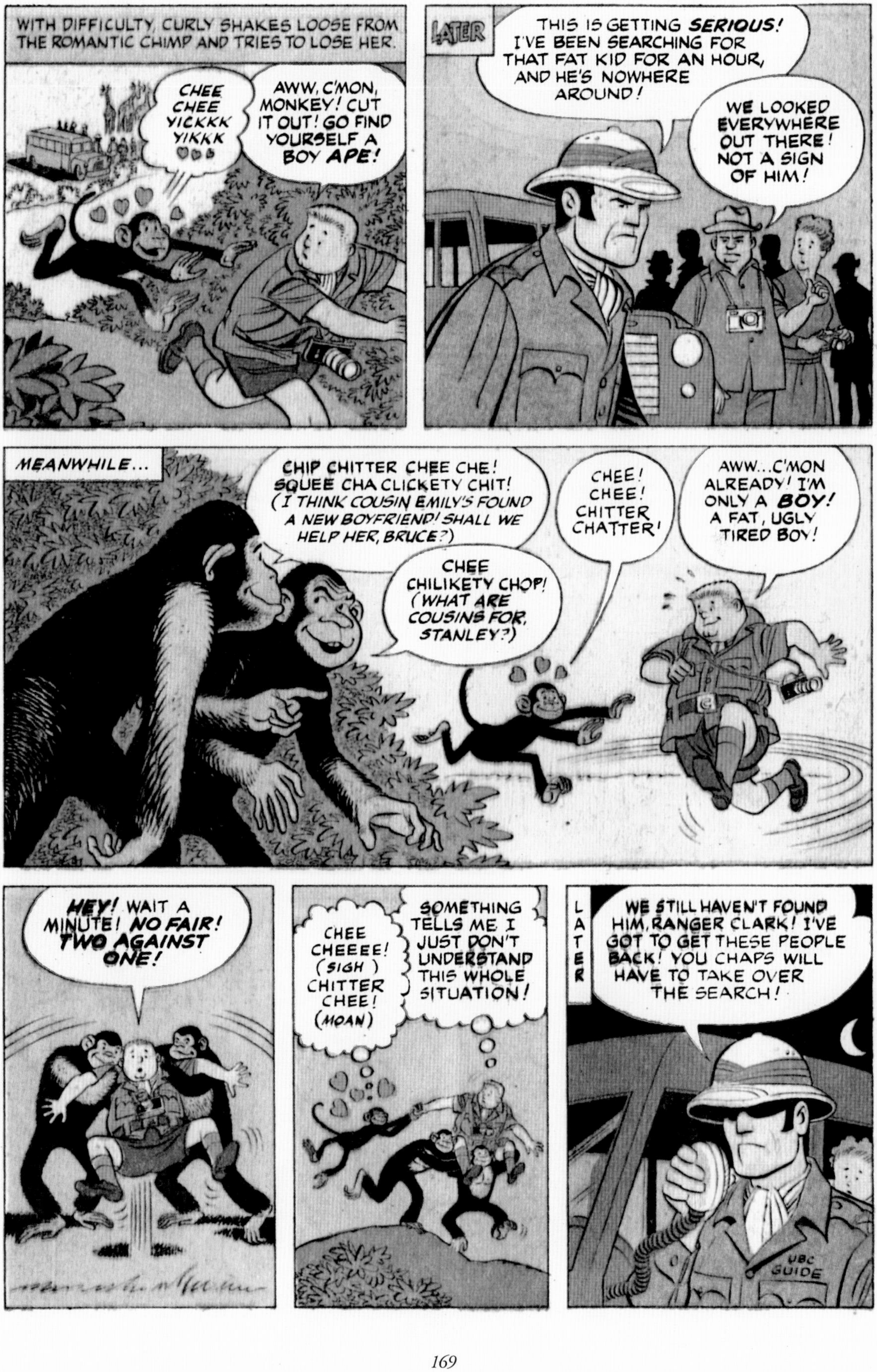
WITH DIFFICULTY, CURLY SHAKES LOOSE FROM THE ROMANTIC CHIMP AND TRIES TO LOSE HER.
CHEE CHEE YICKKK YIKKK
AWW, C'MON, MONKEY! CUT IT OUT! GO FIND YOURSELF A BOY APE!
LATER
THIS IS GETTING SERIOUS! I'VE BEEN SEARCHING FOR THAT FAT KID FOR AN HOUR, AND HE'S NOWHERE AROUND!
WE LOOKED EVERYWHERE OUT THERE! NOT A SIGN OF HIM!
MEANWHILE...
CHIP CHITTER CHEE CHE! SQUEE CHA CLICKETY CHIT! (I THINK COUSIN EMILY'S FOUND A NEW BOYFRIEND! SHALL WE HELP HER, BRUCE?)
CHEE CHILIKETY CHOP! (WHAT ARE COUSINS FOR, STANLEY?)
CHEE! CHEE! CHITTER CHATTER!
AWW...C'MON ALREADY! I'M ONLY A BOY! A FAT, UGLY TIRED BOY!
HEY! WAIT A MINUTE! NO FAIR! TWO AGAINST ONE!
CHEE CHEEEE! (SIGH) CHITTER CHEE! (MOAN)
SOMETHING TELLS ME I JUST DON'T UNDERSTAND THIS WHOLE SITUATION!
LATER
WE STILL HAVEN'T FOUND HIM, RANGER CLARK! I'VE GOT TO GET THESE PEOPLE BACK! YOU CHAPS WILL HAVE TO TAKE OVER THE SEARCH!
UBC GUIDE

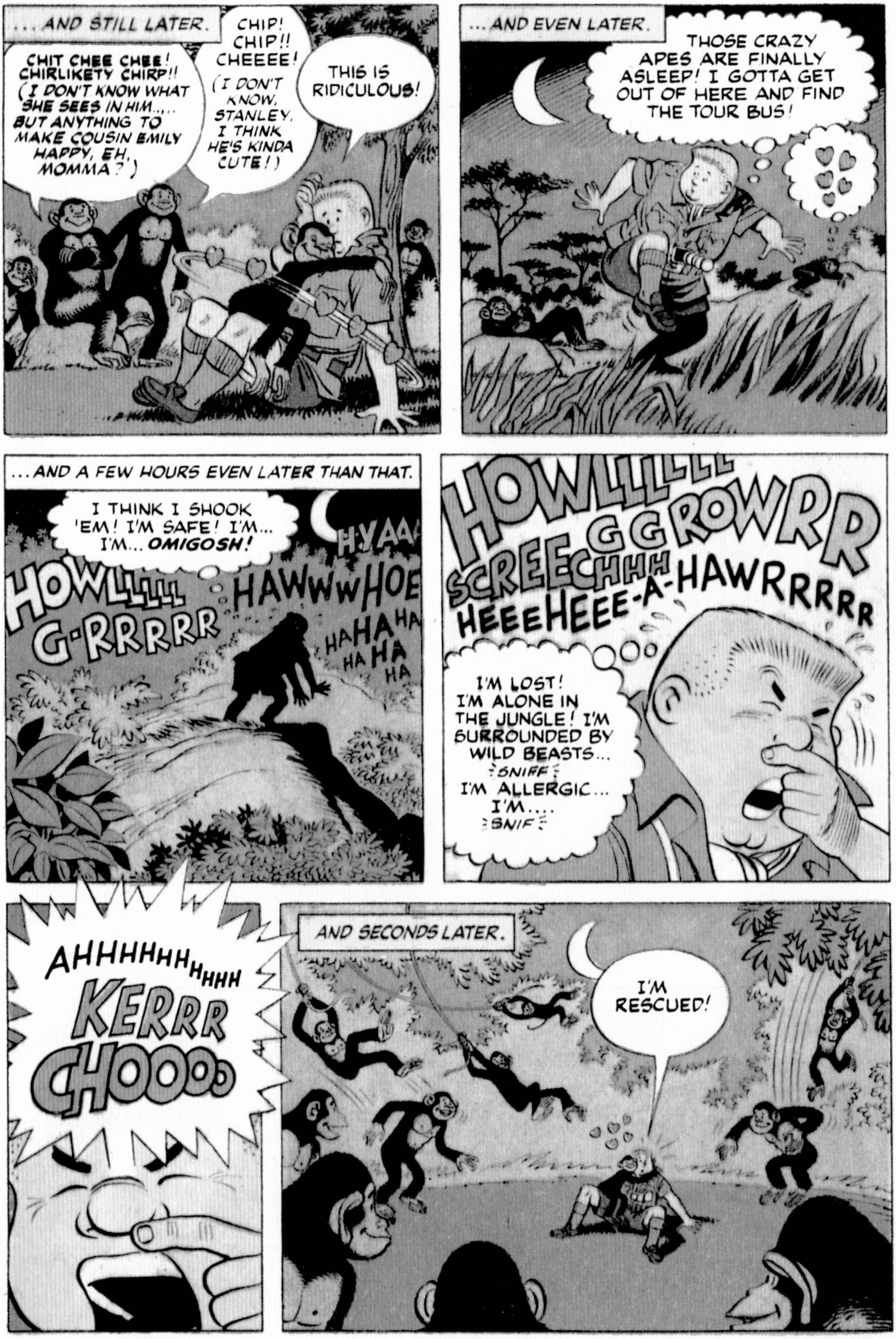
...AND STILL LATER.
CHIT CHEE CHEE! CHIRLIKETY CHIRP!! (I DON'T KNOW WHAT SHE SEES IN HIM..,.. BUT ANYTHING TO MAKE COUSIN EMILY HAPPY, EH, MOMMA?)
CHIP! CHIP!! CHEEEE! (I DON'T KNOW, STANLEY, I THINK HE'S KINDA CUTE!)
THIS IS RIDICULOUS!
...AND EVEN LATER.
THOSE CRAZY APES ARE FINALLY ASLEEP! I GOTTA GET OUT OF HERE AND FIND THE TOUR BUS!
...AND A FEW HOURS EVEN LATER THAN THAT.
I THINK I SHOOK 'EM! I'M SAFE! I'M... I'M... OMIGOSH!
HOWLLLLL G-RRRRR
HAWWWHOE
HYAA
HAHAHA HAHAHA
HOWLLLLLL SCREECHHH GGROWRR HEEEHEEE-A-HAWRRRRR
I'M LOST! I'M ALONE IN THE JUNGLE! I'M SURROUNDED BY WILD BEASTS... SNIFF I'M ALLERGIC... I'M.... SNIF
AHHHHHHHHHH KERRR CHOOOO
AND SECONDS LATER.
I'M RESCUED!

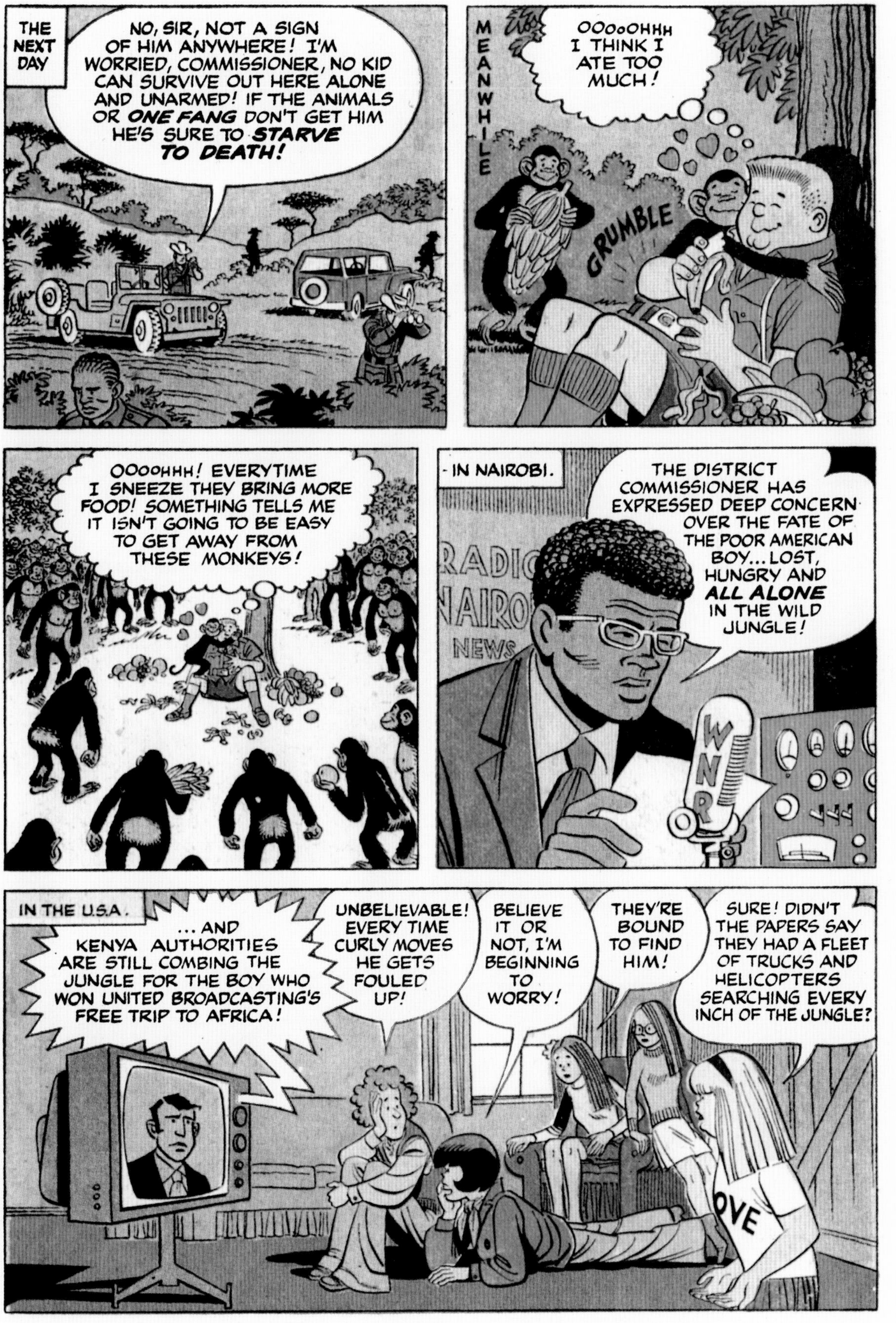
THE NEXT DAY
NO, SIR, NOT A SIGN OF HIM ANYWHERE! I'M WORRIED, COMMISSIONER, NO KID CAN SURVIVE OUT HERE ALONE AND UNARMED! IF THE ANIMALS OR ONE FANG DON'T GET HIM HE'S SURE TO STARVE TO DEATH!
MEANWHILE
OOOoOHHH I THINK I ATE TOO MUCH!
GRUMBLE
OOOoHHH! EVERYTIME I SNEEZE THEY BRING MORE FOOD! SOMETHING TELLS ME IT ISN'T GOING TO BE EASY TO GET AWAY FROM THESE MONKEYS!
- IN NAIROBI.
THE DISTRICT COMMISSIONER HAS EXPRESSED DEEP CONCERN OVER THE FATE OF THE POOR AMERICAN BOY... LOST, HUNGRY AND ALL ALONE IN THE WILD JUNGLE!
NEWS
WNR
IN THE U.S.A.
... AND KENYA AUTHORITIES ARE STILL COMBING THE JUNGLE FOR THE BOY WHO WON UNITED BROADCASTING'S FREE TRIP TO AFRICA!
UNBELIEVABLE! EVERY TIME CURLY MOVES HE GETS FOULED UP!
BELIEVE IT OR NOT, I'M BEGINNING TO WORRY!
THEY'RE BOUND TO FIND HIM!
SURE! DIDN'T THE PAPERS SAY THEY HAD A FLEET OF TRUCKS AND HELICOPTERS SEARCHING EVERY INCH OF THE JUNGLE?
OVE

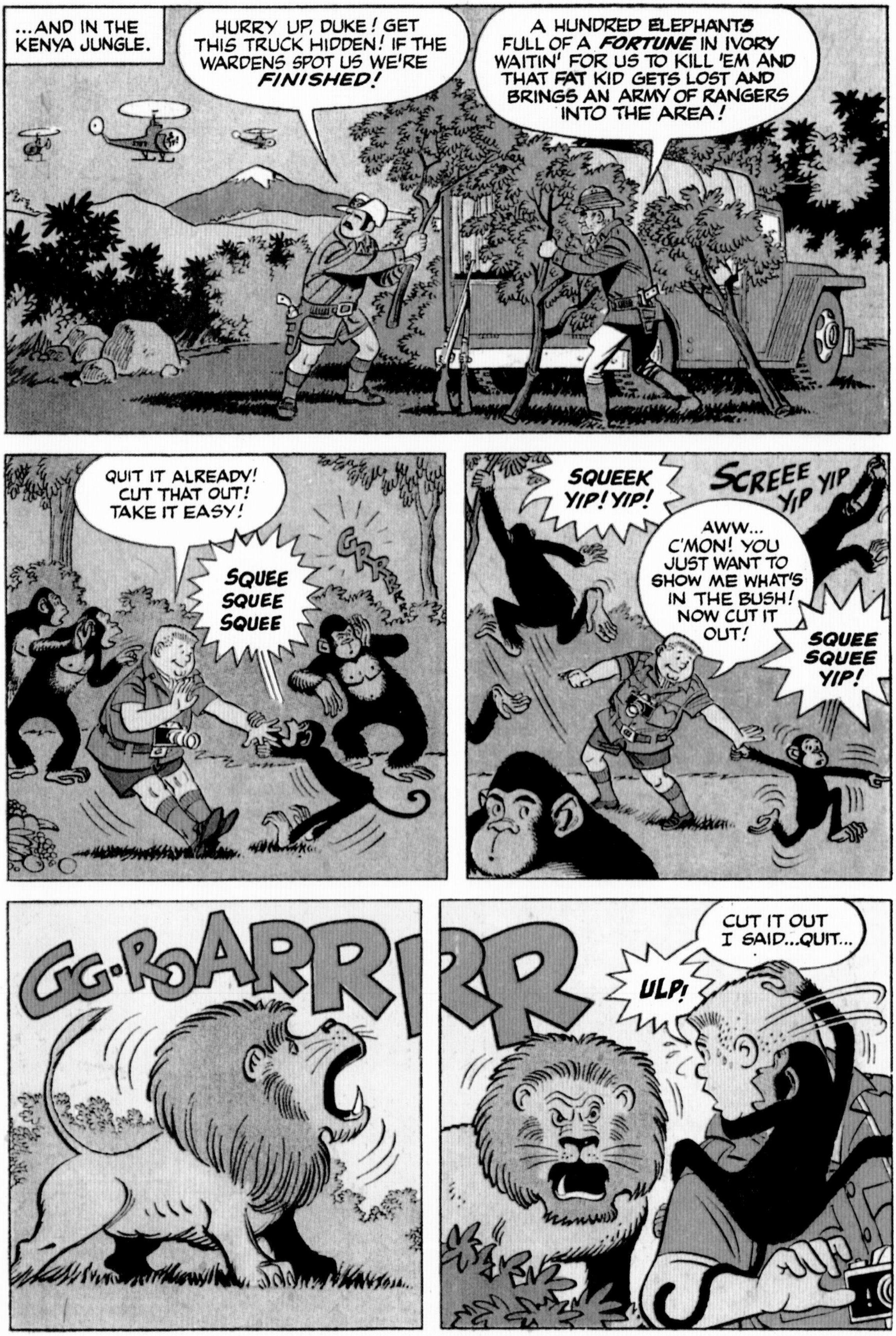
...AND IN THE KENYA JUNGLE.
HURRY UP, DUKE! GET THIS TRUCK HIDDEN! IF THE WARDENS SPOT US WE'RE FINISHED!
A HUNDRED ELEPHANTS FULL OF A FORTUNE IN IVORY WAITIN' FOR US TO KILL 'EM AND THAT FAT KID GETS LOST AND BRINGS AN ARMY OF RANGERS INTO THE AREA!
QUIT IT ALREADY! CUT THAT OUT! TAKE IT EASY!
SQUEE SQUEE SQUEE
GRRRR
SQUEEK YIP! YIP!
SCREEE YIP YIP
AWW... C'MON! YOU JUST WANT TO SHOW ME WHAT'S IN THE BUSH! NOW CUT IT OUT!
SQUEE SQUEE YIP!
GG-ROARRRR
CUT IT OUT I SAID...QUIT...
ULP!

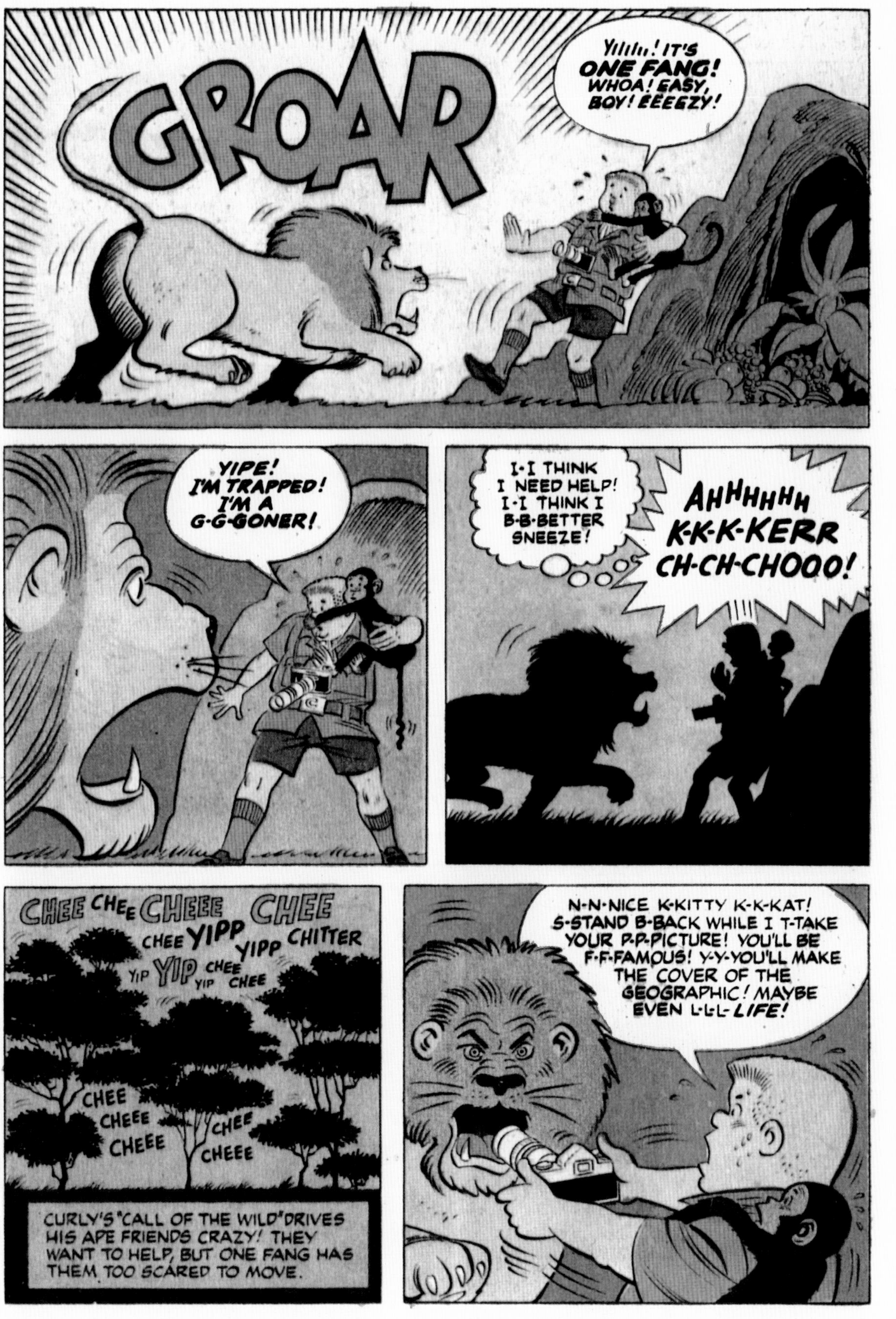
GROAR
YIIII! IT'S ONE FANG! WHOA! EASY, BOY! EEEEZY!
YIPE! I'M TRAPPED! I'M A G-G-GONER!
I-I THINK I NEED HELP! I-I THINK I B-B-BETTER SNEEZE!
AHHHHHH K-K-K-KERR CH-CH-CHOOO!
CHEE CHEE CHEEE CHEE CHEE YIPP YIPP CHITTER YIP YIP CHEE YIP CHEE
CHEE CHEEE CHEEE CHEE CHEEE
CURLY'S "CALL OF THE WILD" DRIVES HIS APE FRIENDS CRAZY! THEY WANT TO HELP, BUT ONE FANG HAS THEM TOO SCARED TO MOVE.
N-N-NICE K-KITTY K-K-KAT! S-STAND B-BACK WHILE I T-TAKE YOUR P-P-PICTURE! YOU'LL BE F-F-FAMOUS! Y-Y-YOU'LL MAKE THE COVER OF THE GEOGRAPHIC! MAYBE EVEN L-L-L-LIFE!

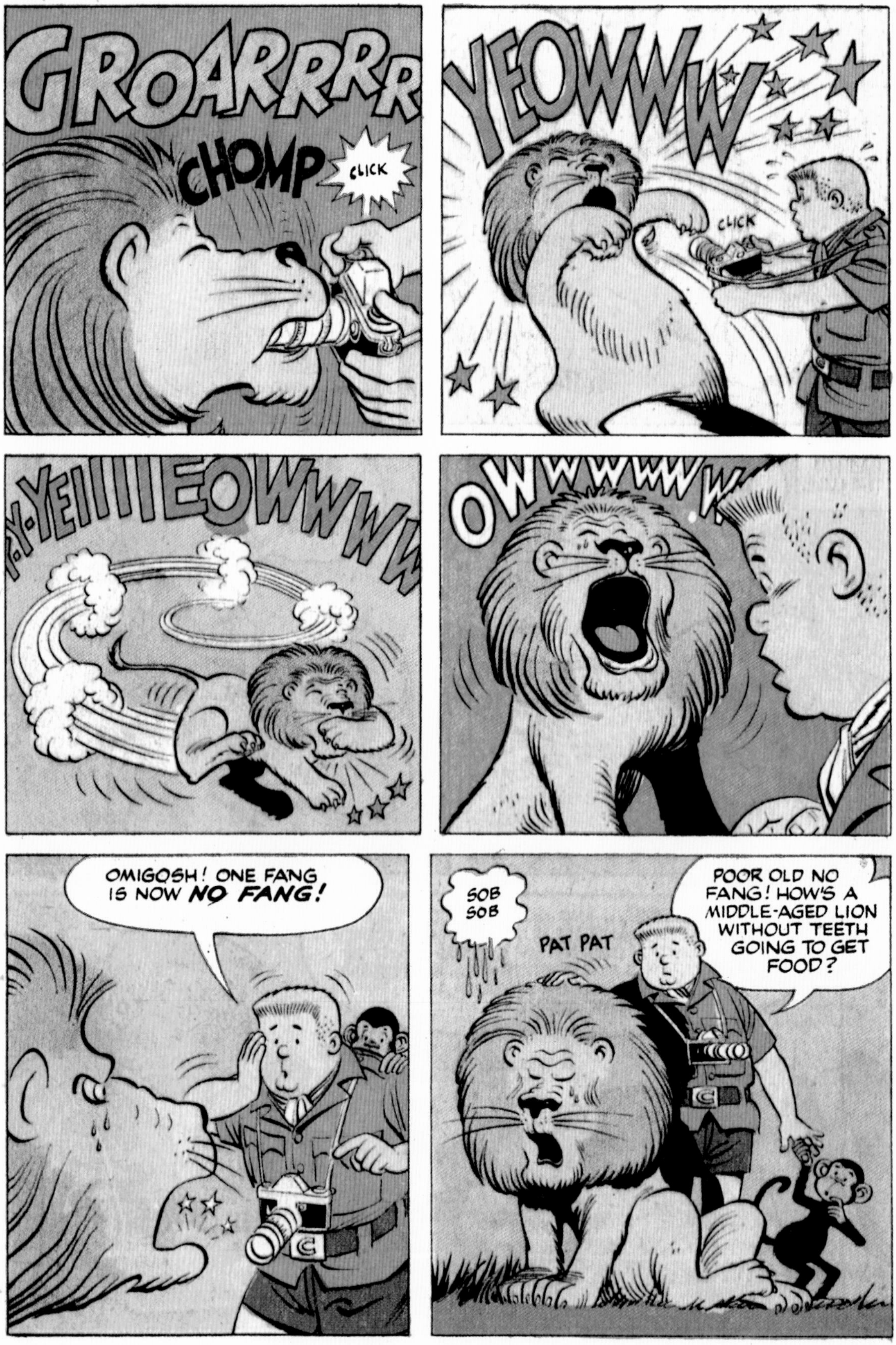
GROARRRR
CHOMP
CLICK
YEOWWW
CLICK
Y-Y-YEIIIIEOWWWW
OWWWWWW
OMIGOSH! ONE FANG IS NOW NO FANG!
SOB SOB
PAT PAT
POOR OLD NO FANG! HOW'S A MIDDLE-AGED LION WITHOUT TEETH GOING TO GET FOOD?

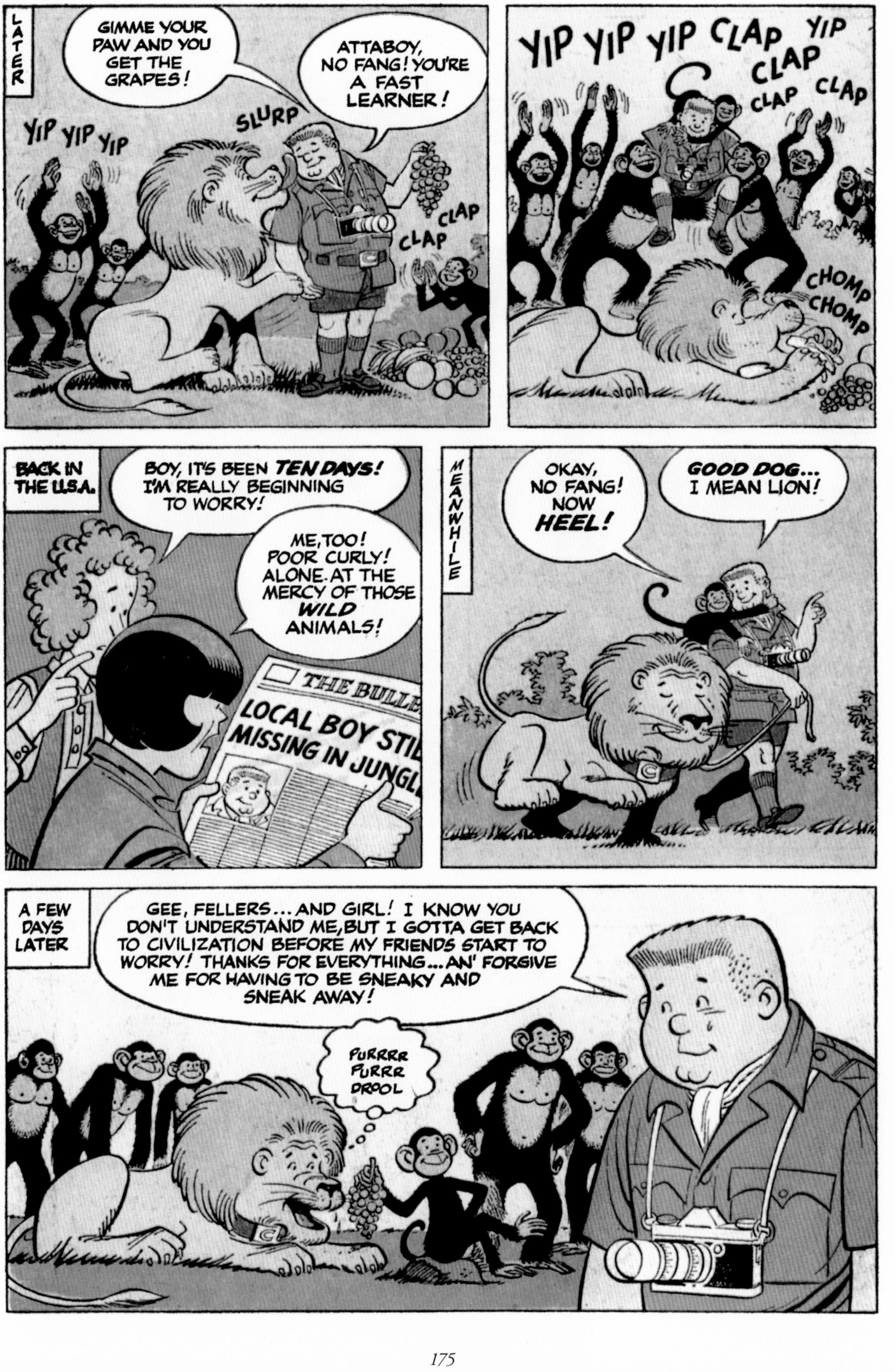
LATER
GIMME YOUR PAW AND YOU GET THE GRAPES!
ATTABOY, NO FANG! YOU'RE A FAST LEARNER!
SLURP
YIP YIP YIP
CLAP CLAP
YIP YIP YIP CLAP YIP CLAP CLAP CLAP
CHOMP CHOMP
BACK IN THE U.S.A.
BOY, IT'S BEEN **TEN DAYS!** I'M REALLY BEGINNING TO WORRY!
ME, TOO! POOR CURLY! ALONE AT THE MERCY OF THOSE **WILD** ANIMALS!
LOCAL BOY
MISSING IN
MEANWHILE
OKAY, NO FANG! NOW **HEEL!**
GOOD DOG... I MEAN LION!
A FEW DAYS LATER
GEE, FELLERS... AND GIRL! I KNOW YOU DON'T UNDERSTAND ME, BUT I GOTTA GET BACK TO CIVILIZATION BEFORE MY FRIENDS START TO WORRY! THANKS FOR EVERYTHING... AN' FORGIVE ME FOR HAVING TO BE SNEAKY AND SNEAK AWAY!
PURRRR PURRR DROOL

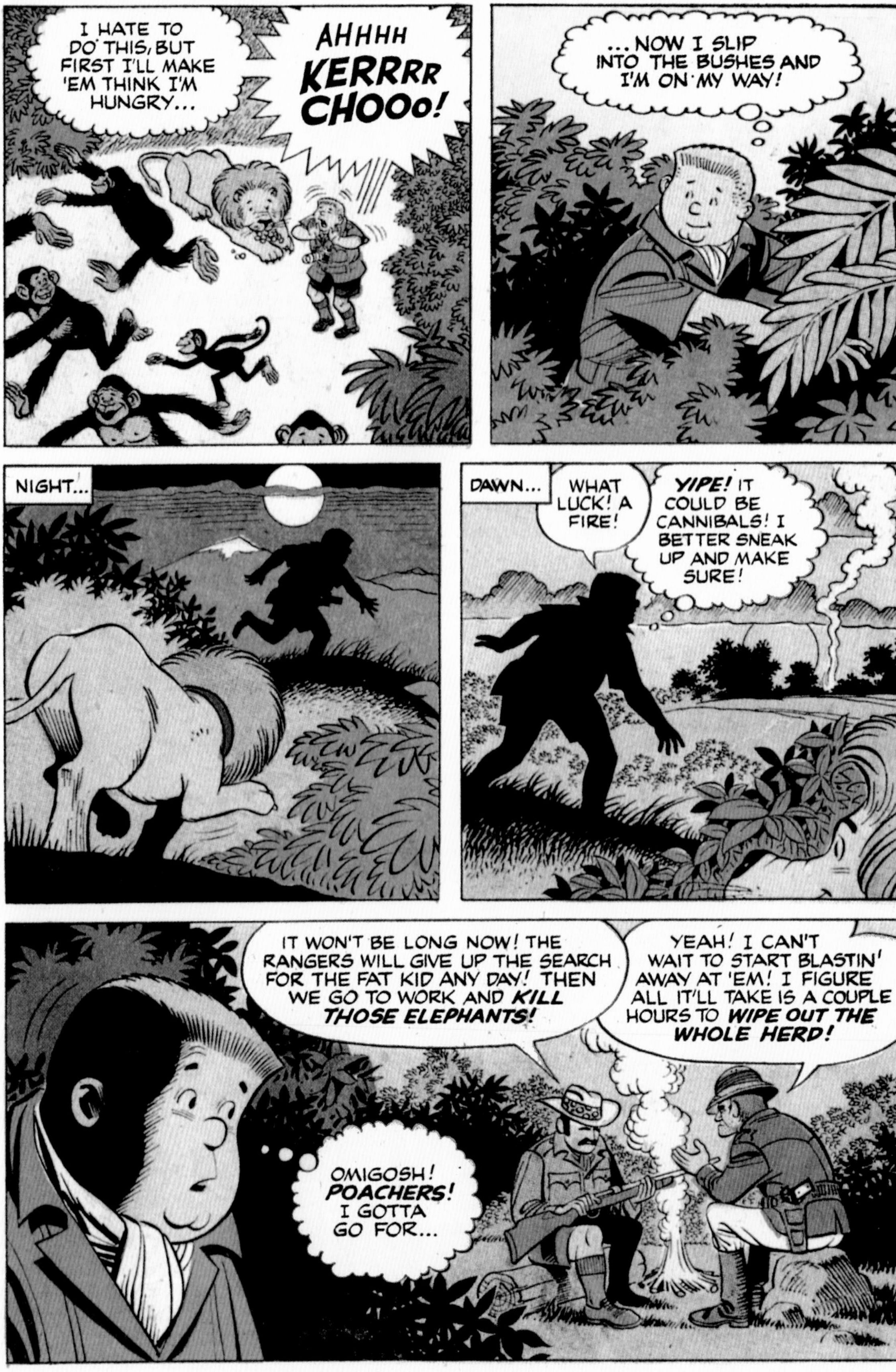
I HATE TO DO THIS, BUT FIRST I'LL MAKE 'EM THINK I'M HUNGRY...
AHHHH KERRRR CHOOo!
...NOW I SLIP INTO THE BUSHES AND I'M ON MY WAY!
NIGHT...
DAWN...
WHAT LUCK! A FIRE!
YIPE! IT COULD BE CANNIBALS! I BETTER SNEAK UP AND MAKE SURE!
IT WON'T BE LONG NOW! THE RANGERS WILL GIVE UP THE SEARCH FOR THE FAT KID ANY DAY! THEN WE GO TO WORK AND KILL THOSE ELEPHANTS!
YEAH! I CAN'T WAIT TO START BLASTIN' AWAY AT 'EM! I FIGURE ALL IT'LL TAKE IS A COUPLE HOURS TO WIPE OUT THE WHOLE HERD!
OMIGOSH! POACHERS! I GOTTA GO FOR...

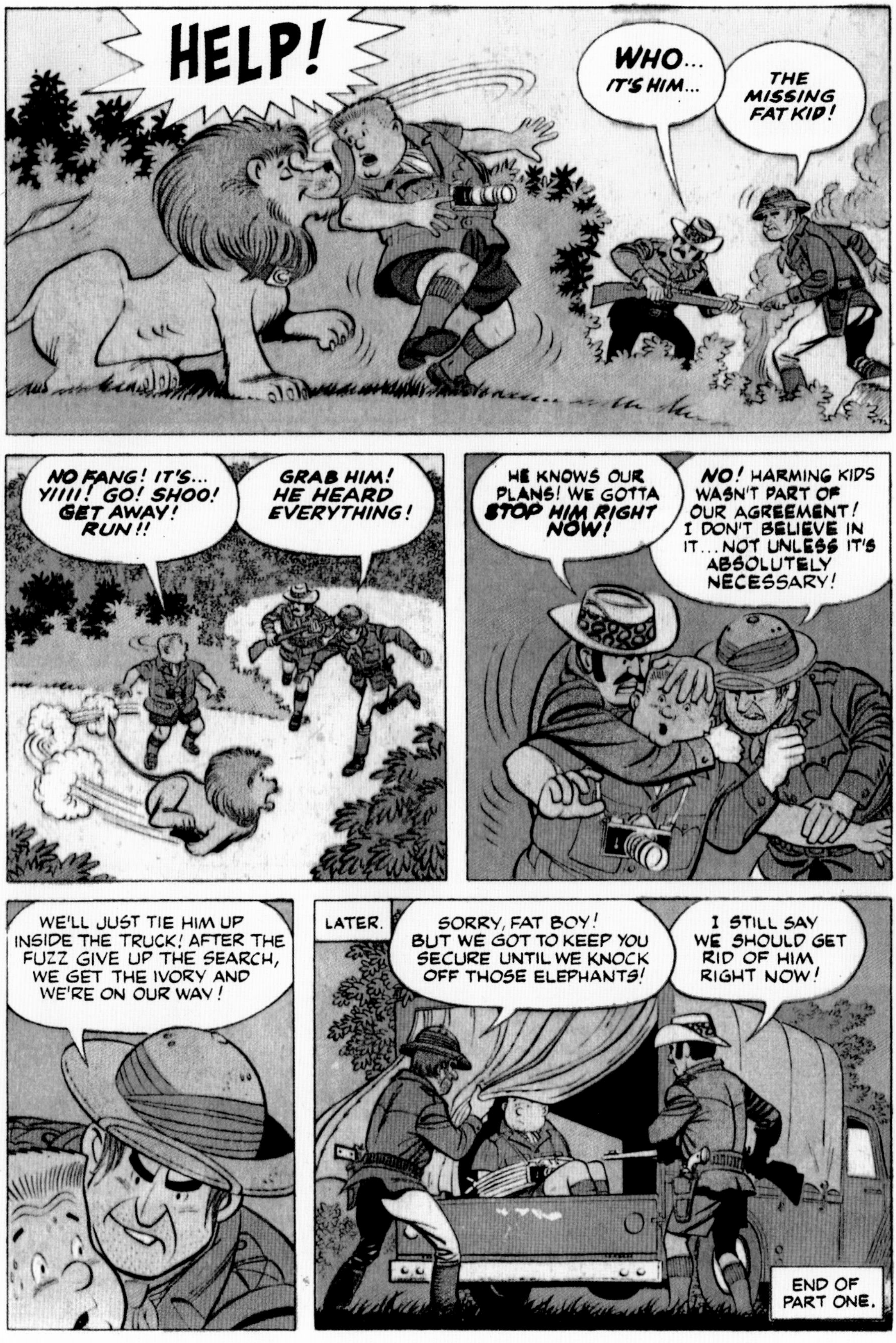
HELP!
WHO... IT'S HIM...
THE MISSING FAT KID!
NO FANG! IT'S... YIIII! GO! SHOO! GET AWAY! RUN!!
GRAB HIM! HE HEARD EVERYTHING!
HE KNOWS OUR PLANS! WE GOTTA STOP HIM RIGHT NOW!
NO! HARMING KIDS WASN'T PART OF OUR AGREEMENT! I DON'T BELIEVE IN IT... NOT UNLESS IT'S ABSOLUTELY NECESSARY!
WE'LL JUST TIE HIM UP INSIDE THE TRUCK! AFTER THE FUZZ GIVE UP THE SEARCH, WE GET THE IVORY AND WE'RE ON OUR WAY!
LATER.
SORRY, FAT BOY! BUT WE GOT TO KEEP YOU SECURE UNTIL WE KNOCK OFF THOSE ELEPHANTS!
I STILL SAY WE SHOULD GET RID OF HIM RIGHT NOW!
END OF PART ONE.

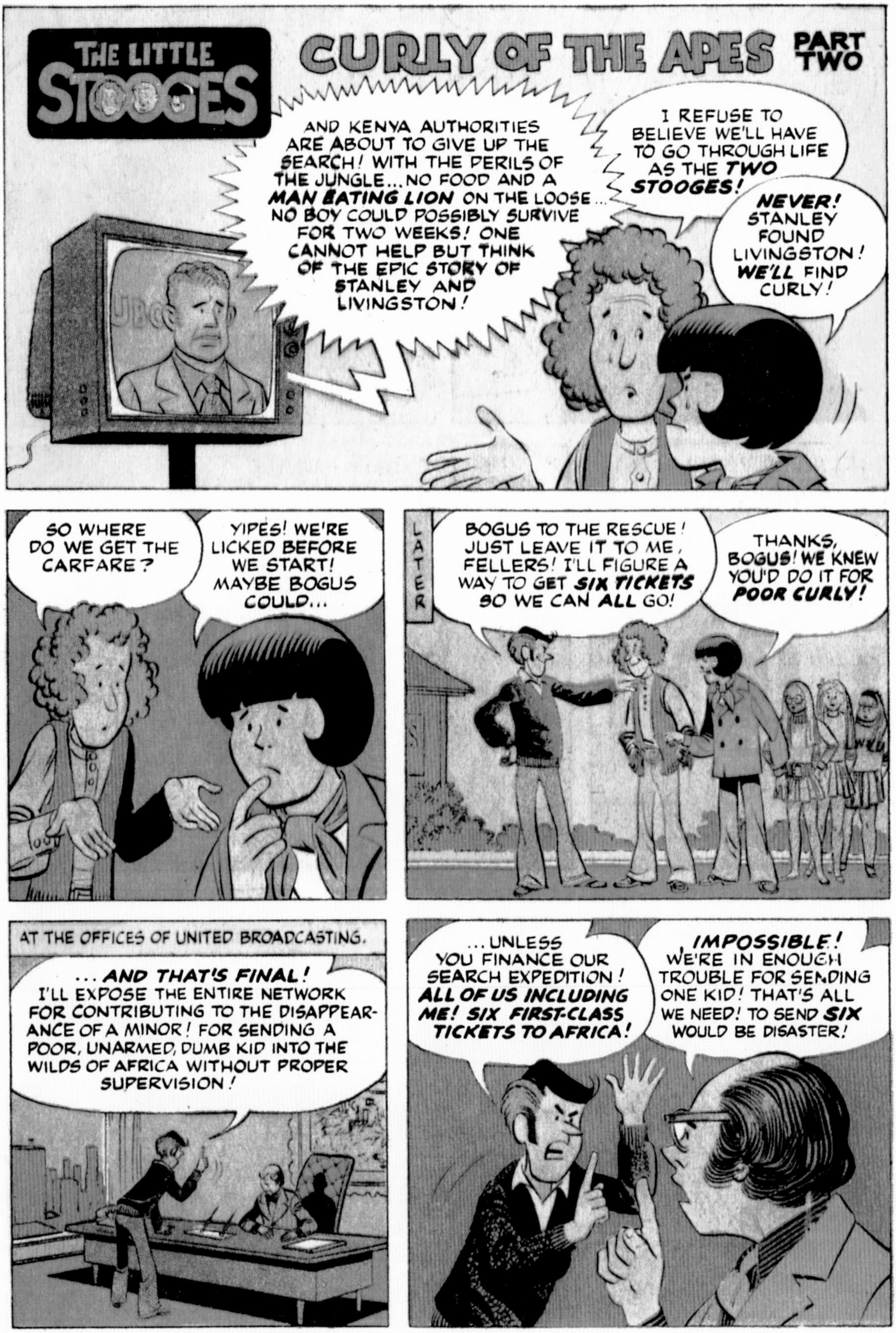
THE LITTLE STOOGES
CURLY OF THE APES PART TWO
AND KENYA AUTHORITIES ARE ABOUT TO GIVE UP THE SEARCH! WITH THE PERILS OF THE JUNGLE... NO FOOD AND A MAN EATING LION ON THE LOOSE... NO BOY COULD POSSIBLY SURVIVE FOR TWO WEEKS! ONE CANNOT HELP BUT THINK OF THE EPIC STORY OF STANLEY AND LIVINGSTON!
I REFUSE TO BELIEVE WE'LL HAVE TO GO THROUGH LIFE AS THE TWO STOOGES!
NEVER! STANLEY FOUND LIVINGSTON! WE'LL FIND CURLY!
SO WHERE DO WE GET THE CARFARE?
YIPES! WE'RE LICKED BEFORE WE START! MAYBE BOGUS COULD...
LATER
BOGUS TO THE RESCUE! JUST LEAVE IT TO ME, FELLERS! I'LL FIGURE A WAY TO GET SIX TICKETS SO WE CAN ALL GO!
THANKS, BOGUS! WE KNEW YOU'D DO IT FOR POOR CURLY!
AT THE OFFICES OF UNITED BROADCASTING.
... AND THAT'S FINAL! I'LL EXPOSE THE ENTIRE NETWORK FOR CONTRIBUTING TO THE DISAPPEARANCE OF A MINOR! FOR SENDING A POOR, UNARMED, DUMB KID INTO THE WILDS OF AFRICA WITHOUT PROPER SUPERVISION!
... UNLESS YOU FINANCE OUR SEARCH EXPEDITION! ALL OF US INCLUDING ME! SIX FIRST-CLASS TICKETS TO AFRICA!
IMPOSSIBLE! WE'RE IN ENOUGH TROUBLE FOR SENDING ONE KID! THAT'S ALL WE NEED! TO SEND SIX WOULD BE DISASTER!

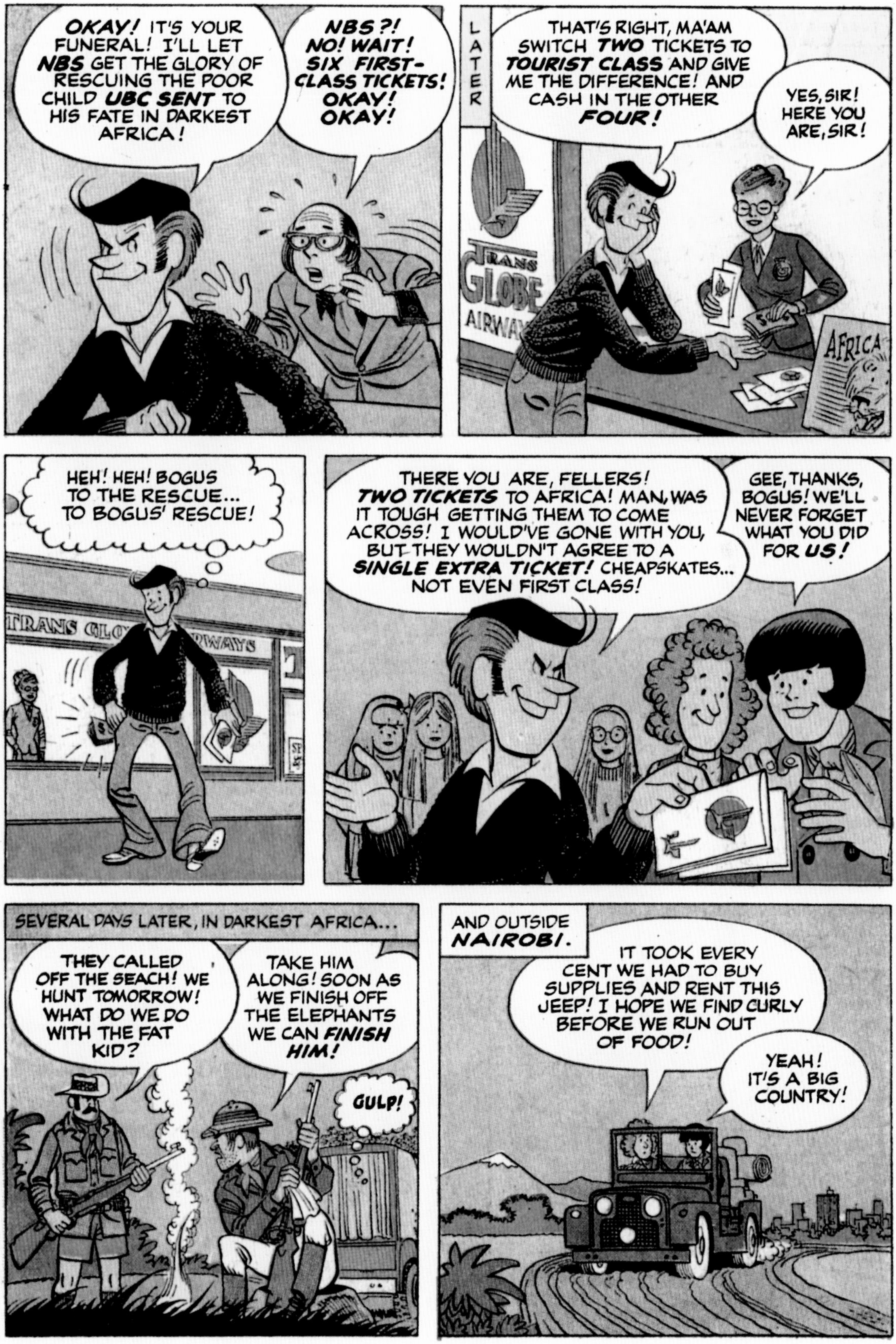
OKAY! IT'S YOUR FUNERAL! I'LL LET NBS GET THE GLORY OF RESCUING THE POOR CHILD UBC SENT TO HIS FATE IN DARKEST AFRICA!
NBS?! NO! WAIT! SIX FIRST-CLASS TICKETS! OKAY! OKAY!
LATER
THAT'S RIGHT, MA'AM SWITCH TWO TICKETS TO TOURIST CLASS AND GIVE ME THE DIFFERENCE! AND CASH IN THE OTHER FOUR!
YES, SIR! HERE YOU ARE, SIR!
TRANS GLOBE AIRWAYS
AFRICA
HEH! HEH! BOGUS TO THE RESCUE... TO BOGUS' RESCUE!
TRANS GLO RWAYS
THERE YOU ARE, FELLERS! TWO TICKETS TO AFRICA! MAN, WAS IT TOUGH GETTING THEM TO COME ACROSS! I WOULD'VE GONE WITH YOU, BUT THEY WOULDN'T AGREE TO A SINGLE EXTRA TICKET! CHEAPSKATES... NOT EVEN FIRST CLASS!
GEE, THANKS, BOGUS! WE'LL NEVER FORGET WHAT YOU DID FOR US!
SEVERAL DAYS LATER, IN DARKEST AFRICA...
THEY CALLED OFF THE SEACH! WE HUNT TOMORROW! WHAT DO WE DO WITH THE FAT KID?
TAKE HIM ALONG! SOON AS WE FINISH OFF THE ELEPHANTS WE CAN FINISH HIM!
GULP!
AND OUTSIDE NAIROBI.
IT TOOK EVERY CENT WE HAD TO BUY SUPPLIES AND RENT THIS JEEP! I HOPE WE FIND CURLY BEFORE WE RUN OUT OF FOOD!
YEAH! IT'S A BIG COUNTRY!

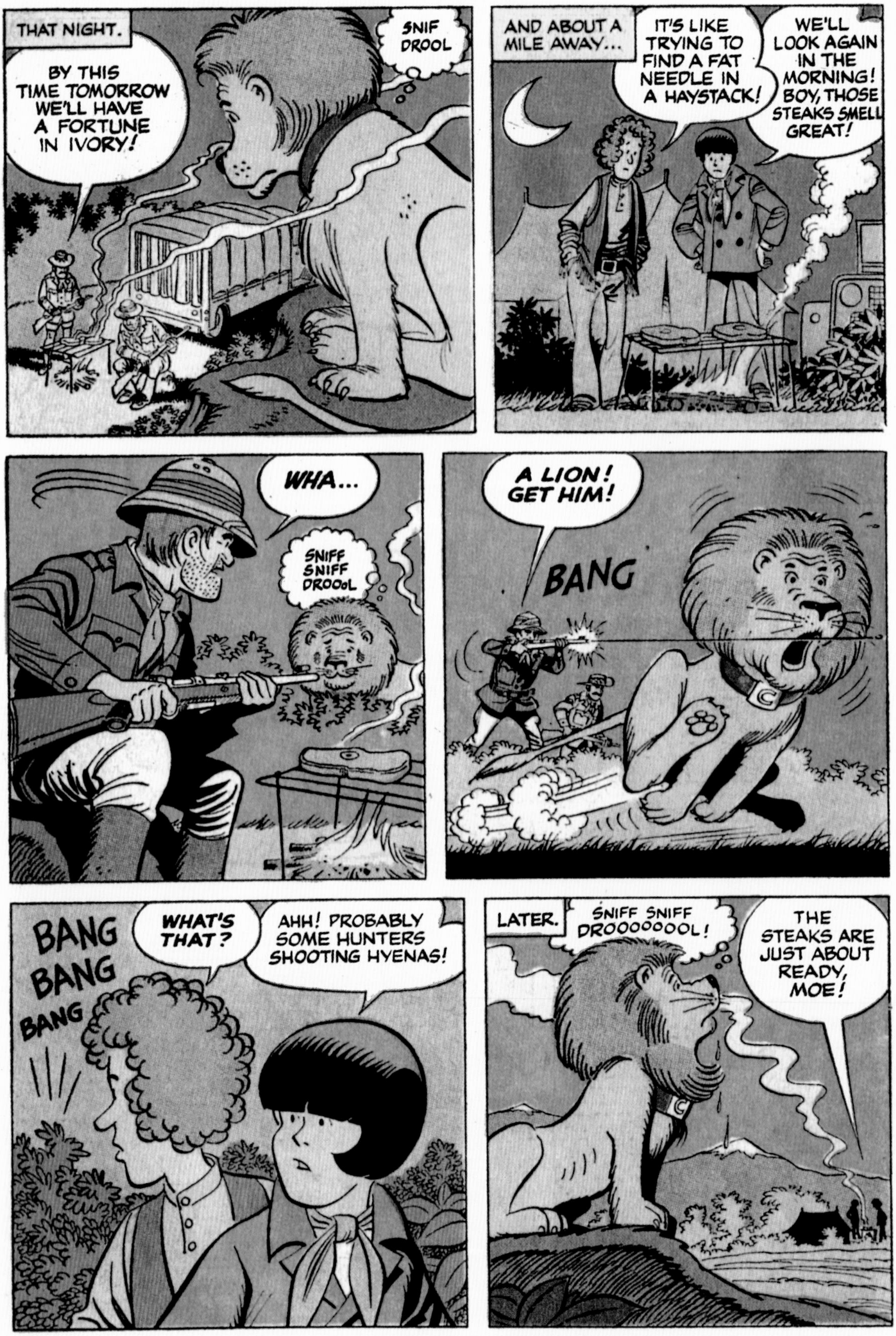
THAT NIGHT.
SNIF DROOL
BY THIS TIME TOMORROW WE'LL HAVE A FORTUNE IN IVORY!
AND ABOUT A MILE AWAY...
IT'S LIKE TRYING TO FIND A FAT NEEDLE IN A HAYSTACK!
WE'LL LOOK AGAIN IN THE MORNING! BOY, THOSE STEAKS SMELL GREAT!
WHA...
SNIFF SNIFF DROOoL
A LION! GET HIM!
BANG
BANG
BANG
BANG
WHAT'S THAT?
AHH! PROBABLY SOME HUNTERS SHOOTING HYENAS!
LATER.
SNIFF SNIFF DROOOOOOOL!
THE STEAKS ARE JUST ABOUT READY, MOE!

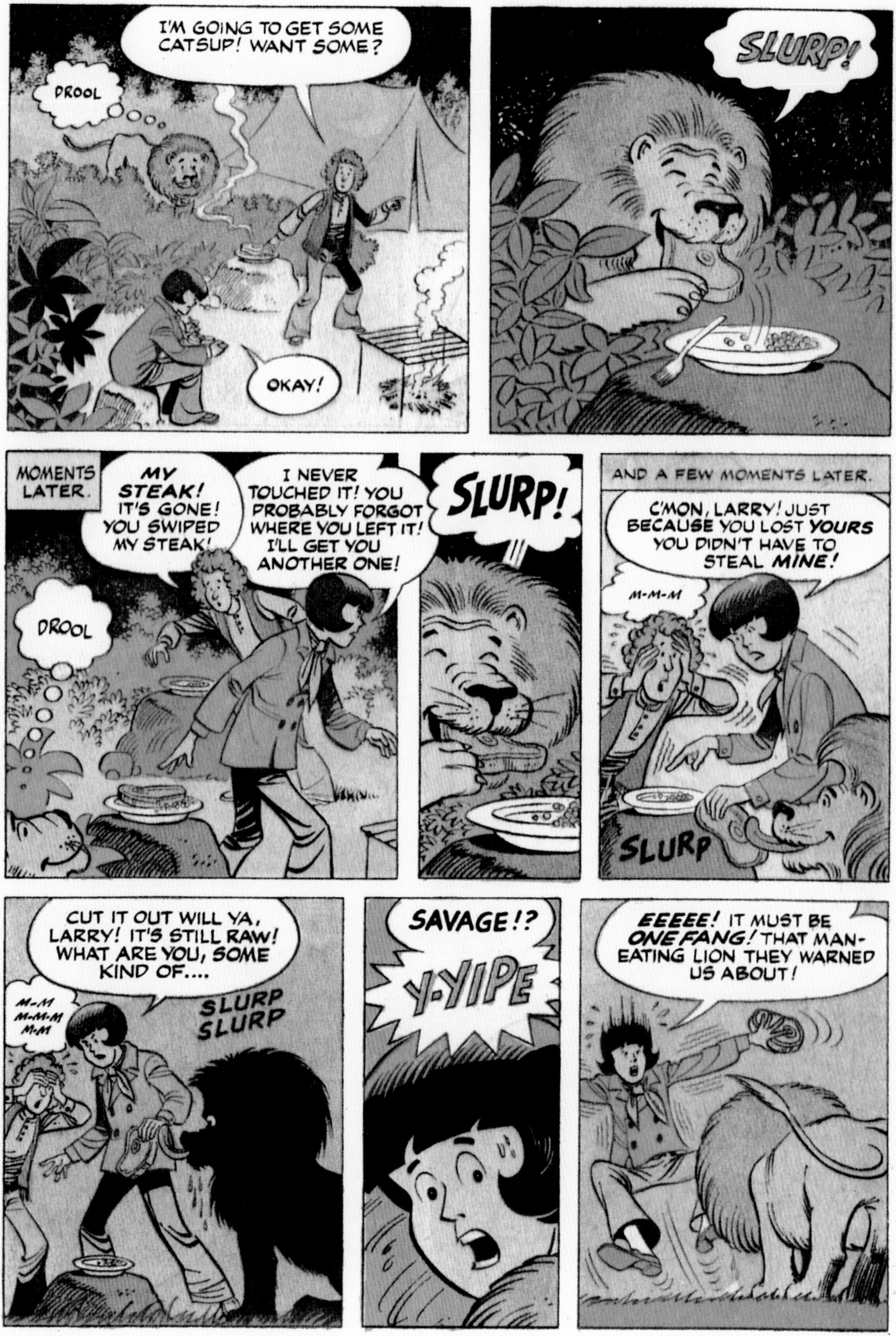
I'M GOING TO GET SOME CATSUP! WANT SOME?
DROOL
OKAY!
SLURP!
MOMENTS LATER.
MY STEAK! IT'S GONE! YOU SWIPED MY STEAK!
I NEVER TOUCHED IT! YOU PROBABLY FORGOT WHERE YOU LEFT IT! I'LL GET YOU ANOTHER ONE!
DROOL
SLURP!
AND A FEW MOMENTS LATER.
C'MON, LARRY! JUST BECAUSE YOU LOST YOURS YOU DIDN'T HAVE TO STEAL MINE!
M-M-M
SLURP
CUT IT OUT WILL YA, LARRY! IT'S STILL RAW! WHAT ARE YOU, SOME KIND OF....
M-M M-M-M M-M
SLURP SLURP
SAVAGE!?
Y-YIPE
EEEEE! IT MUST BE ONE FANG! THAT MAN-EATING LION THEY WARNED US ABOUT!

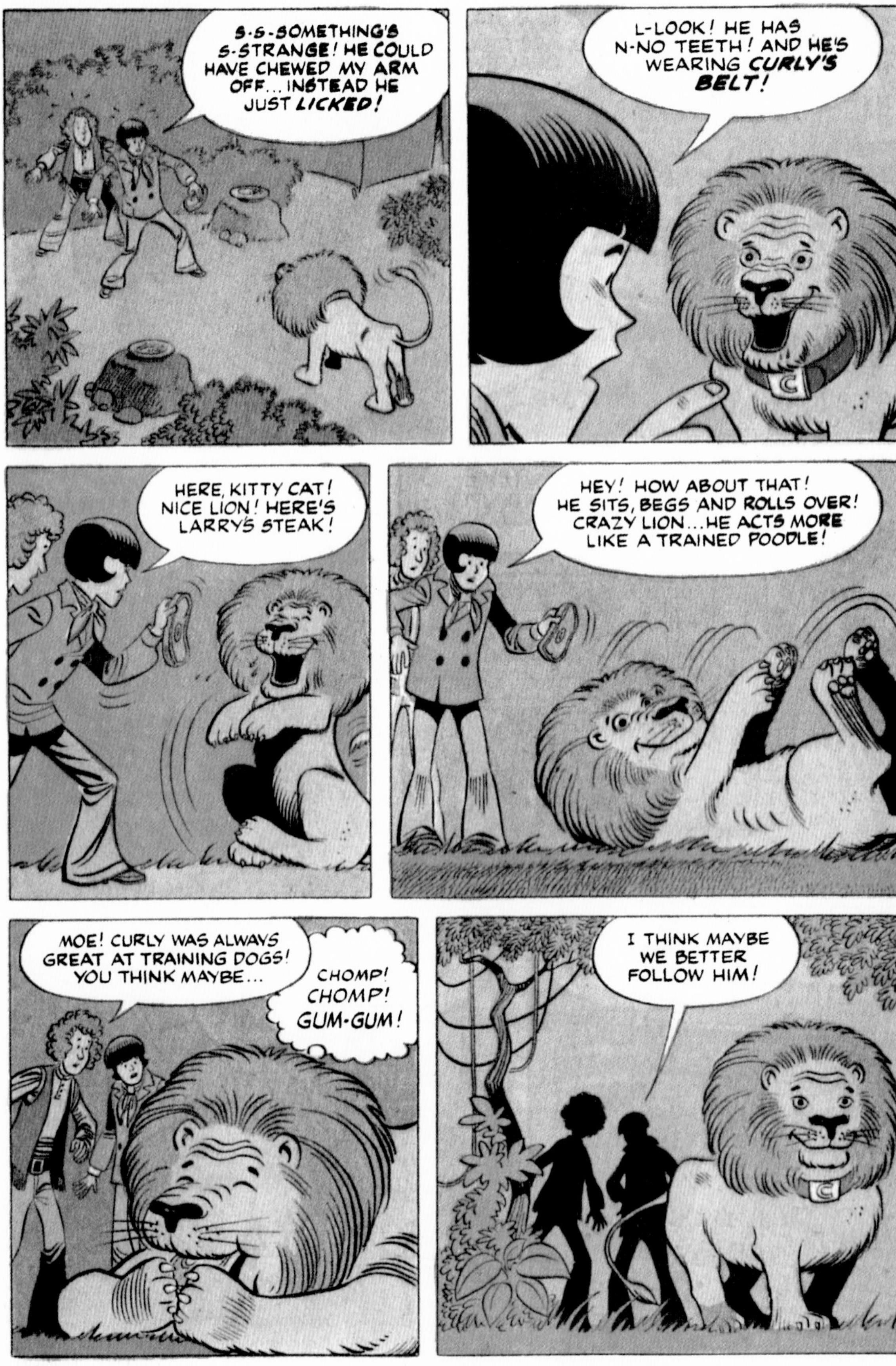
S-S-SOMETHING'S S-STRANGE! HE COULD HAVE CHEWED MY ARM OFF... INSTEAD HE JUST LICKED!
L-LOOK! HE HAS N-NO TEETH! AND HE'S WEARING CURLY'S BELT!
HERE, KITTY CAT! NICE LION! HERE'S LARRY'S STEAK!
HEY! HOW ABOUT THAT! HE SITS, BEGS AND ROLLS OVER! CRAZY LION... HE ACTS MORE LIKE A TRAINED POODLE!
MOE! CURLY WAS ALWAYS GREAT AT TRAINING DOGS! YOU THINK MAYBE...
CHOMP! CHOMP! GUM-GUM!
I THINK MAYBE WE BETTER FOLLOW HIM!

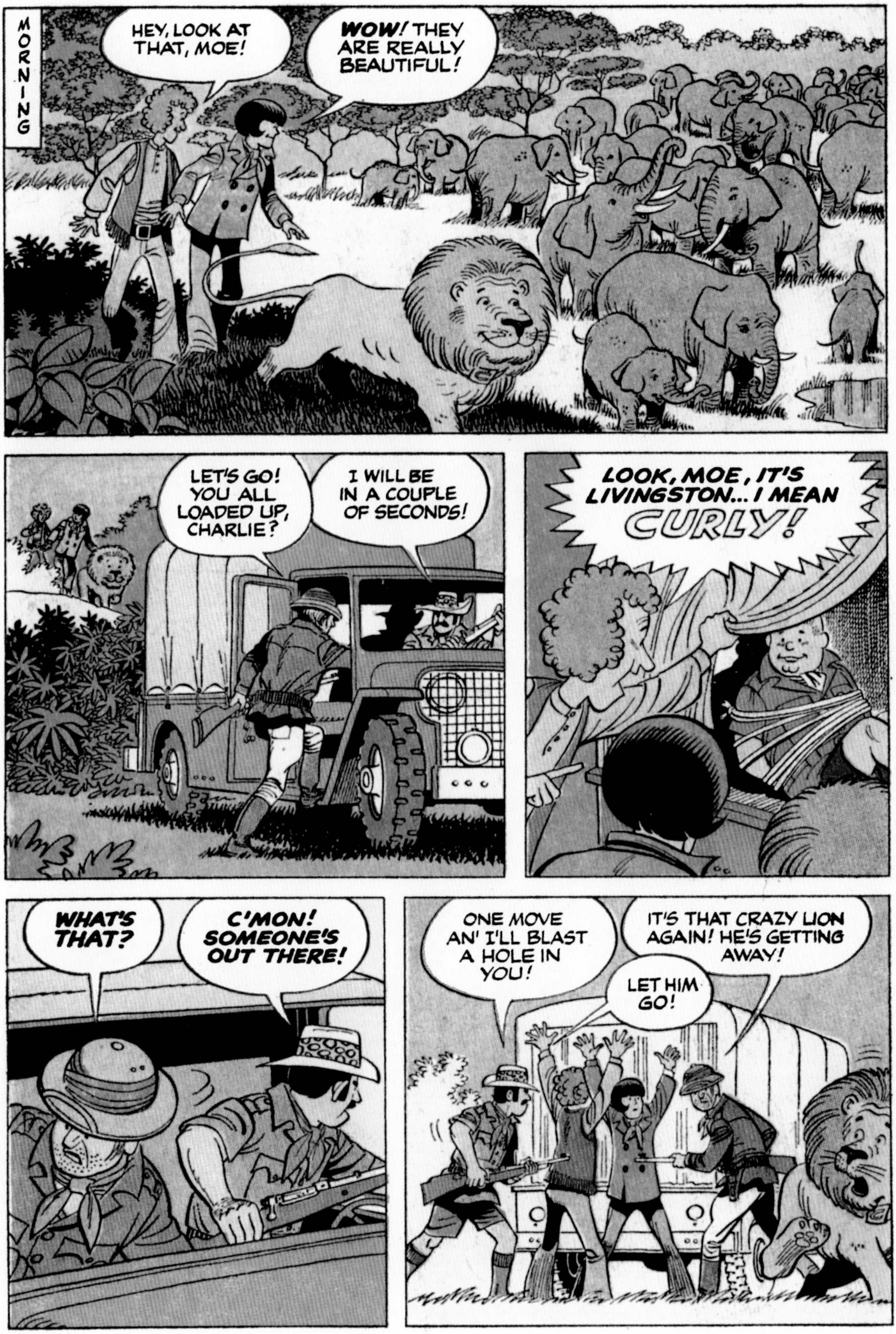
MORNING
HEY, LOOK AT THAT, MOE!
WOW! THEY ARE REALLY BEAUTIFUL!
LET'S GO! YOU ALL LOADED UP, CHARLIE?
I WILL BE IN A COUPLE OF SECONDS!
LOOK, MOE, IT'S LIVINGSTON... I MEAN CURLY!
WHAT'S THAT?
C'MON! SOMEONE'S OUT THERE!
ONE MOVE AN' I'LL BLAST A HOLE IN YOU!
IT'S THAT CRAZY LION AGAIN! HE'S GETTING AWAY!
LET HIM GO!

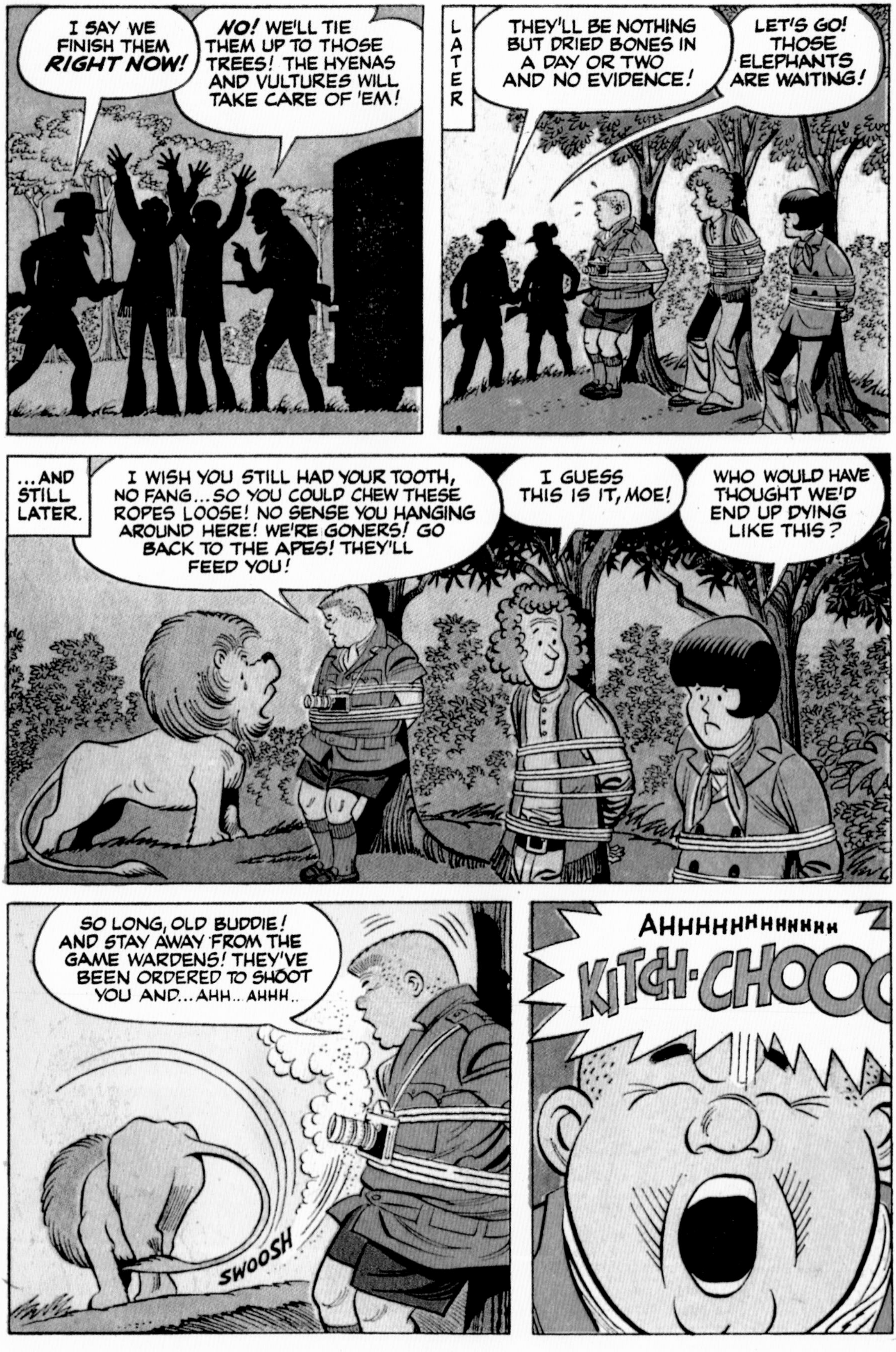
I SAY WE FINISH THEM RIGHT NOW!
NO! WE'LL TIE THEM UP TO THOSE TREES! THE HYENAS AND VULTURES WILL TAKE CARE OF 'EM!
LATER
THEY'LL BE NOTHING BUT DRIED BONES IN A DAY OR TWO AND NO EVIDENCE!
LET'S GO! THOSE ELEPHANTS ARE WAITING!
...AND STILL LATER.
I WISH YOU STILL HAD YOUR TOOTH, NO FANG...SO YOU COULD CHEW THESE ROPES LOOSE! NO SENSE YOU HANGING AROUND HERE! WE'RE GONERS! GO BACK TO THE APES! THEY'LL FEED YOU!
I GUESS THIS IS IT, MOE!
WHO WOULD HAVE THOUGHT WE'D END UP DYING LIKE THIS?
SO LONG, OLD BUDDIE! AND STAY AWAY FROM THE GAME WARDENS! THEY'VE BEEN ORDERED TO SHOOT YOU AND...AHH...AHHH..
SWOOSH
AHHHHHHHHHHHHH
KITCH-CHOOO

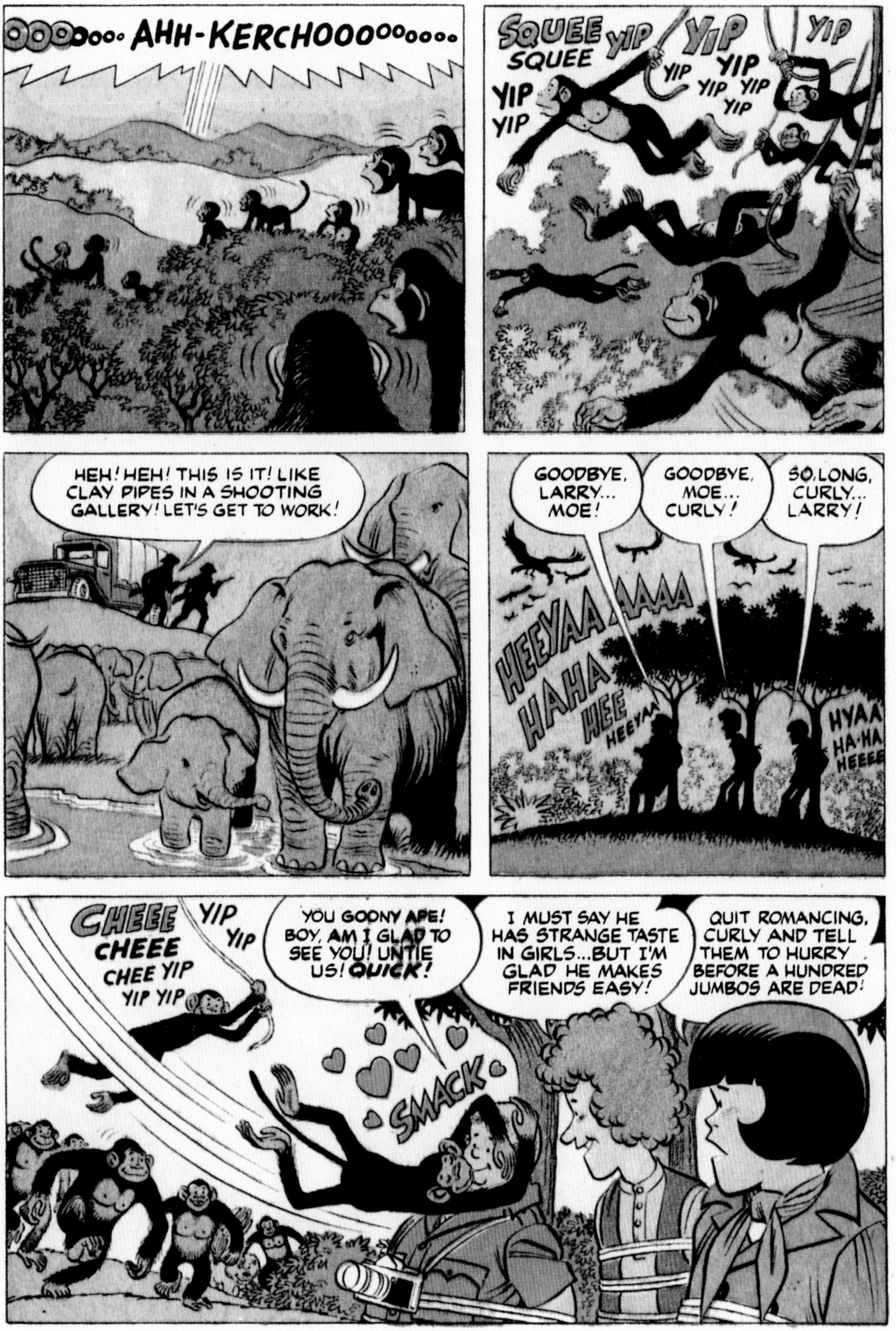
OOOOooo AHH-KERCHOOOooooo
SQUEE SQUEE YIP YIP YIP YIP YIP YIP YIP YIP YIP YIP YIP
HEH! HEH! THIS IS IT! LIKE CLAY PIPES IN A SHOOTING GALLERY! LET'S GET TO WORK!
GOODBYE, LARRY... MOE!
GOODBYE, MOE... CURLY!
SO LONG, CURLY... LARRY!
HEEYAA AAAA HAHA HEE HEEYAA
HYAA HA-HA HEEEE
CHEEE CHEEE CHEE YIP YIP YIP YIP YIP
YOU GOONY APE! BOY, AM I GLAD TO SEE YOU! UNTIE US! QUICK!
SMACK
I MUST SAY HE HAS STRANGE TASTE IN GIRLS...BUT I'M GLAD HE MAKES FRIENDS EASY!
QUIT ROMANCING, CURLY AND TELL THEM TO HURRY BEFORE A HUNDRED JUMBOS ARE DEAD!

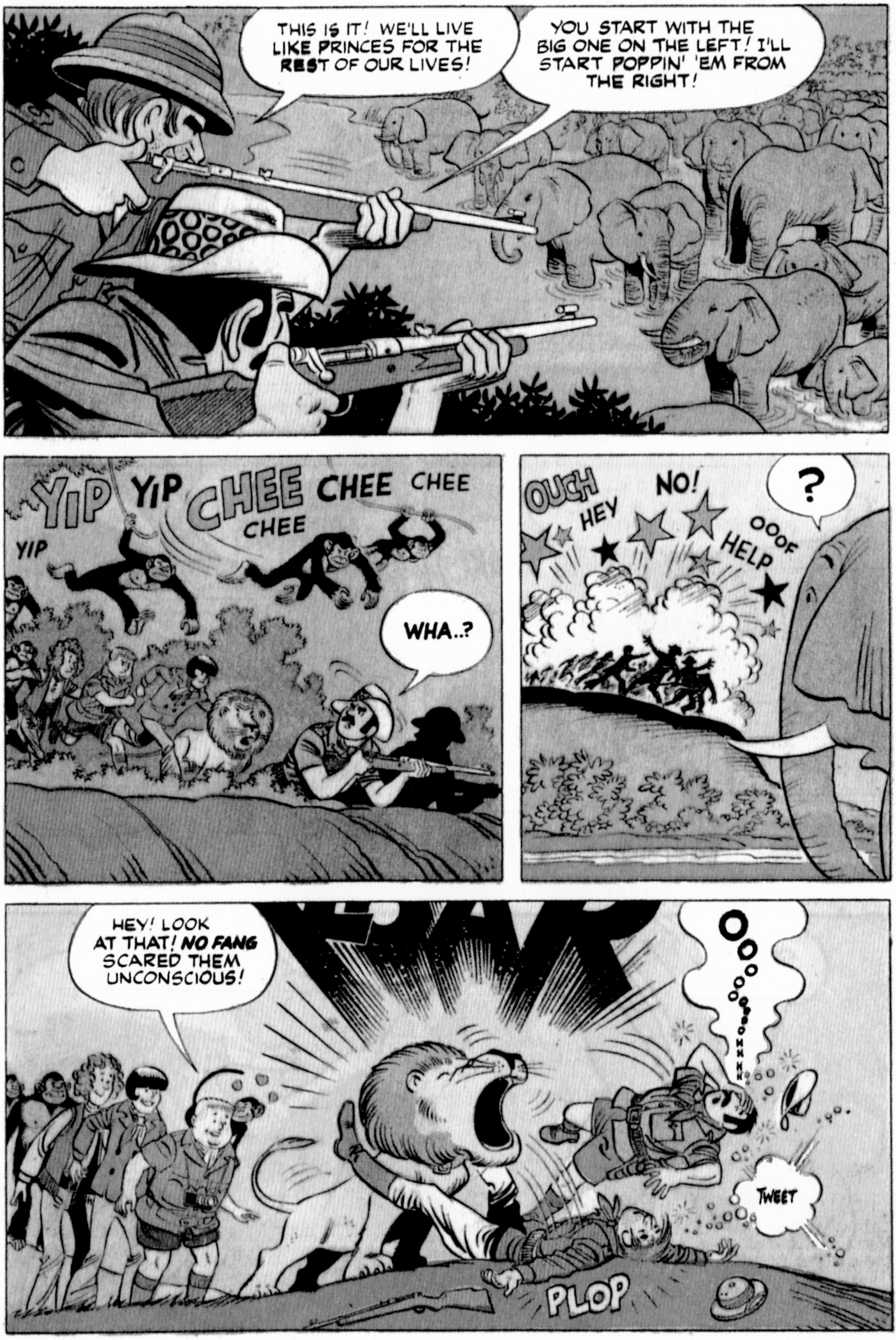
THIS IS IT! WE'LL LIVE LIKE PRINCES FOR THE REST OF OUR LIVES!
YOU START WITH THE BIG ONE ON THE LEFT! I'LL START POPPIN' 'EM FROM THE RIGHT!
YIP YIP CHEE CHEE CHEE CHEE
YIP
WHA..?
OUCH
HEY
NO!
OOOF
HELP
?
HEY! LOOK AT THAT! NO FANG SCARED THEM UNCONSCIOUS!
TWEET
PLOP

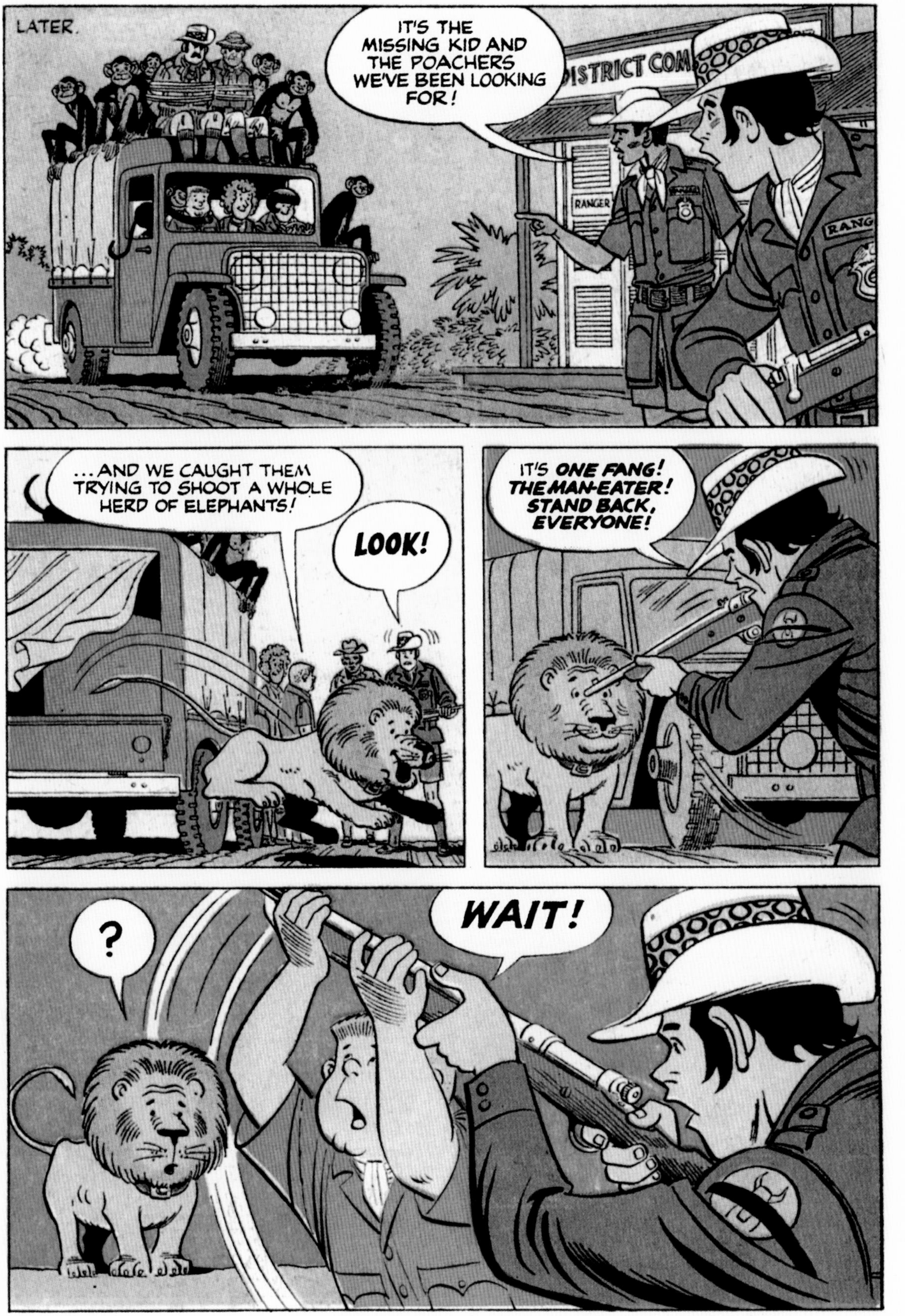
LATER.
IT'S THE MISSING KID AND THE POACHERS WE'VE BEEN LOOKING FOR!
DISTRICT COM
RANGER
...AND WE CAUGHT THEM TRYING TO SHOOT A WHOLE HERD OF ELEPHANTS!
LOOK!
IT'S ONE FANG! THE MAN-EATER! STAND BACK, EVERYONE!
?
WAIT!

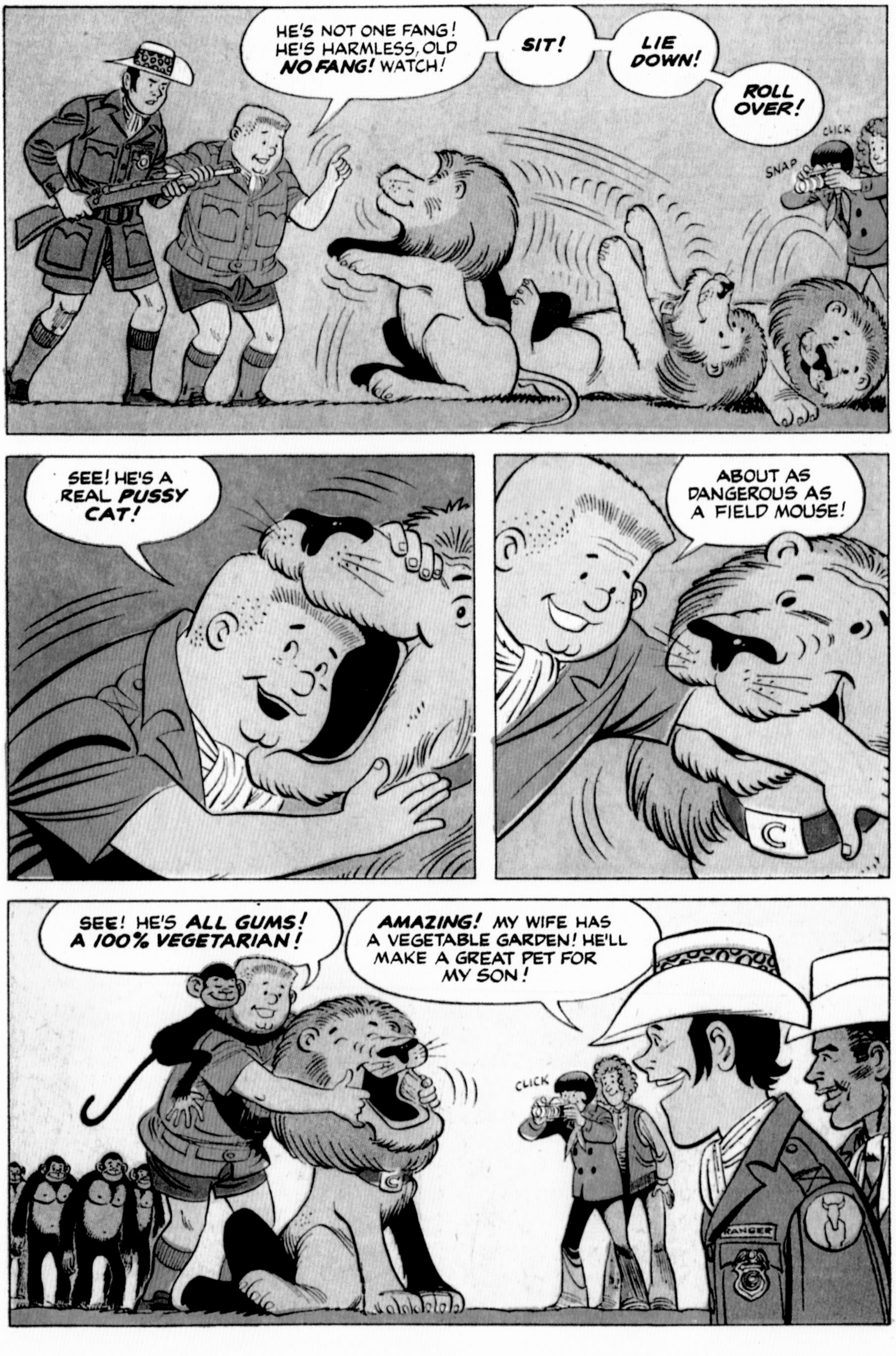
HE'S NOT ONE FANG! HE'S HARMLESS, OLD NO FANG! WATCH!
SIT!
LIE DOWN!
ROLL OVER!
CLICK
SNAP
SEE! HE'S A REAL PUSSY CAT!
ABOUT AS DANGEROUS AS A FIELD MOUSE!
SEE! HE'S ALL GUMS! A 100% VEGETARIAN!
AMAZING! MY WIFE HAS A VEGETABLE GARDEN! HE'LL MAKE A GREAT PET FOR MY SON!
CLICK
RANGER

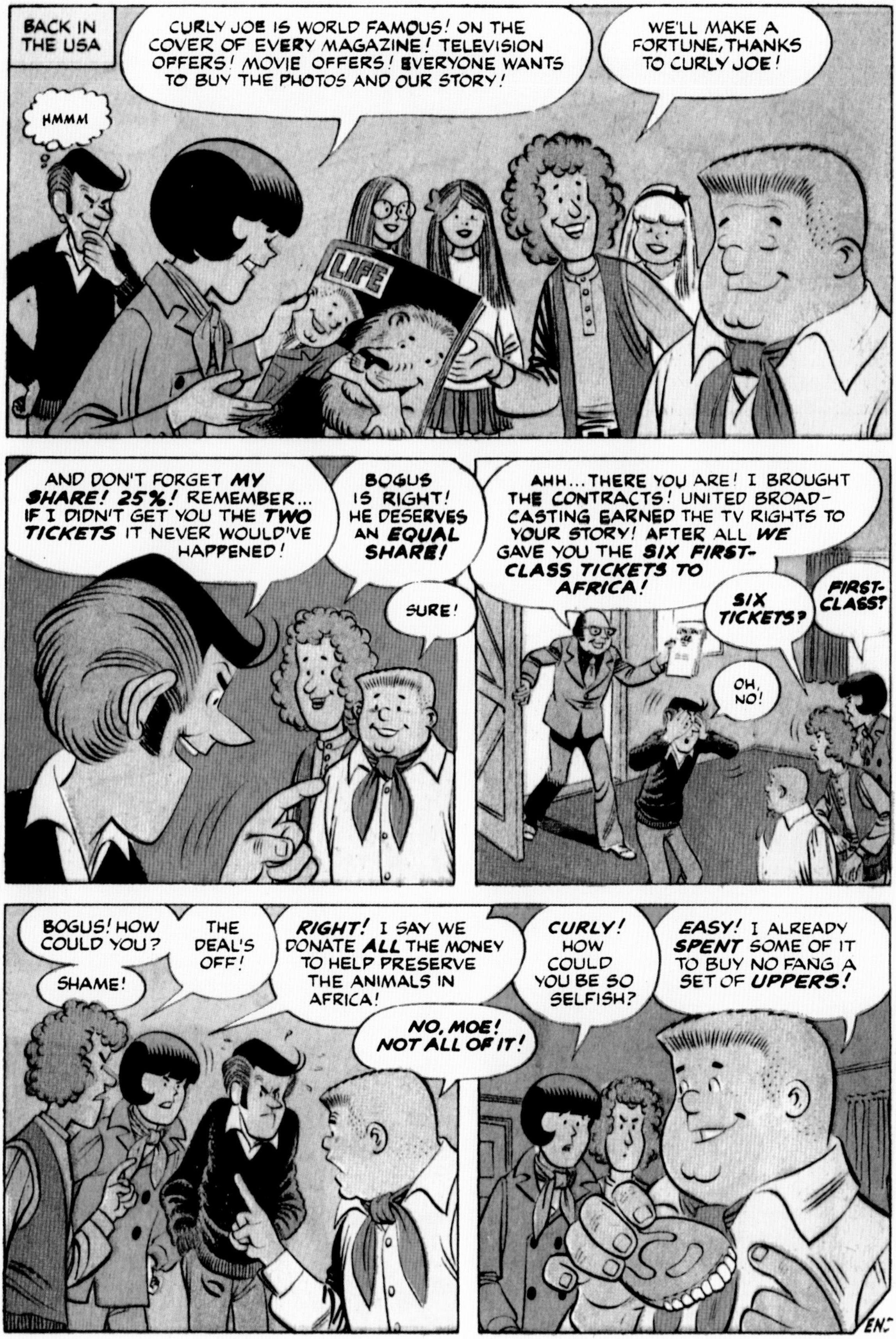
BACK IN THE USA
CURLY JOE IS WORLD FAMOUS! ON THE COVER OF EVERY MAGAZINE! TELEVISION OFFERS! MOVIE OFFERS! EVERYONE WANTS TO BUY THE PHOTOS AND OUR STORY!
WE'LL MAKE A FORTUNE, THANKS TO CURLY JOE!
HMMM
LIFE
AND DON'T FORGET MY SHARE! 25%! REMEMBER... IF I DIDN'T GET YOU THE TWO TICKETS IT NEVER WOULD'VE HAPPENED!
BOGUS IS RIGHT! HE DESERVES AN EQUAL SHARE!
SURE!
AHH... THERE YOU ARE! I BROUGHT THE CONTRACTS! UNITED BROADCASTING EARNED THE TV RIGHTS TO YOUR STORY! AFTER ALL WE GAVE YOU THE SIX FIRST-CLASS TICKETS TO AFRICA!
SIX TICKETS?
FIRST-CLASS?
OH, NO!
BOGUS! HOW COULD YOU?
SHAME!
THE DEAL'S OFF!
RIGHT! I SAY WE DONATE ALL THE MONEY TO HELP PRESERVE THE ANIMALS IN AFRICA!
NO, MOE! NOT ALL OF IT!
CURLY! HOW COULD YOU BE SO SELFISH?
EASY! I ALREADY SPENT SOME OF IT TO BUY NO FANG A SET OF UPPERS!
END

AFTERWORD

by Jim Salicrup

This second volume of THE BEST OF THE THREE STOOGES COMICBOOKS is respectfully dedicated to one of the great pioneers of the comic art world, the legendary Joe Kubert. A case could be made that if it wasn't for Joe Kubert, there would never have been any THREE STOOGES comicbooks, or at the very least, there wouldn't have been THE THREE STOOGES comicbooks by Norman Maurer. As Norman recalls in his interview, presented on page six, and as Joe remembers in his interview presented here, it was during a vacation to California that the idea to do comicbooks based on Norman's father-in-law's world famous comedy team was hatched.

As a young fan, I met Joe Kubert at conventions and was always impressed by his kindness and friendly attitude. I even had a fan letter published in DC's STAR-SPANGLED WAR STORIES #164, which was edited by Joe. Later, as an editor then working at Marvel Comics, I interviewed him for the May, 1984 issue of David Anthony Kraft's COMICS INTERVIEW magazine. Here is an excerpt, that focuses on his relationship with Norman Maurer, from that conversation…

Jim Salicrup: I've heard that you started in comics at an incredibly young age.

Joe Kubert: I was 11 years old.

Jim: Then you actually were a comics professional before you even started high school, right?

Joe: I was still going to junior high school in East Flatbush, in Brooklyn. One of the guys I was going to school with, a kid I used to play ball with, had a relative who owned MLJ, the company that's Archie Comics today. I had been doing cartoon-type drawing since the time I could hold a pencil in my hand, and this friend of mine had seen work that I'd been doing and suggested that I go up and see his relative at MLJ. This sounded absolutely fascinating to me. So I did a couple of drawings, got on the subway, and went to the MLJ office, which at that time was down on Canal Street in lower Manhattan.

Jim: What was it like, a kid from Brooklyn, 10 or 11 years old, going to the Big City to break into comics?

Joe: I couldn't begin to tell you how exciting it was for me. I can still remember the smell of the MLJ office. *(Laughter.)* Not that it stunk, but it had a heady aroma, a combination of ink and paper and pencils. It smelled like a comicbook house is supposed to smell. It held that kind of excitement to me.

Jim: When did you decide you wanted to make your living drawing comicbooks?

Joe: The first day I was up at MLJ.

Jim: What was the reaction of your family?

Joe: My family came from the other side. They were immigrants. The idea of anybody making a living doing these crazy little drawings was probably the furthest thing removed from their minds. But my parents were extremely understanding, and it's a result of that that I'm in this business to this day. Because despite the fact that my parents never figured that I'd be able to make a living wage at this, just seeing that I was so involved and interested in it, and that I wanted to do this more than anything else, was enough for them to say, "Well, go ahead."

Jim: That sounds sensational.

Joe: I was incredibly fortunate. A couple of guys I knew, in Brooklyn, with similar family backgrounds, could draw as well as me, maybe better, but their parents wanted them in the family business—plumbing or whatever—and they had to give it up. Anyway, I was at MLJ when STEEL STERLING and THE SHIELD and those things that are coming out now were really very popular. I never dreamed of going up to a place like DC because DC was, I don't know how many stages beyond MLJ at that time. But I didn't seriously start going around to the different comicbook houses til I started off to high school at Music and Art, where I met my buddy Norman Maurer. And at that time all the comicbook publishers were situated in Manhattan. And Norman and I would play hooky, and we'd meet, before we went into the homeroom class, and say, "Well, do we go to school today, or go to the comicbook houses?"

And two or three days out of the week Norman and I would take our drawings and we would walk from 135th Street, which is where Music and Art was, down to midtown, maybe all the way down to 23rd Street, and we'd hit like five or six places, and ask to speak to the art director. We were perhaps 11 or 12 at the time and would make ourselves as pestiferous and obnoxious as we could. (Laughter.) But everyone was extremely kind to us.

Jim: Didn't you publish your own work – 3-D stuff – in the Fifties?

Joe: I got out of the Army in 1952, and while I was stationed in Germany, I had seen some three-dimensional magazines – magazines that contained 3-D photographs, not illustrations – with the red-and-green glasses. And when I came back, one of the first things my wife and I did – I had gotten married before going overseas – we took a vacation and went out to California. The guy I wanted to see out there was Norman Maurer because he had taken up residence permanently out there, having married the daughter of Moe Howard. I had been out there for their wedding, as a matter of fact, in 1948,

I had driven out there from New Jersey with Irwin Hasen, who was later the artist for DONDI, in my car, a Town and Country Chrysler, a convertible, the top of which we never put up the whole time. Irwin did not drive, so I had driven the whole way and Irwin was my navigator.

Anyhow getting back to 1952, my wife and I took our first vacation in California. I had made contact and had a relationship on-going with St. John Publishing Company, prior to having gone into the Army, and St. John evidenced an interest in a collaboration where we would be producing comics as co-publishers. I had come up with the idea for TOR in 1950 on the troop ship heading out for Europe.

Jim: So, what did you do on your 1952 vacation in California?

Joe: Norman and I were shooting the breeze, and Norman seemed more interested in getting back into comics than what he was doing at the time. He had become the agent for the Three Stooges. And I told Norman that if I could set something up and that seemed reasonable and equitable and interesting to him would he be interested in coming into a deal that I was hoping to set up with St. John. Norman said that he wanted to put out a THREE STOOGES comicbook. When I got back from California and told these things to St. John, they said "Great, let's go with it." I contacted Norman and Norman came out with his wife. At that time he didn't have any children; he left a house in California, and rented a house at Lake Hopacatong in New Jersey, which is not far from where I lived at the time. And we started publishing TOR and THREE STOOGES and one or two other books at the time, with the St. John Publishing Company.

Jim: Were you working out of a studio or at home?

Joe: We had offices in New York, and we could go into the city. At that time we were looking for something new in comics. The competition was pretty heavy. It was about 1953, and we were looking for some really novel idea to push our books ahead. It was at that time that I remembered the 3-D stuff that I had seen in the Army. I said to Norman, "Look, do you think there's any possibility that we could do what I saw in these magazines?" In an illustrated form, as opposed to photographs. At first Norman said that he didn't think it was possible, but after we kind of chewed it around a little bit we felt that it might be feasible. And he and I and his brother Lenny– who I think had more technical knowledge than either Norman or myself– knocked it around, and finally worked out a method whereby we could do a 3-D comic with a price feasible for a comicbook audience. So Norman and I made our first test sketches. One was of TOR, another was of the STOOGES, and we also had a painting– a wash drawing– to see what a painting would look like in 3-D. The painting was done by a person named Bob Bean, who eventually went on to own Transfilm-Wylde Animation, an animation studio, and was very successful. Anyhow, we made these samples and couldn't know whether it had worked or not, because first we had to reproduce these in color and get the glasses to look through and see if they really worked. And you know what we did for the color glasses?

Jim: No, what?

Joe: Well, at one time lollipops used to be sold wrapped with color cellophane. (Laughter.) That's right, that's what we used to make our first test 3-D glasses. We went to an engraver with the pictures, had shots made, set them up the way we felt it should be set up, and made the glasses out of these cellophanes from the lollipops. And the damn thing worked. So that was how we published the 3-D comics, along with TOR, THREE STOOGES, and a whole bunch of other things.

(The full interview with Joe Kubert, where he discusses his countless other comicbook accomplishments, has been republished, along with many other incredible interviews, in *David Anthony Kraft's COMICS INTERVIEW THE COMPLETE COLLECTION Volume 1*, available from co2comics.com.)

A few years ago, I got to hang out again with Joe at a comicbook convention in Spain, and it was indescribably wonderful. Even though he was in his eighties, he still had his famous vice-like grip when shaking hands. It was still a bit of a shock to hear of his passing. As someone who also started working in the comics field at a very young age, I hope I remain healthy enough to keep doing what I love as long as I live, just like Joe did. Thanks, Joe—for everything.

A FEW NOTES ON THIS VOLUME...

"Beach Boo-Boobs," illustrated by Pete Alvarado, which originally ran in Dell's THE THREE STOOGES #3, was squeezed out of Volume 1, so we're happily presenting it here. There is also some debate as to whether Dell's THE THREE STOOGES #4 was illustrated by Pete Alvarado or Joe Messerli. We're going out on a limb and saying it's by Joe Messerli, but we could be wrong. Not many comics ran with credits back in those days, so we're often relying on the best guesses of comics historians and researchers. Furthermore, while it's possible to learn to identify artists' styles, it's a bit trickier to identify writers' styles, especially on licensed material. That's why we don't have writing credits on the Dell comics. Or credits for lettering and coloring for that matter.

Speaking of Joe Messerli, here's some biographical information gleaned from www.joemesserli.com and other places, Joe was born in Texas in 1930. At age 18 he was assisting cartoonist Charlie Plumb on the *Ella Cinders* syndicated newspaper comic strip. He served in the U.S. Army from 1950 to 1952, and was then able to attend the Chouinard Art Institute in Los Angeles, California, on the G.I. Bill. While there he ghosted the *Napoleon and Uncle Elby* comic strip. He later assisted the great Al Wiseman on DENNIS THE MENACE comicbooks in 1956-1957. He worked at UPA Studios (designed the very first TWILIGHT ZONE logo) and NBC Burbank Graphic Arts Department (color illustrations for the BONANZA credits, the "More to Come" cards featured during breaks on THE TONIGHT SHOW *with Johnny Carson*); he was at Cambria Studio when they did CLUTCH CARGO, CAPTAIN FATHOM, SPACE ANGEL etc; for most of the 60s he did the inking and lettering on the FLINTSTONES daily and Sunday strip and YOGI BEAR daily panel and Sunday page for Hannah-Barbera. His comicbook work for Western Publishing in L.A. included THE THREE STOOGES, BUGS BUNNY, PORKY PIG, YOSEMITE SAM, DAFFY DUCK, CAVE KIDS, FLINTSTONES, PINK PANTHER, BABY SNOOTS, WOODY WOODPECKER, ANDY PANDA and others. He spent many years doing coloring and activity books for Western Publishing in New York, L.A., and Racine. Also in New York: Little Golden Books (Warner Bros. characters), Marvel Books (FLINTSTONE KIDS, FOOFUR, SCOOBY-DOO), DC Comics Publications (LOONEY TUNES, TINY TOONS characters); Random House (SESAME STREET). Joe Messerli passed away June 23rd, 2010.

For true comicbook collectors, it should be noted that the comics we've identified as Dell's THE THREE STOOGES #1-5 are technically issues of Dell's FOUR COLOR COMICS, a comicbook series that featured different characters from issue to issue. After appearing in five different issues of FOUR COLOR COMICS, THE THREE STOOGES were awarded their own official comicbook that began with issue #6. For the record, here's the official numbers and dates for THE THREE STOOGES #1-5: #1: 1043-1, October, 1959; #2: 1078-2, February 1960; #3: 1127-3, August 1970; #4: 1170-4, March 1961; and #5: 1187-5, August 1961.

The Norman Maurer Interview, conducted by Shel Dorf, comes to us courtesy of the wonderful folks at the Comics Buyer's Guide, the longest running periodical reporting on the American comics field. For more information go to: http://www.cbgxtra.com. For more information on the 3-D THREE STOOGES comics, we suggest picking up AMAZING 3-D COMICS, edited and designed by Craig Yoe, with a 3-D cover and introduction by Joe Kubert, published by IDW.

We're also thrilled to include the first two issues of THE LITTLE STOOGES in this volume. It marks the return of Norman Maurer to writing, drawing, and editing THREE STOOGES comics after many years. Finally, don't miss the all-new graphic novels from Papercutz starring THE THREE STOOGES. The first two volumes, with work by George Gladir, Stefan Petrucha, and award-winning cartoonist Stan Goldberg, are available now at booksellers everywhere.

—Jim Salicrup
Editor-in-Chief
PAPERCUTZ